WIND RIDER'S OATH

DAVID WEBER

For Megan, Morgan, and Michael, who hold my heart in their hands. And always and especially for Sharon, the center of us all, for making miracles possible.

WIND RIDER'S OATH

This is a work of fiction. All the characters and events portrayed in this book are fictional, and any resemblance to real people or incidents is purely coincidental.

A Baen Books Original

Baen Publishing Enterprises
P.O. Box 1403
Riverdale, NY 10471
www.baen.com

ISBN-10: 1-4165-0895-3
ISBN-13: 978-1-4165-0895-3

Cover art by Clyde Caldwell
Maps by Eleanor Kostyk

First paperback printing, August 2005

Library of Congress Cataloging-in-Publication Number 2004004240

Distributed by Simon & Schuster
1230 Avenue of the Americas
New York, NY 10020

Production & design by Windhaven Press, Auburn, NH (www.windhaven.com)
Printed in the United States of America

CHAMPION, WARRIOR—AND HEALER

Bahzell never paused. He continued to move toward the filly at that slow, steady pace.

"Now, then, Milady," he said gently. "I'll not blame you for distrusting such as me. But I've no least notion of doing you or yours hurt. I'm naught but a friend, whatever it may be you're thinking."

The filly whistled shrilly, the sound deafening inside the stable, and reared. She towered above the hradani, dwarfing even his mountainous stature, and her poison-corrupted madness shook the stable like a storm. The other coursers caught her fury, and all seven of them started forward. Bahzell was about to be trampled under by nine or ten tons of hoofed rage.

He continued toward them and his right hand rose. "*Still*," he said.

It was only a single word, yet it echoed in the bones and blood of every man in that stable. The rearing filly's forehooves thudded back to earth, and she froze, staring one-eyed at the hradani and god-light blazing from his open palm. Behind her, six more coursers stood trembling, all of their defiance and rage frozen inside an unbreakable crystal cocoon that streamed over them from Bahzell.

"*Come*," Bahzell breathed, and a chorus of gasps echoed through the stable as a huge, gleaming sword materialized in his hand. The crossed Sword and Mace of Tomanāk were etched into the shining steel of that superb blade. Bahzell reversed it in his hand, holding the hilt up between him and the strangely frozen filly, and a corona of blue light grew about him. It stretched to the rafters and enveloped the filly.

And in the heart of that silently roaring inferno, Bahzell Bahnakson threw all of his unstoppable drive to do what duty required of him against the strangling shroud of the poison consuming the filly from within. . . .

In This Series:

Oath of Swords
The War God's Own
Wind Rider's Oath

Baen Books by David Weber:

Honor Harrington:
On Basilisk Station
The Honor of the Queen
The Short Victorious War
Field of Dishonor
Flag in Exile
Honor Among Enemies
In Enemy Hands
Echoes of Honor
Ashes of Victory
War of Honor
At All Costs (forthcoming)

Honorverse:
Crown of Slaves
(with Eric Flint)
The Shadow of Saganami

edited by David Weber:
More than Honor
Worlds of Honor
Changer of Worlds
The Service of the Sword

Mutineers' Moon
The Armageddon Inheritance
Heirs of Empire
Empire from the Ashes

Path of the Fury

The Apocalypse Troll

The Excalibur Alternative

Bolos!

with Steve White:
Crusade
In Death Ground
The Stars At War
Insurrection
The Shiva Option
The Stars At War II

with Eric Flint:
1633

The Prince Roger Saga,
with John Ringo:
March Upcountry
March to the Sea
March to the Stars
We Few

CHARACTERS

Alfar Axeblade—Sothōii armsman/horse herder from the holding of Warm Springs.

Balcartha Evahnalfressa—Commander of Five Hundred; the senior officer of the Kalatha town guard.

Brother Relath—an acolyte in the Balthar Temple of Tomanāk.

Cassan Axehammer—Baron Toramos, Lord Warden of the South Riding. Baron Tellian's most powerful political enemy, and someone who does not believe that it is possible or desirable to coexist with hradani.

Cathman the Peddler—an alias of Varnaythus.

Dahlaha Farrier—Triahm Pickaxe's mistress and a worshiper of Shīgū.

Dalthys Hallafressa—the town administrator of Kalatha.

Darhal Pickaxe—previous Lord Warden of Lorham. Trisu Pickaxe's deceased father.

Darnas Warshoe—a trusted spy and agent of Baron Cassan.

Dathgar—Baron Tellian's bonded courser. The name means "Thunder Grass."

Dathian Halberd—Lord Warden of the Fens; one of Baron Tellian's vassals plotting with Duke Cassan against him.

Edinghas Bardiche—One of Baron Tellian's vassals; Lord Warden of Warm Springs.

Eramis Yohlahnafressa—a war maid; one of Maretha's partisans.

Erlis Rahnafressa—Commander of One Hundred; the war maid officer in charge of training at Kalatha.

Ermath Balcarafressa—the head of Housekeeping for Kalatha.

Festian Wrathson—Lord Warden of Glanharrow. Baron Tellian's choice to replace the traitor Mathian Redhelm at Glanharrow.

Forhada Helmcleaver—a wind rider who joins Bahzell's attack on Krahana's servants. His courser is named **Konhandro**, or "Mist Born."

Garlahna Lorhanalfressa—a young war maid assigned by Erlis as Leeana's mentor.

Garthan Warbridle—Lord Warden of Hollow Cave. One of Baron Cassan's vassals.

Gayrfressa —the courser filly Bahzell heals at Warm Springs. The name means "Daughter of the Wind" or "Wind Daughter."

Gayrhalan—Hathan's bonded courser. The name means "Storm Souled."

Gharnal Uthmâgson—Bahzell's foster brother; a member of the Order of Tomanāk.

Gurlahn Morakson—the Horse Stealer warrior commanding the guard assigned to Bahzell in Balthar by his father.

Hahnal Bardiche—the eldest son of Lord Warden Edinghas.

Halahk Arrowsmith—one of Baron Cassan's vassals.

Haliku Koharth—a Servant of Krahana, under the orders of Jerghar.

Hanatha Bowmaster—Baroness of Balthar, wife of Tellian.

Hathan Shieldarm—Baron Tellian's wind brother. Rider of courser Gayrhalan.

Jerghar Sholdan—a Servant of Krahana.

Johlana Ermathfressa—the head seamstress of Kalatha.

Jolhanna Evahlafressa—the war maid who serves as Kalatha's official trade representative to Thalar.

Lanitha Sarthayafressa—the Kalatha librarian and senior schoolteacher.

Layantha Peliath—a Servant of Krahana, under the orders of Jerghar.

Leeana Glorana Syliveste Bowmaster—14-year-old daughter (and only child) of Tellian and Hanatha of Balthar.

Luthyr Battlehorn—a wind rider who is not prepared for a hradani champion of Tomanāk or a hradani wind rider.

Maretha Keralinfressa—the leader of the faction of the Kalatha town council most opposed to any sort of appeasement.

Marthya Steelshank—Leeana Bowmaster's personal maid.

Paratha Kharlan—major in the service of the Church of Lillinara.

Ravlahn Thregafressa—Hundred Erlis' senior assistant for weapons training at Kalatha.

Rulth Blackhill—Lord Warden of Transhar. Political ally and vassal of Baron Cassan.

Saeth Pickaxe—deceased father of Triahm Pickaxe.

Salgahn—a dog brother working with Varnaythus and Jerghar.

Salthan Pickaxe—Lord Warden Trisu's cousin, senior magistrate, and librarian.

Saratic Redhelm—Lord Warden of Golden Vale. One of Baron Cassan's vassals who is working with him against Baron Tellian. He is a cousin of Mathian Redhelm, the disgraced Lord Warden of Glanharrow.

Shalsan Warlamp—a wind rider who joins Bahzell's attack on Krahana's servants. His courser is named **Shaynhara**.

Shardohn—a demon familiar of Krahana.

Sharral Ahnlarfressa—Mayor Yalith's assistant in Kalatha.

Sir Altharn Warblade—captain in the service of Lord Warden Trisu.

Sir Chalthar Ranseur—Saratic Redhelm's military marshal, the commander of his personal troops.

Sir Fahlthu Greavesbiter—commander of Saratic Redhelm's Third Company.

Sir Halnahk Partisan—commander of Saratic Redhelm's Fifth Company.

Sir Jahlahan Swordspinner—Baron Tellian's seneschal at Hill Guard Castle.

Sir Kelthys Lancebearer—Lord of Deep Water, a minor manor of Glanharrow. He is a wind rider and a cousin of Baron Tellian.

Sir Markhalt Ravencaw—The senior Sothōii member of the Order of Tomanāk in Balthar upon the arrival of Bahzell and Hurthang.

Sir Trianal Bowmaster—Baron Tellian's 19-year-old nephew.

Sir Yarran Battlecrow—Lord Festian's scout commander and marshal.

Sofalla Bardiche—wife of Lord Warden Edinghas.

Soumeta Harlahnnafressa—a war maid commander of fifty from Kalatha who opposes any appeasement of the war maids' opponents.

Taraman Wararrow—the senior priest of Tomanāk in Balthar.

Tarith Shieldarm—Leeana's personal armsman.

Tarlan Swordsmith—Lord Warden of High Tranith. One of Baron Cassan's vassals.

Tellian Bowmaster—Baron of Balthar, Lord Warden of the West Riding.

Thalgahr Rarikson one of the hradani warriors assigned to Bahzell's bodyguard by his father.

Tharnha Garhlanfressa—a war maid; one of Maretha Keralinfressa's partisans.

Theretha Maglahnfressa—a war maid artist (glassblower) from Kalatha.

Trebdor Horsemaster—one of Baron Cassan's vassals.

Treharm Haltharu—a Servant of Krahana, under the orders of Jerghar.

Triahm Pickaxe—Lord Warden Trisu's cousin, a bitter enemy of all war maids.

Trisu Pickaxe—Lord Warden of Lorham.

Varnaythus—Master Varnaythus; a black sorceror and priest of Carnadosa.

Walasfro—Sir Kelthys Lancebearer's courser. The name means Son of Battle.

Walsharno—Gayrfressa's older brother, the courser who bonds with Bahzell. His name means Battle Dawn (it could also be translated Dawn of Battle or Battle Sun).

Welthan Handaxe—Lord Warden of Dronhar, one of Baron Cassan's vassals.

Yalith Tamalthfressa—Mayor of Kalatha.

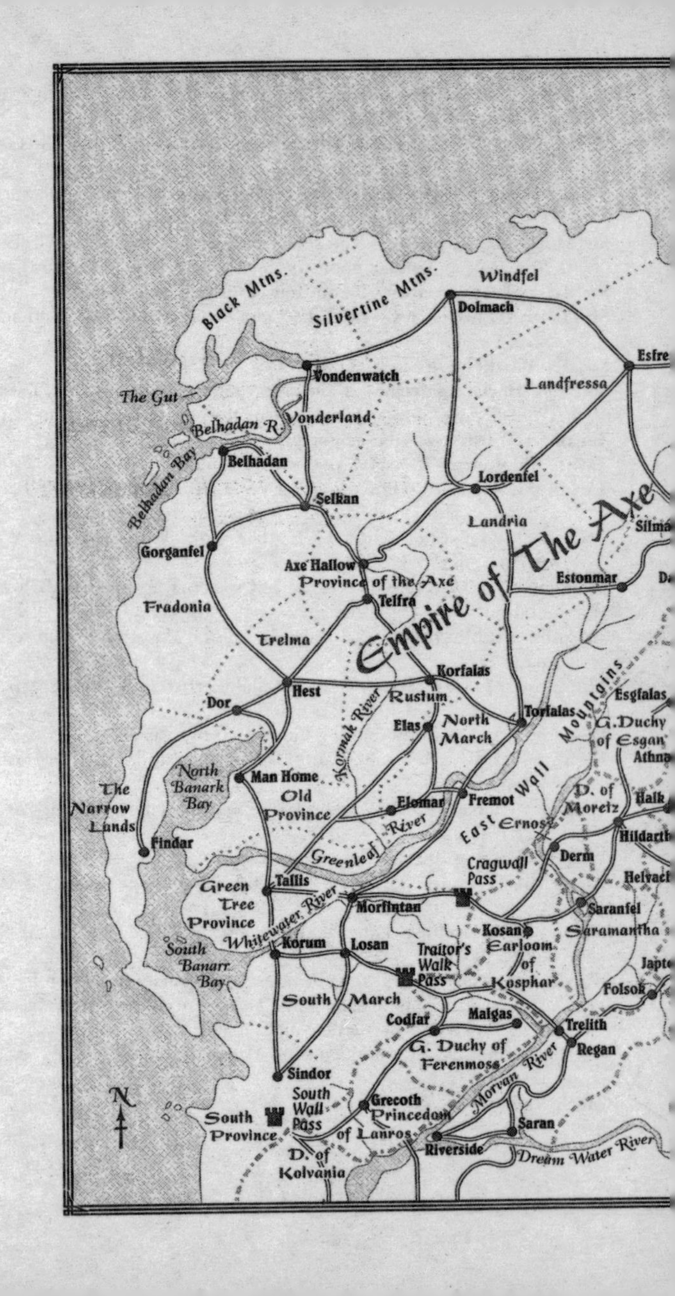

Black Mtns.
Silvertine Mtns.
Windfel
Dolmach
Esfre
Vondenwatch
Landfressa
The Gut
Vonderland
Belhadan R.
Belhadan Bay
Belhadan
Lordenfel
Selkan
Landria
Empire of The Axe
Silma
Gorganfel
Axe Hallow
Province of the Axe
Estonmar
Telfra
Fradonia
Trelma
Korfalas
Hest
Rustum
Esgfalas
Dor
Kormak River
Torlalas
Mountains
G. Duchy of Esgan
Elas
North March
Athna
North Banark Bay
Man Home
Old Province
The Narrow Lands
Elomar
Fremot
Wall
D. of Moretz
Halk
East
Ernos
Hildarth
River
Findar
Greenleaf
Derm
Cragwall Pass
Helvaci
Tallis
Green Tree Province
Whitewater River
Morfintan
Saranfel
Kosan
Saramantha
South Banarr Bay
Korum
Losan
Traitor's Walk Pass
Earloom of Kosphar
Japt
South
March
Folsok
Codfar
Malgas
Trelith
G. Duchy of Ferenmoss
Regan
River
Sindor
Morvan
N
South Wall Pass
Grecoth
Princedom of Lanros
South Province
Saran
Riverside
D. of Kolvania
Dream Water River

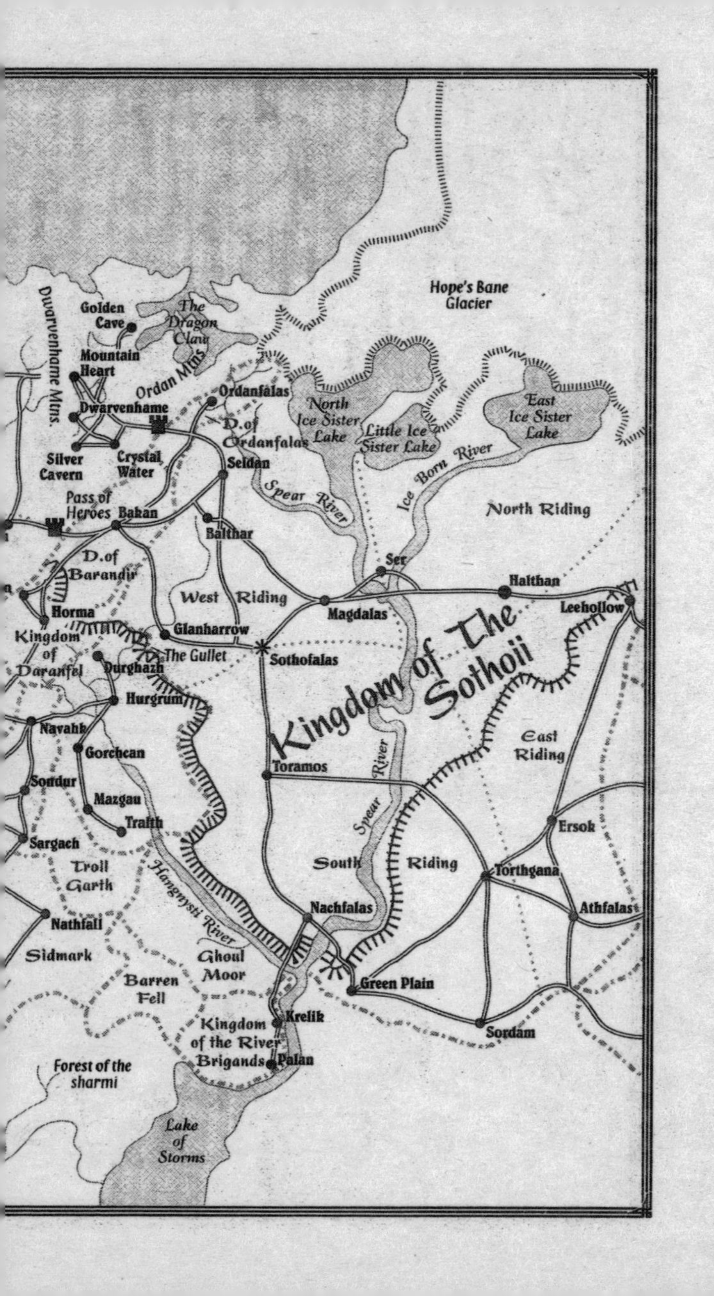

Hope's Bane Glacier
Golden Cave
The Dragon Claw
Dwarvenhame Mtns.
Mountain Heart
Ordan Mtns
Ordanfalas
Dwarvenhame
D. of Ordanfalas
North Ice Sister Lake
Little Ice Sister Lake
East Ice Sister Lake
Silver Cavern
Crystal Water
Seldan
Ice Born River
Spear River
Pass of Heroes
Bakan
North Riding
Balthar
D. of Barandir
Ser
Halthan
West Riding
Magdalas
Leehollow
Horma
Glanharrow
Kingdom of Daranfel
The Gullet
Sothofalas
Kingdom of The Sothoii
Durghazh
Hurgrum
Navahk
East Riding
Gorchean
Toramos
Spear River
Soudur
Mazgau
Traith
Ersok
Sargach
South Riding
Troll Garth
Torthgana
Hangnysti River
Nachfalas
Athfalas
Nathfall
Sidmark
Ghoul Moor
Barren Fell
Green Plain
Krelik
Kingdom of the River Brigands
Palan
Sordam
Forest of the sharmi
Lake of Storms

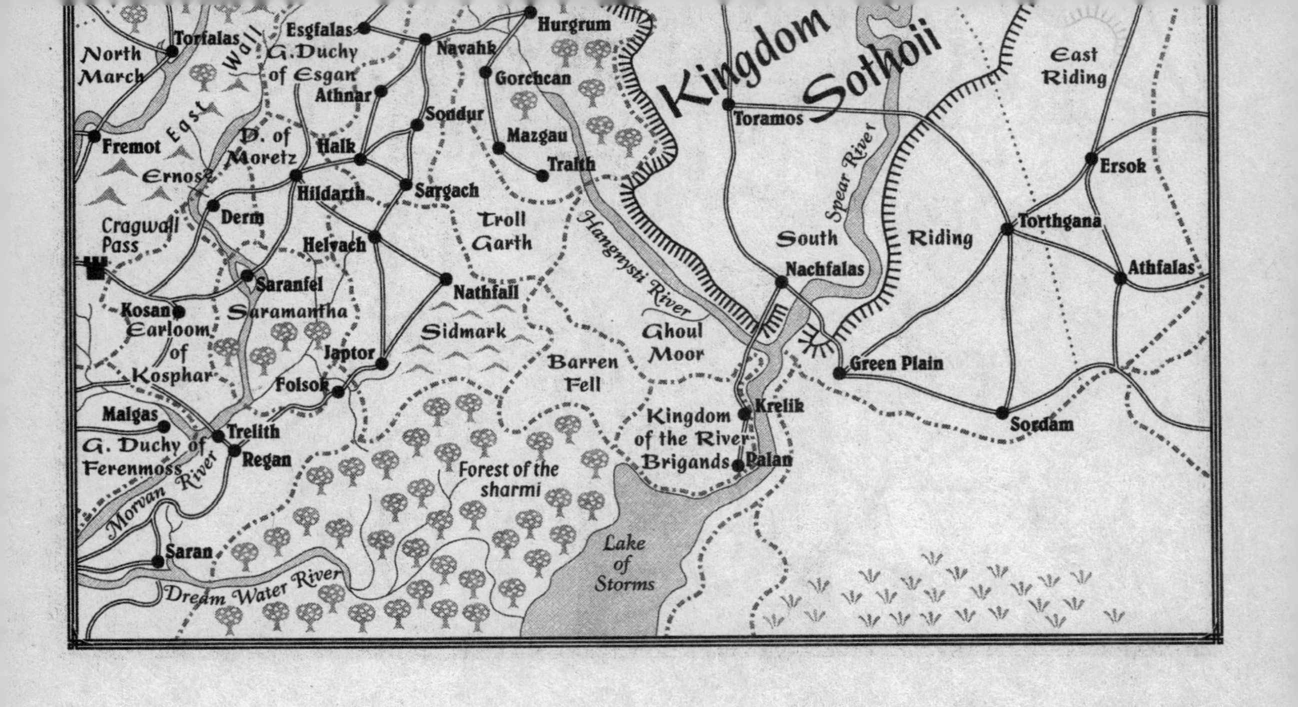

North March
Torfalas
East Wall
G. Duchy of Esgan
Esgfalas
Navahk
Hurgrum
Gorchcan
Athnar
Sondur
Fremot
D. of Moretz
Halk
Mazgau
Traith
Ernos
Hildarth
Sargach
Derm
Cragwall Pass
Troll Garth
Helvach
Saranfel
Nathfall
Kosan
Earloom of Kosphar
Saramantha
Sidmark
Japtor
Folsok
Barren Fell
Ghoul Moor
Hangnysti River
Malgas
Trelith
Regan
G. Duchy of Ferenmoss
Morvan River
Forest of the sharmi
Kingdom of the River Brigands
Krelik
Palan
Saran
Dream Water River
Lake of Storms
Kingdom Sothoii
Toramos
Spear River
South Riding
Nachfalas
Green Plain
Riding
Torthgana
East Riding
Ersok
Athfalas
Sordam

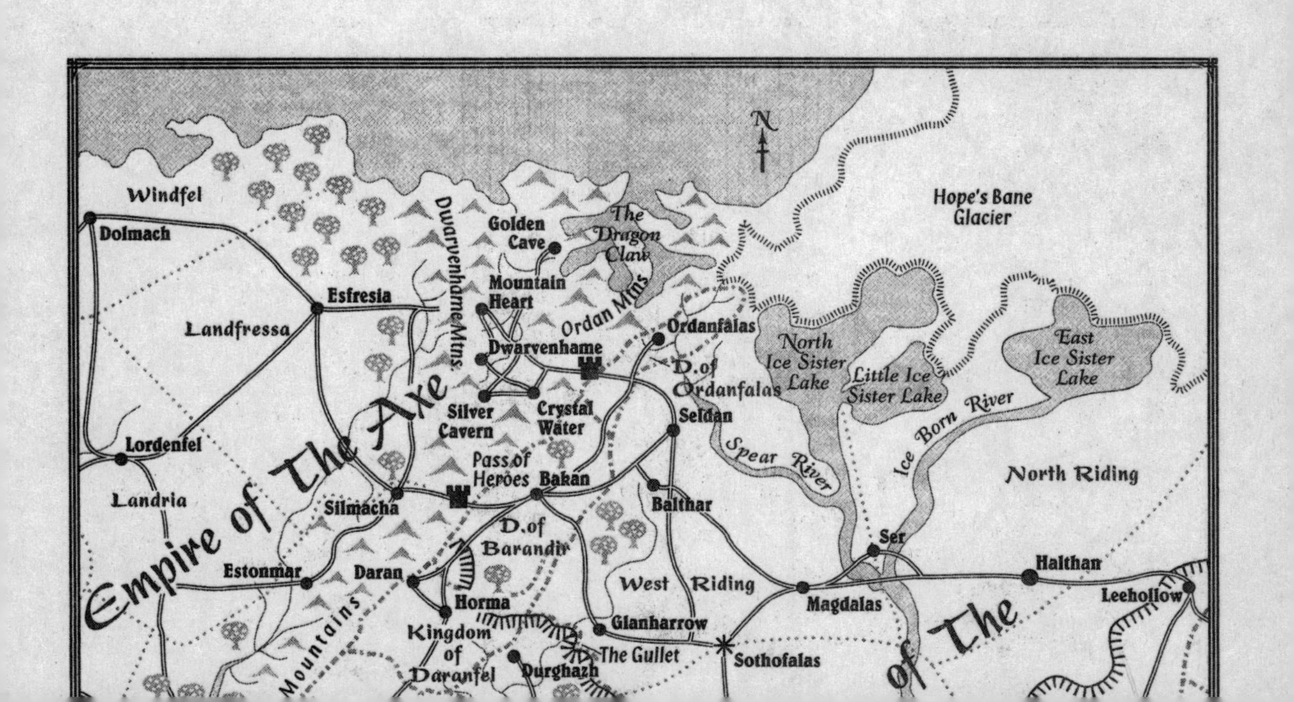
Windfel
Dolmach
Landfressa
Esfresia
Lordenfel
Landria
Empire of The Axe
Dwarvenhame Mtns.
Golden Cave
The Dragon Claw
Mountain Heart
Ordan Mtns
Dwarvenhame
Ordanfalas
D. of Ordanfalas
Silver Cavern
Crystal Water
Seldan
Pass of Heroes
Bakan
Silmacha
Balthar
D. of Barandir
Estonmar
Daran
Horma
Mountains
Kingdom of Daranfel
Durghazh
The Gullet
Glanharrow
West Riding
Sothofalas
Magdalas
Ser
Halthan
Leehollow
of The
N
Hope's Bane Glacier
North Ice Sister Lake
Little Ice Sister Lake
East Ice Sister Lake
Ice Born River
Spear River
North Riding

Prologue

Thunder rumbled overhead like a distant battering ram, pounding at the hasp of heaven. The harsh grumble was muted in the stone-walled room, but the waterfall sound of pounding rain came through the single open window on the windy breath of the chilly spring night. Half a dozen richly dressed men sat around the large wooden table's polished surface. Three of them nursed ruby-hearted wineglasses. Two more quaffed beer from elaborately ornamented tankards. The sixth leaned back in the larger, more heavily ornamented chair at the head of the table. A small glass of Dwarvenhame whiskey sat before him, warm amber in the light of the oil lamps, and he squinted through a cloud of fragrant smoke as he used a flaring splinter to relight his pipe from the lamp at his end of the table.

He waved out the flaming splinter and replaced the lamp chimney. His pipe hissed softly as he drew upon it, then exhaled a single, perfectly formed ring of smoke. More thunder rumbled, a little closer this time, and the darkness outside the window flickered to the distant dance of lightning, far away on the edge of the rainy world.

"I agree that the situation is intolerable, Milord," one

of the beer-drinking men said into the calm stillness created by the comfort of a fire on a night of storm and wind. His hair was the golden red often seen among the oldest of Sothōii noble families, and his expression was unhappy, to say the least. He took another swallow from his tankard, raised hand flickering with the dance of golden rings and reflecting gems. Then he set the tankard back down and shrugged. "Still, we seem to have no option but to accept it."

"I'm afraid Welthan is right about that, Milord," one of the wine-drinkers agreed sourly. "It's an insult to every Sothōii ever born, but as long as Tellian is prepared to swallow it himself, he can force it down all of our throats, as well."

"And as long as the King is prepared to allow him to," another of the wine-drinkers reminded them all darkly. "Don't forget that, Garthan."

"I'm not forgetting anything, Tarlan," Garthan replied shortly. "But does any man at this table believe that His Majesty hasn't been . . . poorly advised in this instance?"

"Ill-advised or well-advised, the King is the King," the pipe-smoking man at the head of the table observed. His voice was well modulated, his tone almost but not quite mild. There was also a faintly dangerous set to his handsome face, and Garthan stiffened slightly in his chair.

"It was not my intent to suggest anything else, Milord." His own voice was deferential, but cored with stubbornness. "Nonetheless, there is a reason His Majesty has a Council, and you *are* a member of it. Is it not the function of a councilor to counsel? And who is more valuable? A councilor who offers his own wisdom, even when it may not be the most popular advice? Or one who will not disagree when he believes that other, more . . . expedient councilors are in error?"

The night outside the chamber was on the cold side of cool, and the breeze blowing through the window was a bit stronger than it had been a moment before. No doubt that accounted for the chill which breathed through the room.

"You're correct, of course," the man at the head of the table told Garthan after a long, still moment, stroking his golden beard with his left hand. "Yet so is Tarlan. And while I may sit on the Council, I'm certainly not the only one who does. Prince Yurokhas also sits there, for example. And at the moment, King Markhos seems prepared to listen to the prince and give Tellian the opportunity to pursue his useless attempt to 'peacefully coexist' with the hradani."

More than one of the men seated around the table looked as if he wanted to spit on the polished stone floor, and there was a low mutter of thunder-washed disgust. Yet none of them could disagree with what their host had just said.

"Well, yes, Milord," the second beer-drinker agreed after several seconds. "We're all aware of that, as I'm sure you realized before you called us here tonight. But I trust you'll forgive my possible bluntness in observing that you didn't choose us for this meeting because of our ardent agreement with Prince Yurokhas' position."

His tone was so droll that more than one of the men at the table actually found themselves chuckling, and even the pipe-smoking man smiled.

"For my own part," the speaker continued, "I readily admit that I have personal as well as patriotic reasons for detesting the present situation. My kinsman Mathian finds himself little better than a beggar, a pensioner in my house, supplanted by a jumped-up, common-born knight without a drop of noble blood in his veins." His tone was no longer droll, and his eyes were dangerous. "Leaving aside the insult to my entire family—and to every true noble house among us—there is such a thing as justice. We have a bone to pick with Baron Tellian, and I, for one, refuse to pretend we don't. Nor, I think, are you prepared to do so, Milord."

Some of the others suddenly seemed to find the contents of their glasses or tankards deeply absorbing. They stared down into them as if consulting fermented auguries, but the man at the head of the table only looked steadily at the one who had spoken.

"I have never pretended I didn't have many bones to pick with Tellian of Balthar, Lord Saratic. I do. And you're quite right to point out that I invited all of you to join me this evening because I felt confident each of you do, as well. Yet it behooves all of us to remember that to openly assail him over this matter risks presenting the appearance of defying the *King*. Before we may deal properly with Tellian and his pet hradani, we must bring King Markhos to realize that, as Garthan says, he has been poorly advised in this matter. Once he withdraws support from Tellian, we may become more . . . direct in our methods. But for the present, as loyal subjects and vassals of the King, we must lend his policies our firm public support."

"Of course, Milord," Saratic agreed. "I would never suggest—and it was never my intention—that we do anything else. As you say, it is our manifest duty to the Crown to make our acceptance of the King's policies clear. And public."

"Precisely." The pipe-smoking man blew another smoke ring while rain pounded down, heavier than ever, outside the window. Burning coal seethed on the hearth behind him, hissing as the occasional raindrop found its way down the chimney and through the flue. He picked up his whiskey glass and sipped with slow appreciation, then set it back down very precisely.

"Still," he said, "just as it is the duty of any subject of the King to accept his policies and abide by his decisions, so it is also the duty of his subjects to consider all the ways in which they might further the true object of those policies. Which, of course, is the peace and security of the entire Kingdom. And, as all of you, I cannot convince myself that Baron Tellian's present actions can ultimately pose anything but a threat to that peace and security."

"I see, Milord," Saratic said. "And I agree with you." Other heads nodded around the table, and if most of the nods seemed less enthusiastic than Saratic's, none of them seemed the least hesitant. "Yet bearing in mind what you've already so rightly said about our responsibility and duty to support the King's policies, it would seem there's little we can openly do to stop Tellian."

"You've fought as many battles as any man here, Lord Saratic," the pipe-smoking man said. "As such, you know as well as I that the most obvious and open tactic is seldom the most effective one. Understand me, all of you. I will not openly oppose His Majesty in this matter, or in any other. I will, as I always have, express my own views before both the King and the other members of his Council, and I will strive to convince him of the wisdom of my arguments. But beyond the limits of debate and the duty to advise which comes with my seat on that Council, I will raise no hand and no voice against His Majesty. It would be not merely wrong but foolish—and perhaps even foolhardy—to do otherwise.

"Yet what I can do to change the factors and limitations which constrain the King's options I will do. And if it proves possible to create circumstances which will make the wisdom of my own views and recommendations apparent, then I will do that, also. Nor—" he let his eyes sweep over their faces in the lamplight "—will I forget those who help me to create those circumstances."

"I see," Saratic murmured once more. He and Garthan looked at one another across the table, and then Saratic turned his gaze back to their host. "And may I ask, Milord, if you've given thought to the best way in which we might aid in the creation of those circumstances to which you just referred?"

"Well, no," the pipe-smoking man said mildly. "I mean, certain possibilities seem obvious enough. For example, this 'Lord Festian' who Tellian convinced the King to install at Glanharrow in place of your kinsman Mathian is scarcely likely to be equal to the sorts of challenges any lord must expect to face and master in safeguarding his lands and the people consigned to his care. Surely it would be appropriate for those in a position to demonstrate his incompetence to do so."

He bared his teeth in a smile any shark might have admired, and equally toothy smiles came back to him from his guests.

"And," he continued, "there's always the matter of this so-called champion of Tomanāk, 'Prince Bahzell.' Perhaps you may have failed to note that while His Majesty is prepared to acknowledge the existence of a chapter of the Order of Tomanāk among the hradani, and even to treat this Bahzell as one of the War God's champions, he has not expressly granted Bahzell ambassadorial status. While I feel certain King Markhos would be horrified if some evil mischance befell Bahzell, it wouldn't be the same as if that mischance had befallen an accredited ambassador from a civilized land."

"Nor does he enjoy the legal immunities of an ambassador," Tarlan said slowly. His thoughtful voice was little more than a murmur, but the pipe-smoking man nodded.

"Obviously not," he agreed. "There *is* the matter of his supposed status as a champion of Tomanāk, of course. But with all due respect to His Majesty and his other advisers, how can anyone honestly believe Tomanāk would choose a hradani—and a *Horse Stealer* hradani, at that—as one of His champions?" He snorted contemptuously. "If this Bahzell wants to claim the privileges and powers of a champion, I think it would be only fair to give him the opportunity to prove he deserves them. And since Scale Balancer's courtroom is the field of battle, there's really only one place he could do that, isn't there?"

One or two of the others exchanged glances of varying degrees of uneasiness as they listened to his last couple of sentences, but no one disagreed. After all, the mere thought of a hradani champion of any God of Light was far worse than merely ridiculous. It verged all too closely upon outright blasphemy, whatever others might think.

"I, for one, agree with you completely, Milord," Saratic said, and Garthan nodded firmly. Tarlan also nodded, only a shade less enthusiastically.

"Thank you, Lord Saratic," the pipe-smoking man said. "I value your support. And it has always been the tradition of my house to remember those who have lent us support when we most needed it."

More than a hint of avarice flickered in Saratic's eyes.

It didn't supplant the anger and vengefulness which already filled them, but it honed and strengthened those preexisting emotions, and the pipe-smoker hid a smile of satisfaction as he saw it.

"It seems to me, Milord," Saratic said after a moment, "that if we really put our minds to it, there ought to be some way in which we might both demonstrate this Festian's inadequacy as Lord Mathian's usurper—I mean, of course, *successor*—and simultaneously provide 'Prince Bahzell' the opportunity to prove his status as Tomanāk's champion once and for all."

"I'm certain there is," the pipe-smoking man agreed. Then he put his hands on the tabletop and pushed to his feet, smiling at the others.

"However," he continued, "I fear the hour has grown quite late. I have a full and demanding day waiting for me tomorrow, and so, with your permission, I will bid you all good night. No, no," he said, shaking his head and raising the palm of one hand as two or three of his guests made as if to stand, as well. "Don't let my departure interrupt your conversation, gentlemen. It would be a poor host who expected his own early retirement to cut short his guests' enjoyment of discussions among themselves." He smiled at them again. "Stay where you are as long as you like. The servants have been instructed to leave you in peace, unless you summon them for additional refreshments. Who knows? Perhaps your discussions will suggest some way in which we might all further the Kingdom's interests and prosperity."

He nodded to them all, and then walked softly out of the room.

Chapter One

Thick mist swirled in slow, heavy clouds on the chill breeze, rising from the cold, standing water and scarcely thicker mud of the swamp. Somewhere above the mist, the sun crawled towards midday, burnishing the upper reaches of vapor with a golden aura that was delicately beautiful in its own way. All thirty of the mounted men were liberally coated in mud, however, and the golden glow did little to improve their tempers.

"It *would* be the Bogs," one of the trackers growled, grimacing at the mounted troop's commander.

"Would you really prefer the Gullet?" the grizzled horseman responded in an equally sour voice.

"Not really, Sir Yarran," the tracker admitted. "But at least I've been down the Gullet before. Halfway, at least."

Sir Yarran grunted a laugh, and so did most of his men. Their last trip down the Gullet had not been a happy one, but the men in this troop were not so secretly delighted by at least one of its consequences. Yet the laughter faded quickly, for like Sir Yarran, all of them were unhappily certain that the mission which brought them to the swamps this morning had been sparked by an effort to undo that consequence.

Sir Yarran rose in his stirrups as if those extra few inches of elevation could somehow help his sight pierce the billowing fog. They didn't, and he growled a mental curse.

"Well, lads," he said as he finally settled back into the saddle, "I'm afraid we've no choice but to keep going for at least a bit farther." He looked at one of his men and pointed back over his shoulder the way they'd come. "Trobius, go back and find Sir Kelthys and his men. Tell him we're pushing on into the swamp." He grimaced. "If he cares to join us, he'll be welcome, but there's little point *his* wallowing about in there, unless he's nothing better to do than freeze his arse off in muddy water along with the rest of us."

"Aye, Sir Yarran." Trobius saluted, reined his horse around, and went trotting off into the mist. Sir Yarran contemplated the swamp ahead of them sourly for a few more moments, then grunted resignedly.

"All right, lads," he said. "Let's be going. Who knows? We might get lucky enough to actually find something to track."

"Aye, Sir," the tracker acknowledged, and urged his horse forward, picking a careful path deeper into the watery muck. "And pigs may fly, too," he muttered to himself, and Sir Yarran glanced at him. Fortunately, his voice had been low enough Sir Yarran could pretend he hadn't heard him. Which suited Sir Yarran just fine. Especially because he was in complete agreement with the other man.

He watched the tracker and his two assistants making their cautious way deeper into the treacherous footing, then sighed and clucked gently to his own horse.

"And of course we won't be able to prove a thing."

Sir Yarran Battlecrow grimaced, then hawked noisily and spat into the fire in disgust. It was a habit Sir Festian Wrathson, Lord Warden of Glanharrow, had been trying to break him of for years. Not because Festian disagreed with the emotions which spawned it, but because Yarran did it with so much energy.

At the moment, however, Festian felt no urge to reprimand Yarran. If anything, he longed to emulate his marshal, the commander of Glanharrow's armsmen. And whatever Festian might long for, Yarran, at least, had earned the right to express himself however he chose.

Steam oozed from the knight's rain-soaked tunic and trousers. His graying blond hair was rough edged and sodden, and although it was obvious he'd wiped down his riding boots, they were still smeared with mud stains. His sodden poncho was draped over the back of one of the hall's chairs, radiating its own steam wisps before the fire, and a servant was busy drying Yarran's cuirass in one corner.

"No, we won't be," Festian said after a moment. "And because we won't, I can't afford to go about making accusations. Especially not about my neighboring lords."

"Aye, that's true enough, and I know it," Yarran agreed in a heavy, resigned tone. "Still and all, though, Milord, you and I both know, don't we?"

"Maybe we do, and maybe we don't," Festian replied. Yarran gave him a skeptical look, and the lord warden waved one hand. "Oh, I know what we both *suspect*, Yarran, but as you say, it's not as if we had proof, is it?"

"No, Phrobus take it," Yarran acknowledged sourly.

"Then let's take it one step at a time and consider what we do know for certain. For example, what direction were they headed when you lost the trail?"

"Phrobus only knows," Yarran growled. A serving woman entered the hall and handed him a steaming mug, and the marshal's expression lightened perceptibly as he detected the rich, strong scent of chocolate. It was an extraordinarily expensive luxury on the Sothōii Wind Plain, and the tough, grizzled warrior had a bigger sweet tooth than any three of Glanharrow's children combined.

He smiled at the serving woman, accepted the mug, and sipped with slow, sensual pleasure. Festian allowed him to savor it for several seconds. Then he cleared his throat rather pointedly, and Yarran lowered the mug and wiped a froth of chocolate from his mustache with an almost sheepish air.

"Beg pardon, Milord," he said. "Took me a bit by surprise, that did."

"You've been working your arse off for me for weeks now, Yarran," Festian said mildly. In fact, as he and Yarran both knew, the other knight had been doing precisely what Festian would once have been doing for the deposed Lord Mathian. Not, as both of them knew, that Mathian would have been rewarding anyone with hot chocolate for his efforts.

"What I'm here for, Milord," Yarran said, which was as close as either of them was ever likely to come to putting their shared knowledge into words.

"Any road," the marshal continued after a moment, "whoever it was started off headed southwest, but there's no damned way that was where he was really going. Nothing that direction but the Gullet, and not even a wizard could get that many cattle down the Gullet." He shook his head. "No, Milord, they started out that way, and I'm guessing they meant to at least make us wonder if they'd headed down it. Wanted us to think it was the Horse Stealers if they could, like as not. But they turned another direction once they hit the Bogs." He shrugged. "Can't prove any of that, of course. We did our best to follow them, but there's too much quicksand and too little solid ground to hold hoof prints. I damned near lost three of my men before we gave it up. I'd have kept going if we'd been able to find any signs at all, but it's soupy enough in there at the best of times. In the spring—especially one as rainy as this?" He shook his head again. "No way at all to say what direction they went."

"And whatever way they headed, there are altogether too many places they can come out of the muck again," Festian agreed sourly.

"Aye, Milord. That's true enough. But what sticks in my mind is that it would take someone who knows the Bogs like the back of his own hand to get a herd of cattle through them."

Festian grunted in agreement. He knew what Yarran was really getting at. "The Bogs" were a treacherous spread of swamp, mud banks, and mire which stretched for miles south and eastward from the narrow passage known as "the Gullet." Once, centuries ago, a river had found its way down the Escarpment, the towering side of the Sothōii Wind Plain, to the grasslands below, through that passage. Then some long forgotten earthquake had changed its course, turning the gorge it had bitten out of the Escarpment's forbidding wall into one of the very few avenues by which the Sothōii and the barbarian hradani could get at one another. It wasn't much of an avenue—more of a tortuous, twisting alley, really—but it had served as an invasion route either way, in its time.

Yet Yarran was correct when he said no one could possibly get a herd of stolen cattle down the Gullet . . . and that only someone with an intimate knowledge of the terrain could have threaded that same herd through the trackless mud where the frustrated river had spread and flowed and soaked to create the Bogs.

Which meant, almost certainly, that whoever had stolen the cattle—and the sheep, and the horses, before them—came from Glanharrow itself. Not that that was very much of a surprise.

"With all due respect, Milord, and I know you don't want to, but I think it's time you called on Baron Tellian for help," Yarran said after several silent seconds. A heavier gust of rain drummed on the hall's roof, and the flames on the hearth danced.

"A lord is supposed to look after his own herds, just as he's supposed to look after the well-being of his own people," Festian said flatly.

"Aye, so he is," Yarran agreed with the stubborn deference of a trusted henchman. "And meaning no disrespect, but just what has that got to do with it?" Festian glared at him, and the marshal shrugged. "Chew my head off if you want, Milord, but you and I both know truth when it bites us on the arse. And so does Baron Tellian, come to that. He knew when he chose you to replace that arse-headed idiot Redhelm that there'd be those as would do all they could to see to it you fell flat on your face. Well, that's what's happening now. I'd bet my best sword that whoever ran those cattle off in the first place is one of our own people. No one else'd know the Bogs well enough to get a herd that size through 'em. But whoever *he* is, he's got to have someone to take them off his hands when he gets to t'other side. Now, I suppose it's possible he could have some bent merchant who could dispose of them for him for a partner. But it's a lot more likely one of your fellow lords is waiting for him. Maybe we can't prove it, but we both know it, and Baron Tellian's your liege lord . . . not to mention the one as dropped you into the pot in the first place. And if another lord is behind this, then like as not he's a close enough neighbor of yours to make the Baron *his* liege, too. Or else he's someone *else's* vassal," Yarran carefully named no names, "in which case you've no choice but to appeal to the Baron. So, either road, it seems to me, it's the Baron's place to be sending help now that someone's declared open war on you."

"Stealing cattle and horses is hardly 'open war,' Yarran," Festian objected, but it sounded weak, even to him. True, there'd been no formal declaration of defiance or hostilities, but among the Sothōii, herd-raiding and lightning border forays were the traditional means of striking at an enemy. Yarran only snorted with magnificent emphasis, which was quite enough to make his own opinion of Festian's objection clear, and the Lord Warden of Glanharrow shrugged.

"Whatever it may be," he said, "Baron Tellian has enough other problems on his plate right now without my adding this one to it."

"Again, with all due respect, Milord, this is something as is supposed to be landing on his plate. And I'm not the only one who thinks so." Festian cocked an eyebrow, and it was Yarran's turn to shrug. "Sir Kelthys thinks it's time, as well."

"You've discussed this with Kelthys?" Festian asked sharply, a thin flicker of anger dancing in his eyes for the first time, and Yarran nodded.

"Wasn't as if I had a lot of choice about it, Milord," he pointed out. "Being as how Deep Water backs right up on the Bogs the way it does. Wouldn't have done for me to be leading more than a score of mounted men across his land without explaining to him just what we were up to."

"The thieves cut across Deep Water?" Festian demanded, his surprise evident.

"No, of course not." Yarran snorted again. "I just said that anyone who knows the Bogs well enough to give me the slip in them has to be from around here, Milord. And anyone from around here knows exactly what would happen to anyone fool enough to try to take a herd of stolen cattle through Sir Kelthys' lands." He shook his head. "No, I cut across Deep Water to try to make up time on them. Did, too. Just not enough.

"Anyway, he turned out a half-score of his own men to help, not that it made much difference in the end. And he spent most of our ride together discussing the raids and their pattern with me."

"I see." Festian frowned unhappily, but much as he might have liked to, he couldn't simply reject Yarran's advice out of hand. Especially not if Sir Kelthys Lancebearer, Baron Tellian's cousin, also thought it was time Festian called upon his liege for assistance. If only it didn't stick so sideways in his craw!

"Milord," Yarran said with the respectful insistence of the man who had been Festian's senior lieutenant when Festian had commanded Glanharrow's scouts for Lord Mathian, "I know it's not something you want to be doing. And I know pigs probably know more about politics than I do. But it's plain as a pimple on Sharnā's arse that whoever is doing this is striking as much at Baron Tellian as at you. I'm not saying whoever it is wouldn't be happy enough to do anything he could to make you look unfit to hold Glanharrow, because we both know that, even as stupid as Redhelm was, there'll always be some as think he ought to be sitting in that chair still. But there's bigger fish to fry this time, and if they make *you* look unfit, then they make *him* look unfit for having chosen you. That's my opinion, anyway, and Sir Kelthys shares it. Which means Baron Tellian won't be thanking you if you wait to call on him until it's too late."

For a taciturn fighting man with a reputation for never using two words when one would do the trick, Yarran did have a way of getting his points across, Festian reflected. And he wasn't saying anything Festian hadn't already thought. It was just—

It's just that I'm too damned stubborn to ask for help easily. But Yarran's right. If I can't solve this problem on my own—and it seems I can't—and I wait too long to ask the Baron for help, it will be too late. And then both *of us will be drowning in horse shit.*

"Well," he said mildly after a moment, "if you and Sir Kelthys both agree so strongly, then I suppose there's not much point in my arguing, is there?" Yarran had the grace to look embarrassed, though it was obvious it took some effort on his part, and Festian grinned crookedly.

"Finish your chocolate, Yarran. If you're so eager for me to go hat in hand asking for Baron Tellian's assistance, then I think you're the best choice to take the message to him."

Another gust of rain pounded on the hall's roof, and Yarran grimaced at the sound.

Chapter Two

"He's certainly *tall* enough, isn't he, Milady?"

"Yes, Marthya, he is," Leeana Bowmaster agreed, and the maid hid a small smile at her youthful mistress' repressive tone. There was a reason for that repressiveness, she thought, and managed somehow not to giggle at the reflection.

"Pity about the ears though, Milady," she continued in an impishly innocent tone. "He could be almost handsome without them."

" 'Handsome' isn't exactly the word I'd choose to describe him," Leeana replied. Although, if she'd been prepared to be honest with her maid (which she most emphatically was not), she would have argued that the man in question was quite handsome even *with* the ears. Indeed, the undeniable edge of otherness they lent him only made him more exotically attractive.

"Well, at least he comes closer to handsome than his friend does!" Marthya observed, and this time Leeana chose to make no response at all. Marthya had known her since childhood, and she was only too capable of putting isolated comments together to divine her charge's thoughts with devastating accuracy. Which was not something Leeana needed her—or anyone else!—doing at this particular moment. Especially not where the current object of their attention was concerned.

The two of them stood in the concealing shadows of the minstrel gallery above Hill Guard Castle's great hall. Below them, Leeana's father and a dozen or so of his senior officers had just risen to greet two new arrivals. Well, not *new*, precisely. They'd been living at Hill Guard for weeks now. But they'd been away for several days, on a visit to their own people, and Leeana was afire with curiosity, among other things. Even her father (who any unprejudiced soul must concede was the best father in the Kingdom) sometimes forgot to mention interesting political information or speculation to a mere daughter. Besides, the newcomers fascinated Leeana. She was a Sothōii. No one had to tell her about the bitter, eternal enmity between her own people and the hradani. But these two were utterly at odds with the popular stereotype of their people, which would have made them interesting enough without all of the political ramifications of their presence.

And, she admitted, Marthya was quite correct about how tall her father's guest—or captor, depending upon one's perspective—was.

"Welcome back, Prince Bahzell. And you, too, Lord Brandark." Tellian Bowmaster, Baron of Balthar and Lord Warden of the West Riding, smiled with a genuine warmth some might have found surprising as he greeted his visitors. Tellian's tenor voice was melodious enough, but it always sounded a bit strange coming from someone who stood six and a half inches over six feet in height. As was true of many of the oldest noble houses of the Sothōii, members of the Bowmaster clan tended to be very tall, for humans, and Tellian was no exception.

"It's thankful for the welcome we are," the taller of the new arrivals replied in a deep bass that sounded not at all strange rumbling up out of the massive chest of a hradani who stood well over *seven* and a half feet in his stockings. "Still and all, I'm thinking you might want to be making that welcome a mite less obvious, Milord."

"Why?" Tellian smiled crookedly as he waved Bahzell and his companion towards chairs at the long refectory table before the fire blazing on the hearth. That hearth was big enough to consume entire trees but, like most fires on the rolling grasslands of the Wind Plain, it burned coal, not wood. "Those who believe I have even the faintest notion of what I'm doing won't be bothered by it. And those who are convinced I *don't* have any notion won't like me any more just because I pretend to sulk when you cross my threshold. That being so, I might as well at least be polite!"

"A succinct analysis, Milord," the smaller of the two hradani observed with a chuckle. At six feet two inches, Brandark Brandarkson was shorter than Tellian, far less Bahzell, and he dressed like someone who was as close to an overcivilized fop as any hradani could hope to come. But he was almost squat with muscle, and the shoulders under his exquisitely cut doublets and waistcoats were almost as broad as Bahzell's. Despite his shorter stature, he was one of the very few people who came close to matching Bahzell's lethality in a fight, which had been a handy thing, from time to time, for he was also a bard. Of sorts.

The hradani language was well suited to long, rolling cadences, and richly evocative verse and song. That was good, for during the darkest periods of their twelve centuries in Norfressa, it was only the oral traditions of their generally illiterate bards which had kept any of their history alive. Even today, bards were more honored among the hradani than among any other Norfressan people, except, perhaps, the elven lords of Saramantha, and Brandark had the soul of a bard. He was also a brilliant, completely self-educated scholar, and a talented musician. But not even his closest friends were willing to pretend that he could actually *sing*, and his poetry was almost as bad as his voice. He yearned to craft the epic poems to express the beauty his soul reached out to . . . and what he actually produced was doggerel. Witty, entertaining, trenchant doggerel, to be sure, but doggerel. Which perhaps explained his habit of writing biting, sometimes savage satire. Indeed, he'd spent years baiting Prince Churnazh of Navahk—something no one else had dared to do—and only the deadliness of the swordsman hiding beneath his foppish exterior had kept him alive while he did it.

Those days were behind him now, but his broad grin suggested that his inner satirist found the entire situation which had engulfed his friend and the Sothōii enormously entertaining.

Which Bahzell did not.

"'Succinct' is all well and good," the Horse Stealer growled at his friend. "But there's enough as would like to see the two of us fall flat on our arses as it is, without us looking all happy to be seeing one another."

"No doubt we should maintain a proper decorum in more public venues," Tellian conceded. "But this is my home, Bahzell. I'll damned well greet anyone I want any way I want in it."

"I can't say as I can fault you there," Bahzell said after a moment. "Mind you, I'm thinking there's more Sothōii would rather see my head on a pike over your gate than my backside in this chair in front of your fire!"

"Not many more than the number of hradani who'd like to see *my* head over your father's gate in Hurgrum, I imagine," Tellian replied with a wry smile. "Although at least you didn't surrender an entire invasion army to a ragtag force of hradani you outnumbered thirty- or forty-to-one."

"But at least Prince Bahzell was also good enough to grant us all parole, Wind Brother," a shorter, stockier Sothōii pointed out.

"Yes, Hathan," Tellian agreed. "And I accepted his offer—which only makes those who would already have been prepared to be disgusted feel that the honor of all Sothōii has been mortally affronted, as well. They just can't decide if they're more furious with me for the 'travesty' of my surrender or with Bahzell for the 'humiliation' of his acceptance of it!"

"With all due respect, Baron," Brandark said, nodding his thanks as he reached for the wine glass Hathan had filled for him, "I'd say let them feel as affronted as they want to feel as long as what you and Bahzell are up to manages to keep your people from one another's throats. And speaking purely for myself, of course, and admitting that it's remotely possible I might be slightly prejudiced, I happen to feel you did exactly the right thing, since any solution which left my personal head on my shoulders was a good one. Which, of course, only underscores the brilliance and wisdom of the people who arrived at it."

Several of the humans seated at the table chuckled, yet their laughter had a darker edge. Tellian's decision to "surrender" the unauthorized invasion force Mathian Redhelm had led down the Gullet to attack the city state of Hurgrum was the only thing which had prevented the massacre of the first hradani chapter of the Order of Tomanāk in Norfressan history. It had also prevented the sack of Hurgrum, the slaughter of innocent women and children, and quite probably a new and even bloodier war between Sothōii and hradani.

Unfortunately, not everyone—and not just on the Sothōii side—had been in favor of preventing all those things.

It's truly remarkable how frantically we all cling to our most treasured hatreds, Brandark thought. *And even though I would have said it was impossible, these Sothōii are even more bloody-minded about that than* hradani *are.*

"You may be prejudiced, Brandark," Tellian said in a more serious tone, "but that doesn't make you wrong. And at least the King seems prepared to go along with us for now."

"For now," Bahzell agreed.

"And while that's true, we need to make as much progress as we can," Tellian continued. "Perhaps we can actually manage to turn his acceptance into enthusiastic support."

"It's certainly to be hoped so," Bahzell said. "And Father is after agreeing with you. I passed on your message to him, and he says as how, if you're willing, he's thinking it might be best for him to be sending another score or so of his lads up the Gullet to fill out my 'guards.'" The towering hradani shrugged, and his foxlike ears twitched gently back and forth. "For myself, I'd sooner not have *any* guards."

"I've explained that before, Bahzell," Tellian half-sighed. "You may not be an *official* ambassador, but that's one of the roles you've got to play. And if you expect a batch of stiff-necked Sothōii to take you seriously as an ambassador, you'd better have a proper retinue."

"Aye, you've explained it, right enough," Bahzell agreed. "And seeing as how Father agrees with you, and he's after being one of the canniest men I've yet to meet, I'll not say you're wrong. But it's in my mind that if I was after being one of those of your folk as don't think this is just the very best idea anyone ever had, then I'd not like to see a jumped up barbarian like me bringing in any more swords to stand behind him."

"You'd need a lot more men than your father is talking about sending before you could pose any sort of credible threat to the Kingdom," Tellian pointed out. "Again, Bahzell. You've *got* to play the part properly, and having your father send you the guards your position demands isn't going to upset anyone who wasn't already prepared to be upset with us. So for Toragan's sake, stop worrying about it!"

Bahzell regarded his host thoughtfully across the table for several seconds, then shrugged. He still wasn't certain he agreed with Tellian, and he *was* certain he wanted to do nothing which might make the Sothōii baron's position any more precarious than he had to. But if Tellian, his father and mother, his sister Marglyth, and even Brandark were all in agreement, it was obviously time for him to close his mouth and accept their advice.

"Well, seeing as you're all so set on it, I'll say no more against it," he said mildly.

"Tomanāk preserve us!" Brandark exclaimed. "My ears must be deceiving me. I could swear I just heard *Bahzell Bahnakson* say something reasonable!"

"Just you keep it up, little man. I'm thinking it should make an impressive funeral."

Brandark twitched his ears impudently at his towering

friend, and another, louder chuckle ran around the table.

"If you keep threatening me," Brandark said warningly, "I'll have you trodden on. It won't be that hard, you know." He elevated his prominent nose with a disdainful sniff. "Dathgar and Gayrhalan both like *me* much more than they like you."

"Oh-ho!" Tellian laughed and shook his head. "That's a lower blow than that song of yours, Brandark! Coursers have memories as long as Sothōii and hradani combined!"

"I prefer to think of it not so much as a matter of remembered past grievances as a case of exquisite and refined present good taste," Brandark replied. Then he shrugged. "Of course, the fact that they've spent the better part of a thousand years thinking of Horse Stealers as their natural mortal enemies *might* play some small part in it, I suppose."

"Aye, that they have," Bahzell rumbled. "And, truth to tell, I'm thinking as how I don't blame them if it should happen as how they're wanting to carry a grudge. At least they've been civil enough."

The baron might have chosen to make a joke of it, but it hadn't always been a laughing matter. And for many Sothōii—and coursers—it still wasn't. The Horse Stealers' "traditional" taste for horseflesh had always been grossly exaggerated—by themselves, often enough. Their habit of eating warhorses killed in combat had been the product of their bitter, unrelenting hatred for the humans who'd sought their extermination when first the Sothōii came to the Wind Plain—a case of striking back at their enemies in the way they knew would hurt them worst. They'd never made a practice of slaughtering *live* warhorses for the pot, however. That particular charge had been the product of Sothōii demonization of their foes, because the Horse Stealers had been right about how they would react. The Sothōii had regarded it as proof of the hradani's subhuman, blood soaked barbarian status. For the *coursers*, however, it had been the equivalent of cannibalism. To the best of Bahzell's knowledge, there'd been only two cases of coursers themselves being eaten in the entire bloody history of his people's endless battles with the Sothōii, and the coursers knew that as well as he did. But as Tellian had just said, coursers had long memories. It was fortunate that they were at least a little less prone than humans or hradani to visit responsibility for the sins of the fathers upon the sons.

A *little* less prone, at any rate.

"Really?" Brandark glanced at him sidelong. "Are you saying you didn't really need that doublet Gayrhalan tore to shreds . . . while you were wearing it?"

"Well, as to that," Bahzell replied with a calmness he'd been very far from feeling on the day in question, "I'm thinking as how Gayrhalan was after being in a bad mood that day. And I'll ask you to be taking note of the fact that he never drew any blood at all, at all. If he'd been so minded, it's an arm I would have been losing, and not just a doublet."

"That really is true," Hathan agreed, and shook his head, grinning wryly at the memory of his companion's fractious mood. "And it was at least partly my fault, too. I was a bit clumsy with my hoof knife that morning."

"No, you weren't," Tellian snorted. "Gayrhalan flinched and tossed you halfway across the stable when that stupid warhorse stallion of Trianal's slammed into the other side of the wall. How you managed to avoid really gashing him is more than I'll ever know. And Dathgar happens to agree with me, however unscrupulously Gayrhalan may try to shuffle the blame off on to you, Wind Brother!"

"You may be right," Hathan acknowledged with a slow smile, then chuckled. "I may have known one or two coursers with tempers worse than Gayrhalan's, but I know I haven't known three of them. There's a reason for his name, you know."

He chuckled again, louder, and Bahzell grinned at him. "Gayrhalan" meant "Storm Souled" in the Sothōii tongue, and the courser seemed to feel an almost Brandark-like obligation to live up to the image it conjured.

"They do say that coursers become more like their riders, and wind riders become more like their coursers,"

Hathan continued, "and since Gayrhalan and I were both already a bit on the obnoxious side before we ever met—"

He shrugged, and the laughter was even louder this time.

"For all that, though," the wind rider continued after a moment, his tone at least marginally more serious, "he truly was just showing his temper, however ungracious of him it may have been."

"Oh, never fear, Hathan! There was never after being any least doubt in my mind on that score! It's battleaxes I've seen with blades less impressive than your outsized friend's teeth." Bahzell shook his head. "It was then and there that I was after making up my mind not to be calling on him—or on Dathgar, for that matter—without I'd been formally invited."

"How uncharacteristically wise of you," Brandark murmured in a mildly maliciously provocative voice.

Bahzell made a rude gesture at him, but the truth was that both Tellian's and Hathan's companions continued to regard all hradani, but especially all *Horse Stealer* hradani, with profound reservations. Given that a courser was one of the very few creatures on the face of the earth who could reduce a Horse Stealer to so much gory, trampled jelly, he was eminently prepared to give them as wide a berth as they desired for as long as they wanted it. However magnificent they might be, and however quickly hradani might heal, now that he'd finally seen them at close quarters, he preferred his bones unbroken.

"I've no doubt we've more than enough other matters to be discussing, Milord," he continued, returning his attention to Tellian. "Just for a beginning, Father says he and Kilthan have been talking over your notion of a three-way trade up the Escarpment, and he's of a mind to agree you've hit on an excellent idea. But I've a few matters that need doing for the Order, as well, and I've messages for Hurthang from Vaijon. Would it be that he and Kaeritha are somewhere about the place?"

"None of us expected you back before tomorrow," Hathan replied for the baron, "and the two of them went over to the temple this morning. They're not back yet, but we can certainly send word for them to return if it's urgent."

"Well, as to that," Bahzell said, pushing his chair back and coming to his feet, "I'm thinking there's no need to be rousting out one of your people to run messages. I need to be dropping by the temple myself, so if it's all the same to you, Milord," he nodded to Tellian, "I'll just be heading over that way."

"Oh! Excuse me, Prince Bahzell! I didn't see you."

"No harm done," Bahzell said mildly, setting the girl back on her feet. She'd emerged from the half-hidden arch with more speed than decorum, but his reflexes had been good enough to catch her before the actual impact that would have bounced her off her feet. Her maid came bustling down the stair behind her, then screeched to a halt as she saw her charge being set effortlessly upright by a pair of hands the size of small shovels.

The maid—Marthya, he thought her name was, if he recalled correctly—was obviously less than enthralled by the sight, but she didn't look especially surprised. Nor was Bahzell, really. One thing he'd discovered early on about his host's daughter was that she was utterly lacking in the sort of bored languor which appeared to be the current, carefully cultivated ideal of most aristocratic young Sothōii noblewomen. It might be too much to call her own accustomed pace headlong, but not by very much.

He smiled down at her—however tall she might be for a human child, she was barely even petite for a Horse Stealer girl—and restrained himself with some difficulty from patting her on the head. She wouldn't have appreciated it if he'd yielded to the temptation, he thought dryly.

Although she had her father's hair and height, she'd thankfully escaped Tellian's hawklike profile. At fourteen, she'd just emerged from the coltishly awkward stage, although there were moments—like this one—when she suffered temporary relapses. She had an insatiable curiosity to go along with an obviously keen mind, and she obviously found Brandark and Bahzell himself exotically intriguing, no doubt because they were the first hradani she'd actually met. He found the obvious intensity of her curiosity amusing, but he'd learned to take her questions seriously, despite the fact that someone her age would have remained firmly immured in the schoolroom, had she been one of his sisters. Leeana's mother and father, on the other hand, had long since begun her formal tutelage as their only heir. The shorter-lived humans often seemed to do things with breakneck speed compared to hradani. So he reminded himself once again that Leeana Bowmaster obviously didn't consider herself the barely-out-of-leading-strings child he saw when he looked at her.

The fact that she was as cute as a basketful of puppies didn't make it any easier for him to remember that she was—or at least thought she was—older than she looked to him. The . . . irritated looks she gave him when he forgot, however, did. So he supposed it was something of a wash.

"It's kind of you to be so understanding," she told him now. "But if I'd been watching where I was going, I would never have come bursting out of the gallery stair and run into you that way. So if no harm was done, it was only a matter of pure luck. Please don't mention to Mother that I did!" She rolled her green eyes. "She already thinks I have the deportment of a stable hand."

"Now, somehow I'm doubtful she'd be putting it quite that way," Bahzell said with a grin. "Not that she wouldn't be after having a few tart things to say, I'm sure. But she'll not hear about it from me, Milady."

"Thank you." She smiled up at him warmly. "And might I ask how your visit home went?" she continued.

"Better than I'd hoped, more ways than not," he replied, and shook his head in something very like bemusement. "Father and Mother are well enough, though I'd not have thought anyone could be as busy as they're after being at the moment."

"I'm not surprised," she said, and chuckled. "Just keeping up with all your sisters and brothers must be challenge enough without settling all the political problems your father's facing right now!"

"Aye, you've got that right enough," he agreed. "Still and all, they've had more than enough experience managing all of us; it's the rest of my folk keeping their hands full just now. My Da's a lot of details to be settling—and some of them ugly ones, too—but I'm thinking things are after beginning to quiet down a mite." He snorted. "Of course, it could be as how that's because there's after being so few left as feel like arguing the fine points with him. The crows have finished picking over Churnazh's head, and his son Chalak's after being so stupid not even the likes of Churnazh's hangers-on will be following him. Arsham's the only one of Churnazh's get with the brains to be coming in out of a thunderstorm, and they must have come from his mother, for they can't have been coming from his father! And the fact that he's bastard-born isn't so very big a thing to be holding against him in the succession amongst our folk. So now he's sworn fealty to Father as Prince of Navahk, the rest of the Bloody Swords are after lining up to do the same." He glanced at Brandark for a moment, his expression half-apologetic, and shrugged. "If I were being a betting man, which I'm not, I'd put my kormaks on the fighting being over for good and all at last."

Leeana cocked her head in thought. Most Sothōii might have considered Bahzell's response to her question a bit odd. Ladies—and especially gently born ones who were still little more than children—should be sheltered from the brutal realities of the difficult problems and solutions which faced rulers. Leeana, though, only weighed what he'd said carefully, then nodded. One thing about her which was not at all childlike, Bahzell thought, was her obviously deep interest in politics. Or her uncanny ability to grasp the ramifications of her father's current, convoluted political problems. For that matter, her grasp of the problems facing *Bahzell's* father was better than that quite a few hradani chieftains could claim.

"Do you think the fighting is over, too, Lord Brandark?" she asked softly after several seconds of consideration.

She looked at the shorter hradani, and Brandark gazed back at her for a long moment, his eyes more thoughtful than Bahzell's, then shrugged.

"Yes, I do, Milady," he said. "And while I won't go so far as to say I'm happy the Bloody Swords have had their feet systematically kicked out from under them by a bunch of loutish Horse Stealers, it's certainly not a bad thing if the fighting really is over." He grimaced. "We've been killing each other over one imagined insult or another for almost as long as the Horse Stealers and *your* people have been doing the same thing. As someone who once wanted to be a bard, I may regret the loss of all those glorious, ballad-inspiring episodes of mutual bloodletting and slaughter. As a historian, and someone who's seen the bloodletting in question firsthand, I'd just as soon settle for the ballads we already have. And all the gods know Bahzell's father is infinitely preferable to someone like Churnazh."

He kept his tone light, but his gaze was level, and she looked back at him for several heartbeats before she nodded.

"I can see that," she said. "It's funny, isn't it? All the songs and tales are full of high adventure, not what really happens in a war. And I've heard lots of songs about splendid victories and defiance even in defeat. But I don't think I've ever heard even one where the side that lost ends up admitting that it's better that they didn't win."

Bahzell's mobile ears cocked, and one eyebrow arched, but Brandark simply nodded, as if unsurprised by her observation.

"It's not an easy thing to do," he agreed. "And the bards who write songs suggesting that it's a good thing their own side got its backside kicked tend to find their audiences less than receptive. Unfortunately, that doesn't mean it isn't true sometimes, does it?"

"No, I don't suppose it does," she said, and looked back at Bahzell. "So from what you and Lord Brandark are saying, Prince Bahzell, it sounds as if you may find yourself an official ambassador for the King of the Hradani after all."

Bahzell's deep, rumbling chuckle could have been alarming if she hadn't heard it before and known what it was. She cocked her head at him, and he grinned.

"Now, that I won't be." He shook his head. "First, I've no least desire to be anyone's 'official ambassador.' Second, Milady, I've even less of a notion how to go about being one! And third, the one thing my Da's least likely ever to be calling himself is 'King of the Hradani.' "

"There I have to agree with Bahzell," Brandark agreed with a slightly less rumbling laugh of his own. "Prince Bahnak is many things, Milady, but one thing he's remarkably free of is anything resembling delusions of grandeur. Unlike Bahzell, he's also a very bright fellow. Which means he understands exactly how hard a bunch of hradani princes would find it to take anyone who called himself 'King of the Hradani' seriously. I have no idea what title he'll finally come up with, but I feel confident that it won't have the word 'king' in it anywhere."

"Perhaps not," she said. "But what he chooses to call himself won't change what he actually is, now will it?" Her tone was a bit tarter, and the green eyes gazing up at the two hradani were a bit harder.

"No, it won't," Brandark agreed. "Which is my real point, I suppose. Just as he's unlikely to rub his recent enemies' noses in their defeat by calling himself a king, he's not going to make your father's position even more difficult by asking him to *officially* accept a hradani ambassador at his court."

Leeana's eyes widened very briefly. Then they narrowed again, even more briefly, before she nodded.

"That does make sense," she said after a moment, and Brandark wondered if the girl realized how completely her thoughtful tone demolished her pretense of having "accidentally" collided with Bahzell. She stood there for a second or two, as if being certain she'd digested the information thoroughly, than shook herself and smiled at Bahzell again.

"Now I've compounded my carelessness in running into you by keeping you and Lord Brandark standing here nattering away," she apologized. "I seem to be going from triumph to triumph this afternoon, don't I?"

"In a manner of speaking, I suppose," he agreed. "Not but what Brandark and I haven't enjoyed the conversation."

"It's kind of you to say so, but I've detained both of you long enough. Marthya?" She looked over her shoulder at her maid and gathered up the older woman with her eyes. Then she gave Bahzell and Brandark a quick, abbreviated curtsy and whisked Marthya off down a connecting hallway.

Chapter Three

The herd stallion was magnificent.

He was coal black, but for a white star on his forehead, and his conformation was perfect. At just over twenty-one hands, he was huge for any horse, and looked even bigger than he actually was, with his still-shaggy coat of winter. But despite that, he was actually of less than average size for a courser stallion, and he lacked the heaviness of build which characterized any breed of horse which even approached his own, massive stature. Indeed, he looked almost exactly like a Sothōii warhorse, with the same powerful quarters, well-sloped shoulders, and deep girth, but for the fact that he was very nearly half again the size of any warhorse ever born. Yet for all his size and magnificent presence, he moved with a delicate precision and grace which had to be seen to be believed.

At the moment, however, that silken-gaited precision was in abeyance. He stood almost motionless on a slight rise, under gray skies and gauzy, drifting curtains of rainy wind, only his head stirring as he gazed out over his slowly moving herd. He ignored the rain, but his gaze was intent, and his ears shifted uneasily. It was still early spring here atop the Wind Plain, and the herd had only recently left its winter pastures. He ought to have been busy sorting out the myriad details of its transition back to full independence, but something else occupied his attention. He didn't know precisely what it was, but he knew it was a threat.

It shouldn't have been. There were very few creatures in the world which could—or would dare to—threaten a single Sothōii courser, much less an entire herd of them. Despite how lightly he moved, the herd stallion weighed over three thousand pounds, with blue-horn hooves the size of dinner plates. He was powerful enough to drop a direcat, or even one of the great white bears of the eternally frozen north, with one well-placed hoof, and unlike lesser breeds, he could place that hoof with human intelligence and forethought.

And he and his kind were equally well bred for flight, at need. For all their mass, they could move like the wind itself, and they could keep it up literally for hours on end. According to Sothōii legend, the coursers had been created by Toragan and Tomanāk themselves, gifted with the impossible speed and endurance to match their incomparable intelligence and courage. According to others—like Wencit of Rūm—they owed their existence to somewhat less divine intervention, yet that made them no less wondrous. They couldn't match the acceleration of the smaller warhorses, but they were (quite literally) magically agile, and their wizardry-modified ancestry let them sustain a pace no mere horse could equal for periods which would have killed that same horse in short order. The only things they lacked were hands and the gift of speech, and those the Sothōii were honored to provide.

The stallion's herd (or most of it, at any rate) had spent the hard, snowy months of winter as guests at the Warm Springs stud farm. Lord Edinghas of Warm Springs was one of Baron Tellian's vassals, and the Warm Springs courser herd had been wintering with his family for generations. Although no Sothōii would ever mistake a courser for a horse, many of a courser's needs matched those of lesser breeds. They could have survived the winter on their own, though they would undoubtedly have lost some of their foals, but the grain and shelter provided by their human friends had brought the entire herd through without a single loss. Now it was time they returned to their summer range.

Under normal circumstances, they would have been accompanied by at least one wind rider, one of the humans who had formed a bond with a particular courser. It was hard to say whether the courser half of such a bond became half human, or its rider became half courser, and it didn't matter which it was. Every spring, wind riders and their coursers returned to the farms and pastures where courser herds had wintered to escort them to their summer ranges. No Sothōii would have dreamed of impeding those yearly migrations, but there were still times when it helped immensely to have a wind rider along to provide the human voice the herd stallions could not.

But this spring, the herd had been impatient, because three of their younger stallions and two youthful mares had elected to remain behind over the winter months. The herd stallion had been opposed, but courser herds weren't like those of normal horses. Courser herd stallions didn't win their positions simply by being stronger and faster and thrashing all competitors, and those stallions who never rose to lead the herd seldom left because they hadn't. Coursers were too intelligent, their society too sophisticated and intricate, for that. Herd stallions couldn't rely on their ability to defeat challengers—they had to be able to convince the rest of the herd to accept their wisdom. And the other stallions were too valuable to the herd, for their minds, as well as their strength and courage, to simply wander or be driven away. Besides, unlike horses, coursers mated for life, and mated pairs normally remained with the mare's herd.

But there were times this herd stallion wished his kind were just a little more like the smaller, frailer horses from which they had been bred so long ago. He would have preferred nothing more than to have been able to drive his quintet of stay-behinds into accompanying the rest of the herd last autumn with a display of bared teeth and flattened ears, or possibly a few sharp, disciplinary nips. Unfortunately, such simple and direct remedies had been denied him.

He remained unable to understand what had inspired the others to stay behind. Occasionally—*very* occasionally—bachelor stallions might choose to remain on the open range for at least part of a winter. It was unheard of for a *group* to linger there, though, and none of the truants had been able to explain their reasoning. It was simply something they'd felt they *had* to do. Which (unfortunately, from the herd stallion's perspective) was a perfectly adequate explanation for almost anything a courser might choose to do. The herd stallion understood that the Races of Man found that frustrating and perplexing, but he couldn't really understand *why* they did, because coursers didn't belong to the Races of Man. Their minds worked differently. For all of the countless things which set them apart from ordinary horses, they were herd-oriented in a way none of the Races of Man was prepared to understand, and they trusted and followed their instincts in a way very few of the Races of Man, with their fixed habitations, were prepared to accept.

Still, the herd stallion had remained uneasy all winter, fretting about the safety of those who had been left behind and wondering what could possibly have possessed them to stay. Nor was he alone in that. Whatever their motivations, the five absentees were members of the herd, and their absence left an aching, uncomfortable void. The other coursers *missed* them, and the pressure to make an early start back to their range, whether or not a wind rider was available to go with them, had been overpowering.

But now . . .

The herd stallion stamped one rear hoof on the soggy grass, and his nostrils flared. The sense of threat grew stronger, and he threw up his head with a high, shrill whistle. The herd slowed, and other heads rose, looking back in his direction. The other stallions, and the childless mares, drifted towards the outer edges of the herd, prepared to place themselves between the foals and nursing mares and any potential threat. Thoughts flickered back and forth, in flashing patterns and without anything any member of any Race of Man—except, perhaps, those telepathic magi gifted with the ability to communicate with animals—would have recognized as words.

The herd stallion's uneasiness communicated itself to the rest of the herd, and every head turned, facing into the fine, misty billows of rain sweeping down out of the northeast. There was nothing to scent, nothing to see, yet those same instincts the coursers trusted so implicitly warned more strongly than ever of approaching threat.

And then, with the suddenness of a lightning bolt forged of arctic fury, the steady wind which had pushed rain into the herd's faces all morning turned into a shrieking hurricane, and the misty raindrops turned into stinging, biting darts of ice. The herd stallion reared, trumpeting his challenge as the vile smell of something long dead swept over him on the teeth of the howling wind. He heard other shrill screams of outrage and defiance, yet he knew the true threat wasn't the wind, or the ice. It was whatever came *behind* the wind. Whatever drove the wind before it like the outrider of its fury . . . and its hunger.

The herd stallion galloped down from the hillock on which he had stood. He thundered into the teeth of the wind, mane and tail streaming magnificently behind him, mud and spray exploding under the war hammer beat of his hooves. The herd's other stallions fell into formation with him, converging from every direction to follow him in an earth-shaking drumbeat of hooves. Courser mares were among the deadliest creatures in Norfressa, but even so, they were smaller and lighter than the males of their species. And coursers were less fertile than horses. Potential mothers were not to be lightly risked, and so the childless mares closed up behind the stallions, forming the inner line of defense for the herd, rather than charging to meet the threat with them.

The stallions slowed their headlong pace as they spread out into battle formation, each making certain he had the space he needed to fight effectively, yet stayed close enough to his companions to cover one another's flanks. The herd stallion didn't need to look back to check their positioning. Unlike horses, coursers relied as much on training as instinct at times like this, and his stallions were a well-drilled, disciplined team. They knew exactly where they were supposed to be, and he knew they did. Besides, one of the things which *made* him herd stallion was the inborn ability to know the precise location of every member of his herd, and despite the instinct-driven fury pounding through him and the terrifying unnaturalness of the sudden, shrieking wind, he felt the confidence of the herd's defenders. And his own. His was not the largest of the courser herds, by any stretch of the imagination, yet there were seventeen stallions behind him, prepared to trample any possible enemies into the Wind Plain's mud in broken ruin.

But then he threw up his head again, eyes flaring wide as that same ability to place the members of his herd shrieked in warning horror.

Screaming whistles of anger and confusion rose behind him, audible even above the howling wind, as the rest of the herd tasted his confusion and revulsion through the intricately fused net of their minds. It was impossible. He couldn't be sensing the members of his own herd who had remained behind—not as the threat beyond the barrier of the icy gale!

Yet he did. And he sensed something else with them, some transcendent horror. It had no name, yet it rode them more cruelly than any spur or whip, for it was part of them. Or they had become part of *it*.

They were dead, he realized. And yet they weren't. He reached out to them, despite his revulsion, but nothing answered. The stallions and mares he had known, watched grow from foals, were no more, yet some splinter of them—some tortured, broken and defiled fragment—remained. It was part of whatever hid behind the wind, sweeping down upon the rest of his herd.

It was . . . recognition. It was the diametric opposite of his own sense of the herd, for his was the sense of a leader, a shepherd and protector, but this was the sense of a predator. A hunter. It was as if the monstrous danger hidden in the hurricane had devoured those he had known and taken their herd sense, their existence as part of the corporate whole, to use as a hound master might use a human's discarded clothing to give his hounds the scent of his prey.

And then the icy clouds of frozen rain pellets parted, and the herd stallion faced a horror which daunted even his mighty heart.

The plain before him was alive. Not with grass, or trees, but with wolves. A huge, seething sea of wolves. Not one or two, or a dozen, but *scores* of them, all of them racing towards his herd in a deadly, profoundly unnatural silence.

No wolf was foolish enough to attack a courser, and no pack of wolves was sufficiently insane to attack a herd of them. They didn't even take down foals who'd strayed, or the sick or the lame, because they'd learned over the centuries that the rest of the herd could and would hunt them down and trample them into ruin.

But this onrushing comber of wolves was unlike anything any courser had ever seen, and that stench of long-ago death clung to them like a curse from an open grave. Eyes blazed with a sickly, crawling green fire; green venom dripped from the fangs bared by their silent, savage snarls; and no wolf pack born of nature had ever been so vast. The herd stallion shook off the momentary paralysis of that incredible sight, rallying the rest of the stallions, who had been just as stunned and shaken as he, and they charged to meet the threat.

The herd stallion reared, bringing his hooves down like flails, and a sound came from the wolves at last—a shriek of hatred-cored agony as he smashed a wolf the size of a small cart pony into splintered bone and torn flesh. His head darted down, and teeth like cleavers, despite his herbivorous diet, bit deep. He caught the second wolf just behind its shoulders, crushing its spine, and gagged at the taste of something which was both dead and alive at once. He snapped his head around, worrying it as a normal wolf might worry a rabbit, until even its unnatural vitality failed, and then threw it from him with a final flip of his head. He sensed another wolf, flowing around him, coming from behind in the ancient hamstringing attack of its kind, and a rear hoof smashed out, catching it on its way in. It flew away from him, dead or crippled—it mattered not which—and he trumpeted his war cry as pounding hooves and tearing teeth harvested his enemies.

Yet there were too many of them. No one of them, no two, or even three, could have been a threat to him. But they came not in twos or threes—they came in *dozens*, all larger than any natural wolf, and all with that same uncanny, not-dead vitality. However many he crippled, however many he killed—assuming that he truly was killing them—there were always more behind them. They swept down on his stallions like a sea crashing against a cliff, but this sea was alive. It knew to look for weaknesses and exploit them, and coursers needed space to fight effectively. Even their closest formation offered openings wolves could wedge their way into, and the herd stallion could not avoid the fangs of them all.

He heard one of his stallions scream in agony as a wolf got beneath him, fastening its teeth in the other courser's belly. Other wolves swarmed over the wounded stallion, ripping and tearing while their companion's grim grip crippled and hampered him, and he screamed again as they dragged him down into the sea of teeth waiting to devour him while he shrieked and thrashed in his death agony.

Other teeth scored the herd stallion's right foreleg, just above the chestnut, and he screamed in anguish of his own. It wasn't just the white bone of fangs rending his flesh. That green venom seared like fire, filling his veins with an ice-cold blaze of anguish. He rose, exposing his own belly dangerously, and arched his spine to bring both forehooves smashing down on the wolf who'd bitten him. He crushed it into tattered hide and broken bones, but that shattered body continued to twitch and jerk. Even as he turned to another foe, the broken wolf continued to move, and its movements were becoming stronger, more purposeful. Slow and clumsy compared to its original lethal speed, yet lurching its way back upright. It staggered towards him, broken bone flowing back into wholeness, hide recovering muscle and sinew, and he lashed out again. He smashed it yet again, and even as he did, another hurled itself through the air, springing up onto his back, despite his height, to bite viciously at his neck.

His attacker got a mouthful of mane, and before it could try again, the stallion covering his right side leaned over the herd stallion's withers. Jaws like axes crunched down on the wolf, tearing it away . . . and two more wolves seized the moment of the second stallion's distraction to tear out his throat in a steaming geyser of blood.

He went down, and the herd stallion smashed his killers, but it wasn't enough. The wolves paid an extortionate price—one no natural pack of wolves would ever have paid—for every courser they dragged down. But it was a price *these* creatures were willing to pay, and the snarling tide of possessed wolves swept forward as inexorably as any glacier.

He should have fled, not stood to fight, he thought as he turned two more wolves into bags of broken bones and a third opened another bleeding wound just above his left stifle. But he hadn't known then. Hadn't suspected the true nature of the threat he faced. And because he hadn't, he and all of the other stallions were doomed. But he might still save the rest of the herd.

The order flashed out from him even as he continued to kick and tear at the endless waves, and the herd obeyed. Mares with foals turned and ran, while the childless mares formed a rearguard, and the remaining stallions prepared to cover their retreat.

Not one of them tried to escape. They stood their ground in a holocaust of blood and terror and death, building a breastwork of broken, crushed wolf bodies that died and yet refused to become—quite—dead. They fought like hoofed demons to defend their mates and children, shrieking and thundering their rage until the inevitable moment when their own bodies joined the wreckage.

The herd stallion was one of the last to die.

He had become a thing of horror, a slashed and bleeding ruin of his beauty and grace. Bone showed in the deepest wounds, and venom pulsed through his body on the broken stutter of his pulse. The remaining wolves closed in upon him, and he made himself turn in a staggering heave to face them. He dimly sensed still more of them sweeping past him, and even through his agony and exhaustion, he felt a fresh, dull horror as more of the "dead" lurched back to their feet and staggered grotesquely by him. They were slow and clumsy, those wolfish revenants, but they joined the others of their cursed kind, flowing around him like a river flowing around a lump of stone, and a fresh and different horror choked him as he saw the missing members of his own herd loom out of the rain.

They moved like puppets with tangled strings, following the wolves—*with* the wolves—and their eyes blazed with the same green sickness, and fiery green froth hung from their jaws. They ignored him, moving past him with the wolves, and torment filled him as his fading herd sense felt the agonized death of the first of his childless mares. The wolves he and the other stallions had "slain" were too crippled, too clumsy, despite their resurrection, to overtake the herd . . . but their undamaged fellows were another matter entirely. Sorrow and grief twisted him with the despairing knowledge that not even the fabled speed and endurance of the coursers would save many of the herd's foals from the unnatural wave of death racing after them like the tide across a mud bank.

The wolves he still faced came at him. He had no idea how many of them there were. It didn't matter. He brought a leaden forehoof down one last time, crushing one more wolf, crippling one more foe who would not murder one of his foals.

And then they foamed over him in a final wave of rending, tearing agony, and there was only darkness.

Chapter Four

"It's about time you were getting your lazy arse back up here."

"And it's a pleasure to be seeing *you*, too, Hurthang," Bahzell said mildly. He wiggled his ears gently at his cousin—one of the very few warriors, even among the Horse Stealers, who was almost as massive and powerfully built as Bahzell himself—and grinned impudently.

"All very well for you to be playing the japester . . . as usual," Hurthang growled as he threw his arms around Bahzell in a kinsman's embrace and thumped him on both shoulders. "But this time round, I'm thinking the midden's getting just a bit riper than any of us might be wishing. If you'd not turned up today or tomorrow, I'd've been shoveling the sh—ah, dealing with it myself."

His voice and manner were both serious, despite his obvious pleasure at seeing his cousin again. He gave Bahzell's shoulders another slap, then stood back and nodded a welcome to Brandark.

"He wanted to start shoveling it yesterday," a soprano voice observed tartly. "So thank Tomanāk you did get back! He's not any more, um, sophisticated than you are, Bahzell, and he's even harder to keep on a leash."

Bahzell turned towards the speaker, a young woman, a human in her very early thirties, with hair so black it was almost blue, sapphire-dark eyes, and a pronounced Axeman accent. She wore matched short swords, one on either hip, her slender hands were strong and callused from their hilts, and her quarterstaff leaned against the pew beside her. Even without the old scars which marked her face (without making it one bit less attractive) it would have been obvious she was a warrior, and one to be reckoned with. She was also tall for a woman, especially one from the Empire of the Axe . . . which meant that the top of her head came almost as high as Bahzell's chest.

"Not that he's necessarily wrong just because he's a simple, direct barbarian," she continued. "As a matter of fact, *I'm* a bit worried, too. But I hope you'll be just a little more careful about local sensibilities this time around." Bahzell looked at her with profound innocence, and she shook her head sternly. "Don't show *me* those puppy-dog eyes, Milord Champion! I've heard all about your enlightened techniques for dealing with Navahkan crown princes, Purple Lord landlords, and scholars in Derm! Or Riverside thugs, for that matter, Bahzell *Bloody-Hand*." She rolled her eyes. "And Hurthang is another chip off exactly the same block. Both of you still think any social or political problems should be solved by hitting them over the head with rocks until they stop twitching."

"We do, do we, Kerry?" Bahzell snorted, reaching out to hug her in turn. Dame Kaeritha Seldansdaughter was broad shouldered and well muscled, yet she seemed to disappear in his embrace. Not that it had any noticeable effect on the tartness of her tongue.

"Yes, you do. In fact, both of you favor *dull* rocks," she shot back.

"Well, that's because we'd most likely be cutting our own fingers off if we were after using sharp ones," he replied cheerfully as he released her.

"You two probably would," she conceded, reaching past him to exchange clasped forearms with Brandark. "Still," she continued more seriously, "I agree with Hurthang. Things are developing a definite potential for turning ugly."

"They've been that way from the beginning, Kerry," Brandark pointed out.

"Of course they have. But in the last few days, it's started to seem that all our lads have targets painted on their backs," Kaeritha replied.

"All our lads?" Bahzell repeated, and she nodded.

"All of them," she said more grimly. "Gurlahn's been keeping most of your father's people fairly close to home up in the castle, but there have been some incidents with them, even so. And it's been worse for Hurthang's men."

"There's been trouble with the Order?" Bahzell turned back to Hurthang, his expression concerned, and Hurthang grimaced.

"Not yet—not open trouble, that's to say," he said. "Truth to tell, Bahzell, I'd as lief follow Gurlahn's example and clap 'em all up here in the temple, but—"

He shrugged, and Bahzell nodded in understanding. Hurthang was the official commander of the detachment from the Hurgrum Order of Tomanāk which had come along to Balthar to establish formal communion with the Church of Tomanāk outside the hradani homeland. Although both Bahzell and Kaeritha, as champions of Tomanāk, technically outranked him, Hurthang was the senior member of the Hurgrum chapter present and the one officially in charge of regularizing its relationship with the Church at large.

Fortunately, Taraman Wararrow, the senior priest of Tomanāk in Balthar, had proved a broad-minded sort of fellow. He'd actually taken the arrival of a clutch of bloodthirsty Horse Stealer hradani claiming to be servants of the War God in stride. And he'd managed to convince Sir Markhalt Ravencaw, the commander of the small detachment of the Order's knights and lay brothers assigned to the Balthar temple, to go along with him, as well.

The Order wasn't as well represented in the Kingdom of the Sothōii as it was in the Empire of the Axe or the Empire of the Spear. It was respected, of course. Indeed, the King's younger brother, Prince Yurokhas, was an outspoken member of the Order, and the temples of

Tomanāk were usually well attended. But the Order itself maintained only two official chapters in the entire Kingdom: one in Sōthōfalas, King Markhos' capital, and one in Nachfalas, where its members could keep an eye on the Ghoul Moor and the river brigands. Those two chapters maintained detachments on semipermanent assignment to the temples in most of the Sothōii's cities and larger towns, but the bulk of their manpower remained concentrated in their home chapter houses. Which meant that the eighteen members of the Hurgrum Chapter who had accompanied Bahzell, Kaeritha, and Hurthang to Balthar actually outnumbered Sir Markhalt's detachment.

Markhalt and Father Taraman might have taken the Horse Stealers' arrival in stride, after the first inevitable moments of eye-goggling shock. One or two members of Markhalt's detachment had found the situation much more difficult to accept, however. And if the members of the Order itself had qualms, it was scarcely surprising that Sothōii who were not members of the Order (and did remember the better part of a millennium of mutual hradani-Sothōii slaughter), had profound reservations about the entire notion.

But despite that, the situation had seemed to be under control when Bahzell and Brandark returned to Hurgrum for their brief visit with Prince Bahnak. If it hadn't seemed that way, Bahzell would never have gone.

"How bad is it?" he asked now.

"Mostly naught but words, although I'll not deny some of 'em have been uglier than I'd've stomached without blood if I'd only myself to be thinking of. But it's in my mind that at least some of them as've been flinging those words about are hopeful some of our lads will slip into the Rage if they goad 'em hard enough."

"That would be just a bit hard on whoever provoked them into it," Brandark observed in a tone whose mildness fooled no one.

"True," Kaeritha agreed. "But I think Hurthang is right. And I've noticed that when the hecklers are at their most provocative, there's usually a crowd around." Bahzell cocked his ears at her, and she shrugged. "They may actually be foolish enough to think that a dozen or so friends would be enough to save them from a hradani in the Rage."

"Maybe some folk would be," Bahzell snorted, "but these people are after knowing hradani better than most. I'm thinking as how it would take a mighty stupid Sothōii to be making that particular mistake."

"And has it been your observation that most blind, pigheaded, dyed-in-the-wool bigots *aren't* stupid?" Kaeritha inquired.

"Not to mention easy to manipulate," Brandark added, and Bahzell nodded unhappily.

"Aye, there's truth enough in that," he conceded. "I'd sooner be able to say there wasn't, but wishing won't make it so." He shook his head. "I've a nasty feeling there's more than one set of manipulators in it, too."

"Likely enough," Kaeritha agreed. "And I doubt it's going to get much better anytime soon."

"Well, at least we're not after having Gharnal to worry about," Hurthang said with a grimace.

"Ah, well, as to that . . ." Bahzell allowed his voice to trail off, and Hurthang looked at him with sudden sharp suspicion.

"Aye?" he prompted ominously as Bahzell's pause stretched out.

"Well, it's just that I've a message for you from Vaijon," Bahzell said, and Hurthang's suspicious eye narrowed.

Sir Vaijon of Almerhas was the youthful knight who'd been assigned to the Belhadan chapter of the Order of Tomanāk when Bahzell arrived there. His anti-hradani prejudices had been so hugely offended by the idea of a hradani champion of Tomanāk that he'd found himself facing Bahzell in trial by combat. He'd entered the combat arrogantly certain of victory only to emerge astonished by his own survival, and somehow the youngster had ended up not only a champion of Tomanāk himself, but the sword brother Bahzell had left behind to oversee the organization of the hradani branch of the Order.

"And just what might it be that Vaijon's after telling me?" Hurthang demanded.

"As to that, most of it's after being routine enough," Bahzell said in a reassuring tone. "He says as how Father's deeded another manor to the Order, at Tharkhul, up on the Hangnysti. And he's been after making progress getting the new Bloody Swords settled in amongst us nasty Horse Stealers. And—"

"And something about Gharnal, I'm thinking?" Hurthang rumbled.

"Well, aye," Bahzell agreed with a slow smile. "There *was* after being something about him."

"Then you'd best be spitting it out while I'm still remembering you're after being a champion and all so I'm not supposed to be thumping your head for you," Hurthang told him grimly.

"It's naught to be worrying about at all, at all," Bahzell said soothingly. "Naught but a little matter of a reassignment, as you might be saying."

"Bahzell!" It was Kaeritha, with a twinkle in her eye. "You're not saying that Vaijon is assigning *Gharnal* to Hurthang?"

"Aye," Bahzell said, with an expression of consummate innocence. "And why shouldn't he be?"

"*Gharnal?*" Hurthang stared at him, then shook his head. Gharnal, Bahzell's foster brother, possessed many good qualities, however . . .

"Bahzell," Kaeritha said for Hurthang, "Gharnal isn't exactly, um . . . how shall I say this? Not exactly the most *tactful* member of the Order. In fact, he's the only person I know who makes you and Hurthang look like effete, overcivilized diplomats. What in the world is Vaijon thinking of?"

"As to that, I'm not so very sure," Bahzell acknowledged. "It was after being Gharnal's very own idea, but Vaijon says as how it 'felt' right when he asked. As to why Gharnal might be wanting to be sent into such as this, I've no least idea what maggot's invaded his brain, and no more does he, as far as I can be telling. But let's us be honest here, Hurthang. Vaijon's been after making less mistakes with the Order than you or I most likely would, so I'm thinking we'd best not quibble here." He flicked his ears and shrugged. "It just might be as how himself is after poking a finger back into the pie. Any road, he'll be arriving tomorrow morning, so we'd best be battening down."

"You think Tomanāk Himself might want Gharnal up here among all these hradani-hating Sothōii?" Clearly, despite her own champion's status, Kaeritha found the possibility difficult to accept.

"And why not?" Bahzell grinned wryly. "It's not as if we've not had proof enough of himself's sense of humor, Kerry! After all, look where *Vaijon* was after ending up!"

"Um." Kaeritha closed her mouth on a fresh objection, then nodded. "You're right," she said after a moment. "If He can send Vaijon of Almerhas to Hurgrum, then there's no reason He couldn't send Gharnal here . . . even if the mere thought of it does send a chill down my spine. On the other hand, I'm afraid that even adding Gharnal to the mess isn't going to make it a lot worse. In fact—"

"Milord Champion!"

Bahzell turned towards the raised voice that wasn't quite a shout, although it seemed like one in the temple's quiet precincts.

Brother Relath, one of Father Taraman's acolytes, hurried up the temple nave towards them, his youthful face screwed up in an expression of deep concern . . . or something worse.

"Milord Champion!" he repeated as he slid to a halt before Bahzell, panting slightly. "Come quickly! There's trouble!"

Relath, Bahzell thought sourly when he reached the temple doors, had a distinct gift for understatement.

Thalgahr Rarikson—one of the Horse Stealer warriors his father had assigned to his official bodyguard, rather than a member of the Hurgrum Order—had accompanied him to the temple as the "official" bodyguard Sothōii protocol demanded of any ambassador, be he ever so unofficial. Like most hradani, Thalgahr had little enough use for any god—of Light or Dark—and so, however much he might respect Tomanāk, he'd chosen to stay outside, sheltering from the misting rain under the portico which protected the temple's main entrance.

Prince Bahnak had handpicked the members of Bahzell's guard. He was perfectly well aware of how delicate a balancing act Bahzell confronted, and he also knew how assiduously Sothōii who disapproved of Tellian's initiative would attempt to provoke incidents designed to joggle Bahzell's elbow. Which was why he'd chosen men whose discipline and ability to control their tempers he could trust.

The men he'd selected had regarded their inclusion among Bahzell's guardsmen as a high honor, proof of their chieftain's confidence in both their loyalty and their capacity to resist the inevitable provocations. At the moment, however, Thalgahr looked as if he was regretting the fact that his Prince's eye had fallen upon him for this duty.

Bahzell swallowed a curse as he took in the tableau. Thalgahr stood with his back to the temple wall, and the set of his shoulders under his chain hauberk suggested that he'd put it there to keep daggers out of it. His right hand was carefully away from his sword hilt, but the way his wrist was cocked told Bahzell he was ready to draw steel instantly. Worse, the half-flattened ears and the fire burning at the backs of his eyes told any hradani that Thalgahr was fighting a bitter battle to restrain the Rage, the berserker curse of his people.

". . . back where your kind belong, you murdering, thieving bastard—away from *civilized* people!" someone shouted from the damp crowd of Sothōii which had assembled itself on the brightly colored pavement as if by magic in the brief time Bahzell had been inside the temple. It was still a crowd, not yet anything which might have been called a mob, but Bahzell felt it hovering on the brink and realized it could go either way with no more warning than an avalanche in snow country. Worse, several of its members seemed more than a little sympathetic to the taunts and vituperation the heckler was spouting.

Thalgahr said nothing in response to the human's invective, but his ears flattened still further.

"Yes!" someone else shouted. "We've had a bellyful of you raping, horse-stealing—horse-*killing*—bastards! Are you really stupid enough to think you can fool us by pretending you're not the sneaking, backstabbing cowards your kind have always been, *hradani*?"

There were more than a few mutters of agreement from the crowd, this time, but Bahzell's eyes narrowed with more than simple anger as they found the two bravos who were doing all the shouting. The pair of hecklers were obviously working as a team, and both of them were better equipped than a typical street tough. They wore traditional Sothōii steel cuirasses, but they wore them over chain hauberks, not the usual boiled leather of the Sothōii cavalryman, and their swords were of excellent, dwarvish work. The straps which ought to have been buttoned across the quillons of those swords to keep them in their sheaths had been unbuttoned, as well, and though they tried to hide it from casual observers, their own expressions and body language were those of men poised on the brink of violence.

"I say the only *good* hradani is one lying in a ditch with his throat slit and his balls in his cold, dead hand! What d'you think of *that*, hradani?" the first heckler sneered, and Bahzell took one stride towards the broad steps leading up to the temple from the roadway below. Then he stopped as a strong, slender hand gripped his elbow.

"If you get involved in this," Kaeritha said to him, too quietly for anyone else to hear through the fresh round of taunting obscenities being flung at Thalgahr, "you give them exactly what they want. And the same goes for Hurthang and Brandark."

"And if I'm *not* after getting 'involved,'" he growled back, "Thalgahr will be flashing over into the Rage and carving those two idiots into short ribs and roasts in about one more minute."

"They're trying to make this a matter of human-versus-hradani," she told him, hanging onto his elbow with steely fingers. "You can't afford to play their game for them. Let *me* handle it."

Bahzell began an immediate, instinctive protest. Not because he doubted her capability, but because Thalgahr was one of Prince Bahnak's troopers, not a member of Tomanāk's Order, and he wanted to keep Kaeritha out of a mess which didn't concern her. He opened his mouth, but the glint in her sapphire eyes closed it again with a click.

"Better, Sword Brother," she told him as she released her grip on his elbow and turned it into an approving pat. "How *wise* of you not to insult me by suggesting that my brother's problems aren't mine."

He glowered at her, and she strolled past him with a chuckle, carrying her quarterstaff in her left hand.

Thalgahr never noticed her presence until she'd stepped past him, but the two hecklers were another matter. One of them nudged the other, pointing at her with his chin, and their suddenly wary expressions said that they knew exactly who she was.

"Excuse me, gentlemen," she said mildly into the sudden silence. "I'm sure you wouldn't want anyone to doubt your respect for Tomanāk, but perhaps you hadn't realized that creating this sort of an uproar on the steps of His house isn't exactly polite."

"I'm a free Sothōii subject," one of the hecklers shot back. "I've the right to speak my mind anywhere!"

"Of course you do," she said soothingly, and gripped her staff in both hands so that she could round her shoulders and lean her weight on it. Her posture was eloquently nonthreatening, and she smiled. "I'm simply suggesting that this isn't the best possible place for this, um, conversation."

"And who are you to suggest anything to *us*?" The spokesman for the pair spat on the paving. "Some kind of hradani-lover? What—you couldn't find a *human* to keep you warm at night?"

One or two onlookers shifted uneasily at the last remark. Kaeritha had drawn almost as much attention in Balthar as Bahzell himself. Sothōii minds seemed to have a great deal of trouble wrapping themselves about the concept of any female knight, much less one who was acknowledged as a champion of Tomanāk *Him*self. But however *outre* or even disgraceful they might find the notion, all of the gossip her arrival had generated at least guaranteed that everyone in that crowd knew precisely who she was. And it would seem that even some of those who approved of hradani-baiting were less prepared to publicly insult a woman . . . and a champion.

"You seem to make a habit of leaping to conclusions, friend," Kaeritha said mildly into the sudden hush. "First you assume humans are somehow better than hradani, and then you compound your initial error by making all sorts of unfounded assumptions about me." She shook her head. "Personally, I think you should be devoting at least a little thought to all of the trouble that sort of impetuosity could end up dropping you into."

"Trouble?" the man laughed scornfully. "Oh, I know who you are now. You're that what's-her-name—Kaeritha, wasn't it? The woman who *claims* to be a knight? *A champion of Tomanāk?* Hah! That's almost as funny as claiming *he* is!"

A contemptuous thumb jerked in Bahzell's direction, and the hradani's eyes narrowed further. They were getting to the nub of it now, he realized, and he suddenly wondered if his own initial assumption had been in error. Was it possible these two actually were operating on their own? The anger in the heckler's voice and face seemed completely genuine, with a degree of passion Bahzell wouldn't have expected to see in the average paid provocateur. And the gods knew there were more than enough humans, and not simply among the Sothōii, who considered themselves true followers of Tomanāk and would still find the very suggestion that the War God might welcome hradani followers rankest blasphemy. Adding that view to the traditional Sothōii antipathy for women warriors could easily produce a blind, driving anger.

Not, he reminded himself, that the fact that they truly were angry meant that they weren't working with—or for—someone else entirely. As Brandark had said, bigots' hatred only made them even easier to manipulate.

"Friend," Kaeritha's tone was still mild, but her eyes were hard, "I don't believe Tomanāk would be particularly pleased by all this shouting and carrying on outside His front door. If you have some sort of problem with me and you'd care to discuss it calmly and in private, like a sensible person, I'm at your disposal. But I'd really appreciate it if you'd stop making such a public nuisance of yourself in front of His temple. In fact, I'm going to have to insist that you do. Now."

" 'Public nuisance' is it?" The heckler pushed closer to her, standing no more than four or five feet away as he looked her up and down, head to toe, with an elaborate sneer. "Better than standing here in His colors like a public whore trying to pretend she's some kind of noblewoman, *I* say!"

The silence behind him was suddenly profound. Even his partner seemed taken aback by his last sentence. However unhappy the average Sothōii might be over the thought of a female champion, he would never have dreamed of addressing such language to a woman of rank in public. The second heckler looked as if he would cheerfully have strangled his friend, but it was too late to disassociate himself from him now.

"There you go, making more of those assumptions," Kaeritha said into the quiet, in a tone compounded of equal parts weariness and resignation. She shook her head. "Me, some kind of noblewoman?" She snorted and thumped the iron-shod heel of her upright quarterstaff lightly on a paving stone. "What sort of 'noblewoman' carries one of *these*?"

She chuckled, and the heckler's expression abruptly acquired an edge of perplexity. Clearly, her reaction was unlike anything he'd anticipated.

"No," she continued, sliding one hand thoughtfully along the staff's use-polished shaft. "I was born a peasant, friend." She shrugged. "There's no point trying to pretend otherwise, and truth to tell, I don't see any reason I ought to. One thing about Tomanāk, He doesn't seem to mind where His followers come from. The Order made me a knight, and He made me a champion, but nobody ever made me a noblewoman. Which is unfortunate for you, I'm afraid."

She smiled thinly at him, and he frowned back uncertainly, obviously confused about where she was headed.

"You see," she explained to him calmly, "if I were a *noblewoman*, I'd probably be all upset and flustered by all those nasty things you said about me. Noblewomen don't approve of public brawls or shouting matches, so I wouldn't have the least idea what to do about them, or how to respond to your rudeness. But if you say things like that to a peasant, she doesn't get upset. No," Kaeritha shook her head again, "she just gets *even*."

He was still frowning at her in confusion when she took one precise step forward, the quarterstaff snapped up, and its iron end cap smashed down on the arch of his right foot in a vicious, vertical blow any piledriver might have envied.

Kaeritha Seldansdaughter might be short compared to a hradani, but she was quite tall—and very, very strong—for a human woman, and the heckler let out an unearthly screech as she brought the staff crunching down with both hands. The soft leather upper of his boot offered no protection against such a blow, and the sound it made was remarkably like the one produced by crushing a wicker basket with a hammer.

Despite himself, Bahzell winced in sympathy, but Kaeritha's expression didn't even flicker as her victim jerked his wounded foot up where he could clasp it in both hands. He hopped on his other foot, howling in precariously balanced anguish, and she whipped the lower end of the staff up in a perfectly timed and placed blow to his left knee. Administered with even the slightest error, that stroke could have crippled her victim for life, but Bahzell had watched Kaeritha working out with her staff too often to worry about that. He had no doubt that the heckler's kneecap, unlike his foot, was intact, whatever it might *feel* like, but the hapless loudmouth went down as if he were a sapling and Kaeritha's staff were an axe she'd just applied to his roots.

He hit the paving with a fresh bellow of agony, and

even before he landed, the staff was back upright before Kaeritha, and she was leaning on it once more. He writhed and twisted on the ground, hands flashing back and forth between foot and knee, clearly unable to decide which source of anguish most required comforting, and Kaeritha shook her head. Her eyes, Bahzell noticed, never left the heckler's companion. The object of her attention seemed as well aware of it as the hradani, and he was very careful to keep his hands away from any weapon.

"There now!" Kaeritha said scoldingly to the writhing man at her feet. "You went and made me forget how important it is for a miserable imposter like me to ape a proper noblewoman's manners if I want to fool anyone!" She sighed and shook her head mournfully while the stunned onlookers began to laugh. "I suppose it just goes to show, you can take the girl out of the peasant village, but you can't take the peasant out of the girl, can you?"

"And I suppose you're thinking as how this was a tactful, diplomatic way to be handling our little problem?" Bahzell asked in a quiet voice, one eyebrow quirked and his ears half-cocked, when she turned her back on the writhing heckler and strolled casually back up the temple steps to him. He shook his head. "I'm thinking it may be *you're* the one to be a mite more careful about 'local sensibilities' and being diplomatic and all."

"Why?" she asked innocently, while the crowd laughed harder than ever behind her. "He survived, didn't he?"

Chapter Five

It was raining again, and no mere drizzle this time, either.

It seemed to do an awful lot of that on the Sothōii Wind Plain, Kaeritha thought.

She leaned one shoulder moodily against the deep-cut frame of a tower window, folded her arms across her chest, and stared out across Hill Guard Castle's battlements at the raindrops' falling silver spears. The sky was the color of wet charcoal, swirled by gusty wind and lumpy with the weight of rain not yet fallen, and the temperature was decidedly on the cool side. Not that it wasn't immensely preferable to the bone-freezing winter she'd just endured.

Thunder rumbled somewhere above the cloud ceiling, and she grimaced as a harder gust of wind drove a spray of rain in through the open window. She didn't step back, though. Instead, she inhaled deeply, drawing the wet, living scent of the rain deep into her lungs. There was a fine, stimulating feel to it, despite the chill—one that seemed to tingle in her blood—and her grimace faded into something suspiciously like a grin as she admitted the truth to herself.

It wasn't the rain that irritated her so. Not really. As a matter of fact, Kaeritha rather liked rain. She might have preferred a little less of it than the West Riding had received over the past several weeks, but the truth was that this rain was simply part and parcel of the real cause of her frustration. She should have been on her way at least two weeks ago, and instead she'd allowed the rain to help delay her travel plans.

Not that there hadn't been enough other reasons for that same delay. She could come up with a lengthy list of those, all of them entirely valid, without really trying. Helping Bahzell and Hurthang steer the Hurgrum Chapter safely through the rocks and shoals of Sothōii public opinion, for example . . . or impressing the error of their ways on the local bigots. Those had certainly been worthwhile endeavors. And so had lending her own presence as another, undeniably human, champion of Tomanāk to Bahzell's diplomatic mission. Unfortunately, she had to admit that however useful her efforts might have been, they were scarcely indispensable. No, her "reasons" for continually postponing her departure were beginning to turn into something entirely too much like "excuses" for her taste. Which meant that, rain or no rain, it was time she was on her way. Besides—

Her thoughts broke off as a tall, red-haired young woman rounded the passageway corner with a hurried stride that was just short of a trot. The newcomer, who came to an abrupt halt as she caught sight of Kaeritha, was both young and quite tall, even for a Sothōii noblewoman. At fourteen, she was already at least six feet tall—taller than Kaeritha herself, who was considered a tall woman, by Axeman standards—and she was also beginning to show the curves of what promised to be an extraordinarily attractive womanhood.

Her expression was a curious blend of pleasure, half-guilt, and semi-rebellion . . . and her attire of the moment was better suited to a second undergroom than an aristocratic young lady, Kaeritha thought wryly. She wore a worn pair of leather trousers (which, Kaeritha noted, were becoming more than a bit too tight in certain inappropriate places) under a faded smock which had been darned in half a dozen spots. It also showed several damp patches, and there were splashes of mud on the girl's riding boots and the thoroughly soaked poncho hanging over her left arm.

"Excuse me, Dame Kaeritha," she said quickly. "I didn't mean to intrude on you. I was just taking a shortcut."

"It's not an intrusion," Kaeritha assured her. "And even if it were, unless I'm mistaken, this is your family's home, Lady Leeana. I imagine it's appropriate for you to wander about in it from time to time if it takes your fancy."

She smiled, and Leeana grinned back at her.

"Well, yes, I guess," the girl said. "On the other hand, if I'm going to be honest about it, the real reason I'm taking a shortcut this time is to stay out of Father's sight."

"Oh?" Kaeritha said. "And just how have you managed to infuriate your father so badly that you find it necessary to avoid his wrath?"

"I haven't infuriated him at all . . . yet. But I'd like to get back to my quarters and changed out of these clothes while that's still true." Kaeritha cocked her head, her expression questioning, and the girl shrugged. "I love Father, Dame Kaeritha, but he gets, well, *fussy* if I sneak out to go riding without half a dozen armsmen clattering around behind me." She made a face. "And he and Mother are both beginning to insist that I ought to dress 'as befits my station.' " This time she rolled jade-green eyes with a martyred sigh, and Kaeritha was hard put not to chuckle.

"However annoying it may be," she said instead, with commendable seriousness, "they probably have a point, you know." Leeana looked at her skeptically, and Kaeritha shrugged. "You *are* the only child of one of the four most powerful nobles of the entire Kingdom," she pointed out gently, "and men like your father always have enemies. You'd make a powerful weapon against him in the wrong hands, Leeana."

"I suppose you're right," Leeana conceded after a moment. "I'm safe enough here in Balthar, though. Even Father's willing to admit that, when he isn't being stuffy just to make a point! And," she added in a darker tone, "it's not as if I'm not a weapon against him anyway."

"I don't think that's exactly fair," Kaeritha said with a quick frown. "And I'm certain that's not how *he* thinks of it."

"No?" Leeana gazed at her for several seconds, then gave her head a little toss that twitched her long, thick braid of damp golden-red hair. "Maybe he doesn't, but that doesn't really change anything, Dame Kaeritha. Do you have any idea how many people want him to produce a *real* heir?" She grimaced. "The entire King's Council certainly goes on at him enough about it whenever he attends!"

"Not the entire Council, I'm sure," Kaeritha objected, her eyes widening slightly as she sensed the true depth of bitterness Leeana's normally cheerful demeanor concealed.

"Oh, no," Leeana agreed. "Only the ones who don't have sons they think are just the right age to marry off to the heir to Balthar and the West Riding. Or don't think they're still young enough for the job themselves—*they* can hardly wait to get their greasy little paws on me." She grimaced in disgust. "All the rest of them, though, use it as an excuse to go on at him, gnawing away at his power base like a pack of mongrels snarling at a leashed wolfhound."

"Is it really that bad?" Kaeritha asked, and Leeana looked surprised by the question. "I may be a champion of Tomanāk, Leeana," Kaeritha said wryly, "but I'm also an Axewoman, not a Sothōii. Tomanāk!" She laughed. "As far as that goes, I'm only even an Axewoman by adoption. I was born a peasant in Moretz! So I may be intellectually familiar with the sorts of machinations that go on amongst great nobles, but I don't have that much first-hand experience with them."

Leeana appeared to have a little difficulty with the idea that a belted knight—and a champion of Tomanāk, into the bargain—could be that ignorant of things which were so much a part of her own life. And she also seemed surprised that Kaeritha seemed genuinely interested in *her* opinion.

"Well," she said slowly, in the voice of one manifestly attempting to be as fair-minded as possible, "it probably does seem even worse to me than it actually is, but it's bad enough. You do know how Sothōii inheritance laws work, don't you?"

"That much I have down, in general terms, at least," Kaeritha assured her.

"Then you know that while I can't legally inherit Father's titles and lands myself, they'll pass through me as heir conveyant to my own children? Assuming he doesn't produce a son after all, of course."

Kaeritha nodded, and Leeana shrugged.

"Since our enlightened customs and traditions won't permit a woman to inherit in her own right, whatever fortunate man wins my hand in matrimony will become my 'regent.' He'll govern Balthar and hold the wardenship of the West Riding 'in my name,' until our firstborn son inherits father's titles and lands. And, of course, in the most unfortunate case that I might produce only daughters, he—or the husband of my eldest daughter—would continue to hold the wardenship until one of *them* produced a son." The irony in her soprano voice was withering, especially coming from one so young, Kaeritha thought.

"Because of that," Leeana continued, "two thirds of the Council want Father to go ahead and set Mother aside to produce a good, strong, *male* heir. Some of them say it's his duty to the bloodline, and others argue that a matrimonial regency always creates the possibility of a succession crisis. Some of them may even be sincere, but most of them know perfectly well he won't do it. *They* see it all as a sword to use against him, something he has to use up political capital fighting off. The last thing he needs, especially now, is to give his enemies any more weapons to use against him! But the ones who are sincere may be even worse, because the real reason they want him to produce a male heir is that none of them like to think about the possibility that such a plum might fall into the hands of one of their rivals. And the third of the Council who don't want him to set Mother aside probably hope they're the ones who will *catch* the plum."

Kaeritha nodded slowly, gazing into the younger woman's dark green eyes. Tellian Bowmaster's marriage eighteen years before to Hanatha Whitesaddle had not simply united the Bowmasters of Balthar with the Whitesaddles of Windpeak. It had also been a love match, not just a political alliance between two powerful families. That had been obvious to anyone who'd ever laid eyes on them.

And if it hadn't been, the fact that Tellian had furiously rejected any suggestion that he set Hanatha aside after the riding accident which had left the baroness with one crippled leg and cost her her fertility would have made it so. But that decision on his part did carry a heavy price for their only child.

"And how does the plum feel about being caught?" Kaeritha asked softly.

"The plum?" Leeana gazed back into Kaeritha's midnight-blue eyes for several silent seconds, and her voice was even softer than Kaeritha's when she finally replied. "The plum would sell her soul to be anywhere else in the world," she said.

The two of them looked at each other, then Leeana shook herself, bobbed a quick half-bow, and turned abruptly away. She walked down the passage with quick, hard strides, her spine pikestaff-straight, and Kaeritha watched her go. She wondered if Leeana had actually intended to reveal the true depth of her feelings. And if the girl had ever revealed them that frankly to anyone else.

She frowned in troubled thought, then shook herself and turned back to the window as fresh thunder grumbled overhead. Her heart went out to the girl—and to her parents, for that matter—but that wasn't what had brought her to the Wind Plain, and it was past time she got on with what *had* brought her here. She gazed out the window a few moments longer, inhaled one more deep breath of rain from her relatively dry perch, and then turned away and walked briskly towards the tower's spiral stair.

✧ ✧ ✧

The library was quiet, the silence broken only by the ticking of the grandfather clock in one corner and the soft, seething crackle of the fire on the hearth. There was no other sound, yet Bahzell looked up an instant before the library door opened. Baron Tellian, sitting across the gaming table from him looked up in turn, and then shook his head as the door swung wide and Kaeritha stepped through it.

"I wish you two would stop doing that," he complained.

"And just what is it the two of us are after doing?" Bahzell inquired genially.

"You know perfectly well what," Tellian replied, using the black pawn he'd just picked up from the chessboard to wave at Kaeritha, still standing in the doorway and smiling at him. "*That.*" He shook his head and snorted. "You could at least *pretend* you have to wait until the other one knocks, like normal people!"

"With all due respect, Milord," Brandark sat in a window seat to take advantage of the gray, rainy-afternoon light coming in through it and spoke without ever looking up from the book in his lap, "I don't believe anyone's ever been foolish enough to suggest that there was anything 'normal' about either of them."

"But they could at least try," Tellian objected. "Damn it, it's uncanny . . . and it worries my men. Phrobus! It worries *me*, sometimes!"

"I apologize, Milord," Kaeritha said with a small smile. "It's not really anything we do, you know. It just . . . happens."

"Aye," Bahzell agreed, and the smile he gave the baron was much broader than hers had been. "And come to that, I've not heard yet that champions of Tomanāk weren't supposed to be after being 'uncanny.'"

"That's because they are," Brandark said in a slightly more serious tone, looking up from his book at last and cocking his foxlike ears. "Uncanny, that is. And the truth is, Milord," he went on as Tellian turned his head to look at him, "that it's so unusual to have two champions as houseguests at the same time that very few people have ever had the opportunity to watch them being uncanny together."

Tellian considered that for a few seconds, then nodded.

"You have a point," he conceded. "But then, everything about the current situation is on the unusual side, isn't it?"

"It is that." Heartfelt agreement rumbled in Bahzell's deep voice as he leaned back in his chair—specially built by Tellian's master woodworker to Bahzell's size and weight—and gazed across the neat ranks of chessmen at the human host who was technically his prisoner. "And I hope you won't be taking this wrongly, Baron, but it's in my mind that those of your folk who'd sooner see my head on a pike are after getting a mite more . . . vocal about it."

"You're talking about those idiots Kaeritha trounced at the temple the other day?" Tellian asked, and Bahzell nodded.

"Those, and those like them who're after being a bit more discreet, as you might be saying," he agreed a trifle grimly. "And I'm not so easy in my mind about those problems biting Lord Festian's backside, either." Tellian raised an eyebrow, and Bahzell shrugged. "I've no doubt there's always enough political infighting to be going around amongst you Sothōii—there certainly is amongst any other lot of noblemen I've ever heard aught about! But I'm thinking that there's more than a few getting behind to push where concern over your taste in houseguests is concerned."

"Of course there are," Tellian agreed. "Surely you didn't expect anything else to happen?"

"Of course not," Bahzell said. "Not that that's after making it any more pleasant—or keeping my shoulder blades from itching whenever daggers are about—now that it's here."

"On the other hand," Kaeritha observed mildly, "nobody ever said being a champion of Tomanāk would be an endless pleasure jaunt, either. Or, at least, no one ever said so to *me*, anyway."

"Nor to me," Bahzell admitted, and his ears twitched in wry amusement as he recalled the conversation in which the god of war had recruited one Bahzell Bahnakson as the first hradani champion of any god of Light in the past twelve millennia. "Pleasure jaunt" was one phrase which had never passed Tomanāk's lips.

"I can well believe that." Tellian shook his head. "It's bad enough being a simple baron without having a god looking over my shoulder all the time!"

"That's as may be," Bahzell said, "but I'm thinking it wasn't all that 'simple' for you, either, when we ran up against each other in the Gullet."

"Oh, I don't know about that." Tellian leaned back in his chair and smiled. "If nothing else, at least I've assured that I'll go down in history. After all, how many men have ever managed to surrender to a force they outnumbered twenty or thirty times over?"

"I have a feeling you'll go down in history for more than just that, Milord," Kaeritha said. "But Bahzell does have a point, you know. Those louts trying to goad Thalgahr into the Rage knew exactly what they were doing. And I don't think they came up with the idea spontaneously all on their own. They weren't bright enough for that! Which suggests that someone is orchestrating events a bit carefully this time. Is it possible you might actually have an enemy somewhere, Milord?" she asked in an elaborately innocent tone.

"Oh, I suppose anything is *possible*," Tellian said wryly. "Do you think I should look into the matter?"

"If you don't have anything better to do," she agreed. "In the meantime, however, I'm afraid it's past time *I* was off on one of those 'pleasure jaunts' Bahzell and I were never promised."

"Ah?" Bahzell cocked his head. "And has himself been talking to you again, Kerry?"

"Not directly." She shook her head. "On the other hand, He doesn't speak directly to me as often as He seems to speak to you."

"Perhaps," Brandark murmured in the tone of one in whose mouth butter would adamantly refuse to melt, "that's because it doesn't require something quite that, um . . . *direct* to get through to you."

"I wouldn't know about that," Kaeritha said primly, and her blue eyes twinkled as Bahzell made a rude gesture at his friend. "But," she went on, "He does have His own ways of getting messages through to me. And the one I'm getting now is that I've been sitting around your house too long, Milord."

"My house has been honored by your presence, Dame Kaeritha," Tellian said, and this time his voice was completely serious. "I would be most pleased for you to remain here however long you like. And while I know a champion's duties take precedence over all other considerations, could you not wait at least until the rain stops?"

"*Does* the rain ever stop on the Wind Plain, Milord?" Kaeritha asked wryly.

"Not in the spring," Bahzell replied before Tellian could. "It may be after pausing a bit, here and there, though."

"Bahzell is right, I'm afraid," Tellian confirmed. "Winter weather is worse, of course. They say Chemalka uses the Wind Plain to test Her foul weather before She sends it elsewhere, and I believe it. But spring is usually our rainiest season. Although, to be fair, this one's been rainier than most, even for us."

"Which I'm sure will be doing wonderful things for the grass and crops, assuming as how it doesn't wash all of them away before ever they sprout. But that won't be leaving you any drier right this very moment, Kerry," Bahzell observed.

"I've been wet before." Kaeritha shrugged. "I haven't melted or shrunk yet, and I probably won't this time, either."

"I see you're serious about leaving," Tellian said, and she nodded. "Well, I'm not foolish enough to try to tell a champion of Tomanāk her business, Milady. But if He insists on sending you out in such weather, is there at least anything I can do to assist you on your way?"

"It might help if you could tell me where I'm going," Kaeritha said ruefully.

"I beg your pardon?" Tellian looked at her as if he half suspected her of pulling his leg.

"One of the more frustrating consequences of the fact that He doesn't talk to me as directly as He does to Bahzell here," Kaeritha told him, "is that my directions are often a bit less precise."

"Well, Bahzell does require as much clarity—not to say simplicity—as possible," Brandark put in with a wicked grin.

"Just you be keeping it up, little man," Bahzell told him. "I'm sure it's an impressive splash you'll make when someone kicks your hairy arse halfway across the moat."

"This castle doesn't *have* a moat," Brandark pointed out.

"It will as soon as I've finished digging one for the occasion," Bahzell shot back.

"As I was saying," Kaeritha continued in the tone of a governess ignoring her charges' obstreperousness, "I haven't really received any specific instructions about exactly what I'm supposed to be doing here."

"I should think that helping to destroy an entire temple of Sharnā and to establish a brand-new chapter of your order amongst Bahzell's people—not to mention playing some small part in preventing that idiot Redhelm from committing all of us to a disastrous war—constitutes a worthwhile effort already," Tellian observed.

"I'd like to think so," Kaeritha agreed with a small smile. "On the other hand, I was already headed this direction before Bahzell ever came along. Not that I knew exactly why then, either, of course. But one thing I do know, Milord, is that He doesn't normally leave His champions sitting around idle. Swords don't accomplish much hanging on an armory wall. So it's time I was about figuring out whatever it is He has in mind for me next."

"You've no clue at all?" Bahzell asked.

"You know Him better than that," Kaeritha replied. "He may not have actually discussed it with me, but I know that whatever it is, it lies east of here."

"With all due respect, Dame Kaeritha," Tellian pointed

out, "three-quarters of the Wind Plain 'lies east of here.' Would it be possible for you to narrow that down just a bit more?"

"Not a great deal, I'm afraid, Milord." She shrugged. "About all I can say is that I'm probably within a few days' travel—certainly not more than a week's or so—of where I'm supposed to be."

"While it would never do to criticize a god," Tellian said, "it occurs to me that if I attempted to plan a campaign with as little information as He appears to have provided you, I'd fall flat on my arse."

"Champions do require a certain . . . agility," Kaeritha agreed with a wry smile. "On the other hand, Milord, that's usually because He's careful to avoid leading us around by the hand." Tellian quirked an eyebrow at her, and she shrugged again. "We need to be able to stand on our own two feet," she pointed out, "and if we started to rely on Him for explicit instructions on everything we're supposed to be doing, how long would it be before we couldn't accomplish anything *without* those instructions? He expects us to be bright enough to figure out our duty without His constant prompting."

"And himself is after having his own version of a sense of humor, as well," Bahzell put in.

"And that." Kaeritha nodded.

"I'll take your word for that," Tellian said. "You two are the first of His champions I've ever personally met, after all. Although, to be honest, I have to admit I harbor a few dark suspicions about how typical the pair of you are." Bahzell and Kaeritha both grinned at him, and he shook his head. "Be that as it may," he continued, "I'm afraid I can't really think of anything to the east of here—within no more than a few days' travel, at least—that would seem to require a champion's services. If I did know of anything that serious, I assure you that I'd already have been trying to do something about it!"

"I'm sure you would, Milord. But that's frequently the way it is, especially when the local authorities are competent."

"I'm not sure I'd consider someone who could let that

idiot Redhelm come so close to succeeding 'competent,'" Tellian said a bit sourly.

"I doubt anyone could have stopped him from making the attempt," Kaeritha objected. "You could scarcely have stripped him of his authority before he actually abused it, after all. And once you discovered that he had, you acted promptly enough."

"Barely," Tellian grumbled.

"But promptly enough, all the same," Bahzell said. "And, if you'll pardon my saying so, I'm thinking that betwixt us it's been effective enough, as well. So far, at least."

"It certainly has," Kaeritha agreed. "But my point, Milord, is that champions frequently end up dealing with problems which have succeeded in hiding themselves from the local authorities' attention. Often with a little help from someone like Sharnā or one of his relatives."

"You think whatever it is you're here to deal with is that serious?" Tellian sat up straight in his chair, his sudden frown intense. "That there could be another of the Dark Gods at work here on the Wind Plain?"

"I didn't say that, Milord. On the other hand, and without wanting to sound paranoid, Bahzell and I *are* champions of one of the Gods of Light. Tomanāk doesn't have that many of us, either, so we tend not to get wasted on easy tasks." She grimaced so wryly that Tellian chuckled. "Of course, a great deal of what we do in the world requires us to deal with purely mortal problems, but we do see rather more of the Dark Gods and their handiwork than most people do. And the Dark Gods are quite accomplished at concealing their presence and influence."

"Like Sharnā in Navahk," Brandark agreed grimly.

"Well, yes, but—" Tellian began, then stopped. His three guests looked at him expressionlessly, and he had the grace to blush.

"Forgive me," he said. "I *was* about to say that that was among hradani, not Sothōii. But I suppose that sort of 'It couldn't possibly happen to *us*' thinking is what does let it happen, isn't it?"

"It's certainly a part of it," Kaeritha said. "But infections are always hard to see before they rise to the surface." She shrugged. "One of a champion's functions is to bring things to a head and clean the wound before it gets so bad that the only alternative is amputation, Milord."

"A charming analogy." Tellian grimaced, but it was obvious he was thinking hard. He leaned back in his chair, the fingers of his right hand drumming on the armrest, and distant thunder rolled and rumbled beyond the library while he pondered.

"I still can't think of anything that *seems* serious enough to require a champion," he said finally. "But as you and Bahzell—and Brandark—have all just pointed out, that doesn't necessarily mean as much as I'd like to think, so I've been trying to come up with anything that may have seemed less important to me than it actually is. If you can delay your departure for perhaps another day or two, Kaeritha, I'll spend some time going over the reports from my local lords and bailiffs to see if there is something I missed the first time around. Right off the top of my head, though, the only ongoing local problem I'm aware of is the situation at Kalatha."

"Kalatha?" Kaeritha repeated.

"It's a town a bit more than a week's ride east of here," Tellian told her. "I realize you said you were within a 'few days' of whatever your destination is, but you could probably make the trip in five days if you pushed hard on a good horse, so I suppose it might qualify."

"Why is it a problem?" she asked.

"Why *isn't* it a problem?" he responded with a harsh chuckle. She looked puzzled, and he shrugged. "Kalatha isn't just any town, Milady. It holds a special Crown charter, guaranteeing its independence from the local lords, and some of them resent that. Not just because it exempts the Kalathans from their taxes, either." He smiled crookedly. "The reason it holds a free-city charter in the first place is because Lord Kellos Swordsmith, one of my maternal great-great-grandfathers, deeded it to the war maids—with the Crown's strong 'approval'—over two centuries ago."

Kaeritha's eyes narrowed, and he nodded.

"The war maids aren't so very popular," he said with what all of his listeners recognized as massive understatement. "I suppose we Sothōii are too traditional for it to be any other way. But for the most part, they're at least respected as the sort of enemies you wouldn't want to make. However much they may be *disliked*, very few people, even among the most convinced traditionalists, are foolish enough to go out of their way to pick quarrels with them."

"And that isn't the case at the moment with Kalatha?" Kaeritha asked.

"That depends on whose version you accept," Tellian replied. "According to the local lords, the Kalathans have been encroaching on territory not covered by the town charter, and they've been 'confrontational' and 'hostile' to efforts to resolve the competing claims peaceably. But according to the war maids, the local lords—and especially Trisu of Lorham, the most powerful of them—have been systematically encroaching upon the rights guaranteed to them by their charter for years now. It's been going on for some time, but there's always something like this. Especially where war maids are concerned. And it's worse in Kalatha's case—inevitably, I suppose. Kalatha isn't the largest war maid free-town or city, but it *is* the oldest, thanks to my highly principled ancestor. I like to think he didn't realize just how much of a pain in the arse he was going to dump on all his descendants. Although, if he didn't, he must have been stupider than I'd prefer to think."

Kaeritha had started to ask another question, but she paused almost visibly at the baron's tone. It would have been too much to call it bitter or biting, but there was a definite edge to it. So instead of what she'd been about to ask, she nodded.

"I agree it doesn't sound like an earthshaking problem," she said. "On the other hand, I have to start somewhere, and this sounds like it might very well be the place. Especially since each of Tomanāk's champions has his—or her—particular . . . specialties, call them."

Tellian's brow furrowed, and Kaeritha chuckled.

"Any of us are expected to be able to handle any duty any of His champions might encounter, Milord, but we each have our own personality traits and skills. That tends to mean we're more comfortable, or effective, at least, serving different aspects of Him. For example, Bahzell here is obviously most at home serving Him as God of War, although he's done *fairly* well serving Him as God of Justice. For someone who's most at home breaking things, anyway."

She grinned at Bahzell, who looked back affably, with an expression which boded ill for the next time they met on the training field.

"My own reasons for joining His service, though," she went on, returning her attention to Tellian, "had more to do with a burning thirst for justice." She paused and frowned, eyes darkening with old and painful memories, then shook herself. "That's always been the aspect of Him I'm most comfortable—or happiest, anyway—serving, and my talents and abilities seem best suited to it. So if there's a legal dispute between this Kalatha and the neighboring nobility, it certainly seems like a logical place for me to start looking. Can I get a map to show me how to find it?"

"Oh, I can do better than that, Milady," Tellian assured her. "Kalatha may hold a Crown charter, but Trisu and his neighbors are my vassals. If you can wait until the end of the week to depart, I'll make some additional inquiries and provide as much background information as I can. And of course I'll send along letters of introduction and instructions for them to cooperate fully with you during your visit."

"Thank you, Milord," Kaeritha said formally. "That would be very good of you."

Chapter Six

"So, *there* you are, Leeana."

Leeana's not quite stealthy progress along the passageway stopped as she paused and looked over her shoulder. Although the dark-haired woman in the open doorway behind her leaned heavily on the silver-worked, ebony cane under her right hand, she also stood very straight. Her left hand held a book, closed on a place-marking index finger, and a pair of gold, wire-framed, dwarvish-made reading glasses had been pushed up onto the top of her head to get them out of the way. It was subtly apparent, despite her full gown, that her right hip was carried higher than her left and her right leg was frailer, less well-muscled and thin. Yet despite that, and despite the faint traceries of silver in her dark hair, she was still a beautiful woman, with a well-formed, high-bosomed figure Leeana had both admired and envied for as long as she could remember. She was taller than Dame Kaeritha, although not quite so tall as Leeana, and her eyes were exactly the same deep, jade-green as Leeana's.

"Good afternoon, Mother," Leeana said with a slight smile. "Ah, I don't suppose I could convince you to go back to your book until I finish sneaking into my room and change, could I?"

"No," Baroness Hanatha said thoughtfully. "I don't believe you could."

"I was afraid of that," Leeana sighed. She turned and walked back towards her mother, still carrying her dripping poncho over one arm.

"Did you enjoy your ride?" Hanatha asked politely as she stepped back through the doorway to her private sitting room and let her daughter past her.

"Yes, I did." Leeana crossed to the wrought iron fire screen in front of her mother's hearth and hung the wet poncho across it to dry. Then she turned back to face Hanatha, who gave her head a small, smiling shake and sank into a pleasantly overstuffed chair under the comfortable chamber's rain-streaming skylight.

"Where did you go?" she asked. The fire's soft noises and the patter of rain on the skylight formed a soothing backdrop for her voice, and Leeana rubbed her hands, holding them out to the fire's warmth.

"Down to the river and up the bank to Highwayman's Height."

"I remember," Hanatha said. She leaned back in the chair, eyes dreamy with memories. "Down that hollow by Jargham's Farm. Are the crocuses still blooming along the bank above the farm?"

"Yes." Leeana paused and stopped herself before she cleared her throat. "Yes, they are. Purple and yellow. Although," she smiled, "it looks as if the rain is trying to wash them away."

"I imagine so. And I imagine the river's running quite high, as well. Do tell me you weren't foolish enough to attempt the ford below the Height."

"Of course I wasn't!" Leeana gave her mother a slightly indignant look. "Nobody would be crazy enough to try that with the river a good twenty yards out of its banks on either side!"

"No?" Hanatha gazed at her daughter for several seconds, then cocked her head and smiled. "Your father and I were, the year before we were married. Although, now that I think about it, it was only about fifteen yards out of its banks when *we* did it."

Leeana stared at her mother in disbelief, and Hanatha looked back calmly.

"I can't believe you two would have done something like that!" Leeana said finally. "Not after the way both of you go on at me about the risk to the succession if anything should happen to me. Father was the heir to Balthar, not just the heir conveyant, you know!"

"Yes," Hanatha said thoughtfully. "I believe I *was* aware of that, now that you mention it. Although, to be fair, there was your Uncle Garlayn, at that point, so he wasn't precisely the only heir. And he did have several sturdy, healthy male cousins who might have succeeded him. But, yes, despite that, it was incredibly foolish of both of us. And, by the way, Leeana, it was my idea."

Leeana sank onto a footstool, facing her mother's chair, and stared at her. She'd heard stories all of her life about her mother's youthful, headstrong defiance of stifling convention. Given the way both her parents fussed over any minor infractions on her own part, she'd always secretly assumed most of those stories were exaggerated. After all, they'd all come to her second- or third-hand, through servants' gossip, and she was only too well aware of how the family retainers tended to embroider the family's adventures. More than that, Hanatha was deeply beloved by all of Duke Tellian's household. That gave all of them, and particularly the older ones, who remembered the laughing young noblewoman Tellian Bowmaster had brought home, a tendency to emphasize what an outrageous, perpetually racing about handful she'd been. Especially since she would never go racing about again.

But if her mother—the same mother who was constantly suggesting that perhaps Leeana might want to moderate her own lifestyle just a bit—had been crazy enough to talk her father into swimming their horses across a river in full springtime flood—!

"Yes," Hanatha said wryly, "I *was* that foolish, dear. And I was three years older than you are now. Which, I suppose, probably does make it seem just a little unfair for me to complain about your own high jinks, doesn't it?"

"I wouldn't say that," Leeana began, and her mother laughed.

"Oh, I should certainly hope not!" Her dark green eyes danced, and she leaned back in her chair. "You're much too good a daughter to throw my own youthful misdeeds into my teeth. But we both know you're *thinking* it, don't we?"

"Well . . . yes, I suppose I am," Leeana admitted, unable not to smile back at her.

"Of course you are. And I often thought your grandmother was dreadfully unfair when she took me to task for some dreadful lapse on my part. And to some extent, I imagine she was—just as I realize that I'm applying something of a double standard when I upbraid you. Unfortunately," she continued to smile, but her voice became more serious, "this business of being a parent sometimes does require us to be a bit unfair."

"I never thought you were really unfair," Leeana told her. "Not like Aunt Gayarla, for example."

"There's a difference between unfair and capricious, dear," Hanatha said. "And worthy as your father's sister-in-law is in many ways, I'm afraid she's always alternated between tyranny and overindulgence where your cousins are concerned. And it's gotten worse since Garlayn died. Indeed, I'm often surprised Trianal managed to turn out so well, although Staphos and— Well. Never mind."

She shook her head and returned to her original thread.

"No, Leeana. What I meant is that sometimes—more often than I would prefer, really—I find myself telling you not to do things since I know just how . . . unwise they are because, when I was your age, I did those very same things. I'm afraid it truly is a matter of experience and the burned hand teaching best. The way parents discover the things their children shouldn't do all too often turns out to be that they did the same things, made the same mistakes, they're trying to prevent their children from repeating. It's messy, and not a very organized way to go about things.

Unfortunately, it seems to be the way that human beings' minds are arranged."

"Maybe it is, Mother," Leeana said slowly, after several seconds of careful consideration, "and I know I may be prejudiced, but I happen to think you turned out pretty well." Her mother snorted softly in obvious amusement, and Leeana smiled. But she also continued in the same serious tone of voice. "You and Father, more than anyone else I've ever met, seem to know exactly who you are and exactly what you mean to one another. And you don't just love each other—you *laugh* with each other. Sometimes just with your eyes, but I always know, and I love it so whenever you do. If making the same 'mistakes' makes me turn out just like you, I can't think of anything I'd rather have happen."

Hanatha's eyes softened, and she inhaled deeply. She studied her daughter's face, seeing the subtle merging of her own features and her husband's in the graceful bone structure and the strong, yet feminine nose, and she shook her head again, gently.

"Knowing you think that makes me a very proud woman, Leeana. But you aren't me. And who you are is a very wonderful person, someone your Father and I love almost more than life itself. I don't *want* you to be another me, like something turned out by one of Cook's cookie cutters. I want you to be *you*, and to live your own life. But even if you and I both wanted you to turn out exactly like me, it wouldn't happen. It can't, because you're your father's daughter . . . and because we can't have any more children."

Leeana bit the inside of her lip, hearing the echo of her own conversation with Dame Kaeritha, and unshed tears burned behind her eyes.

Her mother was still young, despite the silver strands pain and suffering had put into her hair, no more than a few years older than Kaeritha. She'd been only eighteen when she wed her husband, and Leeana had been born before her twenty-second birthday. If there'd been any true justice in the world, Leeana thought bitterly, her mother would have had at least two or three more children by now. For that matter, she would still have had time to have two or three more *now*. If only—

She stopped her thoughts and took herself sternly to task. Perhaps it was unjust, or at least unfair, that her mother had been injured so severely. And it was certainly a tragedy. But most women who'd suffered such injuries would have died. At the very least, they would have been completely crippled for whatever remained of their lives. But Hanatha Bowmaster was the Baroness of Balthar. The finest physicians in Balthar had attended her, and managed to keep her alive until a mage healer had arrived from the Sōtḥōfalas mage academy. And that healer had been escorted to Balthar by a fellow mage, a wind walker, which had gotten her there faster than even a courser might have.

But there were limits in all things, Leeana reminded herself. She'd heard the story of how Prince Bahzell had healed Brandark in his very first exercise of the healing power which was his as a champion of Tomanāk. Yet despite the touch of a very god, Brandark's truncated ear and missing fingers had not magically regrown. And just as they hadn't, the healer who had attended her mother almost four full days after the accident had been unable to restore full mobility to a leg which had been practically dead any more than she had been able to restore Baroness Hanatha's fertility.

"I know that, Mother," she said after a moment. "I wish you could, and not just because of any differences it might have made in my own life."

"Leeana," Hanatha said very gently, "we wish we might have had more children, too. But not because we could possibly have loved them more, or been more satisfied with them, than we've been with you. Yet the fact that you have no brothers is why you can't live your life the way I lived mine, and for that I apologize with all my heart."

Her green eyes glistened, and Leeana opened her mouth to reject any need for her mother to apologize for something over which no one but the gods themselves had any power. But Hanatha shook her head, stopping her before she spoke.

"I ought to have encouraged your Father to seek a divorce and take another wife," she said very softly. "I knew it at the time, too. But I couldn't, Leeana. I wasn't that strong. And even if I had been, I knew in my heart that there was no way I could have convinced him to. And so, whatever you may think, he and I do owe you an apology for the way our own selfish decisions have constrained your life."

"Don't be foolish, Mother!" Leeana said fiercely. "If Father had been able to set you aside so easily, I certainly wouldn't be the person I am now, because I love him. And I wouldn't love a man who could do that. Of course there are things about my life I'd change if I could! I think that must be true of anyone. But I would never, ever have wanted them changed if the price had been to separate you and Father. Never!"

"No wonder I love you so much." Hanatha's tone was light, almost whimsical, but her eyes glowed, and Leeana smiled. They sat for several more moments in silence, and then Hanatha cleared her throat.

"At any rate," she said more briskly, "the reason I was lurking in the hall to intercept you, was to chide you for doing something we both know you love to do and also knew you shouldn't be doing."

"I know that, Mother, but—"

"There are no buts, Leeana," her mother said with stern compassion. "Perhaps there ought to be, but there aren't. You simply cannot do things like taking long, solitary rides. Dressing as you are right now—" she waved one hand at Leeana's leather trousers and worn-out smock "—would be bad enough in the eyes of most of your peers, but that much, at least, I'm not prepared to deny you. I want you to begin dressing more as befits your station and your age for normal wear, or when we have guests. But for stable tasks or garden work, or hacking about the countryside, comfortable clothes—if, perhaps, somewhat less worn out than the ones you have on now—are fine with me."

Leeana let out a deep breath of half-relief, but her mother wasn't done, and she continued in that same gently implacable tone.

"But one thing I am going to insist upon, Leeana. And if you can't agree to accept it, then I'm afraid you won't be taking any rides anywhere except under your Father's direct supervision."

Leeana swallowed apprehensively. She could count on the fingers of her hands the number of times her mother had issued such a flat decree of authority.

"You will never again go riding without at least Tarith in attendance," Hanatha told her. "Never, do you understand, Leeana?"

"But, Mother—"

"I said there are no buts this time," her mother interrupted firmly. "I don't intend to be any more unreasonable than I have to be, but I do intend to be obeyed. I've also spoken to Tarith about it." Tarith Shieldarm was Leeana's personal armsman, and had been since she learned to walk. "He understands that I do not expect him to play the role of informant. I need for you to be able to trust him, as you always have, and so I've instructed him that he is not to discuss your comings and goings with me or with your father so long as he's certain none of those comings and goings are without him. That, I hope I need not add, applies only here in Balthar. Here, everyone knows you and we can be relatively confident of your safety with only Tarith to look after you. We cannot be certain of that elsewhere, however, and I will expect Tarith's duty to safeguard you to take precedence over his responsibility to respect your confidences."

Leeana looked at her mother with dismay. She knew Tarith would die to protect her, and that he would respect and protect her privacy and the confidentiality of anything she said to him up to the very limits of his oath of fealty to her father. He was in every sense except blood itself a member of her family, a beloved uncle whose protectiveness might sometimes be exasperating, but whose devotion and rocklike reliability were beyond the very possibility of question. Yet her mother's decision—and Leeana knew an unyielding decision when she heard one from the baroness—meant an end to any true privacy. Worse, it was a gentle, loving declaration that she would no longer be allowed to fool herself, even briefly, into forgetting that she was the heir conveyant of Balthar and the West Riding.

Tears gleamed on her eyelashes, and her mother sighed.

"I'm sorry, Leeana," she said regretfully. "I wish I could let you ride anywhere you wanted, with or without a guard. But I can't, love. Not even here in Balthar, anymore. The situation with your father, and the Council, and this business with Prince Bahzell and *his* father . . ." She shook her head. "There are too many enemies, Leeana. Too many people who would strike at your father any way they can. And it wasn't so many years ago that abductions and forced marriages were accepted, even if they were looked upon more than a little askance. I honestly don't think anyone would be stupid enough to believe for an instant that your father would allow any man who dared to touch you against your will to live, under any circumstances. But some of his enemies are almost as powerful, or even fully as powerful, as he. Some of them singly, some running as packs. I will not risk your safety at a time like this."

Leeana inhaled deeply as she heard the flat, unwavering determination of Hanatha's last sentence. Her mother was right, and she knew it, however little she liked it. Indeed, any other mother and father in the same position would probably have locked her up in one of Hill Guard's towers long ago. Yet that made the draught no less bitter on the tongue.

"You understand what I'm saying, and why?" her mother asked after a moment, and Leeana nodded.

"Yes, Ma'am," she said. "I hate it, but I understand it. And I don't hate *you* because of it."

"Thank you for that," Hanatha said softly.

"I wish—" Leeana began, then closed her mouth.

"You wish what, dear?" her mother prompted after a second or two.

"I don't know," Leeana said, feeling the hearth fire warm against her back as she sat on the stool at her mother's feet. She closed her eyes and shook her head slowly. "I wish it didn't have to be this way. I wish I could be who I am and still be someone else, someone who could do and be what she wanted to . . . and who didn't have to worry about someone else's using her as a weapon against her family."

"I don't blame you, darling," her mother said with a tiny smile. "But you can't, any more than your father or I can."

"I know." Leeana opened her eyes and returned her mother's smile. "I know, Momma. And I'll try to be good, really I will."

"You've always been good, even when you were *bad*," her mother said with a small, sad chuckle. "I'm not asking for miraculous changes in your behavior or who you are. I'm only insisting that you be careful, as well."

"I'll try," Leeana repeated.

Chapter Seven

"I don't think you should be here," the powerfully built, blond-haired nobleman said. His expression was almost neutral, but his hand lingered near the hilt of his dagger and his voice was dangerously flat. He was a man who neither liked surprises nor was accustomed to—or brooked—disobedience, and it showed.

"It's not as if anyone else knows that I *am* here, Milord Baron," his visitor replied. He was a nondescript little man, brown-haired and brown-eyed, and his clothing was just as unremarkable and easily forgotten as he was. He might have been a tradesman, or a clerk. Possibly a minor functionary, attached to the household of some middle-ranked nobleman. Perhaps even a moderately prosperous physician with a middle-class patient list.

But, of course, the baron thought, he was none of those. Although what precisely he actually *was* remained much less satisfyingly defined than the list of things he wasn't.

The baron listened to the spatter of raindrops and the splash of gurgling downspouts on the terrace outside the study of his private suite and considered pointing out that he was on his way to bed and suggesting that the other come back at a more convenient time. As a matter of fact, he considered the idea very carefully before, in the end, he rejected it.

"And how can you be so certain no one knows?" he asked instead.

"My dear Baron!" The little man sounded affronted, although he was respectful enough about it to satisfy propriety. "We're talking about part of my stock in trade! What sort of a conspirator would I be if I couldn't be positive about things like that?"

The baron clenched his teeth at the word "conspirator." Not because it was inaccurate, but because he disliked hearing it bandied about so casually by a man about whom he knew far less than he liked. And also, perhaps, because a noble of his rank was never party to something so *common* as a "conspiracy."

"I repeat," he said, his voice frosted with a warning edge of chill, "how can you be so certain?"

"Because your armsmen aren't swarming into your chambers even as we speak, Milord," his visitor said in a much more serious tone. The baron arched one eyebrow, and the other man nodded. "If I could get into your personal chambers without *them* noticing me, I think it's safe to say that no one else could possibly suspect I'm here. Besides, I have a few . . . other ways of being certain I'm not under observation."

"I see."

The baron shrugged and crossed the study. He sat in the comfortable chair behind his desk and turned to face his visitor. He had to agree that the point about his armsmen's not having noticed the other's arrival was a good one. And then there was the other man's second point. The baron neither knew nor wanted to know all of the resources his self-proclaimed fellow conspirator might possess. He strongly suspected that sorcery was among them, and if it was, it was most certainly not *white* sorcery. And since the punishment for dark sorcery and blood magic was death, he preferred to have no more direct knowledge than he could avoid. In an ironic sort of way, his very ignorance—however hard he had to work to maintain it—would be his most powerful protection if things ever went far enough wrong for him to face investigation. Even a court-appointed mage could only confirm the truth of his statement when he testified that he didn't *know* that the other was a sorcerer.

"Well," he said, after regarding the nondescript man coldly for almost a full minute, "since you're here, I suppose it wouldn't hurt for you to go ahead and tell me why."

The other man seemed remarkably unaffected by the fishy eye of such a powerful noble. He wasn't precisely insouciant about it, but he strolled across to stand at a corner of the desk, hands clasped behind him while he toasted his backside at the baron's fireplace, and smiled.

"There are a few matters I thought we ought, perhaps, to discuss," he said easily. "And there are also some bits of news about which you probably should be informed. So since I was already in Sōthōfalas, I decided to come on as far as Toramos and share them with you."

"What sort of news?" the baron asked.

"For starters, Festian has decided to formally appeal to Tellian for assistance." The baron grunted in an unsurprised sort of way, and the little man chuckled. "I know, I know—we expected that from the beginning. Indeed, I'm mostly surprised that he's waited this long."

"That's because you're not a lord," the baron said, and smiled thinly as he not so subtly emphasized the gap between his rank and that of his visitor. "Yes, he has both the right and the duty to call upon his liege in a matter like this. But by appealing to Tellian for aid he admits his inability to handle the problem out of his own resources, and among our people, that will constitute a serious blow to his authority and legitimacy in many eyes." He shrugged. "Whatever I may think of Festian and his claim to Glanharrow, I understand the constraints he faces."

"No doubt you're better placed to understand," the little man agreed amiably, unfazed by any effort on his ostensible employer's part to put him in his place. "My question is whether or not you want his messenger—he's decided to send Sir Yarran—to reach Tellian."

"Surely what I want or don't want has little bearing at this point," the baron said, watching the other man's face carefully from behind the untroubled expression of a veteran politician. "Balthar is the better part of a hundred and fifty leagues from where we sit."

"True." The other man nodded and pursed his lips judiciously. "On the other hand, I did just tell you that Festian has *decided* to appeal to Tellian, not that he's already done so. If my . . . sources can get that information to me that promptly, what makes you think I couldn't get instructions back to them just as quickly?"

"Put that way, I don't suppose there's any reason you couldn't," the baron acknowledged, silently taking himself to task for asking the question in the first place. That sort of probe was dangerous to his carefully maintained ignorance. He leaned back in his chair, stroking his beard, and considered the question.

"I think it's best that we leave his messenger alone," he said finally. "While it's tempting to take this opportunity to dispose of Yarran once and for all, it's better to remember that a prudent spider weaves her webs patiently. Yarran is a capable enough man, in a rough-edged sort of way, and he's completely loyal to Festian. As such, he'll have to go eventually. But killing him—or even arranging a perfectly natural seeming accident for him—at this particular moment would only make Tellian even more suspicious than he'll already be."

"In what way?" the little man asked in a tone of mild curiosity.

"Yarran is Festian's senior field commander," the baron said. "If we kill him at this point, we up the stakes all around. It would be a major escalation from simply stealing cattle, or even horses. As I say, we'll have to do it eventually, but I've just launched a little arrow which ought to add significantly to Tellian's distractions. I'd prefer to give that time to work on him before we escalate any further. Especially if the escalation in question might be sufficiently significant for Tellian to justify calling in Crown investigators. Those infernal busybodies are probably just panting to poke their noses in, and half of them are magi, curse them."

His last observation was an exaggeration, but not all that great a one. The Crown's best investigators *were* magi, with the mage talents to make them fiendishly effective at ferreting out the truth, however well it hid itself. King Markhos' father's decision to found the Sōthōfalas Mage Academy and commission almost a quarter of its yearly graduates as Crown investigators was a major reason the Time of Troubles of his own father's reign had not repeated themselves. Cassan knew that, and as Baron Toramos and Lord Warden of the South Riding, he had to approve, in a grudging sort of way. But that didn't keep him from detesting the consequences for his own plans . . . or regarding the Crown investigators with a wariness that verged far more closely than he cared to admit on outright fear.

"That might be unfortunate at this point," the other man agreed, wondering idly what sort of "arrow" the baron might have sent Tellian's way. "But as dangerous as magi are, it's not as if they'd really make that much difference, is it?" The baron frowned, and he shrugged. "I don't wish to appear alarmist, but at the moment, Baron Tellian has not one, but two champions of Tomanāk as houseguests," he pointed out. "I approve of all the precautions you've taken against magi, Milord, and I'm glad I was able to assist in some small way with them. But given my choice between two of Scale Balancer's champions and every mage in the world, I'd probably choose the magi."

"A point," the baron conceded. "But, of course, that assumes the two of them really are champions of Tomanāk." He bared strong, even, white teeth in something no one would ever have called a smile. "Given that we're talking about a hradani and a hradani-lover who's not only a *woman* but who publicly admits she was born a peasant, I sincerely doubt they are."

His visitor's expression didn't even flicker, but it wasn't easy for the little man to keep it from doing so. The baron was a powerful, cunning man who was not unduly burdened by scruples. In his own way, he was easily one of the most intelligent men the little man had ever encountered, as well. But he was also a Sothōii, and a bigot. Armored by his own iron prejudice, he genuinely didn't believe that Bahzell Bahnakson or Dame Kaeritha could possibly be what they claimed to be.

"I can understand why you might doubt their legitimacy," he lied after a moment, "but that doesn't mean they aren't dangerous. If even half the things they say about this Bahzell are true, he has a nasty habit of surviving rather . . . extreme threats. And whatever *we* may believe about them, a significant number of people, especially in Balthar and, unfortunately, Sōthōfalas, accept that they truly are champions. I might point out that even Wencit of Rūm has vouched for them. So whether they are or not, they're going to be allowed to operate as if they were."

"So Wencit of Rūm *vouches* for them, does he? Well, how wonderful!" The baron made a disgusted sound and looked as if he wanted to spit. "Wencit may be impressive to many people, but I'm not one of them," he said.

This time, the little man couldn't keep his shock, even fear, entirely out of his expression, and the baron chuckled harshly.

"Don't mistake me," he said. "I freely acknowledge Wencit's power, and I have no intention of openly challenging him or giving him a visible threat as a target. However, it's been my observation that Wencit is also an inveterate meddler. He works for his own ends and according to his own plans, and he's done it for so long now that I'd be surprised if even he remembers what all those ends are. I don't doubt for a moment that he would 'vouch' for this Bahzell and 'Dame Kaeritha' if it served his purposes. For that matter, I don't doubt that he'd vouch for a three-legged, one-eyed, mangy *dog* if it served his purposes."

His visitor nodded neutrally, but even as he did, he made a mental note to reevaluate all of the plans he and the baron had hatched together. Cunning and intelligent the nobleman might be, but what he'd just said showed an alarming ability to project his own deviousness and inherent dishonesty onto others, whether it was merited or not. The nondescript little man had no objection to deviousness and dishonesty—they, like his ability to suddenly appear places he shouldn't be able to get into—were part of his stock in trade, after all. But automatically assuming that those same qualities were what motivated an opponent, especially a powerful opponent like Wencit of Rūm, was dangerous. Success required that enemies not be underestimated or discounted.

"At the same time," the baron continued, "I recognize that his imprimatur grants this Bahzell and this Kaeritha a certain legitimacy. Fortunately, Wencit himself has already left the Wind Plain. Apparently, he believes he's accomplished whatever goal brought him here in the first place, which may well be true. But what matters for our purposes is that he's no longer here to continue to support their ridiculous claims . . . or to protect them."

"Assuming they require his protection," the other man observed.

"Oh," the baron said unpleasantly, "I think you can rely upon it that they'll require all the protection they can get before too very much longer. I have quite a few little diversions planned for both of them. Especially 'Prince Bahzell.' I believe you'll find they're much too busy just staying alive to spend a great deal of time driving spokes into our wheels."

"I see." The other man nodded again, then stretched and walked slowly across to a chair which faced the baron's desk. He settled into it and crossed his legs, and his mind was busy behind his bland eyes.

Obviously, the baron had plans even he hadn't yet discovered. Well, that had been a given from the outset. Whatever his other flaws, the baron was an experienced and skillful conspirator, and the nondescript man had taken it for granted from the beginning that he would keep his various conspiracies as separated from one another as he could. Which was only fair, since the nondescript man was doing precisely the same thing.

But all of this secrecy and skulking about, however entertaining and profitable it might be, did lead to the occasional moment of uncertainty. For example, what sort of deviltry did the baron have in mind for Bahzell and Kaeritha? And did he began to suspect the deviltry the nondescript man and his other . . . associates had in mind for the two of them? More to the point, would the baron's plans get in the way of the nondescript man's?

He considered the delightfully different possibility of simply asking the baron straightforwardly what he intended, but he was afraid the shock might do his host's health a mischief. Besides, if he asked the baron that, the baron might ask him the same question, and that could lead to all sorts of complications. The nondescript man was confident that the baron was every bit as ambitious and ruthless as he could have hoped, but there were probably limits to the actions and allies he was prepared to contemplate, even so. Given how hard he was working at maintaining his technical ignorance about the nondescript man's own abilities, it seemed safe enough to assume he would definitely balk at direct, knowing association with black wizardry and Dark Gods. For that matter, it was even possible (however unlikely) that if the baron discovered the nondescript man's full intentions and plans he might actually choose to place the well-being of the Kingdom above his own power and position.

"I suppose, since you've obviously already made arrangements to keep both of them occupied, that you're aware Prince Yurokhas seems close to convincing the King to grant official ambassadorial status to Prince Bahzell?"

"I know the Prince would like to convince the King to do so," the baron replied a bit cautiously. "According to my own sources, however, the King remains resistant. And, I should add, that's also been my own observation as a member of his Council."

"The King does remain resistant . . . so far," the other man agreed. "But that doesn't mean he doesn't *want* to grant it, Milord. As you must know even better than I, Markhos is skilled at keeping his own counsel and avoiding any open appearance of commitment until after he's made up his mind to act."

"That's certainly true enough," the baron agreed sourly. "He learned that from his father. Fortunately, however, and with all due respect for the Crown, he's not as intelligent, in some ways, as his younger brother." The baron snorted. "Yurokhas may have a big enough maggot in his brain where religion is concerned to accept that this Bahzell might really be a champion of Tomanāk, but aside from that, he's a dangerous man. We're fortunate so much of his time is taken up with the Order of Tomanāk in Sōthōfalas. If it wasn't, he'd have even more opportunity to lead the King into dangerously foolish policy decisions."

"I thought you just said the Prince was intelligent," the other man said, more to poke the baron with a sharp stick than because he disagreed. A slight gleam in the baron's eye suggested that he understood exactly why the question had been asked, but he chose to answer it anyway.

"He *is* intelligent. Unfortunately, even intelligent people can be wrong, especially when something like religious belief begins to interfere with the pragmatic requirements of governing a kingdom. And when that happens, the more intelligent the believer is, the more damage he can do before someone else stops him. That's why Yurokhas is dangerous. He's not only smarter than the King, unfortunately, but the King knows he is, which is even more dangerous. Markhos doesn't always agree with Yurokhas, and he's quite capable of rejecting his brother's advice. But he doesn't do it out of hand, and it doesn't keep him from trusting Yurokhas and regarding the Prince as his closest, most reliable adviser."

"I see," the little man said again, and nodded. "Actually, Milord, that agrees very closely with my own analysis. Which leads to another perhaps delicate question." He paused until the baron raised his eyebrows politely, then shrugged. "I'm curious, Milord. Have you, by any chance, considered . . . removing Yurokhas from the equation?"

"I am prepared to do many things in the service of

the Kingdom and its best interests," the baron said in a cold, flat voice. "Yet the King is the heart and soul of the Kingdom. It is his person which unites us, and without that unity, we would disintegrate once more into the patchwork of squabbling, warring factions we had become in his grandfather's day. Because of that, his person must be sacrosanct, whatever I may think of his policies of the moment, under any but the most desperate of imaginable circumstances. At present, Prince Yurokhas stands only fifth in the succession, after the King's sons, yet the blood in his veins is the same as that in the veins of King Markhos himself. Mistaken and dangerous though I believe him to be, I will not see it spilled unless there is no other possible way to save the Kingdom."

"I see," the nondescript man said yet again. He leaned back in his chair, steepling his fingers across his chest, and gazed steadily at the baron. *How much of that*, he wondered, *was actually sincere? And how much of it is no more than so much rationalization? Protection not of the all-unifying King or his precious person but of the system and hierarchy which grants the good Baron his own power base?*

Not that it really mattered. He'd been told what he needed to know. Always assuming the baron had told him the truth.

"Very well, Milord," he said finally. "I think we've each given the other enough to chew on for the moment. I'll keep you informed of anything my sources turn up about Festian, Tellian, and the rest. For now, Lord Saratic and his people will keep the pressure on all of them, I feel certain."

He cocked one questioning eyebrow, and the baron nodded in confirmation.

"Excellent! And while they're doing that, my associates and I will be doing our bit to help. And if anything occurs to us which might help to distract or otherwise occupy Bahzell and Kaeritha, I assure you that we'll act upon it. With your agreement, I'll drop back by for another visit in about a week, unless something comes up in the meantime. If something should happen to come to your attention, or if any small way in which we might be of service should occur to you, you know how to get word to me."

The baron nodded just short of curtly, and the nondescript man rose from his chair.

"In that case, Milord, I'll bid you good evening," he said cheerfully, and stepped out of a windowed door onto the rain-swept terrace beyond. One of the baron's most trusted armsmen was responsible for guarding that door, but no shout of alarm or challenge was raised. Not that the baron thought for a moment that any lack of alertness on his armsman's part was to blame for that silence.

He watched his visitor disappear, then snorted in irritation, stood, and crossed the study to close the door behind him. Then he continued his interrupted trip towards his bedchamber, considering the conversation which had just ended.

As the other man had said, he reflected, he had a great deal to chew upon before he dropped off to sleep.

Chapter Eight

"Now remember, Soumeta. We *need* access to Herian and his outlets."

"I *understand* that, Theretha."

"Well, if things are as bad as Jolhanna says they are, then we've got to convince Master Manuar to approve our entry. *And* to enforce the charter's requirements that we be given fair access and the full protection of the law while we're here."

"Theretha," Soumeta said with exaggerated patience, "I was there when Mayor Yalith discussed the entire trip with you. I know why we're here, all right?"

Theretha Maglahnfressa bit her tongue. She knew it was only her own anxiety which made her so insistent. But still—

"Maybe I should come along," she said nervously. "I *have* met Master Manuar before. Maybe I could—"

"Theretha—!" Soumeta began, then visibly made herself stop and draw a deep breath.

"Look," she said, in the tone of someone hanging onto her own composure with both hands, "the Mayor discussed all of this with us before she sent us out here. She and the Town Council made it abundantly clear that the situation's gotten so bad that it's time we took an official position. And I, Theretha, as an officer in the City Guard, have official standing which *you* do not. As such, I will make the initial contact with the market master, and you won't. And I promise that I won't snatch him across the desk and cut his throat, no matter how he provokes me."

Theretha started to say something more, then closed her mouth with an almost audible snap as Soumeta glared at her. The older woman wasn't particularly fond of men, especially those in positions of power, in the first place, and her frustration was only too apparent. But Theretha never doubted that it—like the anger which accompanied it—was directed at the situation which had prompted this trip in the first place, and not at her.

Which didn't make her feel a whole lot better as she nodded acceptance of Soumeta's orders.

"Good," Soumeta growled, and Theretha stood huddled in her cloak, tense and unhappy beside the cart, and watched Soumeta stalk into the market master's office. A couple of townsfolk saw Soumeta coming and got out of her way—promptly. Unlike Theretha, Soumeta wore the war maids' chari and yathu with no cloak or poncho, despite the drizzly chill. She also wore a grimly determined expression . . . along with her swords, garrotte, and bandolier of throwing stars. No one was going to mistake her for anything but what she was—a dangerous individual in an unhappy mood—and Theretha wished she could convince herself that that was a good thing.

Her powers of self-persuasion didn't seem to be up to the task, and she didn't much care for the older war maid's expression herself, either. Nor did the fact that Soumeta had been nominated for this by Maretha Keralinfressa, the leader of the Council faction most in favor of taking a hard line with Trisu of Lorham, make her feel any better. She knew Mayor Yalith herself had wanted to be sure Kalatha sent someone who would stand up to any attempt at intimidation, but Theretha was worried by the politics of the choice. She couldn't escape the feeling that the real reason Yalith had put Soumeta in charge had been to blunt the increasingly vocal criticism of her own, less confrontational policies by Maretha's faction. Theretha was firmly in agreement with the mayor in this instance, and it worried her that Soumeta wasn't. Then again, she knew she'd never liked any sort of confrontation, whether it was physical or purely verbal, so perhaps she was overreacting.

She folded her delicate, skilled hands under the cloak, rubbing them lightly together for warmth. The spring day had been chilly enough at noon, with the sun directly overhead. Now that late afternoon was shading into evening and the omnipresent clouds of this torrential spring were blowing up once again out of the west, Theretha's breath was beginning to steam. It was going to be a wretched night if they wound up having to sleep under the thin protection of the cart's canvas cover, she thought miserably, and from Soumeta's combative expression, it was likely enough that that was precisely what they were going to do.

Not for the first time, Theretha wished she'd shown at least some aptitude for the weapons and self-defense training every war maid candidate was required to undergo. Unfortunately, she hadn't. Her instructors had done their best, but Theretha was a mouse at heart, not a direcat. As Darhanna, a senior instructor had put it, Theretha was one of those people whose best primary defense was to be invisible, because she simply couldn't bring herself to try to actually *hurt* someone, even in self-defense. Darhanna had been as kind as she could about it, and gotten her through the mandatory training somehow, but it had been only too obvious at the end of it that she regarded Theretha as someone who should never be allowed out without a keeper. Like Soumeta, she supposed.

Actually, Theretha agreed with Darhanna. There were times when she still couldn't believe she'd ever found the courage to run away to the war maids in the first place, despite everything her stepfather had done to her. She probably wouldn't have managed it even then, if her younger brother Barthon hadn't agreed to—insisted that she let him, actually—escort her to Kalatha, the nearest war maid free-town. Kalatha's mayor at the time had been deeply surprised to find a male member of her family actively abetting her in her flight. And surprise had turned into astonishment when the mayor discovered that Theretha's escape to the war maids had been Barthon's idea in the first place. In fact, the mayor had been suspicious, and initially disinclined to accept Theretha, as if she'd feared that Barthon was part of some elaborate trap or scheme to discredit the war maids. But then the mayor had received the report from Kalatha's senior physician on Theretha's condition.

It was the evidence of the botched, two-day-old miscarriage which had turned the mayor's suspicious resistance into angry acceptance. To her credit, the mayor hadn't even suggested that it might be Barthon's place to "avenge" Theretha. No doubt a good part of that restraint stemmed from the fact that war maids, like their patron Lillinara, believed it was a woman's own responsibility to seek redress for wrongs done to her. But the horrible, crippling burns Barthon had suffered in the furnace explosion which had killed their father would have prevented him from taking any sort of personal, direct action against their stepfather, and the mayor had recognized that. In fact, she'd offered *Barthon* a place in Kalatha, and Theretha still wished her brother had accepted the offer.

Despite the urging of the mayor and other older war maids, Theretha had steadfastly resisted the suggestion that she go to the courts in an effort to punish her stepfather. The odds against her being believed by the court in her home town were formidable. Those who knew only his public face thought her stepfather was an honest businessman, devoted to his deceased wife's family. They probably thought he liked puppies and small kittens, too, she thought grimly, and even if the magistrate had chosen to believe her, the chance that someone who could call on so many character witnesses—most of whom would actually believe what they were saying—would suffer any significant penalty would have been slight. As far as Theretha was concerned, she had better things to do with her life than to reopen all the old wounds in a futile effort to see her victimizer punished. She sometimes wondered if that belief was a reflection of the mouselike tendencies which had made any possibility of her becoming a warrior like Soumeta laughable.

Fortunately, she'd completed most of her apprenticeship before her father's death, and until her mother died, she'd insisted that Theretha's stepfather continue her training. He'd done so only grudgingly, but until his wife's death, he'd really had no choice, since she'd owned both the workshop and the store. But after Theretha's mother died, he'd taken gloating delight in refusing to sign her journeyman's certificate, no doubt because he'd seen that refusal as a means to deprive her of any independent livelihood and trap her in his power.

The war maids didn't much concern themselves with what sorts of certificates a woman might have received—or not received—before becoming a war maid. They were more concerned with what she could actually *do*, and the glassblower assigned to test Theretha had realized almost instantly what a treasure she represented. At sixteen and a half, Theretha had already possessed the skills her raw talent required to draw both utility and dazzling beauty from the clear, incandescent magic of molten sand. Now, ten years later, she was an acknowledged mistress of her craft, her work sought out and prized by wealthy commoners and aristocrats alike throughout most of the Kingdom of the Sothōii. Her pieces and name were even known to a select few collectors in the Empire of the Axe, and they commanded substantial prices. Very few of the connoisseurs who purchased them for prices Theretha sometimes had trouble believing were real, even now, realized she was a war maid, although it was unlikely many of them would have cared, even if they had.

She accepted an increasing number of commissions these days, but she'd never forgotten her father's admonition. Beauty was to the soul as water was to a fish, but it was the more mundane work of a glassblower's hands, dedicated to the day-to-day sustenance of others, that was his true reason for being. And so Theretha insisted—with the stubborn ferocity of a mouse who had discovered how to become a direcat in this one aspect of her life—upon keeping her hand turned to the merely useful, as well. The glassware, like the pharmacist's bottles and the spice seller's jars, which did nothing at all . . . except save lives or help someone else earn an honest living.

Or like the glassware in the cart she and Soumeta had brought to Thalar.

She hadn't really wanted to make the journey—especially not now, when everything seemed so . . . unsettled and difficult. For that matter, Mayor Yalith clearly had very mixed feelings about it. In a way, Theretha was the "kid sister" of every war maid in Kalatha, and all of them were intensely protective of her. Probably because they realized she was completely unsuited to protect *herself* from anything more dangerous than a crazed chipmunk, she thought.

But she'd decided that she didn't have a choice, and then managed to convince Yalith to see it her way. The bulk of the output from Theretha's workshop and her six employees consisted not of her beautiful art pieces, but of those everyday, practical items. That was what earned the routine revenues Kalatha needed and paid the salaries of the people who worked for her. It was essential to maintain the outlet through which those wares might be sold.

Thalar wasn't a very large or especially wealthy town, but it was the largest and wealthiest in the holding of Lorham. More to the point, it had the biggest, most active market, and Theretha had established what she'd thought were good relationships with the merchants who distributed her more mundane products. Especially with Herian Axemaster, who handled over half of all the glassware and pottery which moved through Lorham. Herian was also a factor for Clan Harkanath, the powerful Dwarvenhame trading house. But those relationships seemed to have suffered serious damage, along with every other aspect of Kalatha's relations with Lord Trisu and all of his subjects. If she wanted to maintain her access to the Thalar market, and through it, to the world beyond, she'd decided, she had to come along and see what she could do to repair them And, as she had somewhat delicately suggested to the mayor, the fact that her Thalar contacts also knew about her art pieces, and that Herian had actually handled the sale of several of them for her, ought to give her a bit more clout than she might have had otherwise.

Unfortunately . . .

Theretha bit her lip as she looked in through the open door of the market master's office and saw Soumeta leaning over Master Manuar's desk. The lamps were already lit in anticipation of the rapidly oncoming evening, and Soumeta's short blond hair gleamed in their mellow light as she stabbed an angry index finger repeatedly onto the desk's top. It was impossible for Theretha to hear anything from here, but from Soumeta's flushed face and Manuar's thunderous expression she strongly suspected that the two of them were shouting at one another.

She stopped rubbing her hands together under her cloak, but only so that she could actively wring them. This was bad. This was very bad! Lillinara knew enough other war maids had experienced difficulties in Thalar's market, just as they had in what seemed to be every town, village, and hamlet throughout Trisu's domain. There'd always been some discrimination against war maid merchants, farmers, and craftswomen, but it had grown much worse over the past several months. In fact, it had reached the point that the market masters, the magistrates whose responsibility it was to oversee the fair and legal operation of the markets, appeared to have washed their hands of it. Some of them actually seemed to be actively harassing any war maid who entered their jurisdiction, or even flatly refusing to sign the permits required to trade in the markets they supervised. But Theretha hadn't been able to believe that Manuar, who'd always been a gruff stickler when it came to the discharge of his duties, could possibly be one of those.

Manuar suddenly shoved himself up out of his chair, and leaned forward over his desk. He braced his weight on the knuckles of his fisted left hand while he shoved his face within inches of Soumeta's and slammed his right palm on the desktop. If he hadn't been shouting before, he obviously was now, Theretha thought glumly, and took two involuntary steps towards his office before her memory of Yalith's instructions stopped her.

Soumeta closed her mouth, muscles bunching along her jaw as she clenched her teeth. She glared at the market master, her anger almost physically visible from where Theretha stood. Then she turned on her heel and stormed out of Manuar's office.

Not good, Theretha thought. *Not good at all.*

"That . . . that . . . that *man*!" Soumeta spat. Rain was beginning to sift over them again, glistening on her hair and the bare skin exposed by her chari and yathu, and she reminded Theretha of nothing in the world so much as a furious soaked cat.

"It looked like it didn't go very well?" Theretha's tone turned the statement into a question. She hated it when she did that. It always made her feel indecisive, more like a mouse than ever.

"You might say that," Soumeta snarled. "Just like you might say it's been a little damp this spring!"

"How bad was it?" Theretha sighed.

"Just for starters, he says *Jolhanna* is the one who's done all of the antagonizing here in Thalar. It wasn't any of the town's merchants—oh, no! For some reason known only to her, our representative—the person whose job it is to keep our access to the market open—has taken it upon herself to pick fights with virtually every important merchant in Thalar!"

"What?!" Theretha shook her head in confused disbelief. "Why in the world would she do something like that?"

"Exactly my point!" Soumeta's voice was harsh. "Jolhanna has—*we* have—no reason to be confrontational. Not here, not about this, and certainly not without provocation. But according to Manuar, that's exactly what she was. And because of her 'misbehavior,' the rest of us are not welcome here."

"He's officially excluded us from the market?" Theretha stared at the other war maid in shock.

"No, not officially," Soumeta replied, almost as if she hated conceding Manuar even that. "But he didn't have to. What he said was that, of course he would sign our permit and see to it that anyone trading with us complies with every requirement of the law and the charter. However, he pointed out, not even the charter requires people to *buy* from us if they choose not to. And apparently," she bared her teeth in a smile totally devoid of humor, "it just happens that every merchant in Thalar has decided not to trade with us. Completely spontaneously, of course."

"I'm sure Herian wouldn't feel that way," Theretha protested.

"Maybe not, but it doesn't matter," Soumeta sighed. "Herian isn't here."

"What?" Theretha blinked. "That's ridiculous. Herian is *always* here!"

"Not according to Manuar, he isn't," Soumeta said, biting off each word as if she were chewing horseshoes. Theretha looked at her in consternation, and she shrugged irritably. "Figure it out for yourself, Theretha. If Manuar's lying and Herian *is* here, then there's no point in even hoping he'll enforce the charter's provisions for us, whatever he says. And if Herian *isn't* here, that may be even worse. It may mean he's chosen to join in this boycott of our people and just doesn't want to openly admit it. Either way, I see no reason to stay here and batter our heads against a wall that isn't going to come down for us!"

"But—" Theretha began, only to have Soumeta cut her off with a sharp shake of her head.

"We're not staying," she said flatly.

"But we must!" Theretha protested. "We need the markets—the income! We can't just—"

"Oh, yes we can," Soumeta told her. "I don't like the feel of this one bit, Theretha. I'm not sure it's even safe here, certainly not sure enough to risk exposing you to danger."

"Me? In danger here in Thalar?" Soumeta seemed to be speaking a foreign language, and Theretha shook her head, trying to understand what the other war maid was thinking. "You should have let *me* talk to Manuar," she said with mingled plaintiveness and frustration. "He *knows* me. For Lillinara's sake, I've eaten lunch in his home, Soumeta!"

"I know you have. And I know that's one reason you were sent along in the first place. But he made it fairly obvious that there are people here in Thalar who are really upset over our supposed demands and Jolhanna's supposed hostility. He seems to think some of those upset people might just try to find someone to take revenge on."

"Revenge for *what*?" Theretha demanded in total confusion and exasperation. "All I want to do is sell some bottles! This doesn't make any sense!"

"That's because no one is feeling particularly sensible just now," Soumeta told her harshly. "And, for the second time, I don't have any idea what started it all. The one thing I'm positive of is that it wasn't *Jolhanna* who went crazy. After that, I don't have a clue. Unless—"

"Unless what?" Theretha asked when the other woman paused.

"Unless Trisu and his cronies are trying to concoct some sort of a bizarre pretext, a justification for the way they've been systematically infringing on our rights and boundaries."

"That's preposterous." Theretha wished she sounded more certain of that than she felt.

"Of course it is. But that doesn't mean it's not happening." The older war maid shook her head. "You know, I didn't want to believe it, myself. Not even when the Voice at Quaysar warned Mayor Yalith that the Mother was uneasy. But now—"

She shrugged, and Theretha nodded slowly and miserably. The Voice hadn't been very specific, or not, at least, in any of the messages from her which Theretha knew anything about. But when a priestess of Lillinara—especially *the* priestess, at the Quaysar Temple of Lillinara—warned a war maid free-town of impending danger, it was best to pay attention.

"But that's why we're getting out of here, now—this evening," Soumeta continued flatly. "If I knew what was going on, I might not be so concerned over whether or not I could handle it. But this whole thing is so crazy, so bizarre, that I can't begin to figure out what's happening, or even what's *already* happened. In the meantime, though, it's my job to be sure you get home safe and sound. You and your art commissions are more important to Kalatha in the long run than opening the local markets, and if Manuar's telling the truth, not just blowing smoke out of his arse because he's pissed at me for calling him on his dereliction of his duties, then there might be a genuine danger of something . . . unpleasant happening to you.

"So climb back up in the cart, Theretha. We're leaving. Now."

Theretha opened her mouth, ready for one, final protest. But Soumeta's expression stopped her. The other woman's face was like a stone wall, a fortress turned against the world in general and Thalar and Master Manuar in particular. There was no point arguing, the glassblower realized.

The rain was falling harder as Theretha clambered up into the cart, in the center aisle between the crates of glassware they'd brought with them so hopefully. She heard the raindrops hitting the taut canvas above her, like an endless series of tiny fists, punching the cover. Here and there, water broke through the fabric, running downward across its inner curve. Some of it seemed to home in on Theretha, and she wrapped her cloak more tightly still about her as Soumeta walked around to the front of the cart and got a good grip on the cart pony's halter. The older woman clucked to the pony, and Theretha grabbed at one of the strapped-up crates for balance as the cart lurched back into motion.

She was going to be cold, wet, and thoroughly miserable by dawn, she thought as the sweet chiming of vibrated glass sang softly to the rain's patter from the crates. And the fact that Soumeta was going to be even wetter and colder only made her feel even more frustrated and obscurely guilty. Soumeta was right—Mayor Yalith had made it clear she was to be Kalatha's official representative, and that she was to "look after" Theretha. Yet Theretha couldn't rid herself of the gnawing suspicion that if she'd only spoken to Manuar herself, she might somehow have made a difference.

But she hadn't, and as the cart jolted and splashed through the rain, she settled into the most comfortable position she could find and wondered just when everything had started going so dreadfully wrong.

Chapter Nine

"That was delicious, Tala—as always," Kaeritha said with a deeply satisfied sigh. She laid her spoon neatly in the empty bowl of bread pudding and patted her flat stomach as she leaned back in her chair, smiling at the sturdy, middle-aged hradani woman who'd been sent along by Prince Bahnak as his son's housekeeper.

"I'm glad you enjoyed it, Milady," Tala said in a pronounced Navahkan accent. "It's always a pleasure to cook for someone who knows good food when she tastes it."

"Or devours it—in copious quantities," Brandark observed, eyeing the empty platters on the table.

"I didn't seem to notice you shirking your share of the devouring, Milord," Tala replied dryly.

"No, but there's more of me to maintain," Brandark replied with a grin, and Kaeritha grinned back at him. Brandark might be of less than average height for even a Bloody Sword hradani, but that still left him a good three inches taller than Kaeritha, and he was far more massively built.

"Aye," Bahzell agreed. "For a sawed-off runt of a hradani who's after sitting on his arse with a pen and a bit of parchment all day, you've a bit of meat on your bones, I suppose."

"I'll remember that the next time you need some obscure Sothōii text translated," Brandark assured him.

"Hush, now, Brandark!" the fourth person at the table scolded. Gharnal Uthmâgson was short for a Horse Stealer, but taller than Brandark and almost as massively built. Which still left him over a full foot shorter than his foster brother, Bahzell. "It's not so very nice of you to be pointing out as how the thin air up where Bahzell's after keeping his head keeps a man's brain from working. It's not as if it was after being his fault he can't be reading for himself."

He grinned at Brandark, without a trace of the vitriolic hatred for all Bloody Swords which had made him Brandark's bitter enemy when the smaller hradani first accompanied Bahzell to Hurgrum.

"Speaking of obscure Sothōii texts," Kaeritha said in the voice of an adult overlooking a children's squabble as a smiling Tala withdrew, "I wonder if you've come across a copy of the war maids' charter in your forays through Tellian's library, Brandark?"

"I haven't been looking for one," the Bloody Sword replied. "I've done a little research on the entire question of war maids since you and Tellian discussed them the other morning, but I've really only scratched the surface so far. I assume there's probably a copy of the charter and its amending documents somewhere, though. Would you like me to take a look for them?"

"I don't know." Kaeritha grimaced. "It's just that I've realized I'm really pretty appallingly ignorant where any detailed knowledge about the war maids is concerned. Tellian's suggestion that whatever I'm supposed to be dealing with concerns them may well be right, but my training in Sothōii jurisprudence is a bit shakier than my training in Axeman law. If I am supposed to be investigating the war maids' claims, it would probably be a good idea to know what their prerogatives are in the first place."

"I'm not so sure laying hands on a copy of their

original charter would be enough to be telling you that," Bahzell put in. He leaned back in a chair which creaked alarmingly under his weight.

"Why not?" Kaeritha asked.

"The war maids aren't so very popular with most Sothōii," Bahzell said in a tone of deliberate understatement. "Not to be putting too fine a point on it, there's those amongst the Sothōii who'd sooner see an invading hradani army in their lands than one of the war maids' free-towns."

"They're that unpopular?" Kaeritha looked surprised, and Bahzell shrugged.

"An invading army is likely to be burning their roofs over their heads, Kerry. But roofs can be rebuilt, when all's said. Rebuilding a way of life, now—that's after being just a mite harder."

"And that's exactly how your typical conservative Sothōii would see having a batch of war maids move in next door," Brandark agreed.

Kaeritha nodded in acknowledgment, yet there was still a baffled edge to her expression. As she'd told Leeana, she'd been born a peasant in Moretz, which was at least as patriarchal a society as that of the Sothōii, but she'd fled that land when she'd been even younger than Leeana was now. And she'd also been educated in the Empire of the Axe, where women enjoyed far broader choices and possibilities then were generally available to Sothōii women.

"Kerry," Bahzell said, "I'm thinking you've too much of the Axewoman in you. You, if any, ought to have realized by now how hard any Sothōii is after finding it to wrap his mind round the very notion of a woman as a warrior."

Kaeritha nodded again, more emphatically, and Bahzell chuckled. If he found his position in Balthar difficult as a hradani, Kaeritha had found hers only marginally less so . . . as the heckler she'd trounced outside the temple made clear. Tellian's men, and those of the city guard, had at least taken their cue from their liege lord and extended to her the same deference and respect any champion of Tomanāk might have expected. Yet it was only too obvious that even they found the concept of a female champion profoundly unnatural.

"Well, for all that our folk've spent the best part of a thousand years massacring one another," Bahzell continued, "there's much to be said for the Sothōii. But one thing no one is ever likely to be suggesting is that they've an overabundance of innovation in their natures, especially where matters of tradition and custom are concerned. Don't let Tellian be fooling you. For a Sothōii, he's about as radical as you're ever likely to meet, and well-educated about foreign lands, to boot. But your typical Sothōii is stiffer-necked than even a hradani, and the real conservatives are still after thinking the wheel is a dangerous, newfangled, harebrained novelty that will never really be catching on."

Kaeritha chuckled, and Brandark grinned.

"Aye, and some of them are stupid enough to be after thinking they invented fire for their very own selves just last week," Gharnal agreed. His grin was a bit sharper than Brandark's, honed on a core of deeply cherished hostility for all things Sothōii, but that represented a tremendous exercise of restraint for him.

"I won't say there isn't an element of the pot and kettle in that pithy description, Kerry," Brandark said after a moment. "But there's a lot of accuracy in it, too. The Sothōii take a tremendous amount of pride in how 'traditional' they are, you know. Their very name—'Sothōii'—is derived from the Old Kontovaran word *sothōfranos*, which translates roughly as 'sons of the fathers.' According to their traditions, they're descended from the highest nobility of the Empire of Ottovar, and they've grown pretty fanatical about protecting that line of descent—intellectually, as well as physically—over the last twelve centuries or so."

"Are they really?" Kaeritha asked. "Descended from the old Ottovarn nobility, that is?"

"That's hard to say," Brandark said with a shrug. "It's certainly possible. But the significant point is that they *think* they are, and that pride in their ancestry is part of what produces those conservatives Bahzell and Gharnal were just talking about. And the very existence of the war maids is an affront to their view of the way their entire society—or the rest of the world, for that matter—is supposed to work. In fact, the war maids wouldn't exist at all if the Crown hadn't specifically guaranteed their legal rights. Unfortunately—and I suspect this is what Bahzell was getting at—calling that royal guarantee 'a charter' is more of a convenient shorthand than an accurate description."

Kaeritha cocked an eyebrow, and he shrugged.

"It's actually more of a bundle of separate charters and decrees dealing with specific instances than some sort of neat, unified legal document, Kerry. According to what I've learned so far, the original proclamation legitimizing the war maids was unfortunately vague on several key points. Over the next century or so, additional proclamations intended to clarify some of the obscurity, and even an occasional judge's opinion, were bundled together, and the whole mishmash is what they fondly call their 'charter.' I haven't actually looked at it, you understand, but I'm familiar enough with the same sort of thing among the hradani. When something just sort of grows up the way the war maids' 'charter' has, there's usually a substantial degree of variation between the terms of its constituent documents. And that means there's an enormous scope for ambiguities and misunderstandings . . . especially when the people whose rights those decrees are supposed to stipulate aren't very popular with their neighbors."

"You have a positive gift for understatement," Kaeritha sighed, and shook her head. "Axeman law is much more codified and uniform than what you're describing, but I've seen more than enough of this kind of melt-it-all-together mess of precedent, statute, and common law even there." She sighed again. "Just what rights *do* the war maids have? In general terms, I mean, if there's that much variation from grant to grant."

"Basically," Brandark replied, "they have the right to determine how they want to live their own lives, free of traditional Sothōii familial and social obligations."

The Bloody Sword scholar tipped back in his chair, folded his arms, and frowned thoughtfully.

"Although they're uniformly referred to as 'war maids,' most of them aren't, really." Kaeritha raised an eyebrow, and he shrugged. "Virtually every legal right up here on the Wind Plain is associated in one way or another with the holding of land and the reciprocal obligation of service to the Crown, Kaeritha, and the war maids are no exception. As part of King Gartha's original proclamation, their free-towns are obligated to provide military forces to the Crown. In my more cynical moments, I think Gartha included that obligation as a deliberate attempt to effectively nullify the charter while pacifying the women who'd demanded it, since it's hard for me to conceive of any Sothōii king who could honestly believe a batch of women could provide an effective military force."

"If that *was* after being the case, then he was in for a nasty surprise," Gharnal put in, and Brandark chuckled.

"Oh, he was that!" he agreed. "And in my *less* cynical moments, I'm inclined to think Gartha included the obligation only because he had to. Given how much of the current crop of Sothōii nobles is hostile to the war maids, the opposition to authorizing their existence in the first place must have been enormous, and the great nobles of Gartha's day were far more powerful, in relation to the Crown, than they are today. Which means his Council probably could have mustered the support to block the initial charter without that provision. For that matter, the measure's opponents would have been the ones most inclined to believe that requiring military service out of a bunch of frail, timid women would be an effective, underhanded way of negating Gartha's intentions without coming out in open opposition.

"At any rate, only about a quarter of all 'war maids' are actually warriors. Their own laws and traditions require all of them to have at least rudimentary training in self-defense, but most of them follow other professions. Some of them are farmers or, like most Sothōii, horse breeders. But more of them are shopkeepers, blacksmiths, potters, physicians, glassmakers, even lawyers—the sorts of tradesmen and craftsmen who populate most free-towns or cities up here. And the purpose of their charter is to ensure that they have the same legal rights and protections, despite the fact that they're women, that men in the same professions would enjoy."

"Are they *all* women?"

"Well," Brandark said dryly, "the real war *maids* are. But if what you're actually asking is whether or not war maid society is composed solely of women, the answer is no. The fact that a woman chooses to live her own life doesn't necessarily mean she hates all men. Of course, many of them become war maids because they *aren't* very fond of men, and quite a few of them end up partnering with other women. *Not* a practice likely to endear them to Sothōii men who already think the entire notion of women making decisions for themselves is unnatural. But it would be a serious mistake to assume that any woman who chooses to become—or, for that matter, is born—a war maid isn't going to fall in love with a man and choose to spend her life with him on her own terms. Or at least to dally with one on occasion. And war maid mothers do tend to produce male children from time to time, just like any other mothers. Of course, those two facts lead to some of the thornier 'ambiguities' I mentioned earlier."

"Why?" Kaeritha leaned forward, elbows on the table, her expression intent, while she cradled her wineglass in her hands, and Bahzell hid a smile. He'd seen exactly that same hunting-hawk expression when she encountered a new combat technique.

"There's always been some question as to whether or not the war maids' charter automatically extends to their male children," Brandark explained. "Or, for that matter, to their *female* children, in the eyes of some of the true reactionaries. When a woman chooses to become a war maid, her familial duties and inheritance obligations are legally severed. Even your true sticks-in-the-mud have been forced to admit that. But a fair number of nobles continue to assert that the legal severance applies only to *her*—that whatever line of inheritance or obligation would have passed through her to her children is unimpaired. For the most part, the courts haven't agreed with that view, but enough have to mean it's still something of a gray area. I suppose it's fortunate most 'first-generation' war maids come from commoner stock, or at most from the minor nobility—the squirearchy, you might call them. Or maybe it isn't. If the higher nobility had been forced to come to grips with the question, the Crown Courts would have been driven to make a definitive ruling on the disputed points years ago.

"At any rate, the exact question of the legal status of war maids' children is still up in the air, at least to some extent. And so is the question of their marriages. Their more diehard opponents argue that since their precious charter severs all familial obligations, it precludes the creation of new ones, which means no war maid marriage has any legal validity in their eyes. And there really is some question, I understand, in this instance. I doubt very much that Gartha had any intention of precluding the possibility of war maid marriages, but Baron Tellian's senior magistrate tells me some of the controlling language is less precise than it ought to be. According to him, everyone knows it's a matter of technicalities and reading the letter of the law, not its spirit, but apparently the problems do exist. And, to be perfectly honest, from what he said—and a couple of things he *didn't* say—I think the war maids have done their own bit to keep the waters muddied."

"Why would they do that?" Kaeritha asked. "Unless . . . Oh. The children."

"Exactly. If war maid marriages have no legal standing, then every child of a war maid is technically illegitimate."

"Which would take them out of the line of inheritance, unless there were no legitimate heirs at all," Kaeritha said with a nod of understanding, but her expression was troubled.

"I can follow the logic," she continued after a moment, "but it seems awfully shortsighted of them. Or maybe like the triumph of expedience. It may prevent their children from being yanked away from them and drawn into a system they wanted out of, but it also prevents them from extending the legal protections of their own families to those same children."

"Yes, it does," Brandark agreed. "On the other hand, their own courts and judges don't see it that way, and for the most part, the charters which create their free-towns extend the jurisdiction of their judges to all of the citizens of those towns. The problem comes with legal cases which cross the boundaries between the war maids' jurisdiction and those of more traditional Sothōii nobles."

"Tomanāk," Kaeritha sighed. "What a mess!"

"Well, it isn't after being just the tidiest situation in the world," Bahzell agreed. "Still and all, it's one the Sothōii have been working at for two or three centuries now. There's those as have some mighty sharp axes to grind, but for the most part, they've learned how to be getting on with one another."

"'For the most part' still leaves a lot of room for potential trouble, though," Kaeritha pointed out. "And somehow, I don't think He'd be sending me off to deal with a crop of Sothōii who were 'getting on with one another.' Do you?"

"Well, as to that," Bahzell replied with a crooked smile, "no."

It was still raining when Kaeritha left Hill Guard . . . of course.

At least it wasn't a torrential downpour, she told herself encouragingly as she started down the steep approach road from Baron Tellian's ancestral keep. The Wind Plain was actually a huge, high plateau which, for the most part, was one vast ocean of grass and occasionally interspersed patches of ancient forest. The terrain might fairly be described as "rolling," but there weren't very many true hills on it, so, over the centuries, those which did exist had exhibited a distinct tendency to attract towns and fortifications. Hill Guard had come into existence in exactly that fashion the better part of eight hundred years ago when Halyu

Bowmaster, the first Lord Warden of Balthar, had looked about for a suitable spot for the capital of his new holding. Now the city of Balthar sprawled out for several miles from the castle which brooded down over it from above.

The Sothōii weren't great city builders. For the most part, their people continued to follow their ancestors' pastoral lifestyle. While the Wind Plain remained the heart of their realm, they'd also acquired extensive holdings to the east, below the towering plateau. Those lower regions enjoyed a far milder climate, and a substantial portion of the vast Sothōii horse and cattle herds were wintered in those more salubrious surroundings. But the huge stud farms where the magnificent Sothōii warhorses were bred and trained remained where tradition insisted they must—atop the Wind Plain. And for whatever reason, the Sothōii coursers flatly refused to live anywhere else.

Horses—and coursers—required a lot of space, and the Sothōii population by and large was scattered sparsely about the Wind Plain, watching over its herds. That produced a lot of villages and small towns, but not very many cities. Which, conversely, meant that what cities there were tended to be quite large.

They were also well maintained, and Kaeritha moved briskly along the wide, straight avenue on the new mount Tellian had insisted upon giving her. She'd argued about accepting it, but not, she was guiltily aware, very hard. Any Sothōii warhorse was worth a prince's ransom, and the mare Tellian had bestowed upon Kaeritha was a princess among her own kind. Smaller and lighter than the heavier cavalry horses of other lands, the winter-hardy Sothōii warhorse was perfectly suited to the swift, deadly, archery-dominated tactics of the people who had bred it. Indeed, only the coursers themselves exceeded its combination of speed and endurance.

And unlike Kaeritha, the warhorses seemed perfectly content with the Wind Plain's soggy spring weather.

She chuckled damply at the thought and reached down to pat the mare's shoulder. The horse flicked her ears in acknowledgment of the caress, and Kaeritha smiled. The mare's dark chestnut coloring, even darker at the moment thanks to the rain, probably accounted for her name, but Kaeritha still felt that naming such an affectionate creature "Dark War Cloud Rising" was just a bit much. She'd promptly shortened it to "Cloudy," which had earned her a rather pained look from Tellian. His stable master, on the other hand, had only grinned, and from the readiness with which Cloudy answered to her new name, Kaeritha suspected that the stable hands had employed a similar diminutive before she ever came along.

A packhorse trotted along at Cloudy's heels. Even he, although far more plebeian than the aristocratic warhorse, was a magnificent creature. He would have been happily accepted as a superior light cavalry mount anywhere but among the Sothōii, and Kaeritha knew she had never been better mounted in her life. Which, she reflected, was saying something, given the care the Order of Tomanāk took when it came to equipping their god's champions.

Despite Balthar's size, there was very little traffic as she approached the city's East Gate. The weather undoubtedly had a little something to do with that, she thought, looking past the open gate to the rain blowing across the road beyond and rippling the endless spring grass of the Wind Plain. Sothōii roads were not, by and large, up to Axeman standards. Few highways outside the Empire itself were, but the Sothōii's efforts came up shorter than most, and Kaeritha felt an undeniable sinking sensation as she contemplated the one before her. It was straight enough—not surprisingly, given the unobstructed terrain of the Wind Plain—but that was about all she could say for the broad line of mud stretching out before her.

The officer commanding the gate guard saluted her respectfully as she passed, and she nodded back with equal courtesy. Yet even as she did, she wondered how the officer might have greeted her if not for the gold and green badge of the Order of Tomanāk Tellian's seamstresses had embroidered across the front of her poncho.

Then she was through the gate, and the gentle pressure of a heel sent Cloudy trotting down the last bit of slope towards the waiting road.

Chapter Ten

"I apologize for intruding, Milord, but someone has arrived to see you."

"Indeed?" Baron Tellian paused with his glass half-raised and looked up at his majordomo with a slight, inquiring frown. "Who is it, Kalan?" His tone added another, unspoken question—*And why is his arrival important enough for you to disturb my lunch?*

"It's Sir Yarran Battlecrow, Milord. He says he carries an urgent message from Lord Warden Glanharrow," the majordomo said, in a calm, unflustered voice, and Tellian's eyes narrowed. Then he nodded.

"Thank you, Kalan," he said. "Please have him shown into my study. See to it that he's offered a chance to wash up first, if he so desires, and that refreshments are available to him. Tell him I'll join him there as soon as I can."

"Of course, Milord," Kalan replied, then coughed gently. "In fact, I'd already given those instructions."

"You're entirely too efficient, Kalan," Tellian said with a smile. "Certainly more efficient than I deserve."

"It's kind of you to say so, anyway, Milord," Kalan murmured, and withdrew with a slight bow.

Tellian gazed down into his wineglass for several seconds, then took a sip and set the glass on the table. He wiped his mouth with a linen napkin and looked around the circle of his family and guests.

"Fortunately, I think we were about finished here," he said.

"And if we weren't," Baroness Hanatha said, "we'd all pretend we were, anyway."

"Of course you would, my dear. And so cheerfully and so well that I would never even suspect how I'd trodden on your enjoyment of the meal for reasons of state."

The two of them shared a smile, but there was more than a hint of anxiety behind the baroness' jade eyes. Tellian saw it, and reached out to touch the back of her hand in brief, wordless reassurance. Then he looked at Bahzell and Brandark.

"It doesn't take a wizard or a mage to divine the reason for Sir Yarran's visit. I think it might be as well for the two of you to join us in the study, if that would be convenient."

"I'm thinking it would be convenient enough for the pair of us," Bahzell rumbled. "But it's in my mind that Lord Festian and Sir Yarran might be minded for him to have a word or two with you in private without such as us listening in."

"It might," Tellian agreed. "On the other hand, the Gullet opens on Glanharrow. That means your father, and so you, Bahzell, have a legitimate interest in anything that happens there. Especially if it concerns the man who was named to replace that idiot Redhelm. Don't tell me you haven't been expecting a messenger like this for weeks, man. Just as I have."

"Well, as to that, I'll admit as how I'm more than a mite surprised he's waited this long to be sending for help. I've no sources to match the ones you've no doubt got, but those I do have have been telling me as how things have been getting steadily worse in Glanharrow. And just as you—and, no doubt, Lord Festian and Sir Yarran—I've no least doubt as how it's the doing of some of your folk who weren't so very happy to be seeing Festian replace Mathian."

"Who would just happen to be the same people who aren't too happy about the novel concept of Sothōii and hradani living in a state which resembles peace," Brandark added dryly.

"Exactly." Tellian nodded. "You have both the right and the reason to know what sorts of problems your neighbor might be experiencing, if only so that you're forewarned if . . . unanticipated changes require you to protect yourselves. More to the point, and selfishly, from my perspective, you may be able to offer some additional insight, Bahzell." Bahzell twitched his ears questioningly, and Tellian chuckled. "I happen to know that your sister Marglyth's agents in Glanharrow considerably outnumber my own, Bahzell, despite that rather diplomatic comment of yours on our relative sources. Which is as it should be, really."

"I suppose it *is* possible I'm after hearing the occasional tidbit, or rumor," Bahzell conceded with a grin.

"I'm sure," Tellian said dryly. "But whether you have anything to add or not, I want you there. And you, too, I think, Trianal," he continued, looking at the dark-haired young man seated at the foot of the table.

Sir Trianal Bowmaster was the oldest son of Tellian's younger brother. Garlayn Bowmaster had married very young, but, then, Garlayn had always been the quintessential, impetuous Sothōii. He'd also *died* very young, in a training accident which had resulted largely from that same impetuosity, leaving three young sons and a daughter behind. Tellian had accepted Trianal for training in the military arts when he was only ten, and he'd just turned nineteen only two months before. Despite his youth, he was a thinker, unlike his father, who'd already demonstrated an insight into tactics beyond his years. He'd earned his knighthood, not simply had it handed to him, although he was still short on experience in the field. But for all of his good points, Trianal was considerably more conservative than his uncle. It had taken him quite a while to come to terms with Tellian's "surrender" to Bahzell, and Bahzell suspected that he still harbored some prickly resentments.

"Me, Uncle?" Trianal sounded surprised, and Tellian nodded.

"You know as much as any of my officers about the situation in Glanharrow, and I trust your discretion. Besides, I think I'd like to get you more actively involved in *supporting* Lord Festian."

"Yes, Milord," Trianal said, and his face flushed just a bit.

So he's after noticing his uncle's tone, Bahzell thought, and hid a mental chuckle as he recalled times his own father had done the same sort of thing to him. "Whacking some wit into him," as Prince Bahnak had described it. *And I never enjoyed it at all, at all*, Bahzell thought, *so more power to the lad that he can be taking his whack without so much as a wince*.

"Good," Tellian said, giving his nephew a nod, then folded his napkin. He set it beside his plate, pushed back his chair, rose, and kissed his wife's cheek. Then he glanced at Leeana and smiled crookedly.

"I'm not inviting you this time, daughter of mine," he told her. Brief disappointment flickered in her eyes, but it came and went so quickly it was more imagined than seen, and she returned his smile. "After all," he continued, "I'm quite sure you have your own sources. Come to the library before bed tonight. Let me know what you've been able to pick up about Sir Yarran's visit on your own."

"Yes, Poppa," she murmured in her most dutiful tone, green eyes glinting wickedly, and Tellian laughed. He stroked one hand over her gleaming, golden-red hair, then returned his attention to Bahzell and Brandark.

"Such a submissive child," he said, shaking his head regretfully. "Not a spark of spirit, not an ounce of spunk anywhere in her."

"Aye," Bahzell said, smiling as Leeana stuck out her tongue at him. "I've noticed as how all of your womenfolk seem to be beaten down, Milord."

"Every one of them," Tellian sighed, and then twitched as his "beaten down" wife poked him shrewdly in the ribs.

✧ ✧ ✧

Sir Yarran climbed out of the comfortable chair with something that looked rather more like a respectful nod than a bow as Tellian, Bahzell, Brandark, and Trianal entered the study. He'd obviously availed himself of the offer of a wash up, and changed out of his riding boots, but there were still traces of the Wind Plain's omnipresent springtime mud on his trousers. A tray on the small table beside his chair bore the remains of a fat sandwich, a bowl of thick, savory vegetable soup, a couple of apple cores, and a mostly empty stein of beer, and he brushed a dusting of crumbs from his tunic as he straightened up.

"Welcome, Sir Yarran!" Tellian said, striding across the study to take the older man's right hand and forearm in a warrior's clasp. "I trust my people have seen to your needs adequately?"

"Oh, aye, that they have." Yarran patted his flat belly with his free hand and grinned. "They wanted to sit me down to an entire meal, but I told them a sandwich and some soup would do me fine, and so it did. Thank you."

"You're quite welcome," Tellian assured him, giving his forearm a final squeeze before he released it. Then the baron settled into a chair of his own, waving an invitation for Yarran to sit back down. The knight was obviously pleased by the gesture, but he chose to remain standing, in a sort of modified version of the Sothōii stand-easy, as the others found seats facing him.

"I have no doubt you bring me less than pleasant news from Lord Warden Festian," Tellian continued, "but you are always welcome in my house, nonetheless. I know from my correspondence with him that he has complete faith in you, and if he does, then so do I."

"Uh, thank you. Thank you, Milord Baron." The gray-haired knight seemed almost flustered, as if the praise were unexpected. Then he drew a deep breath and looked past Tellian to the others.

"This is my nephew, Sir Trianal, Sir Yarran," Tellian said in answer to the unasked question. "He's one of my officers, and he spent the summer before last with Sir Kelthys, so he's familiar with Glanharrow's geography. And I invited Prince Bahzell and Lord Brandark to accompany us for much the same reasons. They, too, are familiar with Glanharrow. In fact, I believe you met both of them there in the aftermath of the previous Lord Glanharrow's . . . expedition down the Gullet?"

"Aye, Milord, that I did." Sir Yarran's lips twitched in a smile, and he flexed his left arm. "As a matter of fact, Prince Bahzell and I met during it." He flexed his arm again. "I was just a mite more fortunate than some of the other poor buggers who met up with him that day."

"No lasting damage, I'm hoping? " Bahzell said politely, watching the knight flex his arm for a third time.

"None the healers couldn't put right, Milord Champion," Yarran replied.

"And no hard feelings, I trust," Tellian said. Yarran looked at the baron quickly, his expression almost shocked.

"Of course not, Milord!" He shook his head for emphasis. "'Twasn't anything personal, for either of us. I was with Sir Festian—well, *Lord* Festian, now—and I never thought that trip was a good idea to begin with. Even if I had, I got off lighter than any man should expect to if he's daft enough to cross swords with a champion of Tomanāk!"

"I'm afraid it *was* personal for quite a few people who were there that day," Tellian said grimly.

"It was," Yarran agreed. "Enough hate can curdle anyone, Milord, and the gods know there's been hate enough from both ends of the Gullet, time to time. Course, only a fool lets hate drive him, especially when there's blood to be spilled if he does."

"A wise observation," Tellian said, glancing ever so briefly at his nephew's profile from the corner of his eye. "I wish more people shared your opinion," he added, and Yarran shrugged.

"Can't do much about people who insist on using stable muckings for brains, Milord," he said philosophically. Then chuckled. "Except, of course, for kicking their arses out of their chairs and putting someone else into them. Which is by the way of bringing me to the reason I'm here."

"Then I suppose we should get to it," Tellian said, and pointed rather more emphatically at the chair Yarran had gotten out of. "Sit yourself back down and tell us what Lord Festian needs."

"As to that, Milord Baron," Yarran replied in a voice which held much less humor than it had a moment before, "I'm afraid what he really needs is something in the way of a miracle."

He sat obediently back down, although Bahzell and Brandark both had the impression that he was uncomfortable sitting in Tellian's presence.

"That bad, is it?" the baron asked with a frown.

"If it's not now, it's headed that way, Milord," Yarran told him frankly. "We've had minor problems, almost pinpricks, from the beginning. That started the day Lord Festian was confirmed in his wardenship, as you might say. But it's gotten worse. In the last couple of weeks, we've had two major cattle raids and a raid on one of our stud farms."

"Cattle and horses both?" Tellian mused aloud.

"Aye, Milord. Before that, it was sheep, but it's clear as the nose on my face they're getting more ambitious. And they're not just thieves, either, whatever they'd like us to think so far. They've already managed to burn a handful of barns, despite the rain, and Lord Festian has started posting armed guards to protect our larger herds and farms. To my mind, it's but a matter of time before they decide to raid one of those herds or farms, and when they do, there's going to be blood on someone's blade. And," he added more grimly, "on someone else's hands."

"I see." Tellian leaned back in his chair and crossed his legs. "I wish I hadn't already come to much the same conclusions on my own," he said. "But from your tone of voice, I suspect you have your own suspicions about who the brains behind this campaign might be. Do you?" he asked bluntly.

"Well, as to that, Milord," Yarran said slowly, obviously considering his words with care, "yes, I do. And so does Lord Festian, though I think he's less eager than I to be naming names." The marshal shrugged. "I'm naught but a common-born fighting man, when all's said—Lord Festian, now, his word carries more weight than ever mine could. I'm thinking he knows that, and he's not wishful to be accusing anyone until he's the proof firmly in hand, as it were."

"Very wise of him," Tellian agreed. "But if you have any suspicions, I want to hear them."

"Well, as you've asked, Milord, it's in my mind that Lord Dathian wasn't so very happy to see Lord Festian named to lord it over him. That's how he sees it, leastwise. And I hope you'll pardon my bluntness, Milord, but for all that Dathian was first in line to kiss your hand—aye, and would've kissed something else of yours, if you take my meaning—when you turned up in the Gullet that morning, he'd also been one of Mathian's hangers-on. Until you did turn up, he'd been breathing fire and farting flame about all he'd been set to do when we reached Hurgrum. Then, all of a sudden, there he was, the very spitting image of peace and reason."

He grimaced distastefully, and Tellian scratched his neatly trimmed beard thoughtfully.

"Dathian, hm?" he mused. Dathian Halberd, Lord Warden of the Fens, was one of his less savory vassals. The man reminded Tellian of a snake crossed with a weasel, and Dathgar, Tellian's courser, couldn't stand him. But in some ways, that only made Tellian less ready to seize upon him as an object of suspicion. It was dangerous for a powerful noble to fall into the trap of spending his suspicion on obvious targets. Even if he was right, and those he suspected *were* up to no good, concentrating on them was only too likely to distract him and keep him from noticing the actions of more outwardly honest and trustworthy traitors until it was too late.

"You met Dathian during your time with Kelthys, didn't you, Trianal?" he asked his nephew after a moment, and the young man nodded.

"Yes, Un— Milord Baron." Trianal cleared his throat, then continued more naturally. "I didn't get to know him well. He didn't have a great deal of time to waste on someone too young to know which end of a sword to hold."

The youngster's voice was absolutely neutral, but Tellian had to raise a hand to hide a smile. He could just hear Dathian saying those exact words, even picture the sneer that would curl his lip as he said them.

"I see," he said, when he was certain he could trust his voice. "But you did meet him?" Trianal nodded. "Very well, did your impression of him match Sir Yarran's?"

"I didn't actually see him when Redhelm headed down the Gullet," Trianal said with scrupulous accuracy. "Not until I arrived with you and Hathan, at any rate. But given what I saw of him summer before last, I'd say Sir Yarran is probably being too kind to him."

"Well, that's blunt enough, at any rate," Tellian murmured, and quirked an eyebrow as Bahzell stirred in his chair. "Yes, Milord Champion?"

"If you'll pardon my sticking my own finger into your pie, Milord Baron," the massive Horse Stealer rumbled, "it's quite a few things I've heard of this Dathian, as well, and not a one of 'em good."

"To be honest, I could say the same myself," Tellian agreed. He stroked his beard for another moment, then cocked his head at Yarran.

"From what I've seen of you, Sir Yarran, I doubt very much that you'd be pointing a finger at someone just because you didn't care for his manner."

"I'd try not to, any road, Milord. But not only was Dathian sucking up to Mathian before you arrived to spoil the party, but whoever's been raiding our cattle and horses has been giving us the slip by disappearing with them in the Bogs. Now, that's as nasty a stretch as you're like to find anywhere on the Wind Plain, all full of mud and water and a few patches of quicksand. Yet whoever's been using it for a highroad for cattle's managed to do it without leaving a single mired beef to point his tracks." The marshal shook his head. "I was second in command to Lord Festian when he commanded Redhelm's scouts, Milord. It was my business to find my way through bad going, and I've spent more time in the Bogs than most of Lord Festian's men. But I'll tell you plain, *I'd* not be able to get through there so slick. It would take someone who knew his way through them like the back of his own hand to get herds that size through at all, much less without losses, and Dathian's holding lies smack in the middle of the Bogs. As a matter of fact, it's one of your border holdings. It backs up against Golden Vale. In the South Riding."

Sir Yarran stopped speaking, but his eyes met Tellian's steadily, and Tellian frowned.

"Golden Vale. That would be Lord Warden Saratic, wouldn't it?" It was a statement, not a question, and Yarran nodded silently.

"That's a nasty thought, Sir Yarran," the baron said after a moment. "Not that that necessarily means you're wrong. Especially given that Saratic was so happy to give his cousin Mathian a refuge after the King stripped him of his wardenship."

"'Happy' might be putting it just a bit strongly, Milord." Yarran said with a grim chuckle. "He was ready enough to take Mathian in, but he wasn't half pleased about it. And he'd some remarkably warm things to say about you—and about you, Prince Bahzell—at the time."

"But he's one of Baron Cassan's vassals, isn't he?" Brandark asked.

"Indeed he is," Tellian agreed. "Which, I'm very much afraid, only means Sir Yarran's point is even better taken. Cassan and I aren't exactly boon companions."

He snorted, and Bahzell and Brandark grimaced. Trianal kept his own expression carefully blank, but the bitter enmity between Cassan and Tellian was proverbial. For almost two decades now, they had been locked in combat for domination of the Royal Council, although, up until Mathian Redhelm's attempted invasion of Hurgrum, Tellian had been slowly but steadily gaining the ascendancy.

"I wouldn't be a bit surprised to find him involved

in something like this," Tellian continued. "In fact, I'm fairly certain he used Saratic to help encourage his cousin Mathian's . . . indiscretion in the Gullet. And whether he had a hand in that particular fiasco or not, I imagine it would be all but impossible for him to resist this temptation. But if he *is* involved, I'm certain he's covered his tracks carefully."

"I don't think I'm after being all that fond of Baron Cassan," Bahzell mused out loud.

"Fair enough," Tellian said. "He thinks the only good hradani is one being used for well-rotted fertilizer."

"Even so," Brandark said thoughtfully, "however carefully he's covered his tracks, he's still running quite a risk if he's involved himself. I know you Sothōii are almost as fond of blood feuds as we hradani are, and I've been told cattle raids and horse stealing are among your minor lord wardens' favorite sports. But if it ever comes to light that one of your barons has been attacking another baron's lands, the consequences could be pretty extreme . . . for everyone."

"You've a way with words, Lord Brandark." Yarran's tone was dust dry. "Take us back to the Troubles, that could, like in King Markhos' grandsire's day, with every lord's hand turned against every other lord."

"I don't think Cassan would take things that far—not intentionally, at any rate," Tellian said, shaking his head. "That's why I'm certain he's covered his involvement very carefully, if he *is* involved. Still, I can see why it would be attractive to him. Especially if Dathian is doing the actual raiding."

"Aye, Milord." Yarran nodded his head vigorously. "If he discredits Lord Festian, then he discredits you, because you're the one who was willing to name a simple knight lord warden in that idiot Mathian's stead. And if he can discredit you there, then he's a wedge to discredit you elsewhere. In the meantime, if anything slips, Dathian's his scapegoat. And if throwing Dathian to the hounds isn't enough, then he's Saratic next in line. And Saratic, as Mathian's cousin and what passes for the head of the House of Redhelm these days, makes a splendid decoy. He's reason enough to hate Festian all on his own, and Cassan has more than enough members of the Council in his pocket to protect Saratic from serious consequences as long as Saratic keeps silent about any involvement of Cassan's."

"You're right, Sir Yarran," Tellian said, and regarded the grizzled warrior with speculative interest. Yarran saw the look in his eyes and it was his turn to snort.

"There's no cause to be looking at me all thoughtful, Milord Baron. It's not as if anyone in the entire Kingdom doesn't know how much Cassan hates you. Maybe it's not my place to be speaking my mind so clear, but it doesn't take a genius to see how he's a whole layered defense in place if any of his plans should slip."

"Perhaps not," Tellian agreed. "But don't sell yourself short, Sir Yarran. There are members of the Council who either can't—or won't—see the same logic."

"Maybe that's because they've not spent their entire lives living down on your border with Cassan," Yarran said with grim humor. "It's an amazing thing how that . . . focuses your thoughts."

Tellian nodded appreciatively, but his gray eyes were distant and the others could almost physically feel the intensity of his thoughts. He sat that way for over two full minutes, then shook himself, like a dog who'd just stepped in from the rain.

"Well, Sir Yarran," he said, his eyes refocusing on the knight. "I can see why Lord Festian sent you. On several levels." He smiled under his brushy mustache as Yarran's eyebrows quirked. "He had to send someone to explain what sort of help he needs, and why," the baron continued. "And since he did, he showed excellent judgment in sending someone who understands the situation as well as you obviously do. I must confess that I already knew some of what you've told me, but I hadn't realized the whole of it. I'm going to require a day or two to think about it before I decide how best to help Lord Warden Festian deal with it. I assure you, however, that it *will* be dealt with."

There was a world of determination in his choice of verbs, and Bahzell felt himself nodding in approval.

"In the meantime," Tellian said, slapping the arms of his chair and then thrusting himself up out of it, "consider yourself my honored guest, Sir Yarran. I'm very pleased to have you here, and I'll ask Trianal to escort you to the suite Kalan has assigned to you. Once you've had a chance to settle in, I think it would be an excellent idea for you to spend some time speaking with my own senior officers. I'd be obliged if you—and you, Trianal—" he glanced at his nephew "would leave Baron Cassan out of it, but feel free to share any of your other information or conclusions with them, including your thoughts about Dathian and Lord Saratic." He smiled thinly. "Most of my people are smart enough to figure out who'd have to be behind Saratic, so there's no need to be any more specific about it. And unlike some nobles, I've discovered that keeping the people who are supposed to help you handle any wars or other little unpleasantnesses which come your way as fully informed as possible is a good idea. At least they're more likely to keep you from stepping on your . . . sword that way."

Chapter Eleven

"So, Prince Bahzell," a youthful voice said, "can I pick your brains for Father's secrets?"

Bahzell turned from where he'd stood on Hill Guard's curtain wall, leaning on the battlements while he stared out across the endless grasslands of the Wind Plain. The morning's overcast had blown away on the winds of noon, and the afternoon sun was settling towards a western horizon of such crystalline blue beauty that it hurt the eyes. The deep, dark green of the reborn grasslands, nourished by the long, soaking rains, spread out below him like the visible proof of the Wind Plain's short-seasoned fertility. The wind blowing out of the northwest was still on the cool side of warm, but Bahzell enjoyed its slight bite as he luxuriated in an absence of raindrops.

Leeana Bowmaster stood behind him, in one of the simple yet elegant gowns her mother had lately begun to insist she wear. The wind molded the fabric to her long legs, and strands of hair which had escaped her braid danced about her face, flickering like gilded serpents in the sunlight. With her green eyes sparkling with mischievous deviltry, she looked even cuter than usual, Bahzell told himself, steadfastly ignoring the fact that "cute" might not be precisely the correct adjective.

"I'm not thinking as how my poor brain is after being all that worth picking, Milady," he told her with a smile.

"Don't be silly, Milord Prince." She walked across to stand beside him, gazing out over the same green vista. "Given how hard you work at it, you really don't do a very good job of hiding your intelligence."

Bahzell looked at her profile sidelong. That was coming to grips with a vengeance, he thought.

"It's not so very bad a thing if those as don't much like you spend their time thinking about how much brighter than you they're after being," he said after a moment. "I'll not claim to be a genius, at the best of times, Milady. Yet for all that, it may be I'm not quite the idiot my old da's been known to call me."

"And I imagine it helps that quite a few people are bigoted enough to listen to the way you Horse Stealers talk rather than to what it is you *say*," Leeana mused.

"Aye, no doubt it does," Bahzell agreed. "If it comes to that, there's plenty of those as are ready to assume *any* hradani, regardless of how it might be he talks, must be a barbarian, and stupid to boot." He gave her a slow smile. "Well, I'm thinking those as call my folk barbarians aren't far wrong, when all's said. But those as think all barbarians are after being stupid . . ."

He shrugged, twitching his ears gently, and she laughed delightedly. It was a lovely sound, like bits of crystal music blown on the wind.

"I can see where that would be a mistake," she agreed. "Especially now that you've demonstrated how smoothly you can avoid answering a simple question."

"Avoid, Milady?" he asked innocently. "What question would that have been?"

"The one about Father's secrets," she said patiently.

"Ah, *that* question!" He nodded. "Well, do you know, Milady, I don't really think as how it's my place to be saying aught about the Baron's confidences." She opened her mouth, but he held up his right hand, index finger extended. "Oh, I was there when he was after challenging you," he agreed. "But I'm thinking as how he wanted you to be using your *regular* sources, not bringing in new ones."

"You're probably right," she said after considering it briefly. "On the other hand, any 'regular source' was a new one, once." She shrugged fetchingly. "I have to recruit them at some point, you know."

Bahzell laughed out loud, and she grinned impudently up at him.

"You're after reminding me of my sister Marglyth," he told her. "Maybe with a bit of Sharkah thrown in for spice. Not a scruple amongst the three of you."

"I do so have scruples!" she told him, elevating her nose with a disdainful sniff. "I just don't let them get in the way of business."

"'Business,' is it?" Bahzell considered her thoughtfully. "I'm hoping you won't take this wrongly, Milady, but are you so very sure as how this is the sort of 'business' as you should be wanting to learn?"

"It's the only one I *can* learn," she said, and the levity had ebbed from her voice. She continued to look up at him, but now those huge, dark green eyes were serious, almost somber. "It's not as if anyone is going to let me train to be a knight, even if that were what I wanted to do—which it isn't. I'm only a daughter, after all. Most people figure a daughter's only job is to become someone's wife and produce babies. Preferably male ones."

There was a pronounced bite in her tone, and Bahzell felt a stir of sympathy.

"At least Father and Mother aren't like some parents," she continued in the voice of someone conscientiously reminding herself to look on the bright side. "A lot of other girls my age—*most* of the daughters of the nobility, I sometimes think—seem to have been taught that catching husbands and producing offspring are the only two things that could possibly matter. And the majority of them seem to think admitting that they're intelligent, possibly even—Lillinara forbid!—more intelligent than the men around them, is the one certain way to guarantee that they'll never catch a husband!"

She rolled her eyes, and Bahzell nodded slowly.

"Aye, I've seen the same often enough, and not just amongst your daughters of the nobility, Milady. And truth to tell, I've always thought as how any girl foolish enough to believe that is after deserving the sort of husband she's likely to be catching. I'll not deny that, often as not, it seems as how there's a point in most young bucks' lives where brains, if you'll be forgiving my bluntness, aren't the very first thing they look for in a girl. Then again, it's always seemed to me as how there's a point in most young bucks' lives when *their* brains aren't good for so very much, so I suppose if a lass is after acting just brainless enough at just the very right moment, she's likely enough to be catching herself *a* husband. Like as not, though, it's not the husband as she'd soonest be keeping down the road."

"Really?" She looked at him very intently.

"Oh, aye," he rumbled, once more gazing out across the grasslands and away from the potential distraction of those green eyes. "It's in my mind that a lass as is looking for a husband worth keeping ought to be doing all in the world she can so as to be scaring off the stupid ones. Any man as has his wits about him ought to be smart enough to know a wife with brains at least as good as his own is a treasure. Best to have someone as can help when life is after throwing problems at you, not someone as can only clasp her hands and look at you worshipfully while she's after waiting for *you* to be solving them all. And if you'd not have the two of you growing tired of one another, best to have someone you can actually be talking to. Why," he looked back down at her at last, smiling another slow smile, "I'd not be admitting this in front of Brandark, you understand, but it might not be so very bad a thing as to be finding yourself one who can actually *read*."

"Oh, I do wish more Sothōii thought like that!" Leeana said with a gurgle of laughter. "Not that it would make all that much difference for someone like me, I suppose," she continued, the laughter fading as she turned back to the vista below the walls. "Mother and Father will be far more understanding and careful about it than most parents in their situation would be, but my inheritance—or, my sons', rather—means politics and alliances are bound to figure in whoever marries me." She gave a thin smile. "On the other hand, I suppose I ought to be grateful that I can be absolutely certain that *someone* will marry me! Now if I could only feel remotely as confident that I'll actually like whoever it is, life would be perfect."

"It might not be so very bad as all that," Bahzell said slowly.

She looked back up at him, her eyes suddenly dark, as if with betrayal, and he shook his head quickly.

"Lass," he said, abandoning the "Miladies" with which he was usually careful to address her, "I'm not after saying that just because I'm after being a great, musclebound *male* lump of gristle who's not the least idea of what it is that's worrying you. I'll not say I've worried the worries you have, or that I've some magical ability to be putting myself inside your head and your life. But 'marriages of state' aren't so very unheard of amongst hradani, either. They're not so common as amongst your folk, no doubt, but it's a concern as shows itself amongst our chieftains and princes and their families often enough. And the thing we hradani have been after learning is that an unhappy 'marriage of state' is dangerous. Not to be dancing around the point, they're like as not to end up biting the arse—ah, I mean to be the saying the *backside*—of whoever was after being stupid enough to arrange them in the first place.

"I'm not saying as how every arranged hradani marriage is after being all sunshine and light, because Tomanāk knows as they're not. But, then, that's after being true of marriages in general, when all's said. And I'm thinking as how your parents are after being smart enough, and loving you enough, not to be letting anyone press you into a marriage as *you're* not wishful to be making."

"I know they'll *try* not to," Leeana agreed after a moment. "But the truth is, Prince Bahzell, that we Sothōii and you hradani look at some things very differently. And whatever Father and Mother may think, the rest of the nobility—and the King's Council—think of sons as heirs and daughters as trading chips." She shook her head sadly. "The pressure on Father to accept *someone's* offer for my hand is already heavy, and it's going to mount steadily. The other Councilors may have different reasons for pressing him, but they'll *all* do it eventually, and that's going to happen sooner rather than later."

"You're right," Bahzell said after a long, thoughtful pause. "Our folk are after being different. Because of the Rage, as much as anything else, I'm thinking."

"The Rage? What does that have to do with arranged marriages?" Leeana asked.

"Why, I'd think that was after being plain enough," Bahzell said with a grim smile. "Think it through, lass. You're after knowing what the Rage is, what it's been costing my folk over the years." Leeana nodded slowly, and he shrugged. "Well, who amongst us does the Rage never touch?"

"Your women," Leeana said softly.

"Aye," Bahzell agreed. "And that's the reason, I'm thinking, why amongst hradani, lasses choose their own lads, and brides choose their own grooms. They've enough to put up with living amongst men the Rage can be touching, and truth to tell, it's our women who've been the backbone of what little stability we hradani have been managing to cling to since the Fall. Unlike some other folk, we've none of us ever been able to shut our eyes to how important that's after being to all of us. I'll not say our women are all of them free to live their lives any way they choose, but they've a sight more freedom than women do amongst you Sothōii. Or amongst most of the human folk I've seen."

"I knew there was something I liked about hradani," Leeana said with a flickering smile. "I only wish it was that way for us, as well."

"From what I've seen, lass," Bahzell said gently, "your father and mother are after thinking more like hradani than most. They've fashioned their own lives out of joy and pain, and they've not forgotten what it was first made them love each other. You be trusting them, Leeana Bowmaster. You be trusting them not to forget that for you, either."

She looked up at him very strangely, and he gazed down into her human eyes, wondering exactly what she was thinking. Then she gave herself a small shake and smiled at him once more.

"Thank you, Prince Bahzell," she said simply. "For listening and not laughing. And for understanding without just trying to pat me on the head and tell me to run along and play. I'll try to remember what you've said, because you're right. Father and Mother will do everything anyone in their position could possibly do to protect me from the sort of marriage I'm afraid of. Of course, that's not quite the same thing as saying I'll be able to make the marriage I *want*, but it's a great deal more than most girls in my position could say."

She looked up at him for a few more seconds, and he wished he could think of something else to say, one more reassurance. But he couldn't—not without resorting to comforting lies, and this young woman deserved better from him than that. And so he simply looked back at her, until she gave him an abbreviated curtsy and walked away, leaving him alone on Hill Guard Castle's walls once more.

Chapter Twelve

Alfar Axeblade sagged in the saddle as his gelding trotted wearily homeward. It wasn't raining at the moment—thank the gods!—but the pastures and paddocks remained soggy sources of spattered mud, and he and his horse were both heartily tired of splashing about in it.

Not that Alfar really begrudged his labors. As one of Lord Warden Edinghas' senior trainers, it was his responsibility to be sure that the home farm's facilities were ready when the horses returned from their winter pastures. Actually, he was quite pleased by what he'd discovered in the course of the day's tour. Of course, he reminded himself, the fact that Warm Springs was one of the holdings which traditionally played host to a herd of coursers over the winter helped. The barns, feedlots, exercise yards, and—for that matter—the farriers, horse leeches, and grooms were kept busy all through the winter, rather than standing idle or simply decamping along with the home farm's studs and mares. So unlike some of the horse farms on the Wind Plain, Warm Springs never shut down, which meant all its myriad bits and pieces were kept running smoothly, all year long.

The unusually early departure of the Warm Springs

coursers had produced something of a lull in the home manor's operations, and Alfar had taken full advantage of the opportunity for a final, meticulous inspection. He anticipated Lord Edinghas' approval of his report, and he was looking forward to a long, hot bath before he turned in for his well-earned rest. Perhaps that was why it took him a second or two to rouse from his reverie when his horse suddenly snorted and shied.

Alfar shook his head, automatically answering the gelding's abrupt lunge with a strong hand on the reins and firm, almost instinctive pressure from his knees. He brought the horse around, facing back in the direction of whatever had caused it to shy, and sudden, icy horror flooded through his veins, blotting away his sense of satisfaction and accomplishment as if they had never existed.

He stared at the sight no Sothōii had ever seen. The nightmare sight no Sothōii would ever have *wanted* to see. And then he was flinging himself from the saddle, slipping and sliding through the mud in his riding boots to catch the exhausted, wounded foal as it collapsed.

"*Toragan!*" Edinghas Bardiche, Lord Warden of Warm Springs, whispered in gray-faced horror. He stood bareheaded in the huge stable, watching in disbelief and shock as grooms, trainers, and healers labored frantically. Unlike them, he was not submerged in the frantic effort to save the two worst-wounded foals or the half-blinded, cruelly ripped and torn filly. That meant there was no distraction to divert him from the utter, unthinkable disaster those exhausted, injured coursers represented.

"Only seven?" he said, turning to the man beside him, and his question was a plea to be told that the number was wrong. "Only *seven*?"

"Five mares and two fillies . . . and eight foals," Alfar Axeblade said grimly. "And two of the mares are bachelors. So five of the foals who got back alive—so far—" there was inexpressible bitterness in the qualifier "—are orphans."

"Phrobus take it, man, there were over forty adult

coursers in that herd! Where are all the others?" Edinghas knew there was no way Axeblade could answer his question, but his horror, grief, and fury goaded it out of him anyway.

"Fiendark seize it, Milord, what in Phrobus' name makes you think *I* know?" Alfar spat back, his own voice riven and harrowed by the same emotions. He glared at his liege lord, shaken to his core by the enormity of the disaster, and Lord Edinghas closed his eyes and inhaled deeply. The lord warden's nostrils flared, and he shook his head, as if trying to shake off the paralysis afflicting his thoughts. Then he opened his eyes again and looked back at Alfar.

"You don't, of course. Not any more than I do," he said heavily. He reached out, resting one hand on the taller man's shoulder, and squeezed. "Forgive me, Alfar. It's my own fear."

"There's naught to forgive, Milord," Alfar replied. He turned his head, looking away from his liege to watch the others work, and his face might have been hammered from cold iron.

"I've had longer to think about it than you have, Milord," he continued after a few seconds, his voice dark and heavy. "There's nothing I know—nothing in nature, leastwise—that could have done this. Those look like bite marks, the sort of thing wolves might have done, but there's no wolf ever born could do *that* to coursers! And there's not a single stallion—not *one*. So whatever it was, it pulled them all down—eighteen of them . . . and fifteen mares, seven colts and fillies, and nine foals, as well." He shook his head. "It's not possible, Milord. *It can't happen.*"

"But it has, Alfar." Edinghas' voice was cold and empty, a thing ribbed with grief and despair, but somewhere in its iron belly hatred and rage met and a furnace heat flickered.

"I know it," Alfar grated, then clenched his fists in frustration. "Gods, how I wish we had a wind rider here—just one! Maybe he and his courser could tell us what in all of Fiendark's hells *happened* out there."

Lord Warden Edinghas nodded, his eyes once again on the tattered, wounded, exhausted survivors of the herd which had departed from Warm Springs barely four days ago. The mares and shivering fillies stood spraddle-legged, heads hanging, as they stared desperately through eyes dark with the echoes of hell at the handful of foals they had somehow gotten back. They watched the humans' ministrations with frantic intensity, yet Edinghas could feel their dreadful exhaustion, sense the hideous battle they'd fought to save even this handful of their children.

He'd never before seen a courser exhausted, he realized. Not in fifty-three years of life and eighteen years as Lord Warden of Warm Springs. Not once. That was bad enough, but he also saw the remembered terror in their eyes, and he knew there was nothing on this earth that could terrify a courser. If only the trembling mares could speak to him!

Alfar was right. They needed a wind rider, and they needed him quickly. And even if they hadn't, this had to be reported. Because, he thought while fresh fear wrapped an icy hand about his throat, if whatever had happened here could happen to one courser herd, then it could happen to *others*. Or, perhaps even worse, whatever had ravaged them out there on the Wind Plain might follow them here. Might seek to complete the herd's destruction. Whatever it had been, it had been no natural attacker. That much was obvious, but what else could it have been? What monster, what hideous wizardry, could have *done* this? With no idea of how to answer that question, he had no idea how to fight or stop whatever it was. He didn't even know if it *could* be stopped from hunting down and killing every victim who had somehow escaped it. But one thing he did know—before Edinghas of Warm Springs saw that happen, he and every armsman he commanded would lie dead, sabers and bows in hand, in a ring around this stable.

"Relhardan!" he snapped, summoning his chief armsman to his side.

"Yes, Milord!"

"Turn out your men. Every one of them, armed and

in full armor! I want the walls manned, and I want a cordon around this stable. Nothing gets into it. Nothing—" His voice wavered, and he made himself inhale once again to steady it. "Nothing gets to *them*," he said then, his wavering voice hammered into ice-cold steel, as he waved at the trembling, half-dead coursers. "*Nothing!*" he hissed.

"Aye, Milord," Sir Relhardan said flatly. "I'll see to it. You've my word for it."

"I know I do," Edinghas said in a voice which was more nearly normal. He clasped arms with Relhardan, and then the armsman was jogging purposefully away, shouting for his subordinates as he went, and Edinghas turned back to Alfar.

"I know you're exhausted, and your horse is, too," he said. "But we must send word to Baron Tellian. Choose the best horse we have—even my own mount. And then ride, Alfar. Ride as you've never ridden before, and tell the Baron everything you've seen."

"Yes, Milord. And you?"

"I'll be right here, in this stable, when you return," Edinghas promised him. "One way or another, I'll be right here."

Chapter Thirteen

This time the collision really was an accident.

Bahzell was walking slowly towards his own quarters, cutting across the passage outside Tellian's library, while he considered the baron's response to Sir Yarran's message from Lord Festian. Tellian had spent three days deciding his course of action, and Bahzell hoped it would do the trick, although he had to admit that he still cherished a few reservations. If people like this Lord Warden Saratic were sufficiently determined to undermine Lord Festian's wardenship, they might not take the hint Tellian was about to send their way. Especially not if Baron Cassan was as deeply involved as all the evidence seemed to suggest. In which case, Tellian's decision to dispatch two hundred of his own men, commanded by his nephew, could end up provoking the very confrontation it was intended to prevent.

The fact that Tellian had selected Trianal to command the reinforcements left Bahzell feeling a bit in two minds. The youngster possessed a disposition as fiery as might be anticipated from someone that young. Yet he'd been better blooded than most his age during the previous year's royal expedition against the Ghoul Moor. He hadn't been in command then, but he'd seen the reality of battle and bloodshed, and for all his native impulsiveness, he had a level head. And if he still nursed any reservations about what Bahzell and his uncle were attempting to accomplish, he wouldn't let them get in the way. Trianal's devotion to Tellian was obvious, and he'd amply demonstrated his basic intelligence. More to the point, perhaps, he'd had it explained to him in detail that he was to defer to the judgment of Lord Festian and Sir Yarran, and he was smart enough to do it.

Still, it was enough to make a man nervous, which probably explained why Bahzell wasn't paying as much attention as he might have as he started up the stair outside the library. If he had been, he might have noticed the sound of the light, quick footsteps pattering down it in his direction before the actual moment of impact.

Unfortunately, he didn't, and the shock of the collision was enough to jar his teeth.

His right hand flashed out as Leeana caromed off of him. She'd been moving at something much closer to a run than a walk, and he caught her elbow just before she tumbled headlong off the stair. He didn't have time to be gentle about it, and she gasped in as much unanticipated hurt as surprise as his fingers snapped tight.

"Here now! I'm hoping I've not dislocated your arm, Milady!" he said quickly, setting her back upright.

"N-no," she said, and his eyebrows flew up and his ears flattened at the strange little break in her voice. She looked away from him as she flexed her wrenched arm.

"I-I'm all right," she said, still keeping her face averted, but Bahzell had too many sisters to be fooled.

"Now, that you're not," he told her gently. Her shoulders jerked, and he heard something very like a smothered sob. "If you're wishful to tell me I should be minding my own business, that's one thing, lass," he said. "But if you're wishful for an ear as has nothing better to do than listen to whatever it may be weighs on you so, well, here I am."

She looked at him at last, unable to resist the gentle, genuine sympathy of his voice. Her jade eyes brimmed with tears, and under them was something more than mere sorrow. It was fear, he realized, and he reached out to her once more. He rested a huge, powerful hand lightly on her shoulder, with a familiarity very, very few Sothōii would have shown to the daughter of such a powerful noble, and met her gaze levelly.

"I— It's just that . . ." She drew a deep breath and shook her head. "That's very kind of you, Prince Bahzell," she said, rushing the words ever so slightly as she forced her voice to hold together. "But it's not necessary, I assure you."

"And who was it said anything about 'necessary'?" he asked, with a crooked smile. "But you're the daughter of a man who's after becoming a friend of mine, lass. And even if he wasn't, I know someone as has an overfull heart when I see her. I'm not saying as how you couldn't be dealing with whatever it is all on your own. I'm only suggesting there's no least reason in the world why you should be."

Her mouth quivered for a moment, and then every muscle seemed to relax simultaneously. She stared up at him, one tear trickling down her cheek, and nodded slowly.

They sat at a stone table on a terrace on the castle's south side. It wasn't exactly concealed, but it was in an out of the way spot where no one was likely to stumble over them. Leeana suspected that Marthya would have been officially horrified at the thought of her creeping off all alone for an "assignation," but her maid's reaction was the last thing on her mind.

She felt horribly embarrassed—not at finding herself alone with Bahzell, but for having so little control that she'd been unable to hide her distress from him in the first place. Now she gazed out over the terrace, studying the formal garden below it, and prayed he didn't think she was as foolish and fluttering as she felt.

He simply sat there, on the far side of the table from her, looming like some sort of ogre, but with a calm, unjudging expression and patient brown eyes.

He seemed prepared to wait until high summer, if that was how long it took, and she managed to smile more naturally at him as he neither pressed her to begin nor filled her silence with assurances that "everything will be all right, little girl."

"I'm sorry, Prince Bahzell," she said finally. "I'm afraid I must seem pretty silly, carrying on this way."

"I'll not say someone as I have to be prying every word out of with a crowbar is 'carrying on,'" he told her, with a slow, answering smile. "Upset and unhappy, aye, that I'll grant. But as for the rest—"

He shrugged.

"I think we have different definitions of 'carrying on,'" she said, but she felt herself relax further, even so. "I don't usually get this upset," she continued. "But Father's had some news that . . . took me by surprise." She felt her lips tremble again and forced them to be still.

"Aye, I thought as much," he said as she paused once more.

"It's just that I always thought there'd be more . . . warning," she said. "I never expected it to just come out of *nowhere* this way."

"What, lass?" he asked quietly.

"A formal offer of marriage," she told him. She looked away as she spoke and so missed the flicker in his eyes and the brief twitch of his ears.

"Marriage, is it?" he said after a moment, his deep, rumbling voice no more than merely thoughtful. "I'm thinking you're a mite young for such as that."

"Young?" She turned back to him, her expression surprised. "Half of the noble girls I know were betrothed by the time they were eleven or twelve years old, Prince Bahzell. It's not unheard of for us to be betrothed before we're out of our cradles, for that matter! And at least half of us are married by the time we're fifteen or sixteen."

Bahzell started to say something, then visibly made himself stop. He gazed at her for a few seconds, then shook his head.

"I suppose I should be remembering the difference betwixt humans and hradani," he said slowly. "I hope you'll not take this wrongly, but amongst my folk a lass your age would be little more than a babe." Something besides distress flashed in her jade eyes at that, and he shook his head quickly. "I'm not so very much more than that myself," he told her. "I'm but thirty-nine, and that's no more than a warrior of eighteen or nineteen years—your cousin Trianal's age—amongst your folk."

Leeana blinked, then cocked her head.

"Really?" she asked.

"Oh, aye." He nodded, then chuckled. "Or were you thinking a man as had come to what you might be calling mature judgment would be after flinging himself into all the harebrained, never-a-thought scrapes Brandark keeps putting into that curst song of his?"

The question surprised a giggle out of her even through her misery, and she shook her head.

"I . . . hadn't thought about it that way."

"Aye, and my da would be saying as *I* hadn't, either—thought about it, I mean. Which, as he'd be pointing out, is by the way of explaining how I come to keep ending up in 'em."

She giggled again, louder, and he nodded in approval.

"Better, lass," he approved. "And now that we've established, in a manner of speaking, as how we're both of us young and foolish, why don't you be after trotting out whatever it is about this offer for your hand as has you this upset? Should I be taking it that you're not so very fond of the proposed groom?"

"I don't even know him," Leeana said. "Not personally, at any rate. Not that that's so unusual in cases like this." She paused, then continued in the voice of one determined to be as dispassionately accurate as possible. "Actually, it *is* unusual. Normally, a man would at least want to meet his potential fiancée before he asks for her hand. And to be fair, most parents would at least insist that their daughter meet him before they even considered accepting the offer."

"But you've not met this fellow?"

"No, I haven't."

"Well, I'm naught but a poor, simple hradani, but it's in my mind that a man as hasn't even met a lass has no business proposing marriage to her."

"Oh, I couldn't agree more!" she said forcefully. "And neither, for that matter, could Father and Mother. Unfortunately, it's not quite that simple, Prince Bahzell."

"And why not?" he asked.

"Oh, for dozens of reasons," she sighed, sitting back on the bench across the table from him. "The fact that Father has no male heir. The fact that Mother can't have more children. The fact that the entire Royal Council hates the thought that the succession hasn't yet been secured *by* a male heir . . . which would have to be a son of mine. And," she looked at him very levelly, "by the fact that this is one more weapon for his political enemies to use against him."

"Aye?" It was his turn to lean back on the bench, his expression thoughtful, and she nodded.

"I . . . think I know who's really behind this offer," she said, "and he's no friend of Father's."

"So you're thinking as how he's after pushing an offer as he knows your father won't accept so very happily as a way to be putting still more pressure on him before the Council?"

"That's exactly what I think, Prince Bahzell," Leeana said flatly.

"Well," he said after a moment, "I can see where such as that might be in his mind. Mind you, *I'd* not like to have a mind like that, but that's not to say as how I can't be seeing how it works. But I've come to know your father pretty well, too, lass." He shook his head. "That's not a man as gives in under pressure, and especially not where those as hold his heart in their hands are concerned."

Leeana blinked again on sudden tears, then gave him a misty smile.

"No, he isn't," she agreed. "But sometimes that's a dangerous quality in a nobleman. One enemies can use against him."

"I can see as how those who're thinking as how this

marriage would be a good thing could be pressing him to say aye to it," Bahzell said. "But surely the decision's after being his, not theirs, when all's said."

"Normally," she said, and her smile turned bitter. "But you're forgetting whose daughter—whose *only* daughter—I am. As Father's liege lord, the King has the power to *require* him to secure the succession." Bahzell stiffened, and she shrugged. "I don't like it, but I have to admit I can understand why the law gives His Majesty that prerogative. The King literally can't afford to have the titles and lands of such a powerful noble fall into dispute." She managed a chuckle that sounded almost genuine. "It can be a bit hard on the occasional only daughter, I suppose. But in the final analysis, one or two unhappy marriages are a small price to pay for the stability of the Kingdom."

"That I didn't know," Bahzell admitted. He sat thinking for several seconds, then grimaced. "I'd no notion the law gave your King such power as that. Still and all, I'm thinking as how Markhos wouldn't be so very happy to be pressuring your da on a matter such as this. There's naught I can think of as would be more likely to drive your father into things the King wouldn't care to see him driven to."

"You're probably right," Leeana said, although he had the distinct impression she was agreeing with him more to keep *him* from worrying than because she actually thought he was correct. "At the same time, though, if Father resists an offer of marriage which so much of the Council will consider is a reasonable way to resolve the succession concerns, it will give his enemies one more club to beat him with. And you know as well as I do how many clubs are already beating on him."

"That I do," he conceded. "Though I'm thinking he's unbowed yet, mind you."

"So far, at least," she agreed.

"So what's really upset you so, lass, isn't that you've any least fear your da will be after forcing you to marry this fellow, whoever he might be. It's that if he *isn't* forcing you to, he'll find himself losing allies on the Council."

"Yes."

"So he might," Bahzell said. "Yet I'm thinking as how your father's one of the most canny men I've yet to meet. It's in my mind that anyone wishful of getting on his bad side will be after finding himself bruised and bleeding in the gutter." He shook his head. "Don't you be panicking, lass. The Baron's more arrows in his quiver than most, and he'll be using all of them where you're concerned."

"I know he will," Leeana replied, and smiled tremulously, her eyes bright once more. "I know he will."

"Have you seen Leeana yet this morning, love?"

Baroness Hanatha looked up at her husband's question and gave him a small, sad smile.

"No, I haven't," she said.

"She's not taking this well," Tellian said fretfully, and Hanatha actually laughed.

" 'Taking this well'?" she repeated. "My dear, that has to stand as the understatement of at least the last decade!"

"Well, I know that," her husband said a bit irritably. "But at least she understands I'd never constrain her to marry anyone—least of all someone like Blackhill!"

"What the heart knows isn't always what the mind knows, when you're fourteen," Hanatha said gently. "And much as I love you, and as good a man as you are, you're still a *man*, dear."

"Which means what, aside from the obvious?" his tone was definitely testy this time.

"Which means that ultimately you can't really understand what it means to know every single important decision in your life lies in someone else's hands."

Hanatha's voice was neither angry nor condemnatory, but it was flat, and Tellian looked at her sharply across the breakfast table.

"Leeana knows how much you love her, just as I know how much you love both of us," his wife told him in a gentler tone. "But the fact remains that we live our lives as we choose only on the sufferance of your love. She's constrained in ways no son of yours would be. In many ways that makes her love you even more, you know."

The baron looked puzzled, and she shook her head sadly.

"Of course it does. She knows how much freedom she's been allowed. And she knows how fiercely you'd protect her. She knows how much you're prepared to sacrifice for her, and she loves you for that. Yet in the end, Tellian, she also knows how much it could cost you . . . and she can never forget that *she* can never truly hold those decisions in her own hands. That she has her freedom only because someone else gave it to her, not because she can secure it—forge her own life—on her own. So is it really any wonder she's not 'taking this well'?"

"No," he said softly, looking down at the eggs and ham on his plate. "No, it's not, of course." He poked at the food with his fork for a moment, then selected a fresh, flaky biscuit and began spreading butter across it. "Do you think I should discuss it with her again?" he asked after a moment.

"No," Hanatha said. "Not right now, at any rate. You two have already said all that needs saying. Whether you've both heard exactly what the other one was really saying may be another matter, but until her emotions—and yours, sweetheart—have had some time to settle down, you're not going to be able to make things any clearer. Best to give her some time to herself. Let her cope with it on her own terms."

"You're probably right," he conceded thoughtfully. He bit into the biscuit and chewed slowly, then frowned. "On the other hand, the fact that she isn't here for breakfast might seem to indicate she isn't coping with it very well yet," he observed.

"I don't expect her to cope with it for at least a day or so," his wife said. "In fact, before she went to bed last night she told me she intended to take Boots out for a ride early this morning. A long ride."

"How long a ride?" Tellian looked up again, his expression concerned, and Hanatha shrugged.

"Probably all day," she said frankly. "That's why I'm not

surprised she didn't join us for breakfast. She intended to make an early start, so she probably dropped by the kitchen when the servants were having breakfast and wheedled something out of Cook, like she used to do when she was a baby."

"What about the Mayor's banquet?" Tellian frowned. "You know we'll have to leave for it by midafternoon."

"I told her she didn't have to attend," Hanatha said. "It's not as if there'll be anyone else there her age, you know. You and I may have to suffer through it, but there's no real reason she ought to be forced to do the same thing. Besides, I know what it's like to need to spend some time away from parties and banquets."

"Still . . ." he said slowly.

"She said she wanted time to think, and she thinks best in the saddle. Like someone else I know." She smiled, and despite his manifold worries, Tellian chuckled.

"At any rate," she continued, "I didn't really have the heart to tell her no. I did ask her if she intended to take her armsmen along. I didn't come right out and tell her that if she didn't, she wasn't going anywhere, but she's not exactly a dummy, your daughter. She only made a face and said she knew perfectly well that she wasn't going riding unless Tarith did, too."

"Tarith, all by himself, isn't exactly her arms*men*," Tellian observed.

"I thought about pointing that out to her," Hanatha agreed. "On the other hand, you didn't pick Tarith as her armsman when she was two whole years old because of how incompetent he is. As long as they stay on our lands, he should be able to look after her just fine. And," for just an instant all of her own love for her daughter put a quiver into her voice, "I wanted to give her at least that much, Tellian. It's not all that much of a victory over tradition and convention, but at least we can let her have that much."

The baron looked at his wife and started to speak. Then he stopped, his own eyes just a bit misty, and nodded.

He sat there for a moment, then drew a deep breath, shook himself, and smiled at Hanatha.

"You're right, of course, love," he said. "On the other hand, this *is* Leeana we're talking about. You know—the daughter who broke her arm when she tried to walk all the way around the north tower across the battlements? The one who took her *pony* across a three-rail fence when she was nine? The one who—"

"All right. All right!" Hanatha laughed and threw a balled-up napkin at him. "And your point is?"

"That as soon as I finish eating, I'm personally going down to the stable to make sure Tarith's horse is gone, too."

"Milady Baroness! *Milady Baroness!*"

Hanatha Bowmaster came awake almost instantly in response to the imploring whisper. It was dark, without even a trace of gray dawn glimmering through her window. She sat up, and Marthya stepped back from the edge of her bed.

"What is it?" Her voice was husky with sleep, but she kept it low enough not to disturb her husband.

"It's—it's Lady Leeana," the maid said wretchedly, her lamp quivering in her hand. "Her bed's not been slept in, Milady!"

"What do you mean?" Hanatha demanded, not because she'd misunderstood Marthya, but because her mind refused to grapple with what the maid had just said.

"I mean she never came in *at all* last night, Milady," Marthya said even more wretchedly. "I know you said she had permission to stay out all day with Tarith, but I should have suspected something when she wasn't back in time for supper. But I didn't—truly, I *didn't*, Milady! I lay down, just to nap until she came in, and then, somehow . . ."

The maid shook her head, and a bright flash of panic flared through Hanatha.

"What's the hour?" she demanded.

"Barely three hours till dawn," Marthya admitted. "I just woke up, Milady, and the instant I did—"

"I understand, Marthya," Hanatha said. She wanted to be furious with the maid, but she couldn't. Not when she hadn't made a point of going to Leeana's room to check on her herself when she and Tellian finally returned from the mayor's banquet. She should have. She'd known at the time that she should have. Yet she'd decided not to—decided to respect her daughter's need for privacy.

"Let me get this straight," she said after a moment. "You're saying no one in Hill Guard has seen her at all since breakfast yesterday?"

"Breakfast, Milady?" Marthya looked at Hanatha in obvious confusion.

"Yes, breakfast—before she went riding with Tarith!" Hanatha's frightened worry sharpened her tone, but Marthya shook her head.

"Milady, she told me she and Tarith would be leaving *before* breakfast. She said they were getting an early start because she planned to ride over to Lord Farith's in time for dinner. She said she could dress herself and there was no need for me to be up even earlier than usual. And she said Cook had already packed sandwiches for an early lunch, so they wouldn't need breakfast."

"*Lord Farith's*?" Hanatha looked at the maid blankly. Farith was Lord of Maldahowe, almost a full half-day's ride north of Balthar. She'd never agreed Leeana could ride that far from home with only Tarith for an escort! Which meant—

The Baroness of Balthar went paper-white and reached for her husband's shoulder.

"There's no question about it," Tellian Bowmaster said harshly. The sun was perhaps an hour above the horizon as he stood staring out a window at the city of Balthar, his face haggard. "I've ordered a door-to-door search through the city, but it's not going to find her. *Damn* the girl! How could she *do* something like this?!"

Love and fear made him furious, and he slammed a fist down on the stone windowsill.

"We don't—we don't know for certain what she *has* done," Hanatha said. He shot a glance at her, and she shook her head. "Well, we *don't*, Tellian. Not really. I know what it looks like she's done, but there's no way

Tarith would help her run away. Wherever she is, he's with her. You know he'd never let her out of his sight once they left Hill Guard!"

"I know. I know!" Tellian drummed on the windowsill with both hands, his shoulders tight and his face clenched with worry. "But no one saw them leaving together, Hanatha. In fact, no one saw Leeana leave *at all*."

"That's preposterous," his wife protested. "She had to have been seen by the sentries!"

"Well, she wasn't," he said grimly. "And Tarith *was* seen leaving—by himself."

"What? When?" Hanatha demanded.

"The evening *before* you gave her permission to stay home from the banquet," he said, and then looked up quickly at her small, choked sound of distress.

She stared at him, her face white, her eyes huge with guilt and fear, and he shook his head sharply.

"No, love!" He turned and drew her into his arms, hugging her tightly. "Don't blame yourself—and don't think for a moment that *I* blame you, either! You asked her exactly the same questions, set exactly the same conditions, I would have. You had no more reason to suspect she might do something like this than I would have had!"

"But . . . but if Tarith left then, and no one saw her at breakfast . . ." Hanatha's voice trailed off, and she turned paler than ever. "Lillinara, Tellian!" she half-whispered. "Marthya put her to bed night before last, but how do we know she *stayed* there?"

"We don't," he said harshly. "In fact, I don't think she did." His wife stared at him mutely, and he shrugged. "She told the stable master to turn Boots out into the south paddock the day before yesterday. He didn't think anything about it, and no one told him she was supposed to be going anywhere yesterday. All he can say for certain is that her riding tack is missing, and Boots hasn't been seen since night before last."

"But how did she—?" Hanatha chopped herself off, and her jaw tightened in sudden understanding.

"Exactly," her husband said. "I've sent riders out in

all directions, searching for her—and for Tarith—but I already know how she did it."

He shook his head, but though his expression was grim, there was something else in it, as well. Something almost like pride.

"She knew we'd give her permission to skip the banquet if she asked for it. So she sent Tarith off on some errand before she ever spoke to you."

"But she promised to take him with her!" Hanatha protested, unable to accept that her daughter had lied to her.

"No, she didn't." Tellian shook his head. Hanatha stared at him, and he grinned sourly. "I'm sure she told the exact truth, love. It just wasn't what you thought she said."

"But—"

"You said she said she knew she couldn't spend the day riding unless Tarith did, too," he told her. "I'll wager she never actually said she couldn't do it unless Tarith rode *with* her. What she meant was that she had to send him riding off on some pretext or another to keep him from stopping her."

"Lillinara protect her," Hanatha whispered. "You're right. She didn't say specifically that he'd be with her. I only assumed that was what she meant."

"Just as she knew you would. And just as I would have done," Tellian said. "But with Tarith out of the way, and your permission to go riding, she knew no one would miss her between breakfast and lunch yesterday. So night before last, she told Marthya she and Tarith had to leave early the next morning for Lord Farith's. Then, as soon as she was confident almost everyone else was asleep, she crept out of her room, went down to the stable with the food she'd tricked Cook into giving her and 'Tarith' for lunch, took her riding tack, and let herself out through the southern tunnel."

Hanatha nodded. Only members of the family and their personal armsmen knew how to find and use the castle's two secret escape routes. They couldn't be opened from the outer end without battering rams, and concealment was their best protection, so guards were never posted except in times of high alert.

"So she went to the south paddock, saddled Boots, and disappeared . . . over thirty-six hours ago."

"But . . . but to where?"

"That much I think I know," Tellian said grimly. "If I'm right, she already has enough of a head start to make overtaking her all but impossible, but I can't go after her until I know for certain that Tarith isn't with her. Or that there isn't . . . some other explanation."

His voice wavered on the last three words, and Hanatha's hand rose to her lips. They stared at one another, paralyzed by lack of information and terror for their daughter's safety, and beyond the window, the sun crept steadily higher beyond the rain-weeping clouds.

Chapter Fourteen

Steam rose gently from the stew pot.

More steam rose from the far from occasional drops of rain which found their way through the open side of the lean-to Kaeritha had erected to protect her cooking fire. Centuries of Sothōii had planted trees along the lines of their roads, mainly to provide windbreaks, but also for the purpose to which Kaeritha had put this thick patch of trees. Although it was still spring, the branches above her were densely clothed in fresh, green leaves, which offered at least some protection to her campsite. And, of course, there was firewood in plenty, even if it was a bit on the damp side.

The blanket-covered packhorse was picketed beside the brawling, rain-fed stream at the foot of the slight rise on which she had encamped. Cloudy wasn't picketed at all—the idea that she might require picketing would have been a mortal insult to any Sothōii warhorse—but she'd ambled over and parked herself on the up-wind side of the fire. Kaeritha wasn't sure whether that was a helpful attempt to shield the fire from the rainy wind or an effort to get close enough to soak up what warmth the crackling flames could provide. Not that she was about to object in either case.

She stirred the stew again, then lifted the spoon and sampled it. She sighed. It was hot, and she knew it was going to be filling, but she was going to miss Brandark's deft hand at the cook fire, and the mere thought of Tala's cooking was enough to bring a glum tear to her eye.

She grimaced and sat back on her heels under the cover of the open-fronted tent she'd positioned with the eye of hard-won experience. The lean-to she'd constructed, and a rising swell of ground, served as reflectors to bounce the fire's warmth back into her tent, and only a little of the smoke eddied in along with it. Given the general soddenness of the Wind Plain, she was as comfortable—and as close to dry—as she was likely to get.

Which wasn't saying a great deal.

She got up and began moving additional firewood under the crude lean-to, where it would be at least mostly out of the rain and the cook fire could begin drying it out. She was just about finished when Cloudy suddenly raised her head. The mare's ears came up, pointed forward, and she turned to face back towards the road.

Kaeritha reached up under her poncho and unbuttoned the straps across the quillons of her short swords, then turned casually in the same direction.

Cloudy's hearing was considerably more acute than Kaeritha's. Kaeritha knew that, yet how even the mare could have heard anything through the steady drip and patter of rain surpassed her understanding. For a moment, she thought perhaps Cloudy *hadn't* heard anything, but then she saw the rider emerging ghost-like from the rainy, misty evening gloom and knew the mare hadn't been imagining things after all.

Kaeritha stood silently, watching the newcomer and waiting. The Kingdom of the Sothōii was, by and large, peaceful and law-abiding . . . these days. It hadn't always been so, though, and there were still occasional brigands or outlaws, despite the ruthless justice nobles like Tellian dealt out to any they caught up with. Such predators would be likely to think of a lone traveler as easy prey, especially if they knew that traveler was a woman . . . and *didn't* know she was one of Tomanāk's champions. As far as Kaeritha could tell, there was only one rider out there, but there might be more, and she maintained a prudent watchfulness as the other slowly approached her fire.

The possibility that the stranger might be a brigand declined as Kaeritha got a better look at his mount's gait. It was too dim and rainy to make out color or markings, but from the way it moved, that horse was almost as good as Cloudy. No prudent horse thief would dare to keep such a readily recognizable and remarked animal for himself, which suggested this fellow wasn't one . . . but didn't bring her any closer to being able to guess what he was doing out here in the rain with night coming on.

"Hello, the fire!" a soprano voice called, and Kaeritha closed her eyes as she heard it.

"Why me?" she asked. "Why is it always *me*?"

The cloudy night vouchsafed no reply, and she sighed and opened her eyes again.

"Hello, yourself, Leeana," she called back. "I suppose you might as well come on in and make yourself comfortable."

The Lady Leeana Glorana Syliveste Bowmaster, heir conveyant of Balthar, the West Riding, and at least a dozen other major and minor fiefs, had mud on her face. Her red-gold braid was a thick, sodden serpent, hanging limp down her back, and every line of her body showed her weariness as she sat cross-legged across the fire from Kaeritha and mopped up the last bit of stew in her bowl with a crust of bread. She popped it into her mouth, chewed, and swallowed contentedly.

"You must have been hungry," Kaeritha observed. Leeana looked at her questioningly, and she shrugged. "I've eaten my own cooking too often to cherish any illusions about my culinary talent, Leeana."

"I thought it was quite good, actually, Dame Kaeritha," Leeana said politely, and Kaeritha snorted.

"Flattering the cook isn't going to do you any good, girl," she replied. "Given that you look more like a half-starved, half-drowned, mud-spattered rat then the heir of one of the Kingdom's most powerful nobles, I was willing to let you wrap yourself around something hot before I began the interrogation. You've done that now."

Leeana winced at Kaeritha's pointed tone. But she didn't try to evade it. She put her spoon into the empty bowl and set it neatly aside, then faced Kaeritha squarely.

"I'm running away," she said.

"That much I'd already guessed," the knight told her dryly. "So why don't we just get on to the two whys?"

"The two whys?" Leeana repeated with a puzzled expression.

"Why number one: why you ran away. Why number two: why you don't expect me to march you straight home again."

"Oh." Leeana blushed slightly, and her green eyes dropped to the fire crackling between them. She gazed at the flames for several seconds, then looked back up at Kaeritha.

"I didn't just suddenly decide overnight to run away," she said. "There were lots of reasons. You know most of them, really."

"I suppose I do." Kaeritha studied the girl's face, and it was hard to prevent the sympathy she felt from softening her own uncompromising expression. "But I also know how worried and upset your parents must be right now. I'm sure you do, too." Leeana flinched, and Kaeritha nodded. "So why did you do this to them?" she finished coldly, and Leeana's eyes fell to the fire once more.

"I love my parents," the girl replied after a long, painful pause, her soft voice low enough that Kaeritha had some difficulty hearing her over the sound of the rain. "And you're right—they are going to be worried about me. I know that. It's just—"

She paused again, then drew a deep breath and raised her eyes to Kaeritha's once more.

"Father's received a formal offer for my hand," she said.

It was Kaeritha's turn to sit back on her heels. She'd been afraid it was something like that, but that didn't make having it confirmed any better. She thought of several things she might have said, and discarded each of them just as promptly as she recalled her earlier conversation with Leeana.

"Who was it from?" she asked instead after a moment.

"Rulth Blackhill," Leeana said in a flat voice. Kaeritha obviously looked blank, because the girl grimaced and continued. "He's Lord Warden of Transhar . . . and he'll be fifty years old this fall."

"*Fifty?*" Despite herself, Kaeritha couldn't keep the surprise out of her voice, and she frowned when Leeana nodded glumly. "Why in the world would a man that age believe even for a moment that your father might consider accepting an offer of marriage on your behalf from him?"

"Why shouldn't he believe it?" Leeana asked simply, and Kaeritha stared at her.

"Because he's almost four times your age, that's why!"

"He's also wealthy, a favorite of the King's chief minister, a member of the King's Council in his own right, and related by both blood and marriage to Baron Cassan," Leeana replied.

"But you said he's almost fifty!"

"What difference should that make to him—or the Council?" Leeana asked. "He's a recent widower with four children, two of them boys, by his first wife, and the youngest is less than a year old. So it's obvious he can still sire sons."

She said it so reasonably that Kaeritha had to bite her own tongue hard. For just a moment, she was furious with Leeana because she *did* sound so reasonable. But then she made herself step back from her own anger. Leeana's tone was that of someone who knew the world in which she had been raised would find what she was saying reasonable, not of someone who *agreed* with it.

"Do you really think," the knight asked quietly after another brief pause, "that your father would let someone that age—anyone, regardless of who he's related to!—have you?"

"I don't think he'd do it willingly," Leeana said in a

very low voice. "In fact, I think he'd probably refuse to do it at all, and I know he won't accept *this* offer. But in a way, knowing that only makes things worse."

She stared into Kaeritha's eyes, her own pleading for something. Sympathy, of course, but even more than that, for understanding.

"What do you mean, 'worse'?" she asked.

"Rulth Blackhill is a greedy, powerful man," Leeana replied. "He also has a reputation I'm not supposed to know anything about as someone who's abused his position as lord warden whenever his eye falls on one of his holder's attractive daughter . . . or wife," she added with a grimace. "But what matters most is that he's both ambitious and closely allied with his cousin and brother-in-law, Baron Cassan. And Baron Cassan and Father . . . don't get along. They don't like each other, they don't agree on most matters of policy, and Baron Cassan heads the Court faction most opposed to anything resembling 'appeasement' of the hradani. In fact, he almost convinced the King to deny Father's petition to strip Mathian Redhelm of his wardenship, and Blackhill supported him. The two of them—and the ones who think like them—would love to see Father's heir married off to one of Cassan's allies."

Her young face was taut with distaste and anger, and Kaeritha nodded slowly. Of course, judging by what Leeana had said about this Rulth Blackhill's reputation, the thought of bedding someone as lovely as Leeana probably figured in his thinking as well, the knight thought sardonically. Indeed, if he'd abused his authority the way Leeana was suggesting, the knowledge that she'd been forced to wed him against her will would only give the thought of forcing himself upon his political enemy's lovely only child a certain added savor for him.

"I'd think Cassan would have realized all of that would have made your father even less likely to accept Blackhill's offer," she said.

"He did," Leeana agreed. "In fact, he was probably counting on it."

"Now you have me really confused," Kaeritha admitted.

"Cassan hates Father, and he wants to discredit him in any way he can. And however I might feel about marrying someone Blackhill's age, it's a perfectly appropriate match by most standards."

"Even given what you just said about his abuse of his holders?" Kaeritha asked, cocking one eyebrow, and Leeana shrugged.

"Most of the Councilors have probably heard the reports about him and the women in his bed, Dame Kaeritha, but he's a lord warden. No one's going to want to bring something like that up, because they won't want their own reputations put under a glass and thrown up to them. So Cassan could be certain there'd be enormous pressure from several Council members for Father to accept, and very little support for him to refuse the offer. And if Father does refuse it, Cassan's supporters will urge the King to overrule him and *order* him to accept it. I know some people think Father's too clever to be caught out that way, but managing to avoid it may cost him dearly in terms of political support. Especially when he's already upset so many people by his 'surrender' to Prince Bahzell."

Kaeritha shook her head.

"That's too complicated and devious for my poor peasant-born brain to wrap itself around," she said. Leeana looked at her, and she snorted. "Oh, I don't say I disbelieve you, girl. And intellectually, I suppose I can even understand the twisty sort of thinking that would go into something like that. I just can't understand it on any sort of personal level."

"I wish *I* didn't," Leeana told her. "Or that I didn't have to, at least."

"I can believe that," Kaeritha said. She put some more wood on the fire, listening to the hiss as flames explored its damp surface. Then she looked back up at Leeana.

"So someone you don't like and certainly don't want to marry has asked your father for your hand, and you're afraid that when he refuses the offer, it will make serious problems for him. That's why you ran away?"

"Yes." Something about that one-word reply made

Kaeritha cock an eyebrow. It wasn't a lie—that much she was certain of. Yet somehow she was certain it wasn't the *entire* truth, either. She thought about pushing harder, then changed her mind.

"And how does running away solve any of those problems?" she asked instead.

"I'd have thought that was obvious, Dame Kaeritha," Leeana said in a surprised tone.

"Humor me," Kaeritha said dryly. "Oh, I think I can figure out your basic strategy. I don't flatter myself that you followed me just to place yourself under my protection, champion of Tomanāk or not. So I suspect that what you're really doing is heading for Kalatha with some scatterbrained, romantic schoolgirl's notion of becoming a war maid in order to avoid your unwelcome suitor. Is that about right?"

"Yes, it is," Leeana said just a touch defensively.

"And have you really considered all you'll be giving up?" Kaeritha countered. "I've been a peasant, *Lady* Leeana. I doubt very much that your lot would be quite as hard among the war maids as mine was in Moretz, but it would be very, very different from anything you've ever experienced before. And there won't be any going back. Your birth and family won't protect you any longer—in fact, for all intents and purposes, you'll be dead as far as your family is concerned."

"I know," Leeana said very, very softly, staring into the fire once more. "I know." She raised her eyes to Kaeritha again. "I *know*," she repeated a third time, jade eyes brimming with tears. "But I also know Mother and Father will always love me, whether I'm still legally their daughter or not. Nothing will ever change that. And if I go to the war maids, I take the decision out of Father's hands. No one can possibly blame him for refusing to allow Blackhill to marry me if I'm no longer his daughter. And," she managed a crooked smile, "the disgrace of what I'm doing should put me so far beyond the pale that not even someone as ambitious as Rulth Blackhill would consider offering me honorable marriage."

"But you're not yet fifteen years old," Kaeritha said.

She shook her head sadly. "That's too young to make this sort of decision, girl. I haven't known your father as long as you have, but I know he'd agree about that. You may be doing this for him, but do you really think he'd *want* you to?"

"I'm certain he wouldn't," Leeana admitted with a sort of forlorn pride. "He'll *understand* it, but that isn't the same as wanting me to do it. In fact, I'm pretty sure he and his armsmen are on the road behind me by now, and if he catches up, he'll believe he doesn't have any choice but to take me home again, whether I want to go or not. Because he loves me, and because, like you, he's going to argue that I'm too young to make this decision.

"But I'm *not* too young, according to the war maids' charter. I have the legal right to make that decision myself if I can reach one of their free-towns before Father catches up, and once it's made, he can't make me go home again, no matter how much he loves me or I love him. And if he can't make me go home, Blackhill and Cassan can't use me against him anymore, ever."

A tear broke free at last, spilling down her cheek, and Kaeritha drew a deep breath. Then she let it out again.

"Then I suppose we'd better turn in," she said. "I'm sure we can both use the sleep . . . and we'll have to make an early start if we're going to see to it that he doesn't catch up with us."

At least the rain had stopped when they broke camp in the morning. That was something, Kaeritha told herself as she swung lightly up into Cloudy's saddle and settled the butt of her quarterstaff into the stirrup bucket in which a more traditional knight would have braced her lance. In fact—she sucked in a deep, lung-filling draft of clear, cool morning air—it was quite a bit.

She'd watched Leeana as unobtrusively as possible as they went about preparing to take the road once more. The girl had been almost painfully ready to undertake any task, although it was obvious she'd never been faced with many of those tasks before in her life.

Like any Sothōii noble, male or female, she'd been thrown into a saddle about the same time she learned to stand up unassisted, and her horsemanship skills were beyond reproach. Her gelding, who rejoiced in a name even more highfaluting than "Dark War Cloud Rising," answered perfectly amiably to "Boots," and Kaeritha wondered if *any* Sothōii warhorse actually had to put up with its formal given name. However that might be, Boots (a bay brown who took his name from his black legs and the white stockings on his forelegs) was immaculately groomed, and his tack and saddle furniture were spotless, despite the wet and mud. Unfortunately, his rider was considerably less adept at others of the homey little chores involved in wilderness travel. At least she was willing, though, as Kaeritha had noted, and she took direction amazingly well for one of her exalted birth. All in all, Kaeritha was inclined to believe there was some sound metal in the girl.

And there had better be, the champion thought more grimly as she watched Leeana swing nimbly up into Boots' saddle. Kaeritha found herself unable to do anything but respect Leeana's motives, but the plain fact was that the girl couldn't possibly have any realistic notion of how drastically her life was about to change. It was entirely possible that, assuming she survived the shock, she would find her new life more satisfying and fulfilling. Kaeritha hoped she would, but the gulf which yawned between the daughter of someone who was arguably the most powerful feudal magnate in an entire kingdom and one more anonymous war maid, despised by virtually everyone in the only world she'd ever known, was far deeper than a fall from the Wind Plain's mighty ramparts might have been. Surviving that plunge would be a shattering experience—one fit to destroy any normal sheltered flower of noble femininity—however assiduously Leeana had tried to prepare herself for it ahead of time.

On the other hand, Kaeritha had never had all that much use for sheltered flowers of noble femininity. Was that the real reason she'd agreed to help the girl flee from the situation fate had trapped her into? A part of her wanted to think it was. And another part wanted to think she was doing this because it was the duty of any champion of Tomanāk to rescue the helpless from persecution. Given Leeana's scathing description of Rulth Blackhill and his reputation, it was impossible for Kaeritha to think of a marriage between him and the girl as anything but the rankest form of persecution, after all. "Marriage" or no, it would be no better than a case of legally sanctioned rape, and Tomanāk, as the God of Justice, disapproved of persecution and rape, however they were sanctioned. Besides, Leeana was right; she *did* have a legal right to make this decision . . . if she could reach Kalatha.

Both of those reasons were real enough, she thought. But she also knew that at the heart of things was another, still deeper reason. The memory of a thirteen-year-old orphan who'd found herself trapped into another, even grimmer life . . . until she refused to accept that sentence.

For a moment, Dame Kaeritha's sapphire-blue eyes were darker and deeper—and colder—than the waters of Belhadan Bay. Then the mood passed, and she shook herself like a dog, shaking off the water of memory, and gazed out through the cool, misty morning. The new-risen sun hovered directly in front of them, a huge, molten ball of gold, bisected by the hard, sharp line of the horizon. The morning mists rose to enfold it like steam from a forge, and the last of the previous day's clouds were high-piled ramparts in the south, their peaks touched with the same golden glow, as the brisk northerly wind continued to sweep them away. The road was just as muddy as it had been, but the day was going to be truly glorious, and she felt an eagerness stirring within her. The eagerness to be off and doing once again.

"Are you ready, Lady Leeana?" she asked.

"Yes," Leeana replied, urging Boots up beside Cloudy. Then she chuckled. Kaeritha cocked her head at the younger woman, and Leeana grinned. "I was just thinking that somehow it sounds more natural when you call me 'girl' than when you call me 'Lady Leeana,'" she explained in answer to Kaeritha's unspoken question.

"Does it?" Kaeritha snorted. "Maybe it's the peasant in me coming back to the surface. On the other hand, it might not be such a bad thing if you started getting used to a certain absence of honorifics."

She touched Cloudy very gently with a heel, and the mare started obediently forward. Leeana murmured something softly to Boots, and the gelding moved up at Cloudy's shoulder and fell into step with the mare, as if the two horses were harnessed together.

"I know," the girl said after several silent minutes. "That I should start getting used to it, I mean. Actually, I don't think I'll miss that anywhere near as much as I'll miss having someone to draw my bath and brush my hair." She held up a dirty hand and grimaced. "I've already discovered that there's quite a gap between reality and bards' tales. Or, at least, the bards seem to leave out some of the more unpleasant little details involved in 'adventures.' And the difference between properly chaperoned hunting trips, with appropriate armsmen and servants along to look after my needs, and traveling light by myself has become rather painfully clear to me."

"A few nights camping out by yourself in the rain will generally start to make that evident," Kaeritha agreed. "And I notice you didn't bring along a tent."

"No," Leeana said with another, more heartfelt grimace. "I had enough trouble coaxing Cook out of a few days worth of sandwiches without trying to bring along proper travel gear." She shivered. "That first night was *really* unpleasant," she admitted. "I never did get a fire started, and Boots needed my poncho worse than I did. He'd worked hard, and I didn't have anything else to rug him with."

"Hard to build a fire without dry wood," Kaeritha observed, carefully hiding a deep pang of sympathy. She pictured Leeana—a pampered young noblewoman, however much she might have wanted and striven to be something else—all alone in a cold, rainy night without a tent or a fire, or even the protection of her poncho. The girl had been right to use it to protect her heated horse, instead, but it must have been the most wretched night of her entire existence.

"Yes, I found that out." Leeana's grin was remarkably free of self-pity. "By the next morning, I'd figured out what I'd done wrong, so I spent about an hour finding myself a nice, dead log and hacking half a saddlebag of dry heartwood out of it with my dagger." She held up her right palm with a rueful chuckle, examining the fresh blisters which crossed it. "At least the exercise got me warmed up! And the next night, I had something dry to start the fire with. Heaven!"

She rolled her eyes so drolly Kaeritha had no choice but to laugh. Then she shook her head severely, returned her attention to the road, and asked Cloudy for a trot. The mare obliged, with the smooth gait which was steadily becoming addictive, and they moved off in a brisk, steady splatter of mud.

Yes, Kaeritha thought, treasuring green eyes that could laugh at their owner's own wet, cold, undoubtedly frightened misery. *Yes, there* is *sound metal in this one, thank Tomanāk.*

Chapter Fifteen

"Father isn't far behind now."

Kaeritha looked up from the breakfast fire. Leeana was standing beside the road, her raised arm hooked up across Boots' withers while she stared back the way they'd come the day before. Her expression was tense, and she stood very still, only the fingers of her right hand moving as they caressed the thick, shaggy warmth of the gelding's winter coat.

"What makes you so certain?" Kaeritha asked, for there'd been no question at all in the sober pronouncement.

"I could say it's because I know he had to have missed me by the second morning and that it's easy to guess he's been pushing hard after me ever since," the girl said. "But the truth is, I just *know*." She turned and looked at Kaeritha. "I always know where he and Mother are," she said simply.

Kaeritha chewed on that for a few moments, while she busied herself turning strips of bacon in her blackened camp skillet. Then she whipped the bacon out of the popping grease and spread it over their last slabs of slightly stale bread. She dumped the grease into the flames and watched the fire sputter eagerly, then looked back up at Leeana.

The girl's face was drawn, and Boots and Cloudy were both beginning to show the effect of the stiff pace they had set. Of course, Leeana and Boots had covered the same distance in twenty-four hours less than she and Cloudy had, but she'd been pushing hard herself ever since the girl caught up with her. However furious and worried he might be, Tellian was too levelheaded to risk riding in pursuit with only Hathan—the Lord Warden of the West Riding would be too juicy a target for the ill-intentioned to pass up—but he and his wind brother would be setting a crushing pace for the rest of his armsmen, and Kaeritha knew it.

"What do you mean, you know where they are?" she asked after a moment.

"I just do." Leeana gave Boots one more caress, then stepped closer to Kaeritha and the fire and accepted her share of the bread and bacon. She took an appreciative bite of the humble repast and shrugged.

"I'm sorry. I'm not trying to be mysterious about it—I just don't know a good way to explain it. Mother says the Sight has always run in her family, all the way back to the Fall." She shrugged again. "I don't really know about that. It's not as if there've been dozens of magi in our family, or anything like that. But I always know where they are, or if they're unhappy . . . or hurt." She shivered, her face suddenly drawn and old beyond its years. "Just like I knew when Moonshine went down and rolled across Mother."

She stared at something only she could see for several seconds, then shook herself. She looked down at the bread and bacon in her hand, as if seeing them for the first time, and gave Kaeritha a smile that was somehow shy, almost embarrassed, before she raised the food and bit into it again.

"Do they always 'know' where *you* are?" Kaeritha asked after a moment.

"No." Leeana shook her head. Then she paused. "Well, actually, I don't know for certain about Mother. I know when I was a very little girl, she always seemed to know just when I was about to get into mischief, but I always just put that down to 'mommy magic.' I do know *Father* doesn't have any trace of whatever it is, though. If he did, I'd have gotten into trouble so many times in the last few years that I doubt I'd be able to sit in a saddle at all! I'd never have gotten away with running away in the first place, either. And I can tell from how unhappy and worried he feels right now that he doesn't realize they're no more than a few hours behind us."

Her eyes darkened with the last sentence, and her voice was low. The thought of her father's unhappiness and worry clearly distressed her.

"It's not too late to change your mind, Leeana," Kaeritha said quietly. The girl looked at her quickly, and the knight shrugged. "If he's that close, all we have to do is sit here for a few hours. Or we can go on. From the map and directions your father's steward gave me, Kalatha can't be more than another two or three hours down the road. But the decision is yours."

"Not anymore," Leeana half-whispered. Her nostrils flared, and then she shook her head firmly. "It's a decision I've already made, Dame Kaeritha. I can't—won't—change it now. Besides," she managed a crooked smile, "he may be unhappy and worried, but those aren't the only things he's feeling. He knows where I'm going, and why."

"He does? You're certain of that?"

"Oh, I wasn't foolish enough to leave any tear-spotted notes that might come to light sooner than I wanted," Leeana said dryly. "Father *is* a wind rider, you know. If I hadn't managed to buy at least a full day's head start, he'd have forgotten about waiting for his bodyguards and he and Hathan would have come after me alone. And in that case, he'd have been certain to catch up with me, even on Boots.

"Since he didn't, I have to assume I did manage to keep anyone from realizing I'd left long enough to get the start I needed. But Father isn't an idiot, and he knows I'm not one, either. He must have figured out where I was going the instant someone finally realized I was missing, and he's been coming after me ever since. But, you know, there's a part of him that doesn't want to catch me."

She finished the last bite of her bread and bacon, then stood, looking across at Kaeritha, and this time her smile was gentle, almost tender.

"Like you, he's afraid I'm making a terrible mistake, and he's determined to keep me from doing it, if he can. But he knows why I'm doing it, too. And that's why a part of him doesn't want to catch me. Actually *wants* me to beat him to Kalatha. He knows as well as I do that the war maids are the only way I'll avoid eventually being forced to become a pedigreed broodmare dropping foals for Blackhill . . . or someone. Mother was never that for him, and he knows *I'll* never be that for anyone. He taught me to feel that way—to value myself that much—himself, and he knows that, too."

"Which won't prevent him from stopping you if he can," Kaeritha said.

"No." Leeana shook her head. "Silly, isn't it? Here we both are—me, running away from him; him, chasing after me to bring me back, whether I want to come or not—and all of it because of how much we love each other."

A tear glittered for an instant, but she wiped it briskly away and turned to busy herself tightening the girth on Boots' saddle.

"Yes," Kaeritha said softly, emptying the teapot over the fire's embers and beginning to cover the ashes with dirt. "Yes, Leeana. Very silly indeed."

"Soumeta is here, Mayor. She says she has an appointment."

Yalith Tamilthfressa, Mayor of Kalatha, looked up from the paperwork on her desk with a grimace. Her assistant, Sharral Ahnlarfressa, stood in the door of her office, with a sour expression which was only too accurate a mirror of Yalith's own emotions.

"What about Theretha?" Yalith asked. "Is she here, too?"

"Theretha?" Sharral shook her head. "It's just Soumeta. And I checked your calendar. If she does have an appointment this morning, *I* didn't write it down there."

"Neither did anyone else," Yalith sighed.

"In that case," Sharral said grimly, "I'll send her packing so fast her head will swim!"

She started to turn to go, but Yalith's quick headshake stopped her.

"No," the mayor said. "Oh, I'd love to turn you loose on her, Sharral, but I can't quite do that."

"Why not?" Sharral demanded.

"You know perfectly well why. As big a pain in the arse as she may be, she's not exactly alone in her feelings, now is she?"

"Yalith," Sharral said, dropping the formal title she normally used when addressing her old friend on official town business, "she's only a Fifty. If you want her jerked up short for insubordination, I'm sure Balcartha would be delighted to take care of it for you."

Yalith leaned back in her chair and smiled affectionately at her assistant. For all practical purposes, Sharral was her unofficial vice-mayor, really, although the town charter provided for no such office. They'd known one another since girlhood, although Yalith had been born in Kalatha and Sharral had been five years old when her mother became a war maid. Ahnlar Geramahnfressa had been luckier than some—Sharral had been an only child. It was always sticky, and often painful, when a woman with children sought out the war maids. It was unusual for a mother to become a war maid, because the war maids' charter didn't provide any legal basis for her to retain custody of, or even the right to visit, her children after she severed herself from her family. It was a very rare, or very desperate, mother who was prepared to risk losing all contact with her children, however intolerable her own life might seem.

Yet a surprising number of them were allowed to take their daughters with them. In most cases, Yalith thought, that said all that needed saying about the fathers of those children. Those men didn't relinquish possession of their children out of gentleness and love; they did it because those children were merely daughters, not something as important as a son. No wonder the women unfortunate enough to be married to them sought any escape they could find!

But however their wives might feel, Yalith often wondered how someone like Sharral felt when she thought about it. How did it feel to know that the man who'd sired you had cared less for you than he did for a pair of old shoes? Did you feel rejected, discarded as something unimportant and easily replaced? Or did you spend every morning thanking Lillinara that you'd escaped having anything to do with a parent who could feel that way about his own child? Yalith knew how *she* felt about anyone who could do that, but she also knew the mind and the heart could be cruelly unreasonable.

"If I thought I could turn Balcartha loose on her, I'd enjoy that even more than handing her over to you, Sharral," the mayor said. "I'd really relish watching that, as a matter of fact. But it might look just a bit extreme to turn a Five Hundred—and the commander of the entire Town Guard, at that—loose on a mere Fifty. Not without clear provocation, at any rate."

"Extreme!" Sharral sniffed. "Balcartha is the Guard commander, and Soumeta is one of her officers—one of her *junior* officers, Yalith. A junior officer who's just lied to me in order to get in to see you without an appointment! That strikes me as a fair to middling offense against good discipline, and if Balcartha can't rake Soumeta over the coals for something like that, then just exactly who *can*?"

"But that's the point, isn't it?" Yalith's mouth quirked in something much too astringent to be called a smile. "Soumeta isn't here just for herself, and she knows I know it. Besides, maybe she's right."

"And maybe she's a dangerous, arrogant, hotheaded, prejudiced, trouble-making idiot with the morals of a mink in heat, the appetites of a praying mantis, and delusions of her own importance, too!"

"You don't have to mince words with me after all these years, Sharral," Yalith said with a harsh chuckle. "Tell me how you *really* feel about her."

"It's not a joke, damn it, Yalith!" Sharral waved both hands in frustration.

"No, it's not," Yalith agreed more soberly. "But whether we like it or not, at this particular moment Soumeta is only saying what a dangerous number of other war maids think. So I can't just let you or Balcartha step on her—not without giving her a little more rope, first, at the very least—without running the risk of further alienating the people who already think I'm being too accommodating. Like Maretha and her crowd."

Sharral's lips tightened as if she wanted to dispute that. Unfortunately, she couldn't.

"All right," she sighed. "You win—or lose, or whatever it is you're doing! I'll show her in."

"Thank you for agreeing to see me on such short notice, Mayor," Soumeta said as Sharral closed the office door behind her and Yalith pointed at a chair on the other side of her desk.

"Did I do that?" Yalith asked pleasantly, arching both eyebrows and steepling her fingers in front of her chest as she leaned back and rested her elbows on the arms of her chair. "That's odd. I could have sworn Sharral just told me that you had an appointment with me."

Soumeta flushed, and Yalith smiled internally. Had the other woman really expected that a meaningless polite formula could somehow convince Yalith to gloss over what amounted to an arrogant demand that the mayor see her?

"I suppose I shouldn't have done that," Soumeta muttered after a moment. "It's just that it's important that I speak to you, and I didn't think Sharral was even going to tell you I was here."

"Sharral tells me about everyone who asks to see me, Soumeta," Yalith said evenly. "Whether she likes them or not."

Soumeta's flush deepened. It was especially obvious in

someone with her fair skin and golden hair, and Yalith let her stew in her own juices for several seconds.

"Very well," she said finally. "You're here. What was so important that you simply had to see me?"

"Mayor Yalith," Soumeta gave herself a visible shake and leaned forward in her chair, "the situation in Lorham is worse than ever, and it's getting steadily worse still. We have to *do* something!"

"And what, precisely, would you like me to do, Soumeta?" Yalith asked with deadly patience.

"We can't just stand there while Trisu and his toadies systematically tear down everything we've accomplished in the last two hundred years!" Soumeta protested. "It's bad enough that he's violating our boundaries with that gristmill of his, or our prerogatives with those road tolls, but now his so-called market master in Thalar is squeezing us completely out." She bared her teeth. "Do you think for one minute that someone like Manuar would dare to do that without Trisu's backing?"

"First," Yalith said levelly, her dark eyes trained on Soumeta like twin ballistae, "we're not 'just standing there.' Second, there seems to be some question as to exactly what Master Manuar is or is not doing in Thalar. Third, when the Council and I specified that you were to be our official representative to him, we also instructed you *not* to be confrontational. The object was to make a firm statement through a spokeswoman official enough to make our concern plain, not to antagonize the man."

"*Antagonize* him!" Soumeta exclaimed. "Mayor, he claimed Jolhanna was responsible for all our difficulties!"

"I've read your report, Soumeta," Yalith said. "It's . . . unfortunate that you excluded Theretha from your meeting with the market master."

"Are you accusing me of misrepresenting what Manuar said?" Soumeta demanded harshly.

"I'm saying a second viewpoint on the conversation would have been useful." Yalith held the younger woman's angry eyes with her own. "And I'm suggesting that Theretha, who knows Manuar personally, might have been able to prevent the conversation from getting so out of hand so quickly. And, frankly, Soumeta, I'm also suggesting that intransigence is often in the eye of the beholder. You went into that meeting with blood already in your eye—and don't pretend to me, or to yourself, that you didn't—and that's hardly the way to evoke a cooperative atmosphere."

"I went into that meeting determined to be just as reasonable as Manuar allowed me to be," Soumeta snapped. "You and the Council had sent me as our *official* representative—was I supposed to just stand there and let him lie to me about Jolhanna without calling him on it?"

"Yes, we sent you as our official representative. We also stressed the importance of being reasonable. Of bending over backward, if that was what it took, to make it abundantly clear that we aren't the ones provoking the problems."

"And letting him shuffle all the blame off on Jolhanna would have made us look 'reasonable'?" Soumeta barked a sharp, angry laugh. "It would have proved to him that we were weak enough to let him get away with a barefaced lie!"

"What you ought to have done was to tell him that you could not believe Jolhanna would have deliberately or knowingly provoked problems between us and the Thalar merchants. You should never have accused *him* of lying about it. Instead, you should have assured him that both I, as Mayor, and the Town Council would look into his allegations most carefully. And you should have pointed out to him that while we were looking into them, it remained his responsibility to ensure that the Thalar market, as opposed to the individual merchants in it, abided by the terms of our charter."

Soumeta muttered something under her breath and looked rebellious, and Yalith suppressed a sudden burning desire to snap the other woman's head off. She settled for glaring at Soumeta for a breath or two before she continued in that same, meticulous tone.

"You should also have listened to Theretha. She wanted

to stay, to look for Herian. For that matter, to speak to Manuar herself. Instead, you bustled her back off to Kalatha."

"The Council charged me with responsibility for her safety," Soumeta grated through clenched teeth. "In my judgment, her safety was at risk in Thalar."

"But it's the soundness of your judgment which is really in question here, isn't it, Soumeta?" Yalith asked softly.

"If you didn't trust my judgment, then you shouldn't have sent me in the first place!" Soumeta shot back.

"You weren't *my* choice," Yalith told her flatly. "I didn't object to it, which I probably should have. But I didn't choose you for the job because, frankly, I was concerned that something just like this might happen."

"It's time we stopped being *afraid* of them!" Soumeta said fiercely. "It's time we pushed back instead of just letting them push *us*! If you can't see that, then others can! We're just lying down for them, reacting to every fresh infringement with one more tearful protest instead of kicking them in the balls, and that's not being reasonable! It's spreading your legs for them and inviting them to—"

"That's enough!" Yalith slapped her desktop so hard her hand stung, and Soumeta's mouth snapped shut in shock. The mayor leaned over the desk towards her, her normally mild eyes crackling with anger, and the younger, taller war maid shrank back in her chair.

"You're young," Yalith told her icily. "Older than Theretha, perhaps, but that's not saying all that much, is it? You're impatient, you're angry, you're not terribly smart, and you're just spoiling for a fight. Well, unless we're luckier than we have any reasonable right to hope, you may have found us one. I don't expect you to understand just how serious the problems you've helped create really are, because you're too busy patting yourself on the back and congratulating yourself on having 'taken a stand.' But I *do* expect you to obey the instructions you're given. I also expect you to keep a civil tongue in your head when you address the Mayor of Kalatha. And you'd better remember both of those things, girl, because if you can't at least pretend to the most basic courtesy or obey the instructions your superiors give you, then I will discuss with Balcartha whether or not you are fit to be trusted with *any* responsibility, including your position as an officer of the Town Guard. Is that perfectly clear, Fifty Soumeta?"

Soumeta stared at her, more terrified and cowed by Yalith's freezing cold precision than she would ever have been by any shouted confrontation. Yalith held her eye for another handful of heartbeats, then nodded very slightly.

"You may go, Fifty Soumeta. And the next time you tell my assistant you have an appointment to see me, you had better have an appointment. Because if you don't, you will never have one again. Is that also clear?"

Soumeta nodded quickly, and Yalith snorted.

"Then go," she said, and Soumeta seemed to levitate up out of her chair. She disappeared through the door much more rapidly than she'd entered, and it closed behind her.

It opened again after a moment, and Sharral stuck her head back into Yalith's office.

"I thought you said we couldn't step on her?" the assistant said mildly.

"No, I said you and Balcartha couldn't step on her."

"Isn't that more or less the same thing?"

"Not even remotely." Yalith grimaced. "What I just did was to personally counsel and reprimand a junior officer because I was dissatisfied with the fashion in which she'd carried out the instructions I'd given her. Well, I did smack her for insubordination, too, but that was on a personal level. What I did not do was to have one of my subordinate minions—that's you, Sharral—whack her, nor did I overreact by having one of her military superiors—that's Balcartha—give her the same reprimand." The mayor shrugged. "Not even her sponsors on the Council can suggest that anything that just transpired in this office was remotely improper on my part. Or that she didn't just give me ample justification for the hammer I did bring down on her."

"And just which member of the Council do you expect to be fooled by all of this dancing around the point?"

"I don't expect to fool anyone," Yalith said. "You know what sort of juggling act I'm already doing with the Council. The sides are pretty clearly drawn, but as long as I stay within the bounds of custom and usage, Maretha's clique doesn't have a pretext to call for an open vote of censure."

"Do you really think it's that bad?" Sharral looked at the mayor, her expression both dismayed and surprised.

"Do I really think that? No." Yalith shook her head. "But that doesn't mean I'm right. And it also doesn't mean the situation can't change. So until I'm positive about exactly what it is Maretha wants—and that I can keep her from getting whatever it is—I'm not planning on taking any chances."

She shook her head again.

"This thing has been building for a long time now, Sharral. I don't like the way the intensity has suddenly started climbing over the last year or two, either. And, to be honest, I'm just as angry as Soumeta or Maretha could possibly be. But right this minute, the situation is hanging on the very brink of going out of control. We don't need some silly confrontation—or anything!—to make things even worse."

Chapter Sixteen

Bahzell Bahnakson stood on the battlements of Hill Guard Castle, gazing off into the distance and worrying. Brandark Brandarkson stood at his left elbow and helped him do it.

"Why do I have the feeling this was a really bad idea?" the Bloody Sword hradani murmured.

"Coming up here?" Bahzell looked down at him and cocked an eyebrow, and Brandark shook his head with a tight grin. It wasn't raining. In fact, the sun shone bright, and clear blue patches showed through fitful breaks in the clouds. But the blustery wind was much stronger up here on the walls, where no obstacles blocked or abated its power, and both hradanis' warrior braids blew out behind them.

"No," Brandark said. He gestured at the road, stretching off to the east. "I meant Tellian's haring off this way."

"It's not as if he'd any other choice, is it now?" Bahzell replied, and Brandark shrugged.

"The fact that something's the only choice someone has, doesn't make it a good idea when he does it," he pointed out. "Especially not when he has as many enemies as Tellian does. I don't like the thought of his dashing about out there with no more than a score of bodyguards, Bahzell."

"First, it's only by the gods' grace that he's any bodyguards at all with him," Bahzell snorted. "Once Tarith turned up and he'd confirmation of all Leeana had done, he was all for heading out with naught but Hathan beside him. Now *that*, I'm thinking, is something as most anyone would think was after being a bad idea."

"You know," Brandark observed, "you're developing quite a gift for understatement, Bahzell."

Bahzell only snorted again, louder, but both of them knew he was right. Even Tellian had known that much, although both Hathan and Hanatha had found themselves forced to sit on him—almost literally—before he'd admitted it. That had been harder for Hanatha than for his wind brother, but frantic as she was over her daughter's safety, she was also the wife of one great noble and the daughter of another. Despite the unmatchable speed with which any wind rider's courser gifted him, the Lord Warden of the West Riding had no business at all putting himself at risk by gallivanting around the countryside unprotected. It was entirely possible that one of his enemies might be keeping an eye on his comings and goings with an eye towards a quiet little assassination, assuming he was foolish enough to offer an opening, and not even a courser could outrun an arrow. Besides, as Hathan had grimly pointed out, Leeana had stolen enough of a lead that it was unlikely even coursers could overtake her short of her destination, so there was no reason to dash out like reckless fools.

"Second," Bahzell continued after a moment, "that's his daughter out there, Brandark. He's a noble and a ruler, aye. But he's after being a father before he's any of those other things." He shook his head. "He'll not give over, no matter what."

"But is that really what's best for Leeana?" Brandark asked more quietly. Bahzell looked at him again, sharply, and the Bloody Sword shrugged. "I know he loves her, Bahzell. And I know he wants her safely home again. But Leeana's no fool. Whatever other people may think, you know—and so do her parents—that she didn't do this on a whim. If she thought it through as carefully as I'm sure she did, perhaps what she's doing is actually for the best."

Bahzell grunted. He'd thought the same thing himself as he remembered the pain, and the fear—and not for herself alone, he realized now—in a pair of jade-green eyes. But he knew that even if Tellian had come to the exact same conclusion, it wouldn't have made any difference to his determination to protect the daughter he loved from the consequences of her own decision.

"It might be you've a point," he said finally. "I'll not deny I've wondered the same. But in Tellian's boots, I'd make the selfsame choice, and well I know it." He shook his head again. "It's a hard thing, Brandark. A hard thing."

They fell silent again, gazing off into the wind, and wondering what was happening out there beyond the eastern horizon.

"Milord Champion!"

Bahzell looked up in surprise. The delicious odors of one of Tala's dinners—rich, hot curry, chicken, beef, and potatoes—drifted tantalizingly upward from the bowls and dishes on the table before him, and evening was busily giving way to night outside the window. He'd invited Gharnal and Hurthang to join him and Brandark for supper, but he hadn't expected any other visitors this night. And he certainly hadn't expected to see Sir Jahlahan Swordspinner turn up in his quarters in person.

"Aye, Sir Jahlahan?" he said mildly, setting down his knife and fork. "And how might it be as I could be of service?"

He waved at a chair on the other side of the table, inviting the human to be seated, but Swordspinner remained standing.

"I apologize for interrupting your supper, Milord Champion. And yours, Milords." He nodded with abrupt, almost spastic courtesy to Brandark and the two other Horse Stealers, and Bahzell's ears pricked as the jagged edges of the other man's voice registered. Sir Jahlahan was the seneschal of Hill Guard Castle. In Tellian's absence, he commanded the garrison not simply of Hill Guard, but of Balthar itself, and Tellian Bowmaster hadn't picked someone who was prone to panic for that post. Yet at this moment, that was what Sir Jahlahan appeared dangerously close to doing.

"There's no need to be apologizing, Sir Jahlahan," Bahzell said after a moment, glancing at the other hradani. "I've no doubt only pressing need could have caused you to."

"You're not wrong there, Milord Champion," Swordspinner agreed in that same, jagged voice. "We've just received a messenger from Lord Warden Edinghas of Warm Springs," he continued. "That's one of the West Riding's smaller holdings, up on the northeast border. Up between the west fork of the Spear River and the shore of the North Ice Sister."

He paused, and Bahzell nodded his understanding of the geography. That meant this Warm Springs was almost as far north as the southern edge of Hope's Bane Glacier, about as far as you could get from Balthar and remain in the West Riding. Yet even as he nodded, he had the odd feeling Swordspinner hadn't paused to be sure Bahzell was following him. It was more as if the seneschal *needed* to pause. As if whatever had brought him here was terrible enough that he needed time to steel himself for the actual explanation.

Sir Jahlahan drew a deep breath, then looked Bahzell in the eye.

"Milord Champion, Lord Edinghas' message is—Well, it's one I don't have the least idea how to answer. I doubt Milord Baron himself would know! But this much I *am* certain of: if any man can know what to do, it's a champion of Tomanāk. Please, Milord. I need your help—badly."

Bahzell's expression was as grim as his thoughts as he and Brandark followed Sir Jahlahan into the seneschal's office. He'd considered bringing Gharnal and Hurthang, as well, but decided against it. This meeting might be difficult enough without piling that many hradani into it. Besides, if what his instincts—and that indefinable link which always connected him, however lightly, to Tomanāk—were telling him was true, someone had needed to go and alert the Order's sword brothers that they might be needed.

Soon.

Swordspinner's was the next door down the corridor from Tellian's own office, and it was only marginally smaller than the baron's. Despite that, and despite the fact that Sothōii were taller than most humans, Bahzell felt cramped and trapped, painfully aware of the ceiling close above his head.

He'd felt that way constantly when he first arrived at Hill Guard, but it was a sensation he'd gotten over with the help of familiarity. Now that comforting sense of the familiar had disappeared. The dreadful message Jahlahan had summarized for him on the walk to his office had stripped it away, and the weight of the castle's stonework seemed to press down upon him.

The human waiting in Swordspinner's office was short for a Sothōii, a good four inches shorter than Brandark, much less Bahzell. But he was a tough, weathered-looking man, with hard muscles and a face wind, sun, and winter had darkened to the hue of old leather. It was impossible for Bahzell to estimate his age accurately, but he was certain the human was at least several years older than he was himself.

And it was also quickly apparent that this was *not* one of Tellian's retainers who approved of hradani.

Lord Edinghas' messenger snapped to his feet, his exhausted face taut with outrage, as soon as he laid eyes on Bahzell and Brandark. His bone-deep weariness had clearly undermined whatever normal reserve he might have, and he opened his mouth angrily. No doubt he intended to demand to know what Swordspinner thought he was doing bringing hradani into his mission to Hill Guard, and Bahzell couldn't honestly blame him. Not given the long and bloody history which lay between the

Sothōii and the Horse Stealer clans. Bahzell didn't begin to have all the details, but the horrifying bits and pieces Swordspinner had shared with him on the walk here were more than enough to explain both the messenger's exhaustion and his anger at suddenly finding himself face-to-face with hradani.

But despite all of that, the man managed to clamp his jaws before his anger found words to express itself. Bahzell was impressed by the other man's self-control. He doubted he could have matched it, had their circumstances been reversed. And he was suddenly glad he'd sent Gharnal off with Hurthang to alert the Order.

"Alfar Axeblade, be known to Prince Bahzell Bahnakson, son of Prince Bahnak of the Horse Stealer Hradani," Swordspinner said, his tone formal. Obviously, he, too, recognized Axeblade's struggle with his emotions, and he kept his own voice carefully under control as he added, "And champion of Tomanāk."

"*Champion of Tomanāk?*" Axeblade repeated. Despite all he could do, there was as much incredulity as surprise in his tone, and his weathered face flushed darker as he realized how he'd given himself away.

"Aye," Bahzell rumbled, his deep voice measured and dispassionate. "And I'll not blame you for feeling a mite . . . surprised, Master Axeblade." He produced a wry smile. "I'm thinking you couldn't possibly be more surprised than *I* was when himself first turned up and told me as how such as I had the makings of a champion! Yet such I am, and if there's aught I can be doing to serve you or Lord Warden Edinghas against the Dark, then that I will be doing."

There was a tang of iron promise in his voice. Axeblade heard it, but so many centuries of mutual hatred couldn't be washed away so quickly.

"I hope you'll not take this wrongly . . . Milord Champion," he said, after a moment. He seemed to have trouble getting the title out, as if the words were sharp-edged enough to cut his tongue. "But Warm Springs isn't exactly what you might call the very heart of the West Riding. Often enough, news takes a while getting to us, and we'd not heard aught about you. So if I could be asking, what's a hradani doing here?"

"And what's a hradani doing pretending as he's a champion of Tomanāk, for that matter?" Bahzell added dryly, and Axeblade flushed again. But he also nodded stubbornly, and Bahzell chuckled.

"Master Axeblade," Swordspinner began stiffly, "Prince Bahzell is Baron Tellian's guest. Under the circumstances, I don't think—"

"Let be, Sir Jahlahan," Bahzell interrupted. The seneschal looked at him sharply, and the Horse Stealer shrugged. "In Master Axeblade's place, I'd not be so polite," he said dryly, and returned his attention to the other man.

"What I'm after doing here is just a mite complicated," he said. "It's glad enough I'll be to explain it all to you, and to Lord Edinghas, assuming as how I have the opportunity. For now, let's just be saying that Baron Tellian and I—aye, and my father, as well—are after doing what we can to be keeping our swords out of one another's bellies for a change. That's what I'm doing here at Hill Guard. But what you're really asking, Master Axeblade, is why a Horse Stealer should be offering to help any Sothōii—or coming within a league or three of any courser ever born. Or, for that matter, why in the world you should be trusting such as me to do any such thing."

"Aye, that I am," Axeblade said after a moment. "Your folk aren't named 'Horse Stealer' for naught . . . Milord. And Tomanāk Himself knows how many of our horses you've stolen, slaughtered, and *eaten*," he continued, matching bluntness to bluntness, and Bahzell smiled more naturally. This man might hate hradani, but Bahzell recognized a kindred soul when he met one.

"That we have," he acknowledged. "And, truth to tell, there's more than enough of my folk as would cheerfully do the same, even now. But my father's not after being one of them, and no more am I. We've done each other harm enough over the years, I'm thinking, Master Axeblade. Time we tried another road, one where neither of us is after raiding the other."

Axeblade looked as if he found the entire concept impossible to grasp, but at least he was polite enough not to call Bahzell insane.

"I can't be undoing all Horse Stealers are having done to the Sothōii," Bahzell continued. "And no more can you—or Baron Tellian, himself—undo a single thing as Sothōii are having done to us. But if we're to stop killing one another once and for all, I'm thinking as how it will have to start somewhere. So why not here, and now? And if it's Tomanāk's little joke to choose such as me to be playing peacemaker to you Sothōii, then it's little choice I have but to be doing the same for the coursers. Or do you think Horse Stealers are daft enough to think we could be after making peace with one and not the other?"

"That sounds mighty fine and reasonable, Milord," Axeblade said in a tone he managed to keep neutral. "I'm not so very sure the *coursers* will think it does, though. They've long memories, too, you know."

"So they do," Bahzell agreed. "And I suppose it's likely enough one of them might like to feel a little Horse Stealer crushed under his toes. Mind you, *I'd* not think it such a marvelous idea, but I can see how it might be having a little appeal for a courser. Still and all, Baron Tellian's courser, and Hathan Shieldarm's courser, have been after being civil enough." He shrugged. "I'll take my chances that other coursers will be being reasonable enough to give one of Tomanāk's champions time enough to at least be saying a few words in his own defense before they're after turning him into Wind Plain mud.

"And whatever it is they may think about the notion," he went on in a voice which was suddenly devoid of any humor at all, "what Sir Jahlahan's told me of your tale is after leaving me no choice. I'll not pretend I've any clear idea of who or what might have been able to do such as you've described. But this I do know, Master Axeblade—whoever, or whatever, it may be, it's flat my business to be stopping it. And stop it I will."

Axeblade started to say something more, then stopped, looking at Bahzell's expression. Several seconds passed in silence, and then Lord Edinghas' messenger nodded slowly.

"I believe you will, Milord Champion," he said. "Or die trying, any road. To my mind, that's the most anyone could ask of any man . . . human or hradani. So if you're daft enough to ride into the middle of a holding full of Sothōii and coursers who're none of them going to be happy to see hradani, now of all times, then I suppose I'm daft enough to take you there."

"Take *us* there, you mean," Brandark put in. Axeblade looked at him, and the Bloody Sword shrugged. "He's not very bright, but he *is* my friend," he said lightly. "I'd never forgive myself if I let him out without a leash and he suffered a mischief."

"As well take two hradani—or a dozen—as one," Axeblade agreed with an answering shrug. "I don't know who's going to explain any of this to the coursers, though!" he added.

"Well, as to that," Bahzell said, "I've taken the liberty of asking Sir Jahlahan to send word to Deep Water. Would it happen you and your lord are after knowing Sir Kelthys and his courser?"

"Aye," Axeblade said slowly, his expression thoughtful.

"So am I," Bahzell said. "And I'm thinking as how Kelthys will vouch for me to you two-legged Sothōii, while Walasfro is after talking fast enough to the other coursers to keep me untrodden on. Besides, like as not we'll be needing him if the surviving coursers are to tell us what happened out there."

"That we will," Axeblade agreed.

"Well, then," Bahzell said. "With Walasfro under him, Kelthys can be making the trip to Warm Springs from Deep Water faster than we can get there from Balthar. Even allowing for the time to be getting word to him in the first place, it's in my mind he'll be there before ever we are, or close enough behind to be treading on our heels. So if you're fit for the saddle, then I'm thinking it's past time we were on the road. You can be telling me the details while we travel."

"Milord Champion, Master Axeblade is—" Sir Jahlahan began, but Bahzell raised one hand.

"It's plain as the nose on my face—or on Brandark's—as how this man's worn himself to the bone getting here, Sir Jahlahan. I'll not let him push himself hard enough to be doing himself in, but no more will I insult him by pretending every hour isn't more precious than gold."

Bahzell held Axeblade's eyes levelly, and the horse trainer nodded slowly.

"I'll ask you to be finding him a fresh horse while I send word to Hurthang, and to be seeing to it as Brandark is mounted and we've supplies for the trip," Bahzell said. "And then we'll be leaving."

Chapter Seventeen

The nondescript man stood gazing moodily out of a second-story inn window with his hands folded behind his back. He was no more remarkable looking than he'd been when he appeared uninvited in Baron Cassan's suite, but the other two people in the room with him watched him attentively. There was deep respect, possibly even fear, in their eyes, and they were careful not to intrude upon his thoughts.

Unlike the weather during his last visit to the baron, the day beyond the window was beautiful. Just a hint of a breeze whispered across the city of Balthar, scarcely enough to set the great standard over the castle above the city gently flapping. Birdsong echoed from the city's towers and eaves, drifting through the rise and fall of voices from the market two blocks over and the rumbling clatter of the wheels and hooves of a heavy freight wagon passing below the window. The early morning sun shone brilliantly from a high blue sky, cradled amid dramatic billows of fleecy white clouds. Like most Sothōii towns and cities, Balthar enjoyed excellent drains and sewers, and the air breathing lightly through the window was remarkably free of the odors it would have carried in many another city the unremarkable man had visited in his time. He drew a deep, lung-filling breath of the fresh spring air . . . which did absolutely nothing to improve his mood.

"Well!" he said finally, turning away from the window. He balanced on the balls of his feet, weight forward, hands still clasped behind him, and both of the other men in the room seemed to shrink ever so slightly away from him. "This is a fine mess, isn't it?"

His tone was almost conversational, but neither of the others appeared inclined to respond, and he smiled thinly.

"Come, now! You know the plan as well as I do. Would *you* say it's proceeding properly?"

"Not exactly according to schedule, no," one of his companions finally replied. The speaker was taller than the nondescript man, with black hair, yet shared something of his lack of remarkability. Except, perhaps, for his dark eyes. There was a peculiar stillness about them, an almost reptilian, unblinking watchfulness. "On the other hand, Master Varnaythus, that's scarcely mine or Jerghar's fault, is it?"

He met the nondescript man's gaze steadily, and it was Varnaythus who finally shrugged irritably.

"I suppose not," he said in a peevish tone. Then he shook his head. "No. No, it isn't," he continued in quite a different tone. It wasn't precisely apologetic, perhaps, but it was at least an admission that his irritation was making him unreasonable.

"Actually," he turned back to the window's open casement, but his shoulders weren't quite so taut and his hands' interlocked grip relaxed slightly, "I think what I'm most frustrated about is having such an unanticipated opportunity slip through our fingers this way."

"If I'd had even a day or two of warning," the black-haired man replied, "I might have been able to put together enough men to do something about it. But Tellian rode out of here like Fiendark's Furies were on his heels. And the armsmen he took with him were all from his personal guard." He shrugged. "I don't have more than a dozen men here in Balthar at the moment—and usually barely half that many, given how low a profile we have to maintain—and I'm not going up against Tellian's handpicked guards, even from ambush, without at least twice their number. We might get Tellian before they killed us all, but the Guild doesn't accept contracts it *knows* are going to be suicidal."

"I understand, Salgahn," Varnaythus said. "I don't like it, but I certainly understand it. And I don't disagree with your analysis. It's just that opportunities to catch Tellian in the open, especially when he's distracted by personal problems and his guard might be down, are so few and far between that I hate to waste one when it comes along."

"A pity you couldn't scry far enough ahead to see it coming," the third man said at that. Jerghar Sholdan was taller than Varnaythus, shorter than Salgahn, and better dressed than either of them. Indeed, he looked like what he was—a wealthy merchant banker who had arrived in Balthar several months before to represent the interests of half a dozen prominent Axeman and Purple Lord merchants. He was well groomed and clean-shaven, with fair hair, manicured hands, and cheerful blue eyes, yet there was something else about him. . . .

Varnaythus knew what that "something else" was, since it was he who had provided the charm which both offset the "banker's" aversion to direct sunlight and prevented others from noticing his minor peculiarities.

"Scrying isn't as simple as people without a trace of the Art at their command sometimes assume, Jerghar," Varnaythus said, still gazing out the window. "And unless I'm mistaken, it was your job to keep Tellian under observation, since that entire portion of the operation is *your* responsibility."

He turned from the window finally, facing Sholdan with a thin smile.

"Scrying takes concentration, a lack of distractions, and enough preliminary information to at least know where to look. Even the best wizard can only employ one scry spell at a time, you know. To watch all of our possible targets by gramerhain, I'd have to concentrate on doing nothing but that, and given the quality of coconspirator currently available to me, I don't seem to be able to find enough time free of distractions to do other people's work for them."

Sholdan's eyes narrowed, and his lips tightened, showing just a flash of sharp, oddly elongated teeth. He started a quick retort, then made himself swallow it unspoken as he remembered who—and what—Varnaythus was.

Varnaythus watched him unblinkingly, then smiled again, even more thinly than before.

"The problem," the black wizard said as if the venomous exchange had never occurred, "is that there are too many cooks busily stirring this particular pot. We know who most of the major players are, but don't delude yourself into believing that we know who *all* of them are. There's no possible way to predict what people you don't even know about are going to do next. That's bad enough, but I prefer it to having someone I do know about take me as completely by surprise as Cassan managed with this little gem."

"Do you think he kept us in the dark because he's begun to distrust us?" Salgahn asked.

"I think he kept us in the dark because he doesn't want his own shadow to know what he's doing, much less anyone else," Varnaythus snorted. "Which, to be fair, doesn't make him so very different from us. And he did at least warn me he'd taken measures to 'distract' Tellian." The wizard twitched his shoulders in another shrug, his smile tart as alum. "He probably wouldn't have given me any specifics, whatever he expected, but I doubt very much that he anticipated a result quite this . . . spectacular. After all, who would have expected the girl to bolt this way?"

"I can see that," Salgahn said thoughtfully. "On the other hand, I wonder what else he's working on that he hasn't bothered to mention to us?"

"He's operating exactly the same way we are," Varnaythus replied. "We're certainly not going to tell him what we actually have in mind, are we?" He took one hand from behind him and waved it in a dismissive gesture. "Our whole object, where he's concerned, is to keep him convinced he's the prime mover and that he's simply using our services. I'm sure he's intelligent enough to assume we have ends of our own in mind, however, and that means he's not stupid enough to trust us. So he'll tell us just enough about his plans to make us useful to him . . . just as we're doing where *he's* concerned. Of course, however much he may distrust us, it's probably never occurred to him that we intend to destabilize the entire Kingdom and let him take the blame for it."

"I'm sure it hasn't," Sholdan agreed, working his way back into the conversation. "After all, he's a baron, and he doesn't know who we're really working for. He sees us only as tools, not anyone who could seriously threaten someone as powerful as he is."

"Which is why They wanted him brought into this in the first place," Varnaythus said. "I only wish I felt more confident that They aren't overreaching."

"Of course They aren't!" Sholdan stared at him, eyes wide in shock. Salgahn seemed much less appalled by Varnaythus' temerity, but dog brothers weren't especially noted for piety even where their own patron, Sharnā, was concerned.

"Oh, don't be an old woman, Jerghar!" Varnaythus snapped. "Of course They can make mistakes! If They couldn't, They'd have finished off the other side twelve hundred years ago. What bothers me this time around is how many balls They expect us to keep in the air simultaneously. If it all works—or even if only half of it works—the results will be all They could hope for. But the more complex the plan, the more opportunities there are for things to go wrong, too. All I'm saying is that, speaking as the person responsible for making it all fit together at the critical moment, I wish They could have kept things a bit simpler."

"All you have to do is follow orders," Sholdan protested, and Varnaythus snorted.

"If that were all I was required to do, They wouldn't need me here at all, Jerghar! But They *do* need me, because someone has to adjust when bits and pieces of the master plan go to your Lady's Seventh Hell in a handbasket! All I have to say is that it's a good thing the other side can make mistakes, too. Especially this time around."

A fine sheen of perspiration dewed Sholdan's forehead. He seemed genuinely horrified by the wizard's attitude.

"If you offend Her—or any of the rest of Them!—Varnaythus, no power on earth—" he began, and Varnaythus laughed.

"I don't intend to offend anyone—certainly not any of Them! But They picked me to oversee this operation—*all* of this operation—because I'm not afraid to use my brain. They need someone who's willing to remember there are at least two sides in any war, and that the other sides work just as hard at beating you as you do at beating them. And do you really think for a moment that Their counterparts are unaware of what They're doing?"

"Well, of course they know She and the others are working against them. But if they really knew all we're doing, surely they would have acted directly against us by now."

"You *do* have a brain, don't you, Jerghar?" Varnaythus asked. The banker swelled with anger, but Varnaythus continued calmly. "I've always assumed you must, because without one, you couldn't be as successful at amassing wealth as you've been, even allowing for all the business your Lady's church throws your way. But when you say something like that, I find myself questioning my basic assumptions. Perhaps it has something to do with your diet."

"And just what do you mean by that?" Sholdan demanded.

"By what? You mean the bit about your diet?" The wizard's smile was deadly, and Sholdan shook his head sharply.

"Not that!" he snapped. "The rest of it. What did you mean by the *rest* of it?"

"I meant that you have a dazzling ability to overlook the obvious when reality isn't to your liking." Varnaythus shook his head. "Both sides are limited in what they can do," he continued in an elaborately patient voice. "Not even They dare to intervene directly and personally very often, and the other side chooses to do it even less frequently. Which—we might as well be honest here, since it's just us plotters—is a very good thing for Them, since the other side is more powerful than They are."

Sholdan's eyes darted around the inn room with more than a hint of true panic. Salgahn, on the other hand, looked faintly amused.

"Oh, calm down, Jerghar," Varnaythus said wearily. "Of course the other side is more powerful! Not only individually, but in numbers, as well. But what of it? How powerful one god or another may be is really immaterial to us mortals." Sholdan goggled at him, and he snorted. "*Any* god could evaporate any one of us with a thought, if he or she decided to," he pointed out acerbically. "Does it really matter if one of them decides to turn us into purple vapor, instead of orange vapor?"

"B-b-b-but—" Sholdan stuttered.

"The point is," Varnaythus said, "that even the weakest god is so much more powerful than any mortal that any differences of power between deities aren't particularly significant. The fact that Tomanāk, say," he watched Sholdan flinch physically at his offhand use of that hated name, "is individually more powerful than any one of Them doesn't matter a solitary damn to you, me, or any other mortal. There's only so much power any deity can apply to the physical universe without smashing the whole thing, which would defeat his own purpose, and either side is perfectly capable of doing that if they get too openly involved. That's why both of them need agents in the first place, to avoid the escalation of direct confrontations that could get out of hand. You know that."

"But—" Sholdan tried again.

"Oh, give it a rest, Jerghar!" Salgahn interjected. "And you stop needling him, Varnaythus!" Both of the others looked at him, and the assassin shrugged. "We can debate about agents, direct divine intervention, and the destruction of the world some other time," he said impatiently. "What matters right now is that the gods on the other side have chosen to restrict their direct intervention, that they believe in free will, and that, unlike certain gods on our side," he carefully named no names, "that they expect their agents to think for themselves. And, as Varnaythus says, Jerghar, even if they wanted to lead someone like Bahzell around by the hand all day long, they can make mistakes, too."

"Salgahn's right, Jerghar," Varnaythus said. "I shouldn't try to goad you that way. But if you want confirmation that the other side isn't whispering the details of all of Their plans into their precious champions' ears—or anyone else's—look at what happened to the coursers. Do you think that precious stallion would have let any of his herd stay behind over the winter if he'd realized my Lady was influencing their minds? Or do you honestly believe the Sothōii would have allowed an entire herd of their precious coursers to walk right into destruction if they'd known what was about to happen?"

"Well, no," Sholdan said.

"Neither do I. And while I'm about it, I might as well acknowledge that your Lady and Her servants succeeded brilliantly in that particular phase of the operation."

"It would have been better if the shardohns had gotten them all," Sholdan grumbled, but Varnaythus shook his head.

"No. It's much better this way—someone had to get home to tell the Sothōii what happened. You'll get all the rest of them in time, if the plan works properly, but for now those poor, pathetic survivors are bound to arouse every protective instinct the Sothōii have. And if there hadn't been any survivors at all, how could we have goaded them into responding?"

"I can see that," Salgahn said. "On the other hand, it was *Tellian* who was supposed to be sucked in, not Bahzell."

"Yes," Sholdan said. "No one suggested we'd have to deal with a champion of Tomanāk!" There wasn't much question that in this case the "we" meant Jerghar Sholdan and his coreligionists, not Varnaythus and Salgahn or any of their associates.

"The possibility was always there," Varnaythus pointed out, his tone less cutting but still a bit impatient. "Ideally, Tellian would have taken his men out himself and been destroyed, of course. But there was always the chance—the distinct probability, really—that Bahzell would insist on accompanying him. It's what those interfering busybodies of Tomanāk's do." He shrugged. "If the plan is sound and it's executed properly, it should be capable of dealing with 'Prince Bahzell.' And even if we don't manage to destroy him, we may manage to kill Brandark. That wouldn't be as good as getting Bahzell, of course, but it's almost as good as getting Tellian."

"I wish They'd tell us *why* it's so damned important to kill two damned hradani," Salgahn muttered. "Tellian, I can understand. For that matter, Bahzell makes sense. But why *Brandark*? He's no prince or champion!"

"I'm sure we'll find out someday, if we don't manage to kill him," Varnaythus said dryly. "Always assuming we survive not killing him in the first place. Which, just between the three of us, is another reason I'm perfectly happy to see Bahzell and Brandark riding off towards Warm Springs without us. I'm just upset because Tellian isn't with them."

"And because you don't know what *else* Cassan might be up to that could disorder our plans," Salgahn put in.

"And because of that," Varnaythus admitted.

"I'll have my people in Toramos see what they can find out," the assassin said. "I know your contacts with Cassan are probably better than mine, but I've got more sets of eyes and ears than you do."

"Good!" Varnaythus grunted. "I'll do what I can, as well, but there are too many magi in Toramos for comfort. Cassan may be more than a bit irrational on the subject, but they really do constitute a threat—to us, at least, if not to him. If you want real honesty, that's the main reason I haven't done more scrying, Jerghar," he admitted. "If I use any of the really effective spells, one of them is likely to catch me at it. They probably wouldn't be able to identify me, but they could certainly tell who I was trying to watch, which could be almost as bad."

"I'd prefer for them not to know we're using wizardry at all," Salgahn said frankly. "Anything that might bring Wencit of Rūm back to the Wind Plain would be a really bad idea, as far as I'm concerned!"

"Amen to that," Varnaythus said fervently, and touched the lump under his shirt and tunic that was the small wizard's wand of wrought silver he wore on the chain about his neck. His clothing hid it, but the simple fact that he possessed it would earn the death penalty if it was discovered. And if *Wencit of Rūm* should happen to discover that Varnaythus wore the amulet of a priest of Carnadosa, death would probably be preferable to his fate.

"What about Kalatha?" Sholdan asked.

"At the moment, everything seems to be proceeding nicely. I'll check with Dahlaha while I'm there, of course but I don't expect any problems to have cropped up since my last visit," Varnaythus told him.

The banker looked as if he wanted to ask more questions, but Varnaythus had made it clear he intended to keep the different aspects of the complex, interwoven operation as compartmentalized as possible. He needed Sholdan's cooperation—or, rather, his cooperation and that of his fellow Servants of Krahana. But however reliable the banker's discretion might have been in matters of business, Varnaythus didn't trust his ability to keep his mouth shut (and his hands off) anything really important. Time enough to let Sholdan know all that was involved at Kalatha when the operation had been crowned with success. For the moment, let him continue to think that nothing else was as important as killing Bahzell, Tellian, and Brandark.

"Very well," the wizard-priest continued, shaking aside his thoughts. "I believe we're all up to date. Jerghar, get word to your Lady's Servants immediately that Bahzell and Brandark are on their way, then get up there and take personal charge of dealing with them. Salgahn, I'll check with your message drop in Sōthōfalas to see what you may have discovered when I get back to the capital. In the meantime, I have a few errands to take care of for Them before I head back."

The other two nodded, and he strode briskly out of the room. One of the advantages of wizardry was how quickly he could cover ground, he thought. He had plenty of time to drop by Lorham and check the Kalathan situation's progress personally before he headed back to Sōthōfalas.

Chapter Eighteen

Although Alfar Axeblade's family came originally from the westernmost edge of the West Riding, he hadn't had any actual personal experience with hradani. One of his grandfathers and two of his uncles had been killed in border clashes with Horse Stealer raiders in the years before Prince Bahnak had been strong enough to forbid such attacks, and his family's modestly prosperous farm and its prized herd of horses had been wiped out in the process. But Alfar himself had been no more than a child when his father relocated to Warm Springs, which was far enough from the Escarpment that no hradani raid had ever penetrated to it. His family history was more than sufficient to reinforce the traditional Sothōii prejudice against all hradani, but unlike men who'd actually fought against them, he was unprepared for the reality of hradani endurance.

He'd become familiar with it over the last several hours, however.

Bahzell had brought along a half dozen members of the Hurgrum chapter of the Order of Tomanāk, all but two of them Horse Stealers. The other two were both Bloody Swords, who, like Brandark, were small enough (by hradani standards) that a sturdy horse might be expected to carry them without too much complaint. All three of the Bloody Swords had brought along an additional horse each, which would at least allow them to switch off when their initial mounts tired, but no horse in its right mind would have consented to carry a Horse Stealer. So Bahzell and his four fellow clansmen, including Hurthang and Gharnal, were on foot.

Alfar had expected that to slow them down, and he'd been prepared to protest that speed was essential. By the time they'd been on the road for two hours, he was just as glad he hadn't let the words out of his mouth. The five Horse Stealers loped along in a sort of half-jog, half-run that easily matched the best pace even a Sothōii warhorse could sustain. Worse, they did it apparently effortlessly. They spent a good bit of their time cheerfully insulting their Bloody Sword brethren over the shorter legs which made horses necessary for them, but Alfar suspected that Brandark and his fellows could have matched their endurance if they'd truly needed to. Possibly not as easily, however. Or, at least, Alfar hoped not. It was bad enough watching the Horse Stealers do it! Bahzell was actually able to run along at Alfar's side, in full armor, and carry on a conversation with him while he did so.

Alfar had never imagined anything like it. The hradani even managed to maintain his side of the conversation almost normally as he probed for more details about the disaster which had sent Alfar to Balthar. His deep, even breathing induced a certain forced rhythm, but that was the only evidence of exertion he showed. It was the most unnatural thing Alfar had ever seen, especially from someone so tall that his head was very nearly on the same level as Alfar's, despite the fact that he was perched on the back of a warhorse who stood just under fifteen hands high.

Finally, after over four hours of it, when the horse Stealers still showed no sign of asking for a rest stop, or even to slow their pace long enough for a breather, Alfar could contain his curiosity no longer.

"Excuse me, Milord Champion," he said gruffly, managing to get the title out with only the smallest hesitation this time, "but would you mind if I asked a question?"

"And why should I be minding?" Bahzell asked with a chuckle. "After all, it's picking your brain about Warm Springs I've been since ever we left Hill Guard. I'm thinking it's only fair exchange if you've a question or two of your own as you'd like answered."

"Thank you." Alfar turned to look into the towering hradani's eyes, and considered how to ask what was on his mind with the least probability of giving offense. In the end, he decided it was best to just go ahead and ask, so he did.

"Milord, you and your friends have been running along at my stirrup iron for the better part of five hours now. And you've scarcely broken a sweat. It's in my mind that you could have run even faster than you have, too, if you'd been so inclined."

"And you're after wondering just how it is we do it?" Bahzell suggested, his ears half cocked in amusement.

"Well, in a word, yes," Alfar admitted.

"I can be seeing why you might," Bahzell said. "And up till the last year or so, truth be told, I'd not have been able to answer you." He shrugged. "We hradani have always been after being the biggest, strongest, and toughest of the Races of Man, and by and large, so far as we'd ever known, that was just the way things were after being. We'd no more notion of *why* we were those things than anyone else. But this past winter, Wencit was kind enough to be explaining it to us, though, to be honest, I'm thinking as how it had slipped his mind that the rest of us are just a mite younger than he is and that it might be we'd simply forgot the answer our own selves."

The big hradani grinned so wryly Alfar had to suppress a chuckle. Given that Wencit of Rūm was *at least* twelve hundred years old, Alfar supposed that just about anyone was "a mite younger" than he.

"Any road," Bahzell continued, "from what Wencit was saying, it seems as how we hradani are after being directly linked to what he's pleased to be calling 'the magic field.' "

"'Magic field'?" Alfar repeated.

"Aye. From what old Wencit's saying, it seems as how everything about us—the entire world, and every last thing in it, living or dead—is truly after being naught but energy. It may *look* solid enough, and if it happens you should be dropping a rock on your foot, it may *feel* solid, but to a wizard, it's naught but a mass of energy, like fire or lightning, and all in the world that wizardry is after being is the ability to be seeing and manipulating that energy."

Alfar looked at him skeptically, and Bahzell flicked his ears in the equivalent of a shrug.

"I'll not blame you if you've doubts about all of that, you understand," he said. "I certainly had 'em in plenty at the time, and I'm still not so very certain in my own mind as how it all makes sense. I'm thinking Brandark could explain it better, if you're minded to ask him about it later, but if Wencit has the right of it—and I'm not so very eager to be telling a man as saw the Fall of Kontovar with his own eyes that he *doesn't*—then what makes my folk as we are is that somehow we're after being physically connected to all of that energy. We've no idea how we do it, but we've the ability to be drawing on that energy to aid our own. In a manner of speaking, I suppose, it's not after being all that different from touching it as a wizard might, though I'm hoping Wencit has a better notion of what he's about when he does! But it's that as gives us our size and our strength, aye, and our endurance, as well. And the reason we heal so much quicker than any of the other Races of Man."

"Really?"

Alfar looked across at the huge man jogging so effortlessly along beside his trotting horse, and something very like wonder warred with his ingrained hatred for all things hradani. If what Bahzell was telling him was the truth, then it was suddenly clear to him why hradani were capable of the casual displays of impossible strength and stamina which, along with the Rage, made them such fearsome foes. Yet what truly woke his feeling of wonder was the thought of all the other things such a link might mean to the hradani. Like virtually all Sothōii, Alfar had never given much thought to the hradani, or their lives, beyond the automatic hate and fear they evoked. Why *should* anyone waste time and effort thinking about a batch of bloodthirsty barbarians whose only interests seemed to be murder, looting, and plundering? But if those same capabilities could be applied to other ends, other objectives . . .

And then it hit him.

His eyes flared wide, and his jaw dropped in sudden consternation. His indrawn breath of shock was so abrupt that it was clearly audible even through the thud of hooves, the creak of saddle leather, and the metal-on-metal jingle of armor and weapons. He stared at Bahzell, and the hradani nodded almost compassionately.

"Aye, Master Axeblade," he said. "Brandark and I have been after discussing the selfsame thing with Baron Tellian, Hathan, and Sir Kelthys. And we've come to conclude that, assuming as how Wencit has the right of it where hradani are concerned, then it's only reason that what sets coursers apart from any other breed of horse is after being much the same thing. I'll not blame you if it's not a thought as you find pleasant to contemplate, seeing what's lain between your folk and mine for so long. But there it is." He smiled with an odd gentleness. "You might be saying as how we hradani and the coursers are after being related."

"Not pleasant to contemplate" was a very pale description of Alfar's reaction to the possibility that hradani and coursers might have *anything* in common. Unfortunately for the comfort of his prejudices, by the time they finally stopped late that evening at a wayside inn, he'd been forced to admit they did. He clung to the possibility that there was a different explanation for the abilities of hradani and coursers, but it was impossible to doubt the huge similarities *between* those abilities.

Alfar himself was reeling in the saddle by the time they stopped, but although Bahzell had finally worked up a hard sweat, it was painfully obvious that it was only

Alfar's and his mount's exhaustion which had led the Horse Stealer to call a halt. Alfar had always considered himself a reasonably tough individual, but compared to the hradani, he wasn't. If he'd been even a little less fatigued, he would have felt humiliated to have been found so wanting in hardihood. As it was, he felt only dull-minded, exhausted gratitude when he finally climbed down out of the saddle. He was worn beyond exhaustion as he had never before been in his life, so utterly drained that he actually allowed another man to see to his horse's care while Bahzell chivied him upstairs to bed.

He had a vague impression of the innkeeper's half-frightened, mostly surly expression when he found himself face to face with eight hradani. If he hadn't been all but dead on his feet, he might have felt compelled to speak sharply to the man. Whatever Alfar himself thought about hradani in general, *these* hradani were driving themselves hard to reach Warm Springs because Lord Edinghas needed help. More to the point, perhaps, Sir Jahlahan, acting in Baron Tellian's name, had ordered Alfar to personally escort them to Warm Springs. That gave him an obligation to see to it that they were at least treated with common courtesy. Unfortunately, he was too exhausted even for that—so exhausted that he was never very clear later on exactly how he got to the proper room. He never did manage to undress completely before he fell across the hard, narrow mattress, either, and he was snoring before his head hit the pillow.

He slept for almost nine hours before his own sense of urgency dragged him back up out of dream-troubled sleep. Despite a lifetime in the saddle, he couldn't stifle a groan as he shoved himself up and forced stiff, abused muscles to answer his demands. He managed a sketchy wash up, then tottered downstairs to the inn's common room.

Bahzell and the rest of their party—all hradani, Alfar thought, truly realizing for the first time that he was the only human in the entire group—sat around one of the trestle tables. There was something about the way they sat that was almost defensive. The table wasn't the largest one available, but it was set in the angle of a corner, and the hradani seated around it could see the entire room and all three of its entrances while they sat with their backs to a solid wall. A smallish fire smoldered on the hearth, and bright morning sunshine spilled through the inn's diamond-paned windows to glitter on the crossed, golden mace and sword of Tomanāk where they badged his servants' surcoats and ponchos, and their personal weapons leaned upright against the wall behind them. The remnants of a truly stupendous breakfast were strewn across the table, and Bahzell leaned back on a bench, bracing his shoulders against the wall while he nursed a tankard of ale.

Alfar's jaw clenched in mingled shame and anger as he gazed out the window.

"What's the hour?" he asked.

Bahzell gazed at him for a moment, one eyebrow quirked, then reached into a belt pouch and withdrew a pocket watch. It was only the fourth or fifth watch Alfar had seen in his entire life, and he recognized a work of art when he saw one. He had no idea how a hradani might have come by it, but he also found himself rapidly passing beyond any sense of surprise at anything this improbable hradani champion of Tomanāk might do. And so he simply waited while Bahzell consulted the beautifully painted ivory face and golden hands.

"It's just passed nine of the morning," the hradani rumbled after a moment. He closed the watch case and returned it to his pouch, and Alfar's jaw tightened even harder. They could have been on the road again at least two or three hours earlier, and it was obvious the hradani were all fresh and rested. It was only his own weakness which had delayed them.

"I could wish you'd waked me earlier, Milord Champion," he said, once he was certain he had command of his voice. It appeared, however, that he'd had less command of it than he'd thought, because Bahzell cocked his ears quizzically, then shook his head.

"Master Axeblade," he said, his deep voice surprisingly gentle, "even if we'd been after waking *you* earlier, I'm thinking as how your horse might not have been so very grateful to have his rest cut short. Now, it's in my mind that we'd not find it so very difficult to be finding you another horse, but that's a fine mount Baron Tellian's seneschal already found you. Probably better than any we might be finding in replacement."

He let Alfar consider that for a few seconds, until the human's own common sense had to admit there was some point to the argument. Then he continued.

"Still and all, though," he said, "I'll admit as how I'd not have waked you any sooner even if we'd a courser waiting to go under your backside. It's half-dead you were, for you'd driven yourself like Fiendark himself was on your heels to be reaching Balthar, and it was little enough rest you'd had since. Aye, and naught but a few mouthfuls of bread and sausage in the saddle for food. I've seldom seen a man as needed rest more than you, and it's naught but sheer stubbornness on your part to be arguing otherwise. I'm thinking we're well ahead of how fast you or Lord Edinghas could have expected us to be moving, and I'll not be letting you kill yourself just to shave an hour or two more from our trip."

His voice was as steady and level as his eyes, and Alfar recognized his tone. He'd simply never expected to hear a *hradani*, of all people, speaking to him as his commanding officer. But that, he realized with a lingering sense of disbelief, was precisely what Bahzell Bahnakson had become. And it shamed him again, in a different way, to realize that he was actually surprised by Bahzell's concern for his own exhaustion.

"No doubt you've a point, Milord," he admitted finally. "But even so, I can't say I don't begrudge every lost minute."

"No more can I," Bahzell said. He looked over Alfar's shoulder, and the human turned to see one of the inn maids walking towards him with a large, heavily laden tray of food. She looked as if there were nowhere in the world she would not have preferred to be, and Bahzell's lips tightened at her manifest unhappiness. But he only nodded to her, and gestured for her to set the tray on the table.

She obeyed quickly and silently, her anxious expression proclaiming her trepidation at finding herself in such close proximity to eight murdering hradani, whatever their leader claimed to be, and Alfar looked back at Bahzell as she turned and scurried away like a frightened rabbit. He felt his face heat, but Bahzell only flicked his ears in the equivalent of a human shrug and gave him a crooked smile.

Alfar wondered if he should say something, but nothing suggested itself to him. Then he wondered if he could get away with declining the substantial breakfast Bahzell had obviously ordered for him. One more glance at the hradani's expression told him there was no point trying, however, and his empty belly's sudden, sharp pangs as he smelled the food's aroma made him just as happy that there wasn't.

"Better," Bahzell said with a broader, less ironic smile as Alfar seated himself and reached for a spoon. "I'd half thought as how I'd find myself force-feeding you, Master Axeblade!"

"If I thought it might have gotten us on our way any sooner, you would have, Milord," he said around a mouthful of stinging hot porridge and honey.

"Ah, a man of wisdom, I see," Brandark put in. The Bloody Sword half-reclined along another bench directly under the window, plucking idly at his balalaika, and Alfar glanced across at him. "I wouldn't call Bahzell the very brightest fellow I've ever met, Master Axeblade, but he's certainly in the running for the most stubborn." Hurthang and the other members of the Order chuckled, and Brandark grinned. But then his expression sobered. "And in this case, he would have been right, too," he said. "You needed food, as well as rest, and you'd not have taken either if Bahzell hadn't made you. Riding with worry and grief can drive a man too hard and kill him as surely as any sword or arrow."

Alfar's spoon paused midway between bowl and lips, frozen there by the understanding in the Bloody Sword's voice. After a lifetime of mutual hatred, compassion was the very last thing he would have anticipated from any hradani.

Which, he suddenly thought, might say more about his own prejudices than it did about Bahzell or Brandark.

"I—" He paused, wondering what might be the right thing to say. Then he cleared his throat. "I know what you mean," he said. "But to see something like that—to know an entire herd of *coursers* could be destroyed that way . . ." He shook his head. "I doubt anyone but another Sothōii could really understand what that feels like, Lord Brandark."

"Just 'Brandark' will do fine, Master Axeblade." The Bloody Sword chuckled. "None of us hradani stand much on ceremony, and even if I'd been inclined to do that, I'd've given up months ago. These Horse Stealer louts are too ignorant and uncivilized to remember proper titles, anyway."

"Just you go right on being civilized, my lad," Gharnal advised him, while another chuckle rumbled through the other Horse Stealers. "Don't you be wasting a moment worrying about what nasty things might happen to a man whose mouth is so smart he can't be keeping it shut."

"You see?" Brandark said plaintively. "All of them are like that, not just him." He pointed at Bahzell with his chin, and the Horse Stealer snorted.

"But as to understanding how this all feels for a Sothōii," Brandark continued more seriously, "no doubt you're right. I can probably come closer now that I've met coursers myself—Sir Kelthys' Walasfro and Baron Tellian's Dathgar—but that's not the same thing as growing up around them." He shook his head, his eyes dark. "All I can say is that I never dreamed I'd meet such magnificent creatures. I wouldn't have believed anything could ravage an entire herd of them the way you've described, but if there's something out there that can, then I want it *stopped*, Master Axeblade."

A dark, almost hungry sound of agreement murmured its way around the table. Agreement, Alfar thought, from hradani. And not just any hradani—from *Horse Stealer* hradani. He'd discovered that he was past feeling surprise, but wonder was another thing entirely.

He started to say something more, then shrugged with

a half-apologetic smile and applied his full attention to the meal Bahzell had ordered for him. He ate quickly, but not so quickly he didn't savor every mouthful. It wasn't the best cooking he'd ever tasted—far from it!—but he discovered that the old saw about hunger being the best seasoning was absolutely correct. By the time he'd finished the porridge, drunk the hot tea, eaten the toasted sausages, and mopped up the last egg yolk with a piece of bread, he felt better than he had in days.

"Thank you, Milord Champion," he said simply, pushing the last plate aside. "I still begrudge the delay, but there's no doubt I needed the food, and you're right. Only a fool drives himself into the kind of blind daze I was pushing myself into."

"I'd not say you'd gone quite that far," Bahzell said with another slow smile. "Still and all, I'm thinking as how we can both agree you'd pushed a mite further and harder than you'd the need to. And now, it's no doubt best we be on our way."

"Of course." Alfar stood, reaching for the belt purse Lord Edinghas had sent with him, but Bahzell shook his head.

"No need for that. The Order's seen to our shot."

"But—"

"Leave off, Master Axeblade," Bahzell advised him. "I've no doubt Lord Edinghas would stand good for it, but it's Tomanāk's business we're on. It may be as how Lord Edinghas might choose to be making a donation to himself's church when all's done, but that's neither here nor there just now."

Alfar started to argue, then stopped himself.

"Better," Bahzell said again, then gathered up his fellow hradani with his eyes. "I'm thinking we'd best be on our way, lads," he said. He drained his tankard and set it on the table, then climbed to his feet.

"Aye," Hurthang agreed. "And not just because we've need of haste on Himself's business." He grimaced. "It's not so very popular we are in these parts."

"What?" Alfar looked at him sharply, remembering his own impression when he first entered the common room. *Had* the hradani actually chosen their table out of defensive considerations?

Hurthang waved one hand unobtrusively, and Alfar's eyes narrowed as he followed the gesture. A balding, broad-shouldered, deep-paunched man in a leather apron stood behind the bar at one end of the common room. Alfar hadn't seen him enter, and he certainly hadn't come near the hradani to see if they had any orders. Instead, he simply stood there, arms folded across his chest, and glowered at Bahzell and his companions. There was as much fear as anger in his expression, and his shoulders hunched sullenly.

"Milord Champion," Alfar demanded, "has anyone—?"

"Don't be worrying yourself, Master Axeblade," Bahzell advised him. "It might be as how there was after being an . . . intemperate word or two last night. But that's something as any hradani minded to travel amongst other folk had best be being thick-skinned enough to deal with. I'll not say as how that's after making it any more pleasant, but people are after being people, warts and all, whatever it might be we'd prefer, and we'll not convince your folk to be setting aside all the blood that's flowed betwixt us overnight. The innkeeper was none too happy to be seeing us, but we'd Sir Jahlahan's sealed warrant as how we're on Baron Tellian's business, and our kormaks spend as well as the next man's."

He shrugged and nodded towards the door. Alfar gazed back at him for a long, thoughtful moment, then nodded in response. Not in agreement, precisely, but in acknowledgment. His own sudden urge to kick the sullen-faced innkeeper's backside up between his ears astounded him. Two days—even a single night—ago, he would flatly have rejected the very suggestion that he might find himself siding with hradani against another human. Now, though . . .

"You're right, Milord Champion," he said, deliberately pitching his voice loud enough for the innkeeper to hear, "there's no point trying to beat wisdom into a fool. You'll only hurt your hand on a skull with that much bone in it."

Chapter Nineteen

"You have to be out of your bloody mind!"

The gray-haired woman on the other side of the desk stared at Kaeritha and Leeana in disbelief. The bronze key of her office hung on a chain about her neck, and her brown eyes were hard, almost angry.

"I assure you, Mayor Yalith, that I am *not* out of my mind," Leeana replied sharply. She and Kaeritha were tired, mud-spattered, and worn to the edge of exhaustion from long days in the saddle, but she was obviously fighting hard to hang onto her temper. Equally obviously, her life as the daughter of the Baron of Balthar had not exactly suited her to dealing with attitudes like Yalith's.

"Madwomen seldom *think* they're out of their minds," the mayor shot back. "But whatever you may think, and however much you may believe that the war maids are a way out of some . . . some *social inconvenience*, there are aspects of this situation which could only lead to disaster."

"With all due respect, Mayor," Kaeritha put in sharply, intervening for the first time, "this girl is not talking about 'some social inconvenience.' She's talking, unless I was very much mistaken when I read King Gartha's original proclamation, about the exact thing you and your people are supposed to guarantee to *any* woman."

"Don't you go quoting the charter to *me*, thank you, *Dame* Kaeritha!" Yalith shot back. "You may be a champion of Tomanāk, but Tomanāk's never done anything for the war maids that *I* ever heard about! And the war maids are scarcely a convenient bolt-hole for some pampered noblewoman—the daughter of a baron, no less!—to use just to avoid a betrothal her family hasn't even accepted yet!"

Kaeritha started to speak again, quickly and even more sharply, despite her awareness that her own anger would only guarantee Yalith would refuse to listen to anything she said. But before she could open her mouth, Leeana laid a hand on her forearm and faced the Mayor of Kalatha squarely.

"Yes," she said quietly, holding Yalith's brown eyes with her own jade stare. "I am avoiding a betrothal my family hasn't accepted. I'm not aware, though, that the war maids are in the habit of asking a woman why she seeks to join them—aside from making certain she isn't a criminal trying to avoid punishment. Was I mistaken?"

It was Yalith's turn to bite off a hot return unspoken. She glared at Leeana for several tense seconds, then shook her head curtly.

"No," she admitted. "We aren't 'in the habit' of asking questions like that. Or, rather, we *do* ask them, but the answers don't—or shouldn't—affect whether or not we grant someone membership. But I trust you're willing to admit that this is not a usual situation. First, I'm quite certain you're the highest ranking young woman who's ever sought to become a war maid, and the gods only know where *that* might end. Second, you're less than fifteen years old, which mandates a probationary period in which you'd technically be neither a war maid nor your father's daughter, and I doubt even the gods know what could happen during that! Third, the most common reason women who later regret asking to become one of us seek us out in the first place is to escape an arranged marriage. We always make a special effort to be positive women like that are certain in their own minds of what they want. And, fourth, this is the worst possible time, from Kalatha's perspective, for us to be antagonizing someone like Baron Tellian!"

"I'll want to speak to you about that later, Mayor Yalith," Kaeritha put in, snapping the mayor's eyes back to her. "For now, though, I don't think you need to fear antagonizing Tellian. I don't expect him to be happy about this, and I don't know what his *official* position is likely to be. But I do know he isn't going to blame you for doing precisely what your charter requires you to do just because the applicant in question is his daughter."

"Oh no?" Yalith snorted in obvious disbelief. "All right, then. Let's say you're right, Dame Kaeritha—about her father, anyway. But what about Baron Cassan and this Blackhill?"

She grimaced in distaste.

"We're close enough to the South Riding that we know Cassan better than we'd like, and we've two or three war maids right here in Kalatha who sought us out after Blackhill abused them. If those two are hunting this young woman—" she jabbed a finger at Leeana "—as greedily as the two of you are suggesting, how do you think they're going to react if the war maids help her slip through their filthy fingers? You think, perhaps, they'll send us a sizable cash donation?"

"I expect they'll be as pissed off as hell," Kaeritha said candidly, and despite Yalith's own obvious anger and anxiety, her earthy choice of words lit a very slight twinkle in the mayor's eyes. "On the other hand," the knight continued, "how much harm can it really do you? From what Leeana's told me, Blackhill and Cassan are probably already about as hostile to you war maids as they could possibly get."

"I'm afraid Dame Kaeritha is right about that, Mayor Yalith," Leeana said wryly. Yalith looked back at her with another, harsher snort, and the young woman shrugged. "I'm not trying to say they won't be angry about it, or that they won't do you an ill turn if they can, if I manage to drive a stake through their plans by becoming a war maid. They certainly will. But in the long term, they're already hostile to everything the war maids stand for."

"Which is a *marvelous* reason to antagonize them further, I'm sure," Yalith replied. Her sarcasm was withering, yet it seemed to Kaeritha that her resistance was weakening.

"Mayor Yalith," Leeana stood very straight in front of the mayor's desk, and her youthful face wore a dignity far beyond her years, "the war maids antagonize every noble like Blackhill or Cassan every single day, simply by existing. I know I'm a 'special case.' And I understand why you feel concerned and anxious at the thought of all the complications I represent. But Dame Kaeritha is right, and you know it. *Every* war maid is a 'special case.' That was exactly why the first war maids came together in the first place—to give all those special cases someplace to go for the first time in our history. So if you deny my application because of my birth, then what does that say about how ready the war maids truly are to offer sanctuary to *any* woman who wants only to live her own life, make her own decisions? Lillinara knows no distinctions among the maidens and women who seek Her protection. Should an organization which claims Her as its patron do what She will not?"

She locked eyes once again with the mayor. There was no anger in her gaze this time, no desperation or supplication—only challenge. A challenge that demanded to know whether or not Yalith was prepared to live up to the ideals to which the mayor had dedicated her life.

Silence hovered in the office, flawed only by the crackle of coal burning on the hearth. Kaeritha sensed the tension humming between Yalith and Leeana, but it was a tension she stood outside of. She was a spectator, not a participant. That was a role to which a champion of the War God was ill-accustomed, yet she also knew that this was ultimately not a battle anyone could fight for Leeana. It was one she must win on her own.

And then, finally, Yalith drew a deep breath and, for the first time since Leeana and Kaeritha had been ushered into her office, she sat down behind her desk.

"You're right," she sighed. "The Mother knows I wish you weren't," she went on more wryly, "because this is going to create Shīgū's own nightmare, but you're right. If I turn you away, then I turn away every woman fleeing an intolerable 'marriage' she has no legal right to refuse. So I suppose we have no choice, do we, Milady?"

There was a certain caustic bite in the honorific, yet it was obvious the woman had made up her mind. And there was also an oddly pointed formality in her word choice, Kaeritha realized—one which warned Leeana that if her application was accepted, no one would ever extend that title to her again.

"No, Mayor," Leeana said softly, her voice accepting the warning. "We don't. Not any of us."

"Baron Tellian is here. He demands to speak to you . . . and his daughter."

Yalith gave her assistant a resigned look, then glanced at Kaeritha with a trace of a "look what you've gotten me into" expression. To her credit, it was only a trace, and she returned her attention to the middle-aged woman standing in her office doorway.

"Was that your choice of verbs, or his, Sharral?"

"Mine," Sharral admitted in a slightly chagrined tone. "He's been courteous enough, I suppose. Under the circumstances. But he's also quite . . . emphatic about it."

"Not surprising, I'm afraid." Yalith pinched the bridge of her nose and grimaced wryly. "You did say he was close behind you, Dame Kaeritha," she observed. "Still, I would have appreciated at least a little more time—perhaps even as much as a whole hour—to prepare myself for this particular conversation."

"So would I," Kaeritha admitted. "In fact, a certain cowardly part of me wonders whether or not this office has a back door."

"If you think I'm going to let you sneak out of here, Milady, you're sadly mistaken," Kalatha's mayor replied tartly, and Kaeritha chuckled.

It wasn't an entirely cheerful sound, because she truly wasn't looking forward to what she expected to be a painful confrontation. On the other hand, once Yalith had made her decision and the initial tension between them had eased a bit, she'd found herself liking the mayor much more than she'd originally believed she might. Yet there was still an undeniable edge there, rather like the arched spines of two strange cats, sidling towards one another and still unsure whether or not they should sheath their claws after all. She wasn't certain where it came from, and she didn't much care for it, whatever its source. But there should be plenty of time to smooth any ruffled fur, she reminded herself. Assuming she and Yalith both survived their interview with Tellian.

"I suppose you'd better show him in, then, Sharral," Yalith said after moment.

"Yes, Mayor," Sharral acknowledged, and withdrew, closing the door behind her.

It opened again, less than two minutes later, and Baron Tellian strode through it. It would have been too much to call his expression and body language "bristling," but that was the word which sprang immediately to Kaeritha's mind. He was liberally bespattered with mud, and—like Kaeritha's own—his bedraggled appearance showed just how hard and long he'd ridden to reach Yalith's office. And in his effort to overcome her own head start on him. Even his courser must have found the pace wearying, and she suspected that most of his armsmen—those not mounted on coursers—must either have brought along two or three horses each to ride in relays, or else rented fresh ones at the livery stables along the way.

"Baron," Yalith said, rising behind her desk to greet him. Her voice was respectful and even a bit sympathetic, but it was also firm. It acknowledged both his rank and his rightful anxiety as a parent, but it also reminded him that this was *her* office . . . and that the war maids had seen many anxious parents over the centuries.

"Mayor Yalith," Tellian said. His eyes moved past her for a moment to Kaeritha, but he didn't greet the knight, and Kaeritha wondered just how bad a sign that might be.

"I imagine you know why I'm here," he continued,

returning his gaze to the mayor. "I'd like to see my daughter. Immediately."

His tenor voice was flat and crisp—almost, but not quite, harsh—and his eyes were hard.

"I'm afraid that's not possible, Baron," Yalith replied. Tellian's brow furrowed thunderously, and he started to reply sharply. But Yalith continued before he could.

"The laws and customs of the war maids are unfortunately clear on this point, Milord," she said in a voice which Kaeritha considered was remarkably calm. "Leeana has petitioned for the status of war maid. Because she's only fourteen, she will be required to undergo a six-month probationary period before we will accept her final, binding oath. During that time, members of her family may communicate with her by letter or third-party messenger, but not in person. I should point out to you that she was not aware upon her arrival that she would be required to serve her probationary time, or that she would not be permitted to speak to you during it. When I informed her of those facts, she asked Dame Kaeritha to speak to you for her."

Tellian's jaw had clenched as the mayor spoke. If there'd been any question about whether or not he was angry before, there was none now, and his right hand tightened ominously about the hilt of his dagger. But furious father or no, he was also a powerful noble who had learned from hard experience to control both his expression and his tongue. And so he swallowed the fast, furious retort which hovered just behind his teeth and made himself inhale deeply before he spoke once more.

"My daughter," he said then, still looking directly at Yalith, as if Kaeritha were not even present, "is young and, as I know only too well, stubborn. She is also, however, intelligent, whatever I may think of this current escapade of hers. She knows how badly her actions have hurt her mother and me. I cannot believe she would not wish to speak to me at this time. I don't say she would look forward to it, or be happy about it, but she is neither so heartless nor so unaware of how much we love her that she would refuse to see me."

"I didn't say she had refused, Milord. In fact, she was extremely distressed when she discovered it would be impossible for her to speak to you in person. Unfortunately, our laws permit me no latitude. Not out of arrogance or cruelty, but to protect applicants from being browbeaten or manipulated into changing their minds against their free choice. But I will say, if you'll permit me to, that I have seldom seen an applicant who more strongly desired to speak to her parents. Usually, by the time a young woman seeks the war maids, the last thing she wants is contact with the family she's fled. Leeana doesn't feel at all that way, and she would be here this moment, if it were her decision. But it isn't. Nor is it mine, I'm afraid."

Tellian's knuckles whitened on his dagger, and his nostrils flared. He closed his eyes for a moment, then opened them again.

"I see." His tone was very, very cold, but for a man who'd just been told his beloved daughter would not even be permitted to speak to him, it was remarkably controlled, Kaeritha thought. Then his eyes swiveled to her, and she recognized the raging fury and desperate love—and loss—blazing within them.

"In that case," he continued in that same, icy voice, "I suppose I should hear whatever message my daughter has been permitted to leave me."

Yalith winced slightly before the pain in his voice, but she didn't flinch, and Kaeritha wondered how many interviews like this one she had experienced over the years.

"I think you should, Milord," the mayor agreed quietly. "Would you prefer for me to leave, so that you may speak to Dame Kaeritha frankly in order to confirm what I've said, and that Leeana came to us willingly and of her own accord?"

"I would appreciate privacy when I speak to Dame Kaeritha," Tellian said. "But not," he continued, "because I doubt for a moment that this was entirely Leeana's idea. Whatever some others might accuse the war maids of, I am fully aware that she came to *you* and that you did nothing to 'seduce' her into doing so. I won't pretend I'm not angry—*very* angry—or that I do not deeply resent your refusal to allow me to so much as speak to her. But I know my daughter too well to believe anyone else could have convinced or compelled her to come here against her will."

"Thank you for that, Milord." Yalith inclined her head in a small bow of acknowledgment. "I'm a mother myself, and I've spoken with Leeana. I know why she came to us, and that it wasn't because she didn't love you and her mother or because she doubted for a moment that you love her. In many ways, that's made this one of the saddest applications ever to pass through my office. I'm grateful that, despite the anger and grief I know you must feel, you understand this was *her* decision. And now, I'll leave you and Dame Kaeritha. If you wish to speak to me again afterward, I will, of course, be at your service."

She bowed again, more deeply, and left Tellian and Kaeritha alone in her office.

For several seconds, the baron stood wordlessly, his hand alternately tightening and loosening its grip on his dagger while he glared at Kaeritha.

"Some would call this poor repayment of my hospitality, Dame Kaeritha," he said at length, his voice harsh.

"No doubt some would, Milord," she replied, keeping her own voice level and as nonconfrontational as possible. "If it seems that way to you, I deeply regret it."

"I'm sure you do." Each word was carefully, precisely spoken, as if bitten clean-edged from a sheet of bronze. Then he closed his eyes and gave his head a little shake.

"I could wish," he said then, his voice much softer, its angry edges blurred by grief, "that you'd returned her to me. That when my daughter—my only child, Kaeritha—came to you in the dark, on the side of a lonely road, running away from the only home she's ever known and from Hanatha's and my love, you might have recognized the madness of what she was doing and stopped her." He opened his eyes and looked into her face, his own eyes wrung with pain and bright with unshed tears. "Don't tell me you couldn't have stopped her from casting away her life—throwing away everything and everyone she's ever known. Not if you'd really tried."

"I could have," she told him unflinchingly, refusing to look away from his pain and grief. "For all her determination and courage, I could have stopped her, Milord. And I almost did."

"Then *why*, Kaeritha?" he implored, no longer a baron, no longer the Lord Warden of the West Riding, but only an anguished father. "Why *didn't* you? This will break Hanatha's heart, as it has already broken mine."

"Because it was her decision," Kaeritha said gently. "I'm not a Sothōii, Tellian. I don't pretend to understand your people, or all of your ways and customs. But when your daughter rode up to my fire out of the rain and the night, all by herself, she wasn't running away from your heart, or your love, or from Hanatha's love. She was running *to* them."

The unshed tears broke free, running down Tellian's fatigue-lined cheeks into his beard, and her own eyes stung.

"That's her message to you," Kaeritha continued quietly. "That she can never tell you how sorry she is for the pain she knows her actions will cause you and her mother. But that she also knows this was only the first offer for her hand. There would have been more, if this one was refused, Tellian, and you know it. Just as you know that who she is and what she offers means almost all those offers would have been made for all the wrong reasons. But you also know you couldn't refuse them all—not without paying a disastrous political price. She may be only fourteen years old, but she sees that, and she understands it. So she made the only decision she thinks she *can* make. Not just for her, but for everyone she loves."

"But how could she *leave* us this way?" Tellian demanded, his voice raw with anguish. "The law will take us from her as surely as it takes her from us, Kaeritha! Everyone she's ever known, everything she ever had, will be taken from her. How could you let her pay that price, *whatever* she wanted?"

"Because of who she is," Kaeritha said quietly. "Not 'what'—not because she's the daughter of a baron—but because of *who* she is . . . and who you raised her to be. You made her too strong if you wanted someone who would meekly submit to a life sentence as no more than a high-born broodmare to someone like this Blackhill. And you made her too loving to allow someone like him or Baron Cassan to use her as a weapon against you. Between you, you and Hanatha raised a young woman strong enough and loving enough to give up all of the rank and all of the privileges of her birth, to suffer the pain of 'running away' from you and the even worse pain of knowing how much grief her decision would cause you. Not because she was foolish, or petulant, or spoiled—and certainly not because she was stupid. She did it because of how *much* she loves you both."

The father's tears spilled freely now, and she stepped closer, reaching out to rest her hands on his shoulders.

"What else could I do in the face of that much love, Tellian?" she asked very softly.

"Nothing," he whispered, and he bowed his head and his own right hand left the dagger hilt and rose to cover the hand on his left shoulder.

He stood that way for long, endless moments. Then he inhaled deeply, squeezed her hand lightly, raised his head, and brushed the tears from his eyes.

"I wish, from the bottom of my heart, that she hadn't done this thing," he said, his voice less ragged but still soft. "I would never have consented to her marriage to anyone she didn't choose to marry, whatever the *political* cost. But I suppose she knew that, didn't she?"

"Yes, I think she did," Kaeritha agreed with a slight, sad smile.

"Yet as badly as I wish she hadn't done it, I know why she did. And you're right—whatever else it may have been, it wasn't the decision of a weakling or a coward. And so, despite all the grief and the heartache this will cause me and Hanatha—and Leeana—I'm proud of her."

He shook his head, as if he couldn't quite believe his own words. But then he stopped shaking it, and nodded slowly instead.

"I *am* proud of her," he said.

"And you should be," Kaeritha replied simply.

They gazed at one another for a few more seconds of silence, and then he nodded again, crisply this time, with an air of finality . . . and acceptance.

"Tell her—" He paused, as if searching for exactly the right words. Then he shrugged, as if he'd suddenly realized the search wasn't really difficult at all. "Tell her we love her. Tell her we understand why she's done this. That if she changes her mind during this 'probationary period' we will welcome her home and rejoice. But also tell her it is *her* decision, and that we will accept it—and continue to love her—whatever it may be in the end."

"I will," she promised, inclining her head in a half-bow.

"Thank you," he said, and then surprised her with a wry but genuine chuckle. One of her eyebrows arched, and he snorted.

"The *last* thing I expected for the last three days that I'd be doing when I finally caught up with you was *thanking* you, Dame Kaeritha. Champion of Tomanāk or not, I had something a bit more drastic in mind!"

"If I'd been in your position, Milord," she told him with a crooked smile, "*I'd* have been thinking of something having to do with headsmen and chopping blocks."

"I won't say the thought didn't cross my mind," he conceded, "although I'd probably have had a little difficulty explaining it to Bahzell and Brandark. On the other hand, I'm pretty sure that anything I was contemplating doing to you pales compared to what my *armsmen* think I ought to do. All of them are deeply devoted to Leeana, and some of them will never believe she ever would have thought of something like this without encouragement from someone. I suspect the someone they're going to blame for it will be you. And some of my other retainers—and vassals—are going to see her decision as a disgrace and an insult to my house. When they do, they're going to be looking for someone to blame for *that*, too."

"I anticipated something like that," Kaeritha said dryly.

"I'm sure you did, but the truth is that this isn't going to do your reputation any good with *most* Sothōii," he warned.

"Champions of Tomanāk frequently find themselves a bit unpopular, Milord," she said. "On the other hand, as Bahzell has said a time or two, 'a champion is one as does what needs doing.' " She shrugged. "This needed doing."

"Perhaps it did," he acknowledged. "But I hope one of the consequences won't be to undermine whatever it is you're here to do for Scale Balancer."

"As far as that goes, Milord," she said thoughtfully, "it's occurred to me that helping Leeana get here in the first place may have been a part of what I'm supposed to do. I'm not sure why it should have been, but it *feels* right, and I've learned it's best to trust my feelings in cases like this."

Tellian didn't look as if he found the thought that any god, much less the War God, should want one of his champions to help his only child run away to the war maids particularly encouraging. If so, she didn't blame him a bit . . . and at least he was courteous enough not to put his feelings into words.

"At any rate," she continued, "I will be most happy to deliver your message—*all* of your message—to Leeana."

"Thank you," he repeated, and the corners of his eyes crinkled with an edge of genuine humor as he looked around Yalith's office. "And now, I suppose, we ought to invite the Mayor back into her own office. It would be only courteous to reassure her that we haven't been carving one another up in here, after all!"

Chapter Twenty

"To what do I owe the pleasure?" the richly dressed nobleman asked sardonically as soon as the servant who had ushered Varnaythus into his study departed, closing the door silently behind him.

"I was merely in the neighborhood and thought I'd drop by and compare notes with you, Milord Triahm," the wizard-priest said smoothly. He walked across to one of the comfortable chairs which faced the other man's desk and arched his eyebrows as he rested one hand atop the chair back. His host nodded brusque permission, and he seated himself, then leaned back and crossed his legs.

"It's possible things will be coming to a head sooner than we'd anticipated," he continued. "And a new wrinkle has been added—one I thought you should know about. I'm not certain how much effect it will have on your own concerns here in Lorham, but the possibilities it suggests are at least . . . intriguing."

"Indeed?"

The other man ignored his own chair and crossed to prop a shoulder against the frame of the window behind his desk, half-turning his back on his guest. He gazed out through the glass at the gathering dusk. Thalar Keep, the ancestral seat of the Pickaxes of Lorham, loomed against the darkening sky, dominating the view, and his mouth tightened ever so slightly. Varnaythus couldn't see his expression with his face turned away towards the window, but he read the other man's emotions clearly in the tight set of his shoulders.

"Indeed," the nondescript wizard confirmed. "Unless my sources are much less reliable than usual, a new war maid will be arriving in Kalatha sometime soon."

"How marvelous," the nobleman growled, then made a spitting sound. "And just why should the arrival of one more unnatural bitch concern me?"

"Ah, but this particular unnatural bitch is Lady Leeana Bowmaster," Varnaythus purred.

For a second or two, Triahm seemed not to have heard him at all. Then he whipped around from the window, his eyes wide with disbelief.

"You're joking!"

"Not in the least, Milord," Varnaythus said calmly. "It's remotely possible my information is in error," actually, he knew it wasn't; he'd been tracking Leeana in his gramerhain for the last several days and witnessed her arrival in Kalatha the day before, "but I have every reason to believe it's accurate. If she hasn't arrived in Kalatha already, it's only a matter of a day or so before she does."

"Well, well, well," the other man murmured. He moved away from the window and lowered himself slowly into his own chair, never taking his eyes from Varnaythus' face. "That *does* present some possibilities, doesn't it?"

"I believe you might reasonably say that, Milord," Varnaythus replied in the voice of a tomcat with cream-clotted whiskers.

"Tellian's always been overly soft where those bitches are concerned," Triahm growled. "Probably because his idiot of an ancestor provided them with the initial foothold to begin their pollution of the Kingdom. Personally, that connection would have been enough to make me feel ashamed, not turn me into some sort of lap cat for them. Maybe *this* humiliation will finally open his eyes!"

"It's certainly possible," Varnaythus agreed. For his part, he'd always found Triahm's blindly bigoted, unthinking hatred for the war maids and all they stood for as stupid as it was useful. He doubted that a man like Tellian would ever fall prey to its like, however.

On the other hand, Tellian *was* a Sothōii, and now that his daughter had succeeded in reaching the war maids before he overtook her, it was at least possible he would react exactly as Triahm anticipated. Which, after all, was one of the reasons Varnaythus had decided against attempting to intercept and assassinate the girl. Kaeritha's presence was the other reason, he admitted frankly to himself. Champions of Tomanāk were hard to kill, even—or especially—by arcane means. Still, he'd felt sufficiently confident of managing it to have justified the risk of a few proxies, at least.

But however badly her death might have hurt and weakened her parents, the Dark Gods would weaken the *Kingdom* far more seriously if their servants could set the Lord Warden of the West Riding openly against the war maids. Even if Tellian managed to avoid that particular trap, having his only child run away to become a despised war maid was going to cost him dearly in political support from the more conservative members of the Royal Council. Not to mention all of the delicious possibilities for destabilizing the war maids' charter when the question of the Balthar succession was thrown into the mix.

The wizard-priest rubbed mental hands together in gleeful contemplation of the possibilities, but he kept his expression composed and attentive.

"Even if it doesn't," Triahm went on, thinking aloud and unaware of his guest's own thoughts, "this is bound to have a major impact. It's going to drag Tellian right into the middle of Trisu's little difficulties." He smiled nastily. "It should be interesting to see which way that pushes my dear, irritating cousin."

"If Tellian does end up at odds with the war maids himself, it's likely to embolden Trisu considerably," Varnaythus pointed out. "I imagine he'll become even more persistent in pressing his claims if he thinks Tellian will openly support him. And I'd be surprised if those claims didn't harden and become more extensive, as well."

"But even if Tellian is gutless enough to swallow the shame, the fact that his precious daughter has seen fit to join one side of the dispute will compel him to be very careful about his own position," Triahm said. "If he supports the war maids, he'll be accused of favoritism."

"Perhaps so," Varnaythus said. "On the other hand, if he openly supports Trisu, at least some people will accuse him of doing so because he's angry with the war maids and wants to punish them."

"Either outcome could be useful to us," Triahm observed, beginning to play with a crystal paperweight from his desk. "His neutrality has worked against us from the start. It throws everything back to the local level and prevents Trisu from acting decisively."

"He won't be able to remain neutral very much longer, whatever happens with his daughter," Varnaythus assured him. "Unless I very much miss my guess, the tension on both sides is rapidly approaching the critical level."

He considered informing Triahm of who had become Leeana's escort to Kalatha, and decided—again—that warning him of the incipient arrival of a champion of Tomanāk in Lorham wouldn't exactly fill him with confidence.

"When it does, it's going to lead to open conflict between Trisu and Kalatha, probably with Quaysar going up in flames at the same time," he said instead, and his smile was even nastier than Triahm's had been. "Once it comes to outright warfare, Tellian's going to be forced to take a position, whether he wants to or not, or be accused of ignoring his responsibility to enforce the King's peace. Under the circumstances, I don't believe he'll have very much choice other than to back his own vassal, Trisu, against Kalatha."

"Only, of course, it won't *be* Trisu, will it?" An ugly light danced in Triahm's gray eyes, and Varnaythus carefully hid a smile of triumph. The man was so predictable it was pathetic.

"Not if our plans succeed, Milord," he agreed.

"And they will succeed," Triahm said flatly, and gave

Varnaythus an ominous glance. "Your man *is* already in position, is he not?"

"Have no fear, Milord," Varnaythus said smoothly. "My agent—" if Triahm wanted to assume that Varnaythus' assassin (well, Salgahn's, if the wizard-priest wanted to be accurate) was a man, that was fine with him "—is ready to strike when the moment is right. But that moment won't come until we can provoke the proper level of violence between your cousin and Kalatha and be sure suspicion is directed where we want it to go."

"Understood, understood," Triahm said in an irritated tone, waving one hand dismissively. "Of course the timing is critical. But once he's gone, and the blame for his death is laid in the proper quarter, there will be no suspicions of *me* when I assume the titles which ought to have been mine. And it will give me the excuse I need to burn that cancer at Kalatha out of the flesh of Lorham once and for all!"

"So it will, Milord," Varnaythus agreed. "So it will."

"He truly is an idiot, isn't he?"

"Triahm?" a soft, throaty contralto said from behind Varnaythus. The contralto's owner laughed. "Are you only just now realizing that?"

"Scarcely, Dahlaha," Varnaythus said dryly. It was his turn to gaze out of a window over the night-darkened streets of Thalar. It was a much nicer window than the one in Triahm's office, although Triahm had paid for both of them.

The wizard-priest craned his neck, gazing up past the luxurious mansion's overhanging eaves at a night sky the color of darkest cobalt and full of stars. There was no moon tonight, which was probably a good sign, he told himself. Then he turned away from the stars and back to business.

His hostess, reclining on the chaise longue across the table from him, was one of the most beautiful women he'd ever seen. He admitted that candidly, yet her beauty didn't really appeal to him. He could appreciate and admire her sleek, golden hair and huge blue eyes, the impeccable bone structure of her graceful, oval face and high cheekbones, and the svelte lines of the richly curved figure which hovered just this side of overripeness. But the pouting mouth that whispered passion to other men whispered to him of corruption.

There was something *too* perfect about Dahlaha Farrier's sensual beauty. Not even Varnaythus could be certain, but he strongly suspected that her natural appearance had been significantly improved upon. Unfortunately, improving the packaging had made no difference to what lived inside it, which was hardly surprising. Women who turned to Dahlaha's chosen deity were already corrupt, with a soul-deep twistedness, because only a woman who was could endure Her service. Priestesses like Dahlaha could count upon being gifted with eye-catching physical beauty, if they did not already possess it, but no amount of enhanced beauty was going to change that inner distortion.

Varnaythus enjoyed the pleasures of the flesh as much or more than the next man, and he had no inherent objection to corruption. But there was a *hunger* to Dahlaha's corruption—one as dark as Jerghar's lust for blood, although it yearned for something quite different. Varnaythus had no illusions about what would ultimately happen to any man who surrendered himself to Dahlaha's power.

"Of course I've always known Triahm is a fool," the wizard-priest continued, settling himself into the more conventional chair he preferred to the chaise longues Dahlaha favored. No doubt so that she could display her indisputable charms to best advantage. "If he weren't a fool, he wouldn't be the tool we need. And if stupidity and ambition didn't blind him to everything but what *he* wants, he might ask himself a few awkward questions about just where and how you were able to find him 'hirelings' with our capabilities. But despite all that, it genuinely annoys me to find myself helping an idiot like that supplant someone who at least has a working brain."

"What's this? The conspirator as philosopher?" Dahlaha laughed again. "Or is it just a case of pragmatic necessity offending your innate sense of artistry?"

"The latter, probably," Varnaythus said. He leaned forward and snagged another apple from the table. It was from the previous fall's harvest, and its skin was wrinkled, but its taste remained pleasantly sweet.

"Say what you will about Cassan," he continued as he chewed, "the man is at least competent within the limits of what he knows is going on. And he has two or three people working for him who are very good at what they do—like Darnas Warshoe." He shook his head and took another bite of apple. "Warshoe's good enough that I actually had to hunt him down and arrange for him to stumble over 'Cathman the Peddler.'"

"Oh?" Dahlaha laughed. "Are you still using that old faker as an alias?"

"It works," Varnaythus replied with a grin. "And even though he's considered a harmless old crank, he does manage to find a few charms and protective amulets that actually work. Fortunately for us, Cassan's one real weakness is an absolute phobia about magi reading his mind." The wizard-priest shrugged. "It's silly of him, of course, but it inspired him to send Warshoe to Cathman for amulets to prevent it as soon as Warshoe reported that Cathman was in Toramos. Amulets of my own design, of course. And the beauty of it is that Cassan insists that all of his closest henchmen wear them at all times, to keep magi from picking their brains, so now I can keep track of all of them without even needing my gramerhain. Which is probably a good thing, given how busy Cassan keeps them—especially Warshoe."

"Well, that's Cassan, not Triahm," she said. "But if it makes you feel better about helping an idiot, just remember how unlikely he is to survive long enough to enjoy his success. As you said yourself, his incompetence was one of the reasons They chose him as Their tool. Do you honestly expect him to be able to navigate the storm we're preparing for him?"

"No, of course not." Varnaythus munched on his apple, then chuckled suddenly. "And you know what? It *does* make me feel better."

Dahlaha laughed yet again and raised her glass in mock

salute. He waved the half-eaten apple at her in response, then applied himself to finishing it off.

"Do you really think that having Tellian's daughter injected into the situation at Kalatha is going to work to our advantage?" his hostess asked after a moment, her tone much more serious, and Varnaythus snorted.

"It's hard to say." He took a last bite of apple, tossed the gnawed core back onto his plate, and then stretched. "With another, more typical Sothōii noble, I'd be more prepared to hazard a prediction. But Tellian is scarcely typical—I suspect that that's the main reason They want him dead, or at least discredited and set at odds with the Crown." He shrugged. "The man loves his wife and his daughter, and I frankly think it's unlikely he'll cut himself off from the girl, whatever she's done. That's the real reason I opposed killing her. If we can get *him* tangled up in our little web—" Dahlaha's eyes flashed at his choice of noun, as he'd known they would "—it would do far more to destabilize the Kingdom as a whole than anything we might achieve locally here in Lorham."

"Don't underestimate what we're doing here, Varnaythus." Dahlaha's husky voice had turned cold and hard, and Varnaythus glanced at her. "My Lady doesn't waste Her efforts on minor projects," she continued. "The web She's weaving here will stretch out to every corner of the Wind Plain. Yes, drawing Tellian into Her toils would make things easier. But in the end, She will achieve her goals even without him."

"And if a champion of Tomanāk interferes?" Varnaythus asked levelly. There was an odd, greenish flicker at the backs of Dahlaha's eyes, and he felt his pulse quicken with a sudden tingle of something much too much like fear for his taste. But he made himself look into those eyes steadily, and reminded himself that he, too, had his patron.

"*Tomanāk!*" Dahlaha hissed the hated name. Her long, graceful fingers with their crimson-painted nails flexed like claws, or pincers, and she spat on the floor. "*That* for your precious champion!" she snarled.

She really didn't look at all beautiful in that moment, Varnaythus reflected.

"That's all very well," he said in a brisk, businesslike voice, "but your Lady is the one who's going to have to deal with this Kaeritha if she gets that far putting things together."

"She won't," his hostess said shortly.

"Dahlaha," he said patiently, "that's exactly the sort of thinking that leads to . . . unfortunate errors. I remind you of what happened to Tharnatus when this same champion and Bahzell came calling in Navahk."

"Tharnatus was a fool, and Sharnā is a coward," she shot back, and her ripe mouth twisted with contempt. "I can't believe your Lady let Herself be roped into that entire mess. One thing Carnadosa has always been is smart, so what was She thinking of to throw good money after bad that way?"

"The Lady of the Wand *is* smart," Varnaythus agreed. "In this case, though, She had no choice. The decision came from Phrobus Himself."

Dahlaha looked up from her wineglass, her expression suddenly taut. Then she shrugged.

"I still don't understand why Phrobus allowed Himself to be convinced to let Sharnā deal with the hradani in the first place. Granted, even *He* should have been able to handle a horde of ignorant barbarians, but His father must have known He'd think small, as usual. And then He chose Tharnatus as His chief priest. *Tharnatus!*" She barked a vicious laugh. "He always was as stupid as Triahm, and he certainly proved it in Navahk! First *he* overestimated his own cleverness and power, and then Sharnā was too terrified of Tomanāk to face him openly when Tharnatus needed Him most. But that won't happen here. *My* Lady fears no one and nothing! When we require Her aid, She'll provide it, and spit in Tomanāk's face, if She must."

Varnaythus gazed at her for several seconds, and his stomach muscles tightened at what he saw in her expression. It was more than possible that she was reading too much into her deity's intentions. But it was also possible that she wasn't. Dahlaha's Lady was noted for neither her sense of restraint nor her willingness to accept any limitations upon her power. Or, for that matter, for what most mortals would have called her sanity. The wizard-priest remembered his conversation with Jerghar, and he felt sweat trying to pop out along his hairline.

"I trust it won't be necessary for it to come to that," he said after a moment, choosing his words and controlling his tone rather more carefully than he usually did in conversation with Dahlaha.

"I doubt very much that it will."

She, too, seemed to have stepped back a pace from the intensity of the moment before. She lifted her wineglass and sipped delicately, then set it gently on the table.

"All of the pieces are in place," she said. "When They decided to place this portion of the plan in Her care, They knew what They were doing." Her smile was a thing of ice and old, dried bone. "We've placed Her agents—including the ones who don't even realize they're working for Her—in all of the critical places."

"Including Trisu's household?" Varnaythus asked in a neutral tone, and she grimaced.

"No," she admitted. "Not there." She shrugged irritably. "There's something about Trisu that bothers me. When I look at him, I don't see what I see in other men's eyes."

She picked up the wineglass once more, but this time only to glower down into its depths, not to drink from it, and Varnaythus watched her expression from behind masklike eyes. It was obvious that she resented Trisu's apparent immunity to the allure of her exquisitely maintained beauty and raw sexuality, but there was more to it than simple resentment. There was also uncertainty, almost a trace of fear, and he cocked his head.

"What *do* you see in his eyes?" he asked finally, and she shrugged again, this time angrily.

"Suspicion," she hissed, like a cat passing a fishbone, and glowered at her fellow conspirator. The green flicker was back in her eyes, although fainter than before, and he could almost physically taste her anger—at him, this time—for forcing her to admit that. But he could stand more than Dahlaha's anger if that was the price of making sure he didn't disappoint Them.

"Suspicion of what?" he asked, quietly, but in a tone whose firmness reminded her that he was her superior—for now, at least—and warned her that he expected an answer.

"I don't know," she admitted, then tossed her head angrily. "I know he knows I'm Triahm's mistress, and he's too straitlaced to care for that. Besides, he likes Triahm's wife, and I'm sure he resents his cousin's infidelity because of that, as well. But there's something else in there, too, and I'm not sure exactly what it is."

She obviously hated confessing that much, but she made herself meet Varnaythus' eyes steadily, and it seemed to him that she was being honest about her concerns. Or, at least, as honest as it was possible for her to be.

"Well, he obviously doesn't know Who you serve," the wizard-priest observed. "If he did, you'd be dead—or at least fled, with his troops in hot pursuit, which would be almost as bad from Their viewpoint. I wonder . . ."

His voice trailed off, and he gazed into the distance at something only he could see, his fingers drumming absently on his thigh while he thought. Dahlaha stood it in silence for as long as she could, then cleared her throat noisily. His eyes popped back into focus and swiveled to her.

"You wonder what?" she demanded.

"I wonder if he's Gifted," the wizard-priest replied.

"Gifted?" Dahlaha sat up on her chaise longue, her expression alarmed. "Is that possible?"

"Of course it's possible." Varnaythus grimaced. "He's a Sothōii. Whatever they may have degenerated into since, they're descended from the oldest, highest noble families of the Empire of Ottovar. Some of them probably have traces of Ottovar and Gwynytha's blood in their veins even today. Most of the surviving wizard lords of Kontovar are descended from exactly the same source, for Phrobus' sake. The Art is bred into their bone and blood, Dahlaha. It's our good fortune that their ancestors turned so completely against all forms of wizardry after their escape to Norfressa. There's a very good chance Trisu's bloodline carries the Gift, but there's virtually no chance at all of his *knowing* it. Still, if it's strong enough, he might well have at least a touch of True Sight. In which case he probably recognizes that there's something hidden behind your outward appearance. There's no way he could know *what*, not without a great deal of training he can't possibly have had. But many people who possess instinctive True Sight rely on it even if they don't know exactly what it is." He shrugged. "Most of them simply assume that they have unusually accurate 'hunches' and let it go at that."

"You never suggested he might have any abilities like that!"

"I don't recall your ever having asked me what abilities he might have," Varnaythus replied coolly. "As you've pointed out to me several times, this end of the operation is yours—yours and your Lady's. I assumed that if you'd had any reason to believe you needed my assistance, you would have asked for it."

Dahlaha glared at him, obviously looking for a fresh line of attack, but his defense was unassailable. The Lorham and Kalatha portions of the master plan to destabilize the Kingdom of the Sothōii and return it to the Time of Troubles were, indeed, her responsibility.

"Very well," she huffed finally, "*be* that way. But at least tell me this—is this untrained Gift of his likely to see through Triahm's role playing?"

"It probably already has," Varnaythus said calmly. "Luckily for us, even if he were trained, he wouldn't be able to read minds. He's not a mage, Dahlaha. I'm sure he realized long ago that his dear cousin Triahm hates his guts and resents the fact that a man ten years younger than he is inherited the title he wants so badly. Trisu doesn't trust Triahm as far as he could throw a courser, but aside from helping to confirm that his general suspicions are justified, the True Sight won't help him anywhere else. Although, it's possible that the combination of his distrust for Triahm and any True Sight he might possess could explain why he should have taken his cousin's mistress in such dislike." He flicked one hand in a throwing-away gesture. "On the other hand, does it really matter? Do you really care how much Trisu may dislike you? I mean, you're planning on having the man *killed*, Dahlaha, so what does it matter if he doesn't particularly care for you?"

"It doesn't matter at all," she said, "except that the eye he keeps on me has prevented me from infiltrating his household the way I managed at Kalatha. I haven't cared to take too many chances, so I've been unable to eliminate or tamper with people like Salthan."

"There's not really any need to put Salthan out of the way," Varnaythus said after a brief consideration. "Or, rather, we can let Triahm deal with it once Trisu's dead. That's the beauty of it. We didn't *have* to change anything at this end."

"I know. I'd still feel better if I had more positive control of the situation, though."

"There's never any such thing as too much control," Varnaythus agreed. "Still, it sounds as if you have things in hand. What truly matters is goading the war maids into providing the proper provocation, not whether or not Trisu responds to it exactly the way we want him to. After all," he leaned back with an expansive gesture and an icy smile, "when the time comes, what will count isn't what actually happened, but what everyone *thinks* happened."

Chapter Twenty-One

"Leeana, this is Garlahna Lorhanalfressa. She'll be your mentor during your probationary period."

Leeana saw a very young war maid, no more than six years older than she was. Garlahna was considerably shorter than Leeana, with brown hair and brown eyes. She looked as if she ought to be smiling, but at the moment her expression and body language were soberly attentive, almost brusquely businesslike. She stood at a sort of parade rest, feet slightly spread and hands clasped behind her, her attention evenly divided between Leeana and Erlis Rahnafressa. Erlis was the fair-haired, brown-eyed Commander of One Hundred—roughly equivalent to the rank of captain in the Empire of the Axe's Royal and Imperial Army—who appeared to be in charge of training new war maid . . . recruits. At forty-three, she was a bit old for her rank, but she looked like a competent, no-nonsense sort of person. Perhaps the left arm she'd lost just above the elbow explained why she'd risen no higher in rank. She reminded Leeana a great deal of a female version of Sir Jahlahan Swordspinner.

The three of them stood in the soggy grass behind the roofed exercise salle, and Leeana felt as if she'd dressed inappropriately for a formal party. She wore the leather trousers and smock her mother had deplored with increasing frequency, yet this time she was the one who seemed dreadfully overdressed for the occasion. Erlis and Garlahna both wore the traditional war maid chari and yathu. The former was a short green kilt which fell barely to mid-thigh, and the latter was something which might have been described (in a moment of extreme charity) as a short, abbreviated—*very* abbreviated—bodice. But it wasn't boned and happened to be made out of fabric-lined, glove-supple leather. Whereas the main support of a regular bodice came from below, with little or no weight actually bearing on the shoulders, the yathu was equipped with buckle-adjustable shoulder straps which crossed on the wearer's shoulder blades. It was shorter, snugger, and stronger than any conventional "bodice" Leeana had ever seen. She could see where that support might come in handy, she supposed, but *she* hardly needed it. Not yet, at least. Garlahna, on the other hand, although shorter than Leeana, was considerably bustier, which her yathu made amply—one might almost have said abundantly—apparent.

Although Leeana had heard tales of the "licentious" and "shocking" war maid garments, she'd never actually seen them until she reached Kalatha, and she found herself somewhat in two minds about them. They certainly seemed *practical* enough, but still . . . The fact that both war maids were also barefoot, despite the chilly spring breeze and the muddy footing, whereas she still wore her riding boots, didn't make her feel one bit less overdressed, either.

"Garlahna, this is Leeana Hanathafressa," Erlis continued calmly, and Leeana's entire body tensed.

Her concern for anything as unimportant as what she might or might not be wearing vanished instantly, and her head twitched as it tried to whip around towards Erlis. She stopped herself in time, but it was hard, hard. It was the first time anyone had ever called her that, and the loss of her father's name hit her like an axe. Yet she'd known it was coming. Every war maid was known legally by her mother's given name, not whatever surname she might have borne before she became a war maid. It wasn't as if Leeana had a choice—she didn't—or as if she didn't love her mother or hated to be known as Hanatha's daughter. But she still felt as if in that moment, when Erlis first used her matronym, she had somehow abandoned her father, and it hurt. Perhaps it hurt even more because, in a way, some small, deeply hidden piece of her insisted that that was precisely what she had done.

But much as it hurt, she refused to let herself look at Erlis in either surprise or pain. And certainly not in anger. She suspected that her reaction to that first, abrupt use of her new name was a test, or at least a part of the training process she was about to begin.

"I'm pleased to meet you, Leeana," Garlahna said after a moment. Her voice was deeper than Leeana's, with a musical throatiness. "I hope I can help you settle in here reasonably comfortably."

Leeana did glance at Erlis this time, out of the corner of her eye, and the Hundred nodded.

"Thank you . . . Garlahna," Leeana said then. "I hope I can fit in quickly, but—" she flashed a small smile "—I wonder if any new war maid ever really settles in *comfortably*."

She heard something suspiciously like a smothered snort from Erlis' direction, and Garlahna grinned. Then she smoothed the smile quickly from her expression and nodded with appropriate sobriety.

"It does come as quite a shock for most of us, whatever we expected ahead of time," she agreed.

"Most of us survive it, though," Erlis put in dryly, and Leeana looked back at her.

"And you'll have your opportunity to begin surviving it first thing tomorrow morning, Leeana," the Hundred continued briskly. "You'll be joining us for calisthenics at dawn. Once you've had a chance to warm up, I'll evaluate the level of your current general physical skills. After breakfast, you'll have your first session with Ravlahn—that's Ravlahn Thregafressa, my assistant arms master—and me. We'll see where you are in terms of self-defense and weapons skills. Then, after lunch," Erlis continued, apparently oblivious to Leeana's reaction, "you'll have an hour or two with Lanitha Sarthayafressa. She's our archivist, but she's also the principal of our school here in Kalatha. She'll evaluate your basic literacy, your math ability, and your general knowledge. That should take you to an hour or so before supper, and you'll be assigned to one of the dining hall crews for that. I'm not sure which of the cooks will be in charge of the kitchen, but Garlahna will be responsible for finding that out and seeing to it that you report in the right place at the right time."

She paused and smiled at Leeana, possibly with a tiny edge of compassion.

"Any questions?" she asked then.

"Ah, no, Hundred Erlis," Leeana replied after a moment spent womanfully throttling the dozens of questions she *wanted* to ask.

"Good." Leeana thought she might detect a trace of approval in Erlis' eyes, but if she had, the hundred let no sign of it show in her voice or expression. "In that case, I'll leave you with Garlahna."

She nodded briskly, turned on her heel, and strode away, leaving the two young women alone.

Leeana stood gazing at Garlahna while butterflies seemed to circle one another in some sort of intricate dance in her midsection. She felt a fluttery-pulsed uncertainty she was not accustomed to, and none of the social formulae or skills she'd been taught as a baron's daughter offered her any hint about what to do next.

"So, Leeana," Garlahna said before the awkward pause could stretch too long. "I suppose we'd better see about your room assignment and getting you settled in." She smiled. "Trust me—you won't have time to do any of it tomorrow!"

"That's how it sounded to me, too," Leeana admitted with a wan smile.

"Oh, don't let Hundred Erlis' act fool you," Garlahna said cheerfully. "It's *lots* worse than she makes it sound!"

"Oh, *thank* you!" Leeana replied, and found herself sharing a tension-soothing laugh with her "mentor."

She stood back mentally to give Garlahna a quick examination. She'd already noted the other young woman's broad, somewhat rustic accent, although Garlahna's grammar was much better than she would have expected from that accent. Garlahna was from somewhere in the eastern part of the West Riding, she guessed, near the Spear River, and her parents had probably been small freeholders, or the retainers of one of her father's minor lords. As such, the social gulf between their births could not possibly have yawned wider, yet Garlahna seemed totally unaware that she was speaking to the only child of the Lord Warden of the West Riding. Which, Leeana conceded, was as it ought to be, because she no longer was her parents' child—not legally, at any rate. But it was still interesting that Garlahna could manage that disassociation between who she now was and who she once had been.

"You're welcome," Garlahna told her, once their shared laughter had eased. Then she waved one hand in a small, dismissive gesture.

"Don't worry about it too much, Leeana. All of us have had to survive it somehow. In some ways, it's almost like a kind of ceremony—a trial by combat, I guess you might call it—before we're really war maids. Actually," she wrinkled her nose as she gave Leeana a critical, evaluating glance, "I kind of suspect you'll do better than most of us. At least you've got the legs for speed, which is more than I ever did. And," she grinned again, "you're nowhere near as top-heavy as I am!"

Leeana felt the very tips of her ears heat and was just as happy her hair covered them. There was, she noted, just a hint of complacency in Garlahna's voice.

"I hope I won't disappoint you," she said after a heartbeat. "But, not wanting to change the subject, or anything, I do have one other question."

"Ask away," Garlahna invited.

"What do I do about my horse?"

"Your horse?" Garlahna sounded surprised.

"Yes," Leeana said. "My horse."

"You've got a *horse*?" Garlahna shook her head.

"What's so surprising about that?" Leeana asked, her voice just a bit cautious.

"Is it really yours?" Garlahna countered, and for some reason, she sounded even more cautious than Leeana had.

"Of course he's mine. Why?"

"I mean, does he belong to *you*, or to Baron Tellian?"

"He—" Leeana began, then paused. "He was a gift from my—from . . . Baron Tellian," she said after a long moment. "On my twelfth birthday."

"Did he actually give you its ownership papers?" Garlahna's tone had taken on more than a hint of sympathy, and Leeana shook her head.

"No," she admitted, feeling tears sting the backs of her eyes. "Boots has been my horse for over two years now. Everyone knew it. I guess . . . I guess the Baron never saw any reason why he had to formally present me with his papers."

"Then he's not legally yours, Leeana," Garlahna said gently. She shook her head and reached out to lay a sympathetic hand on Leeana's shoulder. "It happens, sometimes," she went on quietly. "Most of the time when someone gets here with a horse, there's someone chasing her who can hardly wait to take it away again. And it always turns out that *legally*, she never owned it at all."

Leeana stared at her while she tried to cope with a sudden, vicious stab of pain. She'd known she would be giving up her entire life, everything she'd ever owned and everyone she'd ever known. Yet, somehow, she'd never thought about giving up *Boots*. He was . . . he was part of her life. Her friend, not "just" her horse. And . . . and . . .

And part of all she'd left behind, she thought wretchedly. She'd managed somehow to overlook that. But perhaps she hadn't overlooked it. Perhaps she'd just *pretended* that she had. Because deep inside, she'd known—she'd always known. It was just the suddenness of being forced to confront the knowledge, she told herself. The abrupt amputation.

"I—" She shook herself. "I never thought about that," she said in a valiantly normal tone which fooled neither her nor Garlahna. "Do you think I could have a few minutes to tell him goodbye before they take him away?"

"We can ask," Garlahna promised her. "But I wouldn't get my hopes up too much. Your fa—" It was her turn to stop herself short. Her eyes met Leeana's, and she smiled apologetically. "*Baron Tellian* will probably be in a hurry to head home, Leeana."

She paused again, then looked around, as if to make certain no one was within earshot, before she leaned closer to Leeana.

"I really shouldn't tell you this," she said conspiratorially, "but Baron Tellian was furious when the Mayor told him he couldn't see you because of your probationary status. We're not supposed to know about anything that went on between them, but one of my friends had an errand to run to Sharral for Hundred Erlis. She was in Sharral's office when the Baron got here, and she could hear him through the door."

She grimaced and rolled her eyes.

"Actually, I think everyone in the building could probably hear him! That happens pretty often in a case like this. In fact, when someone from a new war maid's family turns up, they're *usually* spitting lightning and farting thunder—" her eyes twinkled at something in Leeana's expression "—as Hundred Erlis would put it," she finished the sentence demurely. Then she shook her head.

"But that's normally because they're so pissed off that she's run away from them and gotten to one of our towns before they could catch up with her. And that wasn't why the Baron was mad. *He* was mad because they wouldn't let the two of you say goodbye to each other. Or, that's what my friend Tarisha said, anyway."

Tears flooded Leeana's eyes, and Garlahna squeezed her shoulder.

"The thing is," she continued gently, "that I don't

think he's going to stay even overnight. I don't think he'll want to be this close to you when you can't even speak to each other. So I'm afraid he'll be gone before you could say goodbye to your horse, either."

"I see," Leeana half-whispered. Then she wiped her eyes with her hand, quickly, almost angrily. "I see," she repeated more normally. "And . . . thank you for telling me."

"You're welcome," Garlahna said. "Just don't tell Hundred Erlis I did!" She grinned hugely. "She'd skin me out and tan my hide for shoe leather if she knew I was blabbing to a probationary candidate about something like that!"

"Oh, we couldn't have *that*!" Leeana reassured her with a watery giggle.

"Thanks. And, I know it may not make you feel any better about your horse—Boots?—but it's probably actually for the best, you know. I never had a horse of my own, but I know how much work they take. And how much they cost to feed!" Garlahna grimaced. "If you got to keep him, you'd have to take care of him yourself."

Leeana felt herself stiffen slightly, and Garlahna shook her head quickly.

"I'm not saying you didn't already do that at home. Although, I'd be willing to bet you probably didn't have to muck out his stall yourself, did you?" she added shrewdly, and Leeana felt herself forced to shake her head.

"Well, you'd have to do that, too, here," Garlahna told her. "And, believe me, you're not going to have enough time to breathe, much less take care of horses, for the next couple of weeks! And even if you were, I'll bet you don't have any money with you. Or, at least, not enough to pay for a horse's stable space and food."

"No," Leeana admitted, "I don't. But," she added gamely, "I'm sure I could find some way to earn it!"

"Welllll, I suppose it's *possible*," Garlahna allowed. "There's always extra chores that need doing, and we can usually pick up the odd extra kormak for doing them. But like I say, it's not like you'd have time to *be* doing them."

"You're probably right," Leeana sighed.

"No 'probably' about it," Garlahna snorted. "I *am* right about it. But," she continued more briskly, "we shouldn't be standing here chattering away. Hundred Erlis will kick my backside if I don't get you squared away before dinner, so come on! Over to Administration for your room assignment first, and then over to Housekeeping for bed linens. And," she grinned wickedly, "to get rid of those *tacky* clothes you're wearing and get you measured for your own chari and yathu."

Chapter Twenty-Two

At least Chemalka seemed to have decided to take her rainstorms somewhere else.

Kaeritha grinned at the thought as she stood on the porch of the Kalathan guesthouse with a mug of steaming tea and gazed out into a misty early morning. Tellian and his armsmen had refused the war maids' hospitality and departed late the previous afternoon. They probably hadn't traveled far—there was a largish posting inn at the crossroad with the high road to Magdalas, about three miles from Kalatha, and she felt confident they'd stopped there to rest their horses for at least a day or two. However urgently he might want to return to Hanatha at Hill Guard, Tellian was a Sothōii. He would *not* damage a horse if he had any choice at all about it.

She felt equally certain that the baron hadn't declined Yalith's offer out of anger or pique, but it had probably been as well he had. Whatever he might feel, the attitudes—and anger—of several of his retainers would have been certain to provoke friction and might well have spilled over into an unfortunate incident.

Her grin vanished into a grimace, and she shook her head with an air of resignation before she took another sip of tea. Tellian's warning that many of his followers were going to blame Kaeritha for Leeana's actions had proved only too well founded. All of them had been too disciplined to say or do anything overt in the face of their lord's public acceptance of the situation, but Kaeritha hadn't needed the mage power to recognize the hostility in some of the glances which had come her way. She hoped their anger with her wasn't going to spill over onto Bahzell and Brandark when they got back to Balthar. If it did, though, Bahzell would simply have to deal with it. Which, she thought wryly, he would undoubtedly manage in his own inimitable fashion.

She drank more tea, watching the sun climb above the muddy fields which surrounded Kalatha. It was going to be a warmer day, she decided, and the sun would soon burn off the mists. She'd noticed the training field, and an extensive weapons salle, behind the town armory when she passed it on the day of her arrival, and she wondered if Balcartha Evahnalfressa, Yalith's senior guard officer, would object to her borrowing the salle for an hour or so. She'd missed her regular morning workouts while she and Leeana pressed ahead as rapidly as possible on their journey. Besides, from all she'd heard, her own two-handed fighting technique was much less uncommon among war maids. If she could talk some of them into sparring with her, she might be able to pick up a new trick or two.

She finished the tea and turned to step back into the guesthouse to set the mug on the table beside her other breakfast dishes. Then she looked into the small mirror—an unexpected and expensive luxury—above the fireplace. Welcome as the guesthouse bed had been, the communal bathhouse had been even more welcome. She actually looked human again, she decided, although it was still humid enough that it had taken her long, midnight-black hair hours to dry. Most of her clothes were *still* drying somewhere in the town laundry, but she'd had one decent, clean change still in her saddlebags. There were a few wrinkles and creases here and there, but taken all in all, she was presentable, she decided.

Which was probably a good thing. It might even do her some good in her upcoming interview with Yalith.

Then again, she thought ruefully, *it might not*.

"Thank you for agreeing to see me so early, Mayor," Kaeritha said as Sharral showed her back into Yalith's office and she settled into the proffered chair.

"There's no need to thank me," Yalith replied briskly. "Despite any . . . lack of enthusiasm on my part when you handed me a hot potato like Leeana, any champion deserves whatever hospitality we can provide, Dame Kaeritha. Although," she admitted, "I *am* a bit perplexed by exactly what a Champion of Tomanāk's doing here in Kalatha. However exalted Leeana's birth may have been, I don't believe we've ever had a candidate war maid delivered to us by *any* champion. And if that was going to happen, I would've expected one of the Mother's Arms."

"Actually," Kaeritha said, "I was already headed for Kalatha when Leeana overtook me on the road."

"Were you, indeed?" Yalith's tone was that of a woman expressing polite interest, not surprise. Although, Kaeritha thought, there was also an edge of wariness to it.

"Yes," she said. Her left elbow rested on the arm of her chair, and she raised that hand, palm open. "I don't know how familiar you are with champions and the way we get our instructions, Mayor Yalith."

Her tone made the statement a tactful question, and Yalith smiled.

"I've never dealt directly with a champion, if that's what you mean," she said. "I once met a senior Arm of the Mother, but I was much younger then, and certainly not a mayor. No one was interested in explaining to me how she got her instructions from Lillinara. Even if anyone had been, my impression is that She has Her own way of getting Her desires and intentions across, so I assume the same would be true of Tomanāk or any of the other gods."

"It certainly is," Kaeritha agreed wryly. "For that matter, He seems to tailor His methods to His individual champions. In my own case, however, I tend to receive, well, *feelings*, I suppose, that I ought to be moving in a particular direction or thinking about a particular problem. As I get closer to whatever it is He needs me to be dealing with, I generally recognize the specifics as I come across them."

"That would seem to require a great deal of faith," Yalith observed. Then she wrinkled her nose with a snort of amusement at her own words. "I suppose a champion *does* need rather more 'faith' than most people do, doesn't she?"

"It does seem to come with the job," Kaeritha agreed. "In this instance, though, those feelings He sends me already had me headed in this direction. As nearly as I can pin things down at this point, Kalatha was where He wanted me."

"And not just to escort Leeana to us, I suppose."

"No. I had some discussion with Baron Tellian before I left Balthar, Mayor. Frankly, the reports from his stewards and magistrates, which he shared with me, lead me to believe that relations between your town and its neighbors are . . . not as good as they might be."

"My, what a tactful way to describe it." Yalith's irony was dry enough to burn off the morning mist without benefit of sunlight. She regarded Kaeritha without saying anything more for several more seconds, then leaned back in her chair and folded her arms across her chest.

"As a matter of fact, Dame Kaeritha, our 'neighbors' are probably almost as angry with us as we are with them. Although, of course, my Town Council and I believe we're in the right and *they* aren't. I hope you'll forgive me for saying this, however, but I fail to see why our disagreements and squabbles should be of any particular interest to Tomanāk. Surely He has better things to spend His champions' time on than refereeing fights which have been going on for decades. Besides, with all due respect, I'd think matters concerning the war maids are properly Lillinara's affair, not the War God's."

"First," Kaeritha said calmly, "Tomanāk is the God of Justice, as well as the God of War, and from Tellian's reports, there seems to be some question of exactly what 'justice' means in this case. Second, those same reports also seem to suggest that there's something more to this than the sort of quarrels which usually go on between war maid communities and their neighbors."

Yalith seemed less than pleased by the reminder that Tomanāk was God of Justice—or perhaps by the implication that in that capacity he might have a legitimate interest in a matter which she clearly considered belonged to Lillinara. But if that was the case, she chose not to make a point of it. Yet, at least.

"I suppose there may be a bit more to it this time," she conceded with a slightly grudging air. "Trisu of Lorham's never been particularly fond of war maids in general. His father, Lord Darhal, wasn't either, but at least the old man wasn't as bad as his younger brother, Saeth. *No one* was as bad as Saeth Pickaxe, Milady! Talk about your bigoted, contemptuous, stupid—"

Yalith cut herself off and grimaced, then shook her head. She pinched the bridge of her nose and drew a deep breath, then exhaled.

"Forgive me, Dame Kaeritha. I wasn't yet Mayor when Saeth was killed in a hunting accident, but I had my own personal run-in with him, and I wasn't alone. He seemed torn between the belief that every one of us was an unnatural bitch who should be exterminated for the salvation of the Kingdom and the conviction that every one of us was a whore he could tumble whenever he wished. Frankly, I'm astounded that he managed to be killed in an accident instead of ending up with a war maid garrotte wrapped around his throat and tied in a big, neat bow!

"But Lord Darhal was neither oversexed nor an idiot, and if he felt we were 'unnatural,' at least he kept it to himself. In fact, he seemed to realize we were a fact of life he was going to have to learn to live with, so he did, however grumpily. Trisu, on the other hand, only inherited his title three years ago, and he's still young . . . and impatient. He's nowhere near so loathsome as his Uncle Saeth was, but I sometimes think he actually believes he can make himself sufficiently unpleasant to convince us to all just—" she wiggled the fingers of one hand in midair "—move away and leave him in peace."

She grimaced again, less bitterly, and shook her head.

"When I'm not being totally exasperated with him, though, I doubt even Trisu could really be stupid enough to think that's going to happen. Which means he's making such an ass out of himself for some other reason. My own theory is that it's simple frustration and immaturity. I've been hoping he'll simply outgrow it."

"With all due respect, Mayor Yalith," Kaeritha kept her voice as level and uninflected as possible, "from his own reports—and complaints—to Baron Tellian, he seems to feel he has legitimate cause for his unhappiness with Kalatha." She raised one hand in a pacifying gesture as Yalith's eyes narrowed. "I'm not saying you're wrong about his underlying hostility, because from the tone of his letters, you're not. I'm only saying that he clearly believes he has legitimate grievances over and above the fact that he simply doesn't like you very much."

"I'm aware of that," Yalith said a bit frostily. "I've heard about water rights and pasturage complaints from him until, quite frankly, I'm sick of it. Kalatha's charter clearly gives us control of the river, since it passes through our territory upstream of his boundary with us. What we do with it at that point is up to us, not to him. And if he wants us to make a greater share of *our* water available to him, then he's going to have to make some concessions to us, in return."

Kaeritha nodded—in understanding, not agreement, although she wasn't certain Yalith recognized the distinction. Given the quantity of water which had fallen out of the sky over the past several weeks, the thought that Kalatha and the most powerful of the local nobles were at dagger-drawing over the issue of water rights might have struck some as silly. Kaeritha, however, had been born in a peasant farming community. As a result, she was only too well aware of how desperately important such issues could become when soggy spring gave way to the hot, dry months of summer. On the other hand, it was entirely possible—even probable, she suspected—that the quarrel over water was only an outward manifestation of other, more deeply seated animosities.

"From his arguments to Tellian's magistrates," she said after a moment, "it seems evident Trisu doesn't agree that your control of the river is as straightforward and unambiguous as you believe it is. Or that your interpretation of the boundaries set up by Lord Kellos' grant are correct. Obviously, he's going to put forward what he believes are his strongest arguments in that respect, since he's trying to convince the courts to rule in his favor. I'm not saying he's correct or that his arguments are valid—only that he appears to *believe* they are."

Yalith snorted derisively, but she didn't say anything, and Kaeritha continued.

"To be honest, at the moment I'm more interested in those return 'concessions' to which you just referred. Trisu's complained to Tellian that you war maids have been hostile and confrontational and rejected his best efforts to work out a peaceable compromise solution to his disputes with you. As far as I'm aware, he hasn't gone into any specifics about just how you've been hostile and confrontational. Do you suppose that would have anything to do with the concessions you want from him?"

"Hostile and confrontational, is it?" Yalith glowered. "I'll 'hostile and confrontational' *him*! We've been as reasonable as we *can* be with such a pigheaded, greedy, stubborn, opinionated young idiot!"

Despite herself, Kaeritha found it difficult not to smile. Yalith's evident anger made it a bit easier, since it was obvious her resentment of Trisu burned much deeper and hotter than she wanted to admit to Kaeritha . . . or possibly even to herself. At the same time, the knight could see how even a man considerably more reasonable than she suspected Trisu was might feel the war maids were just a trifle hostile toward him.

"I'm sure you have," she said after a second or two, when she was confident she could control her own voice.

"What I need to know before I move on to Lorham is exactly what concessions you've been seeking."

"Nothing that earthshaking," Yalith responded. "Or they shouldn't be, anyway. We want a right-of-way across one of his pastures to a stud farm which was bequeathed to us by Lady Crowhammer six or seven years ago. We want a formal agreement on how the river's water will be divided and distributed in dry seasons. We want a guarantee that our farm products—and farmers—will receive equal treatment in local markets from his factors and inspectors and from the market magistrates. And we want him to finally and formally accept the provisions of our charter and Lord Kellos' land grant—*all* of their provisions."

"I see." Kaeritha sat back and considered what Yalith had just said. The first three points did, indeed, sound as if they were less than "earthshaking." She was only too well aware of how simply and reasonably someone could describe her own viewpoint on an issue which was bitterly contested, yet she was inclined to think it must be the fourth point which lay at the heart of the war maids' current confrontation with the Lord of Lorham.

"What specific provisions are in dispute?" she asked after a moment.

"Several." Yalith grimaced. "King Gartha's charter defines specific obligations to local lords from which war maids are to be exempted, and, to be fair, Trisu and his father and grandfather have generally accepted that. They've been less interested in enforcing the provisions which require those same local lords to grant war maid crafters and farmers equal protection and treatment in their markets.

"That's bad enough, but it's also been going on literally for generations, and we've managed to live with it all that time. But another serious dispute's arisen in the last few years, concerning the water rights I spoke of and the integrity of the surrounding land which Lord Kellos originally granted to us. Lord Kellos' grant defined specific boundaries and landmarks, obviously, but Trisu's family—and, for that matter, some of the other local lords, although not to the same degree—have been encroaching upon those boundaries for years. In fact, Trisu's father built a grist mill on what's clearly our land, and Trisu has refused to acknowledge that Lord Darhal was in the wrong when he did. In fact, Trisu insists that *he* owns that land and always has, despite the fact that the original grant puts the boundary almost half a mile *beyond* the mill. That's just one instance of the way in which our boundaries are being routinely violated.

"Another point is that the grant clearly specifies that we're exempt from tolls on the use of roadways crossing Lorham. Lord Kellos and Trisu's great-great-grandfather did some horsetrading back and forth over the exact boundaries of our holdings, and Lord Rathman gave us the exemption in return for a couple of offsetting concessions from Lord Kellos. But Lord Trisu's father, Darhal, began charging us the tolls anyway about thirty years ago.

"Admittedly, this isn't a point we've made an issue out of before, since the tolls Lord Darhal levied weren't all that high. More to the point, they were clearly intended for the maintenance of the roads in question, and we *were* using them to transport our goods and produce. But Trisu began raising the tolls immediately after he became Lord Warden of Lorham. He's obviously trying to raise additional revenues, over and above the cost of maintaining the roads themselves. We may've been willing to pay a toll we weren't legally obligated to pay so long as the funds were being used to repair and maintain roadways that benefited us, as well as Lorham. But we are *not* prepared to subsidize other parts of his treasury while he's violating our boundaries and attempting to deny us our legitimate water rights.

"There are several other, minor points—most of them procedural, really. Some of them, to be completely honest, probably aren't worth fighting over. But they're part and parcel of our overall quarrel with him. We're not prepared to concede any of them without getting something in return, but that's something that can be worked out in negotiations, assuming that both sides are willing to negotiate."

"I see." Kaeritha nodded, her expression thoughtful. "That's about the size of it?"

"Well, yes. Where our prerogatives and boundaries are concerned, at any rate. But . . . there is one additional, major problem."

The mayor's pause was almost a hesitation, and Kaeritha quirked an eyebrow.

"As I said," Yalith continued, "our charter clearly and unambiguously provides that our craftspeople, farmers, traders, and anyone else who may be a citizen of Kalatha or any of the free-towns which were founded later are guaranteed the same rights as any other citizens of the Kingdom, regardless of whether they're men or women. Trisu doesn't seem to think that applies in Lorham."

"In what way?" Kaeritha asked, leaning forward and frowning intently.

"Our merchants and artisans and some of our farmers have been harassed in local markets, and Trisu's magistrates have done nothing about it," Yalith replied. She waved a hand in a back-and-forth gesture. "That, in itself, isn't all that important. There's always going to be some bigoted farmer or townsman who's going to give women doing 'man's work' a hard time, and war maids can't afford to be too thin-skinned when it comes along. But it's symptomatic of a more serious problem."

"What sort of problem?"

"There have been . . . incidents concerning the temple of Lillinara at Quaysar," Yalith said. It was obvious she was picking her words carefully, and also that she was trying hard to restrain a volcanic surge of anger. She paused once more, and Kaeritha waited for the mayor to be certain she had control of her temper before she resumed.

"Since you follow Tomanāk, not Lillinara, you may not be aware that the temple in Quaysar has special significance to the Mother," she said, after a few moments. "It's not an especially large temple, but it's a very old one. Quaysar itself is a tiny town. In fact, the town proper has pretty much disappeared over the last fifty or sixty years. What's left of it has been effectively absorbed by the temple itself. But the Quaysar Temple has always been especially important to the war maids—just as Kalatha itself has been, despite our small size—because it was at Quaysar that our original charter from King Gartha was first officially and formally proclaimed. You might say Quaysar is the 'mother chapter' of all war maids everywhere and that Kalatha is the 'mother free-town' to match it. Quaysar's also located in Lorham, unfortunately. As a matter of fact, one of the reasons Lord Kellos originally granted Kalatha to the war maids, and why the Crown recognized it as a free-town, was our proximity to Quaysar."

"You're right. I wasn't aware of that," Kaeritha murmured. "Tellian told me Kalatha was your oldest free-town, but I didn't know about Quaysar or its importance to you."

"There's no reason why you should have," Yalith pointed out. "Obviously, we would have preferred to have been able to include Quaysar under our charter. Unfortunately, the lord wardens of Lorham have always been much less sympathetic to us than Lord Kellos was. It didn't seem to matter much, though, given the respect and autonomy enjoyed by any temple. Whether Trisu or his ancestors approved of war maids or not, surely no sane person was going to harass or insult the temple of *any* god . . . or goddess. Or so we thought."

"You mean he *has* done that?" Kaeritha demanded sharply.

"I mean," Yalith said grimly, "that he's repeatedly demonstrated his disrespect—I would even say contempt—for the temple at Quaysar. He's insulted the Voice of Quaysar in personal conversation. He's made it clear to her that he is not impressed by the fact that she speaks for the Mother. For that matter, he's all but openly stated that he doesn't believe she *does* speak for the Mother at all."

Kaeritha was shocked. Different rulers always evidenced different degrees of reverence and respect, and some people seemed to believe that if *they* worshiped one god—or goddess—all of the others were irrelevant. But what sort of idiot openly showed the sort of disdain and contempt Yalith was describing? Regardless of what he himself believed or disbelieved, such an attitude was guaranteed to offend and infuriate his subjects.

"That's all bad enough," Yalith continued in a flat, bitter voice, "but it isn't everything. Two of the Voice's handmaidens were sent from Quaysar to Kalatha with a message from the Voice to me. They never arrived."

This time, Kaeritha was far more than merely shocked.

"Mayor Yalith, are you suggesting—?"

"I'm not prepared to suggest that Trisu personally had anything to do with their disappearance," Yalith interrupted before Kaeritha could complete the question. "If I had any proof—or even strongly suggestive evidence—of that, I can assure you that I would already have charged him with it before Baron Tellian, as his liege, or demanded that the case be investigated by the Crown Prosecutor. But I do believe that whoever was responsible—who must have shared Trisu's attitude towards war maids generally to have done something so insane—probably took his cue from Trisu. And I'm not at all satisfied with Trisu's so-called 'investigation' of the incident. He claims he can find no evidence *at all* to suggest what happened to the Voice's handmaidens. Indeed, he's gone so far as to suggest that they never disappeared at all. That the entire story is a fabrication."

Kaeritha frowned. There'd been no mention of this incident in any of Trisu's correspondence with Tellian or his magistrates. In the wake of what Yalith had just told her, that omission took on ominous overtones.

"The Voice hasn't been able to determine what happened to her handmaidens?" she asked after a moment.

"Apparently not," Yalith said heavily. She sighed. "All the Voice can discover is that both of them are dead. How they died, and exactly where, she can't say."

A chill ran down Kaeritha's spine. The murder of the consecrated servants of any temple, and especially that of two acolytes sworn to the personal service of a Voice of Lillinara, was an incredibly serious matter. The fact that Trisu wasn't tearing Lorham apart stone-by-stone to find the guilty parties was frightening.

And perhaps it's also the reason Tomanāk needed one of His blades involved, she thought grimly.

"How long ago did this happen?" she asked crisply.

"Not very," Yalith replied. She glanced at the calendar on her desk. "A bit less than four weeks ago, actually."

Kaeritha's mood eased just a bit. If the murders had happened that recently, it was at least possible Trisu hadn't mentioned it to Tellian because he was still investigating it himself. After all, if it had happened in Lorham, it was *Trisu's* responsibility to solve the crime, not Tellian's. If he was unable to do so, he had the right—and, some would argue, the responsibility—to call upon his liege for assistance, but he might simply feel he hadn't yet exhausted all of his own resources.

Sure. He might *feel that*, she told herself.

And the fact that it had happened that recently undoubtably explained why nothing had been said to Tellian by Yalith or the Voice at Quaysar. Kalatha held a Crown charter. That meant that, unlike Trisu, Yalith was *not* one of Tellian's vassals, and as such, she had no responsibility to report anything to him. Nor, for that matter, was Tellian legally obligated to take any action on anything she *did* report to him, although he undoubtably would have acted in a matter this serious which involved or might involve one of his vassals. As for the Voice, Trisu was the appropriate person for her to turn to for an investigation and justice. If he failed to provide them, only then was she entitled to appeal to *his* liege.

"Perhaps now you can see why I was surprised to see a Champion of Tomanāk rather than one of the Mother's Arms," Yalith said quietly.

"To be honest, so am I, a little," Kaeritha admitted, although she privately thought the Arms of Lillinara were a little too intent on avenging victims rather than administering justice. All the same, she *was* surprised Lillinara hadn't dispatched one of them to deal with the situation. The Silver Lady was famed for the devastating retribution she was prepared to visit upon those who victimized her followers.

"Perhaps," she went on slowly, thinking aloud, "if Trisu

is as hostile towards you as you're saying—hostile enough to extend his feelings towards the war maids into public disrespect for Lillinara—She and Tomanāk felt it might be better for Him to send one of His blades. The fact that I'm a woman may make me a bit more acceptable to you war maids and to the Voice, while the fact that I serve Tomanāk rather than Lillinara may make me acceptable to Trisu *despite* the fact that I'm a woman."

"I hope *something* does, Dame Kaeritha," Yalith said soberly. "Because if something doesn't bring about a marked improvement in what's happening here in Kalatha and Lorham sometime soon, it's going to spill over."

Kaeritha looked at her, and she grimaced.

"Kalatha's status as our oldest free-town means all war maids tend to keep up with events here, Milady, and I just explained why Quaysar is important to all of us. If Trisu and those who think like him are able to get away with running roughshod over us *here*, then they may be inspired to try the same thing anywhere else. That would be bad enough, but to be perfectly honest, I'm actually more concerned about how the *war maids* will react. Let's be honest. Most of us aren't all that fond of men in positions of authority, anyway. If Trisu proves our distrust is well founded, it's going to cause our own attitudes to harden. I can assure you that at least some of the war maids are just as bitter and just as prejudiced against the Trisus of the world as Trisu could ever be against us, and some of those women are likely to begin acting on their bitterness if they feel we've been denied justice in this case. And if that happens, then everything we've accomplished over the past two hundred and fifty years is in jeopardy."

Kaeritha nodded, blue eyes dark as she contemplated the spiraling cycle of distrust, hostility, and potential violence Yalith was describing.

"Well, in that case, Mayor," she said quietly, "we'll just have to see to it that that doesn't happen, won't we?"

Chapter Twenty-Three

Edinghas Bardiche knew his expression wasn't the most tactful one possible, but there wasn't a great deal he could do about that. He was too busy gazing in disbelief at his newly arrived . . . "guests."

He stood in the muddy paddock outside the main stable, acutely aware of the watching eyes of the Warm Springs armsmen currently on duty, still ringing the building protectively. Alfar Axeblade stood before him, holding the reins of a borrowed horse, and eight hradani stood behind Alfar—seven of them in the colors of the Order of Tomanāk. It was remotely possible, Edinghas thought, that there could have been a more unlikely sight somewhere in the Kingdom. He just couldn't imagine where it might have been. Or when.

Finally, after endless seconds of silent consternation, he succeeded in goading his tongue to life.

"I crave your pardon . . . Milord Champion," he managed. "I must confess that when I dispatched Alfar to the Baron, I didn't anticipate that he might return with a— That is, I didn't expect a champion of Tomanāk."

His attention was focused on the mountainous hradani looming before him, yet a corner of his eye caught the expression on Alfar's face. He couldn't begin to sort out all of the emotions wrapped up in that expression, but embarrassment and something almost like anger seemed to be a part of them. His retainer opened his mouth, but before he could say anything, the hradani glanced at him with a tiny head shake, and Alfar's mouth closed with an almost audible click.

"What you're meaning, Milord Warden," the hradani replied in a deep, rumbling bass perfectly suited to his huge stature, "is that you were never expecting a *hradani* champion."

Edinghas felt his tired face heat, but the hradani sounded almost amused. It might be a dry, biting amusement, but it wasn't the anger the lord warden's self-correction might all too easily have provoked.

"Yes, I suppose that *is* what I meant," he admitted.

"Well," the hradani said, "I won't say as how that's after making me feel all warm and cuddly inside, Milord. On the other hand, I can't be saying as how it's after surprising me, either. Like enough, I'd feel the same, if the boot were on the other foot. Still and all, here I stand, and it's in my mind that what's happened here is after being the sort of thing as one of Himself's champions ought to be looking into."

"I certainly can't argue with that," Edinghas said. "But I hope I won't offend you by saying that my armsmen are likely to be even more . . . surprised than me."

"Milord." Alfar's voice was polite but firm, and Edinghas looked at him, surprised by the interruption. "Milord," Alfar repeated when he was certain he had his liege's attention, "Sir Jahlahan, Baron Tellian's seneschal, personally vouches for Prince Bahzell in the Baron's name and explains how he came to be in Balthar when I arrived there." His wave indicated the still unopened message from Swordspinner in Edinghas' hand. "And for myself," he continued, even more firmly, "I can only say that, hradani or no, these men have not spared themselves for a moment in their determination to reach Warm Springs as quickly as possible. Milord, they *ran* all the way from Balthar."

Edinghas' eyebrows rose involuntarily. Sothōii retainers and freeholders, especially in a northern holding like Warm Springs, were a sturdy, independent lot. It had something to do with endless hours spent all alone on horseback in the grassy immensity of the Wind Plain—or in the howling chaos of a midwinter blizzard. Yet for all that, the note of near rebuke in Alfar's voice surprised him.

He shook himself, then looked back at the hradani. *No*, he told himself, *at* Prince *Bahzell*.

"I crave your pardon once again, Milord Champion," he said, and this time his voice sounded closer to normal in his own ears. "Alfar's right. I ought to at least read Lord Swordspinner's dispatch. And however surprised I may have been by your . . . unexpected arrival, that surprise doesn't excuse my rudeness."

"I'd not be calling it rude," Bahzell replied. He smiled slowly. "I'd not be calling it exactly the warmest welcome I've ever had, but it's not after being the coldest, either. Not by a long road, Milord."

"It's good of you to say so." Edinghas felt himself returning Bahzell's smile. Then he gave himself another little shake. "With your permission, Prince Bahzell, I'll ask Alfar to escort you to the manor house. He can get you and your men settled in there while I repair my error and read what Lord Swordspinner has to say. And," he met Bahzell's eyes levelly, "while I have a few words with my armsmen, as well."

"Aye, I'd not say that was so very bad an idea," the hradani agreed.

"Thank you." Genuine gratefulness for the other's attitude touched Edinghas' tone, and he returned his gaze to Alfar. "Please take Prince Bahzell and his men up to the house," he said. "Tell Lady Sofalla that they'll be our guests for at least the next few days."

Alfar nodded, but Edinghas' attention had already returned to Bahzell. The hradani gazed back at him for a moment, his face almost expressionless. But then he bowed, very slightly, and Edinghas saw the understanding in his eyes. The lord warden's decision against sending even a single armsman along with Alfar, even as only a courteous "escort," on the trip to his family's private home was the strongest possible way for him to express his trust.

"It's grateful we are," Bahzell rumbled, and turned to follow Alfar towards the fortified manor house that was the closest Warm Springs had to a proper keep.

Lady Sofalla Bardiche was a sturdy, attractively plain woman whose chestnut hair was well stranded with silver. Instead of the gown a more highly ranked Sothōii noblewoman might have worn, she wore serviceable (although subtly feminine) trousers under a long, brightly embroidered tunic. The embroidery was a bit finer and more fanciful than a prosperous farmer's wife might have boasted, but it certainly wasn't the silks and satins, pearls and semiprecious gems of a great noble house. She also had a brisk, no-nonsense manner that reminded Bahzell strongly of Tala, and she took the sudden arrival of her husband's henchman with eight hradani in tow far more calmly than might have been expected.

"Well," she said after Alfar had completed his hasty explanation, "I can't say I ever expected to be entertaining hradani, Prince Bahzell. Or not, at least, on *this* side of the manor wall!" She smiled as she said it, and he smiled back. "But if Lord Edinghas wants you put up in guest quarters, that's good enough for me. I'm afraid you'll find things a bit less fine here at Warm Springs than at Balthar, though!"

"Milady," Bahzell replied, "we're after being hradani. A roof as doesn't leak more than a few bucketfuls each night will be doing us well enough."

"Oh, I think we can manage a little better than that," she assured him, and turned to the small gaggle of housemaids huddled behind her and gazing apprehensively at the hradani whose stature dwarfed the manor house's entry hall.

"Stop gawking like ninnies!" Sofalla scolded. "Ratha," she continued, singling out one of the older, more levelheaded-looking maids, "go and tell Gohlan that we'll be putting Prince Bahzell and his people into the south wing."

✧ ✧ ✧

Lord Edinghas' armsmen still looked less than delighted with the situation when Alfar escorted Bahzell back to the stable an hour and a half later, but at least the most overt hostility seemed to have eased. Bahzell didn't know exactly what Sir Jahlahan had included in his letter, or how Edinghas had explained the situation to his wary retainers, but it seemed to have taken. Bahzell wasn't surprised—not after watching Lady Sofalla deal with the household staff. If her husband possessed even half her strength of personality, it would take a braver man than Bahzell to argue with him!

The reflection made Bahzell chuckle as he and Alfar crossed to where Edinghas stood in one of the stable doors.

"Again, welcome, Milord Champion," the lord warden said, and this time extended his right hand. Bahzell clasped forearms with him, and Edinghas produced a much more natural smile.

"I won't apologize again for my first greeting," he said. "I've read Lord Swordspinner's letter, now, and he told me you'd probably understand if we seemed a bit . . . put off, just at first. Doesn't make it any better—I know that—but if you're willing to forgive me for it, I'll try to see it doesn't happen again."

"There's naught to forgive," Bahzell replied with a shrug. "That's not to be saying we'd not all have been happier to've been being greeted with open arms and glad hosannas, but I'm thinking as a man should be keeping his hopes to what's possible, when all's said."

He smiled, and Edinghas smiled back. Then the lord warden's expression sobered.

"Sir Jahlahan wrote that you'd see it that way, Milord. And I'm glad. But I'd also be happier if there'd never been need for a champion of Tomanāk to come to Warm Springs. And especially not for a reason like this."

"Aye, I'll not disagree with you there," Bahzell said somberly.

"Well, I suppose we should get to it, then," Edinghas sighed. "I warn you, Milord, I've no idea how they'll react when *they* meet you. We've still no idea what happened to them out there, but whatever it was, it's marked them more than just physically." His jaw tightened. "I've never seen coursers frightened, Milord. Not before this. But now—"

He sighed again and turned to lead the way into the stable.

Warm Springs' stables had been built to a much larger scale than those of most manors because of the holding's long association with the Warm Springs coursers. The main stable was a high, airy structure, with huge, open-fronted stalls that were well kept and spotlessly clean. And, in spite of everything, Bahzell was unprepared for what he found inside it.

He'd asked Brandark to remain outside, with the other members of the Order. The last thing they needed was to overwhelm the injured coursers with the presence of so many hradani. He knew that, but no amount of logic could keep him from feeling alone and isolated among so many humans, none of whom knew him, and all of whom were his people's hereditary enemies.

He faced that thought, and then put it firmly behind him. He couldn't afford it now, he told himself, and turned his attention to the coursers he'd come to see.

Despite his people's name and reputation, he'd had quite a bit of experience with horses. He'd actually ridden (if not particularly well, and only for fairly brief periods) on several occasions, and the Horse Stealers' traditional enmity with the Sothōii more or less required them to be familiar with cavalry and its capabilities. No Horse Stealer was ever going to be a cavalryman himself, given his people's sheer size, so most of his personal experience had been with draft animals, but like any Horse Stealer, he had an expert eye when it came to evaluating quality horseflesh.

For all of that, he had never come within a mile of any courser until he encountered Baron Tellian and Dathgar and Hathan and Gayrhalan in the Gullet. To a large extent, that was because his father had outlawed raids on the Wind Plain less than five years after Bahzell had earned his warrior's braid. To an even larger extent, though, it had been because it was more than any hradani's life was worth to come within what any courser stallion might consider threatening range of his herd . . . which equated to coming within the stallion's line of sight. The reservations Gayrhalan continued to nourish where Bahzell was concerned even now only underscored the wisdom of remaining safely out of reach of any courser's battleaxe jaws and piledriver hooves.

Dathgar had become rather more comfortable with Bahzell, but even Tellian's companion remained . . . uneasy in close proximity to him. Still, coursers were at least as intelligent as most of the Races of Man, and both Dathgar and Gayrhalan, like Sir Kelthys' Walasfro, had been wise enough to recognize that Bahzell was not the slavering hradani stereotype for which the coursers had cherished such hatred for so long.

Nonetheless, he recognized that it behooved him to approach these coursers cautiously. None of them had ever met him; Sir Kelthys had not yet arrived, so there was no wind rider and his companion to vouch for Bahzell; and these were the brutally traumatized survivors of a merciless massacre. They were unlikely, to say the least, to take the sudden appearance of eight hradani well.

But when he stepped into the stable and saw the condition of those survivors, it was hard—even harder than he had anticipated—to remember the need for caution and distance.

The seven adults were bad enough. Even now, they shivered uncontrollably, as if with an ague, rolling their eyes and flinching away from any unexpected sound or movement. Seeing horses in such a state of terror would have sufficed to break any heart. Seeing *coursers* reduced to such straits was the stuff of nightmare, and not just for Sothōii like Alfar or Edinghas.

Not one of the terrified survivors had escaped unwounded, and one of the fillies had lost her right ear and eye and bore an ugly, ragged, wound that ran from the point of her left hip forward almost to her shoulder. She must have been almost four years old, and it was obvious that her technically "juvenile" status had not kept her out of the heart of her herd's battle. Her right knee was lacerated, with a deep tear extending downward along the cannon. It seemed impossible that it could have missed the extensor tendons, but although she obviously favored the leg, it was still taking her weight.

She bore at least half a dozen other, scarcely less brutal wounds, and there was something *wrong* about all of them. Coursers healed almost as rapidly as hradani, yet those deep, wicked trenches still oozed. Their discharge crusted her shaggy winter coat, and Bahzell could detect the scent of corruption from where he stood, even through the normal stable smells about him. The injured filly's head drooped, and her breathing was labored, yet her outward damages, grievous though they might be, were less deadly than the wounds no physical eye could see.

Bahzell felt every muscle tighten as his vision shifted. It was an aspect of his champion's status that he had yet to become fully accustomed to, and his jaw clenched as he seemed to find himself suddenly able to look *inside* the filly's body. He could "see" the powerful muscles, the tendons and bones, the lungs and mighty heart . . .

And the vile green pollution spreading slowly, slowly through every vein and artery in her body. Any lesser creature, he knew, would already have succumbed to the infiltrating poison, and even the filly was fading fast.

Nausea churned deep in his belly as the sheer evil of the creeping contamination washed over him. It took a wrenching physical effort to tear his eyes from her and turn that same, penetrating gaze upon the surviving foals.

Bahzell Bahnakson grunted, as if someone had just punched him in the belly. The foals had been less rent and torn than the adults who had fought to protect them, but they were also younger and smaller, with less resistance to the poison spreading from the wounds they had taken. The poison, Bahzell realized, which no horse leech, no physical healer, could possibly see or recognize.

"I'd thought you said as how there were after being

eight foals," he said to Alfar, and even to his own ear, his deep voice sounded harsh.

"There were, Milord Champion," Lord Edinghas said grimly before Alfar could respond. "We lost the worst hurt of them, a colt not more than eight months old, yesterday." The lord warden shook his head, his face ashen. "We shouldn't have, Milord. A horse with those wounds, yes, but not a courser. Never a courser."

"He's right," another voice said from Bahzell's right, and the Horse Stealer turned towards the speaker. It was a young man, not yet out of his twenties, whose face and chestnut hair proclaimed his parentage. And whose eyes were hard and hostile as they met Bahzell's.

"My son, Hahnal, Prince Bahzell," Lord Edinghas said.

Unlike his father and the armsmen guarding the stable, Hahnal was neither armed nor armored. He wore a smock, instead, marked with old bloodstains—and some not so old—and his youthful face was haggard.

"Hahnal is one of our best horse leeches," Edinghas continued. "He's snatched an hour or so of sleep here and there, but he's refused to leave the stable since they returned."

"And Phrobus' own good it's done!" Hahnal half-spat. His big, capable-looking hands clenched into fists at his sides, and he turned to stare at the visibly failing coursers with eyes in which despair was finally strangling desperate determination. "We're losing them Father. We're losing all of them."

His voice cracked on the final word, and he turned away, scrubbing at his face with one palm. Bahzell could almost taste his humiliation at his display of "weakness," and, without even thinking about it, he reached out and laid his own hand on the young man's shoulder.

"Don't touch me, *hradani*!" Hahnal wrenched away from the contact, spinning to face Bahzell, and his eyes were fiery.

"Hahnal!" his father said sharply.

"No, Father." Hahnal never looked away from Bahzell, and his voice was icy cold. "You are Lord Warden of Warm Springs. You may grant guest right to anyone you choose. Including a hradani who claims to be a Champion of Tomanāk. That is your right and prerogative, and I will obey your word in it. But I will *not* be touched or petted and cosseted by a *Horse Stealer*, be he ten times a champion!"

"Hahnal," Edinghas said sternly, "you will apologize to—"

"Let be, Milord," Bahzell said quietly. Edinghas looked at him, and Bahzell raised one cupped palm as if pouring something from it. "I'd no business touching or offering aught without Lord Hahnal's let. And any man as has driven himself as hard as it's pikestaff plain your son has here, is after deserving the right to speak his mind. I'll not hold honesty against any man, however little it may be that I like what he's saying."

Edinghas hovered on the brink of saying something more, but Bahzell shook his head, and the lord warden clamped his teeth against any further reprimand.

"Now, Lord Hahnal," Bahzell continued, turning back to the young man and speaking in a voice which was as level and dispassionate as he could make it, "I'm thinking your father said as how the colt died yesterday?"

"Aye," Hahnal said shortly, his tone abrupt, as if he didn't know quite what to make of Bahzell's response to his own anger.

"And what was it you did with his body?"

"We buried it, of course!" Hahnal snapped. "Why, hradani? Did you want to—"

He stopped himself just in time, but the words he hadn't spoken hovered in the stable, and his father's face went white with shock, and then beet-red with fury. His hand twitched at his side, as if to slap his son, and this time even Bahzell's expression tightened.

"No," he rumbled in a voice which flowed like magma over ice, his ears flattened. "No, Milord. I've no desire to be eating such, though I'll admit, if pressed, that there are some as make me remember why my folk were after earning the name 'Horse Stealer' in the beginning. You'll do me the favor of not suggesting such again."

Hahnal started to respond hotly, but then he looked directly into Bahzell's eyes, and what he saw there was a bucket of ice water in the furnace of his rage. Bahzell said nothing more, made no slightest hostile gesture, yet Hahnal—who, however intemperate and exhausted he might be, was no coward—actually stepped back before he could stop himself.

"I—" He began, then paused and shook himself. "For that much, at least, I most truly apologize, Prince Bahzell," he said stiffly. "It was my grief and anger speaking. That cannot excuse my behavior, but it is the only explanation for it I can give you, and I am shamed by it."

"We'll say no more about it." Bahzell's voice was as chill as Vonderland ice, but then he inhaled deeply and continued in a more nearly normal tone. "The reason I was after asking about the body is that I'm thinking as how these coursers are after suffering from more than physical wounds. There's a poison working in them, one as attacks the heart and the soul as much or more than the body. And I'm not so very sure as it's after stopping when the body dies."

Hahnal and his father stared at Bahzell, Edinghas' lingering anger at his son in abatement as the sense of what Bahzell was saying registered. Hahnal started to protest, than stopped himself. It was obvious to Bahzell that he wanted to disbelieve that what he was hearing was possible, but the sick light in his eyes said that however much he'd wanted to, he'd failed.

"*Toragan!*" Lord Edinghas whispered, his face pale with horror. His hands tightened on his wide sword belt with enough force to squeeze the heavy leather almost double, and he stared at the injured, shivering coursers. Then he wrenched his gaze back to Bahzell.

"What can we do?" he asked, and the raw appeal in his hoarse voice submerged any lingering doubts as to who and what Bahzell was. It wasn't because his intellect had overcome them, Bahzell realized. It was because of his desperate need to believe that someone—*anyone*—could avert or undo this nightmare.

"As to that, I'm not so very sure," Bahzell admitted

heavily. Edinghas stared at him, and the hradani flicked his ears in the equivalent of a shrug. "I'm thinking as how the only thing I could be trying would be to heal them," he said. "I've never yet tried to heal aught but those of the Races of Man, and I've no least notion whether or not it's even possible for me to be after healing coursers. Yet it's in my mind that I've no choice but to try."

"*Heal* them?" Edinghas tried to keep his incredulity out of his voice, and he almost succeeded.

"Aye. But the thing is, I'm thinking there's scant time to waste. I'd hoped as how Sir Kelthys and Walasfro would be here to be introducing me to these coursers. Yet if we're after waiting for them to reach us, we'll be losing at least some of them."

"Then you have to try *now*!" Hahnal burst out.

"Aye, and so I'm saying my own self," Bahzell said shortly. "Yet without Walasfro to be telling them who I am, they're not so very likely to be letting me come next or nigh them. And frightened and confused as they are, it's like enough they'll be lashing out at any threat."

Understanding filled Hahnal's expression.

"We could tether them . . ." he began, slowly and manifestly against his will.

"No." Bahzell shook his head. "They're naught but one small slip from madness as it is, and they're none too clear in their minds. And they're after being coursers, Milord. They've known neither halter nor bridle all their lives long. If you're after trying to tie them now, in their state, no matter what your reason, they'll be panicking, and then—"

He shrugged.

"Forgive me, Prince Bahzell," Edinghas said, "but I've never seen a champion heal. Am I corrcct in believing that you have to actually touch the one you intend to heal?"

"Aye, that I must," Bahzell said grimly.

"Then it's out of the question." The lord warden spoke firmly, despite the despair washing across his face. "Weakened they may be, but they're coursers. They'll die on their feet rather than yield to man, demon, or god. And in their state, and with you a hradani . . ."

He shook his head heavily, but Bahzell surprised him with a sound that was halfway between a grunt and a snort. He looked back up at the towering hradani quickly, and Bahzell gave him a taut, crooked grin.

"Lord Edinghas, a champion of Tomanāk is one as does what needs doing. Himself isn't after promising we'll always like what comes of it, or even that we'll be surviving."

"But—"

"It's grateful I'll be if you all be standing back," Bahzell said, and before anyone else could reply, he walked forward towards the coursers.

He kept his eyes on the wounded filly, ignoring Edinghas' half-stifled cry of protest. He had to begin somewhere, see if it was even possible for him to heal the evil consuming them, and she was the one. Her dreadful wounds made her a logical enough place to begin, but that wasn't all that drew him towards her like a filing to a lodestone. It was her, he thought. He didn't know how he knew, but she was the key, the one who could somehow tell them what they needed to know, if only she lived.

The filly's maimed head came up as he approached her. She turned, moving until she could see him with her remaining eye, and bared her teeth. One forehoof pawed at the stable floor, thudding on earth and straw bedding like a mace, and she gave a harsh, ugly sound of challenge.

Bahzell never paused. He continued to move towards her at that slow, steady pace, careful to remain on the side where she could see him. The adult coursers shifted and flowed behind her, whistling and trumpeting their own challenges as they realized one of the hated hradani had somehow penetrated the frail security of the stable's walls.

"All right, Tomanāk," he murmured very softly. "I'm hoping I've understood all this aright, and it's grateful I'll be if you can be after convincing these fine folk not to be trampling me into mud."

Then he looked at the filly, meeting the terrified challenge and hatred in her wildly rolling eye with a steady brown gaze.

"Now, then, Milady," he said gently. "I'll not blame you for distrusting such as me. But I've no least notion of doing you or yours hurt. I'm naught but a friend, whatever it may be you're thinking."

The filly whistled shrilly, the sound deafening inside the stable, and reared. Large as the stable was, there was scant room for so huge a creature to rear, but she towered above the hradani, dwarfing even his mountainous stature, forehooves pawing the air, and her raging terror and poison-corrupted madness shook the stable like a storm. The other adults caught her fury, and all seven of them started forward. Bahzell heard human voices raised behind him, crying out in warning, but he scarcely needed them to tell him he was about to be trampled under by nine or ten tons of hoofed rage.

He didn't stop. He didn't even think. He simply continued towards them, and his right hand rose. The screams of equine rage completely overwhelmed the merely human voices behind him, but then, suddenly, his raised hand flared with a blinding burst of brilliant blue light. It was like an azure sunrise trapped inside the building, illuminating every knothole, every wisp of straw—every drifting dust mote. It was as if Chemalka's lightning had crackled down from the very heavens and exploded in the palm of a hradani's hand, and a mighty wind not quite of this world seemed to sweep the length of the stable, like a hurricane that was sensed rather than felt.

And then, through the tumult and the trumpeting of the terrified coursers, Bahzell Bahnakson's voice rumbled with impossible clarity.

"*Still*," he said.

It was only a single word, yet it echoed in the bones and blood of every man in that stable. It went through them like an earthquake, impossible to ignore or disobey or evade. It caught them like some huge, unseen set of pincers and nailed them where they stood, unable to move, or protest, or scarcely even to breathe.

Yet that was only the echo, the backwash, of that single command's unstoppable force. The rearing filly's forehooves thudded back to earth, and she froze, staring one-eyed at the hradani and the god-light blazing from his open palm. Behind her, six more coursers stilled, as well. They stood trembling, all of their defiance and rage frozen inside an unbreakable crystal cocoon that streamed over them from Bahzell.

"Better, Milady," Bahzell murmured. "Better."

His voice was soft, gentle, almost a caress, yet that same magnificently dreadful note of command reverberated in its depths. The wounded filly's single eye stopped rolling. The anger and fear drained out of it, replaced by stillness and a sort of dreamy acceptance.

"So," Bahzell whispered. "*Sooooo . . .*"

He reached the filly. Despite her youth, she was bigger and more powerful than the largest draft horse Bahzell had ever seen. Even he had to reach up to touch her head, and his right hand, no longer aflame with power, was gentle on the velvety softness of her nose. She flinched ever so slightly at the touch, then stood quiescent, her eye drooping half closed, and he stroked her forehead with his other hand, his eyes dark with compassion as he saw her dreadful wounds so close at hand.

"Now, Milady," he murmured, and held out his right hand, still gently stroking with the left. He never took his eyes from the courser as he flexed his fingers, and then whispered a single word.

"*Come*," he breathed, and a chorus of gasps echoed through the unnatural silence of the stable as a huge, gleaming sword materialized in his hand. The crossed Sword and Mace of Tomanāk were etched into the shining steel of that superb blade, and they flashed in the stable's dimness, damasked in a faery tracery of blue and golden light.

Bahzell reversed it in his hand, holding the hilt up between him and the strangely frozen filly, and a corona of blue light grew about him. It was faint, at first. Little more than a glimmer, more guessed at than seen. But it grew in both brightness and strength. It seemed to flow outward from Bahzell, conforming to the shape of his body, yet pressing ever outward and upward. Huge as he was, that bright, brilliant blue was huger. It stretched to the rafters and spread from stall to stall, reaching out until it completely enveloped the filly, as well.

Hradani and courser stood there, face-to-face, in an impossible tableau not a single Sothōii in that stable would have believed could ever exist. The light wrapped about them grew brighter, and brighter still. Hands rose to shield their eyes, and they turned away, unable to bear the intensity of that cascading brilliance.

And in the heart of that silently roaring inferno, Bahzell Bahnakson threw all of his faith, and all of his stubborn will—his inability to admit defeat, and his unstoppable drive to do what duty required of him—against the strangling shroud of the poison consuming the filly from within. It was unlike any healing he had ever attempted, for the poison he faced was not physical. The wounds themselves, the torn flesh, the shredded hide, those were enemies he'd come to know well. But the poison was something different, something that tore at the filly's spirit and soul, devouring them, turning them into something else—something unspeakably foul and unclean.

He threw himself at it, turning his will and his own spirit—his very self—into a sword blade of light. In a way he knew he would never be able to describe he found himself locked in combat, parrying and thrusting, meeting the poison's attack on the courser and taking it upon the armor of himself and his link to Tomanāk. He thrust himself between it and its victim, prying at it, chopping at it, forcing it back, back. Slowly, steadily, with every ounce of elemental hradani stubbornness. Inch by inch, he clawed at its smothering shroud and peeled it back.

And as he did, as it slowly and spitefully yielded to his attack, he became aware of something else. He *felt* the filly. There was no other way to describe it. The courser was there, in the hollow of his mind's eye, like some exquisite equestrian sculpture emerging perfect and unflawed from a thick, noisome fog. It was the filly as she would have been—*should* have been—in all the glory of her maturity. Unscarred, unwounded, powerful and magnificent, with the wind itself in her hooves and the power of the Wind Plain's summer thunder in her heart.

He'd never seen, never imagined, such perfect balance and heart, such a splendor of matchless strength and indomitable spirit, in any living creature, and he reached out to it. He wrapped it in that silently seething hurricane of light, and as he did, something flowed through him. It was like a braided cable of lightning, reaching through him as he became a conduit for the touch of Tomanāk Himself. And yet, there was more even than godhood in that outpouring. There was also Bahzell Bahnakson, his own spirit, his own will, a giving of himself—of all that he was and knew and believed and hoped to become. It joined the tide of power, taking with it that essence of the filly, demanding that it be restored to her, *making* it real.

The vision snapped into perfect, impossibly intense focus in his heart and mind, and for just an instant, he, the filly, and Tomanāk were one.

It was an instant that could not last. No mortal—not even a courser, or a champion of Tomanāk—could endure that intensity more than momentarily. They fused . . . and then they flashed apart once more, severed into their separate selves, shaken and grieving for the splendor that had been, and yet joyous as they recognized the strength they had shared and the differences which made each of them unique and in his or her own way equally magnificent.

Bahzell staggered back a half-pace and stared at the filly. Not even that cascade of healing energy could undo all the damage she'd suffered. The eye she had lost, was lost. The ear she had lost would never return. But the gaping wounds, the suppurating gouges—those had vanished. Torn muscle was whole once more, rent hide was restored . . . and the poison corrupting from within had vanished.

They stared at one another, no longer joined, yet

both aware that so deep a fusion could never be fully sundered, either. The filly gazed wonderingly upon the enemy who had given her back life, and more than life, and Bahzell met her gaze with a mind full of memories of thundering hooves, of muscles bunching and springing, of manes and tails streaming in the wind, and the high, wild passion of the gallop. He reached out, touching her muzzle, feeling the warmth and the rough, silken softness, and she leaned forward, pressing her nose gently, so very gently, against his chest.

"Well done, Bahzell." The voice came from everywhere and nowhere. It rumbled with the hooves of a thousand coursers thundering across the Wind Plain, and it throbbed with the rolling crash of distant thunder exploding across autumn skies, and yet it was soft, almost gentle.

"Well done, My Sword," the voice of Tomanāk repeated, and throughout the stable, men went to their knees, staring in awe at the champion and courser. "Now you know the cure," Tomanāk continued. "But the cure is not the only answer. Be ready, Bahzell, and be warned. This foe is no mere demon. This foe can slay not simply your body, but your soul. Are you prepared to face that threat to prevent what happened to Storm Daughter's herd from claiming still more victims?"

Bahzell heard the warning and tasted its truth. His god was the God of Justice and of Truth, as well as the God of War, and He did not lie. And the choice of whether or not to face that danger was his own. It was Bahzell Bahnakson's. And because it was, and because of who Bahzell Bahnakson was, it was really no choice at all.

He looked once more into the filly's—into Storm Daughter's—single eye, and let his deity's question roll through him until its echoes had settled into his bones. And then he answered it.

"Aye," he said, in a voice of quiet, hammered iron, "I am that."

Chapter Twenty-Four

Garlahna, Leeana decided, had a pronounced gift for apt description.

"Lots worse" than Erlis had made it sound was *exactly* how her first day had been.

The thought took almost more energy than she had as she dragged herself out of the kitchen. The sun had set over an hour ago, but she'd been up since at least an hour before dawn. And she didn't believe she'd sat down for more than five minutes in a row all day long. Well, maybe with Lanitha. But it still didn't *feel* as if she had.

Yesterday had been bad enough, but today had set a new record.

Garlahna had led Leeana about Kalatha yesterday afternoon like some sort of fresh exhibit in a freak show. Not that the older war maid had treated her like a freak or done anything but her very best to make Leeana feel welcome. Yet that hadn't kept Leeana from realizing that it wasn't just her imagination when she thought that other eyes watched closely. She and Garlahna had found themselves in a bubble of moving silence, surrounded by people—almost all of them women, though no more than half of them wore the chari and yathu—who watched them with almost frightening intensity.

Leeana knew where it had come from, of course. Mayor Yalith had put it into words during their interview, but she hadn't really needed the mayor to do so. Of course her very presence here in Kalatha had to be seen as a threat. She might be certain that the parents and family she'd fled wouldn't hold her actions against the war maids in general or Kalatha in particular, but there was no way the other inhabitants of Kalatha could share her assurance. They had to be wondering how her choice to come here would affect Baron Tellian's decisions if it finally came to a showdown between them and one of his vassals. And at least some of them had to be wondering what could possibly have possessed the daughter of the man who was arguably the most powerful noble of the entire Kingdom to flee to join them. Why would she have given up the wealth, the prestige? The power of a father whose rank would have protected her from the things which had driven *them* into flight? What had he done to her to make her flee from him? What could have made her hate him that much?

She'd wanted to turn around and scream at them. To tell them they were wrong to worry about her father's reaction and fools to believe for one instant that he'd ever hurt her. To shout that she'd run away from Hill Guard not because she hated her parents, but because she loved them so much. But that would only have made things worse—or convinced them she was insane. And so, like Garlahna, she'd pretended not to notice the way they stared or their whispered speculations.

She doubted that she'd fooled very many of them.

She certainly hadn't fooled Garlahna. Her mentor had never commented directly upon the watching eyes, but she'd taken the opportunity to raise her voice in conversation with Leeana from time to time and "let slip" a few, pithy observations about small-minded, small-town gossip-mongers and people with nothing better to do with their time than make idiots out of themselves by gawking at other perfectly ordinary people or events. At least some of the watchers had taken Garlahna's none-too-subtle hints and gone off to find other things to do. Most of them hadn't, but Leeana had appreciated the other young woman's efforts.

Their first stop had been Administration, located in the Town Hall, on the opposite side of the building from Mayor Yalith's office. Leeana had been a bit surprised by the quiet, orderly efficiency of the office. She shouldn't have been, she told herself, but it appeared that, despite herself, she'd absorbed more of the traditional prejudice against the war maids on a subconscious level than she'd thought. The sight of the orderly rows of filing cabinets, each drawer neatly tabbed and filled with folders or note cards, had astounded her.

Baron Tellian was one of the most progressive members of the Sothōii nobility, and he had only begun the transition from the old, cumbersome scrolls on which all important documents had "traditionally" been stored. It was an awkward proposition for him, given how many of his riding's original documents were on those same old-fashioned scrolls, but he was determined to change over as much of his record-keeping and administration as possible. The original idea had come from the Empire of the Axe, like so many administrative reforms, but he'd recognized its manifold advantages as soon as he saw them.

Yet Kalatha must have completed the same process he was only just beginning at least several years ago. Leeana had never expected that. On the other hand, she'd reminded herself, Kalatha had many fewer records and carried far less of an administrative burden than her father's responsibilities entailed. No doubt it had been enormously easier for such a small town, with such a minuscule jurisdiction, to make the transition.

She'd been just a bit shocked at how spitefully she'd told herself that. The strength of her need to "defend" her father by denigrating anyone who'd accomplished a similar task sooner than he had astonished her. It had also made her feel more than a little bit ashamed of herself, but she'd managed to shake that emotion off by the time

Garlahna hauled her in front of Dalthys Hallafressa, the Town Administrator.

"No, not the Mayor," Dalthys had informed her gruffly. Leeana had blinked, surprised by the Administrator's response to the question she hadn't asked. Dalthys, a heavyset woman in her late thirties or early forties, with graying brown hair, had given her a weary yet somehow conspiratorial smile.

"Mayor Yalith has the honor and dubious pleasure of *governing* Kalatha," Dalthys explained. "I only run it. You might think of it as if she were, oh, a baron, say, and I were her seneschal." Her brown eyes had glinted with amusement at Leeana's expression. "Put another way, she has to take all the political headaches, and I get to get on with the everyday business of executing policy. Does that make sense?"

"Uh, yes—yes, Ma'am, it does."

"No need for 'ma'ams,' my girl," Dalthys had told her with a slight frown. "We don't talk to each other that way, and we don't bow and scrape, either. Job titles or given names—or military ranks, for the Guard—work just fine for any war maid," she'd half-growled.

"Yes, Ma—" Leeana had blushed, but she'd also managed to stop herself in time, and Dalthys had snorted.

"Not trying to bite your head off, Leeana," she'd said more gently. "As a matter of fact, the fact that you—" meaning, Leeana had realized, "someone from your background," although Dalthys had been too tactful to put it into so many words "—feel that we incorrigible war maids deserve to be addressed courteously just indicates that you were well brought up. But it's best to get into the proper habits of thought from the outset, don't you think?"

"Yes, Administrator Dalthys."

"Good! I can always spot the smart ones. They're the ones who agree with me!" Dalthys had chuckled, and Leeana had smiled at her.

"All right, all right," Dalthys had said then, opening a huge ledger and frowning at the pages. "We need to find you a room."

"Excuse me, Dalthys," Garlahna had said.

"Yes?" Dalthys had looked up, over the top edge of the ledger, to fix Garlahna with her sharp eyes.

"At least for now, Erlis would like Leeana to room near me. I'm her assigned mentor, and since she's here on a probationary basis, well—"

She'd shrugged, and Dalthys had nodded, slowly at first, then more rapidly.

"That makes sense," she'd agreed, and looked back down at her ledger, flipping pages. Then she'd stopped and studied a column of entries. "I have one room—it's technically a double, but there's no one else assigned to it right now—three doors down the hall from yours, Garlahna," she'd said after a moment. "Is that close enough?"

"That will be fine!" Garlahna had agreed, and Dalthys had looked back at Leeana.

"Most of the people in Kalatha own their own homes, or rent, just like in any other town," she'd explained, "but any war maid is entitled under the charter to one full year of free housing and meals when she first joins us. For someone like you, Leeana, who has to serve a probationary period first, that's extended to a year and a half. And we also try to look after our own people if they find themselves unable to pay their own way through no fault of their own, of course." She'd shrugged. "At any rate, the town owns several dormitories where that free housing is provided. In addition, we rent rooms in the dormitories at what I like to think are very reasonable rates for war maids who've used up their free months. That's what Garlahna's been doing for several years now."

Leeana had nodded her thanks for the explanation, and Dalthys had chuckled.

"Don't get to feeling too grateful for your room till you see it," the administrator advised her. "It's adequate, but not all that huge. Although, now that I think about it, the fact that we're giving you a double with no roommate will tend to offset that somewhat. But however 'free' it may technically be, I assure you that you'll do more than enough work to compensate us for our generosity."

"I understand . . . Dalthys," Leeana had said with a wry smile.

"Well," Dalthys had said with a slow smile, "if you don't now, you will after your first night working in the dining hall!"

She'd chuckled again, then found the key to Leeana's new room and shooed both young women out of her office.

The next stop had been Housekeeping.

Ermath Balcarafressa, who held the title of Housekeeper, was like no "housekeeper" Leeana had ever met. Leeana rather doubted that Ermath had done any manual labor in years, because hers was an administrative title, like Dalthys'. "Housekeeping" was apparently one of Kalatha's larger municipal divisions, with responsibility for a wide range of maintenance, cleaning, and service duties—including the dining hall.

It had been apparent that Ermath discharged her duties efficiently, but Leeana had been unable to warm to her as she had to Dalthys. Physically, Ermath was the antithesis of the Town Administrator in many ways. She was much older, with hair so white it was probably painful to the eye in direct sunlight, and thin as a rail. She was also sharp featured, and had a tongue to match, with little of Dalthys' lurking humor.

"So, you're the one," she'd said as soon as Garlahna delivered Leeana to her office.

Leeana had obviously looked more taken aback then she'd meant to, and Ermath had laughed. It sounded more like a cackle than a laugh, especially compared to Dalthys' warm chuckle.

"The one all the fuss is over, girl!" the Housekeeper had told her. "Lillinara! There hasn't been this much excitement over a new candidate in— Well, in as long as *I* can remember!" She'd cackled again. "*This*'ll hit that bastard Trisu right where he lives. Don't you think for a minute it won't!"

Leeana hadn't had any notion of how to react, so she'd watched Garlahna from the corner of her eye and taken her cue from her mentor's lack of expression. Since she was the one actually talking to Ermath (or, at least, being talked to *by* Ermath), she'd settled for nodding pleasantly and saying as little as she possibly could in response to the Housekeeper's comments and questions. It hadn't actually taken very long, but it had seemed *much* longer, before they got out of Ermath's office with the required vouchers for bed linens, towels, washcloths, and the one year's worth of clothing the charter required the town to provide to any new war maid.

At least Leeana had grown up accustomed to being measured, poked, and prodded by dressmakers and seamstresses. That had helped at their next stop, when Garlahna delivered her into the hands of Johlana Ermathfressa.

Johlana's face would have made it obvious she was the Housekeeper's daughter even without her war maid matronym. But she was no more than half her mother's age, and the bright, humorous intelligence behind her eyes softened her sharp features remarkably. Leeana had been grateful for the difference between mother and daughter as Johlana discussed her wardrobe needs with a cheerfully earthy pragmatism that carried over into things like monthly cycle choices, and from there to homilies about sex, contraceptive techniques, and young women away from watchful families for the first time, even as she measured busily away. She'd seemed mightily amused by Leeana's obvious reservations about the chari and yathu she was expected to wear, but she'd also taken pity upon her.

"Oh, for Lillinara's sake—you won't be expected to wear them *all the time*, Leeana!" she'd scolded. "I know. I know! Scandalous—simply *scandalous*!—until you get used to them. But you'll find they're more practical than you might think just yet. And, when you're not 'in uniform' for physical training or some sort of heavy labor, you can wear whatever you want. In fact, we'll actually provide you with a couple of pairs of trousers and shirts or smocks in the colors you'd prefer. And once you find a way to earn a kormak here or there—and all of our girls do that eventually, don't they, Garlahna?—you can spend them on whatever you want. Including something nice to wear. We may be war maids, but we're still females, too. Trust me, there's *always* a market for pretties of one sort or another here in Kalatha!"

Garlahna had nodded in enthusiastic agreement, and Leeana had smiled. Then Johlana had gathered up her jotted-down notes on Leeana's measurements and needs.

"You're a tall thing," she'd observed. "Good thing charis and yathus are fairly easy to fit!" She'd shaken her head. "The biggest problem's going to be lacing a yathu tight enough until you fill out, girl! At least holding the chari up won't be a problem. Good breeders run in your family?"

Leeana had turned an interesting shade of red—again—at about that point, and Johlana had laughed.

"Don't pay me any attention, Leeana—no one else does, that's for sure! Just run along now. I'll have something for you to face Erlis in tomorrow morning."

She'd made waving motions with both hands, and Garlahna and Leeana had made a hasty escape.

Leeana had been astonished as they emerged from Johlana's office to discover that the sun had already set. But her surprise had faded quickly as she realized just how tired she was. She and Kaeritha had ridden hard all morning to reach Kalatha, and she hadn't really stopped moving from the moment she dismounted here. None of which even considered the sheer emotional stress of all she'd been through in the last twelve hours or so. "Worn out" was a pale way to describe her physical condition, and she'd wanted to weep in sheer exhaustion as she realized she and Garlahna still had to drag her bed linens to her assigned room and make up her bed before she could tumble into it.

She'd concluded later that Garlahna had known exactly how she felt, but her mentor had allowed no sign of that awareness to color her voice or her manner. She'd moved briskly along, simply *assuming* that Leeana would keep trotting along at her side, and because Garlahna had assumed that, Leeana had discovered she had no choice but to meet her mentor's expectations.

Somehow, she'd managed—with a lot more help from

Garlahna than she suspected a "mentor" was supposed to provide—to get her room more or less ready for occupancy. But then Garlahna had refused to allow her to collapse across the thin, hard mattress of the narrowest bed she had ever contemplated sleeping in. Instead, she'd marched a staggeringly tired Leeana to the meal hall, sat her down on one of the benches, and bullied one of the kitchen workers into providing a huge bowl of thick, delicious vegetable soup despite the lateness of the hour. Leeana had never tasted anything so wonderful in her entire life . . . she only wished she'd been awake enough to remember it later.

Things hadn't gotten any better the next morning.

Garlahna turned out to be one of those disgusting people who were bright and cheerful the instant they got out of bed. Leeana had nothing against mornings, but she usually preferred to at least let the sun get up before she did. Garlahna, however, had rousted her out of bed over an hour before sunrise—and *not* with the welcoming cup of hot chocolate Marthya would have brought her—and helped her into the new garments one of Johlana's minions had deposited outside Leeana's door during the night.

There was quite a difference, Leeana had discovered, between seeing the chari and yathu on someone else, or even worrying about how they would feel on her, and actually finding herself dressed—if that wasn't too strong a verb—in them for the first time. She'd been certain she was about to fall right back out of them! And despite the fact that she was far less bountifully provided for by nature then Garlahna, she'd been appalled by the amount of cleavage that showed once the yathu was laced snugly—*very* snugly—into place. If its designed function was to support her bosom during physical exertion, it was admirably fitted to the job, she'd decided. In fact, she'd rather thought that one of her father's steel breastplates had to have more flex to it. She wasn't quite certain how something could be simultaneously so confining and so humiliatingly revealing, but the yathu had managed just fine.

Not that the chari had been any better! The amount of leg it showed was bad enough, and she'd made a firm mental note to be *very* careful how she sat down in it. But she hadn't realized quite how low on the hips it sat, either, and the notion of displaying her navel for the entire world to see had not been a comfortable fit for the girl who had been the daughter of the Baron of Balthar. As for how her *mother* would have reacted to the sight—!

And it had been *cold*! The least they could have done was to provide her with shoes, she'd thought plaintively as Garlahna urged her out into the windy predawn darkness. She'd shivered convulsively as the chill breeze nipped at all that conveniently exposed skin, but that had been little more than a minor inconvenience compared to the wet, muddy, occasionally gravel-strewn ground under her bare feet.

"My feet are *freezing*!" she'd whispered to Garlahna.

"Hah! Only your feet?" Garlahna had laughed. "Sweetheart, *I* came to Kalatha in early winter. I froze my sweet young arse off—not to mention something a bit higher!"

"You would have to mention that!" Leeana had groaned, reaching down to tug uselessly at her chari's hem as another cold breeze blew up it. She was accustomed to long skirts or trousers, and the predawn wind's chilly kisses on places it had no business kissing made her wish desperately that she was wearing them now.

"Oh, stop whining!" Garlahna's cheerful snort had robbed the words of any offense. "I bet you don't even have icicles down there yet!"

"No, but they're forming nicely. And why can't I even wear *shoes*?" Leeana had moaned, too miserable, for the moment at least, to remember her aristocratic pride.

"Anything that doesn't kill you will only make you stronger," Garlahna had replied with an oddly sympathetic chuckle. "That's what they told *me*, anyway! And even if it weren't true, it's a matter of tradition." She'd shrugged. "Personally, I always figured it was just our way of proving how much tougher than mere men we are."

"I'd rather have warm feet and let them sneer at me for being weak," Leeana had muttered back.

"Hush!" Garlahna had said, and Leeana had looked up to discover that they had just joined at least forty or fifty other war maids.

At first, she'd assumed that mandatory morning calisthenics for everyone must be part of the same bizarre, self-mortifying philosophy which had denied her shoes. She certainly couldn't think of any other reason for so many women, of all ages—she even saw Dalthys and Johlana among them—to be standing around semi-naked and barefooted in the icy predawn wind! It had taken her several shivering minutes of listening to scraps of other conversations to discover that most of them had *chosen* to be there. That they actually *enjoyed* these "brisk" morning workouts together.

At that moment, Leeana had begun to seriously consider the possibility that all of those who insisted any woman had to be mad to choose to be a war maid were right.

Unfortunately, unlike the lunatics who'd been there voluntarily, Leeana had had no choice. Nor, she'd discovered, had Garlahna. It didn't seem to bother the other young woman particularly, but as Leeana's "mentor," she was expected to lead by example. Leeana suspected that it would have bothered *her* a great deal, if their roles had been reversed.

She'd still been standing there, shivering as she looked woebegonely about herself in the gray half-light, when Erlis and another, younger, war maid with chestnut hair had come bounding energetically up. Erlis had a whistle, which she had immediately begun to blow with revolting vigor, and thus had begun what was quite possibly the most hideous single morning of Leeana Hanathafressa's life.

Leeana had always been an active girl. She'd ridden virtually every day of her life, from the time she could walk. She'd been an energetic hiker, and she and her maids had enjoyed swimming—at least when it was warm enough for the water not to turn them blue the instant they jumped into it. But she'd never been particularly interested in exercise for exercise's own sake. For her, physical exertion had been a way to get from one point to another, or a secondary cost of doing something that she enjoyed.

Erlis obviously came from a completely different tradition. It had been the first time Leeana had ever encountered a carefully planned exercise regimen, and she'd hated it. And not just because she'd been cold, miserable, and hungry, either. Leeana was accustomed to being *good* at what she did. She most emphatically was *not* accustomed to being clumsy or inept, and she'd felt both of those things as she attempted to emulate the war maids around her.

It had lasted for a seeming eternity, but that had turned out to be just long enough to prepare her for an even more humiliating experience. At least the physical exertion had warmed her up, and it had also loosened up her muscles. Which was fortunate, since Erlis and the chestnut-haired woman, who turned out to be Ravlahn Thregafressa, had descended upon her for the promised "evaluation of her general physical skills."

By the time their exam—finally—came to a close, Leeana had concluded that she *had* no "general physical skills." She'd done her best, and at least her examiners had maintained grave, nonjudgmental façades as she strove to meet their demands. But it had been evident to her that her life as an indolent aristocrat had left her woefully underequipped with the physical skills a war maid required. The only area in which she'd felt she'd performed with something approaching adequacy had been the sprints they required of her. She supposed that she'd done at least semi-adequately in the longer runs, as well, but that was about the best she could say.

At least they'd released her in the end and allowed her to stagger off under Garlahna's guidance, limping on her bruised-feeling, bare feet, to the mess hall for breakfast. Back home in Balthar, Leeana had normally made do with hot chocolate or tea, a croissant or two, butter, some honey, perhaps, and a few pieces of fruit, when it was in season. But here in Kalatha, she'd found herself devouring a third huge bowl of honey-laced porridge, and then wondering where she could find just a little bit more of it for dessert. To her amazement, she'd actually felt almost human again when she finished.

Her relief had been brief, however. They'd given her a half-hour, or so, for breakfast to settle, and then Garlahna—that traitor she'd *thought* was becoming her friend—had borne her off to face Hundred Ravlahn in the training salle. The only real blessing had been that there'd been no one there besides Garlahna and Ravlahn to witness her fresh inadequacy.

It hadn't really been her fault, and she'd known it. She'd never been trained with a bow, although she was an excellent shot with the light crossbows with which Sothōii noblewomen hunted birds and small game. And however radical Tellian Bowmaster might have been, it would never have crossed his mind to have his daughter trained in swordsmanship, or in the most effective way to open someone's belly with a dagger. Nor, for that matter, had it ever occurred to him to teach his only child the finer points of using a garrotte, or throwing a knife or throwing stars.

Her abilities when it came to hand-to-hand combat without weapons had been even more rudimentary—not to say laughable—than her clumsy efforts with the various wooden training weapons with which Ravlahn had provided her. The one thing Leeana had been able to say with a certain forlorn pride at the end of two and a half grueling hours, was that she'd never stopped trying. Her efforts might simply have served to demonstrate that she was about as dangerous to another human being as a newborn kitten, but at least she'd *tried*. And, she thought miserably, she'd ended up with the bruises, the bloody nose, and the split lip to prove it, too.

She'd hobbled off to the mess hall, still under Garlahna's escort, in time for lunch. Which, she'd discovered, she'd needed at least as badly as she had breakfast. She'd ravened her way through three heaping servings of buttered potatoes, baked beans, and fried chicken and been wondering wistfully if she quite dared to ask for a *fourth* helping of the potatoes, when a youngish-looking woman in a neat gray gown came over to her and Garlahna.

"Leeana?"

"Yes?" Leeana had looked up from her mostly empty plate suspiciously, her spoon still clutched in her hand, and something about her expression had made the other woman smile.

"I'm Lanitha," she'd said.

"Oh." Leeana had lowered her spoon. "The archivist?"

"That's one way to put it," Lanitha had agreed. "Personally, I prefer 'librarian,' but I suppose my duties do make archivist a better fit, these days." She'd grimaced. "I'm also, however, the principal of our town school here in Kalatha."

"Oh," Leeana had said in a tone she'd belatedly realized might have been described as less than wildly enthusiastic.

"I see you've been having an . . . interesting day," Lanitha had observed, her voice wavering oddly while she tried not to smile. "I'll try not to make things any more difficult for you than I have to. But I do need to get some feel for your scholastic abilities."

Leeana had hovered on the brink of asking her why, but she'd suppressed the question in time. She'd had no doubt she would discover the answer, probably sooner than she wanted to.

"If you're finished eating," Lanitha had continued in a tone which, for all its politeness, had informed Leeana that she *was* finished eating, "why don't you—and Garlahna, of course—come along with me? This shouldn't take more than two or three hours."

"Of course," Leeana had replied, with only a trace of glumness. Then she'd put her spoon down, given it a regretful pat, and followed Lanitha out of the mess hall.

Lanitha had been almost correct. In fact, her estimate of the time required had been only about an hour short. By the end of her examination, Leeana had felt as exhausted mentally as she'd already been physically, but at least this time she'd felt reasonably confident that she'd acquitted herself well. Her father might not have seen any reason to teach her to lop the heads off of enemies, but he and her mother had both actively aided and abetted her in the pursuit of an intellectual curiosity other nobles might have found most unbecoming in a mere daughter. Leeana spoke six languages—four of them fluently—and could read and write in two more. She had a formidable education in geography, history, and literature, and a practical knowledge of politics—at least as practiced at the highest level of the Kingdom—which was quite astounding in anyone her age, and especially in a daughter.

In fact, the main reason Lanitha's original time estimate had proved overly optimistic was that the archivist/teacher had become too interested in discussing things with the subject of her examination. In the end, she'd sent Leeana back off to the dining hall with Garlahna with the warning that she intended to request at least an hour or two of Leeana's time each afternoon as an assistant instructor.

Any temptation towards a swelled head which Leeana might have taken away with her had evaporated like snow in summer when she and Garlahna arrived almost twenty minutes late for her shift in the kitchen. The excuse that Lanitha had kept her longer than anticipated had done remarkably little to placate the head cook's ire, and neither had the fact that Leeana had effectively no kitchen skills at all. It wasn't exactly Leeana's fault, but she hadn't felt like explaining that she hadn't acquired those skills because her parents had employed others to perform those menial tasks. Partly because she'd had a shrewd suspicion that the cook would not have responded well to the suggestion that her own skills were "menial" ones. But even more because Leeana had agreed that it was time she acquired them.

That willingness to dig right in—enthusiastically, however ineptly—had turned the trick. She'd wondered if perhaps part of the cook's prickliness had resulted from an expectation that someone who'd been so nobly born *would* have dismissed her assigned duties as beneath her. It had seemed as if some of the other war maids assigned to Leeana's work crew had cherished some of the same suspicions, but if they had, their reservations had thawed quickly as her willingness sank in. She'd been restricted by her ignorance to more or less unskilled labor, but most of her fellow workers had paused in passing at least once to drop some little hint or encouragement upon her.

That had helped, but by the time supper was finished, the tables were cleared and scrubbed, the pots and pans and dishes were washed, and the cooking utensils had been laid out in preparation for the breakfast crews, she'd been literally stumbling with exhaustion.

She'd thought her ride from Balthar to Kalatha had been exhausting, and no doubt it had been. But the fatigue she'd felt then, even after that first hideous, sleepless night in the rain, was as nothing compared to what she felt now. She knew with absolute certainty that she had never been this tired in her entire life.

She staggered out of the mess hall towards the dormitory, then shambled to a halt as she realized someone was standing in front of her. It took her a moment or two to focus, then she straightened her aching back as she recognized Mayor Yalith by the light of the lanterns above the mess hall entrance.

"I won't keep you long, Leeana," the mayor said. She smiled, and her voice was gently compassionate and understanding. "I know all you really want to do at this moment is to go fall on your nose and stay there for as long as we'll let you. It may be cold comfort, but just about every war maid has been where you are right now, and most of us survived the experience.

"I just wanted to tell you three things before you go collapse.

"First, I feel confident that you're convinced you were an absolute and utter failure when Erlis and Ravlahn examined you today. Well, you weren't." Leeana blinked in fatigue-foggy disbelief, and Yalith smiled again. "Oh, I won't say you thrilled them with your incredible prowess.

But given your complete lack of training, you actually performed quite well. And both Erlis and Ravlahn feel you have considerable native ability, which they confidently expect to be able to nurture.

"Second, Lanitha was *very* impressed by both your native intelligence and the education you've already received. There are several places where you can probably still use a little polishing, but for the most part, you're already as well qualified—from the perspective of your knowledge, at least—to teach as any of our present teachers. Do try not to let that go to your head, dear," the mayor added with a small chuckle.

"And, third," she said after a moment, in a noticeably different voice, "something happened yesterday which, to the best of my knowledge, has never happened before. Baron Tellian—" even now she did not permit herself the words "your father," and Leeana's eyes fell as she felt a pang of pain "—left something for you."

Leeana looked back up into the mayor's face.

"He left you the title to your horse, Leeana," Yalith said quietly.

Leeana blinked, unable to understand for a moment, but then her heart leapt and incredulous joy blossomed across her exhausted face.

"It's a princely gift," the mayor continued. "To be perfectly honest, I was tempted to refuse it, because no one else in Kalatha has ever so much as ridden a horse half, or even a quarter, as good as that one, much less *owned* one. There's an enormous amount of room for potential resentment in the gift he chose to bestow upon you, Leeana. I want you to be aware of that. But I didn't refuse it in the end for two reasons. First, and I'd like to think most important, was the fact that I had no legal right to refuse it in someone else's name, and I wasn't prepared to violate the law. But, second, was the fact that Dame Kaeritha argued very strongly on your behalf. It speaks well of anyone that a champion of Tomanāk should speak so forcefully on her behalf, and I think I've seen enough of Dame Kaeritha by now to know that however much she might like you, she would never have argued your case so vehemently if she hadn't believed you truly deserved it."

"Oh, thank you—*thank you*, Mayor Yalith!" Leeana whispered, tears spangling her vision.

"*I* didn't do anything," Yalith replied. "And don't think that this won't make problems of its own for you, even if—as I don't expect for a moment—you should be so fortunate as to find that no one else in Kalatha resents your good luck. Baron Tellian left sufficient funds, also as a gift for you, to pay for your horse's feed for at least several months. He did *not*—at Dame Kaeritha's urging, I might add—leave funds to pay its stable fees. *You* will have to come up with some way to cover those expenses yourself."

Leeana looked at her, and Yalith shrugged.

"Dame Kaeritha was there when I worried aloud about possible resentment. She said, and I think she was right, that if you have to work harder and longer than anyone else in Kalatha to keep him, it should go a long way towards defusing the inevitable resentment. And I imagine it will also make you appreciate the Baron's gift even more."

She paused, her gaze level as she looked into Leeana's face.

"Do you understand all of that, Leeana?"

"Yes, Mayor Yalith. I understand," the exhausted young woman replied, jade-green eyes still glistening with tears of joy.

"I believe you do," the mayor said, and nodded in dismissal. She turned away herself, then paused and looked back over her shoulder.

"You know," she observed, "I'm not sure that it's one I'd like to have received myself, but you could look upon Dame Kaeritha's insistence that you earn your horse's stabling fees as a rather profound sort of compliment, Leeana."

Leeana blinked at her, and Yalith chuckled.

"Of course it is! She wouldn't have wanted you to have the horse in the first place if she hadn't felt you deserved it . . . and she obviously has immense faith in you. She must! If she didn't, she never would have wished that much extra exhaustion off on you."

She smiled.

"Goodnight, Leeana. Get some sleep . . . you'll need it."

Chapter Twenty-Five

It was a strange fog.

It hung like a heavy, motionless curtain over the shallow valley between two isolated hills, frozen in place, yet with an odd, internal swirling movement. Although the spring night was cool, the fog was chill as ice and thick as death, and it ignored the stiff breeze that whispered across the endless miles of grass, as if no mere wind could touch it.

There was no moon, and jewellike stars glittered and gleamed in a velvet sky clearer than crystal. Yet for all their beauty, their light seemed to sink into the fog, absorbed and deadened . . . devoured.

The night sounds of the Wind Plain—the sighing song of wind, the counterpointing songs and hums of insects, the distant noise of a small stream chuckling to itself in the dark, the shrill squeaks of bats, and the occasional cry of some nocturnal bird—flowed over the grasslands. But all stopped short at the edge of the fog. None penetrated it, or crossed the unnatural barrier it erected.

Then new sounds added themselves. Not loud ones. Hooves thudding into the soft earth made little more noise than the creak of saddle leather, or the jingle of a bridle.

A single rider came cantering out of the night, straight towards the eerie wall of fog. But the horseman slowed as he neared it. Not because he chose to, but because his mount balked. The horse slowed, tossing its head, then turned sideways. It fought the reins, ears flat, shaking its head and sunfishing while it whistled its protest.

The rider swore and wrenched his mount's head back around, trying to force it onward, but the horse planted its hooves, and when he drove in his spurs, it bucked wildly.

The rider was no Sothōii. That much was obvious when he parted company with his saddle and went flying over the horse's head. Yet however clumsy he might have been on horseback, he displayed an unnatural agility as he flew through the air. He tucked and rolled somehow in midair, twisting his body about, and landed on his booted feet with an impossible lightness. He didn't even stumble, and his right hand flashed up and caught the bridle cheek strap before the startled horse could flinch away from him. There was a dreadful strength in that hand, and the horse whistled in panic, fighting vainly to wrench away from it. But the other hand came up, reaching not for the bridle, but for the horse's throat. It closed, squeezing with that same hideous strength, and the horse's whistle became a strangled sound of terror as it was pulled remorselessly to its knees.

A sound came from the dismounted rider then—a snarling, hungry sound, as animallike as any noise the horse had made, but uglier, more predatory—and his eyes blazed with green fire. The horse's struggles began to weaken, and the rider's snarl took on a vicious note of triumph.

"Cease."

The single word came from the fog bank behind the rider. It was not really very loud, yet it echoed and reechoed with irresistible power, and the other sounds of the night seemed to stop instantly, as if terrified into silence by that infinitely cold, infinitely cruel voice.

The rider straightened, snatching his strangling left hand away from the semiconscious horse's throat, and whirled to face the fog.

"Fool," the voice said, and it was filled with bottomless contempt. *"It is ten miles and more to the nearest habitation. If you wish to walk that far, then finish what you were doing."*

The rider seemed to hover on the brink of saying something in reply, but then he thought better of it.

"Wiser, far wiser, so," the voice said. *"Now come. I will see to it that your beast remains where it is."*

The rider obeyed without so much as a backward glance at the horse which was feebly attempting to climb back to its feet behind him.

He walked into the opaque, blinding fog with the confident stride of one who could see perfectly . . . and as if the charnel stench which infused it did not bother him at all. The stench grew steadily stronger as he moved deeper into it, and then he stepped out of the fog, crossing a dividing line between vapor and clear air as sharp as the line he had crossed to enter it.

If he had believed for an instant that the fog was natural, he would have known better as he stepped out into the wide space it surrounded with its protective barrier. The protected area was at least two hundred yards across, perfectly circular, its air still and calm, and free of any trace of the enveloping mist. The pinprick stars shone down upon it without distortion or obscuration, but for all the clarity of the air, the dreadful stench was stronger and more choking than ever.

A woman—or something shaped like one—stood at the exact center of the circle. She towered above the rider, at least eight feet in height, and clustered about her, like a sea of fur, fangs, and poison-green eyes, lay scores of wolves. They seemed to shift and flow strangely—sometimes wolves, and sometimes crouching, misshapen forms, almost humanoid, but with snouted, pig-like heads and batlike wings folded tight to their spines. Their eyes blazed the same malevolent green the rider's had, regardless of their forms, and that same glare clung to the woman who stood surrounded by them. She wore it as if it were a second skin, and it hung about her like a nimbus of airy ice.

That cloak of dim brilliance illuminated her, despite the moonless night. She stood wrapped in an aura of deadly power and debased beauty. Despite the perfection of her features, despite the long, intricately braided black hair and the exquisite diadem upon her head, there was something about her fit to repulse and terrify any living creature. Something that whispered of violated crypts and the power of corruption. When she turned her head to look at the new arrival, he could see the brilliant green flare of her eyes, like slickly polished ice, and the floating black skulls which were her pupils. They studied him with a cold, dead indifference, and his own head rose. His eyes glowed with a dimmer light than hers, and his nostrils flared hungrily to the scent of death—of long dead flesh rising from an opened grave—as it flowed over him from her like some corrupt perfume.

She and the wolves and not-wolves were not alone. Four other humans (or as "human" as the rider, at any rate) stood dotted about among the wolves, and behind her loomed a herd of shapes. They were indistinct and wavering, those shapes. Impossible for even the rider's unnaturally acute vision to see clearly. But they might almost have been horses—huge horses—standing with hanging heads and ragged manes like an army of slaves.

"*So, you arrive at last, Jerghar,*" she said, and he inclined his head to her in obeisance. His eye-glow dimmed further, banking itself in submission to her greater power.

"I came as rapidly as I could, Milady," he said, his voice fawning.

"*So I already knew . . . and because I did, and because you have arrived in time, however barely, despite your tardiness, you will continue to survive and serve Me.*"

Jerghar bowed more deeply still, saying nothing, but he knew she sensed what would have been the quicker, harder throbbing of a living man's pulse.

"I exist only to obey, Milady," he said.

"*Yes, you do,*" she agreed. "*Only to obey and to feed . . . or to be fed upon. Now come, join your brothers and sister.*"

Once again, Jerghar obeyed, walking through the ranks of her shardohns like a man wading through a waist-deep swamp. They parted to make way, without a sound, gazing at him with those lambent eyes filled with hate, fear, and hunger, and he passed among them to join the other once-human servants standing about his mistress.

"The trap has sprung," she said, speaking to all of them, *"yet it has closed not upon Tellian, but upon the accursed hradani* Bahzell *and his companion."*

Something went through her listeners. In another time and another place, it might have been called a stir of uneasiness. But only a fool would dare to display uneasiness in the presence of that mistress.

"It was not what We wished for, but it will serve Our purposes well," she told them. *"Brandark's death is worth more even than Tellian's, and Bahzell's is worth more than the destruction of the entire Sothōii Kingdom."*

Jerghar stiffened. He'd known his mistress and her allies were determined to destroy Bahzell, Brandark, and Tellian, but he still didn't know why. Nor could he understand how the death of a single hradani, even one who was the son of Prince Bahnak of Hurgrum and a champion of Tomanāk, could be *that* vital to the triumph of the Dark.

"I know that the prospect of facing a champion of My never sufficiently damned uncle is a frightening one," she continued, and this time Jerghar was astonished, for it was not her way to concern herself with anything so insignificant as her servants' hopes or fears. *"So it should be, for of all Our enemies, he is the most powerful, after Orr himself, and by far the most relentless. But his arrogance will be the downfall of his champions, just as it will one day be his own. He sends them out by ones and twos, bragging to himself about their 'strength,' and their 'courage.' And he restricts himself, as his precious Compact requires, limiting his own power only to that which he may channel through them. It may well make each of them more powerful, more dangerous, but they are only a handful, and you are many—just as he is one, and* We *are many. And where his strength is*

limited only to them, and by the amount of his power each can touch and survive, My strength fills you all, just as your service and the souls upon which you feed strengthen My grip upon this mortal world. He will come to you, this Bahzell, and he will bring with him his friend, and his kinsmen, and you—all of you—" her blazing green eyes swept over the wolves, as well as her once-human servants "*—will fall upon them. You will feed, as you have never fed before, upon the blood and the soul of one of* his *champions, and it will be sweet, and rich beyond your dreams.*"

The seductive power of that cold, hungry voice reached out to them all, entwining them in her power, binding them to her will, and behind her, a wave of hopeless desolation and horror swelled up from the torn and tattered shades which had been coursers.

"*You will serve Me, and in the serving you will find such power as even* you *have never before dreamed might be yours*," Krahana Phrofressa, Lady of the Damned, promised her Servants, and she smiled.

"Is your information certain, Darnas?"

Baron Cassan leaned forward in his chair, his handsome face intent. His study's lamplight picked out the gems on his ringed fingers and gleamed on his golden hair, and the buillon embroidery of his black velvet tunic flickered in the mellow glow when he shifted position. The man before him had dark, thinning hair, brown eyes, and a weathered complexion. In contrast to his lord's elegance, his clothing was plain, durable and practical, but cheap. Indeed, he was almost as nondescript as Varnaythus, but unlike the wizard-priest, Darnas Warshoe had been in Cassan's service for almost nine years. At the moment, he looked rather the worse for wear, unshaven and tired, his boots spattered with mud.

"Aye, Milord Baron," he said wearily. "No one made any great secret of it, and I confirmed the stories myself." He gave his liege lord a tired smile. "I've not forgotten how to mend riding tack, Milord, and there's always need for a few extra sets of hands this time of year. That got me into Hill Guard, and there was plenty of gossip amongst the castle's garrison."

"So Tellian sent *Trianal* to Festian," Cassan mused aloud, leaning back in his chair and crossing his legs. He waved Darnas towards the sideboard, with its wine bottles and gleaming decanters, and his henchman accepted the silent invitation with alacrity. Cassan was never niggardly with those who served him well, and Darnas unhesitatingly poured himself a snifter of outrageously expensive Saramanthan brandy. All the same, Cassan noted with dry amusement, it was a rather *small* snifter.

The baron didn't care. As far as he was concerned, Darnas' report entitled the man to the entire decanter. Of course, precisely what Cassan was going to do with that information remained to be seen.

He gazed into the fire—kindled more for custom and emotional comfort than for need, now that spring was moving steadily towards warmer days and nights—and thought hard.

He'd always anticipated that Tellian would send some sort of assistance to Festian. He almost had to, given the pressure Saratic, Garthan, and Dathian were exerting. But Cassan hadn't really considered the possibility that he might send a youngster like Trianal as his proxy. In some ways, it was a most shrewd move on Tellian's part, but in others . . .

Trianal was young, very young, for such a responsibility. The Bowmasters had a tradition of testing members of their clan young, and from all of Cassan's reports, the cub had acquitted himself well in the face of the opportunities which had already arisen. Yet despite all that, he had a young man's judgment and experience. It would be much easier for a youngster his age, especially one eager to make a good impression and justify his uncle's faith in him, to let enthusiasm or overconfidence lead him into disaster an older, wiser head might have avoided.

Cassan had hoped Tellian might have been concerned enough to personally lead a contingent of his troops to Glanharrow. Or, failing that, that he might have sent that infernal, interfering busybody "Prince Bahzell" as his proxy, given the Gullet's proximity to the area of Dathian's raids. In either of those cases, Darnas' expertise with bow and arbalest might have proven most useful.

In the end, not even Saratic would willingly have launched a personal attack upon the Baron of Balthar. Accidents might have happened, had Tellian insisted (as was his wont) upon leading his men in person, but no mere lord warden would be prepared to risk the killing of one of the Kingdom's four barons. The penalty for an "accident" like that would be . . . extreme, and it was almost certain that King Markhos would dispatch his Crown investigators to look into the death of a great magnate like Tellian.

But that was the reason Cassan had infiltrated Darnas into Saratic's employ. The Lord Warden of Golden Vale thought Darnas was only one more skilled scout. He had no way of knowing that before a certain unfortunate lapse in judgment had led to his fall from grace, Sergeant Warshoe had been an instructor in the King's Own Regiment. Darnas could thread a needle with a horsebow at two hundred yards, and he was almost equally skilled with a steel-bowed arbalest. More importantly, Darnas had no qualms whatsoever about putting a yard-long arrow, or a steel-pointed arbalest quarrel, through any baron ever born if Cassan told him to.

It would have been so neat, Cassan thought wistfully. Everyone would have suspected, accurately enough, that Saratic was the primary instigator of the attacks upon Festian's lord wardenship. But everyone who knew him would also have known he would never intentionally kill Tellian. So the only reasonable conclusion would have been that it truly was an accident. In that case, Cassan's protection of his vassal would probably have been enough to preserve Saratic from fatal consequences. And if that protection had proved inadequate, Saratic would not have been an irreplaceable loss, however useful he might have proved if he survived. Indeed, Cassan would cheerfully have cut the man's throat himself if that was what it took to bring about Tellian's death.

Killing Tellian in what was obviously little more than

a border squabble between minor feuding lord wardens would have decapitated the opposing faction on the Royal Council in a way which could never have pointed the finger of suspicion at Cassan. Even better, Tellian's death would have provoked the very succession crisis in Balthar about which Cassan's proxies and cat's-paws on the Council had been warning everyone for years. And when that happened, those same proxies would be prepared to urge the King to give his royal stamp of approval to Rulth Blackhill's offer for Leeana Bowmaster's hand. Under the circumstances, Cassan had estimated that there were at least three chances in four that Markhos would have agreed to marry the girl off to the Lord Warden of Transhar rather than risk seeing the Balthar succession collapse into uncertainty.

The chances of getting Tellian into the open and killing him there had always been problematical, but the prize was certainly worth making the attempt. And if he couldn't kill Tellian, he'd hoped that Darnas would at least manage to get a clear shot at "Prince Bahzell." Killing *him* off would put an end to the entire grotesque sham created by Tellian's shameful and humiliating "surrender" to the horse-murdering barbarians. It would also prove once and for all that no *hradani* could truly be a champion of Tomanāk, no matter who Bahzell and Wencit had managed to fool and manipulate into accepting such a blasphemous absurdity. And with just a little bit of luck, Bahzell's death might very well have provoked the war Tellian's gutless "surrender" had postponed. It might not be as satisfying as removing Tellian and marrying Balthar's heir conveyant off to one of Cassan's kinsmen and allies—especially one who would be as . . . demanding as Rulth. But ending all threat of a united hradani Kingdom on the flank of the Wind Plain before Prince Bahnak was firmly in control was certainly a worthy goal in its own right.

Yet now it seemed neither of those targets was about to come within range of Darnas' bow or arbalest. Cassan wondered if Tellian had been cunning enough to suspect the full depth of his enemy's plans and hopes. Had he been clever enough to send Trianal on the theory that the youngster would have so much less priority as a target that he would be, in effect, protected? Or, conversely, was Tellian cold-blooded enough to send the young man off *expecting* him to be targeted? Trianal was his nephew, yet any military commander worth his salt knew there were times when a diversion was necessary. And for a diversion to succeed, it had to be tempting enough that it might well draw an attack, which meant that sometimes one had to risk—or even knowingly and deliberately accept—that diversion's sacrifice.

"Tell me, Darnas," Cassan said, emerging from his reverie at last, "what do Tellian's armsmen and minor lords think of Trianal?"

"Well, Milord," Warshoe began with slow, obvious thoughtfulness, "I'd say they think well of him. He's handled himself well enough in the field, given how few chances he's had. And although he's young, most of Tellian's people think he's a shrewd and level head on his shoulders. They certainly prefer him to either of his brothers! Indeed, Milord, and bearing in mind Lord Transhar's offer for Lady Leeana, there's quite a few of Tellian's armsmen who think he ought to have settled the succession question by arranging a marriage between Trianal and his daughter."

"The Council would never have stood for it," Cassan said dismissively. "There's much too close a degree of consanguinity."

"I know that, Milord. And so do Tellian's armsmen. But you asked what they thought of him, and I'd say that wishing Tellian *could* arrange that marriage is a fair indication that they think pretty highly of him."

"Um." Cassan rubbed his lower lip, frowning, then nodded. "You're right," he conceded. "And, truth to tell, if I were Tellian, I might be tempted in the same direction, if I thought for a minute the Council might stand for it. Everything I'd heard suggested that Trianal's a likely lad—what you've just said only confirms it."

He thought some more. As he'd told Darnas, there was no way even Tellian's closest allies on the Council would have supported a marriage between Trianal and

Leeana. But if anything happened to Leeana, and the gods knew illness and accident were no respecters of rank or birth, then Tellian might very well select Trianal as his heir adoptive. That would be well within the accepted framework of law and custom. And an heir adoptive that well thought of by Tellian's vassals would make a formidable opponent. Especially if Tellian had another ten or twenty years in which to train him.

"You've spoken with Lord Saratic and Lord Garthan more recently than I," he said aloud after another lengthy moment of consideration. "How willing do you think they would be to risk a little more escalation?"

"You mean over and beyond what you've discussed with them, Milord? Or over and beyond what you've discussed with *me*?"

"Beyond what you and I have discussed," Cassan replied.

"Well, Milord, I'd say Lord Garthan would have second thoughts, or even third thoughts. Not to put too fine a point upon it, Garthan's not only smarter than Saratic, but he's in it only for what he can do to strengthen his own position. Saratic, on the other hand . . ." Darnas shook his head. "That's a man who's being eaten up inside by hate. He wants Festian dead, and even more than that, he wants 'Prince Bahzell' dead. Truth to tell, I doubt he would have been at all upset, whatever he might have said openly, if I'd had the opportunity for the archery practice we discussed. With Tellian not even there to suffer an accident, I think Saratic would be willing enough to risk killing young Trianal."

"Willing enough to commit some of his own armsmen to the 'raids' on Festian's herds and farms?"

"If they were the right men, Milord—men he could trust both for their ability and for their loyalty and ability to keep their mouths closed—then, yes, I think he would."

"And Dathian?"

"There, I'm not so sure, Milord," Darnas confessed with the ability to admit honest ignorance which made him so valuable. "I've not spoken directly to Lord Dathian, and I can't really say I *know* him at all. If you want my best guess, Milord, I'd say he hates Festian enough to be willing to let someone else across his holding to launch an attack on Festian, or even Trianal, directly. He'd not be willing to risk committing his own men to it, but he'd probably go as far as providing guides through the Bogs for someone else's men." The spy-assassin shrugged. "As I say, that's my best guess, Milord, but it's *only* a guess. I'd not want to think you were basing all your plans on something no more positive than that."

"I understand." Cassan nodded, and wished he had two or three more men whose judgment and ability—and, most importantly, loyalty—he could trust as he trusted Darnas'. But he didn't.

"Very well," he said finally. "Get some rest. I'm afraid I'm putting you back on the road tomorrow—early. I'll be sending written messages to Saratic in our private cipher, but the important ones will be making the trip in your brain, not on paper."

"Understood, Milord." It was Darnas' turn to nod.

"Good. And one other thing, Darnas."

"Aye, Milord?"

"Don't forget to take your bow with you."

Chapter Twenty-Six

Sir Kelthys Lancebearer eased himself in the saddle as Walasfro's steady, inexorable gallop brought them over the final rise and they paused, with the home manor of Warm Springs spread out before them at last. The sun was barely above the eastern horizon, shining down across the towering height of Hope's Bane Glacier far to the north, while morning mist hovered like blue fog across the fields and pastures and the white steam of the springs which gave the manor its name rose in motionless, argent plumes.

Walasfro stood for a moment with his head high, breathing deeply. Not even a courser could maintain the pace he'd set without eventually wearing himself out, and Kelthys could feel the stallion's weariness . . . and his own. Indeed, although Walasfro had been doing all the galloping, Kelthys suspected that he felt more fatigued than the courser did. Unlike Walasfro, no one had done any sorcerous improvement of *his* ancestors; he was merely a mortal human being, like any other. Being chosen as a wind rider didn't change that, and he ached as if his entire body had been beaten with cudgels after their long, exhausting ride. They'd traveled over fifty leagues since receiving the horrifying message from Bahzell and Sir Jahlahan, not including a sixty-mile detour to take the same message to the manor of Bear River. Kelthys had begrudged the extra time, but he could never have justified not spending it, for he'd known that the Bear River courser herd had left its winter pastures and stables earlier that week. Only another courser—like Walasfro—could have located the Bear River herd stallion in the immensity of the Wind Plain and taken him warning.

And, he admitted, looking over his shoulder at the fourteen riderless stallions who had paused behind him and Walasfro, nostrils flaring as they blew and tossed their heads, the reinforcements were welcome. Or, he hoped so, at any rate.

Almost half the Bear River adult stallions—including all of the herd's bachelors—had chosen to accompany them to Warm Springs. He'd expected that they would, and under normal circumstances, such a powerful reinforcement would have been priceless. But although the details in Bahzell's and Jahlahan's message had been sketchy, it was obvious that the Warm Springs herd had been unable to resist whatever had attacked it. Which meant he and Walasfro might have brought the other coursers along only to expose them to a danger they could not match. It was virtually impossible for Kelthys to imagine such a threat, but what had already happened seemed grimly sufficient proof that it could exist.

Yet despite that, he'd known he would never be able to justify not giving them the choice of facing it. That was part of what it meant to be a wind rider. No courser had ever answered to the demand of whip or spur, and there were no reins connected to the ornamental hackamore Walasfro wore. Coursers decided where they would go, and when, as *they* chose, and those privileged to share their lives had no choice but to accept that they had the same right as any human to choose what dangers they would face, what sacrifices they would make, as well.

Kelthys had been a wind rider for over twenty years, and there were times—like today—when he still found it difficult to believe he had ever won Walasfro's brotherhood and love. It was not given to everyone, he knew, to experience the fierce exaltation of galloping across open plains on the back of a Sothōii warhorse. To feel the mighty muscles bunching and exploding with energy, the wind whipping into one's face, the stretch and grace of four hooves at the moment all of them were off the ground at once. To feel one's own muscles merging with the movement, weaving into that wild, exhilarating dance. To know that one was hurtling across the face of Toragan's own realm at speeds as high as thirty miles an hour, or even more.

It was those magical moments when man and horse melded, when they fused into one racing being, which truly created the character of the Sothōii. It accounted for their sense of self-sufficiency, their trust in their own capability—their arrogance, if one wanted to put it that way. For the truth was that the Sothōii knew, beyond any possibility of contradiction, that there were no finer, more deadly cavalry than they in the entire world. And in those moments when their mounts' hooves spurned the earth itself, they experienced a freedom and an exaltation that was almost like a taste of godhood.

Yet even those blessed to know the capabilities of the Wind Plain's superb warhorses could only imagine, and that but dimly, the glory of saddling the wind itself. Of feeling a ton and a half or more of muscle, bone, and wild, unquenchable spirit thundering beneath one. Of knowing that not even a warhorse could outsprint the magnificent, four-legged being who had chosen one as his brother. Or of experiencing that same, wild exhilaration not for the fleeting minutes of a warhorse's endurance, but literally for hours at a time. Of being able to actually touch the thoughts of another living, breathing being, and to know beyond a shadow of a doubt that he would die at your side, defending you as you would defend him.

No creature born solely of nature could have matched that incredible performance, but the coursers could, and as many as one in ten of them might bond with a human rider. And those wind riders were the elite of the Sothōii cavalry—paired mounts and riders who *truly* fused into single beings, faster, smarter, more powerful and infinitely more deadly than any mere horseman could ever hope to be.

That was the reason the coursers and the Sothōii existed in an almost symbiotic relationship. Only a very small percentage of Sothōii would ever sit astride a courser, but all Sothōii felt the awe which the coursers' sheer majesty and beauty evoked in any who saw it. And in a way which no other people in Norfressa would ever truly understand, the coursers were as much citizens of the Kingdom of the Sothōii as any human. They lived on the same land. They defended that land against the same enemies. They died with their chosen riders to preserve it. In return for the human hands they required to do what they could not, they offered their incomparable speed and strength and endurance in the service of their common homeland.

That was why what had happened to the Warm Springs coursers filled any Sothōii's blood with icy fear . . . and his heart with fiery rage. No one—*no one*, mortal, demon, or devil—could commit such an atrocity and escape retribution. And if Kelthys felt that way, then how much more did the Bear River coursers feel the same fury . . . and fear? That was why he'd had to tell them. And it was also why, as he looked back over his shoulder at those huge, beautiful creatures behind him and Walasfro, for one of the very few times in his life, Sir Kelthys Lancebearer's apprehension and outright fear fully matched his joy in his courser brother's speeding majesty.

<Do you think we're in time?>

The question in Kelthys' mind was fretful, filled with as much guilt, despite the speed with which they had outraced the wind itself, as with anxiety. Only coursers who had bonded—and then only with their own riders—had the ability to form thoughts into actual words, but their mental "voices" were as expressive as any human speech could hope to be.

"Your guess is as good as mine," Kelthys replied, as Walasfro sprang back into motion—not a gallop, this time, but a distance-devouring canter that was faster than many a horse's full gallop—with the Bear River stallions on his heels. "But if we're not, it's not your fault, my heart."

He knew not even a courser could have physically heard him over the sound of hooves and wind, but he almost always spoke aloud to Walasfro.

<*They should not have gone without a wind brother. What was their herd stallion* thinking?>

Kelthys recognized a rhetorical question, and the gnawing acid of fear which spawned it, when he heard one, and he made no answer.

<*Tellian or Hathan should have come. They're wind chosen, and Dathgar and Gayrhalan could have brought* them *here already. And* they *would have known what to do when they got here,*> the stallion continued, worrying his fears like a dog with a bone, and Kelthys tasted the lingering wariness, hovering on the brink of distrust, in that querulous insistence. The courser had seen as much evidence of Bahzell's champion's status as Kelthys, but he found it even harder than his rider to overcome the fact of Bahzell's hradaniness.

"They weren't there," and Kelthys said firmly. "Walasfro, you know that as well as I do. Just as you know how lucky we are that a champion of Tomanāk *was* there."

<A hradani *champion,*> Walasfro shot back.

"A *champion,*" Kelthys said even more firmly. "If Tomanāk Himself accepts Prince Bahzell as His own, don't you think *we* ought to be able to do the same?"

<*I suppose so,*> Walasfro muttered in the back of Kelthys' brain, and the wind rider sighed.

In the Sothōii tongue, which was much more directly descended from the ancient Kontovaran than most languages in Norfressa, Walasfro's name meant "Son of Battle." It had been given to him by his herd stallion when he was barely a two-year old, and like most of the names herd stallions assigned, it carried a keen insight into the bearer's personality . . . and not just on the field of war. Not even a god's testimonial to a hradani's character was enough to change *his* mind. Not entirely.

"I'm sure he'll do all that *any* champion of Tomanāk could do, once he arrives," Kelthys said now, and watched Warm Springs' outbuildings growing steadily larger as Walasfro thundered towards them.

Lord Edinghas' masonry manor house stood on an artificial mound of earth, surrounded by an outlying earthen wall and rampart which also enclosed all the manor's other critical structures. It had not been designed to resist armies or sieges, but it was more than adequate to stand off raiders, or even sizable detachments, if the attackers lacked proper siege equipment. As Sir Kelthys, Walasfro, and the Bear River stallions pounded through the open gates, they saw far more sentries than usual atop the deep, thick berm. No one challenged them, of course. One of the consequences of being a wind rider or a courser was that one was both highly visible and instantly identifiable.

The senior officer of the watch didn't even speak to Kelthys; he only waved his helmet from atop the rampart in greeting, then pointed at the main stables. Kelthys raised a hand in reply, and he and Walasfro—trotting now, no longer cantering—led the Bear River stallions in the indicated direction.

Their shared anxiety had grown sharper than ever as they neared the end of their journey, and although Kelthys couldn't directly speak to or hear any of the other coursers, he felt the echo of their own tension and uneasiness through Walasfro. The sound of the other stallions' hooves grew louder as they entered the built-up area of the manor, and Kelthys' mouth twitched in a humorless smile as he realized those hooves were falling in a synchronized cadence. The Bear River stallions were closing ranks, forming up as if for battle. But then the stable was close before them, and they slowed even further, dread at what they might find honing their anxiety even sharper.

They moved forward at little more than a walk, past the ring of armsmen surrounding the stable. And then, with a suddenness so abrupt it made even a courser look clumsy and rocked a wind rider in the saddle, Walasfro stopped. The courser's head snapped up, his ears went straight up like exclamation points, and the sheer strength of his surprise hit Kelthys like a fist through their shared awareness.

Seven foals and a filly stood with four mares in the stable paddock. The youngsters huddled close around the mares, wariness and the echoes of remembered terror drawing them into tight proximity. There were scars on all twelve of them, some savage, and yet, as Kelthys looked at them, he could almost *feel* their healthiness. And then he realized he *was* feeling it, feeling it through Walasfro. He'd always known his courser brother had a powerful personality, but until that moment he'd never fully realized how powerful it actually was. Walasfro might well have become a herd stallion himself, had he not chosen to bond with Kelthys, and it was that herd sense that reached out and touched those scarred survivors.

One of the mares raised her head, whickering in response, and Walasfro shook himself, very much as a human might have done, as he tried to recover from his stunned astonishment. It looked much more impressive when a courser did it, but the outward manifestation was as nothing compared to the inward reality Kelthys shared with him.

He heard equally startled equine sounds from behind him as the Bear River stallions realized, albeit more slowly, what Walasfro had already sensed. Bahzell's and Jahlahan's message had warned them that according to the messenger from Lord Edinghas, all of the Warm Springs survivors hovered close to death, but there was no trace of the deathly illness Alfar Axeblade had reported in any of *these* coursers. Scars to mark its passing, perhaps, but no more. Even the shadow of the terror they had endured had been somehow lessened. Not set aside, or erased, but . . . transformed. Transmuted into memory which might frighten but could no longer paralyze or crush the indomitable spirit which was any courser's birthright.

<*How?*>

The single word came to Kelthys from Walasfro. It

was as if the stallion were incapable of forming a more complex thought, and yet that one word carried every nuance of his complicated bewilderment, joy, confusion, gratitude, and rejoicing.

"I don't know." Kelthys knew his own voice sounded almost as stunned as Walasfro's thought had felt. "I—"

He broke off, turning his head and following the direction of Walasfro's gaze as he felt the stallion's fresh surprise. Two more coursers, one of them huge for a mare, and more brutally scarred than any they had yet seen, paced slowly out of the stable. The bigger of the two—and the younger, Kelthys realized as Walasfro's herd sense touched them—had lost an eye and an ear, and her winter-thick chestnut coat bore the bold white lines of what must be wicked scars. She was obviously still adjusting to her half-blindness, but she carried her maimed head with the same regal pride which infused her high-stepping walk.

Walasfro's herd sense identified the older courser beside her as the senior surviving mare of the Warm Springs herd. Not that she was very old. Coursers, unlike horses, routinely lived for as long as sixty years, although they matured at only a slightly slower rate. But this mare—the oldest surviving member of the entire Warm Springs herd—could not have been more than nineteen years old.

That single fact drove home how utterly devastated the herd had been, but that registered only peripherally on Kelthys' awareness. Something else seized upon his attention, and he felt the disbelieving astonishment of Walasfro and the Bear River stallions as they, too, saw the stumbling, utterly exhausted hradani between the two coursers. Saw him scarcely able even to stand, yet forcing himself erect as he came to greet them. And saw his arm across the back of that half-blind, horribly scarred filly as she walked protectively beside him and lent him her strength.

"It's glad I am to be seeing you, Sir Kelthys," Bahzell Bahnakson greeted him in a frail husk of his deep, powerful voice.

✧ ✧ ✧

<I can't believe he didn't wait for us.>

"I'm still trying to accept that he and the others managed to beat us here in the first place!" Kelthys replied, as he moved the dandy brush briskly against the direction of the hair with a strong circular motion.

He stood in Lord Edinghas' stable, carefully grooming Walasfro. All around them, other stable hands performed the same service for the Bear River stallions, and drifting hair from shedding winter coats seemed to be everywhere. In many ways, it was a reassuringly domestic scene, but Walasfro's residual disbelief echoed from all the coursers, hanging in the air like another, invisible cloud of hair.

There had been no time yet for details, and the filly—Gayrfressa—had insisted on sending the exhausted champion off to rest. One of the Bear River stallions, a massive red roan with black mane and tail, had attempted to delay her. Kelthys hadn't been able to hear any of their conversation, but he'd seen Gayrfressa shake her head impatiently, then actually bare her teeth, and the older, bigger stallion had backed off. He and all of his companions had fallen back, flowing apart to open an avenue through their midst for Gayrfressa and Bahzell, and as the hradani half-walked and half-staggered past them, leaning heavily on the filly, they had tossed their heads high, then lowered them in perfect unison. Kelthys' jaw had done its best to drop as he recognized the salute coursers normally reserved only for their own herd stallions.

He very much doubted that Bahzell had had any suspicion of the honor those stallions had bestowed upon him. Even if he'd been a wind rider himself, he was so totally exhausted that very little of what happened about him could have registered. But the sight of coursers bowing—offering their homage, really—to a *hradani* had been so profoundly unnatural that, even now, Kelthys had difficulty believing he'd actually seen it.

But he was obviously the only human in the entire holding of Warm Springs who did, he told himself.

<The speed they made on their journey surprises me,

too,> Walasfro admitted. <*Yet even that is less surprising than that he chose not to wait until we could arrive so that I might speak to the others for him before he approached them.*>

"There was no time for him to wait," Kelthys said. And, as if to underscore his own earlier thought, another human voice spoke quietly.

"No, there wasn't," it said, and Kelthys turned to look at the speaker.

Hahnal Bardiche stood beside him, personally currying the huge roan who had attempted to accost Gayrfressa. The wind rider arched an eyebrow, and Hahnal shrugged.

"I'm not a wind rider, Sir Kelthys, but I've spent all my life around coursers. I can usually tell when a wind rider is talking to himself and when he's talking to his courser. And, under the circumstances, there's really only one thing you and Walasfro are very likely to be discussing at the moment, isn't there?"

"I can't fault your reasoning, Lord Hahnal." Kelthys grinned wryly. "And to be fair to Walasfro, I'm almost as surprised as he is." He shook his head. "First and foremost by the simple fact that they got here so quickly. The gods know the speed of hradani infantry has surprised us often enough to our cost in the past, but not even that prepared me for this. They must literally have run the entire way!"

"They did," Hahnal agreed quietly. "Well, the Bloody Swords rode, but every one of the Horse Stealers ran."

"I know," Kelthys said, and shook his head again. "I'm just having trouble believing it. But over and above that, I've come to know Prince Bahzell well enough to know he must have realized exactly how dangerous it was for a hradani to get that close to wounded coursers. Especially without someone like Walasfro to talk to them for him."

"It was more dangerous than even you can possibly realize, Sir Kelthys." Hahnal's young voice was dark, and he looked away for a moment. "To my eternal shame,

I doubted that Prince Bahzell truly was a champion of Tomanāk. Worse, I was prepared to hate him even if he *were* a champion. But he never hesitated. He knew we were losing them, that none of them would have survived if he'd waited for your arrival . . . and that every one of them was half-mad with terror and pain and the poison working on them. They didn't see a champion of Tomanāk, either, Milord. They saw a Horse Stealer hradani, and I still don't understand how he kept them from trampling him into the mud. But he did."

The young man looked back at Sir Kelthys, his eyes shining with wonder.

"He healed Gayrfressa first. And not just her wounds, Milord." He shook his head slowly. "He healed her *soul*, called her back from the Dark and gave her back herself. I'm no wind rider, but I have a touch—too little to train, but a touch—of the healing mage talent, and I *felt* what he did. It was nothing at all like what a mage healer would have done. It was . . . it was—I don't know the words to describe what it was, Sir Kelthys, but he offered *himself* to whatever was consuming her. He took all of it upon himself in her stead, and then he—and Tomanāk—peeled it away from her and destroyed it."

Lord Edinghas' son shook his head again.

"It took everything he had to channel enough of the God's power to do it, Milord. Any fool—even one like me—could see that. Just as we could all see that he stayed on his feet on nothing but sheer guts and stubbornness after he'd healed her. And then, somehow, he did it all over again. And again, and again—*thirteen* times, Milord. Without stopping to rest. Until he'd healed every . . . single . . . one . . . of . . . them.

"I think it almost killed him," Hahnal said very softly, staring at his hands as they moved across the roan stallion's coat. "I think it *could* have killed him . . . and that he knew it. And he's a hradani. Not a Sothōii, but a *hradani*."

"I know," Kelthys responded after a moment. "And it probably says something we'd rather not hear about *us* that we're so surprised by his actions. Whatever else he may be, Lord Hahnal, he's also a champion of Tomanāk. Somehow I doubt that Tomanāk is in the habit of taking champions, whatever their race, who are anything except extraordinary people."

He was speaking to Walasfro, and the Bear River stallion Hahnal was tending to, as much as to the heir of Warm Springs. And Walasfro's presence in the back of his mind told him that the courser understood that perfectly.

"Aye, Milord," Hahnal nodded soberly, "and that's exactly what he and those other hradani from the Order are—*people*. Alfar was right about them when he told my father how hard they'd driven themselves to get here. And I don't think any of us will ever forget seeing Prince Bahzell heal the coursers."

"No, I don't suppose you will," Kelthys agreed, and looked up as Walasfro turned his head to meet his gaze. "And neither will the coursers, I suspect," the wind rider said.

Chapter Twenty-Seven

Sir Kelthys looked up from the bridle in his lap as Bahzell walked into the stable. The wind rider nodded companionably to the hradani, then returned his attention to the bridle, setting small, neat stitches into the noseband. He sensed Bahzell settling onto a three-legged stool beside him, but he continued to concentrate on repairing the bridle.

"I was thinking," Bahzell rumbled after a moment, "as how wind riders weren't after using bridles."

"We don't," Kelthys agreed. He set another stitch and studied it critically, then flipped the jointed curb bit with a fingertip. "Walasfro would take my arm off at the elbow—and rightly so—if I tried to put something like this into *his* mouth, Prince Bahzell." He shrugged. "As a matter of fact, they only wear hackamores to give them someplace to wear their decorations."

"Aye?"

"Of course." Kelthys chuckled. "Coursers are incredibly vain, you know. Almost as bad as your friend Brandark! That's why all of us go in for those big silver conches on our 'formal wear' saddles. Their hackamores are only an excuse for more silver studding—although some of them, like Walasfro, like to hang bells on them, as well. But we'd never dream of putting *reins* on them! As a matter of fact, that's one of the things that drives other cavalry crazy the first time they run up against wind riders."

He chuckled again, this time with a nastier edge.

"Our coursers know what they're doing as well as we do, and they think with us in battle. We don't even need to tell each other what we have in mind in words. And the fact that we've no use at all for reins just happens to leave both of our hands free for doing . . . unpleasant things to the other side."

"Aye, I can be seeing that," Bahzell told him with an answering laugh. Then he lapsed into silence, and Kelthys returned his attention to the piece of tack he was repairing for Lord Edinghas. Like many Sothōii, he was naturally on the laconic side. But this time there was another reason for his companionable silence. Bahzell had something on his mind, and Kelthys had no pressing engagements. If the champion needed time to get around to whatever was bothering him, that was fine with him.

Bahzell leaned back against the stable wall, crossing his arms across his massive chest, and gazed out the open stable door. The early afternoon sun was bright, but the stable was dimly lit and cool. It was like looking out of a cave, and he allowed himself to savor the sense of calm that it evoked.

Yet that calm was deceptive, and he knew it. He still didn't know everything about what had happened to the Warm Springs herd, but he knew enough. In that moment when he and Gayrfressa had fused, he'd actually seen what she had seen, heard what she had heard . . . and felt what she had felt. And Tomanāk had been at least a little more forthcoming than usual. He'd tucked away more information in handy corners of Bahzell's brain than the Horse Stealer had expected. He certainly possessed a far better idea of what was waiting out there than he'd had when he and Brandark and Hurthang had led the Hurgrum Chapter into Navahk to destroy Sharnā's temple.

None of which made deciding exactly what to do about it any easier. And then there was Gayrfressa. . . .

"Sir Kelthys," he began after a moment.

"Yes, Milord?" the wind rider replied courteously, his nimble fingers still working on the bridle.

"You're after being a wind rider, and you've been such for over twenty years, I'm thinking?"

"Yes, I have," Kelthys agreed.

"Well, it's in my mind as how it's likely you've been after learning a mite more about coursers during that time than ever I have."

"I'd certainly like to think I have," Kelthys agreed again, this time with a slight smile. "Why?"

"It's Gayrfressa," Bahzell admitted after a moment, then paused.

"What about her?" Kelthys pressed gently.

"Well," Bahzell said slowly, "when Himself and I were after healing her, there was a moment when everything was after *flowing* together, as you might say." He grimaced, mobile ears twitching with frustration as he sought unsuccessfully for the exact words he needed. "There was after being a moment—naught but a heartbeat or two, mind you—when she and I were after . . . merging. As if there was naught but the one of us." He turned and looked at the wind rider. "Would it happen as how you've felt such as that, or know someone else as has?"

"I . . . don't think so," Kelthys said, picking his own words as slowly and carefully as Bahzell had. "There's a moment for most wind riders—not all of us, but most—when we first bond with our brothers when we see *each other*. When we know all there is to know about one another. When we can actually almost *see* the other one's thoughts. But we don't fuse, or merge. Not really, although we throw those words around sometimes. We remain separate. Closer than to our own siblings, or even our lovers, but still separate. And that doesn't sound to me like what you're describing."

"Nor to me," Bahzell agreed, and sighed.

"Was it all that terrible an experience?" Kelthys inquired, with a note of gentle teasing, and Bahzell snorted.

"Terrible?" He shook his head. "Not by a long chalk, Sir Kelthys. Mind you, I'd not be wishful as to be doing such as that again any time soon! No, and I'd not wish for any other courser to be experiencing what these have."

His voice had darkened with the last sentence, but then he gave himself a shake.

"Still and all, though, I've no choice but to say as how it's probably after being one of the two or three most wonderful experiences of my life. They're truly after being the gods' own creatures, aren't they just?"

"I think so," Kelthys agreed quietly.

"Aye. But you're after being Sothōii, d'you see, whereas I'm hradani. And there's not a courser ever born as was so very fond of hradani. So you might be saying as how that's after being the relationship as we're both most comfortable with."

Kelthys quirked a quizzical eyebrow, and the huge hradani shrugged, looking almost embarrassed.

"Gayrfressa and I," he said. "We're not after being so very comfortable, anymore. I'll not go so far as to say what's betwixt us is after being the same as betwixt you and Walasfro, but it's not anything as ever existed betwixt *another* courser and hradani, you can lay to that! I—"

"Forgive me, Prince Bahzell," Kelthys asked gently, "but is it really so difficult for you to admit that the two of you love one another?" Bahzell gave him a sharp look, and Kelthys waved one hand in the air. "I doubt very much that anyone besides a wind rider has ever experienced anything remotely like what you've described to me, Milord Champion. But it's not at all unheard of for coursers to form deep, intensive friendships with humans who aren't wind riders—to love them, Prince Bahzell. Think of Dathgar and Baroness Hanatha, or Lady Leeana. Those who don't know them well tend to forget, if they ever truly realize it in the first place, that coursers are at least as intelligent as any of the Races of Man. And they have far, far greater hearts than most of *us* have."

"Aye, I can be seeing that," Bahzell murmured. "Yet I'm not so very sure as how any other coursers, as weren't here and didn't see, will be accepting that Gayrfressa could be feeling such for a hradani like me. And, truth to tell, there's those among my folk as would find it even more unnatural than hers."

"I don't think you need to worry about how the other coursers are likely to react," Kelthys reassured him. "They communicate with one another in ways I don't think anyone, including the wind riders, has ever truly understood." He shook his head. "Trust me, Prince Bahzell. If Gayrfressa is prepared to feel about you as you've described, then any other courser she ever meets will understand why. That's not to say they'll all *agree* with her, you understand, but I doubt very much that any of them will ever question her feelings or fault her for them."

"Well, to be speaking the truth," Bahzell said after a moment, "that's after being the least of my concerns just this very moment. You see, it's in my mind as how she's not going to be so very willing to be being left behind."

"Excuse me, Prince Bahzell, but are you saying that you and Gayrfressa are still linked somehow?"

"I'd not be calling it 'linked,'" Bahzell replied. "Yet it might be as how it's after being something in that direction." He tapped his forehead with an index finger. "It's not so much as if I'm after 'hearing' her, or as if we're after living inside one another's minds still. And yet, there's not the least tiniest question in my mind as how I know what it is she's after thinking. Or, come to that, where she's after *being*."

Kelthys' eyes widened suddenly, and he laid the bridle aside for the first time since Bahzell had entered the stable. The hradani's eyes narrowed as he saw the human's expression, but he said nothing, only waited.

"Milord Champion," Kelthys said after several seconds, obviously choosing his words even more carefully than before, "is Gayrfressa the only courser whose location you know?"

"Ah?" Bahzell gave him a look which combined surprise and disbelief at being asked such a ridiculous question. But then he frowned and closed his eyes, cocking his head as if he were listening to a distant sound. He stayed that way for several seconds, and then his expression went blank and his eyes popped back open.

"She isn't, is she?" Kelthys murmured, watching him very intently.

"No," Bahzell said. He waved a hand in the general direction of the paddock to the south of the stable, completely invisible from where the two of them sat. "It's the entire herd I can be feeling," he said. "All of them—from Gayrfressa to the youngest foal."

"Tomanāk!" Kelthys whispered. He stared at Bahzell for what seemed like forever, then shook himself vigorously. "I don't understand it, Prince Bahzell," he said. "Perhaps it's because you're a champion of Tomanāk. But whatever the reason, it *sounds* to me as if you've somehow acquired a form of the courser herd sense."

"That's after being ridiculous!"

"Oh, I agree—I *definitely* agree! And if you think it sounds ridiculous to you, wait until *Walasfro* hears about it! But, tell me—can you sense any of the other coursers? Or only the Warm Springs survivors?"

"Only Gayrfressa and her family," Bahzell replied. But then he shook his head. "No, that's not after being exactly right. There *is* one other courser as I can sense. That big, roan fellow with the black mane and tail."

"Only him?" Kelthys frowned in surprise. "None of the others?"

"Naught but him," Bahzell confirmed, and then he smiled slowly. "And now I think on it, I'm thinking as how I might be knowing why. I'd not realized it until this very moment, but now it's plain as the nose on Brandark's face! He's after being her brother, Sir Kelthys."

"Her *brother*?" Kelthys blinked at the hradani.

"Aye, he'd a mate among the Bear River mares, but he was after losing her to an accident these three years back."

"And how do you know all that, Milord?" Kelthys asked in fascination.

"As to that, I don't really know. But I'm thinking as how he might be after telling us himself in not so very long."

"He might wh—?" Kelthys began, then cut himself off as the light from the stable entrance was abruptly obstructed. He looked up, and his face lost all expression as he recognized the huge stallion pacing slowly into the stable. It was the Bear River roan.

"Aye, so he might," Bahzell continued quietly, his own eyes locked to the oncoming courser, "for unless I'm after missing my guess, he's after having just discovered as how *he* can be sensing *me*, too."

The roan might very well have been the largest courser Kelthys had seen in his entire life. The stallion had to stand over twenty-four hands—more than eight feet tall at the shoulder—and he carried his majestic head almost eleven feet above the stable floor. He towered over Bahzell, well over two tons of majesty and power, managing to do what no other creature ever had and reduce the hradani to merely mortal stature. It seemed as if the very earth should tremble when he trod upon it, and his presence seemed to fill not simply the stable, but the world.

He stood there, magnificent in the remnant of his winter coat, and his huge eyes—amber-gold, not brown—were fixed upon Bahzell.

Bahzell stood, slowly, as if he were being drawn to his feet by another hand, not rising of his own volition. He stood less than five feet from the courser, and then, even more slowly than he'd stood, he stepped forward.

The courser stood motionless for a second, possibly two. And then he lowered his head, and his impossibly soft nose touched the hradani's broad chest. The nostrils flared, the amber-gold eyes slipped shut, and the stallion blew heavily. Bahzell's hands rose, as if they belonged to someone else. They stroked up the stallion's muzzle, gently, gently. They found the ears—the ears that pricked sharply forward, as if listening for the sound of the hradani's heart—and caressed them with a delicacy that seemed impossible for such powerful, sword-callused fingers.

Kelthys stared, unable to believe even now, despite everything that had happened, that he was seeing what he saw. A thousand years of history said this moment *could not* occur, and he held his breath, waiting to see if a thousand years were wrong.

"His name," Bahzell half-whispered, "is Walsharno."

A thousand years, it seemed, *were* wrong.

Sir Kelthys Lancebearer leaned against a paddock fence, Walasfro standing beside him like a warm, black wall, and watched the Wind Plain's newest wind rider trying not to fall off of his courser.

<This *is going to cause problems,*> Walasfro observed in resigned tones.

"Tell me something I didn't already know, Twinkle Hoofs," Kelthys replied mildly, then winced as Bahzell almost lost his seat. The hradani looked ridiculous perched on top of what was probably the only "horse" in the world that could make *him* look like a child on his first pony. Of course, the fact that Bahzell's riding style could best be summed up in two words—"*very* bad"—probably helped create that image.

<*He'll break his neck the first time Walsharno breaks into a trot,*> Walasfro predicted glumly.

"Nonsense!" Kelthys said bracingly. "Hradani are tougher than that. Besides, he'll probably fall off *before* Walsharno hits a trot."

<*This isn't funny, Brother,*> Walasfro said reprovingly. <*Whatever some people may think,*> he added as Bahzell grabbed at the saddle horn and Brandark and Gharnal burst into loud guffaws. The Bloody Sword, and every member of the Order of Tomanāk who'd accompanied Bahzell to Warm Springs, sat along the top rail of the paddock, watching Bahzell and Walsharno "get acquainted." From Bahzell's expression, he would have been far happier without the audience.

"Actually, you know, it *is* funny," Kelthys told his courser. Walasfro snorted heavily, shaking his head in equine disgust, but Kelthys was unmoved.

"I'm not saying it isn't going to . . . upset a few people," he conceded. "On the other hand, only the most dyed-in-the-wool bigot is going to be able to argue Bahzell didn't do one hell of a lot more to *earn* Walsharno's companionship than most wind riders ever manage. Dear heart, I certainly never did anything that worthy of your love, but you gave it to me anyway."

<*As you gave me yours, Brother,*> Walasfro replied gently.

"Well, of course." Kelthys smiled and reached up to stroke Walasfro's shoulder.

"Still," he continued after a moment, fighting not to grin as Walsharno circled patiently around the paddock, "it *is* just a trifle unusual for any courser to choose someone who just plain can't ride worth a damn. I suppose it comes of Bahzell's never having had much opportunity to practice."

<*Practice?! And, pray tell me, Two Foots, just where was a hradani his size going to find a* horse *capable of carrying him?*> Walasfro snorted again. <*Not to mention the fact that his people don't exactly have the best possible relationship with us or the lesser cousins—historically speaking, of course,*> the stallion corrected himself with exquisite irony.

"You can be so cynical sometimes," Kelthys scolded with a chuckle. Walasfro poked his nose at him, and Kelthys smacked it.

<*All jesting aside,*> Walasfro said more seriously, <*he and Walsharno will need weeks to truly settle into their bond. And he'll probably need at least that long—or longer!—before* I'd *feel comfortable about his chances of staying in the saddle in a serious fight.*>

"You're probably right," Kelthys agreed. Indeed, there was usually no better judge of a human's—or, he supposed, a hradani's—horsemanship than a courser. "Still," the human added hopefully, "he's getting better faster than almost anyone else I've ever watched."

<*You may be right about that,*> Walasfro conceded thoughtfully. <*I wish we understood more about whatever sort of "herd sense" he's apparently acquired. I wonder . . .* >

"You wonder what?" Kelthys prompted after several seconds.

<*I wonder if whatever it is is allowing him to link*

with Walsharno on a deeper level than the rest of us can match outside battle? Watch him, Brother. He is *getting better faster than he ought to be. Do you think he could be using his version of the herd sense to anticipate Walsharno's movements?*>

"Now that is a very interesting thought," Kelthys murmured softly. "And while we're having interesting thoughts, here's another one for you. Have you ever heard of a champion of Tomanāk bonding with a courser before?"

<*No,*> Walasfro replied after a moment—a very long, thoughtful moment. <*Have* you, *Brother?*>

"No, I haven't," Kelthys said. "Because it's never happened before. And I find myself wondering how Bahzell's relationship with Tomanāk is going to affect Walsharno."

<*I couldn't begin to guess,*> Walasfro admitted frankly. Then he laughed. <*Still, it might be less of a change than you may be anticipating, Brother. After all, his name is certainly appropriate for a champion's companion!*>

"Yes, it is," Kelthys agreed, laughing with him. "I wonder if his herd stallion knew something when he gave it to him?"

<*Stranger things have happened. And whether he knew something or not, the name certainly fits.*>

"Yes, it does. For that matter, it fits *Bahzell*, too."

Walasfro tossed his head in a gesture of agreement coursers had long ago picked up from humans. In the Sothōii tongue, "Walsharno" meant "Sun of War," although it might also be translated as "Battle Dawn."

"At any rate," Kelthys continued, "I suppose that even without Bahzell's status as one of Tomanāk's champions, the mere fact that a hradani's been chosen as a wind rider at all should suggest that we'd all better be as open-minded as possible about their bond."

<*Easier for some than for others,*> Walasfro thought dryly. <*But however quickly he may be learning, do we truly have time for the two of them to complete the bonding? Whatever attacked Gayrfressa's herd is still out there. What if it attacks another herd? Or Warm Springs itself?*>

"I don't know," Kelthys admitted frankly. "I do know that Bahzell is worrying over the same questions. But I don't think he'll be ready to move for at least another two or three days, anyway."

<*Why not?*>

"Because I asked him not to," Kelthys said calmly. Walasfro swung his head around to look at him, and Kelthys shrugged. "Yes, we have to move. And, yes, the fundamental responsibility has to be Bahzell's—well, his and the Order's. But whatever's happening out there, it's on the *Wind Plain*, Walasfro. It's on *our* land, and it's attacked and killed *our* coursers, and at the moment, you and I—well, you and I and Bahzell and Walsharno—are the only wind riders here. That's why I sent out the dispatches before we left Deep Water. By now, there must be over a dozen other wind riders on their way to Warm Springs. I expect to see the first of them no later than tomorrow. Don't you think that our own honor and responsibility require that the wind borne and our brothers ride with Tomanāk's warriors at a time like this?"

Walasfro had started to interrupt, but then he'd stopped to listen to what Kelthys had to say. And at the end, he snorted once again, and tossed his head in agreement.

<*There are probably enormous holes in your logic, Brother,*> he said, <*but there are no holes in your heart. I think we can give our fledglings another day or two of practice.*>

"Begging your pardon, Milord, but are you certain about this?"

Saratic Redhelm, Lord Warden of Golden Vale, glared at his marshal. Sir Chalthar Ranseur met his glare with a level look of his own. Chalthar had served Saratic for over ten years, and he'd begun as a common armsman under Saratic's father, almost twenty years before that.

Saratic reminded himself of that as he fought his own temper back under control. There was no doubt in his mind that Chalthar was completely loyal—as only a Sothōii armsman could be—to Saratic personally and to Golden Vale. But the man's long service gave him the right to offer advice when he thought his liege lord was about to commit a serious error. And he obviously thought that was what was about to happen.

And I'd probably be less angry with him if a part of me wasn't worried that he's right, Saratic thought grimly. But he wasn't about to admit that to Chalthar.

"Yes, I *am* certain about it," he said instead, and held Chalthar's eyes with his own. There was no expression on the dark-haired, grizzled knight's weathered face, but he bobbed his head in an abbreviated bow.

"Very well, Milord," he said. "In that case, I'd recommend that we send the Third and Fifth."

Saratic pursed his lips while he considered the advice carefully. It was as shrewd as he would have expected from Chalthar, although the Third and Fifth Companies were very different from one another.

Sir Fahlthu Greavesbiter's Third Company was actually the largest in Saratic's service. At two hundred men, it was almost twice the size of Sir Halnahk Partisan's Fifth Company. But Fahlthu was also the most mercenary of Saratic's officers. He was very good at his trade, if a bit inclined towards brutality as the solution to most problems, but his loyalty went to the man who *paid* him, and he'd recruited his oversized company up to strength with men very like himself.

Sir Halnahk was almost the diametric opposite. His loyalty was given to his liege lord because he'd sworn fealty to him. After Chalthar himself, his was probably the most reliable allegiance of any of Saratic's field commanders.

"An excellent suggestion, Chalthar," Saratic mused aloud. "Of course, Fahlthu and Halnahk hate each other's guts."

"To be honest, Milord, that consideration is one reason I feel they'd be the best choices."

"Ah?" Saratic leaned back in his chair, squinting his eyes against the bright sunlight streaming into his study through the windows behind Chalthar.

"Of course, Milord." Chalthar waved a blunt-fingered hand. "To be honest, it we're going to risk someone,

I'd sooner lose Fahlthu than anyone else. But he's only as reliable as his next payday, and I wouldn't trust him not to betray you in a heartbeat if a better offer came along—or if he thought it would keep his own skin safe." The marshal paused, then grimaced. "Actually, Milord, that's not quite fair, I suppose. Fahlthu's brave enough once it actually comes down to blows. It's in his planning *before* the fighting starts that his thinking depends on what he expects to get out of it."

Saratic nodded. That attitude of Fahlthu's was one reason he'd recruited the man in the first place. There were times when a lord warden needed the proper tool for fishing in murky waters.

"Halnahk, on the other hand, isn't much going to like his orders," Chalthar continued with blunt honesty, "but he's your man and always has been. He'll carry 'em out, whatever they are, and he's senior to Fahlthu. So, Milord, I think we should put him in command of this affair. His seniority would make it logical, but even more importantly, we can tell him your full intentions and rely upon him to act in accordance with them. In the meantime, let me tell Fahlthu a *part* of what you intend—the part he'll have to know—but not enough details to make betraying us strike him as being worth the risk. We can trust Halnahk to make the best use of him . . . and if it should chance that my concerns prove to have been justified, he'll make Halnahk a rear guard none of us will miss. Not to mention," the marshal smiled thinly, "the fact that everyone *knows* Fahlthu's little better than a common mercenary. If something unfortunate should befall him, I think it would not be unreasonable for Baron Cassan to conclude that Sir Fahlthu had been bribed by Lord Warden Dathian—who's *Tellian*'s vassal, not the Baron's—to vastly exceed any orders *you* might have given him."

"As always, your reasoning is acute, Chalthar," Saratic purred. "See to it. And see to it that Baron Cassan's man, Warshoe, is attached to Sir Fahlthu." Chalthar looked a question at him, and Saratic shrugged. "Something about the man worries me, Chalthar. Not enough to offend

Baron Cassan by refusing his services, and the gods know he's proved capable enough in everything we've asked of him so far. But if he's a blade that's likely to turn in our hands, I'd rather have him chopping off Fahlthu's fingers than Halnahk's. And having him safely among those 'bribed by Dathian' might not be a very bad thing, either."

"There's a messenger from Sir Jahlahan, Milord."

Baron Tellian looked up from the breakfast campfire beside the Balthar high road at the sound of Tarith Shieldarm's voice.

He and his armsmen were still two days' travel—for those on warhorses, instead of coursers, at least—from Hill Guard. They'd been setting an easy pace, allowing the horses from whom they had demanded so much in their pursuit of Leeana to recover somewhat. Even so, it had not been a pleasant journey, and especially not for Tarith. The burly, dark-haired and dark-eyed armsman had been assigned as Leeana's personal armsman even before she could walk, and when she'd been a baby, she'd held his heart in her two pudgy hands. Nor had she ever released that grip. Of all Tellian's armsmen, Tarith had taken his daughter's loss to the war maids hardest, and he continued to blame himself for it. It was nonsense, and Tellian knew it, but Tarith stubbornly insisted that he should have disobeyed Leeana's direct orders and refused to let her send him away. The fact that she'd constructed a totally plausible errand for him to run seemed lost upon him, and Tellian only hoped time would heal his grief and blunt that draining sense of guilt.

"From Sir Jahlahan?" the baron said after a moment, shaking off his reverie.

"Aye, Milord," Tarith said, and extended a sealed message pouch.

Tellian took it with a grunt of thanks that partially concealed a pang of anxiety. He'd deliberately avoided sending any messages ahead to Balthar. Despite the relatively moderate pace he'd set, he and his armsmen would reach Hill Guard no more than two days—two and a half, at most—after a messenger from Kalatha could have arrived. He refused to subject Hanatha to a written confirmation that they had lost their daughter forever when the delay to tell her in person, and hold her in his arms as she wept, would be so brief.

But Jahlahan had to know Tellian must be well on his way back to Balthar by now, whether with Leeana, or without her. So what could be so urgent that the seneschal hadn't felt able to wait and report it to him directly?

He gazed down at the message pouch for a moment, then drew a deep breath and broke the seal. He extracted the message inside, opened it, and sat back on his haunches to read it.

But then the report's second sentence wrenched him upright with a jerk and a white-faced oath of disbelief.

He felt all his armsmen staring at him, knew his expression was giving away entirely too much, but he couldn't help it. He read the short, horrifying message all the way through, then made himself reread it to be certain there'd been no mistake.

There hadn't been, and he felt his shoulders slump.

"Milord?" a voice asked. "Wind Brother?!" it said more sharply, and he shook himself.

"Yes—yes, Hathan," he said, looking across to meet his wind brother's anxious eyes.

"What is it? Surely not the Baroness—?!"

"No." Tellian shook his head again, sharply, as if trying to shake his mind back into functioning. "No, Hanatha is well. It's—"

He looked back down at Jahlahan's message, then crushed it into a ball in a white-knuckled fist.

"It's not anything at Hill Guard or Balthar," he said hoarsely. "There was an . . . emergency at Warm Springs. Prince Bahzell has gone to deal with it."

"I see," Hathan gazed at him for a moment, and Tellian flicked a thought to Dathgar.

<Brother, ask Gayrhalan to ask Hathan to ask no more questions. Ask him to tell him that I will explain everything shortly.>

<Of course,> his courser replied. *<And may I hope*

that you'll explain it to me *at the same time?*> Dathgar continued dryly.

<*Of course I will,*> Tellian assured him, and felt a familiar sense of comfort from Dathgar's attitude. Although, he reflected more grimly, even Dathgar was going to be horrified by *this* news.

"All right, Tarith," he said aloud, turning back to the senior armsman. "As I'm sure you've already figured out, Sir Jahlahan's note is scarcely good news. All's well at Balthar and Hill Guard, though. The problem lies further north, and as I told Hathan, Prince Bahzell and Lord Brandark have already left Hill Guard to deal with it. However, *I* am the Lord Warden of the West Riding. It's my responsibility, not Prince Bahzell's, to respond to my lord wardens' requests for help. There's nothing that any of you—" he swept the listening armsmen with his eyes "—could do to help with this . . . particular problem, however. So Hathan and I are going to leave you here and go on ahead."

"Milord—!" Tarith began an instant, automatic armsman's protest, but Tellian shook his head firmly.

"We're not going to argue about this, old friend," he said. "Hathan and I *are* riding ahead. And I don't want you laming the horses trying to catch up with us, either!" He eyed the armsman sternly. "There's no way your mounts could keep up with us, so there's no use trying. Is that understood?"

Tarith clearly wanted to continue the argument, and he had all of a life-long retainer's stubbornness to continue it with. But he'd also served the Bowmasters of Balthar since boyhood. He recognized his Baron's seriousness . . . and he knew when it was time *not* to argue.

"Aye, Milord," he acknowledged unhappily.

"Thank you," Tellian said, punching him lightly on one armored shoulder. Then he turned to Hathan.

"Let's ride, Wind Brother," he said simply.

Chapter Twenty-Eight

Thalar Keep, the home of Lord Warden Trisu of Lorham and the ancestral seat of the Pickaxes of Lorham, was a considerably more modest fortress than Hill Guard Castle. Then again, the town of Thalar (calling it a "city" would have been a gross exaggeration) was far, far smaller than Balthar. Still, the castle, with its two curtain walls and massive, square central keep, was of respectable antiquity. Indeed, it looked to Kaeritha's experienced eye as if the outer walls were at least a couple of centuries younger than the original keep.

There was nothing remotely like finesse about the castle's architecture or construction. It was uncompromisingly angular, laid out with an obvious eye for fields of fire for the archers expected to man its battlements in time of emergency. Whoever had designed it, though—assuming anything like an actual "design" process had been part of its construction—had clearly been less concerned about what an enemy with capable siege engineers might have done to it. It was dominated by a higher ridge to the east, beyond accurate bow range but well within reach for the sort of ballistae someone like the Empire of the Axe might have deployed. Nor was the castle moated. It was built on what appeared to be an artificial mound, too, rather than bedrock. That raised it above the town proper and gave its parapets a greater command of its surroundings, but the earthen mound would have been highly vulnerable to mining operations.

Of course, she mused as Cloudy carried her up the very slight slope towards Thalar just over a week after she'd reached Kalatha, the people who'd built that castle had probably had their fellow Sothōii, or possibly Horse Stealers, in mind. Neither the cavalry-oriented Sothōii nor the relatively unsophisticated hradani would have been in much of a position to take advantage of the weaknesses evident to Kaeritha. And according to Mayor Yalith, Thalar Keep had withstood serious attack at least three times during the Sothōii's Time of Troubles.

Despite its small size, compared to Balthar, Thalar appeared to be relatively prosperous. There were few houses over two stories in height, but all of the dwellings Kaeritha could see appeared to be well maintained and clean. Despite the incessant spring rains, the local farmers had managed to get their fields plowed, and the first blush of green crops showed vividly against the furrows' rich, black topsoil. And, of course, there were the endless paddocks, training rings, and stables of Trisu's home stud farm.

There were laborers in the fields, and most of them paused to look up and study Kaeritha as Cloudy trotted past. Like Thalar itself, they seemed to be sturdy and well fed, if not wealthy, and almost despite herself, Kaeritha was forced to concede that first appearances suggested that Trisu, whatever his other failings, took excellent care of his people and his holding.

The road up to Thalar Keep was at least marginally better maintained than the muddy track Kaeritha had followed across the Wind Plain. She was grateful for that, and so was Cloudy. The mare picked up her pace as she recognized journey's end. No doubt she was looking forward to a warm stall and a bucketful of oats and bran.

Kaeritha chuckled at the thought, then drew rein as she approached the castle's outer gatehouse and a bugle blared. Her eyebrows rose as she recognized the bugle call. It was a formal challenge, a demand to stand and be recognized, and it was unusual, to say the least, for a single rider to be greeted by it. On the other hand, she could see at least six archers on the wall. Under the circumstances, she decided, compliance was probably in order.

She and Cloudy stopped just beyond the gatehouse's shadow, and she looked up as a man in the crested helmet of an officer appeared on the battlement above her.

"Who are you? And what brings you to Thalar Keep?" the officer shouted down in a nasal bass voice. It was unfortunate that his natural voice made him sound querulous and ill-tempered, Kaeritha thought.

"I am Dame Kaeritha Seldansdaughter," she called back in her clear, carrying soprano, carefully not smiling as his helmeted head twitched in obvious surprise at hearing a woman's voice. "Champion of Tomanāk," she continued, fighting not to chortle as she pictured the effect *that* was likely to have upon him. "Here to see Lord Warden Trisu of Lorham on the War God's business," she finished genially, and sat back in the saddle to await results.

There was a long moment of motionless consternation atop the battlements. Then the officer who'd challenged her seemed to give his entire body a shake and whipped around to gabble orders at one of the archers. The archer in question didn't even wait to nod in acknowledgment before he went speeding off. Then the officer turned back to Kaeritha.

"Ah, you *did* say a champion of Tomanāk, didn't you?" he inquired rather tentatively.

"Yes, I did," Kaeritha replied. "And I'm still waiting to be admitted," she added pointedly.

"Well, yes—" the flustered officer began. Then he stopped. Clearly, he had no idea how to proceed when faced with the preposterous, self-evidently impossible paradox of a woman who claimed to be not only a knight, but a champion of Tomanāk, as well! Kaeritha understood perfectly, but she rather hoped the average intelligence level of Trisu's officers and retainers was higher than this fellow seemed to imply.

"I'm getting a crick in my neck shouting up at you," she said mildly, and even from where she sat in Cloudy's saddle she imagined she could see the fiery blush which colored the unfortunate man's face.

He turned away from her once more, shouting to someone inside the gatehouse.

"Open the gate!" he snapped, and hinges groaned as someone began obediently heaving one of the massive gate leaves open.

Kaeritha waited patiently, hands folded in plain sight on the pommel of her saddle, until the gate was fully open. Then she nodded her thanks to the still flustered officer and clucked gently to Cloudy. The mare tossed her head, as if she were as amused as her mistress by the obvious consternation they'd caused, then trotted forward with dainty, ladylike grace.

The unfortunate officer from the battlements was waiting for her in the courtyard beyond the gatehouse by the time she emerged from the gate tunnel. Seen at closer range, he was rather more prepossessing than Kaeritha's first impression had suggested. Not that that was particularly difficult, she thought dryly.

His coloring was unusually dark for a Sothōii, and he stared up at her, his brown eyes clinging to the embroidered sword and mace of Tomanāk, glittering in gold bullion on the front of her poncho. From his expression, he would have found a fire-breathing dragon considerably less unnatural, but he was at least trying to handle the situation as if it were a normal one.

"Ah, please forgive my seeming discourtesy, Dame . . . Kaeritha," he said. There was a slight questioning note in his pronunciation of her name, Kaeritha noticed, and nodded pleasantly, acknowledging his apology even as she confirmed that he had it right. "I'm afraid," the officer continued with a surprisingly genuine smile, "that we're not accustomed to seeing champions of Tomanāk here in Lorham."

"There aren't that many of us," Kaeritha agreed,

amiably consenting to pretend that that had been the true reason for his confusion.

"I've sent word of your arrival to Lord Trisu," he continued. "I'm sure he'll want to come down to the gate to greet you properly and in person."

Or to kick me back out of the gate if he decides I'm not a champion after all, Kaeritha added silently. *On the other hand, one must be polite, I suppose.*

"Thank you, Captain—?"

"Forgive me," the officer said hastily. "I seem to be forgetting all of my manners today! I am called Sir Altharn."

"Thank you, Sir Altharn," Kaeritha said. "I appreciate the prompt and efficient manner in which you've discharged your duties."

The words were courteously formal, but Sir Altharn obviously noticed the gently teasing edge to her voice. For a moment he started to color up again, but then, to her pleased surprise, he shook his head and smiled at her, instead.

"I suppose I had that coming," he told her. "But truly, Dame Kaeritha, I'm seldom quite so inept as I've managed to appear this morning."

"I believe that," Kaeritha said, and somewhat to her own surprise, it was true.

"Thank you. That's kinder than I deserve," Sir Altharn said. "I hope I'll have the opportunity to demonstrate the fact that I don't always manage to put my own boot in my mouth. Or, at least, that I usually remember to take my spurs off first!"

He laughed at himself, so naturally that Kaeritha laughed with him. There might be some worthwhile depths to this fellow after all, she reflected.

"I'm sure you'll have the chance," she told him. "In fact, I—"

She broke off in midsentence as four more men, one of them the messenger Altharn had dispatched, arrived from the direction of the central keep. The one in the lead had to be Trisu, she thought. His stride was too imperious, his bearing too confident—indeed, arrogant—for him to be anyone else. He was fair-haired, gray-eyed, and darkly tanned. He was also very young, no more than twenty-four or twenty-five, she judged. And as seemed to be the case with every male Sothōii nobleman Kaeritha had so far met, he stood comfortably over six feet in height. That would have been more than enough to make him impressive, but if his height was typical of the Sothōii, his breadth was not. Most of them tended—like Sir Altharn or Baron Tellian—towards a lean and rangy look, but Trisu Pickaxe's shoulders were almost as broad in proportion to his height as Brandark's. He must, she reflected, have weighed close to three hundred pounds, none of it fat, and she felt a twinge of sympathy for any warhorse which found itself under him.

He was unarmored, but he'd taken time to belt on a jewel-hilted saber in a gold-chased black scabbard, and two of the men behind him—obviously armsmen—wore the standard steel breastplates and leather armor of Sothōii horse archers.

"So!" Trisu rocked to a halt and tucked his hands inside his sword belt as he glowered up at Kaeritha. She looked back down at him calmly from Cloudy's saddle, her very silence an unspoken rebuke of his brusqueness. He seemed remarkably impervious to it, however, for his only response was to bare his teeth in a tight, humorless smile.

"So you claim to be a champion of Tomanāk, do you?" he continued before the silence could stretch out too far.

"I do not '*claim*' anything, Milord," Kaeritha returned in a deliberately courteous but pointed tone. She smiled thinly. "It would take a braver woman than me to attempt to pass herself off falsely as one of His champions. Somehow, I don't think He'd like that very much, do you?"

Something flashed in Trisu's gray eyes—a sparkle of anger, perhaps, although she supposed it was remotely possible it might have been humor. But whatever it had been, it went almost as fast as it had come, and he snorted.

"Bravery might be one word for it," he said.

"Foolishness—or perhaps even stupidity—might be others, though, don't you think?"

"They might," she acknowledged. "In the meantime, however, Milord, I have to wonder if keeping a traveler standing in the courtyard is the usual courtesy of Lorham."

"Under normal circumstances, no," he said coolly. "On the other hand, I trust you will concede that women claiming to be knights and champions of the gods aren't exactly normal travelers."

"On the Wind Plain, perhaps," Kaeritha replied with matching coolness, and, for the first time, he flushed. But he wasn't prepared to surrender the point quite yet.

"That's as may be, Milady," he told her, "but at the moment, you're *on* the Wind Plain, and here what you claim to be is not simply unusual, but unheard of. Under the circumstances, I hope you'll not find me unduly discourteous if I request some proof that you are indeed who and what you say you are." He smiled again. "Surely, the Order of Tomanāk would prefer that people be cautious about accepting anyone's unsubstantiated claim to be one of His champions."

"I see." Kaeritha regarded him thoughtfully for a long moment. It would have been handy, she reflected, if Tomanāk had seen fit to gift her with a sword like Bahzell's, which came when he called it. It was certainly an impressive way to demonstrate his champion's credentials when necessary. Unfortunately, her own blades, while possessed of certain unusual attributes of their own, stayed obstinately in their sheaths unless she drew them herself, no matter how much she might whistle or snap her fingers for them.

"I've come from Balthar," she said, after a moment, "where Baron Tellian was kind enough to offer me hospitality and to gift me with this lovely lady." She leaned forward to stroke Cloudy's neck, and smiled behind her expressionless face as the first, faint uncertainty flickered in those gray eyes. "He also," she continued blandly, "sent with me written letters of introduction and, I believe, instructions to cooperate with me in my mission." Those eyes were definitely less cheerful than they had been, she noted with satisfaction. "And if you should happen to have anyone here in the Keep who is injured or ill, I suppose I could demonstrate my ability to heal them. Or—" she looked straight into Trisu's eyes "—if you insist, I suppose I might simply settle for demonstrating my skill at arms upon your chosen champion, instead. In that case, however, I hope you won't be requiring his services anytime soon."

Trisu's face tightened, its lines momentarily harder and bleaker than its owner's years. The people who'd described him as "conservative" had been guilty of considerable understatement, Kaeritha thought. But there appeared to be a brain behind that hard face. However angry he might be, his was not an *unthinking* reactionism, and he made his expression relax.

"If you bear the letters you've described," he said after a moment, with what Kaeritha had to concede was commendable dignity under the circumstances, "that will be more than sufficient proof for me, Milady."

"I thank you for your courtesy, Milord," she said, bending her head in a slight bow. "At the same time—and I fear I owe you an apology, because I did make the offer at least partly out of pique—if there are any sick or injured, it would be my pleasure as well as my duty to offer them healing."

"That was courteously said, Milady," Trisu replied, still more than a bit stiffly but with the first genuine warmth she'd seen from him. "Please, Dame Kaeritha—alight from your horse. My house is yours, and it would seem I have a certain unfortunate first impression to overcome."

Kaeritha's initial impression of Sir Altharn had been misleading. Her first impression of Lord Trisu, unfortunately, and despite his promise to overcome it, had not.

It wasn't that there was anything wrong with Trisu's brain; it was simply that he chose not to use it where certain opinions and preconceptions were concerned. Kaeritha could see only too well why Yalith and the war maids found it so difficult to work with him. However determined one might be to be diplomatic and reasonable, it must be hard to remember one's intention when all one wanted to do was to strangle the stiff-necked, obstinate, bigoted, prejudiced, quintessential young Sothōii reactionary on the other side of the conference table.

His obvious native intelligence never challenged his opinions and prejudices because it was enlisted in their support, instead. That might not prevent him from being an excellent administrator, as was obvious from the condition of his lands and the people living on them. But it was a serious handicap when he was forced to deal with people or events he couldn't hammer into submission to his own biases.

On the other hand, perhaps it's time someone jerked him up short, she thought as she settled into her place at his right hand at the high table in Thalar Keep's great hall.

"I fear Thalar's hospitality must appear somewhat modest compared to that of Balthar." Trisu's words were courteous enough, as was their tone, but there was a challenging glint in his eyes. Or perhaps there wasn't. It was always possible, Kaeritha reminded herself conscientiously, that her own prejudices were unfairly ascribing false attitudes and motives to him.

"Balthar is considerably larger than Thalar, Milord," she replied, after a moment. "But it's been my experience that simple size has less to do with hospitality and the gracious treatment of guests than the graciousness of the host. Certainly no attention to my own comfort has been omitted here in Thalar."

She hid an inner wince at the stiltedness of her own turn of phrase. Trisu seemed to have that effect on her. But what she'd said had been only the truth, at least in physical terms. The fact that Trisu's retainers and servants took their lead from their lord's own attitudes probably explained why there had been a certain lack of genuine welcome behind their courteous attentiveness, but good manners forbade her from mentioning that.

"I'm pleased to hear it," Trisu said, looking out across the crowded tables below them as serving women began bringing in the food. Then he returned his attention fully to Kaeritha.

"I've read Baron Tellian's letters, Dame Kaeritha," he said. "And I will, of course, comply with his wishes and instructions." His smile was thin, and his gray eyes glittered. "Lorham stands ready to assist you in any way we may."

"I appreciate that," she replied, forbearing to observe that it was marvelous that it appeared to have taken him no more than the better part of seven hours to work his way through all two of the letters Tellian had sent along.

"Yes. But that's for tomorrow. For tonight, allow my cooks to demonstrate their skill for you." A serving maid deposited a stuffed, roasted fowl before him, and he reached for a carving knife. "Would you prefer light meat, or dark, Milady?" he inquired.

Chapter Twenty-Nine

"Is that crate about ready, Leeana?"

"Almost, Theretha!" Leeana called back up the stair. She finished wrapping the last piece of glassware in its protective braided straw and slipped it into the proper pigeonhole in the crate's top tray. Then she scooped up an armful of loose straw and sifted it down over the tray, making certain that every piece was packed snugly into place yet padded and cushioned against unexpected impacts.

The straw caught on her fingers, and she grimaced with wry humor as she looked down at them. Her hands were as slender as they had always been, with the same long, aristocratic fingers, but now they were work-roughened, nicked, and chapped, as well. They were also bruised, she noted, and two of her fingernails had been gnawed back to the quick after she broke them practicing unarmed combat against Garlahna under Ravlahn's supervision. And they'd developed a nicely growing crop of calluses from mucking out stalls and sweeping up in the municipal stables.

She patted the last of the straw down into a smooth layer, then laid the top slats of the crate across the frame and reached for the tack hammer. Quick, crisp strokes tacked each slat neatly into place, and she set the hammer back down, dipped the paintbrush into the pot of paint, and inscribed the crate's number from the bill of lading on both side panels.

"It's done, Theretha!" she called, stepping to the foot of the stair and looking up it.

"Oh, good!" Theretha replied as she appeared at the head of the stair, smiling down at her helper. "I don't know how I would have gotten this shipment packed in time without you," she continued gratefully, and Leeana grinned.

"Be sure you remember my efficiency the next time you need an assistant!" she said cheerfully.

"Oh, I will—I will!" Theretha assured her. The glassblower came down the stair into her shop's basement and patted the final crate of the consignment with a proprietary air.

"Good! I can use the money."

"Can't we all?" Theretha grimaced humorously, and Leeana laughed. She liked Theretha, and it had been an unanticipated surprise to discover her mother's favorite glassblower lived and worked here in Kalatha. The fact that she'd recognized Theretha's work when she saw it in the shop's display window had emboldened her to answer the other war maid's advertisement when she saw it posted on the Town Hall notice board.

It had worked out quite well, she thought with a certain satisfaction. Recognition of Theretha's work had made her feel as if the shop were somehow connected with the home she'd left behind forever. She treasured that feeling. But perhaps even more importantly, it was what had given her the confidence to approach someone else in search of work for the first time in her entire life.

Theretha was about as little like Leeana's pre-Kalatha vision of a war maid as it was possible to be. She was shy—though not at all timid, a distinction it had taken Leeana a day or two to recognize—and very much on the retiring side, except where her art and her shop were concerned. She was petite, and Leeana doubted

Theretha had reported for a single morning's calisthenics since the day she thankfully finished her required physical training period and escaped the mandatory workouts. She wore a pair of wire-framed glasses for close work, and her favorite article of clothing was a burn-spotted smock improbably decorated with butterflies embroidered in blue, red, and gold. She appeared to have no special passions, aside from her obvious love for glass and the somehow fanatical absentmindedness which seemed to take possession of her the instant she touched her glassblower's pipe. On first acquaintance, she seemed like the sort of person who would always have a mousehole to hide in and would probably spend every night curled up in bed with a book.

Despite that, Theretha was one of the most popular citizens of Kalatha. She seemed to know literally everyone, and everyone who knew her, liked her. She was perpetually helpful, unassuming, yet cheerful, and something about her made everyone want to look after her. It was almost like some protective coloration or natural defense mechanism, although it clearly wasn't anything Theretha did. It was simply who she *was*. Even Leeana, who was certainly the newest war maid in town and at least ten years younger than Theretha, to boot, felt the protective urge which made Theretha a sort of surrogate kid sister for everyone.

There was nothing childlike about Theretha when it came to business, however, and she was an exacting taskmistress. She'd already been through three part-time workers before Leeana walked through her shop door, and none of them had been satisfactory. Which had been fortunate for Leeana . . . who *had* been. After the first afternoon, Theretha had agreed to pay her on a piece basis, rather than an hourly one, despite the glassblower's initial fear that haste would increase breakage. It hadn't, and Leeana had discovered that if she really concentrated, she could earn half again as much in the same period of time—or earn the same amount and still get to her scheduled class with Hundred Ravlahn on time.

Which, she reminded herself as the Town Hall clock struck the hour, was not a minor consideration.

"I've got to run, Theretha!" she said. "I'm going to be late for Hundred Ravlahn. Can I pick up my pay tomorrow morning? I've got to pay the stable master for next week."

"Of course you can," Theretha assured her. "And, trust me, you *don't* want to be late for Ravlahn." She rolled her eyes. "So scoot!"

"On my way!" Leeana assured her, and darted out of the shop door.

"Hi, Leeana!" a voice called as she went bounding down the pedestrian walkway beside the town's main street. "We're all going over to the Green Maiden after dinner, and we—"

"No time, Besthrya," Leeana called back over her shoulder, never slowing her pace. "Sorry! And I'm going to be mucking out stalls again after dinner!" She made a face, waved, and disappeared around the corner.

She kept running, and it occurred to her that the last week had made some major changes in her life. Garlahna had been her lifeline for the first day or so, and Leeana had clung to her desperately . . . whenever she wasn't collapsed in bed trying to catch up on that half-mythic thing called "sleep." But rather to her own surprise, she'd found herself adjusting to her new life with remarkable speed. Or perhaps it wasn't so remarkable. She'd never had the opportunity to watch any other war maids adapting to the same changes, but Hundred Erlis and her assistants—like Hundred Ravlahn—must have taken scores or hundreds of war maid candidates through the same process over the years. Their confident, competent briskness was immensely reassuring, despite their demanding expectations. And after the first day or so, Leeana had realized that, unlike her, they knew exactly what they were doing. Which meant all she had to do was whatever they told her to.

So she had, and in the process, she'd discovered she truly did have at least some aptitude for the physical training they subjected her to. That had come as a pronounced surprise for her, and she'd been just a bit piqued by the fact that it hadn't seemed to surprise *them*. She supposed she ought to take that as a compliment, but the occasional pigeon-eating-cat looks she surprised on their faces made it a bit difficult.

They'd started rather gently with her (though it certainly hadn't seemed that way to her at the time!), but they'd also designed a program whose rigor mounted steadily. Leeana had too little experience with deliberate physical conditioning to realize just how grueling a pace they were actually setting for her, however. No one had ever told her she should be collapsing in exhaustion or whimpering that they were pushing her too hard, and so she'd simply buckled down to the challenge of meeting their expectations and discovered she was actually having *fun*, in an exhausting sort of way. She was even beginning to make some progress in her combat training, although she was still considerably short of the tyro level. At least she was learning to trust her ability to move, and Ravlahn and Garlahna had gotten her past the "Oh, I couldn't possibly *hit* anyone!" stage.

Of course, she grinned at the thought, her tongue gently probing at a loosened tooth, *until my guard gets a lot better,* I'm *not the one who's going to be doing most of the hitting!*

At that, though, she was doing far better in physical training than she was when it came to her kitchen skills. She was perpetually nicking herself peeling potatoes, cutting up onions, or chopping carrots. It had gotten to the point that she'd acquired the nickname "Leeana Bloody Finger" and one or two of the permanent kitchen staff had taken to referring to tomato-based soups as "Leeana juice." Personally, Leeana hadn't found either witticism all that hilarious (despite a certain amusement at the unintended echo of Prince Bahzell's cognomen), but she treasured them anyway. Especially the night one of Kalatha's resident bards, Filkhata Yanakfressa, had unveiled "The Lay of Leeana Bloody Finger" to near-universal gales of laughter. It was a sign that she was finding true acceptance as who she'd become, unshadowed by who she once had been.

Now if there'd only been about five more hours in a day! What with her morning calisthenics, two sessions a day with Ravlahn, an hour or so as an assistant teacher with Lanitha, and the daily work crew assignments—usually, but not always, in the stable (because of Boots) and the kitchen—required of any new war maid in return for the free housing the town furnished to her, it was all but impossible to find the time to care for Boots.

At least the stable's attached paddocks were large enough for the gelding to get some self-provided exercise trotting around and exploring or playing follow-the-leader with other horses. But while that might have been sufficient for a sedentary horse, or one who'd been retired, it certainly wasn't sufficient for Boots! He needed regular workouts if he was going to stay healthy, and somehow she had to find time to at least work him regularly on a lunging line. Taking him out for a brisk ride was even better, of course, but it also ate much more deeply into her time. Given that she had to personally muck out his stall, in addition to grooming, feeding, watering, and exercising him, time was not something of which she had a surplus. Especially not when she factored in the need to do enough odd jobs to earn the money she needed to pay the portion of his stabling fees not covered by her work as one of the stable master's part-time grooms.

Money wasn't something Lady Leeana Bowmaster had ever worried about particularly, but it had become a matter of rather burning urgency to Leeana Hanathafressa.

Fortunately, Leeana had discovered one area in which she could save some of the time she needed so badly elsewhere. It wasn't as if she really *needed* more than five hours of sleep a night, after all.

She turned another corner and picked up her pace a bit more as she saw the weapons salle before her. Garlahna was waiting on the wooden porch, and she looked up and waved as Leeana pounded down the last dozen yards or so and dashed up the steps to the porch.

"Running late, girl!" Garlahna observed, and Leeana

stuck out her tongue at her mentor. "Go ahead," Garlahna shrugged. "Make faces at *me.* But I'll bet you Ravlahn works you a bit harder than usual for it!"

"Hah!" Leeana snorted, passing her friend at a dead run. "That's an empty threat if I ever heard one—she *can't* work me any harder than she's already doing!"

"Oh, can't I?" another voice inquired, and Leeana skidded to a halt with an almost comical expression of dismay as Ravlahn Thregafressa smiled at her. The assistant training mistress stood just inside the salle door, hands propped on her hips, and Leeana managed to give her a smile that was only slightly sickly.

"Uh, I hope you aren't going to take any silly jokes I may have made to Garlahna seriously?" she said.

"Oh, of *course* not," Ravlahn agreed with a broad, toothy smile, and waved Leeana courteously past her into the salle.

"Dear gods," Leeana groaned to Garlahna as she dragged herself into the welcoming steam of the training salle's attached baths. "Remind me to never, ever say *anything* Ravlahn could take as a challenge again!"

"She did seem just a tad inspired," Garlahna agreed with a chuckle. She stopped Leeana by one of the big, communal tubs and began helping to unlace her yathu. Leeana sagged bonelessly, leaning gratefully back against the raised, masonry lip of the poollike tub.

"Yes, she did," someone else observed, and Leeana turned to look at the speaker. It was a war maid she'd seen once or twice before, but hadn't actually been introduced to. The other woman was probably a few years older than Ravlahn, with short blond hair. She was soaking in the slightly cooler tub beside the one Leeana was leaning against, and it was obvious from her hard-trained muscles and scars—most of them small, but including one or two which were fairly spectacular—that she was one of the true *war* maids.

"Soumeta Harlahnnafressa," the other woman introduced herself with a lazy smile, then raised one arm from the water to wave a dripping hand at the other two women—

both somewhere between her own age and Leeana's—who shared the tub with her. "Tharnha Garhlanfressa," Soumeta said, indicating the dark-haired, dark-complected woman to her right, "and Eramis Yohlahnafressa."

Eramis' complexion was as fair as Tharnha's was dark, and the long hair, temporarily done up in a knot atop her head, was a platinum blond so pale it was almost white. All things considered, Soumeta and her companions made a striking trio, Leeana thought.

"Leeana—Leeana Hanathafressa," she said, politely introducing herself in return. It still took her a moment or two to remember to use her matronym, and she felt her face go just a little pink over the embarrassing hesitation.

"I know," Soumeta said with a smile. "Everyone in Kalatha's been talking about you ever since you arrived, you know."

"Oh." Leeana felt her blush darken. She half-turned away from the other woman and busied herself peeling out of the rest of her clothing. She'd spent enough time undressed in front of maids and seamstresses and in Hill Guard's women's baths not to be particularly bothered by her nudity under normal circumstances. At the moment, however, she felt sufficiently embarrassed by Soumeta's comment to climb into the water more quickly than usual.

And, of course, the water is hotter *than usual,* she thought, trying not to squeal and leap back out as the stinging tide enveloped her. She managed to settle down almost normally, up to her neck in steaming water, and after the first second or two, the liquid heat began its magic and started sucking the aches and pains out of her muscles.

Garlahna joined her a moment later, considerably more cautiously.

"I did notice that they've built the fire under the water heater a bit higher than usual today," Soumeta commented to no one in particular. Leeana darted a look at her, and then found herself forced to chuckle at the older woman's knowing expression.

"Yes, they have," she confirmed feelingly, and Soumeta smiled at her.

"Actually," Leeana continued in a more normal voice, "it's probably a good thing they did. I can use the extra heat after the way Hundred Ravlahn just spent the last decade or so chasing me around the salle. And beating me senseless whenever she caught up with me!"

"Oh, I think you may be being a bit too hard on yourself," Soumeta replied. Leeana blinked at her in surprise, and Soumeta laughed. "I'm not saying you're ready to go out and begin slaying brigands—not by a long chalk! But I've seen quite a few new girls do a lot worse than you were doing out there today."

"Like me, for example," Eramis agreed with something like a cross between a giggle and a chuckle. She shook her head. "It took me *weeks* to get to the point of actually swinging back at Erlis—she was still doing all of the training herself, one arm or not, when I arrived. At least you were trying, Leeana!"

"And she actually got through Ravlahn's guard—once, anyway," Garlahna pointed out.

"I noticed," Soumeta agreed with a nod.

"Oh, she just let me do that!" Leeana protested, turning pink all over again. *And*, she thought, looking down at her half-submerged breasts, *I really am pink* all over. *Wonderful*.

"The Hundred doesn't 'just let' people get a pop in past her guard," Soumeta told her. "I won't say you didn't have the element of surprise on your side, but you're quick, Leeana. Very quick." She considered the younger woman appraisingly. "I think you could work out very well in the Guard after you've completed your probationary period."

Leeana looked up, certain Soumeta was teasing. But the older war maid's expression was completely serious.

"Oh, I don't think—" Leeana began, then stopped herself, suddenly aware that she didn't have any idea what she wanted to say.

The last thing she'd ever wanted to be was some sort of female warrior. Not out of any sort of physical fear, but because it had simply never occurred to her that she might. And, she added honestly, because the fact was that the thought of hurting other people frightened her much more than the thought of being hurt herself. Nor did she cherish many illusions about the "glory" of combat. She was the daughter and granddaughter of warriors—heir of a tradition of women who'd sent generation after generation of husbands and sons off to war . . . and all too often never gotten them home again. The notion of charging into battle held very little allure for Leeana Hanathafressa.

Yet the truth was that she'd discovered she was one of those cheerful lunatics who actually enjoyed physical exercise. Not only that, but she found a strange, obscure, but solid enjoyment in the challenge of Hundred Ravlahn's instruction. They were working almost entirely without weapons at the moment, but she'd also discovered that she was looking forward to the day that that changed.

And, she thought, *there really are some things important enough to fight for. "Glory" might not be one of them, but that doesn't mean they don't exist.*

"Well, it's not as if you have to make up your mind tomorrow," Soumeta pointed out. "For that matter, it's not as if Five Hundred Ermath was going to invite you to take over her duties next week!"

"I'm sure she'll wait at least, oh, a month or two," Tharnha agreed with a laugh, and Leeana had to grin back.

"But aside from your physical training," Soumeta continued, "how are you settling in, Leeana?"

"Better than I expected," Leeana admitted.

"It must have been hard, coming from your family," Tharnha murmured,

"I imagine it's hard coming from *any* family," Leeana said, and kicked herself mentally as she heard the edge of chill which had crept into her voice.

"Tharnha isn't exactly the most tactful person in the world," Soumeta observed with a grin, and gave the dark-haired war maid a friendly clout on the back of her head. Then the blonde looked back at Leeana. "Still, she didn't say anything the rest of us haven't thought, I suppose. In fact, we're all wondering about why you came and whether or not you're glad you did." She cocked her head, gazing thoughtfully at Leeana. "You have to admit, Leeana—we don't exactly see the heir of a baron wandering around in a chari and yathu every day!"

"Well, no. I guess not," Leeana said, then shrugged and looked at Tharnha. "I'm sorry if I sounded offended or something, Tharnha. It's just sort of a sore point with me."

"Where we came from and why is a 'sore point' for a lot of us," Tharnha agreed. "And I should have kept my big mouth shut about it."

"Well, yes," Eramis agreed. "But like Soumeta says, we're all being eaten to death by little bugs trying *not* to ask you, Leeana." She flashed a smile at the younger woman. "I mean, if you tell us to shut up and mind our own business, we will, of course. But you have to know we'll go right on wondering, whatever you say." She waved both hands over her head. "We shouldn't, but we're only human, you know!"

"Yes, I suppose I do," Leeana sighed. She considered it for a few seconds, frowning down into the water of her tub, then sighed.

"Let me put it this way. I didn't leave my family because of anything they did, all right? It was a political—" She paused. "My father received an offer for me—one I didn't want to accept." She made a face. "*No one* would have wanted to accept it, actually. Father wouldn't have made me, but there would have been a lot of political pressure on him to accept it, or something like it. So I decided I'd rather be a war maid."

She considered that for a few seconds, frowning, and decided it was accurate enough to go on with.

"As for whether or not I'm glad I came, ask me again in a month or so! I should have at least caught my breath by then."

Soumeta laughed, and both of the other war maids with her chuckled.

"I don't think it'll take that long," Soumeta said. "You

seem to be adjusting better than most candidates do. And I hear you've already found some extra work to help pay for your horse?"

"And *what* a horse!" Tharnha said, rolling her eyes in appreciative envy.

"Well, yes," Leeana admitted a bit uncomfortably, remembering Mayor Yalith's warnings about resentment from other war maids.

"I envy you the horse," Soumeta said, as if she'd read Leeana's mind, "but I definitely *don't* envy you all the extra work!"

"Of course you don't!" Eramis snickered teasingly. "It would cut into your . . . social calendar."

"You can just leave my social calendar out of this, Mistress Gossip," Soumeta told her with a mock-serious glower.

"Why? It's not as if everybody in Kalatha doesn't know all about your red-hot sex life, Soumeta." Tharnha rolled her eyes again, as enviously as she had over Leeana's possession of Boots.

"Well," Soumeta acknowledged a bit complacently, "I do try to do my bit to balance the scales."

"Balance the scales?" Leeana blushed as the question popped out of her, apparently of its own volition, and Soumeta's eyes swung lazily back to her. She hadn't intended to say a single word, she told herself furiously. What other people did with their own lives was their business, not hers! But, still . . .

"Sure," Soumeta said, after a moment or two during which she seemed to find Leeana's blush enormously entertaining. "Think of all the years and years and years men have been chasing after women like we were mares in season and they were all stallions in rut. Of course, if we ever let any of them *catch* us—outside a nice, legal marriage bed, at least—then *we* were the 'loose women'—" she made what Leeana considered was a fairly obvious decision not to use a few other, cruder terms "—for opening our legs for them. And Lillinara help us if we actually got *pregnant* without a wedding bracelet!"

She rolled her eyes theatrically and her friends laughed,

but there was an undeniable flicker of anger under the humor in Soumeta's voice, and the others' laughter had a hard edge.

"Given how long that's been going on," Soumeta continued after a moment, "I figure it's time we started evening things up a little. I think we ought to be chasing *them* for a change. And if one of them decides he wants to spend an evening cozying up to me, well fine. But if he thinks he's going to nail me down like a good, obedient little girl afterwards, he's got another thought or two coming. Funny how few of them seem to realize it's going to be that way, though. And it may show a nasty streak, but I have to admit, I sort of *like* looking back over my shoulder to watch their faces when they realize I *mean* 'No' and walk away wiggling my sweet arse at them."

She'd watched Leeana's face while she spoke, and the younger woman had the distinct impression Soumeta was gauging her reaction carefully. But was that because Leeana was younger, and Soumeta wanted to see how sheltered her pre-Kalatha existence had truly been? Or was there another reason?

Leeana felt a sudden urge to look at Garlahna and see how *she* was reacting to the conversation, but she decided that wouldn't be a good idea. So, instead, she shrugged.

"I don't think that's something I'm going to have to worry about for a while," she said lightly. "I've got my probation to complete, and Erlis and Ravlahn waiting to work my backside off while I do it. Between that, chores, working for Theretha, and mucking out Boots' stall—oh! and helping Lanitha at the school, too!—I'm not going to have enough time to eat and sleep by myself, much less with anyone else!"

"But it's such a waste to actually *sleep* with someone when there are so many other interesting things you could be doing," Soumeta said with a wicked smile, then laughed at Leeana's expression. "Sorry! I didn't meant to tease you. And I think you're probably right about how much free time you're likely to have, at least for the next few weeks. But this is something you're going to have to think about sooner or later, you know, Leeana," she went on in a more serious tone. "You're a war maid now—or you will be, when you finish your probation, anyway—and that means the decisions will be yours. Not your father's, or your family's, or anyone else's: *yours*. That's the reason most of us became war maids in the first place, to make those decisions for ourselves."

"I know," Leeana agreed, remembering her first day's conversation with Johlana.

"And it's the fact that we want to make them which pisses off people like Trisu of Lorham," Eramis said darkly.

"Among other things," Soumeta agreed, still looking at Leeana. "But there's more to it in his case, too, Eramis. You know how hard he's been pushing us about *everything* ever since he inherited the title. Of course he resents the fact that we don't all ask 'How high?' any time he says 'Jump!' But he's after more than just changing that." She glowered. "He's one of those bastards who wants to turn the clock back two or three hundred years and just pretend the war maids never existed. That we never had a charter at all. And until someone kicks him right in those great big balls he's so proud of having, he's going to go right on pushing, and pushing, and pushing until we give him what he damned well wants or—"

She stopped abruptly and gave her head a short, angry shake that sloshed water over the lip of her tub.

"Sorry, Leeana," she said after a heartbeat or two, with a smile that looked almost natural. "Didn't mean to climb up on my personal hobbyhorse. It just really pisses me off to see someone like him pushing us around—again!—as if we were all still meek little female mice living in a world full of male cats. Or obedient little puppets waiting till they get around to coming home and hauling us off to bed by our hair! Well, we're not, and it's time someone pointed that out to him . . . and all the men like him."

"I'm sure D—" It was Leeana's turn to stop herself short. Dame Kaeritha hadn't told her she was free to discuss the mission which had brought the knight to

Kalatha in the first place. She hadn't told her she *wasn't* free to do so, either, of course, but a champion's business was a champion's business, not a subject for bathhouse gossiping.

"I'm sure Mayor Yalith and the Town Council know what they're doing," she said instead, and hid a mental wince. What she'd just said was probably true enough, but it sounded like the sort of fatuous thing a schoolgirl without two thoughts to rub together would have said.

"Hmph!" Soumeta snorted, flouncing in the water. "Maybe they do, and maybe they don't. Well, at least *some* of them do, I'm sure," she corrected herself. "But this is a war maid free-town, you know. We all get a voice—and a vote—when it comes to deciding what we should be doing. And if this keeps up, Trisu may just find his precious claims starting something he won't like the finish of!"

"And about time, too," Tharnha muttered.

"In a lot of ways," Eramis agreed, then stretched and yawned elaborately. The motion arched her spine and brought her shapely bosom free of the water, and she preened like a cat, with a shameless sensuality which Leeana had never before encountered. "*I* think you're right about who should be chasing who, too, Soumeta," she said lazily. "Let's get what we want from them and let *them* have the broken hearts for a change."

"Hah! Broken *something*, anyway," Tharnha agreed with a chuckle.

"Well, I'm already doing my bit," Soumeta reminded her with a predatory smile. "But whether or not I can keep on doing it depends on whether or not interfering bastards like Trisu can squeeze us all back into their little toy boxes and lock us up there. And I, for one, plan on chopping a few of them up for dog meat before they manage to do that."

"That's sort of what the Voice said at the Temple when I was at Quaysar last fall," Tharnha said. Everyone looked at her, and she shrugged just a little defensively. "Well, she did!" she insisted.

Leeana blinked. She'd heard of the Temple of Lillinara

at Quaysar, though she'd never been there. But she'd never heard of a Voice getting involved in secular affairs unless the very lives of women were involved and the situation was close to desperate.

"The *Voice* said we should stand up to Lord Trisu more strongly?" Garlahna said in a voice which showed she'd found the idea as disturbing as Leeana had.

"Not in so many words," Tharnha admitted. "But she did say she was concerned. That the Mother's daughters should always oppose and fight people who try to make all women victims, and who else do you think she could've been talking about right now?"

"Voices don't send people off to war, Tharnha," Soumeta said. "Or not very often, anyway. She probably just meant we should stand our ground." The guardswoman snorted. "A Voice can't go around telling us to push back even harder than he's pushing us, whatever she might *want* to say. Not without provoking all kinds of complaints from every lord warden—every *male* lord warden—in the Kingdom, anyway. Which doesn't mean it wouldn't be a good idea, of course. Just that a Voice is a little too visible to tell people that."

"Maybe not, Soumeta," Eramis said, "but you know the Voice thinks we shouldn't let anyone push us around the way we always have before. You know that."

"I never said she didn't," Soumeta replied. "I just said she has to be careful about any official position she takes because of who she is. If you want me to admit she's given her support to people like Maretha and her supporters on the Town Council, then I will. I'm just saying that she's smart enough and subtle enough to do it in ways that aren't going to drag her, the temple, or the Mother into open conflict with a lord warden."

"You're probably right," Tharnha agreed. She didn't sound as if she really did agree, but she smiled and shrugged anyway.

"In the meantime, though," she said more brightly, "did any of you see that good looking blond armsman who rode in with the wine merchant this afternoon? *Yummmmmm!*"

She batted her eyes at the others, and Eramis giggled.

"I wouldn't mind getting to know *him* a little better, I can tell you that!" Tharnha went on with a cheerful leer. "Look at that arse of his—and those shoulders! You know what they say about puppies growing up to match the size of their feet?" She leered again, harder. "Well, if certain other portions of *his* anatomy have grown up to match those shoulders—!"

Chapter Thirty

Lord Warden Trisu's office was on the third floor of his family's somewhat antiquated keep. Kaeritha had been surprised when she discovered that, since his father had built a much more palatial suite of offices into Thalar's relatively new Town Hall. Once she saw it, however, her initial surprise faded as quickly as it had come. The choice was part and parcel of the man's entire character, she realized. Its narrow windows—the glass which had been added later couldn't disguise the fact that they'd been designed as archery slits, as much as a way to admit light, when they were built—looked down on the city of Thalar, below, letting him survey his domain whenever he chose. Besides, one look at the office itself, with its spartan, whitewashed walls decorated without softening with shields and weapons, made it clear no other place could possibly have been as comfortable for Trisu, however much more spacious it might have been.

The armsman who'd ushered her into Trisu's presence, withdrew at his lord's gesture, and the office door closed quietly behind him. Sunlight spilled in through the diamond-pane windows behind Trisu's desk, and for all its trophy-girt walls, the square, high-ceilinged room did have a certain airy warmth.

"Good morning, Dame Kaeritha. I trust you slept well? That your chambers were comfortable?"

"Yes, thank you, Milord. I did, and they were." She smiled. "And thank you for seeing me so promptly this morning."

"You are, of course, welcome, although no thanks are necessary. Duty to my liege lord—and to the War God, as well—requires no less." He leaned back in his high-backed chair and folded his hands atop one another on the desk before him. "At the same time," he continued, "I fear Baron Tellian's instructions, while clear, were less than complete. In what way may I assist you?"

"The Baron *was* less than specific," Kaeritha conceded. "Unfortunately, when he wrote those letters, before I set out, neither he nor I were certain what I would discover or what sorts of problems I might find myself dealing with."

He raised an eyebrow, and she shrugged.

"Champions of Tomanāk often find themselves in that sort of situation, Milord. We get used to dealing with challenges on the fly, as it were. Baron Tellian knew that would be the case here."

"I see." Trisu pursed his lips as he considered that. Then it was his turn to shrug. "I see," he repeated. "But may I assume that since you've sought me out and presented the Baron's letters, you now know what problem you face?"

"I believe I've discovered the nature of the problem, at least, Milord." Kaeritha hoped her tone sounded more courteous than cautious, but she was aware that his obvious prejudices had awakened a matching antipathy in her and she was watching her tongue carefully. "It involves your ongoing . . . dispute with Kalatha."

"*Which* dispute, Milady?" Trisu inquired with a thin smile. His response was just a bit quicker than Kaeritha had expected, and her eyes narrowed. "Several matters stand in contention between the war maids and me," he continued. The words "war maids" came out sourly, but Kaeritha would have expected that. What she didn't care for was something else in his tone—something which seemed to suggest he anticipated less than complete impartiality out of her.

"If you'll forgive my saying so, Milord," she said after a moment, "all of your disputes with Kalatha—" she carefully refrained from using the apparently incendiary words "war maids" herself "—are the same at the heart."

"I beg to differ, Dame Kaeritha," Trisu replied, his jaw jutting. "I am well aware that Mayor Yalith chooses to ascribe all of the differences between us to my own deep-seated prejudices. That, however, is not the case."

Kaeritha's expression must have revealed her own skepticism, because he gave a short, barking laugh.

"Don't mistake me, Milady Champion," he said. "I *don't* like war maids. I wouldn't say that I *dis*like them as much as, say, my cousin Triahm, but that's not saying a great deal. I think their very existence is an affront to the way the gods intended us to live, and the notion that women—*most* women at any rate—" he amended as Kaeritha's eyes flashed, although his tone remained unapologetic "—can be the equal of men as warriors is ridiculous. Obviously, as you yourself demonstrate, there are exceptions, but as a general rule, the idea is ludicrous."

Kaeritha made herself sit firmly on her temper. It wasn't easy. But at least the young man sitting across the desk from her had the courage—or arrogance—to say exactly what he thought. And, she admitted after a moment, the honesty to bring his own feelings openly to the table rather than attempt to deny them or dress them up in fine linen. In fact, and although she found herself hesitant to rush to assign virtues to him, that honesty seemed to be an integral part of his personality.

Which undoubtedly makes him even more difficult to live with, she thought wryly. *But it also makes me wonder how he can be maintaining his position so strongly now, when he must know inside that he's in the wrong. Unless his prejudices against war maids are strong enough to overcome that innate honesty of his?*

"I don't much care for 'general rules,' Milord," she said when she was certain she could keep her own tone level. "I've found that, for most people, 'general rules' are all too often little more than an excuse for ignoring realities they don't care to face."

She held his eyes across the desktop, and neither gaze flinched.

"I'm not surprised you should feel that way," he said. "And I imagine that if our positions were reversed, I might feel much as you do. But they aren't reversed, and I don't." The words weren't—quite—as challenging as they might have been, Kaeritha noted. "Because I don't, I choose to say so openly. Not simply because I believe I'm right—although, obviously, I do—but so that there should be no misunderstanding on your part or mine."

"It's always best to avoid misunderstandings," she agreed in a dust-dry voice.

"I've always thought so," he said with a nod. "And having said that, I repeat that my . . . difficulties with Kalatha have very little to do with my opinion of war maids in general. The fact of the matter is that Kalatha is clearly in violation of its own charter and my boundaries and that Mayor Yalith and her town council refuse to admit it."

Kaeritha sat back in her chair, surprised despite herself by his blunt assertion. He'd taken the same position in his correspondence with Tellian's magistrates, but Kaeritha had read the relevant portions of Kalatha's original charter and Lord Kellos' grant in Yalith's library before riding to Thalar. The mayor and Lanitha had pointed out the specific language governing the points in dispute, and Kaeritha had been grateful for the archivist's guidance. Her own command of the written Sothōii language was far inferior to Brandark's, and the archaic usages and cramped, faded penmanship of the long-dead scribe who'd written out Gartha and Kellos' original proclamations hadn't helped. But she'd been able to puzzle her way through the phraseology of the relevant sections eventually, and it was obvious that Yalith's interpretation was far more accurate than Trisu's assertions.

"With all due respect, Milord," she said now, "I've read King Gartha's original proclamation, and the terms of Lord Kellos' grant to the war maids. While I realize many of the subsequent points in dispute between you and Kalatha have arisen out of later customary usages and practices, I think the original language is quite clear. On the matters of water rights, road tolls, and the location of your father's grist mill on land which belongs to Kalatha, it would appear to me that the war maids are correct."

"No, they aren't," Trisu said flatly. "As any fair reading of the documents in question amply demonstrates."

"Are you suggesting that a champion of Tomanāk would *not* read evidentiary documents fairly?" Kaeritha was aware that her own voice was both colder and harder than it had been, but she couldn't help it. Not in the face of his bald denial of the documents she'd read with her own eyes.

"I'm suggesting that the documents clearly say the opposite of what Mayor Yalith claims they say," Trisu replied, refusing to back down. Which, Kaeritha, admitted to herself, required a certain moral courage on his part. Whatever reservations he might cherish about women warriors, he'd had ample proof when she healed three of his sick and injured retainers that she most certainly was a champion of Tomanāk. And only a man absolutely certain of his own ground—or a fool—would so flatly challenge a direct, personal servant of the God of Justice.

"Milord," she said after a pause, "while I would normally hesitate to contradict you, in this instance I fear you are incorrect." His mouth tightened and his eyes narrowed, but he said nothing, and she continued. "Once I reached Kalatha and realized where the dispute lay, I took particular care to examine the originals of the relevant documents. Admittedly, my command of your language is less than perfect, but as a champion of Tomanāk, I've been well trained in jurisprudence. It took me quite some time to feel confident I'd read the documents correctly, but I must tell you that, in my opinion, Mayor Yalith is correct . . . and you aren't."

A silence hovered between them. It was very quiet in the sun-filled, whitewashed room, but Kaeritha sensed the fury blazing incandescently within her host. Yet for all his prejudices, he was a disciplined man, and he kept that fiery temper securely leashed. For the most part.

"Milady Champion," he said at length, and despite his control, there was a bite in the way he pronounced "champion" which Kaeritha didn't care for at all, "I make all due allowance for the fact that our language is not your native tongue. As you yourself just pointed out. However, I, too, have copies of the original charter and grant—made at the same time, by the same scribe, as the documents you examined at Kalatha—in my library. I am quite prepared, if you so desire, to allow you to examine them, as well. I am also prepared to allow you to discuss—freely, and in private—my interpretation of them with my senior magistrate. Who is also my librarian and, I might point out, served my father before me, and whose interpretation is identical to my own. As I say, any *fair* reading not prejudiced by . . . differences of opinion as to proper ways of life, let us say, must come to the same conclusion."

Kaeritha's jaw clenched, and she was forced to throw a leash onto her own temper at the pointed emphasis of his final sentence. Yet even through her anger, she felt a fresh sense of puzzlement. As she'd told him, she was at least as thoroughly trained in matters of law as most royal and imperial judges in the King Emperor's service. To be sure, she was more familiar with Axeman law than that of other countries, but the Code of Kormak was the basic foundation of *all* Norfressan law, not just the Empire's. And there was no way in the world that anyone could possibly stretch and strain the language of the documents in question to support Trisu's unvarnished contention. Yet she'd already come to the conclusion that he was an intelligent man, despite his prejudices. He must know the language *wouldn't* support his position . . . so why was he offering—indeed, almost demanding—that she examine them?

She made herself sit very still and draw a deep, tension-cleansing breath. Trisu's anger was resonating with her own, threatening to undermine the impartiality any champion of Tomanāk must maintain when called upon to consider matters of justice. She knew that, and so she knew she must proceed carefully and cautiously. Besides, she reminded herself as she felt the white-hot heat of her own initial anger cool ever so slightly, he had a point. She'd examined Kalatha's documents; she had a moral obligation to examine his, as well, and to listen to his magistrate's construction of the language involved. The chance that she'd misunderstood or misinterpreted the originals was minuscule, but it did exist, and it was her responsibility to be absolutely positive she had not.

"Milord," she said finally, keeping her voice very level, "you've assured me that your own opinions—or prejudices—are not the basis for your disagreements with Kalatha and the war maids. I, in turn, assure *you*, that any 'differences of opinion' I may hold have not been and will not be permitted to influence my reading of the law or of the evidentiary documents. I will examine them again, if you so desire. And I will discuss them with your magistrate. In the end, however, my interpretation of them will be based upon *my* reading of them, not yours. And if I come to the conclusion that they support my original belief that Mayor Yalith's reading of them is correct, then I will so rule as champion of Tomanāk."

Trisu's gray eyes glittered. There was anger in them, but not nearly so much as she'd expected. Indeed, that hard light seemed born of confidence, not temper. Which only increased her sense of confusion.

If she ruled formally in this case as Tomanāk's champion, her decision was final. That was one reason champions so seldom made formal rulings. Most of them, like Kaeritha herself, preferred simply to investigate and then to make recommendations to the appropriate local authorities. It prevented bruised feelings, and it allowed for local compromises, which any champion knew were often a truer path to justice than cold, unparsed legalism. Yet Trisu seemed unfazed by the possibility of an adverse decision which would absolutely and permanently foreclose any revisiting of the dispute. Indeed, he seemed to welcome the possibility of a ruling from her, and she wondered if he had deliberately set out to goad her into exactly this course of action.

"The ruling of Scale Balancer's champion must, of course, be final," he said at length. "And, to be honest, Milady Champion, even if you should rule against me, simply having the entire matter laid to rest once and for all will be a relief of sorts. Not that I believe you will."

"We'll see, Milord," Kaeritha said. "We'll see."

Chapter Thirty-One

"Here it is, Dame Kaeritha."

Salthan Pickaxe was some sort of distant cousin of Trisu, although he was at least twice Trisu's age. That kind of relationship between a lord and his chief magistrate was scarcely unheard of, but Kaeritha had been more than a bit surprised by Salthan. He was much more like Sir Altharn then his liege, with a lively sense of humor hiding behind bright blue-gray eyes and a thick, neatly trimmed beard of white-shot auburn. He was also, she'd been amused to note, much more gallant then his cousin. Indeed, he seemed quite taken by the combination of Kaeritha's dark black hair and sapphire eyes. Which, to be fair, was such an unusual combination among Sothōii that she'd become accustomed to their reaction to her exotic attractiveness.

But Salthan was also at least as intelligent as Trisu, and he seemed just as mystifyingly confident.

Now he took a heavy wooden scroll case from its pigeonhole and eased its contents out into his hand. He was obviously well accustomed to dealing with documents which were no longer in their first youth, but it was unhappily apparent that not all keepers of Lorham's records had been. Kalatha's documents were, by and large, in much better shape than Lorham's, and it showed in the care Salthan took as he slowly and gently unrolled the scroll.

Age-fragile parchment crackled, and Kaeritha felt a tingle of that unease any archivist feels when her examination of ancient materials threatens them with destruction. But Salthan got it open without inflicting major additional damage. He laid it out on the library table, then adjusted the oil lamp's wick and chimney to provide her with the best possible light.

It was as well he had, Kaeritha thought, leaning forward and squinting at the document before her. It was, as Trisu had said, a duplicate copy of Lord Kellos' original grant to the war maids, and it was even more faded and difficult to read than the original. No doubt because of the indifferent care it had received, she thought. Still, she could make out the large numeral "3" in the margin, which indicated that it was the third copy made, and she recognized the crabbed, archaic penmanship of the same scribe who'd written out the original.

She ran her eyes down the section which set forth the boundaries of the grant, looking for the language which defined the specific landmarks around the river and the disputed gristmill. It was the least ambiguous and archaic of the entire document, and she might as well start with the parts that were easiest to follow. Besides, the exact boundaries were at the heart of the issue, so—

Ah! Here they were. She bent closer, reading carefully, then stiffened.

That can't be right, she thought, and reread the section. The words remained stubbornly unchanged, and she frowned in puzzlement. Then she opened the document pouch she'd brought with her and extracted the notes she'd written out so meticulously in Kalatha's library. She opened them and laid the neatly written pages on the table beside the scroll, comparing the passage she'd copied with the document before her on a word-for-word basis. It was absolutely clear and unambiguous.

". . . and the aforesaid boundary shall run from the

east side of Stelham's Rock to the corner of Haymar's holding, where it shall turn south at the boundary stone and run two thousand yards across the River Renha to the boundary stone of Thaman Bridlemaker, which shall be the marker for the boundary of the Lord of Lorham."

That was the exact language from the original grant at Kalatha. But the language in the document Salthan had just laid before her said—

". . . and the aforesaid boundary shall run from the east side of Stelham's Rock to the corner of Haymar's holding, where it shall turn south at the boundary stone and run one thousand yards to the north side of the River Renha, the agreed-upon boundary of the Lord of Lorham."

It wasn't a minor ambiguity after all, she thought. It was a flat contradiction. If the document before her was accurate, then Trisu was completely correct—the disputed gristmill on the southern bank of the Renha was on his property and always had been. For that matter, Kalatha's claim to undisputed control of the river's water rights was also nonexistent, since the river would lie entirely within Trisu's boundaries, not Kalatha's. But how *could* it be accurate? Surely the original grant must supersede any copy in the event of differences between them, and the one before her could only represent a bizarre mistake.

Yet that was preposterous. True, it was a copy, not the original, yet it was scarcely likely that the same scribe who'd written out both documents would have made such a mistake. And it was even less likely that such an error could have been missed in the intense scrutiny all copies of the original grant must have received by those party to it.

Unless one copy was a deliberate forgery, of course. . . .

But how could *that* be the case? If this was a counterfeit, it was a remarkably good one. Indeed, it was so good she couldn't believe anyone in Lorham could have produced it in the first place. However good Salthan might be as a librarian, turning out such a flawless false copy of a document over two centuries old must be well beyond his capabilities. So if a forgery had been produced, who had produced it, and when?

She carefully hid a grimace at the thought, wondering how in the world anyone would ever be able to answer those questions. But answering them could wait at least until she'd determined that they were the only ones which required answers.

She considered her options for a few more seconds, then looked up at Salthan with a painstakingly neutral expression.

"Thank you," she said, tapping the scroll very carefully with a fingertip. "This is exactly the section of Lord Kellos' grant I wanted to see. Now, if you please, Lord Trisu also mentioned that you have a copy of King Gartha's proclamation, as well."

"Yes, we do, Lady," Salthan replied. "In fact, it's in rather more readable condition than Kellos' grant. Let me get it for you."

"If you would," she requested, and leafed through her other notes for the sections of the war maid charter relevant to the other points in dispute between Trisu and his neighbors that she'd copied in Kalatha.

Salthan opened the proper case and unrolled a second scroll, just as carefully as he'd unrolled the first one. He was right; this document was much more legible than the Kalatha land grant, and Kaeritha bent over it, eyes searching for the sections she needed.

She read through them one by one, comparing the language before her to that she had copied in Kalatha, and despite all of her formidable self-control, her frown grew more and more intense as she worked her way through them. Then she sat back and rubbed the tip of her nose, wondering if she looked as perplexed as she thought she did.

Well, she thought, *it just may be that I'm beginning to understand yet another reason He sent me to deal with this instead of Bahzell or Vaijon. He does have a way of choosing His tools to fit the problem . . . even when we poor tools don't have a clue why it has to be us. Or exactly where we're supposed to go next.*

"I appreciate your assistance, Sir Salthan," she said after a moment. "And I think I may be beginning to understand why your and your lord's interpretation of the documents is so fundamentally different from that of Mayor Yalith. There does seem to be a degree of . . . discrepancy now that I've had a chance to lay my notes side-by-side with your copy. I don't pretend to understand where it came from, but it's obvious that until it's resolved, it will be impossible for anyone to rule definitively in this case."

"I couldn't agree more, Milady," Salthan said soberly. Trisu's magistrate was sitting across the table from her now, his blue-gray eyes intent . . . and troubled. "Unlike you, I haven't had the opportunity to compare the documents to one another, but I *know* these copies have been here in this library from the day they were first penned. Under the circumstances, I think My Lord and I have no alternative but to believe they're accurate, and, unlike his late father, Lord Trisu is not the sort of man to tolerate the infringement of his rights or prerogatives. Which is why, after he'd asked me to research the language and had seen the relevant passages for himself, he began to press Kalatha over these matters."

"No doubt you're right," Kaeritha said. "On the other hand, Sir Salthan, I can't quite escape the suspicion that he's a little more irritated over the apparent violation of his rights or prerogatives when the suspected violators are war maids."

"Probably—no, certainly—you're right, Dame Kaeritha. And he's not alone in that regard, either. We've had other disputes with Kalatha over the years. Indeed, when Lord Trisu's Uncle Saeth—his father's younger brother; Lord Triahm's father—was killed in a hunting accident some ten years ago, there were those who claimed to have evidence that it was no accident at all. That the war maids arranged it because of his outspoken condemnation of their chosen way of life. I personally always found that a bit hard to swallow, but the fact that it could gain such wide credence clearly suggests that Lord Trisu is far from alone in his dislike for them. Yet even if he were, would that truly have any bearing on whether or not our interpretation is correct in the eyes of the law?"

"No," she said, although she was guiltily aware that part of her wished it did. On the other hand, champions of Tomanāk were still mere mortals. They had their prejudices and opinions, just like anyone else. But they also had a unique responsibility to recognize that they did and to set those prejudices aside rather than allow them to influence their decisions or actions.

"Are you familiar, Sir Salthan," she continued after a moment, "with the sorts of abilities Tomanāk bestows upon His champions when he accepts Sword Oath from them?"

"I beg your pardon?" Salthan blinked, clearly surprised by the apparent *non sequitur*. Then he shrugged.

"I'm scarcely 'familiar' with them, Milady. I doubt very many people are, really. I've done some reading, of course. And to be honest, I did a little more research when Lord Trisu told me a champion had come to visit us. Our library, unfortunately, isn't especially well stocked with the references I needed. The best anything I had could do was to tell me that Tomanāk is less . . . consistent from champion to champion than many of the other Gods of Light are."

"'Less consistent,'" Kaeritha murmured, and smiled. "That may be as concisely as I've ever heard it put, Sir Salthan. There are times when I wish He was more like, oh, Toragan or Torframos. Or Lillinara, for that matter. *Their* champions all seem to get approximately the same abilities, in greater or lesser measure. But Tomanāk prefers to gift each of His champions with individual abilities. For the most part, they seem to mesh with abilities or talents we already had before we heard His call, but sometimes no one has any idea why a particular champion received a specific ability. Until, of course, the day comes when he—or she—*needs* that ability."

"And is this such an occasion, Milady?" Salthan asked, his eyes more intent than ever.

"Yes and no." Kaeritha shrugged. "I've had the need for almost all of the abilities He's granted me at one time or another already. But I have to admit that I should have begun to suspect there was a specific reason He'd sent me to deal with this problem. Especially when Lord Trisu reminded me that the controlling language itself is in dispute."

"I wish I'd had the opportunity to examine the Kalathan originals," Salthan said a bit wistfully. "It's been obvious from the beginning that there's a fundamental contradiction between what I was reading here and the language Mayor Yalith and her magistrates have been citing. But without the chance to see the originals for myself, there was no way for me to judge how accurate—or, for that matter, honest—their citations were."

"Well, I have had the opportunity to examine them," Kaeritha told him. As she spoke, she stood and crossed to another table, under the library window, where she'd placed her sheathed swords when she and Salthan entered. No champion of Tomanāk ever left the sword—or swords—which was the emblem of her authority behind when engaged upon official duties. Now she unbuttoned the retaining strap on the sword she normally wore at her left hip and drew the glittering, two-foot blade.

Salthan raised an eyebrow in surprise as she drew steel, and then she smiled, despite the gravity of the moment, as his other eyebrow rose to match it when her sword suddenly began to glow with a blue nimbus bright enough to be clearly visible even in the well-lit library.

"As I say," she continued in a deliberately blasé tone, "I have had the opportunity to examine them. Unfortunately, it didn't occur to me then just how *thoroughly* I should have 'examined' them."

She sat back down, facing him over the original table once more, and laid the sword flat before her, its glittering blade across both the scrolls Salthan had located for her.

"And now, Sir Salthan," she said in a far more formal voice, "I have a request to make of you as champion of the Keeper of the Scales."

"Of course, Milady," the Sothōii said quickly, and

Kaeritha noted his tone and manner carefully. She was gratified by his prompt acquiescence, but she was even more gratified when she was unable to detect any sign of hesitation or indecision. Clearly he felt no more reservations about accepting her authority than he would have felt accepting the authority of any male champion.

"This is primarily for the record," she told him, "because you are the primary custodian of these documents." She turned her sword slightly, angling the hilt in his direction. "Please place your hand on the hilt of my sword."

He obeyed, although she felt dryly amused by the fact that this time he did hesitate ever so slightly. Not that she blamed him. This was undoubtedly the first time anyone had ever invited him to lay hold of a sword wrapped in the corona of a god's power.

She waited for his initial, ginger touch to settle into something a bit more confident when no lightning bolt sizzled down from the rafters to incinerate him where he sat. Then she nodded.

"Thank you," she said, as encouragingly as she could without stepping out of her own magisterial role. "And now, Sir Salthan, will you attest for me, in the presence of the God of Justice, that to the best of your personal knowledge, these are the original copies of the proclamation of King Gartha and the Kalathan land grant of Lord Kellos which were originally placed in the custody of the Lords of Lorham?"

"To the best of my personal knowledge, they are, Milady," Salthan said in a calm, formal voice, his eyes never wavering under her intent regard. The blue light clinging to her sword never wavered, either, she noted. In fact, it grew stronger.

"And also to the best of your personal knowledge, they are authentic and unchanged. There have been no additions, no deletions, and no alterations?"

"None, Milady," Salthan said firmly.

"Thank you," she repeated, and nodded for him to remove his hand. He did so, and if he sat back in his chair with a bit more alacrity than he'd shown leaning forward, Kaeritha didn't blame him a bit.

She looked down at the documents before her, then lifted her sword across her open palms, holding it between her and the scrolls.

All right, she thought, closing her eyes while she reached out to that ever-present link connecting her to the blazing power of Tomanāk's presence. *It took me a while to get the hint. I'm sorry about that, although I suppose I* could *point out that having Leeana along was enough to distract anyone. But now that I'm here and You've more or less used Salthan to rub my nose in it, suppose You tell me whether or not these documents are forgeries.*

She sensed a distant, delighted rumble of divine laughter . . . and approval. Then she opened her eyes again and looked down at her sword.

Which, she was no longer the least bit surprised to see, continued to glow a bright, steady blue.

Chapter Thirty-Two

Kaeritha Seldansdaughter sat in the chamber Lord Trisu had assigned to her in Thalar Keep and gazed out the window at a cloudless sky of midnight blue spangled with the glitter and glow of Silendros' stars. It was a clearer sky than she'd seen any night since arriving on the Wind Plain, and she had never seen the stars brighter or larger than they looked tonight. A crescent nail-paring of a new moon glowed purest silver in the eastern sky, and she studied it with an intent frown, wondering what Lillinara thought She was doing to let this situation get so out of hand.

Well, she told herself scoldingly, *that's probably not entirely fair. It's not as if She were the only god with an interest in mortal affairs, and I suppose not even a god can be expected to keep up with everything Her worshipers need. But these are war maids, for Tomanāk's sake!* Her *war maids—so what in the world is She* thinking *about? And why hasn't She spoken to Her Voice at Quaysar about it?*

That was the heart of the entire question. Of course, it would have helped if it had occurred to Kaeritha to test the authenticity—or, at least, the accuracy—of the documents at Kalatha. She should have, if only in the name of thoroughness, although to be fair to herself, she'd had absolutely no reason to doubt them. And even now she was certain Yalith and her council saw no reason to question them. And why should they? They knew they had the original, controlling documents in their possession.

Unfortunately, Tomanāk Himself had seen fit to assure Kaeritha that the copies in Trisu's possession were most definitely not forgeries. One of those special abilities she'd mentioned to Salthan was that no one could lie successfully to her while touching her sword, and that no false or deliberately misleading document or evidence could evade her detection when she held the blade and called upon Tomanāk to determine its accuracy. Which meant Trisu's documents were not simply genuine, but that they accurately set forth the original language and *true intent* of both Gartha and Kellos. Kaeritha had seen enough in other investigations she'd conducted to be unwilling to rule very many things categorically out of consideration, but she was not prepared to question His personal assurances.

Which meant that somehow, impossible as it manifestly must be, the *original* documents at Kalatha were the forgeries.

Kaeritha hadn't shared that conclusion with Trisu. And she had invoked her champion's authority to extract Sword Oath from Salthan to keep the results of this afternoon's examination and investigation to himself. Which meant that so far no one but she knew where the unpalatable chain of evidence was leading her. Nor did she intend to share that with anyone else until she saw a clearer path through the maze before her.

She let her mind wander back an hour or two to this evening's after-dinner conversation with Trisu.

"And has your investigation thrown any fresh light on my differences with Mayor Yalith?" Trisu asked as he toyed with his glass. Like many Sothōii nobles, he was particularly fond of the expensive liqueurs distilled in Dwarvenhame and the Empire of the Axe. Kaeritha liked them just fine herself, but she also entertained a lively respect for their potency. Which was why she had contented herself with wine rather than the brandy Trisu had offered her.

"Some, Milord," she said.

He leaned back, cocking an eyebrow, and regarded her thoughtfully.

"May I take it that whatever you and Salthan discovered—or discussed, at least—this afternoon has at least not inspired you to immediately rule against me?"

"It was never my intent to 'immediately rule' for or against anyone, Milord," she said mildly. "I would prefer, at this point, not to be a great deal more specific than that, although honesty and simple justice do compel me to admit that, so far at least, the situation is considerably less cut and dried than I had assumed initially."

"Well," he said with a slight smile, "I suppose I must consider that an improvement, given your original comments to me." Kaeritha's temper stirred, but she suppressed it firmly, and he continued. "And I must admit," he went on, "that I'm gratified to see exactly the sort of impartiality and willingness to consider all the evidence which I would have expected out of a champion of Tomanāk. The more so because I have something of a reputation for stubbornness myself. I know how difficult it is for anyone, however honest or however good his—or her—intentions, to truly consider fresh evidence which appears to contradict evidence he's already accepted as valid."

For a moment, Kaeritha wondered if somehow Salthan's oath had slipped. But even as the thought crossed her mind, she dismissed it out of hand. She didn't believe the magistrate would have knowingly or intentionally violated it under any circumstances. More than that, even if he'd been inclined to do so, he couldn't have been able to break an oath sworn on a champion's sword, which, in the moment of swearing, actually *was* the very Sword of Tomanāk. It was simply a fresh warning to her never to underestimate Trisu's intelligence just because she detested his opinions and attitudes.

"It's not always easy, no," she agreed. "But it *is* a trick any of Tomanāk's champions has to master. I imagine the lord of any domain has to be able to do much the same thing if he's going to administer justice fairly."

She smiled affably, hiding her amusement—mostly—as his eyes flashed when her shot went home.

"On the other hand, Milord," she continued more briskly, "I feel I'm definitely making progress where the documents and their interpretations are concerned. At the moment, I have more questions than I have answers, but at least I believe I've figured out what the questions themselves are. And I feel confident Tomanāk will lead me to their answers in the end.

"But there is one other matter which doesn't relate to the documents or, actually, officially to Kalatha itself in any way."

"Indeed?" he said coolly when she paused.

"Yes, Milord. When I spoke with Mayor Yalith, it was clear to me that more was involved than the simple legalities of your disagreement could explain. There was, quite frankly, a great deal of anger on the war maids' part. And, to be equally frank, it became quite apparent in speaking with you that the same is true from your perspective."

Trisu's gray eyes were hard, and she raised one hand in a slight throwing away gesture.

"Milord, that's almost always the case when a dispute reaches the point this one has. It's not necessarily because either side is inherently evil, either. It's because the people on both sides are just that—people. And people, Milord, get angry with other people they feel are wrong or, even worse, out to cheat them in some way. It's a fact of life which any judge—or champion of Tomanāk—simply has to take into consideration. Just as you have to take it into consideration, I'm sure, when you're forced to adjudicate between the conflicting claims of two of your retainers or tenants."

It would have been too much to say that Trisu's anger dissipated, but at least he nodded grudgingly in an admission that she'd made her point.

"Quite often," she continued, "there are additional causes for anger and resentment. When people are already unhappy with one another, they're seldom as interested as they might otherwise be in extending the benefit of the doubt to the people they're unhappy with."

"I understand that you're attempting to prepare me for some point you intend to raise and think I'll find objectionable, Lady Champion," Trisu said with a thin smile which actually held a trace of genuine amusement. "Shall we simply agree that you've done that now and get on with it?"

"Well, yes, I suppose we could." Kaeritha gave him an answering smile and nodded her head in acknowledgment.

"Where I was going, Milord, is that the Mayor's share of the . . . intransigence in this dispute seems to be fueled in no small part by her belief that you've shown insufficient respect for the Voice of Lillinara at Quaysar."

"What you truly mean, Milady," Trisu responded in a flat, hard voice, "is that she believes I have shown *no* respect for the Voice. And, while we're on the subject, that she bitterly resents my failure to solve the disappearance—or murder—of the Voice's handmaidens."

Once again, Kaeritha was surprised by his blunt, head-on attitude. Not that she should have been, perhaps, she reflected. Trisu was in many ways the quintessential Sothōii. He might be capable of tactical subtlety on the battlefield, but he disdained anything that smacked of the indirect approach in his own life.

She felt a fresh flicker of anger at the confrontational light in his eyes, but she reminded herself once more never to underestimate this intolerable young man's native intelligence. Nor was she about to forget that the evidence she herself had turned up that afternoon strongly suggested that there was more than a little merit to his interpretation of the actual legal disputes.

"I suppose that is what I mean," she conceded after a moment. "Although that's considerably more . . . pointed than the manner in which I would have chosen to express it."

He looked at her long and steadily, then dipped his head in a small bob of acknowledgment. He even had the grace to blush ever so slightly, she thought. But one thing he didn't do was retreat from the point he'd just made.

"No doubt it was more confrontational than one as courteous as you've already proven yourself to be would have phrased it to her host, Milady. For that, I apologize. But that was essentially what she said, was it not?"

"Essentially," she acknowledged.

"I thought it would be," he said and gazed at her speculatively for a few more seconds. "Given your willingness to consider and examine the evidence Salthan and I offered you, I would assume you've raised this point in order to hear my side of it directly."

His tone made the statement a question, and she nodded.

"Dame Kaeritha," he began after a moment, "I won't attempt to pretend that I'm not more uncomfortable dealing with Lillinara and Her followers than I am with other gods and their worshipers. I don't understand Lillinara. And I don't much care for many of the things Her followers justify on the basis of things She's supposed to have told them. To be perfectly honest, there are times I wonder just how much of what She's supposed to have said was actually invented by people who would have found it convenient for Her to tell them what they wanted to hear in the first place."

Kaeritha arched her eyebrows.

"That's a . . . surprisingly frank admission, Milord," she observed.

"No sane man doubts the existence of the gods, Milady," he replied. "But no *intelligent* man doubts that charlatans and tricksters are fully capable of using the gods and the religious faith of others for their own manipulative ends. Surely you wouldn't expect someone charged with the governance of any domain to close his eyes to that possibility?"

"No, I wouldn't," she said, and felt a brief flicker of something very like affection for this hard-edged, opinionated youngster. "In fact, that sort of manipulation is one of the things champions spend a lot of their time undoing and repairing."

"I thought it probably would be." Trisu sipped brandy, then set down his glass, and his nostrils flared.

"I brought up my . . . discomfort with Lillinara intentionally, Milady. I wanted you to be aware that *I* was aware of it. And because I am aware of it, I reminded myself when I met Lillinara's newest Voice that the fact that I don't like what someone tells me She wants me to do doesn't *necessarily* make that someone a liar. But in this instance, I've come to the conclusion that the so-called 'Voice' at Quaysar is one of those manipulators."

"That's an extremely serious charge, Lord Trisu." Kaeritha's voice was low, her expression grim, yet she wasn't remotely as surprised to hear it as she should have been.

"I'm aware of that," he replied with unwonted somberness. "It's also one which I haven't previously made to anyone in so many words. I would suspect, however, that Mayor Yalith, who—despite our many and lively differences—is an intelligent woman, knows that it's what I think."

"And why *do* you think it, Milord?"

"First and foremost, I'm sure, is the fact that I don't much care for this particular Voice. In fact, the day I first met her, when she arrived to take up her post at Quaysar, she and I took one another in immediate and intense dislike."

"Took *one another* in immediate dislike?" Kaeritha repeated, and Trisu chuckled sourly.

"Milady, I couldn't possibly dislike her as much as I do without her disliking me right back! I don't care how saintly a Voice of Lillinara is supposed to be."

Despite herself, Kaeritha laughed, and he shrugged and continued.

"It's not unusual, I imagine, for the lord of any domain to have differences of opinion with the priests and priestesses whose spheres of authority and responsibility overlap with his. Each of us would like to be master in his own house, and when we have conflicting views or objectives, that natural resentment can only grow stronger.

"But in this case, it went further than that."

He paused, and Kaeritha watched his face. It was as hard, as uncompromising, as ever, yet there was something else behind his expression now. She didn't know quite what the emotion was, but she knew it was there.

"How so, Milord?" she asked after the silence had stretched out for several breaths.

"I don't—" he began, then stopped. "No, Dame Kaeritha," he said, "that's not true. I started to say that I don't really know how to answer your question, but I do. I suppose I hesitated because I was afraid honesty might alienate you."

"Honesty may anger me, Milord," she said with the seriousness his tone and manner deserved. "It shouldn't, but I'm only the champion of a god, not a god myself. But this much I will promise you, on my sword and His. So long as you give me honesty, I will give you an open ear and an open mind." She smiled without humor. "As you've been honest with me, I'll be honest with you. You hold certain beliefs and opinions with which I am as uncomfortable as I'm sure you are with the war maids. No doubt you'd already realized that. But whether or not I agree with you in those matters has nothing to do with whether or not I trust your honesty."

"That was well said, Milady," Trisu said with the first completely ungrudging warmth he'd displayed. Then he drew a deep breath.

"As I'm sure Mayor Yalith told you, the original town of Quaysar has effectively been absorbed by the temple there. In the process, the office of the Voice of the temple has merged with the office of the mayor of Quaysar, as well. By tradition, the same person has held both of them for the past seventy-odd years. Which means the Voice isn't simply the priestess of the temple, but also the secular head of the community. In that role, she's one of my vassals, which has occasionally created uncomfortable strains between the various Voices and my own father and grandfather. Inevitably, I suppose, given the unavoidable difficulties the Voices must have faced in juggling their secular obligations to the Lord of Lorham with their spiritual obligations to his subjects. And, of course, to the war maids over whom my house has no actual jurisdiction.

"My father had seen to it that I would be aware such difficulties were only to be expected from time to time. I think he was afraid that without such an awareness I would be unwilling to consider the sorts of compromises which situations like that might require. He'd seen enough of that attitude from my Uncle Saeth, I suspect, and even as a child, I'm afraid I wasn't exactly noted for *cheerful* compromises." He snorted a sudden laugh of his own and shook his head when Kaeritha looked a question at him. "Your pardon, Milady. I was just thinking about how fervently my tutors and arms instructors would have endorsed that last statement of mine."

Kaeritha nodded. At least he was able to laugh at himself sometimes, she thought.

"At any rate," he continued, "I was prepared for the possibility that the new Voice and I might not exactly take to one another on sight. What I wasn't prepared for was the . . . well, the wave of *wrongness* that poured off of her."

"'Wrongness'?" Kaeritha repeated very carefully.

"I don't know a better word for it," Trisu said. "It was as if every word she said rang false. *Every* word, Milady. I've met other people I simply didn't like, and I'm sure other people have had that reaction to me. But this was like a dog and a cat closed into the same cage—or perhaps a snake and a ferret. It was there between us from the instant she opened her mouth, and although it shames me to admit it, something about her frightened me."

He looked squarely at Kaeritha, and his gray eyes were dark.

"If you want the full truth of it, Milady," he said very quietly, "I wasn't at all sure which of us was the ferret . . . and which the serpent."

✧ ✧ ✧

Kaeritha stared up at the heavens, recalling Trisu's expression and tone, and a chill ran down her spine like the tip of an icicle. Trisu of Lorham might be a pain in the arse. He might be opinionated, and he was certainly stubborn. But one thing she did not believe he was was a coward. For that matter, no true coward would have been prepared to admit to a champion of Tomanāk that he'd been frightened by anyone. Especially not if he was also a thorough-going conservative of Trisu's stripe admitting he'd been frightened by a woman.

But Yalith had shown no sign of any similar feelings towards the Voice. It was tempting, dreadfully so, to put the difference down to all of the other differences between Kalatha and the Lord of Lorham. Yet tempting or not, Kaeritha knew that simple answer was insufficient.

Which was why she knew she had to travel to Quaysar herself. And why she felt an icy edge of fear of her own at the thought.

Chapter Thirty-Three

"I wish you didn't have to go."

"I'd rather not go myself, dear heart," Tellian said. He put an arm around Hanatha and hugged her gently. "What I wish I could do is stay here with you. If I can't bring Leeana home to you—and I can't—then if the gods were fair, I could at least be here with you while we adjust to the emptiness."

"The gods are never unfair," Hanatha said. She rose on tiptoe to kiss his cheek and smiled sadly at him. "We mortals make our own decisions, and we must live with their consequences."

"I don't remember deciding that an unmitigated bastard like Cassan, with the morals of a pimp and the mind of a weasel, had any right to propose a lecherous dog older than I am, who's little better than a common rapist, as our only daughter's husband!" Tellian replied, just a bit more warmly than he'd intended to.

"No," she replied, and her own quiet tone was a gentle rebuke, "but I don't remember saying we had to live only with the consequences of our *own* decisions. It wouldn't be proper for me to agree with your description of Cassan or Blackhill," she continued primly, "but since only a most undutiful wife would *disagree* with her husband, and I, of course, am far too beaten down and intimidated to be anything but dutiful, I'll let that deplorable language pass. If, however, the opportunity to introduce Cassan's parents to one another should ever come your way, I trust you will do so."

Despite his own frustration and anger, Tellian felt his lips twitch as he tried to suppress a smile.

"But whatever we may think of the two of them," Hanatha continued more seriously, "they, too, have power to make decisions, and their decisions carry consequences not simply for them, but for others. Including us. And however much it may pain us, *Leeana's* decisions also carry consequences for all of us. It seems to me that it would be asking a bit much of the gods to sort out that incredible snake's nest of mutually conflicting decisions just so they could make you and me happy. Mind you, I wouldn't object if they decided to do exactly that, but I'm afraid the best any of us can do is cope with our own decisions—and responsibilities—as best we may."

"There are times, love—many times—when I feel the wrong one of us was born male. You would have made a superb baron."

"Perhaps. But as it is, I get to give my advice knowing the ultimate responsibility is yours, not mine." She smiled. "That means I feel less pressure, so I suppose it's only natural that it should be easier for me to take a long view."

"Perhaps," he agreed, and turned, his arm still around her, to look down from the upper terrace at the armsmen waiting patiently for him to join them. Breastplates flashed under the morning sun, brass and leatherwork gleamed, and the blue-and-white gryphon banner of Balthar and the personal standard of its Baron stirred in the gentle breeze. His eyes rested on the gryphon—the ancient emblem of Ottovar's vanished empire in Kontovar, carried only by the Sothōii here in Norfressa—and his mouth tightened.

"I should be going to Warm Springs, as I'd intended," he said, and Hanatha sighed. She was the one who had pointed out why he should change his mind, yet she knew he wasn't really arguing against *her*. It was the inescapable fact that there was only one of him which he really hated.

"You can go to only one place at a time, Tellian," she said patiently, in a we've-already-had-this-discussion sort of tone. "Prince Bahzell, Hurthang, Gharnal, Brandark, and Kelthys have all gone to Warm Springs. If *they* can't be trusted to deal with whatever happened there, just who do you think can?"

"Yes, but—"

"Oh, no, Tellian!" She shook her head, then turned to wave a finger under his nose. "You are *not* going to double- and triple-think your way into belaboring yourself with a guilty conscience this time! You have responsibilities in Glanharrow, as well as in Warm Springs, and the most experienced, most competent people you could possibly have chosen have already gone to Warm Springs. Trianal, on the other hand, is probably your *least* experienced senior officer, and he's all alone at Glanharrow as your direct representative." She half-glared at him. "Now, given all of that, how can you possibly even doubt where you ought to be going?"

He started to open his mouth again, then thought better of it and simply shook his head, instead.

"Better," she said, a twinkle lurking in the eyes which had been so shadowed with sorrow ever since his return from Kalatha without Leeana. Those eyes narrowed for just an instant as she wondered how much of his apparent indecisiveness was no more than a ploy to distract her from their shared grief by inciting her to take him to task.

"Yes, dear," he said meekly. Then he drew a deep breath and squared his shoulders.

"Speaking of Trianal," he began. "I've been thinking—"

"Yes," she said, and he blinked in surprise at the interruption.

"'Yes,' what?" he asked.

"Yes, you should go ahead and write Gayarla and His Majesty about our formal adoption of Trianal."

He looked down at her, his eyes suddenly soft, and she

gazed back up at him with a serenity she was surprised to discover was almost entirely genuine.

"Of course it hurts to think that in some way we would be 'replacing' Leeana with such indecent haste," she went on. "But after her, he's the only logical heir, anyway. The Royal Council would certainly name him as your heir if you died tomorrow! So the sooner it's done and the matter is officially settled, the sooner people like Cassan will be unable to meddle in the succession. And that was the entire reason Leeana . . . left us. Besides, Trianal is a wonderful boy. I couldn't love him more if he'd been our son from birth. And—I know you won't take this wrongly—despite everything your sister-in-law did wrong raising him, he's grown into a fairly wonderful young *man*, as well. One who will make an excellent baron and lord warden after you."

"I feel sure Gayarla would point out that it was you and I who lost a daughter to those unnatural, depraved war maids, which clearly proves who was the superior parent. As it happens, however, I agree with you that Trianal represents a special miracle, under the circumstances. But are you certain, love, that you're ready to do this so quickly?"

"Tellian, is there some reason your softening brain is causing you to forget who my father and grandfather were? The Whitesaddles aren't exactly strangers to politics or the responsibilities of rulers. It's not as if we have a great deal of choice about it . . . which is why I'm so glad Trianal is someone we already love." She shook her head. "Write the letters, Tellian. But do it from Glanharrow! You've wasted enough time dithering about leaving me behind already!"

"Yes, Milady," he said. But then he took her in his arms, standing high on the terrace where every one of his waiting armsmen could see them, and kissed her long, lingeringly, and passionately. He took his time to do it properly, and he left her panting for breath when they finally straightened.

"Lout!" She smacked him on the breastplate with a balled-up fist, her eyes shining. "How dare you insult my dignity so publicly! My husband will know how to deal with your familiarities, Sirrah!"

"I don't know about that," he said, his eyes devouring her face with bright, passionate tenderness, "but I know how eager I'll be to get back home to you. And," his eyes twinkled, and he brushed her lips lightly with his own once more, "whether your husband will know how to deal with *me* or not, Milady, I will most assuredly know how to deal with *you*!"

Chapter Thirty-Four

"You're walking better than I expected," Brandark said with a smile as Bahzell stepped out onto the manor house's veranda in the gathering dusk.

"And aren't you after being just the most humorous little man in the world?" Bahzell rumbled, easing himself down to sit—gingerly—on the veranda's wide rail.

"If I'm not, it's not because of lack of effort or native talent," Brandark replied, his smile slipping over into a grin as Bahzell grimaced in evident discomfort. "Is your backside very sore, Milord Champion?"

"Well, as to that, it's not so much my arse as my legs." Bahzell snorted, and then rotated his left shoulder with obvious caution. "And I'll not deny as how that last tumble wasn't after being the very most pleasant experience a man might have enjoyed."

"No, I could see that," Brandark said, gazing at him judiciously. "On the other hand, I don't believe I've ever seen anyone attempt to pack a six-month course of riding lessons into less than a week before, either. Especially not a Horse Stealer." He tilted his prominent nose upward and sniffed audibly. "Unlike us compact and skilled Bloody Swords, you poor, oversized amateurs look like sacks of dried horse dung in the saddle. You don't think you and Walsharno might be overdoing things just a bit, given your native disadvantages, do you?"

"It's not as if we were after having much choice about it," Bahzell pointed out, his tone far more serious than Brandark's had been. "If we're to be honest about it, we've spent too long on it already."

"You promised Kelthys," Brandark riposted.

"Aye, that I did," Bahzell acknowledged, his subterranean bass voice heavy. He rose and walked across to the outer edge of the veranda, his footsteps heavier than usual in the new riding boots Lord Edinghas' cobbler had finished only the day before. He gazed up at the stars, and they gleamed back down at him with distant, emotionless beauty while the thin crescent of the Maiden's fragile new moon hung low on the horizon.

"I did promise," he said, his eyes on the stars, "yet I'm thinking it might have been best if I'd not listened to him. There's a foulness here, Brandark—one such as you and I have never faced yet, not even in Sharnā's temple. I've no least business taking others into such a stench of evil as this. There's death in it, and worse than death could ever be."

"I know," Brandark said very quietly, his voice for once untouched by any hint of levity.

Bahzell turned to look at him, ears cocked and eyebrows arched, and the Bloody Sword shrugged.

"Chesmirsa may have told me I'll never be a bard, Bahzell, but I spent all those years studying every ballad, every lay, every epic poem I could get my hands on. And, with all due modesty, I think I've demonstrated that I'm a fair hand as a researcher. As soon as Tomanāk warned you—warned all of us, really—about what's out there, I knew what he was talking about. Did you think I didn't?"

"No," Bahzell admitted, and shook his head. "No, little man. I might be after wishing you hadn't, but there was never the least tiniest chance you wouldn't. But that's not to say as how I'm eager to be seeing you in the midst of such as this."

"I suppose that sort of thing happens to people foolish enough to hang about with champions of Tomanāk," Brandark replied lightly. Then he cocked his head, ears half-forward curiously. "All the same, I have to admit that I'm just a bit surprised that if it is Krahana—" a chill breeze seemed to blow across the verandah as the name was spoken at last "—she hasn't already put in an appearance here. I'd think that for someone like her, this whole place—" he jerked a thumb over his shoulder at the manor house's lamplit windows "—would be like one huge cookie jar she could hardly wait to get her claws into.

"Well, as to that," Bahzell said, "it's in my mind that it's not so very likely she's after being here herself. Or, at least, not that she'll be feeling all that eager to draw himself into meeting her personally." He smiled, a thin smile, remarkably devoid of humor. "Krahana isn't after being the very smartest of the Dark Gods. She's nowhere near the brain of Carnadosa, for example. But she's not so stupid as some, and she's seen what was after happening to Sharnā when *he* crossed swords, in a manner of speaking, with himself.

"I'll not say she's not after being willing to risk a bit of a confrontation, but it will be in her mind as how it will be on her terms, not himself's. So I'm thinking as how what we're most likely to be after seeing will be her Servants. What you might be calling *her* 'champions.' And they're not so very likely to be attacking us here."

"And just why aren't they?" Brandark asked.

"Because I've asked himself to see to it that they can't," Bahzell said simply, and Brandark blinked at him.

"You can do that?" he asked.

"Aye," Bahzell said dryly. "It's after being called prayer, I'm thinking."

"Prayer!" Brandark snorted. "Bahzell, even Kaeritha has to admit that you have your own, thankfully unique way of speaking to Tomanāk. For that matter, I've seen—and heard—it myself, you know. And I'm not so sure that anyone except you would ever describe it as 'prayer.'"

"It's good enough for himself and me to be going on

with," Bahzell informed him. "And after I'd seen what Gayrfressa and her folk had been after enduring, I asked himself if he'd be so very kind as to see to it as how those as attacked them wouldn't be doing it again here. And after I'd asked, he showed me how to be seeing to it myself."

He shrugged, and Brandark's eyebrows rose.

"He showed *you* how to do it?"

"Oh, aye," Bahzell said in a casual, offhand sort of tone belied by the twinkle in his eye. "It's not so very difficult, once you've been shown the way of it."

"Which is?" Brandark was practically quivering with the burning curiosity of a scholar, and Bahzell smiled.

"Little man, your nose is all a-twitch with questions, and isn't that just a frightening thing to see when a man's so proud and fine a nose to twitch about?"

Brandark shook a fist ferociously and took a stride towards him, and the Horse Stealer held up his hands in mock terror.

"Now, don't you be after offering violence to a mild-mannered fellow like myself!" he scolded. Brandark growled something under his breath, and Bahzell laughed.

"Aren't you after being just the most predictable fellow in the world when a man's after knowing the right lever to pull?" he asked with a smile. "But I'd not like you to burst, or do yourself a mischief, so, in answer to your question, it's not so very different from healing a wound or an illness."

"You mean you act as Tomanāk's channel?"

"In a manner of speaking. It's not just himself—there's after being a mite of me in there, as well—but that's the bones of it. It's like . . . like healing a *place*, not a person. I'll not say as how it's a protection strong enough to be after standing against all the forces of hell, but it's set a circle about Lord Edinghas' home manor as nothing short of Krahana herself is going to want to be crossing. Yet it's not something I can be taking with us when we go, Brandark. And it won't be after lasting forever once I leave."

"So that's why you were willing to promise Kelthys you'd wait," Brandark said, rubbing his chin thoughtfully.

"Aye." Bahzell agreed. "It was in my mind as how Krahana's lot would be after coming here, to be finishing what they'd once begun. And, truth to tell, I was minded to *meet* them here, with the other lads from the Order and himself's protections in place to be giving us an edge. But now I'm thinking that if they'd been minded to be coming this way, we'd already have been after seeing them." He shrugged, then frowned. "And since it seems they'll not be coming here, then it's no choice I have but to be going there."

"And once we ride out of Warm Springs, we'll be leaving its protection behind us," Brandark said, nodding slowly. "That's why you're so unhappy you didn't try to stop Kelthys from calling in his wind riders after all."

"Aye, for it's not just a matter of the protections here that we'll be leaving behind," Bahzell said somberly. "I've no way of knowing just what sort of 'champion' Krahana may have been after sending here. For aught I know whoever—or whatever—he is, he may have been after summoning up his own version of a protected circle from her. And if that's the way of it, Brandark, then I've no way at all, at all, of knowing what those as try to cross it may find themselves facing."

"I understand that, Bahzell," Brandark said quietly. "But you have to understand that there's not a one of us—not me, not the Order's lads, and not Kelthys and his wind riders—who hasn't thought long and hard about this. You may not know what we'll find, and we certainly *can't* know, until we've done it. But it's not as if all of us don't know that going in."

"Brandark, this is nothing a man should be facing out of friendship," Bahzell said, speaking just as quietly as Brandark. "Tomanāk knows I've never had a friend so close as you've somehow gotten. I'll not embarrass either of us by pounding what that friendship's after meaning to me into the ground. But this I will be telling you, Brandark Brandarkson—there's naught in this world I'm wanting less than to see you riding north beside me."

"I'm sorry to hear that," Brandark said levelly, "because you don't have much choice about it."

"Brandark—"

"Just what makes you believe you have the right to tell me, or anyone else—including Kelthys and the other wind riders—what we have the right to face? You're a champion of Tomanāk, Bahzell. We all know that. And we all know that facing Krahana is the sort of challenge Tomanāk chooses His champions to confront. We know the brunt of it is going to fall on you and the other lads of the Order, and that nothing we can do will change that. And so what?"

"And so it's not making any sense at all, at all, for the lot of you to be running up against the like of Krahana. If Hurthang and Gharnal and I have it to do, then what's the sense in risking others alongside us?"

"Are you going to try to tell Walsharno that *he* can't go along? If so, then you've just spent the last four days wearing the seat out of your breeches and pounding your arse flat for nothing!"

"Well, as to that," Bahzell began, "Walsharno is after—"

"Don't start any circumlocutions with me, Bahzell Bahnakson! You're not leaving him behind because you know he wouldn't stay, whatever you tried to insist upon. And, in the second place, because the two of you each know exactly what the other is thinking and feeling—really thinking and feeling."

The shorter hradani held his massive friend's eye almost defiantly in the lamplight streaming out of the manor house windows to throw their black shadows across the veranda. And this time, it was Bahzell who looked away.

"You know he *wants* to go . . . and why. And it's not just because the two of you have bonded with one another. He wants to go because he hates and despises and loathes Krahana as much as any of us. Because he wants vengeance for the herd he grew up in before he left for the Bear River herd. And because it's his right—his *right*, Bahzell—to choose to fight evil when he sees it.

"Well, that's *my* right, too. And Kelthys'. And the right of the other coursers, and of the other wind riders. All that good men have to do to allow the Dark to triumph is to do nothing to stop it when they find it before them."

Brandark stopped speaking and drew a deep breath, then chuckled with something approaching his normal insouciance.

"I hope you took notes, Bahzell," he said lightly. "Because unless you did, I doubt very much that you'll manage to keep it all straight later. And also because you're not going to hear *me* getting that sloppy and emotional very often."

"No," Bahzell said softly. "No, that I'm not." He looked back up at the stars again for several endless seconds, then inhaled deeply, nodded to the nail-paring moon, and slapped the Bloody Sword lightly on the shoulder.

"All right, little man," he rumbled. "You've the right of it, when all's said. And even if you hadn't, Tomanāk knows you're nigh as stubborn as a Horse Stealer."

"*Please!*" Brandark gave him a very pained look. "No one, this side of a Sothōii or a lump of granite is as stubborn as a Horse Stealer hradani! It's a law of nature—a physical impossibility. It's a well known and clearly demonstrated fact that nothing short of six solid inches of skull bone can produce your genuine Horse Stealer stubbornness. I refer you to the treatise by—"

His tone of lordly superiority disappeared into a sudden squawk as two shovel-sized hands plucked him easily off the veranda, despite his own two hundred and seventy pounds of solid muscle and bone. He flailed wildly as he sailed through the air, but it was a relatively short journey which ended in a tremendous splash as he alit far from gracefully upon the surface of Lady Sofalla's fishpond.

"So tell me again just why you're here?" Sir Fahlthu Greavesbiter growled, glowering suspiciously at the man in front of him.

"Because Lord Saratic told me to be," Darnas Warshoe replied with a shrug.

"Let's try this again," Sir Fahlthu snorted. "I know Lord Saratic assigned you to ride with my company. And I know you're supposed to be some sort of expert guide and scout. I even know that Lord Dathian is supposed to've personally asked for you because of your knowledge of the Bogs and Glanharrow generally. But, d'you know, Master 'Brownsaddle,' I don't *quite* believe that that's all there is to it."

"And why shouldn't you believe the truth?" Warshoe asked patiently.

"Because I've known a great many guides, and a great many scouts, Master Brownsaddle. A lot of them have carried bows, and some of them have carried crossbows. One or two of them have even carried arbalests. But you, Master Brownsaddle, are the only scout I've ever met who carries both a Sothōii bow *and* a hradani arbalest at the same time. I can't help wondering why you do that. I mean, a man can fire only one bow or one arbalest at a time, unless you possess even more hidden talents than I believe you do."

"You know," Warshoe said, "I do believe that I somehow managed to overlook that, Sir Fahlthu. Thank you for bringing it to my attention."

Cassan's agent snorted with obvious amusement at the absurdity of the knight's suspicions, but it was an amusement he wasn't particularly close to feeling. Fahlthu was obviously brighter than he'd assumed, and Warshoe wondered if he was also brighter than Saratic and Sir Chalthar had assumed. If so, that mistaken estimate might have unfortunate consequences over the next couple of weeks or so.

"Milord Knight," he said after a moment in an even more patient tone, "I'm not sure what sort of flea you have in your ear, but I assure you that I'm exactly who and what I say I am. I'm flattered that Lord Dathian asked for me. And I'm even more flattered by it when I think about the extra kormaks he's paying me for acting as your own personal guide through the Bogs. On the other hand, if you have a problem with who's been assigned to do that, you're certainly welcome to discuss it with Sir Halnahk, or Lord Dathian, or even Lord Saratic. It genuinely doesn't matter to me."

He shrugged, watching Fahlthu's face narrowly from

behind guileless, bored-looking eyes, and hoped the knight didn't decide to take him up on the suggestion. He wasn't particularly concerned about Halnahk or Saratic, but Dathian was a little too weasellike for his taste. The traitorous lord warden might just decide there was some profit for him in telling Fahlthu about the weeks Warshoe had spent acquiring his familiarity with the pathways through the Bogs. It was fortunate that Warshoe's eye and memory for terrain had always been good enough to make that familiarity convincing to someone who didn't know the Bogs himself.

"As for my choice of weapons," he continued, "of course I can only use one of them at a time. But I'm a *scout*, Sir Fahlthu. Sometimes that means I'm going to be riding on a horse, when a *horse*bow is likely to come in a bit handy. Other times, I'm going to be sneaking around in the grass, where a weapon—like, say, an arbalest—that a man can fire while lying prone in the bushes might come in handy. And this is *not* a hradani arbalest." He held the weapon in question out and tapped the dwarfish proof mark on the steel bow. "This is Axeman work, Sir Fahlthu, and it cost me a pretty kormak. I do seem to have . . . ah, acquired some hradani *bolts* for it, but unless I'm mistaken, weren't we supposed to be muddying the water by suggesting that Bahnak's Horse Stealers might be involved in all of this?"

Fahlthu frowned ferociously, obviously angered by Warshoe's withering irony, but Warshoe didn't really care about that. Or, rather, he *did* care—a man like Fahlthu would be perfectly capable of arranging an accident for someone who had sufficiently irritated him—but he preferred the cavalry commander's anger to his undiverted suspicions. It might be unlikely that Fahlthu could figure out everything Saratic and Baron Cassan had in mind, but it wasn't impossible. And if he *did* figure out what Warshoe's true mission was, there was no telling what he might do about it. Except, of course, that a man like Fahlthu would have absolutely no interest in being saddled with the blame for the death of the Kingdom of the Sothōii's first noble.

"All right," the knight growled finally. "I don't believe for a minute that you're the innocent, simpleminded sort you'd like me to believe, 'Master Brownsaddle.' But whatever you may be is no concern of mine. Except for this." He fixed Warshoe with a cold, angry eye. "While you ride with my company, you ride under my orders. And I would not advise you to violate them in any way. Is that clear, 'Master Brownsaddle'?"

"Of course it is," Warshoe replied. "Whatever you may believe, Sir Fahlthu, I never had any intention of violating your instructions."

"Why do you think they've been so quiet lately, Sir Yarran?"

"I beg your pardon?" Sir Yarran Battlecrow looked up from the tankard of ale the serving maid had just plunked down in front of him. "Did you say something, Milord?"

"Yes," Sir Trianal Bowmaster said, then grimaced and waved one hand through the pipe smoke-thickened air. The mess hall attached to Lord Warden Festian's barracks was packed with Glanharrow's own armsmen and almost half of the ten troops of Balthar armsmen who had accompanied him here. That many raised voices, one or two of them already beginning to bawl out the words of a ribald song with more than a trace of tipsiness, made it hard enough for a man to hear his own thoughts, much less what the fellow sitting beside him might have said aloud.

"I asked," he said more loudly, "why you think they've been so quiet lately?"

"Well, as to that, Milord," Sir Yarran said as thoughtfully as a man could when he had to half-shout to be heard, "I'm inclined to be thinking it's a matter of weather and your uncle's reinforcements."

Trianal arched an eyebrow and curled the fingers of the one hand in a drawing motion, inviting him to continue. Sir Yarran grinned, then took a long pull at his tankard, and shrugged.

"The weather's finally clearing, Milord," he pointed

out. "That's probably making it easier for them to get in and out of the Bogs, with or without stolen cattle or horses. But at the same time, it's taken away the cover of all those nice, thick fogs they used to run about inside, and we've moved every cattle and horse herd in the area of their original operations out to the west. That means they'll have to range further out, and the dryer, harder ground—and the fact that the rain doesn't come along and wash out any hoof prints five minutes after they're made—means we'd find it far easier to track them back to their ratholes. They'll know that as well as we do, so when you add to that the fact that Milord Baron's seen fit to send in his own armsmen—which both raises the number of bows and sabers we can send after them and simultaneously says he's minded to take this whole business a mite seriously—I'd say it's fairly plain what they're thinking."

"I see." Trianal pushed the remnants of his supper—exactly the same food any of his armsmen might have expected—around his plate with a spoon and frowned. Sir Yarran watched him and very carefully allowed no sign of his inner smile to show. Sir Yarran was inclined to think that all the good reports he'd had about Trianal had been accurate. The lad was conscientious, hard-working, and determined not to disappoint the uncle he clearly idolized. He was also not only smart but willing to actually use that intelligence . . . which all too many young nobles of Sir Yarran's experience had not been.

But for all of that, he was still only nineteen years old, and he couldn't quite hide his disappointment at the thought that his adversaries' caution—or cowardice—might deny him the opportunity to show what he could do.

"Do you think they've given up for good, then?" he asked after a moment, trying valiantly (though with imperfect success) to conceal his disappointment.

"No, Milord." Sir Yarran leaned closer to his titular commander so that he could speak without shouting—and with less chance of being overheard.

"Milord," he continued in the patient voice he and Festian had used to train generations of eager young armsmen, "there's two sides in any fight, and neither one of them's got any real interest in losing. Which means that whatever you may want the oily bastards to do, *they're* going to be trying to think up something you *won't* want them to do.

"Now, we know that whoever these . . . people are—" he avoided mentioning any names, despite the voice-drowning background hubbub "—they've already shown us as how they're pretty damned determined to make Lord Festian look like he can't find his arse with both hands, and to make your uncle look foolish for having picked him to replace Redhelm in the first place. I'm thinking it's not so very likely that they'll just decide it was all a bad idea and that they ought to go home and behave themselves. And even if it happened that they—or some of them—were beginning to lose their nerve, we've a pretty fair idea of who they are, and you know your uncle better than I do. D'you really think he's going to be inclined to *let* them go home and pretend as how butter wouldn't melt in their mouths?"

Trianal barked a laugh at the very thought, and Yarran nodded.

"Aye, and if you and I think that, don't you think those on the other side might be thinking the same? Which means their best chance to get out of this with their skins whole is to succeed in what they started out to do in the first place. And they'll not do that by sitting home on the other side of the Bogs and letting Lord Festian put Glanharrow back in order.

"So I'm thinking that what they're doing right this minute is either sitting back and waiting to see just how long Milord Baron is prepared to leave you and your armsmen here to support Lord Festian, or else thinking about whether or not they want to reinforce *their* side. Or it might be they're doing both of those at the selfsame time."

He shrugged, and his expression was noticeably more grim as he drank another large mouthful of his ale.

"So the answer to your question, Milord," he said finally, letting his tankard thump back down on the plain, plank tabletop, "is that, aye, I think we'll be seeing them again. Maybe sooner than we'd like."

"Well, at least we're rid of her at last," Dahlaha Farrier said. She pouted into the mirror above her dressing table, leaning close to examine her faultless complexion critically, and her golden hair gleamed under the lamplight.

"*You're* rid of her," Varnaythus corrected. He sat comfortably slouched in an armchair, watching her primp for an evening with Trisu's cousin Triahm. The first evening they'd spent together since Dame Kaeritha's arrival at Thalar Keep.

"What do you mean?" Dahlaha's eyes shifted, gazing at his reflection in her mirror, and there was an edge of something—petulance, perhaps—in her tone.

Varnaythus simply looked back at her blandly. She'd already made it obvious that she resented his return to Thalar, and he saw no reason to let her guess that he resented it as well, probably more than she did. And although he had no intention of admitting it to her, he'd been more than a little frightened when he got the instructions that sent him back. He'd had no desire at all to get any closer to a champion of Tomanāk than he had to, and especially not at a time when that champion's suspicions might well have been aroused. So he'd been delighted to discover that Kaeritha had left Thalar several hours before he himself arrived back there.

"I only meant that Dame Kaeritha hasn't indicated that she's about to resign her interest in Trisu's dispute with Kalatha," he said. "Unless I very much miss my guess—" which, he knew from his gramerhain, he did not "—she's on her way back to Kalatha to reexamine their copies of the documents. After all, the fact that she didn't denounce either side as forgers and liars before she left suggests to me that she isn't prepared at this point to uncritically accept the validity of either side's documents."

"Well, of course not," Dahlaha agreed a bit snippily. "Obviously one set has to be false. But that's fine. My Lady's webs are carefully woven, Varnaythus. In the end, it won't really matter which side Tomanāk's precious champion condemns for creating the forgery. I'll admit, it will work out better if she blames Trisu, especially because she's a woman herself, but either outcome will suit Her needs and plans quite well."

"I know that," Varnaythus said, watching her with unobtrusive intensity, "but my point is that she hasn't blamed anyone. She hasn't even so much as whispered to anyone here in Thalar that she might suspect that *anyone's* committed forgery. To me, that suggests that she isn't about to leap to any conclusions, or issue any hasty rulings."

"And what of it?" Dahlaha asked, hunching one shoulder impatiently. "It doesn't matter to Them if she takes a few days, or weeks, to make her decision. In the end, she *has* to decide for one side or the other, Varnaythus."

"It does make a difference in at least one sense, Dahlaha," Varnaythus said patiently. "Their plan requires a certain degree of synchronization. You do recall that They have multiple strands to their web, don't you?" Dahlaha's blue eyes were dagger-sharp as she glared at his reflection, and he smiled ever so slightly. "It would be nice if your Lady and Krahana could see both of Their plans come to fruition at as close to the same time as possible. Otherwise," his smile disappeared, "it's possible that if either plan fails, the champion of Tomanāk that one should have snared will be available to reinforce his—or her—fellow. Do you really want Bahzell Bloody Hand down here supporting Dame Kaeritha?"

Dahlaha's face had lost all expression at the mention of Bahzell, rather to Varnaythus' amusement. Not that he would have been any happier than she at the prospect of confronting him. For all of Dahlaha's contempt for Sharnā and the deceased Tharnatus, the brutal effectiveness with which Bahzell had dispatched not simply one, but two of Sharnā's greater demons made the prospect of facing him a frightening one. Varnaythus knew that as well as Dahlaha did; what amused him was the obvious twinge of fear she'd felt at the words "Bloody Hand." However fitting they might be, Varnaythus knew the song the cognomen derived from . . . and who its author was.

"No, of course I'd rather not have to deal with two champions instead of one, regardless of who they might be!" Dahlaha said tartly after a brief pause. "But if Krahana's Servants do their jobs properly, it won't come to that, will it?"

"No," Varnaythus agreed in the same obviously patient tone. "At the same time, however, you do realize, don't you, that Jerghar is thinking exactly the same thing about *your* Lady and you." He grimaced. "I don't suppose I can really blame either of you for that, but I do wish you could remember that it's my job to keep both of you running in harness. Not to mention keeping an eye on Baron Cassan and *his* little plots."

"All right," she said with a shrug. "You're right, I should remember this is a web with more than one strand. And that They chose you to look after all of them. On the other hand, I also know you enjoy being a pain in the arse, Varnaythus. Don't bother to deny it—you and I both know it's true."

"Of course I do," he confessed cheerfully. "It's one of the few small pleasures I can allow myself, especially now. But my real reason for dropping by to see you is to ask you exactly what you expect Dame Kaeritha to do when she returns to Kalatha?"

"Do?" Dahlaha turned from the mirror to look at him with obvious surprise. "She's going to reexamine their documents, exactly as she told Trisu she would."

"I meant *after* that," Varnaythus explained in the voice of someone manifestly asking his deity for strength. Dahlaha's eyes hardened again, and he shrugged. "We both know what she's going to find when she compares the documents," he pointed out. "Even They can't—or, at least, haven't—told me whether or not she'll be able to determine which of them are false, but even if she can't, she's going to confirm that they disagree with one another. So, what will she do *then*?"

"I don't know," Dahlaha said irritably. She twitched her shoulders again. "Probably she'll decide to go to Sōthōfalas and the Royal Archives in order to see what the Crown's copy of the original says."

"Dahlaha," he said wearily, "I don't think it's very wise to make any assumption of that nature. Or to assume Kaeritha is a fool who can't see beyond the point of her own sword, just because she follows Tomanāk."

Dahlaha glared at him, and he sighed.

"You yourself just pointed out to me that in a very real sense, it doesn't matter for your Lady's plans which side she accuses of committing the forgery. Hasn't it occurred to you that the same thought might cross *her* mind? Or that she might wonder whether or not the forgery is the work of a third party out to damage both the war maids *and* the Kingdom at large?"

"Well, of course she might," Dahlaha said, her glare fading just a bit as her mind—which, Varnaythus was forced to admit, was actually quite a good one . . . when she chose to use it—began to consider his point.

"In that case," Varnaythus continued patiently, "isn't it possible that instead of simply haring off to Sōthōfalas to confirm, as well as she can, which document was forged, she might decide to concentrate on who did the forging? After all, if it was a third party and she can unmask whoever actually did it, then she can avoid issuing a ruling which is bound to ignite a firestorm by accusing either Trisu or Kalatha. If she could demonstrate that both of them were the victims of someone else's plot, wouldn't that change the entire focus of their confrontation?"

"Yes, she *might* do that," Dahlaha conceded in a tone which was becoming steadily more thoughtful. "But in that case—"

"In that case, she's going to spend some additional time poking around in Kalatha, exactly as she did here," Varnaythus pointed out. "And she's going to be looking very hard for any clue which might point to that hypothetical third party's identity. And she's a *champion of* Tomanāk, Dahlaha. Whatever else you may think of them, you have to admit they have the instincts of a bloodhound once they start nosing around."

"Yes, they do, the Spider take them," Dahlaha growled.

"So I'd say it's entirely possible that she's going to ask

a lot of questions in Kalatha, and that after she's asked them, she's going to continue on not to Sōthōfalas, but to Quaysar. After all, if she's wondering about those sorts of questions, then she's going to need to talk to the only other real authority involved in the dispute. And that's the Quaysar Voice."

"Yes. Yes, it is," Dahlaha said, blue eyes narrow and intent as the keen brain Varnaythus had—finally!—goaded into action went to work.

"I realize there are already contingency plans in place to deal with that possibility," he said. Actually, he knew there were *supposed* to be contingency plans in place, but he had a less than lively faith that Dahlaha had really given them the attention they required. "Nonetheless, I thought it would be worth my time to drop in on you to remind you that they might be needed. And," he held her eyes very steadily, "to suggest that They might feel that it was time you double-checked your plans . . . just in case."

Chapter Thirty-Five

"Welcome back to Kalatha, Dame Kaeritha." Mayor Yalith's voice was much warmer than it had been the first time Kaeritha entered her office, and her smile was broad. "How may we serve you this time?"

"Actually, I'm more or less just passing through on my way to Quaysar," Kaeritha replied, watching the mayor's expression with carefully hidden attentiveness. "I've spoken to you, and to Lord Trisu. Now I think it would be just as well for me to speak to the Voice and get her perspective on the disputes between your town and Trisu. Not to mention her temple's own . . . difficulties with him." It seemed to her watchful eyes that Yalith's quick nod of approval for her last comment was automatic, almost unconscious. "I hadn't realized from our previous discussion that she was also the secular head of the Quaysar community. The fact that she is means she's probably had much more direct contact with him than I'd previously assumed."

"I'm sure she has," Yalith said a bit sourly. "I doubt she's enjoyed it any more than I have, though." The mayor shook her head. "I realize that the Voice is Lillinara's personal servant, but it would take a saint, not merely a priestess, to endure that man as her liege."

"He can certainly be one of the most irritating people I've ever met," Kaeritha acknowledged even as she mentally filed away Yalith's tone and body language. Clearly, the mayor, at least, had no reservations about the Voice. Kaeritha wished the same were true for her.

"If he's irritating to a visiting champion of Tomanāk, you can probably begin to imagine how 'irritating' he can be as a permanent, inescapable neighbor!" The mayor shook her head again, with a grimace.

"I doubt that proximity makes him any *easier* to deal with, anyway," Kaeritha agreed. The mayor snorted a laugh and waved for Kaeritha to take one of the chairs facing her desk.

The knight seated herself in the indicated chair and leaned back, crossing her legs.

"Before I move on to Quaysar," she said in a tone which was as everyday-sounding as she could keep it, "I wonder if you could tell me a little more about the Voice." Yalith's eyebrows rose, and Kaeritha shrugged. "I understand she's almost as new to her office as Trisu is to his lord wardenship," she explained, "and I'd like to have a little bit better feel for her position and personality before I walk into her temple and start asking questions some priestesses might consider impertinent or even insulting. Especially coming from a champion of someone else's god."

"I see." Yalith rested her elbows on the arms of her chair and leaned back comfortably, steepling her fingers under her chin. She pursed her lips for several seconds, clearly marshaling her thoughts, but Kaeritha saw no evidence of any uneasiness or misgivings.

"The present Voice is younger than the last one," the mayor said finally. "To be honest, when I first met her, I thought she might be *too* young for the post, but I was wrong. Now that she's been in it for a while, and I've had a chance to see her in action, as it were, I think she may seem to be younger than she truly is."

"You do? Why?" Kaeritha asked.

"She's an extraordinarily attractive woman, Dame Kaeritha, but she has one of those faces that will look young until she's at least eighty." The mayor smiled. "When I was younger myself, I would have cheerfully traded two or three fingers from my left hand for her bone structure and coloring. Now I just envy them."

"Oh." Kaeritha smiled back. "One of *those*."

"Definitely one of those," Yalith agreed. Then she shook her head. "But she doesn't really seem aware of it herself," the mayor continued more seriously. "I sometimes wonder if her appearance was an obstacle for her in her pursuit of her calling, but her vocation is obvious once you've spent even a very few minutes with her. There's a . . . a presence to her I've never experienced with any other Voice. Once you've met her, I think you'll understand why the Church assigned her to Quaysar."

"I'm sure I will," Kaeritha replied. "At the same time, Mayor, a spiritual vocation doesn't always translate into effectiveness when it comes to managing the more mundane affairs of a temple. I'd imagine that would be even more the case for a priestess who's also a mayor. How would you evaluate her in that regard?"

"I've only been to Quaysar myself once since she became Voice there," Yalith said. "She's visited us here four times since then, but most of the contact between us has been through her handmaidens. So my impressions of her abilities as an administrator are all secondhand, as it were."

She arched an eyebrow, and Kaeritha nodded her understanding of the qualifier.

"Well, having said that," the mayor continued, "I would have to say she seems to be at least as efficient and effective as her predecessor was, which is pretty high praise all by itself. I certainly haven't heard about any internal problems, at any rate. And given my own experiences, I can't say the difficulties she's apparently had with Trisu of Lorham give me any cause to question her ability to work comfortably with an unprejudiced secular lord."

"I see." Kaeritha considered that for a moment, then cocked her head to one side. "Given what you've said about how relatively little direct contact you've had with her, I suppose that's probably as definitive an opinion as anyone could expect you to have formed. Did you know the previous Voice better than that?"

"Oh, yes!" Yalith smiled. It was a broad smile, warm, yet touched with sadness. "The old Voice came from right here in Kalatha. She was born here, actually, and I knew her long before she heard Lillinara's call. In fact, we grew up together."

"You did? Somehow, I had the impression she was older than that."

"*Old?* Shandra?" Yalith snorted, then grimaced. "I suppose I shouldn't call her that. I know any Voice gives up her old name and takes a new one in religion. But she was actually a year or two younger than I was, and I'll always think of her as the blond-haired kid who insisted on tagging along when I went fishing in the river."

"So she was actually *younger* than you," Kaeritha mused. "And from your manner and tone, she sounds as if she were an extraordinary person."

"Indeed she was," Yalith said softly.

"How did she come to die?" Kaeritha asked. "Because I thought she was older than she was, I'd simply assumed it was old age, or perhaps some illness. But if she was as young as you are . . ."

"No one is really sure," Yalith sighed. "Oh, it *was* an illness, but it came on extraordinarily suddenly, and I think it took her and her physicians by surprise because she'd always been so healthy. The constitution of a courser, she always used to joke with me when we were girls." She shook her head sadly. "But that wasn't enough this time. She became ill one day, and she was gone less than three days later. I didn't even realize she was seriously ill in time to get to Quaysar to tell her goodbye."

"I'm sorry for your loss," Kaeritha said softly. *Even sorrier than you can guess, given what I'm beginning to suspect*, she added silently to herself. "But you'd say you're pleased with the job the new Voice is doing as her successor?"

"As pleased as anyone could be after losing someone like Shandra," Yalith agreed firmly. "We were extremely lucky to have two such strong Voices in succession. In fact, I think possibly our present Voice may even be better suited to the . . . less pleasant aspects of our disputes with Trisu than Shandra would have been. Her faith is obviously just as deep, but Shandra always shied away from confrontation. She wasn't *weak*, or anything like that, but she preferred finding a consensus or arriving at compromises. Which is fine, as long as the person on the other side of the dispute is equally willing to be reasonable. Our present Voice is a bit more willing to remember that she speaks as the *Mother's* Voice when it comes to rebuking Her children's misbehavior."

"So she's been supportive of Kalatha's position against Trisu, not simply concerned by his failure to adequately investigate the deaths of her handmaidens?"

"Oh, yes." Yalith nodded emphatically. "She hasn't made any secret of her feelings in that regard. In fact, she saw this round coming even before we did."

"She did?"

"Yes. Actually, she preached a sermon about the need to prepare for the coming storm some months before our relations with Trisu really started going into the chamber pot. I don't think that she knew what was coming, or she would've been more specific, but she clearly sensed that something was about to go wrong in a big way. Once our . . . disagreements with Trisu surfaced, she spoke out strongly about the need for all the Mother's daughters to be strong and vigilant, and she's a strong supporter of our decision to stand fast, at least until we get some sort of reasonable offsetting concessions from Trisu in any compromise settlement. Although she did insist on reviewing the original documents herself before she took any official position."

"She did examine them? Here?"

"No, not here. She was unable to leave Quaysar at the moment, so she sent two of her handmaidens to fetch them back to the temple."

"Just two handmaidens to transport them?" Kaeritha sounded surprised, and Yalith chuckled in harsh understanding.

"We're just as aware as you are of how . . . convenient

some people might find it for those documents to disappear, Dame Kaeritha. I sent along an escort of fifteen war maids, and Lanitha went along to care for the records themselves personally." She shrugged. "But there weren't any problems. That time, at least."

"I see." Kaeritha frowned thoughtfully. "I'm glad you did send an escort, though," she said. "Just from a purely historical perspective, those documents are priceless. I imagine the war maids have always seen to it that they were properly looked after whenever they left Kalatha."

"That was the only time they ever have left Kalatha," Yalith replied. "But I'm sure any of my predecessors would have been just as careful about protecting them."

"Oh, I'm sure they would," Kaeritha agreed. "I'm sure they would."

"Hello, Dame Kaeritha."

Leeana Bowmaster had changed a great deal. Or, no, Kaeritha decided. That conclusion might still be a bit premature. Her *appearance* had certainly changed a great deal; it remained to be seen how much the young woman under that appearance had changed.

"Hello, Leeana," the knight replied. "You're looking good."

"Different, you mean," Leeana corrected with a smile, almost as if she'd read Kaeritha's mind.

"Well, yes. But in your case, I think, 'different' and 'good' may mean the same thing. And, no, I'm not talking just about outward appearances, young lady. The last time I saw you, you weren't exactly the happiest young woman I'd ever seen."

"Oh." Leeana looked down at her bare toes and actually wiggled them. "I guess maybe you have a point," she admitted after a moment.

The two of them stood on one of the training salle's covered porches. The porch's plank flooring was rough and unfinished under Kaeritha's boots, and must have felt even more so to Leeana's bare feet. But the girl didn't seem to notice that. Nor did she appear aware of how the fine garments, rich embroidery, and semiprecious stones of a great baron's daughter had vanished forever.

Kaeritha was. She hadn't actually seen Leeana in over two weeks, not since she'd carried Tellian's reply to his daughter's message to her the afternoon she and Kaeritha had arrived in Kalatha.

The knight had anticipated changes after that long a period, and she hadn't expected to find Leeana lounging about in the sorts of gowns her mother would have approved. But the leather breeches and smocks Leeana had favored as casual, get-your-hands-dirty clothing back home at Hill Guard Castle when her mother wasn't looking had also disappeared, and Kaeritha wondered what Leeana's parents would have had to say if they'd seen her at the moment.

"There *do* seem to have been some changes in your appearance, though," she acknowledged with a smile. She cocked her head. "Are you comfortable with them?"

"'Comfortable' is such a . . . flexible word," Leeana said with a grimace. She reached up and slid an index finger under the shoulder strap of her snugly laced yathu. "I've seen heavy draft harnesses that were probably more 'comfortable' for the horses wearing them! Besides," she grimaced again and withdrew her finger to indicate her bosom with a wave of her hand, "it's not as if *I* really need it."

"*Ha!* You may think that now, girl, but I think your opinion will change in a year or two." She eyed the young woman consideringly for a moment, then chuckled. "As a matter of fact, and bearing your height in mind, I expect you'll end up appreciating it even more than I would. And it probably won't take any 'year or two,' either, now that I think about it!"

"Really?" Leeana looked at her quickly, then blushed and looked back down at her toes. But she also grinned, and Kaeritha shook her head.

"I'd say the odds are in favor of it," she said judiciously. "You're already taller than I am, and you're not done growing. I'd say you've still got a bit of filling out to do, and it looks to me like you're probably going to be built a lot like your mother. So wait a few years before you start complaining."

"If you say so, Dame Kaeritha," Leeana murmured obediently, and Kaeritha suppressed another chuckle. She rather suspected that the war maids had designed their traditional garments at least partly for their shock effect. And whether the war maids' intentions had been solely to provide proper support or to combine that with a poke in respectable Sothōii society's eye or not, she felt certain that neither Baron Tellian nor Baroness Hanatha would have approved of the yathu's undeniable brevity and snug fit . . . or of the way that their daughter's shapely form (and navel) were exposed for all the world to see.

"Don't go fishing for compliments, young lady," she said now, her tone severe, and Leeana produced a sound suspiciously like a giggle.

That giggle, and the girl's entire body language, did a great deal to reassure Kaeritha. Leeana had been called away from self-defense training to speak with Kaeritha, and the war maids' physical training regimen was as demanding as any Kaeritha herself had ever experienced. It was certainly more rigorous than anything *Leeana* had ever experienced before leaving Balthar. Not that the girl had ever been indolent or lazy. But the war maids believed in pushing their new recruits—especially the probationary ones—hard. Not just to make the difference between their old lives and their new ones clear on an emotional as well as an intellectual level, but also as a testing process designed to identify the young women with the potential and mindset to become *war* maids.

The great majority of those who went on to become the war maid community's warriors would serve as the light infantry, scouts, and guerrillas most Sothōii thought of whenever they thought about war maids at all. That combat style required speed and stamina more than sheer size or brute strength, and the physical training required to provide those qualities was demanding and unremitting. It had been Kaeritha's observation that most people—including most men, she thought sardonically—

didn't much care to invest the focus and sweat required to maintain that high pitch of physical conditioning.

From what she could see so far, it looked as if Leeana was actually enjoying it.

"Are you happy, Leeana?" she asked quietly after a moment, and Leeana looked up quickly. Her smile disappeared, but she met Kaeritha's eyes steadily.

"I don't know," she said frankly. "I've cried myself to sleep a night or two, if that's what you're asking." Her shoulders moved in what could have been called a shrug if it had been a little stronger. "I can't say I didn't expect that, though. And it's not because life here in Kalatha is so hard. I'm running my backside off and working an awful lot harder than I ever did before, and half the time I think I'm about to drop dead of exhaustion. But I don't really mind that, either, or the fact that I'm not a baron's daughter anymore." She shook her head. "I think the only thing that really hurts is that I'm not legally *Father and Mother's* daughter anymore. Does that make sense?"

"Oh, yes, girl," Kaeritha said softly, and Leeana drew a deep breath.

"But aside from missing Mother and Father—and being miserably homesick from time to time—I'm actually enjoying myself. So far, at least." Her smile returned. "Ravlahn—she's the Hundred in charge of physical training—has been running me hard ever since I got here. Sometimes I just want to stop running long enough to drop dead from exhaustion, but I'm learning things about myself that I never knew before. Now if only her demands on my time could excuse me from more 'traditional' classes."

"Traditional classes?" Kaeritha repeated.

"Oh, yes." Leeana's smile turned into a wry grin. "I have to admit that I'd hoped running away to the war maids would at least rescue me from the clutches of my tutors. Unfortunately, it turns out that the war maids require all of their members to be literate, and they 'strongly encourage' us to continue with additional education." She snorted. "Except, in my case, they've dragooned me as one of the tutors, instead!"

"I see," Kaeritha said, hiding a smile of her own as she recalled the team of strong horses it had required to drag *her* into a classroom when she'd been Leeana's age.

"What matters most, though," Leeana continued quietly, "is that by coming here I've done the most important thing. Father's enemies can't use me against him anymore, and I have the chance to be something besides an obedient little mare dropping colts for some fine stallion who completely controls my life."

"Then I'm glad you have the opportunity," Kaeritha said.

"So am I. Really." Leeana nodded firmly as if to emphasize the mere words.

"Good." Kaeritha rested one hand lightly on the girl's shoulder for a moment. "That was what I wanted to know before I leave for Quaysar."

"Quaysar? You're going to visit the Voice?"

Something about the way Leeana asked the question narrowed Kaeritha's eyes.

"Yes. Why do you ask?"

"No reason," Leeana said, just a bit too quickly. "It's just—" She broke off, hesitated, then shook her head. "It's just that I have this . . . uncomfortable feeling."

"About what?" Kaeritha was careful to keep any suggestiveness out of her own tone.

"About the Voice," Leeana said in a small voice, as if she were admitting to some heinous fault.

"What sort of feeling? For that matter, why do you have any 'feelings' about her at all? I didn't think you'd even met her."

"I haven't met her," Leeana admitted. "I guess you could say that what I've got is a 'secondhand feeling.' But I've talked to some of the other war maids about her. A lot."

"You have?" Kaeritha's eyes narrowed. Her discussion with Yalith hadn't suggested that the Kalatha community was quite as heavily focused on the Voice as Leeana seemed to be implying.

"Yes," the girl said. "And to be honest, Dame Kaeritha, it's the way they've been talking to me about her that worries me most."

"Suppose you explain that," Kaeritha suggested. She stepped back and settled her posterior onto the porch's railing, leaning back against one of the upright roof supports and folding her arms across her chest. The morning sunlight was warm across her shoulders as she cocked her head.

"You know I'm the most 'nobly born' person in Kalatha," Leeana began after a moment, and Kaeritha raised one eyebrow. The girl saw it and grimaced. "That's not an 'oh-what-a-wonderful-person-I-am' comment, Dame Kaeritha. What I meant to say is that even though I was only Father's daughter, not his real heir, I've seen a lot more political backbiting and maneuvering than most of the people here have."

"All right," Kaeritha said slowly, nodding as Leeana paused. "I'll grant you that—on an aristocratic level, at least. Don't make the mistake of assuming that peasants can't be just as contentious. Or just as subtle about the way they go about biting each other's backs."

"I won't. Or, at least, I don't *think* I will," Leeana replied. "But the thing is, Dame Kaeritha, that the way people here are talking about the Voice strikes me as, well, peculiar."

"Why?"

"First," Leeana said very seriously, her expression intent, "there's exactly which of the war maids seem to be doing most of the talking. It isn't the older ones, or the ones in the most senior positions—not people like Mayor Yalith, or Administrator Dalthys, or Hundred Erlis, for example. And it isn't the very youngest ones, like Garlahna, except in a sort of echoing kind of way."

"What do you mean, 'echoing'?"

"It's almost like there's an organized pattern," Leeana said, obviously choosing her words with care. "I think that's what drew my attention to it in the first place, really. There've been enough whispering campaigns against Father over the years for me to be automatically suspicious when I seem to be seeing the same thing somewhere else."

"And you think that's what you're seeing here?"

"I think it *may* be," Leeana said, nodding slowly. "It took a while for my suspicions to kick in, and the thing that made me start wondering in the first place was that I seemed to be hearing exactly the same sorts of things, in almost exactly the same sorts of words, from half a dozen or more people."

Kaeritha's blue eyes narrowed even further.

"Would you care to tell me just which half-dozen people it was?" she asked.

"I'd rather not name any specific names" Leeana said uncomfortably. Kaeritha gazed at her coolly, and the younger woman looked away for a moment. It was interesting, Kaeritha thought. For all of her intelligence and insight, Leeana seemed to be afflicted with the eternal teenager's aversion for the role of informer.

"All right," the knight said after a moment. "I won't press you for names—not right now, at any rate. But you do understand, don't you, Leeana, that the time may come when I'll have no choice but to?"

"Yes, Milady." Leeana nodded, although it was obvious she wasn't very happy about the thought.

"Good." Kaeritha nodded back, soberly, the gesture a promise that she wouldn't ask unless she felt she truly must. "In that case, go on with what you're saying. What made you notice these people in the first place?"

"The fact that what they were saying wasn't just a matter of people expressing the same general opinions, Dame Kaeritha. They were making the same *arguments*. And the way they were doing it—the way they were choosing their words, and who they were talking to—makes me think it's an organized effort, not something that's happening spontaneously."

It was an enormous loss to the Kingdom of the Sothōii in general that its invincible cultural bias against the possibility of female rulers had deprived the Barony of Balthar of Leeana Bowmaster as its liege lady, Kaeritha thought. She'd known from the outset that Leeana was keenly intelligent, but the brain behind those jade-green eyes was even better than she'd suspected. How many young women Leeana's age, the knight wondered, thrown into a world and facing a future so radically different from anything they had ever experienced before, would have had enough energy to spare to think analytically about what people around them were saying about anything, far less about someone as distant from her own immediate—and exhausting—experience as the Voice of Quaysar?

"Tell me more," she invited, still keeping her own voice as neutral as she could.

"The thing that struck me most about what the war maids talking about the Voice were saying," Leeana continued obediently, "was that they all agreed that the new Voice had changed the policies of the old Voice. Changed them for the better, in the opinion of whoever was doing the talking, that was. I know you never actually discussed with me what took you to Kalatha in the first place, Dame Kaeritha, but I knew the sort of research you'd asked Lord Brandark to do before you left. And—" she glanced away for a moment "—I heard Prince Bahzell and Father discussing it a little. So I know you're really concerned about the disputes between Lord Trisu and the war maids."

Kaeritha frowned, and Leeana shook her head quickly.

"I haven't discussed it with anyone here, Dame Kaeritha! I know you and Mayor Yalith talked about it—or talked about something, anyway—and if Tomanāk Himself sent you here, then it's not my place to be blabbering away about it. But that's part of why what I was hearing bothered me, I think, because the same people who were talking about how much they approved of the Voice were talking about Trisu. And what they were saying was that the new Voice, unlike the *old* Voice, understood that the war maids couldn't put up with the way lords like Trisu were trying to turn the clock back. She understood that it was time the war maids stood up to people like him. That when someone pushed the war maids, the war maids had to push back—hard. Maybe even harder than they'd been pushed in the first place, since they had so little ground they could afford to surrender.

"That was enough to get me started listening to the

way they were saying things, not just *what* they were saying. And when I did, I realized they were suggesting, or even saying outright, in some cases, that it was the Voice, not Mayor Yalith or her Council, who'd really pulled Trisu up short."

"They may believe that," Kaeritha said, forbearing any attempt to pretend Leeana hadn't accurately deduced her purpose in traveling to Kalatha, "but I've spoken to both the Mayor and Lord Trisu. From the way both of them speak about the disputes—and about each other—the Voice has definitely played a secondary role, at most."

She watched the girl carefully. There were some thoughts—and suspicions—she wasn't prepared to share with anyone just yet. Besides, she was curious as to how closely this acute young woman's analysis would parallel her own.

"That's just it," Leeana said. "From what they were saying, the Voice didn't charge right in and begin speaking in Lillinara's voice or anything like that. Instead, they were saying—bragging, almost—that she was too subtle and wise to be that openly 'confrontational' herself. They said it was because she had to maintain the 'neutrality' of her office as Voice. But I've seen and heard about too many 'subtle and wise' noblemen who adopted the same sort of tactics. As far as I can tell, most of them were only avoiding open confrontations so they could hide in the shadows better when it came time to plant a dagger in someone else's back. Either that, or they were setting someone else up to do what they wanted done for them. Preferably someone gullible enough that they could convince him the idea had been his own in the first place."

"Are you suggesting that a Voice of Lillinara is doing that in this case?"

"I'm suggesting that it's possible," Leeana said, undeterred by the slight chill frosting Kaeritha's tone. "And that's not the only thing I think is possible. The way the war maids who seem to approve of the Voice are talking is also undercutting the authority of Mayor Yalith and the majority of the Town Council. Not directly, and not openly, maybe, but that's the effect it's having, and I don't think that's an accident. Every time they talk approvingly about how insightful the Voice is, and how clearly she sees what needs to be done, the implication is that *without* the Voice, Mayor Yalith and the Council *wouldn't* have seen how important it was to stand up to Trisu. Well, except for Councilor Maretha, maybe. But she and the Voice seem to agree about a lot of things, and the war maids who support one of them, tend to support the other, as well.

"The main thing that struck me, though, was that most of the war maids who most admire the Voice and Councilor Maretha are careful to emphasize that the Mayor and the rest of the Council are 'doing their best,' or 'well-intentioned, but mistaken.' Unlike the Voice, of course. I've seen that before, too. Not personally, but I did pay attention to my history lessons, Dame Kaeritha. I think this is an attempt to undermine the authority of the people who are supposed to be governing Kalatha. And I think the Voice is either actively involved in it herself, for some reason, or else that some third party is using her, as well."

"I see." Kaeritha contemplated Leeana for several more moments, then shrugged. "Is there anything else?" she asked.

"Well," Leeana said, and looked away again. She seemed uncomfortable for some reason, almost a bit flustered. "There's the fact that the ones I'm worried about seem to be actively recruiting from among the younger war maids. I think that's one reason I've heard so much about it in the relatively short time I've been here. The fact that I used to be Father's daughter—still am, really, until my probationary period is over—might make me more valuable in their eyes, and they might figure I'd be young and new enough to be easily impressed and convinced.

"And," she turned to look back at Kaeritha, "some of the other things they've been saying about the Voice make me . . . uncomfortable."

"Like what?" Kaeritha asked.

"It's just . . . well, I suppose—" A faint flush of color brushed Leeana's cheeks. "I never expected to hear someone suggesting that a Voice of Lillinara would be so . . . promiscuous."

"Promiscuous?" Kaeritha fought successfully not to grin, but Leeana's blush darkened anyway.

"I'm not all *that* innocent, Dame Kaeritha," she said just a touch huffily. "For that matter, I grew up on one of the Kingdom's biggest stud farms, for goodness' sake! So I'm quite familiar with what goes on between men and women, thank you. Well," she added hastily as Kaeritha chuckled despite herself, "as familiar as I can be without actually—That is, as—Oh, you know what I mean!"

"Yes, Leeana," Kaeritha said, her tone just a bit contrite. "I do know what you mean."

"Well," Leeana went on in a slightly mollified voice, "what bothers me, I guess, is that the people who seem so fond of the Voice's political views are also talking about how 'liberated' her views are on . . . other things."

"Leeana," Kaeritha said carefully, "Lillinara doesn't require celibacy of any of Her Voices. Some of them take individual vows of celibacy when they decide they have a vocation to serve Her, but that's different. A personal decision to free them from other needs and desires in order to concentrate solely on Her. And there's actually some disagreement as to whether or not She really approves of it even then. In fact, her High Voices *can't* be virgins. She is the Goddess of Women, you know—*all* women, not just the patron of maidens—and She feels that Her church—and Her priestesses—need to have experienced the things they're going to be counseling Her worshipers about."

"Really?" Leeana considered that for several seconds, her expression intent, then nodded. "That makes sense," she pronounced with the definitiveness of the young.

"I'm glad you approve," Kaeritha murmured, and the girl blushed again. Then she grinned.

"On the other hand," Kaeritha continued, "it sounded to me like you were talking about something you feel goes a bit far even bearing that in mind."

"Well, yes," Leeana agreed, but her expression remained

thoughtful, and she cocked her head at Kaeritha. "Can I ask *you* a question, Dame Kaeritha?"

"Of course you may," Kaeritha said, but the girl hesitated a moment, despite the reassurance.

"I was wondering," she said finally, slowly, "about how the other gods feel about that." She looked away, gazing out over the training salle's grounds. "For example, you're a champion of Tomanāk. How does *He* feel about it?"

"About celibacy?" Kaeritha chuckled. "Let's just say that as the God of Justice, He wouldn't exactly think it was 'just' to require His followers to forswear something that fundamental to the mortal condition. Like Lillinara, He expects us not to be *casual* about it, and He expects us to recognize and meet any responsibilities which might arise out of it. But all of the Gods of Light celebrate life, Leéana, and I can't think of anything much more 'life-affirming' than the embracing of a loving, shared physical relationship."

"Really?" There was something about that single word which made Kaeritha wonder exactly what the girl was thinking. But then Leeana shook herself, and turned back towards her.

"That makes sense, too," she said. "But it doesn't sound like what the people who worry me are saying, either."

"What do you mean?" Kaeritha asked intently.

"The loving and sharing part seems to get left out a lot," Leeana said simply. "And so does the bit about responsibility." Kaeritha frowned, but she didn't interrupt, and the young woman continued. "There were a couple of other parts that surprised me a little, just at first. They shouldn't have, but I guess that despite everything, I've got a lot more 'conventional' leftovers in my attitudes then I realized I did. I mean, the war maids are a community of women who've chosen not to live in a society run by men. Under the circumstances, I should have been surprised if many of them *hadn't* chosen other women as their partners, not the other way around.

"But even if that surprised me, at first, it didn't take me long to understand it. And what *bothered* me, Dame Kaeritha, wasn't who someone chose to fall in love with.

It was the way these particular war maids were talking about what the Voice thought about the proper 'freedom' when it comes to choosing lovers, whether they're men or women."

She didn't seem a bit flustered by her subject matter now, Kaeritha noted. It was as if her concentration on explaining what she meant had banished such mundane concerns.

"Why?"

"Because the sort of commitment and responsibility you're talking about doesn't seem very important to them. They talk about it as if it were, well, *only* physical. As if it's all about selfish pleasure, or just a momentary fling. Like . . . like the other person doesn't really matter, or isn't really real. Just a *convenience*. I'm not naive enough to think there aren't a lot of people in the world who feel that way anyway, Dame Kaeritha. But these women were laughing—almost snickering—about it, like they knew what they were suggesting was wrong and that only made it better, somehow. Some of them actually look forward to hurting someone else—using sex as a weapon to 'get even' for everything men have ever done to women. And every time I heard one of them saying something like that, I thought about all of the people who *already* believe all war maids think that way."

Kaeritha frowned, and her thoughts were grim. It was possible Leeana was overreacting to a few chance words. As the girl had said, she was the product of a Sothōii upbringing herself. Perhaps not quite as conventional as most, but even an 'unconventional' Sothōii rearing was bound to leave a few footprints.

Yet Kaeritha didn't think that was the case. Not only was Leeana keenly intelligent and observant, but the situation she described fitted only too well into the pattern *Kaeritha* had begun to discern. Or that she was afraid she had, at any rate.

"Do you think I'm imagining things?" Leeana asked, once again almost as if she could read Kaeritha's mind, and the knight shook her head.

"No. I'm certain you're not imagining things, Leeana.

It's possible you're reading more into what you've heard than was actually intended, but I don't believe you've imagined anything."

"Oh," Leeana said in a voice which was suddenly so tiny that Kaeritha looked at her in surprise.

"I'd hoped I was," the young woman said softly.

Chapter Thirty-Six

The morning sun's heat lay golden on the rolling grassland as a reinforced company of cavalry in the mingled colors of Glanharrow and Balthar swept steadily southeast. The wind blew—more than a breeze, but still gentle—from the south, and if it was cooler than it would become once full summer arrived, the day was already warmer than the day before had been. The cavalry sweep was approaching the perimeter of the Bogs, riding along one of the marshy streams that drained the rich but empty pastureland toward the swamps, still some miles away, and hordes of insects sent outriders of their own to scout the horsemen for possible targets.

Sir Trianal Bowmaster grimaced as the first stinging insect lighted on his warhorse's neck. The black stallion's skin shuddered, sending the insect zipping away, but the young man knew it would be back. Along with its brothers, sisters, and cousins . . . and all of their assorted uncles, mothers, fathers, and aunts. And, of course, they would find their way under hardened leather greaves and vambraces. And steel breastplates. Although, he reflected, he wasn't certain that even a horsefly under a breastplate wasn't preferable to a mosquito inside a helmet.

Funny, he told himself, *how the bards somehow forget to mention gnats and midges—or trapped sweat—when they talk about battle and glory*.

He snorted at the thought, then chuckled as he contemplated the response Brandark might have made to his observation. Whatever reservations Trianal might still nurse about hradani in general, he found himself forced to admire the Bloody Sword's intelligence and sharp, biting sense of humor. His views on bardic oversights might well have been profane, but they would certainly have been amusing.

He stood in the stirrups for a moment, stretching his leg muscles, then settled back. He and his men had been in the saddle, but for brief, occasional halts, since well before dawn. Their pace had been slow enough to conserve their mounts, but that hadn't given them any more sleep before they left the barracks, and his backside ached. Fortunately, it wasn't all that bad yet, and it *was* a sensation to which he was well accustomed, despite his youth. And although Chemalka's amusement with the spring rains seemed to have worn itself out, the ground was not yet dry enough for his troopers to be raising the clouds of dust which would have risen, even from grassland like this, later in the summer.

He wondered how many of his armsmen thought they were wasting their time. Whoever—he conscientiously avoided the names Dathian and Saratic—was behind the raids appeared to be doing exactly what Sir Yarran had suggested they might and adopting a waiting posture. There had been no reports of additional raids in almost two weeks now, and Trianal's patrols had found no sign of raiding parties during that time. He had other, smaller groups of scouts out searching for those signs even now, but he'd chosen to lead this larger sweep in person. In no small part that had been to get himself out into the open air and away from the office Lord Festian had assigned him in the keep at Glanharrow. It was also the sweep most likely to encounter something, assuming that Lord Dathian was, in fact, one of those responsible for the attacks. Although, if Trianal wanted to be honest with himself about it, he didn't really anticipate that they were going to run into anything exciting, even so. But at least it was getting him some exercise.

And the opportunity to sweat . . . and worry about horseflies and breastplates.

He chuckled again and reached for his water bottle. He took a sip—little more than enough to rinse his mouth out—then restoppered it and looked up as one of the riders scouting ahead of his main force came cantering back towards him.

"Do you suppose they've actually found something?" he asked the older man beside him skeptically.

"I'd say it's possible," Sir Yarran replied, squinting against the sun which hovered in the vicinity of the eastern horizon against a sky of blue and dramatic white clouds. "If they have, they don't think it's urgent, though." Trianal looked a question at him, and the senior knight shrugged. "If it was urgent, he'd be moving faster than that," he pointed out, and Trianal nodded.

"You've got a point," he conceded. Then he chuckled bitterly. "Of course, if they've found *anything*, they're doing better than we've done for the last two weeks!"

"Patience, Milord. Patience," Sir Yarran advised with a half-grin. "That's what it's all about, most times. Patience, I mean. Knowing when and how to wait is harder than charging behind the bugles, when all's said. Guts or a thirst for glory can get a man through battle and bloodshed, but it's discipline and patience keep him from dashing off to find them—and get his people killed—when there's no need. And they're also what get him through the time between the battles he *does* have to fight without letting boredom dull his edge."

Trianal cocked his head, considering what Yarran had said. The older knight watched him for a moment, then shrugged.

"Boredom's what's killed more sentries—and scouts—than anything else, Milord. A man who's bored is one as doesn't keep his eyes open and his wits about him for that one second when there truly is someone waiting out there with a bow, or creeping up behind to slit his throat with a knife."

"And I imagine it's killed more than a few men whose commander was too bored to be paying attention to his duties," Trianal said after a thoughtful pause, his eyes once again on the cantering scout.

"Aye," Yarran agreed, pleased that the youngster had explicitly made the connection. "Aye, it has."

The returning scout spotted Trianal beside his bugler and standard-bearer and cantered up to him and saluted.

"Sir Stannan's respects, Milord. He thinks we may have found something."

"Such as?" Trianal asked dryly when the armsman paused.

"Pardon, Milord." The armsman gave a wry grimace and shook his head. "Didn't mean to go to sleep on you, Sir. The Captain said to tell you we've struck the tracks of a party of horsemen."

"How large a party?" Trianal's eyes narrowed.

"It looks to be at least a score of horses, Sir. Might be as much as a score and a half. And most of 'em are wearing war shoes."

Trianal nodded acknowledgment and glanced at Sir Yarran. The older knight looked back, his own eyes thoughtful, but said nothing. Every young falcon must learn to fly, and it was as much his job to let Trianal try his wings as it was to keep the youngster from making too many mistakes.

Trianal understood that, and, to his credit, didn't resent it. He returned his attention to the scouts, but his voice was at least half directed towards Yarran when he spoke again.

"War shoes don't *necessarily* mean anything," he said, emphasizing the adverb slightly, "but that large a number of riders in one party is interesting. How far ahead is Sir Stannan?"

"Just over half a league, Milord," the messenger replied, turning in the saddle to point back the way he'd come. "There's a ravine just over the slope yonder, then another line of hills, up against the edge of the Bogs. There's a creek in the ravine—this one here joins it, and from the looks of things, it was a river a week ago—that cuts through the hills. It's not very straight, though. Sir Stannan says his map shows it drains into the Bogs, eventually. The tracks follow the ravine."

"They do, do they?" Trianal murmured, and the messenger nodded. "What's the ground like in the ravine," the young knight asked, rubbing his clean-shaven chin thoughtfully.

"Not good, Sir," the messenger said with a grimace. "Like I say, it looks as if it was filled to the brim with runoff last week, and it's twisty. It's marshy and soft, too, and there's places where the runoff's dumped gravel beds, or even a boulder or two. A man who wasn't careful could break a horse's leg in spots."

"But the going is firm and clear over the hills?" Trianal asked. "And they're not too steep?"

"Aye, Milord." The messenger nodded. "They're just hills, Sir—fairly rolling, dirt and grass, not even any trees. Well, there's some bushes here and there, especially up along the crest line. Such as it is, and what there is of it."

"I see." Trianal looked back at Sir Yarran. "War shoes might not mean very much," he said, "but when a party that size chooses to thread its way through that kind of terrain instead of going over the hills . . ."

"Aye." Yarran nodded, and cocked his head at Stannan's messenger. "How fresh would those tracks be?" he asked.

"Fresh, Sir." The messenger scratched his chin consideringly. "The sun's not been on them long, not down in the ravine like they are. But even saying that, the wet dirt hasn't dried where it was kicked up." He scratched again and squinted. "I'd say they're not more than an hour or so old—two at most."

Trianal's eyes brightened, but he made himself nod thoughtfully. Then he opened the hard leather case attached to his saddle and extracted a map. It was already folded to the proper section, and he beckoned for Yarran to move his horse closer so that they could both see it.

It wasn't as detailed a map as the King Emperor's surveyors could have provided one of the Empire of the Axe's commanders, but it was far better than most maps of the Wind Plain. Baron Tellian had made it a priority to import surveyors from the Empire, and they'd been working their way through the West Riding for several summers now, one section at a time (as he could budget for their fees and weather permitted). Fortunately for Trianal, he'd begun with Glanharrow because of its proximity to the Horse Stealers.

"What do you think?" Trianal ran a fingertip along the course of what had to be Stannan's ravine. According to the map, it wound its way through the line of hills in a serpentine series of twists and turns until it finally emerged on the rather indeterminate edge of the Bogs. There were very few details, aside from one or two larger, more prominent hills, once the map crossed over into the Bogs proper, unfortunately.

"From this," he continued, tapping the map, "it looks as if the ravine comes out well into Lord Dathian's lands."

"Aye," Sir Yarran agreed. Then he shrugged. "Come to that, though, Milord, we've been on Dathian's lands at least since sunup."

"I know. But this," Trianal tapped the map again, on top of the ravine, "leads much further in. In fact, his keep is less than three leagues away from where it hits the Bogs."

"Three leagues might be thirty across ground—or mud—like that," Yarran pointed out.

"Unless a man happened to know a way *through* the Bogs."

"Aye, there is that," the older knight agreed.

"But if following the ravine means they don't have to worry about skylining themselves or leaving tracks out in the open, it also comes near to doubling how far they have to go. And it probably triples their riding time. Whereas if we were to push our pace a bit and cut directly across the hills *here* . . ."

"It's a good thought," Yarran said. "All the same,

Milord, it's not likely we'll be there before them," he warned. "Not if those tracks are nearer two hours old than one."

"I know. But it's worth a try. And even if we don't get there before them, we may get there close enough on their heels to be able to follow them through the Bogs before the mud sucks their tracks under."

"That's true enough," Yarran agreed, and Trianal waved for their troop commanders to join them.

The sun was much higher—past noon, in fact—and the day was hotter as the reinforced company topped the final hill and started down the slope towards the deep-green barrier of the Bogs. The insects which had irritated Trianal earlier had been nothing compared to the swarm of gnats, midges, and mosquitoes which rose from the swamps and whined towards them, and he swatted morosely as a particularly large mosquito lighted briefly on his breastplate. His palm caught the insect before it could move, and he grimaced when the red splotch it left behind on the blackened cuirass indicated that it had already dined.

He grimaced again as he considered the terrain and recalled his own observation that his map wasn't as detailed as the sort a Royal and Imperial Army commander might have had. The ravine and hills were where it had said they would be; it simply hadn't indicated the density of the scrub trees and underbrush which fringed the Bogs and extended inward from its edges. The ravine cut a way through the green barrier, but he was a Sothōii. A horseman at heart, by both training and inclination, and accustomed to the long, clean sight lines of the Wind Plain. He didn't like the way that band of vegetation blocked his view deeper into the swampy land beyond.

He pressed his horse with his right knee, turning it to the left, and the steady pressure of his heels pushed it to a trot as he moved down the slope towards the ravine. It had grown broader and shallower as it approached the Bogs, and as he approached it, he could see the churned earth of the horses they'd been tracking. Sir Stannan, the captain who commanded his troop of scouts, was waiting with his senior sergeant.

Trianal drew up beside Stannan, Yarran and his standard-bearer and bugler at his heels, and the captain and noncom saluted. Trianal returned the salute with a quick brush of his breastplate, then nodded his head at the tracks.

"They look fresher, Captain," he observed.

"That they do, Milord," Stannan agreed. He was a rangy, brown-haired man, perhaps eight years older than Trianal, with a droopy mustache. He jerked his head at the ravine. "We've made up time on them, as you'd hoped," he continued. "But there's more of them than there were."

"I wonder if they had friends waiting for them?" Trianal mused aloud, gazing farther to the east, where the ravine disappeared into the green shadows of the Bog's thickets. The wind had strengthened and hissed softly in the grass about them, then danced on the gently tossing branches of the undergrowth.

"They might have," Sir Yarran said. "Or it may be that there was more than one detachment of them out there, Milord. It's possible they were doing what we're doing—out scouting for targets. We've been moving herds out of the area steadily, so it's been getting emptier. They may be heading home after spending the night ranging out further, looking for something to pounce on."

"Or keeping watch for *us*," Trianal responded. "I know this would be a lot of men if all they were doing was scouting, but they know we're looking for them. It would only make sense for them to want to keep an eye peeled for us to avoid surprises. And they could be sending out bigger scouting parties to give them more strength in case they run into one of our patrols."

"Aye, there's that," Yarran agreed. "Any road, it's reasonable enough that they'd arrange to be meeting up before they went traipsing into the Bogs. Especially if they've only so many men who know their way about in there."

"How many, do you think, Captain?" Trianal asked Sir Stannan.

"Hard to say, with so many hooves churning it up on top of each other, Sir," the mustachioed officer replied. "I'd be surprised if it's less than threescore now. And I'd not be surprised if it was as much as four, or even five."

Trianal pursed his lips, controlling his expression with care. It was hard. Eighty or ninety men—very nearly an entire company of cavalry—moving about in a formed body had to be up to something. It was also, by a considerable margin, the largest single force they or any of Lord Festian's scouts had yet tracked, and they were closer behind their quarry than anyone else had so far come. With the portion of his own command attached to the Glanharrow company Sir Yarran had brought along, he had eight troops—a hundred and sixty men, or almost twice the numbers Sir Stannan was estimating. If he could lay the force they'd been pursuing by the heels . . .

"It would be a fine thing to make a hole in the bastards, Milord," Sir Yarran observed. Trianal glanced at him and nodded, and the older knight continued in a thoughtful tone. "All the same, we've no evidence they've done aught but ride about. And if it should happen they're in Lord Dathian's colors, they've every right to be moving about his lands."

"They do," Trianal agreed. "But if they're *not* in Dathian's colors, or if it should happen that they're in . . . someone else's colors, then we'd certainly have a responsibility to ask them who they are and why they were here, wouldn't we?" He smiled with predatory humor. "After all, Lord Warden Dathian is also my uncle's vassal. It's clearly my responsibility to ensure that strange armsmen aren't violating his territory or threatening the security of his holding."

"Aye, that it is," Sir Yarran said with a toothy smile of admiration for the youngster's pious tone.

"Well, in that case," Trianal said, "let's see if we can't just catch up to ask them."

Chapter Thirty-Seven

"They're back there, all right, Sir," Sergeant Evauhlt said.

The Golden Vale armsman was perched in one of the sturdier trees, peering back to the east through a spyglass at a winking point of light. The long-barreled glass was much heavier and clumsier than the Axeman double-glass in the case hanging from Sir Fahlthu's weapons harness. It was, however, almost as powerful and far cheaper, and Fahlthu had no intention of trusting his prized glasses to any clumsy-fingered cavalry trooper. Even a signaler like Evauhlt.

"How many of them?" he asked, gazing up into the oak.

"The scouts say six or seven score, Sir," Evauhlt reported, still watching the flash of the heliograph from the steep hill further into the swamp. The lookouts atop it could see over the trees sheltering Fahlthu's troopers and their waiting position to the line of hills beyond. They'd been diligently keeping watch on their crests since dawn, in anticipation of his scouting parties' return, and passing their reports to the signal post located far enough down the hill for the swampland's low-growing trees and brush to hide its heliograph's flash from anyone to the west.

Fahlthu grunted in acknowledgment of Evauhlt's report and drummed the fingers of his right hand on the hilt of his saber. That estimate of the enemy's numbers was higher than he'd hoped it might be when the scouts watching his back trail first reported that his tracks were being followed. On the other hand, the other side thought they were still chasing mere horse thieves. They didn't know the rules of the game had changed. . . .

"Well, Master Brownsaddle," he observed to the man beside him. "So much for hiding our tracks."

He knew the criticism implicit in his tone was less than fair, but he really didn't care very much at the moment. The more he saw of "Brownsaddle," the less he liked. Not because the man wasn't competent—in fact, he was almost irritatingly capable. Indeed, much of Fahlthu's unease where "Brownsaddle" was concerned stemmed from the fact that the man was too capable for who and what he claimed to be. Fahlthu had the instincts of a successful mercenary, and they insisted that "Brownsaddle" proved there was even more going on here than Sir Chalthar had explained when he issued Lord Saratic's orders.

"If it were still raining, that would be one thing, Sir," Darnas Warshoe replied—respectfully, but with enough patience in his voice to show his opinion of Fahlthu's critical tone. "As it is—" He shrugged. "You can't hide the tracks of that many horses in weather like this, whatever you do. All you can do is try to put them somewhere no one will look for them—like the bottom of a ravine."

Fahlthu grunted again. This time he sounded remarkably like an irritated boar as he considered his options. Those same instincts which distrusted "Brownsaddle" urged him to avoid any closer contact with his pursuers. It wasn't as if that would be difficult to do, although Sir Trianal had made considerably better time to this point than Fahlthu had anticipated. The boy had reacted quickly and pressed hard, the Golden Vale armsman acknowledged. Not hard enough to tire his horses as much as Fahlthu had hoped for, unfortunately, but that might be Sir Yarran's doing.

And however quickly they'd gotten here, and however fresh their mounts might be, Sir Fahlthu still had the advantage of position. Not to mention guides who knew their way through this miserable, mucky swamp. Still, Trianal's force was considerably larger than Halnahk had anticipated when he issued the detailed instructions which gifted Fahlthu with responsibility for this initial operation. Fahlthu would have been far happier if the youngster's command had been closer to the small, isolated scouting forces he'd expected to encounter during the opening phases of the new campaign.

Unfortunately, now that contact had been made at all, Halnahk's orders—and, worse, Sir Chalthar's—were explicit.

"Milord, there's something wrong," Sir Yarran said.

Trianal turned in the saddle, eyebrows arching in his open-faced helm.

"What?" he asked his adviser.

"That's more than I can say," Yarran replied slowly. He frowned and swiveled his head, sweeping the steadily approaching belt of woodland with his eyes, wondering what had set his instincts so abruptly on edge. "It's just—"

Then he had it, and his eyes narrowed.

"Look there, to the left!" he said urgently. "There—by that clump of oaks!"

"Which oaks? The ones on that hill?"

"No, Sir—further left. Another thirty yards!"

"All right," Trianal said. "What about them?"

"Look at the birds," Yarran said, waving one hand at the small flock—no more than ten or fifteen—which had just launched into the air and now gyrated sharply above the trees. Trianal looked puzzled, and the older knight shook his head.

"Lad," he said, forgetting formality in his need to make the youngster understand, "*something* made them decide to take off just now. Something that spooked them."

Trianal looked at him, then back at the trees from which the birds had come, and his mind raced. There might be any number of perfectly ordinary explanations for their behavior, including an abortive pounce by one of the wildcats who made the Bogs their home. But he couldn't discount Yarran's veteran distrust of coincidence.

Yet the trees were a good hundred yards from where the ravine entered the woodland. If there was someone in there, then they were a long way from the only reasonably clear path through the tangled brush. But the oaks weren't very far back from the edge of the undergrowth. Just far enough for the dense brush and saplings to screen anyone hiding behind them, but not far enough to prevent a horseman from forcing his way out of them . . .

"Bugler," he snapped, "sound 'Column, Halt'!"

"Damnation!" Fahlthu muttered viciously as the sweet notes of a bugle sounded and the column trotting down the bank of the ravine slowed in instant response. He slammed his right fist down on his kneecap, hard enough to startle a twitch out of the horse under him, but it was too late to change his plans now. The underbrush which had concealed his spread-out troops from his enemies' approaching scouts also prevented the quick lateral passage of orders down the length of his formation. He'd had to give his men their instructions before he sent them to their positions, and he couldn't change them now—not without using his own bugles, which would have given away the game just as surely as what was about to happen.

And not in time to stop it, anyway.

Trianal watched his column of fours slow to a walk, then stop. His lead scouts had already been sixty or seventy yards in advance when the bugle call sounded. Now they were almost to the edge of the woods, still opening the gap, and he saw two of them turning in their saddles to look back towards the main body even as they continued trotting forwards.

And then a deadly storm of arrows exploded out of the brush.

✧ ✧ ✧

Darnas Warshoe didn't curse. He was too disciplined for that, despite the provocation, but it was tempting. He couldn't really blame Fahlthu's men. They'd had their orders, and they'd obeyed, firing as soon as the lead Glanharrow scouts reached the specified range. But the bugle call which had abruptly stopped the main column had opened the interval between them and the rest of their force. Not a single scout survived the sudden, overwhelming onslaught, yet their very proximity had drawn a heavy concentration of fire away from their more distant comrades. Coupled with the greater range to the column, that meant the main force's casualties had been far lower than they ought to have been.

Even more irritating from Warshoe's perspective, it meant the range to Sir Yarran and Sir Trianal was much greater than it should have been. Still, there *was* a chance, he reflected, and tucked the butt of the arbalest firmly against his shoulder.

Wounded men and horses screamed under the sudden, surprise onslaught, and Trianal's heart seemed to stop as he watched the wall of arrows sweep his scouts from their saddles. At least a dozen warhorses were down, as well, half of them screaming and kicking, and his mind seemed stunned into frozen immobility.

Which made it even stranger when he heard his own voice barking orders.

"Sound 'Fall Back,' then 'Skirmish Order' and 'Guide on Me'!" that voice which sounded so much like his own said. Something whizzed viciously past him, but he paid it no heed. "Standard, follow me!"

The bugler began to sound the commands, and as the sweet notes flared behind him, Trianal turned his horse and sent the stallion thundering back up the hillside they'd just ridden down. It wasn't easy. Every instinct shouted for him to press forward, get in among the trees and find the archers who had just slaughtered his scouts and were still firing at the rest of his men. But from the sheer volume of fire, plus the wide frontage from which it had come, the force in front of them was obviously far larger than the one they'd been tracking . . . and there was no way to tell how *much* larger.

He didn't know if the trail they'd followed had been designed from the beginning as a bait to lure them into a deliberate ambush, but that was what had happened. If he tried to drive a charge home into that kind of terrain, against a possibly superior force of prepared archers spread out over such a wide frontage, all he would achieve was the massacre of his own command. And if he spurred forward, joining his men as they fought to obey the bugle's commands, he would simply be one more armsman—one more target for the hidden archers.

He needed to stay out of that confusion and chaos if he meant to exercise any sort of control. And he had to keep his standard—the visual orienting guide his troop commanders would look for as they pulled back into their new formation—out of those plunging, screaming horses and cursing armsmen.

He pulled up, turning his horse once more, as he reached the military crest of the hill, and his jaw clenched. The bugler was on his heels, with the standard-bearer just behind him, and the blue-and-white gryphon standard writhed and danced. The wind of the standard-bearer's passage blew in through the large, open beak of the screaming gryphon's head, and the silken, wind-tube body flared wide and proud to its pressure. Sunlight glittered on the gryphon's golden head in a splendid show of martial glory, but the truth was hard and cold beyond its bearer.

All of Trianal's scouts were gone, and at least twenty more men lay scattered where the head of his column had been ravaged. With the scouts added, that was almost a quarter of his entire command. Many of those men lay motionless, but others writhed and screamed, curled around the arrows buried in their flesh. He wanted, more than he'd ever wanted anything in his life, to ride to their aid. They were *his* men, his responsibility, and he should be down there, seeing to their wounds, not abandoning them.

But he couldn't throw away still more lives, and he

forced his jaw to unclench as he saw the rest of his command falling back as he'd ordered. The column had unraveled, but not into the confusion and rout such an onslaught might well have produced. And that, he realized, was because of the brief warning his command to halt the column had given his men. His troopers hadn't known what was about to happen, but they'd been warned that *something* was not as it ought to be. That warning had blunted, however slightly, the surge of panic which even the most experienced armsmen must feel under totally unexpected attack.

His order to fall back in skirmished formation had been the right one, too, he realized, although he still had no idea whether reason or instinct had prompted him to give it. In either case, it had opened the column, making it a more spread-out target, less vulnerable to massed archery, even as the same order pulled it back, opening the range. And, just as importantly, it had been proof there was still someone in command, someone providing the authority to hold them together as a cohesive force.

Now he had to find out what he'd held them together to face.

This time, Darnas did swear, albeit in a deceptively mild tone. He hadn't missed by much, but his arbalest bolt had gone flashing by the figure in Balthar's colors which had to be Trianal Bowmaster. At that range, even the powerful arbalest would most probably have been defeated by the youngster's breastplate . . . but it might not have been, too. And it almost certainly would have penetrated if it had hit anything but his cuirass or helmet.

There was nothing Warshoe could do about that now, so he pulled out the crank of the cocking windless built into the dwarvish arbalest's stock and began respanning the steel bow. It wasn't a speedy process, but that was all right with him. He had no intention of getting directly involved in what was going to happen next.

Sir Fahlthu jerked a hand angrily at his bugler, and the armsman raised his bugle. It sang out, sounding the command to mount and advance, and his outsized company and the three troops Lord Dathian had assigned to him moved forward.

It wasn't what Fahlthu wanted to do. Not without having killed more of the enemy, or at least broken them as an organized force, before he engaged. But his orders from Chalthar and Halnahk left him no choice. He doubted that there was any real chance of killing every single one of Trianal's armsmen, whatever Lord Saratic wanted. Yet he could hardly pretend he hadn't attacked them, and the men he'd already killed had upped the stakes enormously from simple cattle or horse-stealing raids. Now that he'd effectively declared war on Glanharrow, his orders left him and his "brigands" no option but to kill as many more as he could.

Sir Yarran's belly muscles tightened as he watched the woodline spawning armsmen in the plain, unmarked leather and cuirasses of outlaws or unemployed mercenaries—if there was a difference. There were far more than there'd been in the party they'd been pursuing. At least ten-score, he estimated, and possibly as much as half again that number. Even without their opening losses, Trianal's men would have been seriously outnumbered.

He darted a look at his commander. The youngster had reacted with more speed than most grizzled veterans would have shown. And he'd done the right thing by halting the column. Maybe not the perfect thing, but the *right* thing. Yarran knew Trianal would always blame himself for not having halted the scouts, as well. In his position, Yarran would have blamed himself just as bitterly, but stopping them in their tracks would have been unjustifiable with no more than disturbed birds as the vague indicator of something possibly out of the ordinary.

The critical thing was that Trianal had held the command together. Many a formation would have shattered like glass on an anvil under that sudden attack. If it had been composed of veterans, their troop commanders and sergeants would probably have rallied them . . . eventually. But in the meantime, their attackers would have sought to take ruthless advantage of their confusion. Yet Trianal's orders had stilled that automatic, instinctive urge towards flight before it could take effect, and the armsmen Baron Tellian had sent with him to Glanharrow were hand-picked veterans themselves. Like Yarran's own men, they knew the difference between an officer who had a firm grip on his command and one who did not, and they were responding to Trianal's mastery like the well-drilled troops they were.

Now to find out if the young man beside him knew what to do with them.

Trianal watched the main body of his men spread out as they fell back towards his standard. Sothōii tactical doctrine had taken over, and each troop commander knew exactly what to do. His troopers swirled in what anyone who had never faced Sothōii cavalry would undoubtedly have thought was utter confusion, but Trianal's eye saw the underlying pattern. His men had their bows out now, and they sent their own shafts hissing back in reply to their attackers.

The ugly, bickering battle which had sprung so suddenly into existence was developing into a classic clash between light cavalry units. All was movement and speed, bursts of archery followed by sudden wheels away from the enemy while another twenty-man troop dashed up to rake the flank of anyone who followed the withdrawal too closely. Neither side was scoring a high percentage of hits now, for galloping horses, swerving evasively, were difficult targets.

Half a dozen of his troopers who'd been dismounted when their horses were wounded or killed were racing back towards his standard on foot. He saw some of their still-mounted companions swoop up beside them, reaching down a helping hand and offering them a stirrup as they galloped further back from the front of the combat. Riderless horses were also galloping back from the fray. Many of them, as well trained to the bugles as the riders they'd lost, were falling back, not simply running in panic. His double-strength command troop, which formed his only real reserve, let the panicked beasts go, but Captain Steelsaber had detached a sergeant and half a dozen men to scoop up the others and add them to the company's remounts. Trianal wondered if he ought to order them not to, to stay concentrated. But the way things were going, he thought grimly, they were probably going to need every horse they had.

"Pigeons!" he snapped, and a wizened little trooper appeared as if by magic at his elbow. Soft, anxious cries and the flutter of worried wings came from the wicker carrying cage on the other man's packhorse, but he laid a hand atop the cage and made soft, soothing noises to its inhabitants.

Trianal fumbled a block of thin, expensive paper and a stubby pencil out of his map case. He gazed out at the intensifying battle—damp as the ground was, dust was beginning to rise here and there, a thin haze breathing into the air as pounding hooves dashed back and forth over the same dryer pieces of grassland—and made himself think hard for several seconds. Then his pencil scribbled furiously. He had to make the best possible use of the few lines for which he had room, and he wrote quickly, then paused long enough to reread what he'd written. He grunted in satisfaction. It wasn't perfect, but it would have to do.

"Send it," he said, and handed the tightly folded message to the pigeon-keeper. The wizened man had already coaxed one of the pigeons out of the cage. Now he quickly but carefully fitted Trianal's message under the band on the bird's leg and threw it into the air. It circled twice, then headed off, straight as an arrow, into the west.

Trianal had no time to watch its flight. He had turned back to Sir Yarran even before the pigeon-keeper launched the bird.

"We'll fall back towards Shallow Cross," he told the older knight quickly, stabbing the air towards the northwest as he spoke. "I don't want to let them force us into a close action, but I don't want to break contact completely, either."

Sir Yarran glanced at the swirling wave of combat

falling steadily back towards them. Although horses were moving at breakneck speed in every direction, the actual westward movement of the combat itself was much more gradual, moving little more quickly than a single horse might have covered the same distance at a slow trot. That would probably change once the other side was completely free of the tangled underbrush and could begin to make its full numerical advantage felt, but both sides were Sothōii, and no one was better than the Sothōii at this sort of fight. The attackers would be wary of pressing too hard, too quickly, of letting themselves be drawn into fighting piecemeal. They would settle for a more cautious pursuit, using their greater number of bows—and, even more importantly, the greater number of *arrows* so many men could carry—to wear down Trianal's command. They would nibble away, killing and wounding men and horses, exhausting the remaining mounts, and forcing Trianal's troopers to expend their own arrows beating off attacks until, quite abruptly, the moment would arrive. The moment both sides would recognize, when mounting casualties, fatigue, and lack of ammunition shifted the momentum suddenly in the stronger side's favor and the time came for it to finish its opponents off.

The only true counter to that eventual outcome was for the weaker side to break contact and pull away as quickly as possible. He knew it, and so did Trianal. But he also knew what the youngster had in mind, and it might just work. The odds were against it, but Trianal had the audacity of youth, and the superb quality of the troopers under his command might just let him pull it off.

Might.

Sir Yarran Battlecrow weighed the options and alternatives, considered his responsibilities as Trianal's adviser and mentor, and made his decision.

"Aye," he said grimly. "Shallow Cross should do fine, Milord."

Chapter Thirty-Eight

Sir Fahlthu broke out of the undergrowth and guided his own horse up the northern bank of the ravine to the grassland above. It wasn't the best vantage possible, but it meant he could finally see at least some of what was happening with his own eyes. He pulled his double-glass from its case and raised it, adjusting the knurled wheel between the twin tubes until the standard at the crest of the hill to the west snapped into focus. He couldn't make out as much detail as he might have liked, even with the double-glass, but the figure on the tall, black stallion beside the standard wore the blue and white of Balthar, and the white bow and crimson-headed, green-fletched arrows of the House of Bowmaster showed clearly against the breastplate of his blackened cuirass. That had to be Trianal. And the other rider beside him, the one in the gray of Glanharrow and the plain, battered breastplate, was probably Yarran.

He lowered the double-glass and let his unaided eye sweep the seeming chaos of galloping horsemen. Trianal and Yarran would have a much better view of the action from their higher location, but Fahlthu was experienced enough to read the tempo of the battle from the smaller portion of it he could see. And as he absorbed it, he smiled grimly.

The fiery young hothead on top of that hill had made a serious error. Perhaps he'd underestimated the total strength Fahlthu could throw at him. Or perhaps he'd simply reacted with the stubborn inflexibility of youth. Either way, he'd made the wrong choice. He ought to have fallen back immediately, riding hell for leather to break contact while Fahlthu's greater numbers were still occupied making their way clear of the tangled brush and woodland which had concealed them. Instead, he'd accepted battle. No doubt he'd hoped the numbers were close to equal, or—depending on his optimism—even in his favor. In either case, he'd clearly believed he could skirmish successfully, even against superior numbers, and break off if the engagement grew too hot. But this was a game Fahlthu had played before, and he began giving orders to his bugler.

Trianal could see the moment when the enemy commander began once more asserting control over his troopers. Trianal couldn't actually hear the bugle calls across the noise and tumult of the battle between them, but he could see a third or so of the total opposing force falling back in response. The other two-thirds continued to press the attack, volleying arrows from their powerful composite bows and taking slower, more deliberate return fire from Trianal's men.

It was impossible to form any precise assessment of his own losses so far. Only one troop's swallow-tailed guidon had disappeared, but most of those which remained had less than the original twenty men following them, and troopers continued to fall by twos and threes on both sides. At a guess, he was down to perhaps a little over a hundred men, but by his rough count, the attackers showed at least a dozen guidons, which meant they had over two hundred—probably closer to three. So the other commander could afford to pull a third of his men back, resting their horses and conserving their ammunition until the critical moment, while the other two-thirds kept the pressure on Trianal's troopers and forced him to expend his own arrows and exhaust his own horses.

He felt a moment of almost paralyzing doubt, then gave himself a savage mental shake.

If whoever that is knew what I really had in mind, he wouldn't have pulled back a reserve, he thought. *He'd have thrown everything he had at me and accepted his losses to overwhelm me quickly. He can still win this kind of running battle—and more cheaply than a frontal assault, if it goes his way. But if he's willing to let me prolong it . . .*

"I wonder if they know about the pigeons," he said to Sir Yarran quietly while the sounds of distant combat became less distant by the minute.

"Likely not," the older knight said back, just as quietly. "Dathian probably knows at least a little about 'em, but this fellow's too aggressive to be one of Dathian's commanders. Besides, this whole ambush—and that's what it was when we got here, Milord, whatever the other fellow might have intended when he set out this morning—is something Dathian would avoid like the plague. Open warfare with Baron Tellian? He'd never agree to that—not if he thought it could ever be traced back to him, any road. And s'far as I know, nobody outside your uncle's riding knows he's been trying out the birds."

"We can hope, anyway," Trianal grunted, then looked the older man squarely in the face.

"I'm going to need all the help you can give me, Sir Yarran," he said frankly. "Maybe I should have picked a spot further east than Shallow Cross, but I don't just want to drive them back into hiding and leave us to find them all over again." He shrugged. "I know what I *do* want to do, but I don't know that I have enough experience to pull it off. If you have any suggestions—or if you see me making any mistakes—tell me. And be as loud and as blunt as you think necessary!"

He finished with a tight smile, and Sir Yarran returned it in kind.

"Milord—lad—you've done just fine so far. I'll be ready enough to fetch your head a clout, if it seems necessary.

But for now I've little to suggest . . . unless it might be as it's time for you to be pulling a mite further back."

"You're right," Trianal agreed, but before he moved, he beckoned to Yardan Steelsaber.

"Yes, Sir?" the captain of his command troop said in a voice which Trianal strongly suspected must sound much calmer than the other man actually was.

"You and your men, and anyone who gets back here on foot to remount, are our reserve," Trianal said bluntly. "You don't commit any of them without my personal approval, or Sir Yarran's."

"Aye, Sir."

"For right now, though, I need three messengers. I want them to go out into that mess and find Sir Rikhal, Major Helmscrest, and Sir Kallian. Tell them we're falling back to Shallow Cross and that I want them to stay oriented on my standard and keep those people following us until we get there. We'll fight a slow retreat to the top of the hills, get their teeth set into the notion that they're pushing us, we're not pulling them. Then, once we clear the hills, on my signal, it's time to show them just enough of our heels to keep them chasing us. Is that clear?"

"They're to keep contact and fall back to Shallow Cross. Slow retreat up the hills, then go to a gallop at your command. It's a feigned retreat to draw 'em after us. Aye, Sir, it's clear," Steelsaber acknowledged, striking his breastplate with a fist in salute. He seemed remarkably composed for someone who'd just received the orders of a lunatic, Trianal thought. But if anyone could get couriers through to his three senior subordinates, Steelsaber would get it done.

"Very well, see to it. And after you've sent the messengers, I think we'll pull back to that cluster of aspens on the far side of the hill. But slowly! I want our people to see the standard on the crest line here long enough to know we're falling back, not running!"

Fahlthu watched the standard of Balthar retreat towards the very top of its hill, then disappear over the crest. Any hope he might have had that the opposing force would dissolve in the belief its commander had abandoned it quickly faded. The troops of armsmen continued their intricate dance, giving ground steadily, but in a controlled retreat that sent stinging counterattacks to punish any of Fahlthu's own men who got too far ahead. The loss ratio was in his favor—it had to be, when even the portion of his force actively engaged outnumbered the enemy almost two-to-one—but not by very much, and his own losses were painful enough. On the other hand, the young fool's stubbornness might give him the opportunity to carry out his orders for a complete massacre after all.

He grimaced at the thought. Some of his men had already balked at finishing off Trianal's wounded. Indeed, one sergeant had flatly refused to obey the order, and his own captain had cut him down for mutiny. Fahlthu understood the necessity, and he was prepared to be as ruthless as his orders required, but he didn't much care for them himself. And he detested what a campaign like this was likely to do to Third Company's discipline.

And now that we've begun slaughtering the enemy's wounded, he thought grimly, *it would be a very good idea not to lose. Funny how it's the armsmen who carry out the orders, not the lords who gave them the orders in the first place, who always seem to end up paying the penalty for "atrocities" after the campaign. Still, the money's good, and I can always use the kormaks.*

"What the hell does Captain Hathmin think he's playing at?" he growled aloud, shrugging aside his morose thoughts in favor of fresher irritation as he watched the captain's troop go charging up a steep slope toward the enemy's left.

"I don't know, Sir," his standard-bearer replied to the rhetorical question, then cringed under the look Fahlthu gave him for his temerity. The company commander glared at him for a moment longer, and then turned the same glare on the distant Hathmin. It wouldn't do any good, but at least it made him feel a little better.

He could see why Trianal had been willing to weaken that flank, for the hillside was wet, watered by a series of springs the seasonal rains had filled brimfull. Its sodden grass had been largely churned to slick mud by the Balthar and Glanharrow horsemen who'd already ridden over it two or three times, and Hathmin's horses' footing wasn't good. They floundered, forced to move at little more than a walk, and two troops of Festian's men poured fire into his flank as his advance slowed. And then at least another troop worth of archers, all in Balthar's colors, came sweeping up from the back side of the hill and sent a horizontal hail of arrows sleeting into Hathmin's face.

The Sothōii horsebow was a powerful, deadly weapon, and men screamed as point-blank fire punched pile-headed arrows through leather armor, and even breastplates, at such short range. Horses shrieked as they took arrows of their own, and kicking, writhing warhorses went down on the awkward slope as Trianal's men closed with the saber to finish off the remnants. None of Hathmin's troopers got free, and Fahlthu swore vilely as the last of them fell, dead or wounded, in a pointed illustration of why pushing ahead too recklessly was . . . unwise.

Still, the other side had expended a lot of arrows massacring Hathmin, and that was the other side of the equation. When their arrows were gone, they were doomed, for why should Fahlthu close to saber or lance range when his bows could still fire and theirs couldn't? And at this rate, it might take even less time than he'd originally hoped.

He watched the reserve which had finished off Hathmin pull back across the crest of the hill. Then he grunted and sent his horse cantering forward, his chastened standard-bearer and bugler at his heels, following the carpet of dead or writhing men and horses back the way Trianal Bowmaster had retreated.

"Sound the gallop!" Trianal commanded as the main body of his dwindling command topped the line of hills and headed down their western face towards him.

The bugle calls rose perfect and forceful, as if their insistent beauty had nothing to do with the carnage and stink and blood littering the ground between the hills and the Bogs. But the officers his messengers had reached understood what he intended, and they wheeled their men quickly. Their horses were less fresh than they'd been when the engagement began, but they answered to their riders' demands and came pounding down the hillside dangerously quickly. At least one horse and rider went down with a smashing impact and rolled in an ugly, mutually lethal heap. But most got clear, and he exhaled a deep breath of relief as he watched his winnowed troops following the narrow, forked banners of their guidons clear of the slope at last. Only the very front ranks of the enemy's skirmishers had topped the hills behind them by the time his men were settling back into formation, reorganizing on the run as they thundered into the west.

"And now," he told Sir Yarran, swinging his own horse and urging the stallion to a gallop, "we see how fast Golden Vale horses are!"

"They're up to something," Fahlthu heard someone say, and turned his head. "Master Brownsaddle" had appeared out of the chaos, like the proverbial bad kormak, and the knight glowered at him.

"Of course they are!" he snarled back. "They're trying to get out of the chamber pot they shoved their heads into! And," he continued in a grimmer voice, "to kill as many of my lads as they can in the process."

"That's not what I mean." Darnas Warshoe grimaced impatiently, cantering along at Fahlthu's side. "They started out fighting a serious rearguard—now they're galloping away like hares before hounds, when they must know our horses are fresher than theirs are."

"Do you always have to look for the crookedest possible answer to any question?" Fahlthu demanded disgustedly. "Did it ever occur to you that they may simply have had enough? That they've seen enough of their friends killed that they're breaking at last? Men who finally panic and rout seldom stop to think about whose horse is freshest!"

"Milord," Warshoe said as patiently as he could, "if

they were going to panic, they should have done it at the outset. And if their morale's finally broken, why in all the gods' names did it happen *simultaneously* for their entire formation? Hasn't it been your experience that when a force routs, it usually at least begins breaking one subunit at a time?"

"And just how in Phrobus' name do you know they *didn't* start breaking that way?" Fahlthu demanded harshly. "I couldn't see through the solid top of a hill to watch the exact pattern of it—could *you*?"

Warshoe ground his teeth together and managed not to scream at the idiot. *Gods above, this fool wouldn't have lasted three months in the King's Own! He's made his mind up about what's happening, and he's not about to let any inconvenient little* facts *interfere now.*

"Milord," he tried once more, "what if it's a feigned retreat?"

"And what if it's Hirahim Lightfoot's long-lost mother?" Fahlthu shot back sarcastically. "No, Master Brownsaddle. You tend to your responsibilities—whatever they really are—and I'll tend to mine. And right now, mine are to go finish off an overconfident young whippersnapper who let guts and determination get the better of good sense!"

He urged his horse from a canter to a gallop, and Warshoe let his mount fall back. He watched Fahlthu spurring up the hill, waving his sword and shouting at his more laggardly men, and shook his head.

It was always possible Fahlthu's analysis was correct and Warshoe's was wrong. In that case, the cavalry commander had more than enough men to finish off Trianal and Yarran, and Warshoe could leave the brute labor up to him. Even if Fahlthu was wrong, it didn't necessarily follow that Trianal's plan—whatever it was—would succeed. But whether it did or not, Warshoe had no desire to find himself embroiled in the sort of melee that was going to ensue when Fahlthu finally closed for the kill. He was a specialist these days, not a common trooper. And if Fahlthu failed—or even if he succeeded, but Trianal himself escaped death—a specialist in the right place might accomplish more later on than all of

Fahlthu's cavalrymen put together in the wrong place could manage now.

Or, for that matter, a specialist might be required to see to it that Fahlthu himself wasn't around to . . . discuss his orders with Lord Festian or Baron Tellian. It would be most inconvenient for Baron Cassan if the Golden Vale captain were to be taken alive, and Darnas Warshoe wasn't in the habit of inconveniencing his patron.

He smiled unpleasantly at the thought and began dropping back from the front ranks of the pursuit.

Trianal Bowmaster's entire body ached. He supposed that he'd probably been nearly this tired sometime before in his life; he just couldn't remember when.

He drew rein, and the stallion beneath him blew harshly, a deep, heaving sound of fatigue and gratitude. The warhorse's nostrils flared, patches of crusty lather splotched his dark shoulders and flanks, and Trianal could feel the powerful muscles quivering with exhaustion. He leaned forward, patting the coal-black neck and whispering endearments. If he and his surviving men were reeling with fatigue, their horses were even further spent, and every one of them owed his life to his mount.

Not that there were very many of them, he thought bitterly.

He turned and looked back. The enemy had pursued them doggedly for almost three hours now, and the sixty or so of his troopers who remained couldn't stay in front of them much longer. It was fortunate that they'd come so close to breaking contact when they fell back across the hills. That blessed pause while the enemy's main body came up had let them open the range still further. Even more important, it had allowed Trianal's battered troops to reorganize themselves on the fly. Holes in the chain of command had been plugged, formations had been beaten back into order, and his entire surviving force had emerged as a compact formation readily responsive to his bugle commands.

And it was as well that it had, because the grueling pursuit had been even more costly than he'd allowed himself to believe it might. Captain Steelsaber would not send any more messages for Trianal; he lay somewhere miles behind, with an arrow through the base of his throat, and eight of his troopers lay scattered along the track of their retreat with him. Nor had Trianal been able to stay out of the fray, whatever Sir Yarran would have preferred. One of his two saddle quivers was completely empty; the other contained his last five shafts, and at that, he had more arrows than most of his men.

The moment had come, he thought, looking back at the irregular lines of horsemen sweeping across the grass behind him. The sun was sliding down the western sky as the short, northern spring day wound towards twilight. There was no more than an hour and a half—two hours at the outside—of daylight left. Long enough for a fight to the finish before darkness let the weaker side escape, but only if the fight began soon.

And it would, he told himself grimly. One way or the other, whether his desperate plan worked or not. His men's mounts were stumbling, and their quivers were empty. They were a beaten force, fleeing at the best pace their stumbling horses could still maintain while the reserve the enemy commander had pulled back and ruthlessly maintained gradually accelerated its pace. Its horses were scarcely what one could have called fresh, but despite their fatigue, they were far closer to that than the staggering creatures under Trianal's men, and they were pounding closer with every passing moment.

Trianal gazed at them for a moment longer, then sent the stallion back into motion. The big horse responded with a gallantry that made Trianal want to weep, but there was no time for that. His tattered survivors' wavering course was leading them directly towards a shallow river valley.

It wasn't much of a river—little more than a large creek, which normally disappeared entirely at the height of the summer. For now, it still chattered cheerfully in its shallow, gravel bed, singing with the strength which was the gift of the final rains of spring. Its valley was at least a bit more impressive than the "river" itself, if not a lot. It was little more than fifty yards across at its widest, narrower in most places than the ravine they'd followed that morning, but willows and short, brushy trees marked its course, drinking thirstily from the stream. The slope down into the streambed was shallower on this side, and steeper to the west, and Trianal could almost feel the triumph which suffused their pursuers as they realized what that steeper bank would mean for the exhausted horses they pursued.

Assuming that any of Trianal's men made it to the top of the far bank, they would at least have a long, gradual downslope on the far side. Not that it was likely any of them would make it up out of the valley before the pursuit caught up with them.

Trianal leaned forward into his horse's mane like a jockey, urging the stallion on with hands and voice, melding with the driving motion of the powerful, straining muscles between his thighs. Feeling the horse's gasping fight for air as the stallion's eyes blurred with exhaustion and he ran his mighty heart out at his rider's demand.

The sky was clear, yet for a moment anyone with the concentration to spare would have sworn that he'd heard thunder. Then it came again—a dull, rolling, throbbing sound, more sensed than heard . . . but not imagined. Never imagined.

Trianal looked up, his eyes wide with sudden hope, and then the western bank of the streambed disappeared under a line of galloping horses.

Sir Fahlthu didn't hear the thunder; but he saw it. Saw the rolling storm of cavalry coming straight at him. They must have had observers perched up there, waiting, timing the moment perfectly. He didn't know exactly how the terrain laid out beyond the river, but he knew it had to break downward to the west. It was the only way the oncoming troopers in the colors of Balthar and Glanharrow could have gotten their mounts all the way up to a full gallop without being seen.

How? he wondered almost calmly. *How did the little bastard get word to them? They're still an hour's hard ride from Glanharrow Keep. How could they possibly get here in time—and with their horses rested this way?*

And the fact that those horses were rested was painfully obvious as the charging horsemen came down the bank like an earthquake. The shallow water of the stream exploded in white wings of spray under the driving hooves of their mounts, bugles sang wild and fierce, sounding the charge over the deep, hungry bay of voices shouting Trianal's name like a battle cry, and Fahlthu's pursuit slithered to a halt in broken bits and pieces.

Some of his men turned in a vain effort to flee back to the east, towards the illusory sanctuary of the Bogs. But they would never reach the safety of the swamps, and Fahlthu knew it. The tables had just been brutally reversed. However much fresher than Trianal's staggering mounts his horses might have been, they were nowhere near so fresh as the rested, galloping warhorses coming towards them. Warhorses under vengeful troopers who were also fresh . . . and who had full quivers.

He stared at his company's onrushing doom, watching the gryphons at its head—blue and white of Balthar, and the gray of Glanharrow—writhe and dance, and despair was bitter in his mouth. There was no point trying to surrender his men, not after the way they'd massacred Trianal's wounded, and he knew it. But it was impossible to escape that thunderous, vengeful wave, either, and he loosened his saber in its sheath.

He was still staring at the dancing gryphons when the arbalest bolt smashed through the backplate of his cuirass and shattered his spine.

Darnas Warshoe watched from his motionless warhorse as Fahlthu tumbled from the saddle. He grimaced in satisfaction, then dropped the heavy arbalest, wheeled his horse, and went racing away. He would miss the weapon, and only its long range had let him take the shot from so far behind the Golden Vale captain, but his horse would miss its weight even more, and at this particular moment, that was what mattered. Warshoe was far enough back to have an excellent chance of staying ahead of the pursuit until darkness, especially if overrunning the rest of Fahlthu's men slowed it up a bit.

He might have to run his horse to death to do it, he reflected philosophically, but new horses were easier to find than new heads.

Trianal sobbed for breath as the rolling-thunder onslaught crashed past him. It seemed in that moment as if there were literally thousands of armsmen in Balthar's blue and white and Glanharrow's gray. There weren't, of course. There were only the other six troops he'd brought from Hill Guard and the seven more in Lord Festian's service. Only thirteen troops—scarcely two hundred and sixty men—all told. But they might as well have been a thousand as their fresh, tight formation smashed into the men who'd pursued Trianal for so long behind a hurricane of arrows.

"We did it!"

It took him a moment to realize that that exultant scream of triumph had come from his own throat, and when he did, his face blazed with humiliation. But even as he cursed the outburst as a sign of his own youthful lack of maturity, he heard someone laughing uproariously. He turned his head with a glare, and found himself face to face with Sir Yarran. Somehow, the older knight had managed—along with Trianal's standard-bearer and bugler—to cling to Trianal like a cocklebur, and now his face wore an enormous grin.

"Aye, we did, lad—*you* did." Yarran shook his head. "Truth to tell, lad—I mean, Milord—I thought you'd maybe one chance in three of pulling it off. But you did. You actually did!"

Yes, I did—we *did*, Trianal thought, gazing back the way they'd come at the swirling cloud of death as the relief force rampaged through their exhausted pursuers like a battering ram. He brought the stallion down from a hard gallop to a walk, and he could hear bugles, screams, even the crash and clash of steel.

We did it. But we only managed it because of the carrier pigeons, and my own estimate of the odds was lower than yours, Yarran. Gods, *how I wish there'd been some way for Lord Festian to tell us he'd received the message in time!*

"Let's get the men together and the horses cooled, Sir Yarran," he said, meeting his mentor's eyes, and the older man nodded with almost paternal pride.

"Aye, Milord," he said. "Let's be doing that."

Chapter Thirty-Nine

Bahzell stepped up onto the mounting block and clambered into the saddle on Walsharno's back.

He still felt ridiculous.

Someone his height wasn't supposed to need a mounting block—an *outsized* mounting block—just to get him high enough to cram a toe into the stirrup. And a champion of Tomanāk wasn't supposed to heave himself into the saddle as if he had only the vaguest notion of how it was supposed to work. And, to top it all off, Bahzell Bahnakson wasn't accustomed to looking (and feeling) clumsy, whatever he might be doing.

<*If you think this is embarrassing for* you, *think about what I'm going to go through in the field when you don't* have *your precious mounting block,*> a mellow voice said in the back of his brain. <*Now stop worrying and start concentrating on staying put up there.*> The voice was much deeper than Brandark's, but it carried an acerbic tartness that reminded Bahzell strongly, one might almost say painfully, of the Bloody Sword.

"And aren't you the fine one to be giving advice?" he muttered. "You, with all four feet on the ground! I'm after being a hradani, not a blasted sideshow acrobat!"

<*Really?* A hradani? *Perhaps I should be rethinking this partnership.*>

"You'll be finding more than enough to agree with you there, my lad," Bahzell assured him even as he settled fully into the saddle. "But while we've the topic of staying put before us, it's happier I'd be if I were after having more to hang onto up here."

<*You have the saddle horn, the cantle, and—if you* really *feel the need for security—the fighting straps,*> Walsharno said tartly. <*You do* not *need reins, as well.*>

"All very well for you to be saying!" Bahzell shot back with a grin, knowing Walsharno could taste his humor as if it were the stallion's own.

<*Besides,*> Walsharno continued, <*it's going to be years yet before I'd trust you to steer a* horse, *much less risk distracting me at a critical moment.*>

"Ah, well, it might be as there's a mite of sense in that," Bahzell acknowledged with a chuckle. "But seeing as how you're the one who's after doing the steering and all, would you be so very kind as to be moving off sharpish now?"

Walsharno snorted, and Bahzell felt powerful muscles twitch under him. That deliberate, preliminary twitch was the only notice he received before the courser bucked . . . playfully, he thought. At least it was sufficient warning for him to tighten his knees, grab the high cantle of his war saddle with both hands, and hang on as the stallion landed with sufficient energy to jar his teeth. The sight of two tons of "horse" arching its back and kicking up its heels was one which had to be seen to be believed, and his spine felt an inch shorter when Walsharno finished with him.

<*I trust that was sufficiently "sharpish" for you?*>

"Oh, aye, you might be saying that," Bahzell assured him, still clinging to the cantle like grim death, just in case.

<*Good,*> the stallion said silently, then moved off as sedately as a child's first pony.

The hradani heard the courser's silent laugh somewhere deep in his mind, and shared it. It seemed the most natural thing in the world to do, although he'd never imagined he might be that close to another living creature. He understood now why every wind rider called every other wind rider "brother," regardless of birth or rank, for anyone who had shared the intensity of communication with a courser had been forever set apart.

In Bahzell's case, his conversations with Tomanāk had, in an odd sort of way, provided a kind of preliminary training for the bond with Walsharno. It wasn't the same, of course, and yet there were undeniable similarities. More importantly, perhaps, Tomanāk had accustomed Bahzell to the idea that he wouldn't always be alone inside his own skull.

<*And a good thing, too,*> Walsharno agreed sardonically, following Bahzell's thoughts. <*There's so much empty space in here you'd probably get lost without a roommate. Or possibly a little boy with a lantern to lead you about by the hand.*>

"You just be keeping your comments to yourself," Bahzell told him, and Walsharno snorted another laugh.

Bahzell laughed with him, despite the grim reality behind their departure from Warm Springs. He couldn't help it as he tasted the stallion's vibrant personality and strength and felt the way they fused with his own. He knew how desperate a struggle lay before them, yet he had never felt more magnificently alive, except perhaps, in a very different way, in those rare moments when a portion of Tomanāk's power and personality flowed through him. And with that sense of shared strength and power came the knowledge, the absolute certainty, that he would never face this danger—or any danger, any loss—alone again.

"So, you're ready, Longshanks," a familiar voice observed dryly as Walsharno carried him out of the stable yard.

Bahzell looked across at Brandark, whose warhorse looked oddly shrunken, almost toylike, from the Horse Stealer's perch. Even he wasn't accustomed to looking *down* at a warhorse.

"Aye, so I am, if you're all still after being daft enough

to be coming along," he said, his eyes sweeping over the others assembled with Brandark.

"We are," Kelthys said before Brandark could reply, speaking for himself and the fourteen wind riders who had arrived in Warm Springs over the last two days. Hurthang, Gharnal, and the other members of the Order didn't bother with even that much. They only looked at Bahzell, waiting, and beyond them were the thirteen courser stallions who had accompanied Walsharno, Kelthys, and Walasfro to Warm Springs.

"Well then," he said, and Walsharno turned without another word from him and headed away from Warm Springs along the track the Warm Springs herd had taken on its doomed journey north.

"I don't suppose," Brandark said, as his horse trotted along beside Walsharno, looking like a yearling frisking beside its sire, "that you've developed a more, ah, *sophisticated* campaign plan since you and I last talked?"

<I like him,> Walsharno said. *<He* is *a bit of a pain in the arse, though, isn't he?>*

<Aye,> Bahzell agreed silently. *<He is that. In fact, he's after reminding me of a certain courser I know.>*

"As to plans," he continued aloud, "it's not as if there were all that much planning as we could be after doing." He shrugged, then raised a hand and pointed approximately north-by-northeast. "What we're hunting lies in that direction, Brandark. Aside from that, I've no more information than what I've already shared with the lot of you."

"Oh, joy," Brandark murmured, and Bahzell gave a short, harsh laugh.

"You were the one as wanted to come along, my lad," he pointed out.

"Not the only one, Milord Champion," Sir Kelthys said from Bahzell's other side, and the Horse Stealer turned to look at the Sothōii knight who had become his wind brother.

"Aye, it did seem as how there'd been a sudden shortage of brains in Warm Springs," Bahzell agreed affably.

"And then," he continued, looking past Kelthys to the other fourteen wind riders and coursers, "not content, you had to be after importing more idiots fool enough for such as this."

Most of the other wind riders chuckled, but two or three of them looked less than amused, and one of them glowered as if on the brink of an angry retort. But then his expression blanked, and he looked away quickly.

Bahzell hid a mental snort. The wind riders who'd funneled into Warm Springs hadn't known what to expect when they arrived. Certainly none of them had been prepared for the bizarre notion of a *hradani* wind rider. All of them, and their coursers, had reacted with incredulity, and for some of them, that initial reaction had been followed by disbelief, anger, and even outright rejection.

It wasn't the first time since becoming a champion of Tomanāk that Bahzell had experienced that sort of response. And, he admitted, this time there was more excuse for it than usual. Unlike all too many he'd met in the Empire of the Axe and the human-dominated Border Kingdoms along its frontiers, the Sothōii—and coursers—had an actual history of mutual slaughter with the hradani. He could handle and allow for hatred better when there was some basis besides *ignorant* bigotry behind it.

And, fortunately, there was another difference this time, as well—Walsharno, his sister, and the other surviving Warm Springs coursers.

Wind riders, Bahzell had discovered, could be just as stubborn and just as determined to deny an unpalatable reality, as any other humans (or hradani). He suspected that coursers could be even more stubborn, but they did it in different ways. Perhaps the differences had something to do with their herd orientation. He didn't know about that—not yet—but he'd already discovered that when one courser told another something was true, that settled matters. As far as he could tell from his efforts to date discussing it with Walsharno, the concept of lying, or even simply exaggerating, to another courser was completely incomprehensible to them. They simply didn't do that—didn't even know *how* to do it. They might be mistaken about something, and they might not always agree on how to interpret an event or an idea, but they did not fabricate.

Bahzell could already foresee some potentially uncomfortable consequences of that invincible candor, but it did have its advantages. The coursers' *riders* might doubt his champion's status, or question his fitness as a wind rider; the coursers themselves did not. And as Luthyr Battlehorn's sudden change of expression indicated, a courser's patience with his rider was not unlimited.

Not that it seemed likely to change Battlehorn's mind any time soon. Indeed, the dark-haired, burly wind rider couldn't seem to make up his mind which concept he found more offensive—hradani wind riders, hradani champions, or an entire hradani chapter of the Order of Tomanāk. If his courser, Sir Kelthys, and at least three more of his fellow wind riders hadn't ganged up to twist his arm, he probably would have been still sitting in a corner somewhere in Lord Edinghas' manor house and sulking.

Which, Bahzell admitted, somewhat to his own chagrin, would have suited him clear down to the ground. Battlehorn had not made himself one of the Horse Stealer's favorite people.

"Well," Kelthys said, "if I imported additional idiots, it was only because I needed to find people you'd have something in common with, Milord Champion."

"That's probably after being fair enough," Bahzell acknowledged with a smile. "But even if it's not, I've still no more plan than I was after having last night."

"Should we send out scouts?" That was blond-haired, dark-eyed Shalsan Warlamp, another of the recently arrived wind riders, and one who'd done a better job than most of accepting Bahzell for who and what he was.

"Against another foe, aye," Bahzell replied. "Against this one—?" He shook his head, ears half-flattened. "I've all the 'scouts' we should be needing right here." He tapped his forehead. "And I'll not have any of our people out in front where such as we're hunting could be taking them down one at a time."

Warlamp looked skeptical, but before he could say anything else, Brandark spoke up. The Bloody Sword's normal insouciance was absent, and his voice was very serious.

"Bahzell's right, Shalsan," he said. "I know it sounds ridiculous, but I've seen this before, when he went hunting for Sharnā. If Bahzell Bahnakson tells you he knows where to find the Dark, take his word for it. He does."

"Well," Warlamp said after a moment, "I suppose that's an end to the matter, then." He rolled his shoulders, like a man feeling a chill breeze explore his spine, then shrugged. "It's just that it doesn't feel right to not have scouts out when we know the enemy's waiting up ahead somewhere."

"No more it does," Bahzell agreed. "But this isn't the sort of enemy as you're after being used to hunting, Shalsan."

"They come, Master."

The being who had once been a man named Jerghar Sholdan opened his eyes and sat up at the sound of the servile voice. He hadn't really been asleep, of course—he hadn't needed sleep in a long, long time—but it took him a moment to brush aside the memory of the dark, windy void where he had drifted amid tongues of invisible black flame on the wings of a roaring tempest. There was a Presence somewhere beyond those walls of icy fire, a Name lost in the bellow of the battering wind. He knew both of them, and worshiped them, yet the very thought of them simultaneously filled him with hatred and fear.

But that, too, had been true for a very long time, he reminded himself, the tip of his tongue teasing gently at the razor-sharp canines which were the outward indication of what he had become. And hatred and fear, like the knowledge of his own enslavement, were paltry prices to pay for immortality and the power that sustained it.

Although, he admitted to himself, very quietly, in the most deeply hidden recesses of his mind, there were times . . .

"Where?" he demanded harshly.

"Still south," the creature which had roused him said obsequiously. "Far south, but coming!"

It rubbed its misshapen paws together, bobbing its head and fawning before him, silhouetted against the sunlight outside the cave. Jerghar regarded it with contempt, yet there was more than a trace of fear under the contempt. Not of the creature, but of the similarity, the parallel, between them which all his denial could not erase.

The shardohn's long, slick tongue flicked out like a wet, black serpent to lick its piglike tusks, and it crouched still lower as it felt his eyes upon it.

"Please, Master," it whined, and he reached down and cuffed it viciously as his edge of fear spawned anger. That blow would have shattered human bone, but the shardohn only squealed—in fear, more than in pain—and fell onto its side, raising its wings to cover its head. Jerghar drew back his hand to strike it again, then let his arm fall to his side.

"Get up," he snarled, and the shardohn scrambled to its feet and stood hunched into a crouch before him, staring down and refusing to meet his eyes.

"Where 'south' are they?" he growled, and the creature seemed to fold in on itself. It whimpered, and Jerghar forced himself not to cuff it yet again. It was hard, but he reminded himself of its limitations. Night and darkness were the province of Krahana and her creatures. Jerghar himself could tolerate the light, although direct sunlight was painful and remained mildly disorienting, despite the charm Varnaythus had provided to protect him against that weakness and prevent others from noticing his oddly elongated teeth. But the shardohns were far more strongly affected than he, and even when they were shielded from the sun itself, daylight made them clumsy and slow . . . and stupid.

"Tell me the place at which they are located now," he said, speaking very slowly and distinctly, and the shardohn visibly perked up, as if the question had finally been rendered down into words it could understand.

"Perhaps one league south of where we feasted on horses, Master," it said eagerly, reaching out one taloned paw as if to touch his knee. It thought better of the familiarity and jerked its hand back, and Jerghar grunted in grudging approval.

"Very well," he said after a moment. "Rejoin your pack. I'll summon you when I require you."

"Yes, Master—yes!" the shardohn babbled, bobbing and bowing, and then scurried off, scuttling deeper into the shadows of the cave. Jerghar watched it go, then settled down on an outthrust of rock to think.

If the shardohn's report was accurate—which it probably was—then he still had at least three or four hours before Bahzell could arrive. Long enough for the sun to set.

His lip curled at that thought, yet even so, he wished he had better tools with which to work. In their own element, under the cover of darkness, shardohns were far less stupid than the one which had just reported to him might suggest. They were also fearsome opponents for any mortal creature, armed with envenomed claws and tusks, and able to shift into the forms of wolves. They could not be "killed" by most mortal means, and it was extraordinarily difficult even to destroy their physical bodies. Worst of all, from the perspective of living foes, they partook of the essence of their mistress, Krahana. They were virtual extensions of Her—separate and infinitely weaker, true, yet a portion of whatever they fed upon also fed Her. Those they pulled down they devoured, and they did not settle for feasting upon flesh, bone, and blood alone.

Yet for all that, they were paltry creatures, individually, compared to the greater demons Sharnā controlled. Indeed, Jerghar often thought that their greatest value was as food themselves. The essence which filled them was far less sweet and satisfying than the uncorrupted life force of mortals, but it could sustain one like Jerghar. And like all of Krahana's creatures, the lesser existed to be feasted upon by the greater at need . . . or even upon a whim.

He considered summoning the messenger back to him,

pictured the moment his fangs sank into the creature's noisome flesh and the essence of its being flowed into him like the very elixir of life. But then he put the thought firmly aside. He would need all the shardohns he had, and he suspected he would wish he had more of them, before this night was done. Besides, the temptation reminded him that should he fail in this mission, there were those higher than he in Krahana's hierarchy and that his life would taste far sweeter to them than a mere shardohn would to him.

No, it was time to concentrate upon what his Lady demanded of him.

He closed his eyes again, longing to return to the comforting darkness of the void until the sun blazing outside the cave disappeared. Much as he might despise shardohns, he was forced to admit that his thoughts, too, were slower, less acute, during the hours of daylight than in darkness. Varnaythus had scarcely bothered to conceal his own contempt for Jerghar in Balthar, and the wizard-priest's scorn had grated on him. But Varnaythus had never encountered Jerghar in the blackness of night, when he was at the height of his powers. There were times Jerghar hungered to welcome Varnaythus into his embrace then, show him the price of contempt. It would not happen, not so long as Varnaythus was valuable to Carnadosa, for Krahana had decreed that Her sister's chosen Servants were not to be touched. Yet if the wizard-priest should fall from favor, if Carnadosa should withdraw Her protection . . .

He put that thought aside, too, with a mental curse for the way it proved how his mind wandered under the influence of the accursed sun even here, under fifty feet of solid earth and stone.

He knew what he had to do, and he knew what powerful weapons the Queen of the Damned had gifted him with. But despite that, and despite the fact that his enemies were coming to him on ground of his choosing and preparation, he felt what a mortal man would have called a shiver of fear as he contemplated his mission.

It would have been so much better if he'd dared to

attack Warm Springs, to swoop down upon the manor with the shardohns and slaughter every living thing in it. But his mistress' plans had forbidden the shardohns to carry through against the manor after the initial attack on the courser herd. Warm Springs, as much as the attack on the coursers who wintered there, had been the bait in the trap which would close upon Baron Tellian. In the end, Lord Edinghas' entire holding would be taken and devoured slowly, lovingly. But not until after Tellian had been drawn in so that he might be included in the feast.

Only . . . Tellian hadn't come. He'd been sucked away to Kalatha, instead, lured away from Krahana and into the Spider's web. Jerghar wasn't supposed to know the details of what Dahlaha and her mistress intended to happen, but he knew many things he wasn't supposed to. If Varnaythus was too confident of Jerghar's stupidity to realize his attempts to prevent that had failed miserably before one who commanded *his* Lady's resources, so much the worse for him.

Yet the substitution of Bahzell Bahnakson for Baron Tellian threatened to disorder even Her plans, and it was Jerghar's responsibility to make certain it did not. He'd been gravely tempted to proceed with the attack on Warm Springs which had always been part of the original plan, but the speed with which Bahzell and his companions had reached Lord Edinghas from Balthar had taken him by surprise. Bahzell had already arrived and healed the coursers of the shardohns' lingering venom—something Jerghar hadn't believed would be possible, even for a champion of Tomanāk—almost a full day before Jerghar had anticipated his arrival. By the time Jerghar himself had assumed direct command of the shardohns and the additional Servants awaiting him and gotten his forces properly organized, Bahzell had done far more than simply heal the coursers. He'd also been given one full priceless day of sunlight in which to recover from that ordeal; and he'd used his respite well.

Jerghar had required only the gentlest probe by one of his fellow Servants to know that the accursed hradani had erected a defensive perimeter impossible to cross. In fact, the sheer strength of the barrier Bahzell had managed to throw up was more than merely frightening. The Horse Stealer had been a champion for less than one year, yet the seamless, impenetrable power of that barrier—blazing incandescently with the terrifying blue light of Tomanāk for those with the eyes to see it—surpassed anything Jerghar had ever encountered. Thank the Lady he couldn't bring that fixed, focused rampart with him! It must have cost him hours of concentration to erect it in the first place, and he had to have anchored it in the very soil of the Warm Springs home manor.

But it appeared that the hradani was confident enough to come out from behind its protection at last. Which was either a very good thing . . . or the very worst thing that could possibly have happened. And if the shardohn's report was correct, Jerghar should discover which it was this very night.

Chapter Forty

<*Are you prepared, Bahzell? And you, Walsharno?*>

This time, the deep, rolling voice echoing through Bahzell's mind wasn't a courser's. It was the voice of Tomanāk Orfro, God of War and Chief Captain of the Gods of Light.

Bahzell didn't even blink, but his mobile ears twitched, moving in perfect parallel with Walsharno's to point forward. The hradani felt the courser's reaction like an echo of his own, yet Walsharno took the cascading, musical thunder of that voice far more calmly than Bahzell had taken his own first conversation with Tomanāk. There was a flavor of intense respect to his emotions, a touch of wonder and delight, but not one of awe.

<*And isn't that after being a silly question?*> Bahzell thought back at his deity. <*And here was I, thinking as how we were all after riding out for a picnic lunch!*>

Walsharno didn't share the apprehension bordering on horror which Bahzell's tart exchanges with his god tended to evoke in two-legged audiences. He continued to trot briskly forward, swishing his tail to discourage a particularly irritating fly, and looked on with amused interest, perched like another viewpoint in Bahzell's mind.

<*Bahzell,*> the deep, resonant voice observed with a sort of pained amusement of its own, <*I realize you're not exactly the most conventional Sword I've ever had, but you might want to work on your social skills for the moments when we have these little conversations.*>

<*So I might, but I'm thinking that if ever I did, you might be after getting all confused and wondering if you'd the right fellow on the other end.*>

<*Oh, I doubt that, Brother,*> Walsharno's thought put in. <*I doubt very much that He could possibly have* two *champions as irritating as you are.*>

<*Just like you to be after making up to himself just because he's a god, and all,*> Bahzell retorted, and the earthquake rumble of Tomanāk's chuckle rolled through him. Then the god continued, but his voice was softer, somehow.

<*I see that you two are as well suited to one another as any of us of the Light could have hoped, my children. That's good. You have far to go together. Be glad in one another and treasure what lies between you.*>

<*Aye, that we will,*> Bahzell replied, his own "voice" gentler than it had been a moment before. He felt Walsharno's unspoken agreement behind his own, then gave himself a mental shake. <*Still and all,*> he pointed out in something much more like his normal style, <*that sounds as if it's after suggesting we've a way to go yet* after *this little unpleasantness as is waiting up ahead of us somewhere.*>

<*I wish I could promise you that, Bahzell,*> Tomanāk said seriously. <*Unfortunately, I can't. Not even a god can tell you what will be. All we can say is what* may *be.*>

<*Indeed?*> Walsharno's ears shifted. <*Forgive me,* Tomanāk, *but I had always assumed a god could see the future as readily as the past.*>

<*The problem, Walsharno,*> Tomanāk said, <*is that in reality, there is no future or past. All time, all events, coexist. Mortals live in what you might think of as a moving window that briefly illuminates what they conceive of as separate moments in that single reality. It is a factor of their mortality that they cannot see it whole and entire,*

and so they order what they do see and experience into a past, a present, and a future.>

Bahzell frowned, intrigued almost despite himself. A portion of his awareness remained firmly focused on the movement of Walsharno's muscles under him, the caress of the late afternoon breeze as the day wound towards twilight, the jingle of mail and weapons harnesses, the creak of saddle leather, and the slightly dusty smell of grass crushed under the hooves of coursers and warhorses alike. But most of his attention was focused on the question it had never occurred to him to ask and on the answer he would never have anticipated, if he had asked.

<*I'm not so very sure as I understand any of that,*> he put in, <*but I'm mortal positive I'm not understanding* all *of it.*>

<*Nor do I,*> Walsharno agreed. <*Are You saying gods* can *see all of time in a single sweep? Because, if that's the case—if You see what we call the past and the future simultaneously—then why do You also say You can only tell us what may be, and not what will?*>

There was no disrespect or challenge in the courser's question. He accepted what Tomanāk had said, as a yearling accepted the decrees and explanations of his herd stallion. He was simply seeking explanation, not demanding that Tomanāk justify what he had already said.

<*Mortals think in terms of causes and effects,*> Tomanāk replied. <*And insofar as mortal affairs are concerned, that's a useful and effective way to visualize what they experience. But the truth is that a given cause does not have one fixed, inevitable result, as mortals persist in thinking that it does. All possible outcomes of an act, or an event, are equally real and valid, Walsharno. Mortals observe and experience only one as their moving window travels across the moment of resolution, but all are present and real . . . both "before"* and *"after" that perception and experience mortals define as "now."*>

<*My brain is after hurting,*> Bahzell observed dryly, and Tomanāk chuckled again in the back of the link he and Walsharno shared. <*If I'm understanding you aright, then are you after saying that whatever it may be we're*

thinking happened didn't? That we're only after imagining it did because we've not the eyes—or the minds—to be seeing what truly did?>

<*No,*> Tomanāk replied. <*The problem is that mortals lack the proper frame of reference to visualize all that's bound up in what you think of as "now," or "the present." In a way, that's the very thing that makes you so valuable in the struggle between the Light and the Dark, Bahzell. In a fashion I can't explain to you because of the difference in our frames of reference, mortals* define *events and will ultimately define whether the Light or the Dark triumphs in this universe by the framework they impose upon the reality they cannot fully observe.*>

He obviously recognized Bahzell's and Walsharno's confusion, for he went on.

<*Think of it this way. "History" is a mortal creation, a procession of mortal experiences which moves through the interconnected past and future. It . . . selects which single outcome "occurs" out of the collision of all possible causes and all possible effects for each given event. The word "until" is another mortal creation, a consequence of the way in which you perceive time and events, but "until" that moment of mortal experience of an event, all of its possible outcomes happen. Indeed, if you wish to think of it this way, the perception of each individual mortal creates its own individual universe for every outcome of every event.*>

<*But in that case,*> Walsharno thought slowly, <*there must be as many universes as there are possible outcomes.*>

<*Precisely,*> Tomanāk replied simply, as if the staggeringly complex and preposterous implication were perfectly reasonable. <*As I told you once before, Bahzell, the Light and the Dark are engaged in a struggle across more universes than you can possibly imagine. You simply didn't realize that it is you mortals who create those universes. And, in the "end," it will be the balance of all those universes, the preponderance of them, in which Light and Dark have triumphed which determines the fate of them all.*>

<*Now I know my head is after hurting,*> Bahzell thought after a moment. <*But if I've puzzled out even the least tiniest bit of what it is you're after saying, then you can't be telling us what will be after happening because we've not yet reached that moment with our "window"?*>

<*Exactly,*> Tomanāk agreed, <*and yet not complete. Mortals believe we gods see all of time and space and that, if we chose, we could tell them what will happen. But they're only partly correct. We do see all of time and space, and because we see all possible outcomes, we cannot tell you which one of them you will experience. We could tell you which outcomes are more likely, or less, but we cannot tell you which one will be for you, because all of them will happen somewhere.*

<*Yet that's only fair, my children, because only you can tell us what the ultimate fate of all of us will be. Because in the moment that we reach the final end of all mortal perceptions of all mortal events and the decision is rendered in favor of the Light or the Dark, then all other possible outcomes will disappear, as if they never were. Ultimately, your fate lies in your own hands, not ours. What you choose, the struggles you wage, the battles you win and lose—those are what determines the fates of the gods themselves. And that, Bahzell, to answer the question you asked me once, is why you and all other mortals, and why each and every one of all those infinite universes, are "so all-fired important" to us gods.*>

Bahzell and Walsharno were silent, stunned by the immensity of the concept Tomanāk had just laid before them. The idea that there were an infinite number of Bahzells paired with an infinite number of Walsharnos, each fusion experiencing its own outcomes, fighting its own battles and meeting its own fate, might have made them feel small, and insignificant. No more than two single grains of sand upon an endless beach. Yet they were anything but small and insignificant. The exercise of their free will would determine their fates, and their fates would be not grains of sand on a beach, but stones in an avalanche thundering to a grand conclusion which would determine the fate of all universes and of every creature who had ever lived . . . or ever would.

<*That's . . . after being quite a mouthful for a man to be digesting,*> Bahzell said after a long, thoughtful pause.

<*It is,*> Tomanāk agreed. <*And it isn't a mouthful most mortals are prepared to bite off and chew. Not everyone has the capacity to understand and accept the implications, and many of those who do refuse to accept them. The fact that you can both understand and accept, and find in that understanding strength for the battle, rather than hopelessness in the face of such immensity, is one of the things which make you a champion, Bahzell. And you, as well, Walsharno.*>

<*I?*> Walsharno came to a sudden halt, his ears straight up and his eyes wide. <*I, a* champion? *I'm no such thing!*>

<*Oh, but you are,*> Tomanāk said almost gently. <*Not by yourself, perhaps, but a champion nonetheless. The first courser champion, as Bahzell is the first hradani champion in over twelve centuries.*>

<*But—*> Bahzell began.

<*Don't worry, Bahzell,*> Tomanāk said gently, <*no one will constrain Walsharno to be or do anything against his will, any more than I could compel you to become my champion except by your own free choice and decision. Yet coursers are not like the Races of Man. When humans or hradani make choices, they make them as individuals. Each and every one of you is alone in that moment of decision. But coursers are part of a herd, part of an interconnected whole where thought calls to thought, and mind speaks to mind. Walsharno, like all coursers who choose brothers from among the Races of Man, is different in that he reaches beyond the herd. His sense of who and what he is transcends that rich, flowing river of joined thought and experience. In a way, it makes him greater than the whole, and yet less, for until the moment that his soul met yours there was something missing within him. Something the herd could not provide and whose absence he had not recognized*

until he met you. But it was that sense of the herd, that awareness of himself as one who was unique, yet a part of more than one, which let him know you when he met you and to join with you willingly. And in that joining, which made you both the two separate individuals you had always been and also the single entity you become when your bond joins and focuses you, he partook of your champion's status.>

<*Here now!*> Bahzell protested, oblivious to the other coursers and warhorses halted in puzzlement about him and Walsharno. <*Here now—I'll not have it! I'll not be dragging Walsharno like some lamb to the slaughter into whatever might be after waiting for me!*>

The complex linkage between hradani, courser, and deity trembled with the force of his protest.

<*Peace, Brother,*> Walsharno said, shaking off his own shock at Tomanāk's calm announcement as he recognized the pain—and guilt—suffusing Bahzell's mental cry of denial. <*You will never drag me* anywhere *against my will. When I chose you, I chose knowing you were a champion, knowing where that might lead. I was surprised, but He's right, and if you think upon it, you'll see that He is. I willingly and gladly chose to partake of whatever fate awaits you—whatever fate we make for ourselves—in the full knowledge that you were a champion . . . and that few champions perish in peace, surrounded by those who love them. It simply never occurred to me that in doing so I might have stepped so close to the power of the Light myself.*>

<*But you have, Walsharno,*> Tomanāk said gently. <*And it is so like you—and Bahzell—to have made a decision that profound so quickly, so fearlessly. Great heart knows great heart when they meet, as you have met. And yet, Bahzell has the right to fear for you, to seek to protect you—to be certain he has not "dragged" you to a fate you did not willingly accept. And so I ask you, will you take sword oath to me as the first courser champion?*>

<*I will,*> the courser's voice rang in the vaults of Bahzell's mind. A part of the hradani wanted desperately

to forbid it, to prevent Walsharno from binding himself so inescapably to whatever fate awaited Bahzell himself. But another part recognized that it was too late to prevent that. That from the moment Walsharno willingly linked himself to him, their fates had been joined. And another part of him recognized that he had no right to forbid Walsharno this. That it was the courser's—his brother's—right to make the choice for himself.

<Do you, Battle Dawn, son of Summer Thunder and Pride of Morning, swear fealty to me?>

<I do.> Walsharno's "voice" was as deep, as measured, as that of Tomanāk himself, filled with all the certainty and power of his mighty heart.

<Will you honor and keep my Code? Will you bear true service to the Powers of Light, heeding the commands of your own heart and mind and striving always against the Dark as they require, even unto death?>

<I will.>

<Do you swear by my Sword and your own skill in battle to render compassion to those in need, justice to those you may be set to command, loyalty to those you choose to serve, and punishment to those who knowingly serve the Dark?>

<I do.>

<Then I accept your oath, Walsharno, son of Mathygan and Yorthandro. May you bear yourself and your brother always in the service of the Light.>

A deep, resonant bell rang somewhere deep in the depths of Bahzell Bahnakson's soul. A single musical note enveloped him, wrapped itself about him and Walsharno, and as it sang like the voice of the universe itself, Walsharno's presence blazed beside him like the very Sun of Battle for which he was named. The power and essence of Tomanāk himself was infused into that glorious heart of flame, and Bahzell felt all of the myriad connections between the three of them. It was unlike anything he had ever felt before, even in that moment when he and Kaeritha had felt and experienced with Vaijon the moment that Tomanāk accepted *his* sword oath.

<Done—and well done!> The deep voice sang through the depths of their joined souls, deep and triumphant, joyously welcoming and shrouded in the thunder of coming battle. *<Tremble, O, Darkness! Tremble before the coming of these, my Swords!>*

Chapter Forty-One

"The Mistress was right—they *are* fools!"

Treharm Haltharu, who looked as human as Jerghar Sholdan—and was—exposed razor-sharp teeth in a vicious smile. Stars twinkled overhead, their jewellike beauty uncaring, and the crescent new-moon hung low on the eastern horizon. He stood beside Jerghar atop the low hill over the cave in which they had spent the daylight hours, and his eyes glittered with the deadly green light of his true nature.

"Of course the Mistress was right," Jerghar replied harshly, "but She never called them fools."

"Of course She did!" Treharm snarled. "Are you as big a fool as they? Are your mind and memory failing like a shardohn's? Or do you call me a liar?"

He glared at Jerghar, fingers flexing, and raw fury hovered between them. Then Jerghar's right hand came up and across in a terrible, crashing blow. The sound of the impact was like a tree shattering in an icy forest, and Treharm's head snapped to the side as its savage force flung him bodily from his feet. He flew backward for almost ten feet before he hit the grassy hilltop and skidded, and his high-pitched shriek of rage tore the night like the very dagger of the damned.

He bounded back up with the impossible speed and agility of what he had become, but even that unnatural quickness was too little and too late. Jerghar had already moved, and the fingers of his right hand tangled in Treharm's hair. He fell to one knee and heaved brutally, yanking the other Servant's spine into a straining bow across the bridge of his other thigh, and Treharm's scream of rage turned into something more frantic, dark with fear, as Jerghar's left arm pinned his own flailing arms. And then even that whimpered into silence as Jerghar's fangs flashed scant inches from his arched and straining throat.

"You said something, pig?" The words were malformed, chopped into lisping pieces by the teeth which had suddenly elongated into deadly white scimitars, and the green glare flowed out of Treharm's eyes like water. The unnatural strength of a Servant of Krahana went with the emerald light, and Jerghar held his grip for another ten seconds, grinding that surrender deep into Treharm's mind and soul. Then, slowly, he released the other Servant, and allowed him to crouch on the grass at his feet. Had Treharm been a dog, he would have rolled to expose his belly in submission, and Jerghar's mouth curled in a snarl of dominance.

"Defy me, or anger me, once more, and I will take you." The words hissed and eddied past his fangs, and his eyes glared with a brighter, stronger green than Treharm's ever had.

"Yes, Master," Treharm whimpered, and Jerghar spat into grass that hissed and smoked as his emerald spittle struck it.

"Better," he said, then straightened. Had he still been a living man, he would have drawn a deep breath. But he wasn't, and so he simply forced his spine to unbend and his hands to unclench, then jerked his head impatiently at his trembling second in command.

"Get up," he said coldly, and Treharm pushed himself shrinkingly to his feet once more. Jerghar watched him, tasting his own anger, his own contempt, then closed his glittering eyes and forced the last of his rage to yield to self-control.

It took several seconds, but when he finally opened his eyes once again, his expression was calm. Or as close to it as any Servant ever came when he put off his cloak of seeming mortality. The simmering rage spawned by the insatiable hunger and need to feed which was always near the surface of any Servant in the hours of darkness could be useful when he hunted by himself. But, he reminded himself once again, it could be something very different when two or more Servants were forced to work together.

"Now," he said to Treharm, his ice-cold voice more nearly normal as his fangs dwindled once again, his dominance reasserted, "it may be that they're fools, and it may be that they aren't. What the Lady said was that their patron was *arrogant*, and that they partook of his arrogance. But that isn't the same as being fools, Treharm. It may lead them into acts which appear foolish, but to assume that they'll act in that fashion is to give them a dangerous advantage. And this is a champion of the accursed sword. Only an axe of Isvaria could be more dangerous to such as us. Do not forget it."

"No, Master," Treharm promised abjectly, still in full submission mode. Jerghar gave him a menacing glare to see to it that his subordinate stayed that way, although he cherished no illusions that it would last longer than this very night. But that was as long as it truly had to.

"However," he continued after a moment, allowing some of the ice to flow out of his tone, "there *are* times when arrogance and stupidity become indistinguishable, and it's possible—*possible*, I say—that this may be one of those times."

Treharm's submissively bowed head rose slightly, a tiny rim of green glittering once again around the edges of his eyes, and Jerghar nodded.

"It is, at the very least . . . audacious for him to challenge us in the hours of Her darkness. I'd looked for wiser tactics from the champion who so easily defeated Sharnā not once, but twice. To confront us now, when our strength is greatest, is to give us an advantage I never dared to plan upon. And since he's been so obliging as to come to us at the place and time of our choosing, we will meet him and crush him."

The green fire in Treharm's eyes flickered and grew brighter, and he dared to smile at his superior. Treharm had never really liked Jerghar's original plan to harry their enemies' flanks, picking off the weakest first and weakening the strong steadily with the despair of their comrades' destruction, until the time came to take them all. He'd argued that such an attack would take too long, spend too many precious hours of night. In the end, it might allow Bahzell and Brandark, the two enemies who, among all others, must perish, to escape.

Jerghar had been prepared to risk that, despite the penalty he knew his mistress would inflict upon him if he failed, because he had never anticipated that Bahzell would be so rash as to come directly to him in his own prepared place of power. It was no carefully concealed temple, hidden away, depending for its security upon secrecy, as Sharnā's Navahkan temple had. The life force the shardohns had ripped from the slaughtered coursers had provided Jerghar with all the power he needed to raise a fortress around this hill against any champion of the Light. It was a heady, exhilarating power, a tide of stolen strength such as no Servant of Krahana had tasted in centuries, if ever. Jerghar had never suspected the true nature of the coursers, never guessed that draining them would produce such a prodigious well of strength. It had been necessary to reclaim them from the shardohns—temporarily, at least—so that he might use them as burning glasses, reaching through them into their unsuspected link with the energy of the entire world about them.

The shardohns had hated it. Two of them had actually tried to resist Jerghar, and been destroyed and devoured themselves for their impudence. That had been enough, and the others had disgorged their prey, yielding up the taken souls of the courser herd to Jerghar as they would ultimately have yielded them to the Lady Herself.

Oh, but that had been a moment of ecstasy and deadly temptation. As all those souls, all that power, had flowed through him to lie in his hand, ready for his use, he had touched the very edge of godhood himself. As Treharm had been foolish enough to challenge his own authority, he had felt his own momentary power seducing him into thoughts of how he might have used it for himself, *kept* it for himself, and not as his mistress had commanded.

In the end, it had been only temptation, for he'd known too well what vengeance Krahana would have taken upon him. All of that life force, all of that additional power, was his only to borrow for use against Her enemies. In the end, it was *Her* prize, not his. She would have it, harvest it from her shardohns, and woe betide any who dared to stand between Her and it.

And so, instead of claiming it for himself, he'd used it, and the result hovered in the darkness about him. He felt the coursers' souls, reclaimed—however briefly—from the creatures who had slain them, screaming silently. They had tasted what awaited them, and the horror of that taste swirled through them like a cyclone of terror. And that was good, for their fear, their effort to escape the hideous dissolution awaiting them, only made it easier for him to manipulate their essences. They were his focuses, the anchors of the glittering web he'd woven, and his smile was ugly in the darkness. It would make their despair complete, and the taste of their broken life energy so much sweeter, when they realized that it had been they—their souls, and the power stolen from them—which had trapped and destroyed one of Tomanāk's hated champions.

"Go to Haliku and Layantha," he told Treharm now. "Tell them both that our enemies will be here within the hour. And tell Layantha to join me here . . . and that when the time is right, she will have what she requires.

"We're after being close now."

Bahzell's voice was low as his companions—hradani, human, and courser alike—gathered about him and Walsharno. He sensed their tension, their dread of what awaited them. But he also tasted their grim determination and their hatred for the evil they'd come to find.

"How can you tell?" It was Battlehorn. Even now he

sounded sullen, resentful, yet the question was genuine, not a challenge or statement of skepticism.

"It's a sense himself is after giving his champions," Bahzell replied levelly, answering the question with the honesty it deserved. "It's not something as I can be putting neatly into words, but I'm after sensing the presence of the Dark much as you'd see a cloud against the sun. And what it is that's waiting up ahead there is after being the very stormfront of Krahana herself."

Muscles tightened, and jaws clenched, but no one looked away.

"What is it you want us to do?" Kelthys asked simply.

"It's little I know of exactly what we'll be facing," Bahzell said grimly, "but this much I do know. There's after being two battles waiting for us—one as will attack physically, with claw and fang or blade, and one as won't be using weapons most of you will be so much as seeing. I've a nasty enough sense of what's ahead to know as there won't be anything of the mortal, natural world about it, physical or not. But anything as is solid enough to be after hurting you is solid enough that you can be hurting *it*. I'll not say as how you can be *killing* it, but at the least, you can be after holding it in check."

He paused for a moment, surveying his allies, then flicked his ears.

"I'll not be lying to you. It's in my heart and soul to wish as how you'd none of you come, beyond us of the Order, but you'd have none of it, and I knew it. And, truth to tell, I can't but be admiring the guts as brings each and every one of you to this. You've made us sword brothers all, by your courage. Yet men—and coursers—are after dying in battle, brothers, and it's in my mind as how some of us will be doing that this night."

Dozens of eyes looked back at him, levelly, despite the tension ratcheting higher and tighter behind them.

"There's a part of this battle as will be mine to fight," he continued. "It's not one as any of the rest of you can be after joining. But what you can be doing is to keep the rest of whatever it is we're facing off of me while

I've the fighting of it. Will you be watching my back for me, brothers?"

"Aye." It was Luthyr Battlehorn, his voice cold and hard with promise despite the dislike still showing in his eyes. "Aye, Milord Champion, we will."

"Now, Layantha."

Jerghar's command was a sibilant hiss as he crouched atop his hill, and the once-woman beside him smiled a terrible smile. Layantha Peliath was something vanishingly rare among the Servants of Krahana—a mage who'd actually sought the service of the Queen of the Damned. And not just any mage, for she'd been an empath. Not a receptive empath. Most of those went into healing, either of the mind or the body, and the very nature of their talent was enough to make any fate like Layantha's unthinkable. Had she been a receptive empath, her talent would have carried the predatory cruelty of Krahana and her Servants too clearly to her for her to have voluntarily yielded. She might have been taken by a Servant, or a shardohn, or even Krahana herself, but she would not have *yielded*, and so could not have become what she now was.

But Layantha had been a *projective* empath, able to project her own emotions, but unable to sense those of others. It was one of the mage talents of extremely limited utility, and perhaps that had been a factor in the choice she'd made. Layantha had never had the sort of personality which was prepared to accept that she was not the center of everyone's universe as she was of her own.

She hadn't realized in time that to accept Krahana was to become no more than one more satellite of the voracious void which she had made her mistress. The fact that she remained anything but the center of the universe was bitter poison on her tongue, but that only fanned her hatred of all still-living beings even higher. And the mage talent which had survived her surrender to Krahana was no longer a thing of limited utility.

Now, as her enemies crested the last undulating swell of the Wind Plain before their hill, she reached out to that portion of the reservoir of focused power Jerghar was prepared to make available to her, and her smile was a hideous thing to see.

A wave of sheer terror curled across the night-struck grassland like a tsunami.

Terror was no stranger to Bahzell Bahnakson. He'd faced wizards, cursed swords, and demons, and no man, however great his courage, was immune to fear. But he had never tasted a deeper terror, one with a darker core of horror . . . or one which had no apparent source at all.

Layantha's tidal bore of darkness crashed over him, and he heard stricken cries and high-pitched, equine squeals as it fountained over his companions, as well. It smashed down on them, vast and noisome and more crippling than any physical wound. He sensed them behind him, and knew that the only reason they hadn't fled was that the terror which had invaded them was so totally overwhelming that they were paralyzed. Frozen helplessly, like mesmerized rabbits waiting to be taken by a gamekeeper.

Bahzell was trapped with them, but the black river of ice which had sucked them under could not—quite—reach his core. That indomitable core of elemental hradani stubbornness, buttressed by his link to Tomanāk . . . and to Walsharno.

He and the courser stood motionless, as frozen as any of their companions, as the night took on a hideous unlife of its own. He could see the darkness coming alive with the pustulant green sores of hundreds of glittering eyes. They came towards him, and he recognized them. Not because he'd ever seen them with his own eyes, but because Gayrfressa had seen them. Had felt the fangs and poison, and the terrible, lustful hatred which lived behind them. He had experienced Gayrfressa's experiences as his own, and beyond that, he was a champion. The true nature of the shardohns could not hide itself from him, and so, even more than Gayrfressa, he understood what he faced and the true horror of what awaited any who fell to them.

The creatures closed in slowly, made cautious by their dread of Tomanāk and his power despite the quicksand of projected terror which had frozen their enemies. And that caution was a mistake.

They should have flung themselves upon Bahzell. They should have ripped the life and soul out of him and Walsharno instantly, brutally, while Layantha held them paralyzed. But instead, they hesitated, and in that moment of hesitation, Bahzell reached deep.

He didn't think—he simply acted. Despite the vicious wave of emotion sweeping over him he reached both deep within himself and without. It was as if he stretched out both of his hands, one to Tomanāk and one to Walsharno, and answering hands closed upon his in clasps of living steel. He was an acrobat, arcing through empty air in the unwavering knowledge that hands he could trust even more deeply than he trusted his own would be waiting to catch him, and the electric shock when they did rocked through his soul like cleansing sunlight.

And even as his god and his courser brother caught him in that three-part fusion, Bahzell summoned the Rage. Summoned the wild whirlwind of berserker bloodlust which had been the curse of his people for twelve centuries, until time and healing had transformed it into something else—into elemental determination and deadly, ice-cold concentration.

The mighty cables of hopeless horror Layantha had cast about him snapped like cobweb, shredded by the rushing wind of Walsharno's fierce strength and shriveled by the blazing presence of Tomanāk. And at the heart of that focus of Dark-rejecting Light stood Bahzell Bahnakson in the dreadful exaltation of the Rage, like the rock on which the tide of terror broke and recoiled in baffled foam and rushing confusion.

"Tomanāk!"

The deep, bull-throated bellow of his war cry split the darkness, and Walsharno's wild, fierce scream of rage came with it. Bahzell's sword leapt into his right hand, summoned by a thought, glaring so bright a blue that even mortal eyes were dazzled by its brilliance, and the shardohns froze, squealing with a terror even deeper than the one Layantha had conjured to paralyze their foes.

Layantha screamed. Her hands rose to her head, balled into fists, pounding her temples, and she staggered back. She writhed, shrieking as the terror she'd projected recoiled upon her. In all her mortal life she had never received the emotions of another. She'd been as blind to them, despite her empathy, as any non-mage. But now, at last, her mind was opened, its barriers and defenses ripped wide by a talon of azure power, and all the hatred and black despair she had leveled against her intended prey lashed through *her*.

She shrieked again, fighting frantically to stop the pain. But she wasn't permitted to. She couldn't stop projecting, with all of the stolen energy Jerghar had funneled to her. And not just because Tomanāk and his champions would not allow it. The slaughtered victims of the Warm Springs courser herd had been dragged back to face the desecration of being made to serve their destroyers. But those tormented souls were the souls of coursers, and as Lord Edinghas had told Bahzell, coursers would not yield to demon, devil, or god. They refused to take back their power. They writhed, shrieking in torment as terrible as Layantha's own as Jerghar flailed them with the power of his own will, beating at them with whips of fire as he commanded them to stop pouring their stolen life energy through her mage talent. They writhed . . . but they did not relent.

Layantha screamed again and again, jerking, her green eyes blazing like fiery suns, and then Jerghar leapt back from her, stumbling and clumsy in the haste of sudden fear, as she began to burn.

It was only smoke, at first, rising from her. But then, in the flicker of an instant, smoke became flame. A terrible flame that mingled the blue glory of Tomanāk and the green pollution of Krahana into a towering furnace. A column of fire roared into the night, and Jerghar cowered away from the shrieking presence trapped at its heart. There was no heat, yet Layantha shriveled, consumed and blazing in a holocaust which did not even dry the dew from the grass on which she stood.

She screamed once more—a terrible, quavering sound that trailed away into infinite time and distance—and then she was gone, leaving not so much as a trace of ash to mark her destruction.

The paralysis which had held Bahzell's companions vanished as abruptly as the light of a snuffed candle. He heard and sensed them as they fought to shake off the lingering effects, but there was no time for him to explain what had happened. Jerghar had sent Treharm and two other Servants to command the shardohns, and even as he shrank away from the vortex of destruction consuming Layantha, his mind screamed orders at them, whipping them into the attack.

"Now, sword brothers!" Bahzell shouted, and the night came alive with the snarling howl of unnatural wolves.

The shardohns hurled themselves forward, howling with a fury that blazed hotter and hungrier than ever because of their own terror. The blazing blue radiance spilling from Bahzell's sword filled them with panic as paralyzing as anything Layantha could have produced. But the deeper, darker terror of their mistress and her Servants goaded them, lashed them and drove them forward in a madness to rend and tear.

Swords and sabers and Hurthang's daggered axe glittered in the light pouring from Bahzell's blade, and the battle screams of coursers answered the voracious howl of wolves. Walsharno sprang forward, going to meet the rolling wave of attackers, and he and Bahzell were the tip of a wedge, driving into the heart of their enemies.

Horror collided with edged steel and war-hammer hooves. Shrieks of fury, howls of hunger, screams of pain, and the crunch of steel cleaving undead flesh and shattering undead bone filled the night. Scores of more than mortal demon-shapes flung themselves forward in near mindless hunger, and there were too many of them. One of the Bear River stallions screamed as he was dragged down, a ton and a half of fighting fury submerged under a wolf pack that ripped and tore and shredded.

Another courser stumbled and went down, spilling his rider. The courser lurched back to his feet, shrieking with fury and hate as three shardohns descended upon his rider. The wind rider's saber flashed desperately, and one of the shardohns screamed as the blade severed its spine. It fell, writhing in its agony, but the other two got through. The wind rider died without a sound as fangs ripped away his throat, and his courser brother screamed like a demon himself. He reared, crushing the killers, and then screamed again as a tidal wave of wolves rolled over him.

Hurthang's axe came down like a thunderbolt, glaring with an echo of the blue flame spilling from Bahzell's sword. A shardohn squealed in agony as that blazing steel clove through it and it discovered—fleetingly—that it *could* be killed. Gharnal's sword flickered with the same light as he disemboweled another unnatural wolf, and Brandark's warhorse screamed with terror as yet another shardohn lunged at it. The Bloody Sword wrenched its head to one side, spinning it away from the attack, and lashed out with his sword. His blade didn't share the blue flame of Tomanāk's presence, but his target was flung aside, headless and kicking. It wasn't "dead," but, then, it hadn't really been "alive," either, and it lurched back to its feet, staggering in a questing parody of life as the tide of battle surged past it.

"Tomanāk! *Tomanāk!*"

The deep-throated thunder of Bahzell's war cry rose through the hideous tumult, beating down all other sounds, echoing through the night like the war horn of the god he served. He and Walsharno fought like one being, so tightly fused that neither could have said where the thoughts of one ended and the other's began.

Bahzell's huge sword, five feet and more of blue-blazing blade, was a two-handed weapon for any lesser mortal, but he wielded it one-handed, as if it weighed no more than a fencing foil, and any shardohn which came within its sweep was doomed. That same light blazed about

Walsharno, and each forehoof was the heart of an azure explosion as he brought it crashing down. There was no sign of Bahzell's normal clumsiness in the saddle—not now. He was a *part* of Walsharno, not simply a rider, and the two of them forged unwaveringly towards the hilltop on which Layantha's pyre had blazed.

Jerghar shoved himself back upright and tore his eyes away from the unmarked grass where Layantha had perished, and fear as dark as anything the undead mage might ever have projected pounded through him. Nothing had ever suggested to him that what had just happened to her was even possible. And if Bahzell could do *that* . . .

No! Jerghar shook himself viciously. It had been the coursers, seeking vengeance on their killers, as much as anything Bahzell had done! And now that he knew what had happened, he could allow for it. He was the master of those damned souls, and he scourged them with a white-hot strength forged from all of his fury and panic. There was no time to savor their silent screams of agony properly, but he battered their power back under his control. Even then, he felt them fighting him, defeated but not subjugated, yet they could not resist him as he drew deep upon his reserves of corrupt energy.

He looked up from that brief, titanic struggle, and his green-lit eyes widened in disbelief. His enemies had cut deep into his outer perimeter, battering their way through the surging sea of shardohns. It wasn't possible. *Bahzell* might be a champion of Tomanāk, but the others were mere mortals. They should have been chaff in the furnace, easy prey, yet they were not.

He could trace every yard of their progress by their blood and bodies. Coursers and humans and hradani were dying, but they were not dying alone . . . or easily. Almost a third of his shardohns had been crippled or destroyed outright, and still those madmen and coursers hammered their way deeper and deeper into a battle which could end only in their own deaths. And at their head, wrapped in that deadly blue glare of power, was the biggest courser of all and the fiery sword of Bahzell Bahnakson.

✧ ✧ ✧

"Bahzell!"

Gharnal's frantic shout of warning cut through the tumult and chaos, and Bahzell's head snapped around as something arced through the air towards him. It looked like a human, but no human ever born could move like that, with such speed and unnatural agility. It had come out of the grass, out of the tangle of snarling, heaving wolves on Bahzell's left side, and he twisted in the saddle, trying to meet the attack even as Walsharno tried to wheel to face it.

But there was no time. The attacker hit the ground and bounced impossibly, flinging itself at Bahzell's unguarded side, but then an arm flashed out.

Gharnal Uthmâgson caught Treharm's ankle with his left hand, and Krahana's Servant howled in shocked fury. No mortal he'd ever faced had been quick enough to do that, and certainly none of them had been strong enough. But Treharm had never before faced a hradani who had summoned the Rage, and Gharnal jerked him away from Bahzell with a strength which very nearly equaled his own.

Treharm wrenched around, lashing out with taloned fingers, and chain mail shredded as they ripped through it. Gharnal grunted as they ripped flesh, as well, but his blade came hissing back with all the flashing speed of his Rage, and Treharm howled again as that blue-lit steel sheared through his right arm like an axe.

Panic erupted through the Servant, worse than any physical agony, as his severed arm flew away. That wound would have been mortal—or at least disabling—to any mortal being. But Treharm wasn't mortal. The lost limb would regrow in time, and the shock which would have paralyzed a living man had virtually no effect on him at all.

No *physical* effect. Yet there were other forms of shock, and the wound was a terrifying warning that perhaps he *was* mortal still, after all. He squealed, twisting and slashing with his remaining arm, striking out at Gharnal in a desperate frenzy, and Bahzell's foster brother's spine arched as a supernaturally powerful hand punched straight through his breastplate and drove deep into his chest. Ribs splintered and their fragments stabbed jagged ends into his lungs and heart.

Gharnal was a dead man in that moment, but he was also a sword of Tomanāk, and a hradani exalted by the power of the Rage. He didn't fall, and Treharm had a final, flashing instant to gawk in disbelief, his left fist closed upon the beating heart of his foe, before Gharnal's blade came slashing up in one last, perfect stroke and Treharm's head went flying away into the night.

"No!"

Jerghar screamed in denial. Not because he cared about Treharm's fate, but because Treharm's death meant he'd lost two-thirds of his fellow Servants, and with them, their power. And because if Layantha and Treharm could be killed, then so could he.

A dreadful premonition of doom echoed through him, and panic urged him to flee. But the greater terror of Krahana overruled his panic. Tomanāk and his champion might destroy Jerghar, but if he fled Krahana would do far worse than that. And so he stayed nailed to his hilltop, watching the swirling confusion of combat crunch towards him.

Brandark's warhorse screamed again, this time in agony, as a shardohn exploded up under the Bloody Sword's guard and ripped out his mount's throat. The stallion went down, collapsing in blood-spouting ruin, and Brandark kicked frantically clear of the stirrups. He hit hard, but he managed somehow to hang onto his sword, and he rolled upright almost instantly.

Yet fast as he was, he wasn't quite fast enough. The same shardohn which had killed his horse sprang at his own throat, and two more came at him from the sides.

The first met a deadly thrust that drove a foot of steel through its belly. It shrieked in agony, folding up around the blade, snapping at it with its wolfish fangs, and he wrenched the sword free in a spattering fan of blood and whirled to face the shardohn flashing in from his right. The blood and venom-streaked steel came down with all the elegance of a cleaver, driven by the desperate strength of an arm almost as mighty as Bahzell's own . . . and the ferocious precision of the Rage. It crunched through the shardohn's spine, just behind the shoulders, and the shardohn collapsed with a scream. It was back up in a moment, scrabbling forward on its forelegs, yet its crippled hindquarters dragged uselessly behind, and it was too slow to reach him.

But if it could not, the third demon could. It flung itself on Brandark's shoulders, ripping and tearing at the backplate of the Bloody Sword's cuirass. Steellike fangs snarled and savaged their way across the armor, gouging viciously at it, and he twisted his shoulders frantically, trying to hurl the creature off even as he wrenched around to face it.

For a moment, he almost succeeded, but then the shardohn lunged again, and Brandark grunted in anguish as envenomed jaws punched spikelike teeth through the left arm of his haubergeon. The shardohn's fangs pierced the tough, dwarf-forged rings effortlessly, mangling muscle and crushing bone, and its dreadful, baying howl of triumph vibrated agonizingly into his flesh. It tasted his life force, sucking at it even as its poison flooded into him, and it knew he was his.

But he was a hradani, tougher than any other prey the creature had ever taken. And he was empowered by the Rage, with all the terrible, driving energy of his people's ancient curse. And he was Brandark Brandarkson. No champion of Tomanāk he, no servant of the War God's order. Only a man who had longed to be a bard . . . only a poet who had faced greater demons at Bahzell's side and spat defiance in the face of Hell.

He snarled through the icy fury of the Rage, feeling his strength flooding into the shardohn, and twisted his shoulders. He bared his teeth at the soaring spike of agony as broken bone and torn muscle shifted in the creature's maw, and the shardohn's howl of triumph wavered as it felt itself being dragged around. It tried to release its grip, but it was caught, its fangs trapped in shredded chain mail and its victim's very flesh. It couldn't escape as Brandark shortened his right arm, raised his left arm from the shoulder, suspending the shardohn's full, heavy weight from his shattered upper arm, and drove his blade home. It rammed into the "wolf's" belly, and he twisted his wrist, disemboweling the creature.

The shardohn squealed, fighting and bucking with the agony of its wound, heaving until—finally!—its fangs ripped free of its victim. It landed on all fours, flinging its head up in torment . . . and Brandark's sword came down on the back of its neck like an axe.

The shardohn fell, and Brandark thudded to his knees, left arm hanging limp, as pain and blood loss, poison and the icy suction of his soul pulled him down at last. His sword sagged and his head drooped, and yet another shardohn sprang for his throat. He tried to get his blade up, eyes glaring with the defiant fire of his Rage even from the lip of the grave, but his ripped and bleeding body had given all that even a hradani's could. He couldn't raise the weapon in time, and he watched the shardohn's fangs glisten with emerald corruption as they came for him.

And then a daggered battleaxe, its blade shrouded in cleansing blue flame, came smashing down like a thunderbolt.

"Tomanāk! *Tomanāk!*"

Hurthang was there, his axe blazing like a beacon, and Brandark collapsed at last.

Bahzell's heart twisted as he saw Gharnal collapse over the body of his killer, saw Hurthang standing astride Brandark's body while the howling pack converged upon him. But there was no time for grief, no room for fear. Gharnal and Brandark were not the only brothers he had lost this night, and the dying was far from over. And yet . . .

His head snapped up, and his eyes narrowed. The tide of combat had carried him and Walsharno steadily forward. There was so much Dark power abroad in the darkness that even his champion's senses had been unable to cut through it and find its heart. But he was close enough now. His dying sword brothers had brought him close enough at last to sense the focus of the enormous, deadly tornado of twisted energy howling invisibly above the hilltop before him. He felt Walsharno beside him, and tasted the courser's raging grief as Walsharno felt the agony and terror of the damned coursers trapped in Krahana's power. And as they both recognized the heart and core of the vortex waiting to engulf them and all their companions, they knew what they had to do.

Bahzell took Walsharno's fury at the fate of the Warm Springs coursers and melded it with his own grief for Gharnal and Brandark and everyone else who had perished this hideous night. He combined them, wrapped them about his Rage, and gave them back to himself and to Walsharno as determination harder than steel, not despair, and his great voice rose above the tumult.

"*Tomanāk*!" he bellowed, and Walsharno charged.

Jerghar heard that world-shaking shout even from the top of his hill, and the terror he'd felt when Treharm was destroyed swept through him like a black, choking sea. Yet he fought it down—not with courage, but with desperation—and tightened his grip upon the power he had stolen.

Another Servant of Krahana, the once-man called Haliku, surged to his feet, bursting up from the thinning ocean of shardohn wolf-shapes like a hare bounding out of a thicket, as Walsharno erupted in a volcano of blue light. Yelping shardohns, who seemed to have forgotten that they were not in fact the wolves whose shapes they'd taken upon themselves, exploded away from the courser's charge. They flew in all directions, like mud spattered from a noisome puddle by the azure thunderclaps of his enormous hooves. One of them was too slow, and a stupendous hoof came down like the Mace of Tomanāk itself. It caught the squealing shardohn squarely in the center of its spine and its unnatural body vanished in a blinding flash of Tomanāk's light.

The steadily accelerating courser thundered across the night-dark grasslands like a moving holocaust of brilliant blue. That crackling corona clung to him, blew behind him like streamers of lightning on the wind of his passage, and no shardohn could withstand him. They fled into the night, howling, their terror of Tomanāk overpowering, however briefly, their older terror of their mistress.

Haliku looked back over his shoulder, green eyes glaring in the dark, and the shardohns' terror was etched into his own distorted expression. He swerved, trying to break away from the direct line of Walsharno's charge, and Bahzell leaned from the saddle. His left hand gripped the saddle horn, the sword in his right hand swept in a blinding arc, like sheet lightning, and the Servant had an instant to shriek in horrified denial before that deadly blade crunched entirely through his body.

A column of blue flame erupted from the grass, consuming what had been a Servant of Krahana, and then Walsharno was through the final fringes of the shardohn pack. His head went forward, his mighty muscles tightening and exploding as he thundered onward in a gallop only another courser could possibly have matched.

A meteor of green fire, glittering and loathsome with the all-consuming hunger of Krahana, arced up from the hilltop before him. It came screaming out of the night, but Bahzell raised his sword, holding it horizontally above his head, one hand on the hilt and the other wrapped around the blue-blazing blade.

"*Tomanāk!*" he cried, and an actinic flash flared outward from him and Walsharno. The expanding ring of light swept across the grass like a high wind, pounding the stalks flat, and the night rocked to a thunderous concussion as Jerghar's bolt of flame struck Tomanāk's shield . . . and vanished.

Jerghar went to his knees, shuddering, as the backlash of his parried attack ripped through him. His control of the coursers' souls wavered under the agony, but he hadn't been chosen for this task because he was weak. He hammered them back, reforging his control, and raised his head.

His eyes burned like green fire, and desperation blazed deep within him. The shardohns and his subordinate Servants had killed at least a third of Bahzell's companions, but now all of the other Servants had been destroyed and the shardohns were a broken force, fleeing and scattered in Bahzell's wake. There was nothing between Tomanāk's champion and Jerghar—nothing except his final, inner line of defense. The wall of focused energy powerful enough to stop any champion who had ever lived. That much Jerghar was sure of . . . yet even as he told himself that, deep inside he remembered all the *other* things he had been sure of before he'd had to face the reality of Bahzell Bahnakson's assault.

Bahzell reeled in the saddle under the soul-shaking impact of Jerghar's attack. But unlike Jerghar, Bahzell was not alone. He was supported by Tomanāk, linked to Walsharno, and sustained by his own iron determination and his Rage.

He straightened, and his ears flattened and his lips drew back in a snarl as he sensed the final barrier, rising like a wall of invisible steel in the darkness before him.

"*Now*, Brother!" he called to Walsharno, and a voice answered deep within his own mind.

<Take what you need, Brother!>

And Bahzell did. He reached deep, deep—deeper than he had dreamed even now that he *could* reach. He touched his own link to Tomanāk, and to Walsharno, and Walsharno's link to him and Tomanāk alike, and then, in the fusion of hradani, courser, and deity, he touched a vast, seething sea of wildfire energy he had never before perceived. A sea, he knew instantly, which Wencit of Rūm had tried to describe to him and Brandark on a snowy winter night long before.

He had no idea how to manipulate that energy. He was no wizard, and never would be. But he *was* a champion, and he reached out fearlessly to the lethal, crackling beauty.

He laid his hand upon it, and was not consumed, and for just an instant Bahzell Bahnakson's eyes blazed with the same eldritch, wild wizard's fire that had replaced Wencit's eyes so many endless centuries before.

He raised his empty hand, and crackling prominences of writhing fire—not simply the blue of Tomanāk, but blue and silver and every color ever made, all intermingled—blazed about his fist as he clenched it.

"Tomanāk!"

Jerghar's eyes widened in stunned recognition as the wild magic burned above the hradani's fist amid the consuming fury of Tomanāk's wrath. *Impossible*. It couldn't happen! No one but a wizard—and a *wild* wizard, at that—could do what Bahzell had just done!

But his enemies were close enough now. His sense of the unseen was less acute, less keen, than Bahzell's had become, but it was keen enough to scream belated warning as Bahzell and Walsharno charged suicidally towards his unbreachable wall of power.

Impossible, his brain repeated again. *Impossible!*

Not one champion, but *two*—two so deeply linked and fused that they were one!

Bahzell's fist stabbed forward, thrusting at the barrier before him, and lightning crackled. A solid, forked cable of power erupted, reaching out before him and Walsharno like a lance of flame. It struck Jerghar's wall and mushroomed out in a coruscating tornado of clashing energies. There was heat, this time, and the green, damp grass of spring flashed into fire, red tongues of flame and white spires of smoke rising in a billowing curtain.

There was an instant of titanic conflict, of powers far beyond the fringes of the mortal world locked in combat. And then a final, cataclysmic concussion jarred the universe as Bahzell's lightning bolt crashed through Jerghar's last line of defense.

Jerghar screamed in anguish as the fringes of that explosion ripped over him and flung him from his feet as if he were a toy. He skidded across the ground, bouncing through the tough grass of the Wind Plain like a stone thrown from the hand of a spiteful child, and fire enveloped him. The blue fire of Tomanāk, consuming, consuming . . .

He shrieked again and again, tearing at his own undead flesh as the agony of Tomanāk's touch gnawed inward. But there was no escape, no evading that torture. It ate inward, slowly—*so* slowly! —destroying him one agonizing fraction of an inch at a time.

Hooves the size of dinner platters came slowly, remorselessly across the grass to him, and he stared up through the agony of his merciless blue shroud as Walsharno, son of Mathygan and Yorthandro, stopped before him, towering into the night against a backdrop of lurid flame and choking smoke.

"Please!" he managed through his agony. "*Please!*"

"We'll have those coursers free of you and your bitch goddess, first," a deep, rumbling voice, colder than Vonderland ice told him.

"Yes—*yes!*" he shrieked, and released his hold. The coursers' souls exploded out of his opened grasp, fleeing the taint of Krahana, and the eyes of the courser standing above him flashed with the blue glory of Tomanāk.

"Please," Jerghar whimpered, twisting in the dirt, gripped by an agony greater than he had ever imagined. "Oh, please!"

"You'd best be giving me a reason," that infinitely icy voice told him, and he sobbed.

"Your friend," he gasped out. "That bitch champion!" He locked his teeth against another scream and shook his head fiercely.

"What of her?" Bahzell grated.

"Promise," Jerghar got out somehow. "Promise . . . you'll kill me. *Promise!*"

"Aye, you've my word," Bahzell rumbled.

"South," Jerghar sobbed. "A trap—not just Kalatha. They arranged it. Don't know more—I swear!"

"You've set a trap for Kerry?" Bahzell's voice sharpened.

"Not me—others," Jerghar gasped. "Don't know all of them. They want you and her . . . and Tellian. But that's all I know! I swear, I swear!"

Bahzell glared down at him, his face etched with hatred, and Jerghar sobbed.

"You promised," he whimpered. "*Promised!*"

For one more endless, seething moment of agony, nothing happened. And then—

"Aye, I did," Bahzell agreed harshly. "Sword Brother?"

In his torment, Jerghar didn't understand. But then he did, and a terrible gratitude transfigured his face as Walsharno raised one massive, blue-flickering hoof. His eyes clung to it with desperate hunger as it reached its apogee directly above his head.

Then it fell.

Chapter Forty-Two

Kaeritha left Kalatha seven days after her return from Thalar.

She hadn't intended to stay that long, but her conversation with Leeana had suggested there might be more that needed looking into at Kalatha than she'd thought. Conducting her own discreet investigations took more time than she'd allowed for. But that was all right . . . it also took her longer than she'd expected to secure another opportunity to examine the original charter and land grant.

Sharral was as helpful and efficient as ever, but it turned out to be extraordinarily difficult for her to nail Lanitha down and arrange the visit to the town's archives this time around, which seemed just a bit . . . odd. Although Lanitha was relatively new to her position as librarian and archivist, and more than a bit young for responsibilities of such magnitude, she'd also struck Kaeritha as attentive and determined to discharge those responsibilities to the very best of her ability. And her assistance during Kaeritha's first visit to Kalatha had made it obvious that ability was quite high.

This time, though, Lanitha, although she made it obvious

she was trying her very best, found it difficult to schedule an opportunity for Kaeritha to consult the required documents. Given their importance to the town of Kalatha itself, and to all war maids in general, Kaeritha wasn't surprised that the young woman responsible for their security and proper care wanted to be present whenever they were consulted. If their positions had been reversed, Kaeritha would have felt exactly the same way. Not only that, but Lanitha had been a great help to her and Yalith when she first examined them. Still, she could have wished for it to take less than three days for Lanitha to clear her schedule sufficiently to allow her to offer Kaeritha the degree of personal assistance the champion of any god, and especially of the God of War and Justice, deserved. And then, on the fourth day, when Kaeritha arrived at the archives, she was surprised (although probably less so than she should have been) to discover that Lanitha had been called away by an unanticipated personal emergency. She'd left her profound apologies and promised she would be available the next day—or the day after that, at the very latest—without fail, but it had been simply impossible for her to keep her scheduled appointment.

Despite the undeniable frustration she'd felt at the delays, Kaeritha had put the time she found on her hands to efficient use. Most casual observers might have been excused for not noticing that, but Kaeritha had been a champion of Tomanāk for quite a few years. And one thing champions of Tomanāk learned—*well, most of His champions, at any rate*, Kaeritha had corrected herself with a smile—was how to conduct an unobtrusive investigation. It helped that most people expected a champion's methods to be flashy and dramatic. As, indeed, some of the tools in Kaeritha's arsenal were, she cheerfully admitted. But there were times when it was far better to be discreet, and this seemed to be one of them. Which was why none of the war maids of Kalatha noticed that the visiting champion of Tomanāk sharing their meals, working out with them in the exercise salle, or training in weapons craft with them, managed to pick up an amazing amount of information.

Some of it was entirely open and aboveboard, and no less valuable because it was. Kaeritha's own two-sword technique was one she had evolved almost entirely on her own. The fact that she'd been born ambidextrous helped explain why it had occurred to her, but there'd been few weapons masters (or mistresses) in the Empire of the Axe who taught a combat technique which used a primary weapon in each hand. Many of them taught sword and dagger, or sword and dirk, and even more of them taught techniques for fighting with one's off hand, since it was always possible for one's normal weapon hand or arm to be wounded. But all of that was quite different from fighting with matched short swords in both hands simultaneously.

Quite a few of the war maids, however, used a technique which, despite many differences in detail, was very similar overall. As it happened, Hundred Ravlahn was one of them, and Kaeritha looked forward to her opportunities to match her own skills against the Hundred's. Ravlahn appeared to enjoy their training matches just as much as Kaeritha did, although it quickly became apparent to both of them that for all her own experience and skills, the war maid was thoroughly outclassed. But that, as Ravlahn pointed out herself, was as it ought to be when the person she was measuring her abilities against was a chosen champion of the God of War.

But in addition to adding some new wrinkles to her own combat repertoire, Kaeritha found the opportunity to spend time with Kalatha's war maids in informal surroundings invaluable. It wasn't so much what they said to her, as what they said to one another . . . or *didn't* say to her when she asked carefully casual questions. Kaeritha's natural hearing was more acute than that of most humans, although it fell far short of the sensitivity of a hradani like Bahzell. But one of her abilities as Tomanāk's champion was to "listen" to conversations she couldn't possibly have overheard otherwise. It wasn't like the telepathy many magi possessed, and she could only "listen" to conversations she knew about and could see with her own eyes. But it meant that even across a crowded ballroom—or a noisy training yard—she could sit in unobtrusively while other people spoke.

It was an ability she employed only sparingly, because it would have been so easy to misuse. But it was also one which was extraordinarily helpful to any investigator.

She used it to good effect during her extended stay in Kalatha, and what she heard confirmed her unhappy suspicion that Leeana hadn't been an alarmist young woman seeing shadows where none existed. In fact, if anything, the girl had underestimated what was happening.

There was nothing overt enough that Kaeritha could have taken it to a magistrate, but the pattern was clear. There were at least three factions in Kalatha.

One was Mayor Yalith's, which—for the moment, at least—was the most numerous and the most important and influential one. As Yalith herself, its members were angry with Trisu and determined to force him to admit his transgressions. They were gratified by the Quaysar Voice's strong support, but they were still essentially prepared to allow the system to work. Partly because they were convinced of the rectitude of their own positions and believed that, ultimately, the courts must decide in their favor. But also because they accepted that it was incumbent upon them to *prove* they and their demands had been reasonable from the outset. It wasn't because they were any less angry than anyone else, but they were only too well aware that the subjects of the Kingdom of the Sothōii were predisposed to view all war maids with disapproval. They were determined not to provide that prejudice with any fresh ammunition to use against them.

The second faction Kaeritha had identified consisted of most of the townsfolk who weren't firmly behind their mayor. Their view of the disputes was that the mayor and her council were pushing too hard. It wasn't that they doubted Yalith's arguments or her judgment of the technical legalities of the situation; they simply didn't feel the confrontation with Trisu was ultimately worth what it was likely to cost. Whatever else they might think of him, he was the most powerful noble in the vicinity, and they were going to have to deal with him—and his sons—for years to come, regardless of what any judge in a court might decide. Very few people in that faction, however, were upset enough to actively oppose Yalith. They simply didn't *support* her, except with a certain disgruntled sense of civic responsibility, and there appeared to be significantly fewer of them than there were of the mayor's strong partisans.

But it was the third faction, the one headed by Maretha Keralinfressa, which worried Kaeritha. The smallest of the three, it was also the angriest. Maretha's position was clear and unambiguous—she was not simply furious with Trisu and those like him in Lorham but believed it was time to confront *all* of the war maids' critics. Too much time had been wasted on fruitless efforts at compromise and conciliation, in her opinion, and all it had done was to encourage the continuation of the abuse of the war maids' rights. Instead of the war maids proving that their demands were reasonable, it was time to become *unreasonable*, and make it clear to all of their opponents that they would no longer tolerate any infringement, however minor, of their prerogatives.

Maretha herself was in a distinct minority on the Town Council, but she was a charismatic speaker, and it was obvious that she was rapidly becoming Mayor Yalith's strongest rival. Indeed, there were signs that she was contemplating challenging the mayor for office at the next election, although Kaeritha still judged her chances of winning were substantially less than even. Although her supporters on the council itself were vocal and intensely loyal, there weren't many of them.

Yet the impact of her opposition to the mayor spread far beyond the council. In particular, it appeared to have aroused the fervent support of a small but determined group which consisted primarily, although not exclusively, of younger war maids and those too junior in Kalatha's hierarchy to force their own opinions upon the Town Council. They seemed to consider Maretha their titular leader, yet they were even more vociferous and angry than she was.

The most senior of them whom Kaeritha had identified so far was a Soumeta Harlahnnafressa, and she was a mere commander of fifty, but that didn't necessarily mean they weren't influential, and their fervor was frightening. They were the ones who were most furious with Trisu, most militant in their insistence that their rights, and those of all war maids, must be defended. They were impatient with any argument which suggested they must be cautious, or appear reasonable. It was time for someone *else* to be reasonable, as far as they were concerned, and in all honesty, Kaeritha found it easy to sympathize with them in that view.

But many of the conversations she overheard went beyond that. There were no more than ten or fifteen women whom Kaeritha would have considered "ringleaders." The vast majority were no more or less than understandably outraged and angry women reacting to endless years of prejudice and bigotry. But those ten or fifteen Kaeritha had picked out clearly had an organized agenda. They weren't simply angry; they were *manipulating* the anger of others and using it to subtly undermine the traditional figures of authority in the Kalathan war maid community.

That was bad enough, but Leeana had also been correct about the rest of what they were saying. Whether they were actually taking their cue directly from the Voice at Quaysar or not—and at this point, whatever her suspicions, Kaeritha had no way of knowing whether they were—they were using the Voice's supposed statements and views to assert that Lillinara Herself supported self-centered, narcissistic life choices which appalled Kaeritha. And which she was grimly certain would be equally appalling to Lillinara. It wasn't just the denial of responsibility, or the notion that it was morally acceptable to *use* someone else for one's own advantage or pleasure. It was the fact that they justified that denial and notion at least in part on the basis that it was time the war maids "got even" for all the indignities and oppression they had ever suffered.

Kaeritha knew, from brutal personal experience, the

difference between vengeance and justice, and she knew what bitter tang she tasted in the low-voiced, vitriolic conversations she listened to about her.

Unfortunately, all she had were suspicions. It was nothing she could really take to Yalith, and even if it had been, Yalith was angry enough herself that she might not have listened. Besides, there was something about the mayor's own position that bothered Kaeritha. Yalith's tenure as Mayor of Kalatha predated the beginnings of the current confrontation with Trisu. If, as Kaeritha had come to suspect, the original documents at Kalatha had been tampered with somehow, Yalith ought to have been aware of it. Which suggested, logically, that if something nefarious was going on in Kalatha, Yalith was a part of it. But Kaeritha didn't think she was, and she'd done a little subtle probing of the mayor's honesty—enough to be as certain as she could, without the same sort of examination she'd given Salthan, that Yalith honestly and sincerely believed she was in the right.

Which suggested to Kaeritha that something more than mere documents might have been tampered with in Kalatha.

"I am *so* sorry about the delay, Dame Kaeritha," Lanitha said as she ushered Kaeritha into the main Records Room. "I know your time is valuable, to Tomanāk as well as to yourself, and I hate it that you sat around cooling your heels waiting for me for almost an entire week."

She shook her head, her expression simultaneously harassed, irritated, and apologetic.

"It's like there was some sort of curse on my week," she continued, bustling around the Records Room to open the heavy curtains which normally protected its contents and let the daylight in. "Every time I thought I was going to get over here and pull the documents for you, some fresh disaster came rolling out of nowhere."

"That's perfectly all right, Lanitha," Kaeritha reassured her. "I imagine everyone's had weeks like that, you know. I certainly have!"

"Thank you." Lanitha paused to smile gratefully at

her. "I'm relieved that you're so understanding. Not that your sympathy makes me look any more efficient and organized!"

Kaeritha only returned her smile and waited, her expression pleasant, while the archivist finished drawing back the curtains and unlocked the large cabinet which contained the most important of Kalatha's official documents.

"Mayor Yalith—or, rather, Sharral—didn't tell me exactly which sections you're particularly interested in this time," she said over her shoulder as she opened the heavy, iron-reinforced door.

"I need to reexamine the section of Kellos' grant where the boundary by the grist mill is established," Kaeritha said casually.

"I see," Lanitha said. She found the proper document case, withdrew it from the cabinet, and set it carefully on the desk before the Records Room's largest eastern window. Her tone was no more than absently courteous. But Kaeritha was watching her as carefully and unobtrusively as she'd ever watched anyone in her life, and something about the set of the archivist's shoulders suggested Lanitha was less calm than she wanted to appear. It wasn't that Kaeritha detected any indication that Lanitha was anything but the honest, hard-working young woman she seemed to be. Yet there was still that *something* . . . almost as if Lanitha had some inner sense that her own loyalties were at odds with one another.

The archivist opened the document case and laid the original copy of Lord Kellos' grant to the war maids of Kalatha on the desktop. Kaeritha had done enough research among fragile documents to stand patiently, hands clasped behind her, while Lanitha carefully opened the old-fashioned scroll and sought the section Kaeritha had described.

"Here it is," the archivist said finally, and stepped back out of the way so that Kaeritha could examine the document for herself.

"Thank you," Kaeritha said courteously. She moved closer to the desk and bent over the faded, crabbed handwriting. The document's age was only too apparent, and its authenticity was obvious. But the authenticity of Trisu's copy had been equally obvious, she reminded herself, and rested the heel of her hand lightly on the pommel of her left-hand sword.

It was a natural enough pose, if rather more overly dramatic than Kaeritha preferred. The last time she'd been in this room, she'd taken both swords off and laid them to one side, and she hoped Lanitha wasn't wondering why she hadn't done the same thing this time. If the librarian asked, Kaeritha was prepared to point out that last time, she'd been sitting here for hours while she studied the documents and took notes. This time, she only wanted to make a quick recheck of a single section. And, as Lanitha's own profuse apologies had underscored, she was behind schedule and running late.

There it was. She leaned forward, studying the stilted phrases more intently, and ran the index finger of her right hand lightly along the relevant lines. Only a far more casual archivist than Lanitha could have avoided cringing when anyone, even someone who'd already demonstrated her respect for the fragility of the documents in her care, touched one of them that way. The other woman moved a half-step closer, watching Kaeritha's right hand with anxious attentiveness . . . exactly as the knight had intended.

Because she was so focused on Kaeritha's right hand, she failed to notice the faint flicker of blue fire which danced around the *left* hand resting on the champion's sword hilt. It wasn't very bright, anyway—Tomanāk knew how to be unobtrusive when it was necessary, too—but it was enough for Kaeritha's purposes.

"Thank you, Lanitha," she said again, and stepped back. She took her hand from her sword as she did so, and the blue flicker disappeared entirely. "That was all I needed to see."

"Are you certain, Milady?" Lanitha's tone and expression were earnest, and Kaeritha nodded.

"I just wanted to check my memory of the words," she assured the archivist.

"Might I ask why, Milady?" Lanitha asked.

"I'm still in the middle of an investigation, Lanitha," Kaeritha reminded her, and the other woman bent her head in acknowledgment of the gentle rebuke. Kaeritha gazed at her for a moment, then shrugged. "On the other hand," the knight continued, "it's not as if it's not going to come out in the end, anyway, I suppose."

"Not as if what isn't going to come out?" Lanitha asked, emboldened by Kaeritha's last sentence.

"There's a definite discrepancy between the original documents here and Trisu's so-called copies," Kaeritha told her. "I have to say that when I first saw his copy, I was astonished. It didn't seem possible that anyone could have produced such a perfect-looking forgery. But, obviously, the only way his copies could be that different from the originals has to involve a deliberate substitution or forgery."

"Lillinara!" Lanitha said softly, signing the Mother's full moon. "I knew Trisu hated all war maids, but I never imagined he'd try something like that, Milady! How could he possibly expect it to pass muster? He must know that sooner or later someone would do what you've just done and compare the forgery to the original!"

"One thing I learned years ago, Lanitha," Kaeritha said wearily as she watched the archivist carefully returning the land grant to its case, "is that criminals *always* think they can 'get away with it.' If their minds didn't work that way, they wouldn't be criminals in the first place!"

"I suppose not." Lanitha sighed and shook her head. "It just seems so silly—and sad—when you come down to it."

"You're wrong, you know," Kaeritha said quietly, her voice so flat that Lanitha looked quickly back over her shoulder at her.

"Wrong, Milady?"

"It isn't silly, or sad," Kaeritha told her. "Whatever the original motivation may have been, this sort of conflict between the documents here and those at Thalar is going to play right into the hands of everyone else like Trisu. It isn't the sort of minor discrepancy that can be explained away as clerical error. It's a deliberate forgery, and there are altogether too many people out there who are already prepared to think the worst about you war maids. It won't matter to them that you have the originals, while he has only copies. What will matter is that they'll assume *you* must have made the alterations."

"Then I suppose it's a good thing a champion of Tomanāk is on the spot, isn't it, Milady? Even the most prejudiced person would have to take *your* word for it that Trisu or someone working for him is the forger."

"Yes, Lanitha," Kaeritha said grimly. "They certainly would."

The sentry's report had assured that Tellian Bowmaster was waiting in the courtyard of Hill Guard Castle when Bahzell rode in on Walsharno. He didn't look as if he believed what he was seeing.

Bahzell smiled grimly at the baron's expression as he listened to the sound of heavy hooves on the courtyard's stone paving. The sound came not simply from Walsharno but from the hooves of no less than twenty-one other coursers . . . only ten of them with riders.

"Welcome back, Milord Champion," Tellian said with an odd note of formality as Walsharno halted beside the wind rider's mounting block.

"Thank you." Bahzell swung out of the saddle and stepped down onto the mounting block. He reached out to clasp Tellian's forearm firmly, and the baron's eyes searched his face intently, with more than a hint of anxiety.

"Brandark?" he asked quietly, and Bahzell gave him a small, quick smile.

"The little man's after being well enough," he said. "He was a mite nibbled upon about the edges, but hradani are tough, and there was naught wrong with him that couldn't be healed. But however well, or willing, he might be, there was no way at all, at all, as how his warhorse could be after keeping up on the ride here."

"Is that why Gharnal and Hurthang aren't with you?" Tellian asked, and Bahzell's smile vanished.

"No," he said quietly. "Hurthang will be after arriving in a week or so, but not Gharnal. And not Farchach, nor Yourmak, nor Tharchanal or Shulhârch."

"Dead, all of them?" Tellian asked softly, and Bahzell nodded.

"Aye," he said, his voice flat with pain. "We were after being the head of the spear. Not one of the Order's lads but Hurthang survived, and him half-dead before I was after reaching him. They're every one of them gone, Tellian . . . and five wind riders and eight more coursers, with them."

"Tomanāk." Tellian's right hand moved in the sign of Tomanāk's Sword. "May Isvaria keep them as her own," he added.

"She will that," Bahzell said, and drew a deep breath. "If there's ever a soul she'll be keeping, it's theirs. It was Krahana's get that was after attacking the coursers. And but for the lads as died watching my back, I'm thinking as how she'd have had us all."

"But she didn't," Tellian said firmly, reaching out to lay his hand on Bahzell's forearm. "And you wouldn't be back here if you hadn't dealt with the situation."

"No, that I wouldn't," he agreed, and produced a crooked smile. "I'm not after being quite as certain positive of that as I might be wishful, so I left Hurthang and Brandark to keep an eye on things. Still and all, I'd not be here without I felt confident as I'd finished pissing on that particular grass fire. Not but what I've not got enough other problems to be going on with."

"Well, in that case, I suppose you'd best come inside and tell me how I can help."

" . . . so by the time we got to Glanharrow, Trianal, Yarran, and Lord Festian had already dealt with matters," Tellian said, leaning back in his chair and quaffed deeply from his tankard of dark beer. His voice was light, but his eyes were intent as he watched Bahzell's weary face. Hanatha sat with them, sipping more moderately from a delicate, silver-chased tankard of her own, and her eyes, too, were on Bahzell.

"I suspect the matter is going to turn even uglier in the next few months," Tellian continued, "but not because the raiding's going to continue. We took enough prisoners to prove the entire force that attacked Trianal was in Saratic's service, although by the strangest turn of fate, his field commander wound up dead with what appears to be a Horse Stealer quarrel in his back . . . fired from a Dwarvenhame arbalest we found lying about out there."

His acid smile could have been used to etch steel.

"Still and all, we have enough other prisoners—with enough incentive to talk to us to avoid the rope or the block—that we should be able to prove whose colors they should have been wearing. And I think it's only a matter of time before we demonstrate that Dathian was up to his eyebrows in it, as well. Once we do, I'll take care of Dathian myself, and I take a certain amount of pleasure in contemplating what's going through his head while he waits for the axe to fall."

He smiled again, even more nastily.

"In the meantime, I've already dispatched a messenger to the King to petition for an investigation under Crown authority. Under the circumstances, I would've been justified in moving against Saratic myself, immediately, but I chose instead to appeal to the Crown, and I was very patient about it all in the petition, too. King Markhos and Prince Yurokhas should be very impressed by my forbearance—they'll certainly play it up for all it's worth when they have to deal with Cassan, at any rate. Whatever the King may think of my efforts to improve relations with your father, Prince Bahzell, he is *not* going to be amused by the discovery that one of his barons has been instigating open warfare against another one. We had enough of that during the Troubles, thank you. And however well Cassan may have covered his tracks, I don't think there's going to be any question in His Majesty's mind that that's exactly what's happened here. So I expect Cassan is going to discover that he's just incurred a certain degree of royal disfavor which is going to cost him dearly in the long run. Meanwhile, Trianal is doing just fine sitting there in Glanharrow as a pointed suggestion to Dathian and Saratic that this would be a very bad time to push the matter any further."

Bahzell nodded slowly, his eyes thoughtful, and took a long pull from the tankard in his own fist. Tellian drank a little more beer himself, then leaned forward and set his tankard down on the table.

"And that's enough about Festian and Trianal, Milord Champion," he said firmly. Bahzell arched an eyebrow, and his ears cocked. Tellian saw it and snorted. "It was as plain as the nose on Brandark's face when I clapped eyes on you that you were worn to the bone, hradani or not, Bahzell. And, if you'll pardon my saying so, that more even than grief for the people you lost is weighing on you. So Hanatha and I have chattered away for the last half-hour, bringing you up-to-date on everything from Leeana to Trianal and the King's approval of our petition to adopt him as our heir. Now that you've had a chance to settle down a bit, suppose you tell us what it is that brings the first hradani wind rider in history, ten other wind riders and their coursers, and eleven coursers with no riders at all here to Balthar."

"Well," Bahzell said after a moment, "I'm thinking as how it's going to take longer than we're like to have if I'm to explain all that was after happening in Warm Springs. For now, let's just be saying that Walsharno's after having peculiar taste in riders. Oh, and while I'm speaking of Walsharno, that big filly out in your stable's guest quarters is after being his sister and a special friend of mine, as you might be saying."

Tellian blinked, then looked at his wife before returning his attention to their guest.

"I trust that you realize that all you've done is to suggest still more questions to us," he observed.

"Aye." Bahzell smiled wearily. "But truth be told, I've no business at all, at all, sitting on my backside drinking your beer. Mind you, even a hradani can be getting just a mite tuckered, and I'll not deny that all of us—riders and coursers alike—are after needing a breather. But I've no time to waste."

"That much we'd already guessed," Tellian said with a slight edge of impatience. "It's obvious that you've ridden from Warm Springs as if Fiendark's Furies were on your heels. Why?" he finished bluntly.

"Because Kerry's after being in trouble," Bahzell said, equally bluntly.

"How?" Tellian leaned forward in his chair once more, resting his elbows on his knees, his expression intent.

"As to that, I've no way of knowing for certain," Bahzell admitted. He drank more beer, his eyes unhappy, then lowered the tankard again. "All in the world I have to be going on is fragments from a Servant of Krahana and this." He tapped his temple with an index finger. "If it were only the Servant, then I'd not be quite so worried. But this . . ."

He shook his head, ears half-flattened, and his expression was bleak as his finger tapped again.

"So you're headed to help her, Bahzell," Hanatha said, her tone making the statement half a question.

"Aye." His expression eased a bit, and he chuckled. "And not alone, either. I've no least idea how the rest of my folk would be reacting to the company I'm after keeping these days! But after we'd dealt with Krahana's lot, not a single one of those wind riders as had ridden with us but was bound and determined as how he and his courser would be after riding along for this, too. And then Gayrfressa—Walsharno's sister—was after insisting she and the Bear River stallions who'd lived would be doing the same."

"The wind riders I can understand, Bahzell," Tellian said soberly. "Those of us who are wind borne seem to absorb some of our courser brothers' herd sense. Whenever we see another wind brother with a trouble, we all get this itch we can't quite scratch until we pitch in to help solve it."

"So I'd noticed," Bahzell snorted.

"Yes, but what I *don't* quite understand is why the other coursers came along."

"Well, as to that, it's after being Gayrfressa's fault," Bahzell said with a crooked grin. "She's this strange notion that the coursers are after owing me a little favor or two. So after she'd put her head together with the other coursers, the stallions all agreed as how they'd come along and—just this once, mind—see if there were after being a few more of our lads from the Order as they could be carrying along with me."

"They *what*?" Tellian came half out of his chair in astonishment, and Hanatha set her beer abruptly back down on the table. Bahzell only smiled at them again, and Tellian settled back slowly. He shook his head.

"Bahzell," he said, "I don't believe there have been more than three times in the entire history of the Kingdom when coursers have agreed to carry *anyone* other than their own chosen wind riders. And I know that they've never, ever, agreed to carry hradani. And you're telling me they've agreed to carry *Horse Stealer* hradani?"

"Aye." Bahzell took another sip of his beer with elaborate enjoyment, looking as if he'd just said the most reasonable thing in the world. Tellian stared at him, then leaned all the way back in his chair.

"There is," he observed, "a particularly nasty fate reserved for people who get too full of themselves, Milord Champion."

"Aye?" Bahzell cocked his ears impudently at his host, then sobered. "That's all after being very well, yet I've still the little problem of knowing just where it is they're to be carrying us. I'm thinking as how the best I could be doing would be to ride to Kalatha and see what I could be finding out there. Yet there's this—" he tapped his temple yet again "—as is insisting that wherever it may be her trouble lies, it's not Kalatha." He grimaced in obvious frustration. "It's a maddening thing to know as how there's not so very much time, yet not to be knowing where in Tomanāk's name she is."

"Well, Bahzell," Hanatha said, with a slow smile, "you really don't deserve this, after teasing Tellian that way about the coursers, but it just so happens that I'm fairly sure that *I* know where you need to go."

Chapter Forty-Three

The road to Quaysar ran almost due east from Kalatha, and the morning sun shone brightly into Kaeritha's face as Cloudy trotted briskly along it two days after her appointment with Lanitha. Birds soared and dipped overhead, calling to one another against the impossibly blue sky as they rode the brawny wind gusting out of the northwest, and the endless sea of young grass rippled and hissed musically as the stiff gusts pushed waves across it. The morning was still cool, but there was a sense of life and energy wrapped up in the wind and the high, beautiful cries of the birds, and Kaeritha drew that energy deep into her lungs.

It was tempting to abandon herself to the sensual enjoyment of the new day, but the dark suspicion which had first whispered to her in Trisu's library had hardened into something even darker which cast its own ominous shadow across the morning.

She still had altogether too many questions and far too few answers, she reminded herself. Yet even as she conscientiously bore that in mind, she knew which way the facts she'd been able to test all pointed. What she didn't begin to know was how all this could have happened, or why Lillinara and Tomanāk seemed to have agreed that it was *her* job to deal with it.

Not that she was tempted even for a moment to pretend it *wasn't* her job. This was exactly the sort of task which had attracted her to Tomanāk's service in the first place. The fact that she wished with all her heart that someone like the war maids had been available to her mother—or to her—when she was a child only stiffened her resolve still further. She had no clear idea exactly what she was going to encounter at Quaysar, yet there was a stink of Darkness about this entire business. It was only too probable that she was riding directly into that Dark, but it was one of a champion of Tomanāk's functions to carry Light into even the deepest Darkness.

Of course, sometimes the Light failed.

Dame Kaeritha Seldansdaughter knew that, just as she knew how few of Tomanāk's champions ever died in bed. But if that was the price to hold off the Dark which had claimed fallen Kontovar, it was one she would pay. And if worse came to worst, the letter she had dispatched to Bahzell under Sword Seal contained all of her suspicions, discoveries, and deductions. If it should happen that this time she was fated to fail, she knew with absolute certainty that her brother would avenge her and complete her task as surely as she would have done that for him.

She smiled warmly at the thought, then shook off her dark musings and raised her head, turning her face more fully to the sun and luxuriating in its warmth.

Quaysar was impressive.

The temple's original architects had found one of the few genuine hilltops the Wind Plain offered. It was obvious as Kaeritha approached that the upthrust knob upon which the temple and the town which supported it stood was basically a solid plug or dome of granite. It was nowhere near as towering as it had seemed at first glance, she realized as she drew closer. But it didn't have to be, either. The low, rolling flatlands of the Wind Plain stretched away in every direction, as far as the eye could see, and even Quaysar's relatively low perch allowed it to command its surroundings effortlessly.

The old town of Quaysar, which had been folded into the temple community, was surrounded by a low but defensible wall. Newer buildings and outlying farms spread out from the old town along the arms of the crossroads which met beside the sizable pond or small lake at the base of the granite pedestal which supported the temple, and Kaeritha saw workers in the fields as Cloudy trotted past them.

The temple itself had its own wall, which was actually higher than that of the old town and rose sheer from the very lip of the temple's stony perch. That sort of security feature was no part of the temples of Lillinara in the Empire of the Axe, but the Empire was the oldest, most settled realm of Norfressa. Things had been far less orderly on the Wind Plain when Quaysar was first constructed. For that matter, they still were, she supposed. Or they had the potential to be, at any rate; the Time of Troubles wasn't that far in the past. Given that history, she didn't blame the original builders for seeing to it that their temple was not simply located in the most defensible position available but well fortified, to boot.

She couldn't see much of the temple buildings with the wall in the way, but the three traditional towers of any temple of Lillinara rose above them. The Tower of the Mother, with its round, alabaster full moon, was flanked by the slightly lower crescent moon-crowned Tower of the Maiden and the Tower of the Crone, with its matching globe of obsidian. The added height of the prominence upon which the entire temple stood lifted them even higher against the blue sky and high-piled, snow-white clouds to the south, and Kaeritha felt her imagination stir as she realized how they must look against the night heavens when the silver-white glow of Lillinara touched their stonework. Quaysar was far from the largest temple of Lillinara Kaeritha had ever seen, but its location and special significance gave it a majesty and a sense of presence she'd seldom seen equaled.

Yet as she drew closer still, the imagined image of towers, burning with cool, radiant light against the star strewn heavens faded, and an icy chill touched her heart. No silver Lady's Light clung to those towers or those walls under the warm sunlight of early afternoon, but Kaeritha's eyes weren't like those of other mortals. They Saw what others didn't, and her mouth tightened as an ominous, poison-green light flickered at the corner of her vision.

She knew that stomach-churning green. She'd Seen it before, and her mind went back to a rainy day in Baron Tellian's library when she'd told him how unhappily familiar with the presence of the Dark champions of Tomanāk were.

She inhaled deeply and gazed up at the temple, trying to isolate those elusive flickers of green. She couldn't, and her jaw clenched as she failed. Each of Tomanāk's champions perceived evil and the handiwork of the Dark Gods in his or her own, unique fashion. Bahzell received his "feelings"—an impression of things not yet fully perceived, yet somehow known. Another champion she'd known heard music which guided him. But Kaeritha, like some magi to whom she'd spoken, Saw. For her, it was the interplay of light and shadow—or of Light and Dark. That inner perception had never failed or deceived her, and yet today, the meaning of what she Saw was . . . unclear. She couldn't pin it down, couldn't even be positive that the green light-devils dancing at the edges of her vision were coming from the temple, and not the town clustered below it.

That shouldn't have happened. Especially not when she'd come already primed by her suspicions and earlier investigations. The revealing glare of evil should have been obvious to her . . . unless someone—or some*thing*—with enormous power was deliberately concealing it.

She made herself exhale and shook her head like a horse bothered by a fly. The concealment wasn't necessarily directed specifically against *her*, she told herself. Whatever was happening in Quaysar was clearly part of a years-long effort, and the very thing which would make

Quaysar such a prize in the eyes of the Dark was its importance to Lillinara and, specifically, to the Sothōii war maids. But that also meant Quaysar was more prominent, and more likely to draw pilgrims and visitors, than most other temples of its relatively modest size. And with pilgrims came those besides Kaeritha whose eyes might See what the Dark preferred to keep hidden.

Yet logical as that conclusion was, the fact remained that it required tremendous power to so thoroughly obscure the inner sight of a champion of Tomanāk. Indeed, such power must have completely blinded the perceptions—whether of sight, or hearing, or sensing—of anyone less intimately bound to the service of her god.

Which meant that somewhere atop that timeworn tooth of granite waited a servant of the Greater Dark.

Yes, she told herself grimly. *And it's probably the 'Voice' herself. In fact, it would almost have to be. There's no way anything this Dark and powerful could hide itself from an uncorrupted Voice. But whatever it is, it doesn't have complete control. Not even a Dark God himself could keep me from Seeing if that were the case. Great!* She snorted in harsh mental laughter. *It's not* everyone *in Quaysar. Marvelous. All I have to do is assume that* anyone *I meet serves the Dark until she proves differently!*

She closed her eyes and drew another deep breath.

All right, Tomanāk, she thought. *You never promised it would be easy. And I suppose I'd be riding off in search of reinforcements instead of riding in all by my fool self, if my skull wasn't just as thick as Bahzell's. But it is. So, if You don't have anything else to do this afternoon, why don't You and I go call on the Voice?*

"Well, she's almost here, Paratha."

Varnaythus stood on the town wall of Quasar and watched the single rider approaching the town.

"Fine," the tall woman standing beside him said almost indifferently. She sounded so blasé about it that Varnaythus turned his head to glare at her.

"I know Dahlaha is . . . confident, let us say, Paratha.

But I'd hoped it was at least remotely possible that your confidence might not be quite as, ah, exuberant as hers. This is a champion of Tomanāk, you know."

"So she is," the tall woman agreed. She turned away from the wall and leaned her back against it while she looked at Varnaythus with an expression which mingled confidence, contempt, and something else. Hunger, Varnaythus decided. Or perhaps not hunger—perhaps *eagerness*.

"You do remember that you weren't supposed to be seeing *any* champions—and especially not any champions of Tomanāk—here at Quaysar, don't you?" he asked in a tone of withering irony.

"No, we weren't," she agreed. "On the other hand, it's not something I haven't made preparations for. The Spider knew what She was doing when She recruited me, Varnaythus. With all due modesty, I'm the best there is. I'll take care of your little champion for you."

Varnaythus stared at her in disbelief.

"Are you insane?" he asked flatly, and anger flickered in her eyes. Her hand twitched near the hilt of her sword, and her upper lip curled back from her teeth. She opened her mouth to speak, but the index finger jabbed in her face stopped her.

"Don't you say a word," he hissed in a voice like silk sliding on a dagger's blade. "Not one word."

She closed her mouth again, with an almost audible click, and the wizard-priest drew a deep, deep breath and forced his anger back under control.

"Now you will listen to me," he told her, each word chopped off like a separate chip of ice. "Cassan's plan to weaken Tellian is busy ending in what looks like unmitigated disaster. Jerghar and every one of his fellow Servants have been destroyed. And Tellian, Bahzell, and Brandark are all still alive. The entire plan, with the exception of this one, single aspect, has already failed. If your overconfidence causes this part of it to miscarry as the other parts already have, you had better pray that you die here in Quaysar. Because if you don't, They will make you wish you had for the rest of eternity."

A shadow of fear crossed the tall woman's face, but there was as much resentment as fear in her expression, and her nostrils flared.

"I won't fail," she said flatly. "No, we weren't *supposed* to see a champion of Tomanāk here. I'll grant that. But Her plans always provided for the possibility that we might lose our foothold here in Quaysar. Indeed, they *depended* on our losing it at a time and in the fashion of our own choosing." She shrugged. "Perhaps that time is here, and perhaps it isn't. We'll soon see. But I tell you this, Varnaythus, you and Jerghar and your precious Baron Cassan may have failed, but *we* won't. And even if every other aspect of the plan's failed—for now, at least—*this* is the most important one, and you know it. You and Dahlaha told me at the outset that you wanted the Troubles back. Well, you'll have them, damn you! We'll take this terrifying little champion of yours, and the Spider will suck the life and soul out of her and make her serve our ends."

"Our record of successes against champions of Tomanāk doesn't exactly inspire me with unbounded faith in your confidence, Paratha," Varnaythus said coldly. "And you might want to consider this, too. A year ago, there were seventeen champions of Tomanāk in all of Norfressa. Now there are twenty, and four of them—*four*, Paratha; *twenty percent* of the total—are here on the Wind Plain or in Hurgrum. Do you think that's just some sort of minor coincidence? Or do you think there might just be a reason? Because *I* don't think it's an accident, and I do think there's a reason our track record against them has been an unmitigated disaster."

"Oh, no, Varnaythus—not *our* record, but yours. And, in fairness to Jerghar, he had to deal with the Bloody Hand. And, or so the Spider tells us, with a second champion. A *courser* champion, no less." She shook her head. "Against someone as powerful as the Bloody Hand, anything might be possible. And if Jerghar had no reason to expect that he faced not one, but two champions, then small wonder he lost. But we face only one, and the weakest of the three." She snorted and spat contemptuously over the wall. "This one is a lawyer at heart, Varnaythus. She craves to serve *Justice*, to look after the 'little people.' If it were the Bloody Hand, then I might worry, for he, at least, is a foe to respect. But this one—this Kaeritha—!" She barked a harsh laugh of scorn. "This one we'll *eat*, and use the leftover meat to feed the very flames we set out to ignite."

Varnaythus looked at her for several long, silent seconds, then shrugged.

"Very well. I hope you're right. But whether you are or not, the responsibility is yours, Paratha—yours and Dahlaha's. I've warned you, as I warned her. I hope your preparations are adequate."

"They are," she said with flat assurance.

"I'm delighted to hear it," he said. "But in the meantime, I've done everything I can. From here on, you're on your own. If your confidence is justified, I'll see you again in a few days."

Paratha opened her mouth again, but before she could speak, he was gone. She stood on the battlements, glaring at the empty flagstones on which he'd stood, then growled a curse under her breath and turned to look back out at the road from Kalatha once more.

The trotting rider was much closer now, and Paratha gazed at her for two long minutes with a dark, hungry smile. Then she laughed once, a sound like a frozen branch shattering under the weight of winter ice, and turned away.

"Of course, Dame Kaeritha! Come in, come in! We've been expecting you."

The officer in command of the temple's largely ceremonial gate guard bowed deeply and swept his arm at the open gate in a welcoming gesture. He straightened to find Kaeritha gazing down at him from Cloudy's saddle with a quizzical expression and frowned ever so slightly, as if surprised she hadn't ridden straight past at his invitation.

"Expecting me?" she said, and he cleared his throat.

"Uh, yes, Milady." He shook himself. "The Voice warned us several days ago that you would be coming to visit us," he said in a less flustered tone.

"I see." Kaeritha filed that information away along with the officer's strong Sothōii accent and the warmth which had infused his own voice as he mentioned the Voice. It was uncommon for a temple of Lillinara in the Empire of the Axe to have its gate guard commanded by a man. It wasn't precisely unheard of, even there, however, given the small percentage of Axewomen who followed the profession of arms, and she supposed it made even more sense here in the Kingdom of the Sothōii, where even fewer women were warriors. Yet she also saw two war maids in chari and yathu standing behind him, with swords at their hips, crossed bandoliers of throwing stars, and the traditional war maid garrottes wound around their heads like leather headbands. Given the special significance Quaysar held for all war maids, she found it . . . interesting that the temple's entire guard force didn't consist solely of them.

The way the guard commander had spoken of the Voice was almost equally interesting, especially from a native Sothōii. He seemed completely comfortable in the service of a temple not simply dedicated to the goddess of women but intimately associated with the creation of all those "unnatural" war maids. Granted, anyone who would have accepted the position in the first place must be more enlightened than most of his fellow Sothōii males, but there was more than simple acceptance or even approval in his tone. It came far closer to something which might almost have been called . . . obeisance. For that matter, Kaeritha didn't much care for the look in his eyes, although she would have been hard put to pin down what it was about it that bothered her.

"Yes, Milady," the officer continued. "She knew you'd visited Kalatha and Lord Trisu, and she told us almost a week ago that you would be visiting us, as well." He smiled. "And, of course, she made it abundantly clear that we were to greet you with all of the courtesy due to a champion of the War God."

Kaeritha glanced at the rest of his guard force: the two war maids she'd already noticed and three more men in the traditional Sothōii cuirass and leather. They were too well trained to abandon their stance of professional watchfulness, but their body language and expressions matched the warmth in their commander's voice.

"That was very considerate of the Voice," she said after a moment. "I appreciate it. And she was quite correct; I have come to Quaysar to meet with her. Since she was courteous enough to warn you I was coming, did she also indicate whether or not she would be able to grant me an audience?"

"My instructions were to pass you straight in, and I believe you'll find Major Kharlan, the commander of the Voice's personal guards, waiting to escort you directly to her."

"I see the Voice is as foresightful as she is courteous," Kaeritha said with a smile. "As are those who serve her and the Goddess here in Quaysar."

"Thank you for those kind words, Milady." The officer bowed again, less deeply, and waved at the open gateway once more. "But we all know only serious matters could have brought you this far from the Empire, and the Voice is eager for Major Kharlan to escort you to her."

"Of course," Kaeritha agreed, inclining her head in a small, answering bow. "I hope we meet again before I leave Quaysar," she added, and touched Cloudy gently with her heel.

The mare trotted through the open gate. The tunnel beyond it was longer than Kaeritha had expected. The temple's defensive wall was clearly thicker than it had appeared from a distance, and the disk of sunlight waiting to welcome her at its farther end seemed tiny and far away. Her shoulders were tight, tension sang in her belly, and she was acutely conscious of the silent menace of the murder holes in the tunnel ceiling as she passed under them. This wasn't the first time she'd ridden knowingly into what she suspected was an ambush, and she knew she appeared outwardly calm and unconcerned. It just didn't feel that way from her side.

Major Kharlan was waiting for her, and Kaeritha raised a mental eyebrow as she realized the major was accompanied only by a groom who was obviously there to take care of Cloudy for her. Apparently, whatever the Voice had in mind included nothing so crude as swords in the temple courtyard.

"Milady Champion," the major murmured, bending her head in greeting. "My name is Kharlan, Paratha Kharlan. Quaysar is honored by your visit."

The major had a pronounced Sothōii accent, and stood an inch or so taller than Kaeritha herself, but she wore a cuirass over a chain hauberk much like Kaeritha's own and carried a cavalry saber. If she was a war maid, she was obviously one of the minority who'd trained with more "standard" weapons.

That much was apparent the instant Kaeritha glanced at her, just as it would have been to anyone else. But that was all "anyone else" might have seen. The additional armor Kharlan wore was visible only to Kaeritha, and she tensed inside like a cat suddenly faced by a cobra as she Saw the corona of sickly, yellow-green light which outlined the major's body. The sensation of "wrongness" radiating from her was like a punch in the belly to Kaeritha, a taste so vile she almost gagged physically and wondered for a moment how anyone could possibly fail to perceive it as clearly as she did.

"The Voice has instructed me to bid you welcome and to escort you to her at your earliest convenience," the tall woman continued, smiling, her voice so bizarrely normal sounding after what Kaeritha had Seen that it required all of Kaeritha's hard-trained self-control not to stare at her in disbelief.

"I appreciate your gracious welcome, Major," she replied pleasantly, instead, after she'd dismounted, and smiled as if she'd noticed nothing at all.

"How else ought we to welcome a champion of Lillinara's own brother?" Paratha responded. "Our Voice has bidden me welcome you in her name and in the name of her Lady, and to assure you that she and the entire temple stand ready to assist you in any way we may."

"Her graciousness and generosity are no less than I would expect from a Voice of the Mother," Kaeritha said. "And they are most welcome."

"Welcome, perhaps," Paratha said, "yet they're also the very least we can offer a servant of Tomanāk who rides in search of justice. And since you come to us upon that errand, may I guide you directly to the Voice? Or would you prefer to wash and refresh yourself after your ride, first?"

"As you say, Major, I come in search of justice. If the Voice is prepared to see me so quickly, I would prefer to go directly to her."

"Of course, Milady," Paratha said, with another pleasant smile. "If you'll follow me."

Chapter Forty-Four

Well, Kaeritha thought as she followed Paratha into the temple complex, *at least I can be sure where to find* one *of my enemies.*

It took a physical act of will to keep her hands away from the hilts of her weapons while she trailed along behind the major. Paratha seemed to glow in the temple's hushed, reverent dimness, and tendrils of the sickly radiance which clung to her reached out to embrace others as they passed. There was something nauseating about the slow, lascivious way those dully glowing light serpents caressed and stroked those they touched. Most of them gave no indication that they realized anything had touched them, but as Kaeritha walked past them behind Paratha, she Saw tiny, ugly spots, like a leprosy of evil, upon them. They were so small, those spots—hardly visible, only a tiny bit more intense than any normal, fallible mortal might be expected to bear. Yet there were scores of them on most of the acolytes and handmaidens she and Paratha passed, and they blazed briefly stronger and uglier as the major's corona reached out to them. Then they faded, sinking inward, until not even Kaeritha could See them.

That was bad enough, but those who *did* feel something when Paratha's vile web brushed over them were worse. However hard they tried to conceal it, they felt the caress of the Darkness draped about Paratha, and a flicker of pleasure—almost a twisted ecstasy—danced ever so briefly across their faces.

Kaeritha's pulse thudded harder and faster as they moved deeper and deeper into the temple. They'd entered through the Chapel of the Crone, which was not the avenue of approach Kaeritha would have chosen in Major Kharlan's place. Whatever crawling evil had infested Quaysar, this was still a temple of Lillinara. To defile its buildings and, even more, its inhabitants and servitors might be an enormous triumph for the Dark, but the stones themselves must remember in whose honor and reverence they'd been raised. However great the triumph, it could not pass undetected forever, and of all Lillinara's aspects, it was the Crone, the Avenger, whose fury Kaeritha would least have liked to face.

And yet, there was also a sort of fitness, almost a logic, to Paratha's chosen course, for the Crone *was* the Avenger. She was the aspect of the goddess most steeped in blood and vengeance. Her Third Face, most apt to merciless destruction. There were those, including one Kaeritha Seldansdaughter, who felt that the Crone all too often verged upon the Dark Herself, and so perhaps there was a certain resonance between this chapel and the shadowy web which rode Paratha's shoulders and soul.

"Tell me, Major Kharlan," she asked casually, "have you been in Lillinara's service long?"

"Almost twelve years, Milady," Paratha replied.

"And how long have you commanded the Voice's guards?"

"Only since she arrived here," Paratha said, glancing back over her shoulder at Kaeritha with another smile. "I was assigned to the Quaysar Guard eight years ago, and I commanded the previous Voice's guards for almost a year and a half before her death."

"I see," Kaeritha murmured, and the major returned her attention to leading the way through the temple.

They passed through the chapel, and Kaeritha felt the accumulation of Darkness pressing against her shoulders, like a physical presence at her back, as she moved deeper and deeper into the miasma of corruption which had invaded the temple. She was afraid, more afraid than she'd believed she could be even after she'd deduced that Quaysar must be the center of it all. Whatever evil was at work here, it was subtle and terrifyingly powerful, and it must have worked its weavings even longer than she'd believed possible. The outer precincts of the temple, and those members of the temple community furthest from the centers of power, like the gate guards who'd greeted her upon her arrival, were least affected. She wondered if that was deliberate. Had they been left alone, aside from just enough tampering to keep them from noticing what was happening at Quaysar's core, as a part of the corruption's mask? Or had whatever power of the Dark was at work here simply left them for later, after it had fully secured its grasp on the inner temple?

Not that it mattered much either way at the moment. What mattered were the barriers she sensed going up behind her. The waiting strands of power, snapping up, no longer threads but cables. The fly had entered the web of its own volition, arrogant in its own self-confidence, and now it was too late for escape.

She glanced casually over her shoulder and saw more than a dozen other women, the ones who'd reacted most strongly to the touch of Paratha's Darkness, following behind. They looked as if they were merely continuing whatever errands had been theirs before Kaeritha's arrival, but she knew better. She could See the latticework of diseased radiance which bound them together, and the shroud about Paratha was growing stronger, as if it were less and less concerned about even attempting to conceal its presence.

They passed rooms and chambers whose functions Kaeritha could only guess at, and then they entered what was obviously a more residential area of the temple. She had a vague impression of beautiful works of art, religious artifacts, mosaics and magnificent fabrics. Fountains sang sweetly, water splashed and trickled through ornate channels where huge golden fish swam like lazy dreams, and a cool, hushed splendor lay welcomingly all about her.

She noticed all of it . . . and none of it. It was unimportant, peripheral, brushed aside by the tempest of Darkness gathering all about her, sweeping towards her from all directions. It was a subtler and less barbaric Darkness than she and Bahzell and Vaijon had confronted in the Navahkan temple of Sharnā, and yet it was just as strong. Possibly even stronger, and edged with a malice and a sense of endless, cunning patience far beyond that of Sharnā and his tools.

And she faced it alone.

Paratha opened a final pair of double doors of polished ebony inlaid with alabaster moons, and bowed deeply to Kaeritha. The major's smile was as deep and apparently sincere as the one with which she'd first greeted Kaeritha, but the mask had grown increasingly threadbare. Kaeritha Saw the same green-yellow glow at the backs of Paratha's eyes, and she wondered what the other woman Saw when she looked at *her*.

"The Voice awaits you, Milady Champion," Paratha said graciously, and Kaeritha nodded and stepped past her through the ebony doors.

The outsized chamber beyond was obviously intended for formal audiences, yet it was equally obviously part of someone's personal living quarters. Pieces of art, statues, and furniture—much of it comfortably worn, for all its splendor—formed an inviting focus for the vaguely thronelike chair at the chamber's center.

A woman in the glowing white robes of a Voice of Lillinara sat in that chair. She was young, and quite beautiful, with long hair almost as black as Kaeritha's own and huge brown eyes in an oval face. Or Kaeritha thought so, anyway. It was hard to be certain when the poison-green glare radiating from the Voice blinded her so.

"Greetings, Champion of Tomanāk," a silvery soprano, sweeter and more melodious than Kaeritha's, said. "I have yearned for longer than you may believe to greet a champion of one of Lillinara's brothers in this temple."

"Have you, indeed, Milady?" Kaeritha replied, and no one else needed to know how much effort it took to keep her own voice conversational and no more than pleasant. "I'm pleased to hear that, because I've found myself equally eager to make *your* acquaintance."

"Then it would seem to be a fortunate thing that both of our desires have been satisfied this same day," the Voice said.

Kaeritha nodded and bent her head in the slightest of bows. She straightened, rested the heel of her right hand lightly on the hilt of one of her swords, and opened her mouth to speak again.

But before she could say a word, she felt a vast, powerful presence strike out at her. It slammed over her like a tidal wave, crushing as an earthquake, liquid and yet thicker and stronger than mortar or cement. It wrapped a crushing cocoon about her, reaching out to seize her and hold her motionless, and her eyes snapped wide.

"I don't know what you intended to say, Champion," that soprano voice said, and now it was colder than a Vonderland winter and sibilant menace seemed to hiss in its depths. "It doesn't matter, though." The Voice laughed, the sound like fragments of glass shattering on a stone floor, and shook her head. "The arrogance of you 'champions'! Each of you so confident he or she will be protected and guided and warded from harm! Until, of course, the time comes for someone like your master to discard you."

Kaeritha felt the power behind the Voice pressing upon her own vocal cords to silence her, and said nothing. She only gazed at the Voice, standing motionless in the clinging web of Dark power, and the Voice laughed again and stood.

"I suppose it's possible you truly have found a way to interfere with my plans here, little champion. If so, that will be more than a mere inconvenience. You see? I admit it. Yet it isn't something I haven't planned against and allowed for all along. The time had to come when someone would begin to suspect my Mistress was playing Her little games here in Quaysar. But, oh, *Dame*

Kaeritha, the damage I've done to your precious war maids and their Kingdom first! But perhaps you'd care to dispute that with me?"

She made a small gesture, and Kaeritha felt the pressure on her vocal cords vanish.

"You had something you'd care to say?" the Voice mocked her.

"They aren't *my* 'precious war maids,'" Kaeritha said after a moment, and even she was vaguely surprised by how calm and steady her voice sounded. "And you're scarcely the first to try to do them ill. Some of the damage you've inflicted will stick, no doubt. I admit that. But damage can be healed, and Tomanāk—" it seemed to her that the Voice flinched ever so slightly at that name "—is the God of Truth, as well as Justice and War. And the truth is always the bane of the Dark, is it not, O 'Voice'?"

"So you truly think these stone-skulled Sothōii will actually believe a word of it? Or that the war maids *themselves* will believe it?" The Voice laughed yet again. "I think not, little champion. My plans go too deep and my web is too broad for that. I've touched and . . . convinced too many people—like that pathetic little puppet Lanitha, who believes Lillinara Herself commanded her to help safeguard my minor alterations so the war maids get what should have been theirs to begin with. Or those angry little war maids, each so eager to 'avenge' herself for all those real and imagined wrongs. Or your darling Yalith and her Council, who don't even remember that their documents used to say anything else. As you yourself told their fool of an archivist, those who already hate and despise the war maids—those like Trisu—will never believe that *they* didn't forge the 'original documents' at Kalatha. And the war maids won't believe they're forgeries either. Not after all my careful spadework. And not without a champion of Tomanāk to attest to the legitimacy of Trisu's copies . . . and to explain how *Kalatha's* come to have been altered without the connivance of Yalith and her Town Council. And I'm very much afraid you won't be around to tell them."

"Perhaps not," Kaeritha said calmly. "There are, however, other champions of Tomanāk, and one of them will shortly know all I know and everything I've deduced. I think I could safely rely upon him to accomplish my task for me, if it were necessary."

The Voice's brown eyes narrowed and she frowned. But then she forced her expression to smooth once again, and shrugged.

"Perhaps you're correct, little champion," she said lightly. "Personally, I think the damage will linger. I've found such fertile ground on both sides—the lords who hate and loath everything the war maids stand for, and the war maids whose resentment of all the insults and injustices they and their sisters have endured over the years burns equally hot and bitter. Oh, yes, those will listen to *me*, not your precious fellow champion. They'll believe what suits their prejudices and hatreds, and I will send my handmaidens forth to spread the word among them. *My* handmaidens, little champion, not those of that stupid, gutless bitch this place was built for!"

She glared at Kaeritha, and the knight felt the exultant hatred pouring off of her like smoke and acid.

"And to fan the flames properly," the false Voice continued, her soprano suddenly soft and vicious . . . and hungry, "Trisu is about to take matters into his own hands."

Kaeritha said nothing, but the other woman saw the question in her eyes and laughed coldly.

"There are already those who believe he connived at—or possibly even personally ordered—the murder of two handmaidens of Lillinara. He didn't, of course. For all his bigotry, he's proven irritatingly resistant to suggestions which might have led him to that sort of direct action. But that isn't what the war maids think. And it won't be what they think when men in his colors attack Quaysar itself. When they ride in through the gates of the town and the temple under his banner, coming as envoys to the Voice, and then butcher every citizen of Quaysar and every servant of the temple they can catch."

Despite herself, Kaeritha couldn't keep the horror of the images the false Voice's words evoked out of her eyes, and the other woman's smile belonged on something from the depths of Krahana's darkest hell.

"There will be survivors, of course. There always are, aren't there? And I'll see to it that none of the survivors anyone knows about were ever part of my own little web. The most attentive examination by one of your own *infallible* champions of Tomanāk will only demonstrate that they're telling the truth about what they saw and who they saw doing it. And one of the things they'll see, little champion, will be myself and my personal guards and the most senior priestesses, barricading ourselves into the Chapel of the Crone to make our final stand. Trisu's men will attempt to break into it after us, of course. And I will call down the Lady's Wrath to utterly destroy the chapel's attackers . . . and everyone inside it. Of course, it may not be the Wrath of the precise Lady everyone will assume it was, but no matter. The blast and fires will neatly explain why there are no bodies. Or, at least, none of *our* bodies."

She shook her head in mock sorrow.

"No doubt some of Trisu's fellows will be horrified. Others will be charitable enough to believe he simply ran mad, but some of them will feel he was justified in burning out this nest of perversions, especially when the question of forged documents comes to the fore. And whatever Tellian and the Crown may do, little champion, the damage will be done. If Trisu is punished while protesting his innocence and flourishing his proof of forgery, then his fellow lords will blame his liege and the King for a miscarriage of justice. And if he isn't punished—if, for example, some interfering busybody champion of Tomanāk should examine him and find he's telling the truth and had nothing to do with the attack—then the *war maids* will be convinced it's all part of a cover-up and that he's *escaped* justice. And so will be many within the Church of Lillinara."

"Was that your plan all along?" Kaeritha asked. "To sow dissension and hatred and distrust?"

"Well, that and to enjoy the pretty fires and all the lovely killing, of course," the false Voice agreed, pouting as she studied her polished fingernails.

"I see." Kaeritha considered that for a moment, then cocked an eyebrow at the other woman. "I imagine it wasn't too difficult to assassinate the old Voice once Major Kharlan became the commander of her bodyguards. I don't know whether you used poison or a spell, and I don't suppose it matters much, either way. But I would like to know what you did with the Voice who was supposed to replace her."

The false Voice froze, staring at her for just a moment. It was only an instant, almost too brief to be noticed, and then she smiled.

"What makes you think anyone did anything 'with' me? There was no need. It's not as if I were the first oh-so-perfect, straight and narrow priest or priestess to realize the truth, you know. Or would you pretend that no others have ever joined me in transferring my allegiance to a goddess more worthy of my worship?"

"No," Kaeritha acknowledged. "But it's not as if it happens very often, either. And it's never happened at all in the case of a *true* Voice. Nor has it in your case. You were never a priestess of the Mother—or did you truly think you could fool a champion of Tomanāk about that?" She grimaced. "I knew the moment I Saw you that you were no priestess of Lillinara. In fact, I'm not entirely certain you were ever even human in the first place. But the one thing I'm positive of is that whoever—or whatever—you may be or look like, you are not the Voice the Church assigned here."

"Very clever," the false Voice hissed. She glared at Kaeritha for several seconds, then shook herself. "I'm afraid that sweet little girl suffered a mischief before she could take up her duties here," she said with pious sorrow. "I know how dreadfully it disappointed her—in fact, she told me so herself, just before I cut her heart out and Paratha and I ate it in front of her." She smiled viciously. "And since it bothered her so, and since I was in some small way responsible for her failure, I thought it incumbent upon me to come and discharge those responsibilities for her. A duty which I am now about to complete."

"Ah." Kaeritha nodded. "And just where do *I* fit into these plans of yours?" she inquired.

"Why, you *die*, of course," the false Voice told her. "Oh, not immediately—not *physically*, that is. I'm afraid we'll have to settle for just destroying your soul, for the moment. Then I'll replace it with a little demon whose essence I happen to have handy. He'll keep the flesh alive until 'Trisu' gets around to attacking. Who knows?" She smiled terribly. "Perhaps he'll enjoy experimenting with some of my guards. I'm afraid you won't be around anymore to observe the way he broadens your sexual horizons, but no doubt *he'll* be amused. And then, when Trisu attacks, you'll die gallantly, fighting to defend the temple against its desecrators. I think that will add a certain artistic finish to the entire affair, don't you? With a little luck, it will bring your entire church into the fray against Trisu. Won't that be lovely? The church of the god of *justice* helping to destroy the innocent man who didn't have a thing to do with your fate? And whether that happens or not, the opportunity to treat one of Tomanāk's little pets to the experience she so amply deserves would make this entire investment of effort worth while in its own right."

"I see," Kaeritha repeated. "And you believe you can do all of this to me because—?"

"I don't *believe* anything," the false Voice told her flatly. "You've been mine to do with as I chose from the instant you stepped into this chamber, you stupid bitch. Why do you think you haven't been able to so much as move your head, or shift your feet?"

"A good question," Kaeritha conceded. "But there's a better one."

"What '*better* one'?" the false Voice sneered disdainfully.

"Why do *you* think I haven't been able to?" Kaeritha asked calmly, and both swords hissed from their sheaths as she catapulted towards the other woman.

The sudden eruption of movement took the false Voice completely by surprise. She'd never even suspected that Kaeritha had simply *chosen* not to move or speak when she became aware of the power crushing down upon her. Whoever—or whatever—the "Voice" might be, she'd never before tried to control a champion of Tomanāk. If she had, she would have realized that no coercion, no spell of control or compulsion, even backed by the power of another god's avatar, could hold the will or mind of one who had sworn herself to the War God's service and touched His soul as He had touched hers. And because the false Voice hadn't realized that, she was still staring at Kaeritha—gawking in disbelief—as two matched short swords wrapped in coronas of brilliant blue fire drove through her heart and lungs.

A scream of agony cored with fury ripped through the audience chamber as the creature masquerading as a Voice of Lillinara fell back in a scalding gush of blood. Kaeritha twisted her wrists before the swords slid free, and even as she did, she went forward on the ball of her left foot while her right foot flashed up behind her. The heel of her heavy riding boot smashed into the person she'd sensed charging up behind her. It wasn't the clean, central strike she'd hoped for, but it was enough to deflect the attack and send the attacker crashing to the floor with a whooping cry of anguish.

Kaeritha let the force of her kick pivot her on her left foot so that she faced Major Kharlan and the Voice's other servitors. The crackling blue aura of a champion of a God of Light roared up like a volcano of light, blasting through the audience chamber like a silent hurricane. It clung to her, flickering between her and the rest of the world like a thin canopy of lightning. But she could see through it clearly, and her eyes found Paratha with unerring speed. The major's saber was still coming out of its scabbard, and at least half of the others seemed stunned into momentary paralysis. But that paralysis wouldn't hold them for long, and Kaeritha knew it.

Every champion of Tomanāk had his or her own preferred combat style. Kaeritha's was totally unlike Bahzell's, except for one thing; neither of them was ever prepared to stand on the defensive if they had any choice. And since there was no one to watch her back or coordinate with, Kaeritha Seldansdaughter decided to make a virtue of the fact that there was only one of her.

She charged.

There was no doubt in her mind that Paratha was the most dangerous of her remaining opponents. Unfortunately, Paratha seemed disinclined to face her in personal combat. The major dodged swiftly, darting behind one of the corrupted priestesses, who shook herself and then charged to meet Kaeritha with no weapon besides a dagger and the naked fury blazing in her eyes.

Kaeritha's right blade came down with lightning speed and all the elegance of a cleaver. It lopped off her opponent's right hand like a pruning hook removing a branch. The woman shrieked as blood spouted from the stump of her wrist, and then Kaeritha's *left* blade went through the front of her throat from right to left in a backhanded fan of blood. Some of the blood splashed across Kaeritha's face, painting it like a barbarian Wakūo raider's.

"Tomanāk! *Tomanāk!*"

Kaeritha's war cry echoed in the chamber as another dagger grated on her breastplate, and a short, vicious thrust put one of her swords through her attacker's belly. The mortally wounded priestess fell back, writhing and screaming, and Kaeritha's champion's healing sense cringed as she realized all of the daggers coming at her were coated in deadly poison.

She slashed a third priestess to the floor with her right hand even as her left sword darted out to engage and parry yet another dagger. She twisted between two opponents, killing one and wounding the other as she passed, and then she was behind them all and spun on her toes like a dancer to charge once more.

"Tomanāk!"

Her foes seemed less eager to engage her this time, and she smiled like a direcat, teeth white through the blood on her face, as she slammed into them once more. Two more priestesses went down, then another, and finally Kaeritha heard alarm bells ringing throughout the temple complex.

Her jaw tightened. She had no doubt at all that the

Voice and Paratha had drawn upon their patron's power to make certain Quaysar's guard force was loyal to them, whether or not those guards knew what they truly served. And even if there'd been no tampering at all, any guardsman who entered this audience chamber and saw the Voice and half a dozen or more of her priestesses dead on the floor was unlikely to assume that the person who'd killed them was the intended victim of an ambush by the Dark. She had no more than seconds before a veritable flood of guardsmen and war maids came pouring in upon her, and her swords flashed like lethal scythes as she slashed her way through the dagger-armed priestesses towards Major Kharlan.

The bodies between them flew aside, screaming or already dead, and Paratha was no longer falling back. The major still declined to rush forward, watching with no more apparent emotion than a serpent as her allies fell like so much dead meat before Kaeritha's blades. But she made no effort to flee, either, and as Kaeritha looked at her, she Saw something she'd never Seen before.

A cable of vile yellow-green energy linked Paratha to the corpse of the false Voice, and even as Kaeritha watched, something flowed along that cable. Something coming from the dead Voice to the living Paratha. And there were other cables, reaching out to the fallen priestesses, as well. The web of sickening luminescence centered on Paratha, sucking greedily at whatever flowed along it. Kaeritha didn't know what it was, but the corona which had clung to Paratha from the outset suddenly blazed up, fierce and bright as a forest fire to Kaeritha's Vision. And as it did, Kaeritha knew at last which of the Dark Gods she faced, for a huge, hideous spider wrapped in flame arose behind Paratha.

The spider of Shīgū, Queen of Hell and Mother of Madness. Wife of Phrobus and mother of all his dark children. Far more powerful than her son Sharnā, with a foul and twisted malice none of her offspring could equal, and Lillinara's most bitter enemy for the way in which her parody of womanhood perverted and fouled all that Lillinara stood for.

Chapter Forty-Five

The flame-wrapped spider towered up, compound eyes ablaze with hatred and madness. Its mandibles clashed, dripping with venom that flamed and hissed, bubbling on the polished stone floor as it burned its way into it. Claws scraped and grated, and the vilest stench Kaeritha had ever imagined filled the audience chamber. The hideous apparition loomed over her, reaching for her with more than mere claws and pincers, and a black tide of terror lapped out before it.

Even as Kaeritha recognized the spider, Paratha seemed to grow taller. The false Voice hadn't been Shīgū's true tool, Kaeritha realized; *Paratha* had. The Voice might even have believed that she was Shīgū's chosen, but in truth, it had always been Paratha, and now the major no longer hid behind the camouflage of the Voice. She was drinking in the life energy—probably even the very souls—of her fallen followers, and something more was coming with it. Potent as all that energy might be, it was only a focus, a burning glass which reached out for something even stronger and more vile and focused it all upon the major.

Paratha's face was transfigured, and her entire body

seemed to quiver and vibrate as Shīgū poured energy into her chosen. Kaeritha remembered Bahzell's description of the night he'd faced an avatar of Sharnā, and she knew this was worse. Harnak of Navahk had carried a cursed blade which had served as Sharnā's key to the universe of mortals. Paratha carried no key; she *was* the key, and Kaeritha's mind cringed away from the insane risk Shīgū had chosen to run.

No wonder she'd been able to penetrate Lillinara's church, tamper with scores of people in Kalatha, and kill Lillinara's priestesses and Voices and replace them with her own tools! For all the endless ages since Phrobus' fall into evil, no god of Dark or Light had dared to contend openly with one of his or her divine enemies on the mortal plane. They were simply too powerful. If they clashed directly, they might all too easily destroy the very universe for whose dominion they contended. And so there were limits, checks set upon their power and how they might intervene in the world of mortals. It was why there were champions of Light and their Dark equivalents.

Yet Shīgū *had* intervened directly. She'd moved beyond the agreed upon limits and stepped fully into the world of mortals. Paratha was no champion. She was Shīgū's focus, her anchor in this universe. She wasn't touched by the power of Shīgū—in that moment, she *was* the power of Shīgū, and Kaeritha felt a terrifying surge of answering power pouring into her from Tomanāk.

"So, little champion," Paratha hissed. "You would contend with *Me*, would you?"

She laughed, and the web of her power reached out to her living minions, as well as the dead. Kaeritha heard their shrieks of agony—agony mingled with a horrible, defiled ecstasy—as Shīgū's avatar seized them. They didn't die, not right away, but that was no mercy. Instead, they became secondary nodes of the web centered upon Paratha. They blazed like human torches to Kaeritha's Sight as the same power crashed through them, and the will which animated Paratha—a will Kaeritha realized was no longer mortal, if it ever had been—fastened upon them like pincers. All nine of the remaining priestesses moved as one, closing in to form a deadly circle about Kaeritha with Paratha.

"So tasty your soul will be," Paratha crooned. "I'll treasure it like fine brandy."

"I think not," Kaeritha told her, and Paratha's eyes flickered as she heard another timbre in Kaeritha's soprano. A deeper timbre, like the basso rumble of cavalry gathering speed for a charge. The blue corona flickering around Kaeritha blazed higher and hotter, towering over her as the luminously translucent form of Tomanāk Orfro, God of War and Justice, Captain General of the Gods of Light, took form to confront the spider of Shīgū. The priestesses caught up in Shīgū's web froze, as if stilled by some wizard's spell, but although Paratha drew back ever so slightly, her hesitation was only brief and her mouth twisted like the snarl of some rabid beast.

"Not this time, *Scale Balancer,*" she—or someone else, using her voice—hissed venomously. "This one is *mine*!"

Her body tensed, and, on the last word, a deadly blast of power ripped from her. It screamed across the audience chamber like a battering ram of yellow-green hunger, and the entire temple seemed to quiver on its foundations as it slammed into Kaeritha. Or, rather, into the blue nimbus blazing about her. The nimbus which deflected its deadly strength in a score of shattered streamers of vicious lightning that cracked and flared like whips of flame. Small explosions laced the chamber's walls, shattered fountains, and incinerated two of the living priestesses where they stood, and Kaeritha felt the staggering violence of the impact in her very bones. But that was all she felt, and she smiled thinly at her foe.

"Yours, am I?" she asked, and a strange sense of duality swept through her on the tide of Tomanāk's presence. "I think not," she repeated, and Paratha's face twisted in mingled fury and disbelief as Tomanāk's power shed the fury of her attack.

Kaeritha's smile was hard and cold, and she felt the

call to battle throbbing in her veins. She was herself, as she had always been, and the will and courage which kept her on her feet in the face of Shīgū's hideous manifestation were her own. But behind her will, supporting it and bolstering her courage like a tried and trusted battlefield commander, was Tomanāk Himself. His presence filled her as Shīgū's filled Paratha, but without submerging her. Without requiring her subservience, or making her no more than His tool. She was who she had always been—Kaeritha Seldansdaughter, champion of Tomanāk—and she laughed through the choking stench of Shīgū's perversion.

Paratha's entire face knotted with livid rage at the sound of that bright, almost joyous laugh, and the spider snarled behind her. But Kaeritha only laughed again.

"Your reach exceeds your grasp, Paratha. Or should I say Shīgū?" She shook her head. "If you think you want me, come and take me!"

"You may threaten and murder my tools," that voice hissed again, "but you'll find *Me* a different matter, little *champion*. No mortal can stand against My power!"

"But she does not stand alone," a voice deeper than a mountain rumbled from the air all about Kaeritha, and Paratha's face lost all expression as she and the power using her flesh heard it.

"If we two contend openly, power-to-power, this world will be destroyed, and you with it!" Paratha's mouth snarled the words, but the entire audience chamber shook with the grim, rumbling laugh which answered.

"This world might perish," Tomanāk agreed after a moment, "but you know as well as I which of us would be destroyed with it, Shīgū." Paratha's lips drew back, baring her teeth like a wolf's, but Tomanāk spoke again before she could. "Yet it will not come to that. I will not permit it to."

"And how will you stop it, fool?!" Paratha's voice demanded with a sneer. "This is My place now, and *My* power fills it!"

"But you will bring no more power to it," Tomanāk said flatly. "What you have already poured into your tools you may use; all else is blocked against you. If you doubt me, see for yourself."

Paratha's eyes glared madly, but Kaeritha's heart leapt as she realized it was true. She had never faced such a terrifying concentration of evil, yet that concentration was no longer growing.

"If I am blocked, then so also are *you*," Paratha grated. "You can lend no more power to your tool, either!"

"My Swords are not my tools," Tomanāk replied softly. "They are my champions—my battle companions. And my champion is equal to anything such as you might bring against her."

"Is she *indeed*?" Paratha laughed wildly. "I think not."

Her saber seemed to writhe and twist. The blade grew longer, broader, and burned with the same sick, green radiance as the giant spider and its web.

"Come to me, *champion*," she crooned. "Come and die!"

She leapt forward with the words, and even as she did, the remaining priestesses charged with her. They came at Kaeritha from all sides, a wave of deadly blades, all animated and wielded by the same malign presence.

Unlike the priestesses, Kaeritha was armored. But there was only one of her, and she dared not let them swarm over her with those envenomed daggers. Nor did she care to face whatever unnatural power had been poured into Paratha's blade while the priestesses came at her back. And so she spun to her left, away from Paratha, and her twin blades struck like serpents, trailing tails of blue fire as she ripped open the belly and throat of the nearest priestess. She vaulted the body, lashing out with her right-hand sword, and another priestess staggered away as the backhand stroke slashed the tendons behind her knee.

Paratha—or Shīgū, if there was any difference—shrieked in wordless, enraged fury. Her remaining tools pursued Kaeritha, charging after her madly, and Kaeritha laughed coldly, deliberately goading Paratha with the sound.

She supposed some idiots who'd paid too much attention

to bad bard's tales might have thought it cowardly, or unchivalrous, to concentrate on her unarmored, dagger-armed foes rather than go directly for the opponent who was also armored and armed. But although Kaeritha might be a knight, she'd been born a peasant, with all a peasant's pragmatism, and Tomanāk's Order believed in honor and justice, not stupidity. She turned again, once she was clear of the closing perimeter, and two more of Paratha's priestesses caught up with her . . . and died.

Paratha's shriek was even wilder than before, but the two surviving priestesses fell back. The sole unwounded one bent over and seized the crippled one's arm and dragged her to one side, and Kaeritha turned once again—slowly, calmly, with a direcat's predatory grace—to face Paratha and the flaming spider form of Shīgū.

The glaring light web still connected Paratha's body to those of the false Voice and all of the others except Kaeritha herself, living or dead, in the audience chamber. But there was a difference now. The strands connected to the dead women glared with a brighter, fiercer radiance that flared high, then faded and died. And as they died, the nimbus about Paratha blazed more brilliantly still. The bodies themselves changed, as well. They went in an instant from freshly slain corpses to dried and withered husks. Like flies in a true spider's web, Kaeritha thought, sucked dry of all life and vitality.

Tomanāk had blocked Shīgū from pouring still more strength into her avatar, and so she had ripped everything from her dead servants, devouring even their immortal souls and concentrating that power in Paratha.

"Come on, 'Major Kharlan,'" Kaeritha invited softly. "Let's dance."

Paratha screamed wordlessly and charged.

Whatever else Paratha might have been, she was an experienced warrior. She had the advantage of reach, and her armor was every bit as good as Kaeritha's. But she also realized she had only one weapon to Kaeritha's two, and for all her shrieking fury, she was anything but berserk.

Kaeritha discovered that almost too late, when Paratha's

headlong charge suddenly transmuted into a spinning whirl to her left. The demented shriek had very nearly deceived Kaeritha into thinking her foe truly was maddened by rage, attacking in a mindless fury. But Paratha was far from mindless, and she pivoted just beyond Kaeritha's own reach, while her longer, glowing saber came twisting in in a corkscrew thrust at Kaeritha's face.

Kaeritha's right hand parried the thrust wide, and their blades met in a fountaining eruption of fire. Blue and green lightning crackled and hissed, exploding against the chamber's walls and ceiling, blasting divots out of the marble floors like handfuls of thrown gravel. She gasped, staggered by the sheer ferocity of what should have been an oblique, sliding kiss of steel on steel. No doubt Paratha had felt the same terrible shock, but if she had, it didn't interrupt her movement. She was gone again, fading back before Kaeritha could even begin a riposte.

Kaeritha's entire right arm ached and throbbed, and sweat streaked her face as she turned, facing Paratha, swords at the ready, while alarm bells continued to clangor throughout the temple complex.

"And what will you do when the other guards come, little champion?" Paratha's voice mocked. "All *they* will see is you and me, surrounded by the butchered bodies of their precious priestesses. Will you slay them, as well, when I order them to take you for the murderer you are?"

Kaeritha didn't reply. She only moved forward, lightly, poised on the balls of her feet. Paratha backed away from her, eyes lit with the glitter of hell light watching cautiously, alertly, seeking any opening as intently as Kaeritha's own.

Kaeritha's gaze never wavered from Paratha, yet a corner of her attention stood guard. She'd always had what her first arms instructor had called good "situational awareness," and she'd honed that awareness for years. And so, although she never looked away from her opponent, she was aware of the remaining unwounded priestess creeping ever so cautiously around behind her.

Paratha gave no sign that *she* was aware of anything

except Kaeritha, but Kaeritha had almost allowed herself to be fooled once. Now she knew better. And she also knew she had only one opportunity to end this fight before the guards Paratha had spoken of arrived. If the major stayed away, settled for simply holding her in play until the guards burst in on them, she would be doomed. So somehow, she had to entice the other woman into attacking her *now* . . . or convince the major that she'd tricked Kaeritha into attacking on *her* terms.

Paratha slowed, letting Kaeritha close gradually with her. Her saber danced and wove before her, its deadly, glowing tip leaving a twisting crawl of ugly yellow-green light in its wake, and Kaeritha's nerves tightened. The priestess with her poisoned dagger was close behind her, now, and Paratha's glittering eyes narrowed ever so slightly. If it was going to happen, Kaeritha thought, then it would happen—

Now!

The priestess sprang forward, teeth bared in a silent, snarling rictus, dagger thrusting viciously at Kaeritha's unguarded back. And in the same sliver of infinity, with the perfect coordination possible only when a single entity controlled both bodies, Paratha executed her own, deadly attack in a full-extension lunge.

It almost worked. It *should* have worked. But as Tomanāk had told Shīgū, his champion was the equal of anything the Spider might bring against her. Kaeritha had known what was coming, and she'd spent half her life honing the skills she called upon that day. Perfectly as Paratha—or Shīgū—had orchestrated the attack, Kaeritha's response was equally perfect . . . and began a tiny fraction of a second *before* Paratha's.

She twisted lithely, turning her torso through ninety degrees, and lunged at Paratha in a consummately executed stop-thrust. Her left-hand blade met the longer saber, twisting it aside in another of those terrible explosions of light and fury, then slid down its glaring length in a deadly extension that punched the blue caprisoned short sword through Paratha's breastplate as if its hardened steel had been so much cobweb. And even as she lunged towards Paratha, her right-hand sword snapped out *behind* her, and the priestess who'd flung herself at Kaeritha's back shrieked as her own charge impaled her upon that lethal blade.

For one instant, Kaeritha stood between her opponents, both arms at full extension in opposite directions, her sapphire eyes locked with Paratha's hell-lit eyes of brown. The other woman's mouth opened in shocked disbelief, and her saber wavered, then fell to the floor with a crackling explosion. Her left hand groped towards the cross guard of the sword buried in her chest and blood poured from her mouth.

And then the instant passed. Kaeritha twisted both wrists in unison, then straightened, withdrawing both her blades in one, crisp movement, and the bodies of both her opponents crumpled to the floor.

Chapter Forty-Six

The alarm bells continued to sound, and Kaeritha turned from her fallen enemies to face the audience chamber's double doors. Foul smelling smoke drifted and eddied, and small fires burned where the reflected bursts of contending powers had set furniture and wall hangings alight. The walls, ceilings, and polished floors were pitted and scorched, and the windows along the eastern wall had been shattered and blown out of their frames. Bodies—several as seared as the chamber's furnishings—sprawled everywhere amid pools of blood and the sewer stench of ruptured organs.

The blue corona of Tomanāk continued to envelop her, and she knew any priestess who saw it—and who was prepared to think about it—would recognize it for what it was. Unfortunately, it was unlikely that most of the temple's regular guards would do the same. Worse, she knew that although Shīgū's avatar had been vanquished, the spider goddess' residual evil remained. Shīgū might have been considerate enough to concentrate most of her more powerful servants here in the Voice's chambers for the attack on Kaeritha. But she hadn't concentrated *all* of them, and even if her remaining servants hadn't hungered for revenge, they must know that their only chance of escaping retribution lay in killing or at least diverting Kaeritha.

Her jaw tightened. She knew what she'd do, if she'd been one of Shīgū's tools faced by a champion of Tomanāk. She would feed the uncorrupted members of Quaysar's guard force straight into the champion's blades, and the chaos and confusion and the fact that none of the innocents knew what was really happening would let her do exactly that. Any champion would do all she could to avoid slaying men and women who were only doing their sworn duty, with no trace of corruption upon their souls. And if, despite all she could do, that champion found herself forced to kill those men and women in self-defense, the Dark would count that a far from minor victory in its own right.

But Kaeritha had plans of her own, and her sapphire eyes were grim as she kicked the chamber's doors wide and stalked through them, swords blazing blue in her hands.

The bells were louder in the corridor outside the Voice's quarters, and Kaeritha heard sharp shouts of command and the clatter of booted feet. The first group of guards—a dozen war maids and half that many guardsmen in Lillinara's moon-badged livery—came around the bend at a run, and Kaeritha gathered her will. She reached out, in a way she could never have described to someone who was not also a champion, and seized a portion of the power Tomanāk had poured into her. She shaped it to suit her needs, then threw it out before her in a fan-shaped battering ram.

Shouted orders turned into shouts of confusion as Kaeritha's god-reinforced will swept down the corridor like some immense, unseen broom. It gathered up those who were responding to what they thought was an unprovoked attack upon the temple and its Voice and simply pushed them out of the way. Under other circumstances, Kaeritha might have found the sight amusing as their feet slid across the temple's floor as if its stone were polished ice. Some of them beat at the invisible wall shoving them out of Kaeritha's path with their fists. A few actually hewed at it with their weapons. But however they sought to resist, it was useless. They were shunted aside, roughly enough to leave bruises and contusions in some cases, but remarkably gently under the circumstances.

Yet some of the responding guards were *not* pushed out of Kaeritha's way. It took them precious seconds to realize that they hadn't been, and even that fleeting a delay proved fatal. Kaeritha was upon them, her blue eyes blazing with another, brighter blue, before they could react, for there was a reason her bow wave hadn't shunted them aside. Unlike the other guards, these were no innocent dupes of the corruption which had poisoned and befouled their temple. They knew who—or what—they truly served, and their faces twisted with panic as they found themselves singled out from their innocent fellows . . . within blade's reach of a champion of Tomanāk.

"*Tomanāk!*" Kaeritha hurled her war cry into their teeth, and her swords were right behind it. There was no way to avoid her in the corridor's confines, nor was there room or time for finesse. Kaeritha crunched into them, blazing swords moving with the merciless precision of some dwarvish killing machine made of wires and wheels.

Those trapped in front of the others lashed out with the fury of despair as they saw death come for them in the pitiless glitter of her eyes. It did them no good. No more than three of them could face her simultaneously, and all of them together would have been no match for her.

Those in the rear realized it. They tried to turn and flee, only to discover that the same energy which had pushed aside their fellows caught *them* like a tide of glue. They couldn't run; which meant all they could do was face her and die.

Kaeritha cut them down and stepped across their bodies. She continued her steady progress through the temple's corridors, retracing her path towards the Chapel of the Crone, and sweat beaded her brow. Another group of guards came charging down an intersecting passageway from her left, and once more her battering ram broom reached out. Most of the newcomers gawked in disbelief and confusion as they were shunted firmly aside . . . and those who were not gawked in terror as Kaeritha stalked into their midst like death incarnate, brushing aside their efforts to defend themselves and visiting Tomanāk's judgment upon them in the flash of glowing blades and the spatter of traitors' blood.

She resumed her progress towards the chapel, and felt a fatigue which was far more than merely physical gathering within her. Forming and shaping raw power the way she was was only marginally less demanding than channeling Tomanāk's presence to heal wounds or sickness. It required immense concentration, and the drain upon her own energy was enormous. She couldn't keep it up long, and every innocent she pushed out of her way only increased her growing exhaustion. But she couldn't stop, either. Not unless she wanted to slaughter—or to be slaughtered by—those same innocents.

Her advance slowed as her fatigue grew. Every ounce of willpower was focused on the next section of hall or waiting archway between her and her destination. She was vaguely aware of other bells—deeper, louder bells, even more urgent than the ones which had summoned the guards to the false Voice's defense—but she dared not spare the attention to wonder why they were sounding or what they signified. She could only continue, fighting her way through the seemingly endless members of Quaysar's Guard who had been corrupted.

And then, suddenly, she entered the Chapel of the Crone, and there were no more enemies. Even the innocent guards she had been pushing out of her way had disappeared, and the clangor of alarm bells had been cut short as though by a knife. There was only stillness, and the abrupt, shocking cessation of combat.

She stopped, suddenly aware that she was soaked with sweat and gasping for breath. She lowered her blades slowly, bloody to the elbows, wondering what had happened, where her enemies had gone. The sounds of her own boots seemed deafening as she made her way slowly, cautiously, down the chapel's center aisle. And then, without warning, the chapel's huge doors swung wide just as she reached them.

The bright morning sunlight beyond was almost blinding after the interior dimness through which she had clawed and fought her way, and she blinked. Then her vision cleared, and her eyes widened as she saw a sight she was quite certain no one had ever seen before.

She watched the immense wind rider dismount from the roan courser. Despite his own height, his courser was so enormous that it had to kneel like a Wakūo camel so that he could reach the ground. He wore the same green surcoat she wore, and the huge sword in his right hand blazed with the same blue light as he turned and the courser heaved back to its feet behind him. She stared at him, her battle-numbed mind trying to come to grips with his sudden, totally unanticipated appearance, and his left hand swept off his helmet. Foxlike ears shifted gently, cocking themselves in her direction, and a deep voice rumbled like welcome thunder.

"So, Kerry, is this after being only for those with formal invitations, or can just anyone be dropping in?"

She shook her head, unable to make herself quite believe what she was seeing, and stepped out through the chapel doors two of the Quaysar war maids had swung wide. The temple courtyard seemed impossibly crowded by the score or so of coursers and wind riders behind Bahzell. Most of the wind riders were still mounted, interposing with their coursers between the remainder of the Quaysar Guards and the chapel. Two of them weren't. Baron Tellian of Balthar and his wind-brother Hathan had dismounted behind Bahzell, and Kaeritha shook her head in disbelief as she realized that over half of the still mounted "wind riders" were *hradani*.

"Bahzell," she said in a voice which even she recognized was far too calm and remote from the carnage behind her, "what are *you* doing here? And what are you—or any hradani—doing with a *courser*, for Tomanāk's sake?"

"Well," he replied, brown eyes gleaming with wicked amusement, "it's all after being the letter's fault."

"Letter?" She shook her head again. "That's ridiculous. My letter won't even arrive at Balthar for another day or two!"

"And who," he asked amiably, "said a thing at all, at all, about *your* letter?" It was his turn to shake his head, ears tilted impudently. "It wasn't from you, being as how it's clear as the nose on Brandark's face that you've not got the sense to be asking for help *before* you need it. No, this one was after coming from Leeana."

"Leeana?" Kaeritha parroted.

"Aye," Bahzell said a bit more somberly. "She'd suspicions enough all on her own before ever you came back to Kalatha from Thalar. She'd written a bit about them to her Mother, but it was only after you and she spoke that she was sending the lot of her worries to the Baroness. I was away—I'd a bit of business in Warm Springs as needed looking after—but I'd had a hint as you might be after needing a little help. So when I returned to Hill Guard, the Baroness showed me Leeana's letters."

He shrugged.

"As soon as ever I read them, it was pikestaff clear as how I'd best be on my way to Quaysar. I'm hoping you won't be taking this wrongly, Kerry, but charging in here all alone, without so much as me or Brandark to watch your back, was a damned-fool hradani sort of thing to be doing."

"It was my job," she said, looking around for something to wipe her blades on. Tellian silently extended what looked like it had once been part of a temple guard's surcoat. She decided not to ask what had happened to its owner. Instead, she simply nodded her thanks and used it to clean her swords while she continued to gaze up at Bahzell.

"And I never once said as how it wasn't," he replied. "But I'm thinking you'd be carving bits and pieces off of my hide if I'd gone off to deal with such as this without asking if you'd care to be coming along. Now wouldn't you just?"

"That's different," she began, and broke off, recognizing the weakness of her own tone as Bahzell and Tellian both began to laugh.

"And just *how* is it different, Kerry?" another, even deeper voice inquired, and Kaeritha turned to face the speaker.

Tomanāk Himself stood in the courtyard, and all around her people were going to their knees as His presence washed over them. Wind riders slid from their saddles to join them, and even the coursers bent their proud heads. Only Kaeritha, Bahzell, and Walsharno remained standing, facing their God, and He smiled upon them.

"I'm still waiting to hear how it's different," He reminded her in gently teasing tones, and she drew a deep breath as His power withdrew from her. It left quickly, yet gently, flowing back through her like a caress or the shoulder slap of a war captain for a warrior who'd done all that was expected of her and more. There was a moment of regret, a sense of loss, as that glorious tide flowed back to the one from Whom it had come, yet her contact with Him was not severed. It remained, glowing between them, and as He reclaimed the power He had lent her, she found herself refreshed, filled with energy and life, as if she'd just arisen in the dawn of a new day and not come from a deadly battle for her very life and soul.

"Well, maybe it's not," she said after a moment or two and with a fulminating sideways glower for Bahzell. "But it still wasn't *Leeana's* place to be telling you I needed help!"

"No more did she," Bahzell said. "All she wrote was what she suspected—not that it was after taking any geniuses to know what such as you were likely to be doing about it if it should happen as how she was right." He shrugged.

"All right," Kaeritha said after another pregnant moment. "But that still leaves my other question."

"And which other question would that be?" Tomanāk asked.

"The one about him and *him,*" she snapped, jabbing an index finger first at Bahzell and then at the huge stallion who stood regarding her over her fellow champion's shoulder with what could only be described as an expression of mild interest. She glared back at him, and then her eyes widened as she Saw the glowing tendrils of blue light that linked the immense stallion not simply to Bahzell, but directly to Tomanāk. She opened her mouth, then changed what she'd been about to say. There were some questions, she thought, that needed to be discussed in private first.

"The question," she said instead, "of what a hradani—*any* hradani, but especially a *Horse Stealer* hradani—is doing with a courser? I thought they, um, didn't like one another very much."

"Ah, now, I don't think it's my business to be telling that particular tale," Tomanāk told her with a slow smile. He chuckled at the disgusted look she gave Him, then turned His head, gazing about the temple courtyard. There were dozens of bodies lying about, Kaeritha realized—all that was left of the corrupted members of the Quaysar Guard who'd tried to prevent Bahzell and his wind brothers from fighting their way to her aid. Tomanāk gazed at them for several seconds, then shook His head with a sad sigh.

"You've done well, Kaeritha. You and Bahzell alike, as I knew you would. I believe this temple will recover from Shīgū's interference, although you'll still have your work cut out for you in Kalatha. My Sister will be sending two or three of her Arms to aid you in that work, but this is still a matter of Justice, and so falls under your authority . . . and responsibility."

"I understand," she said quietly, and he nodded.

"I know you do. And I know I can count upon you and Bahzell to complete all the tasks you've been called to assume. But for today, my Blades, enjoy your victory. Celebrate the triumph of the Light you've brought to pass. And while you do," He began to fade from their sight, His face wreathed in a huge smile, "perhaps you can get Bahzell to tell you how a Horse Stealer became a wind rider. It's well worth hearing!" He finished, and then He was gone.

"Well?" Kaeritha turned to her towering sword brother and folded her arms.

"Well what?" he asked innocently.

"Well you know perfectly *well* what!"

"Oh," Bahzell said. "That 'well.'" He grinned toothily at her. "Now that's after being a mite of a long story. For now, let's just leave it that while you've been off enjoying your little vacation in Kalatha and Thalar, there's some of us as have been doing some honest work a bit closer to home."

"Work?" Kaeritha repeated. "*Work?* Why, you hairy-eared, overgrown, under-brained, *miserable* excuse for a champion! I'll give you *work*, Milord Champion! And when I'm done with you, you'll wish you'd never—"

She advanced upon him with fell intent, and Bahzell Bahnakson demonstrated once again the sagacity and tactical wisdom which were the hallmarks of any champion of Tomanāk.

He took to his heels instantly, and despite the carnage all about them, Baron Tellian, the other wind riders, and every member of the Order of Tomanāk burst into laughter as Kaeritha paused beside a planter only long enough to snatch out a handful of ornamental river stones suitable for throwing at him before she went speeding off in pursuit.

The Gods of Norfressa

The Gods of Light

Orr All-Father

Often called "The Creator" or "The Establisher," Orr is considered the creator of the universe and the king and judge of gods. He is the father or creator of all but one of the Gods of Light and the most powerful of all the gods, whether of Light or Dark. His symbol is a blue starburst.

Kontifrio

"The Mother of Women" is Orr's wife and the goddess of home, family, and the harvest. According to Norfressan theology, Kontifrio was Orr's second creation (after Orfressa, the rest of the universe), and she is the most nurturing of the gods and the mother of all Orr's children except Orfressa herself. Her hatred for Shīgū is implacable. Her symbol is a sheaf of wheat tied with a grape vine.

Chemalka Orfressa

"The Lady of the Storm" is the sixth child of Orr and Kontifrio. She is the goddess of weather, good and bad, and has little to do with mortals. Her symbol is the sun seen through clouds.

Chesmirsa Orfressa

"The Singer of Light" is the fourth child of Orr and Kontifrio and the younger twin sister of Tomanāk, the war god. Chesmirsa is the goddess of bards, poetry, music and art. She is very fond of mortals and has a mischievous sense of humor. Her symbol is the harp.

Hirahim Lightfoot

Known as "The Laughing God" and "The Great Seducer," Hirahim is something of a rogue element among the Gods of Light. He is the only one of them who is not related to Orr (no one seems certain where he came from, though he acknowledges Orr's authority . . . as much as he does anyone's) and he is the true prankster of the gods. He is the god of merchants, thieves, and dancers, but he is also known as the god of seductions, as he has a terrible weakness for attractive female mortals (or goddesses). His symbol is a silver flute.

Isvaria Orfressa

"The Lady of Remembrance" (also called "The Slayer") is the first child of Orr and Kontifrio. She is the goddess of needful death and the completion of life and rules the House of the Dead, where she keeps the Scroll of the Dead. Somewhat to her mother's dismay, she is also Hirahim's lover. The third most powerful of the Gods of Light, she is the special enemy of Krahana, and her symbol is a scroll with skull winding knobs.

Khalifrio Orfressa

"The Lady of the Lightning" is Orr and Kontifrio's second child and the goddess of elemental destruction. She is considered a Goddess of Light despite her penchant for destructiveness, but she has very little to do with mortals (and mortals are just as happy about it, thank you). Her symbol is a forked lightning bolt.

Korthrala Orfro

Called "Sea Spume" and "Foam Beard," Korthrala is the fifth child of Orr and Kontifrio. He is the god of the sea but also of love, hate, and passion. He is a very powerful god, if not over-blessed with wisdom, and is very fond of mortals. His symbol is the net and trident.

Lillinara Orfressa

Known as "Friend of Women" and "The Silver Lady," Lillinara is Orr and Kontifrio's eleventh child, the goddess of the moon and women. She is one of the more complex deities, and extremely focused. She is appealed to by young women and maidens in her persona as the Maid and by mature women and mothers in her persona as the Mother. As avenger, she manifests as the Crone, who also comforts the dying. She dislikes Hirahim Lightfoot intensely, but she hates Shīgū (as the essential perversion of all womankind) with every fiber of her being. Her symbol is the moon.

Norfram Orfro

The "Lord of Chance" is Orr and Kontifrio's ninth child and the god of fortune, good and bad. His symbol is the infinity sign.

Orfressa

According to Norfressan theology, Orfressa is not a god but the universe herself, created by Orr even before Kontifrio, and she is not truly "awake." Or, rather, she is seldom aware of anything as ephemeral as mortals. On the very rare occasions when she does take notice of mortal affairs, terrible things tend to happen, and even Orr can restrain her wrath only with difficulty. It should be noted that among Norfressans, "Orfressa" is used as the name of their world, as well as to refer to the universe at large.

Semkirk Orfro

Known as "The Watcher," Semkirk is the tenth child of Orr and Kontifrio. He is the god of wisdom and mental and physical discipline and, before The Fall of Kontovar, was the god of white wizardry. Since The Fall, he has become the special patron of the psionic magi, who conduct a merciless war against evil wizards. He is a particularly deadly enemy of Carnadosa, the goddess of black wizardry. His symbol is a golden scepter.

Silendros Orfressa

The fourteenth and final child of Orr and Kontifrio, Silendros (called "Jewel of the Heavens") is the goddess of stars and the night. She is greatly reverenced by jewel smiths, who see their art as an attempt to capture the beauty of her heavens in the work of their hands, but generally has little to do with mortals. Her symbol is a silver star.

Sorbus Kontifra

Known as "Iron Bender," Sorbus is the smith of the gods. He is also the product of history's greatest seduction (that of Kontifrio by Hirahim—a "prank" Kontifrio has never quite forgiven), yet he is the most stolid and dependable of all the gods, and Orr accepts him as his own son. His symbol is an anvil.

Tolomos Orfro

"The Torch Bearer" is the twelfth child of Orr and Kontifrio. He is the god of light and the sun and the patron of all those who work with heat. His symbol is a golden flame.

Tomanāk Orfro

Tomanāk, the third child of Orr and Kontifrio, is Chesmirsa's older twin brother and second only to Orr himself in power. He is known by many names—"Sword of Light," "Scale Balancer," "Lord of Battle," and "Judge of Princes" to list but four—and has been entrusted by his father with the task of overseeing the balance of the Scales of Orr. He is also captain general of the Gods of Light and the foremost enemy of all the Dark Gods (indeed, it was he who cast Phrobus down when Phrobus first rebelled against his father). His symbols are a sword and/or a spiked mace.

Toragan Orfro

"The Huntsman," also called "Woodhelm," is the thirteenth child of Orr and Kontifrio and the god of nature. Forests are especially sacred to him, and he has a reputation for punishing those who hunt needlessly or cruelly. His symbol is an oak tree.

Torframos Orfro

Known as "Stone Beard" and "Lord of Earthquakes," Torframos is the eighth child of Orr and Kontifrio. He is the lord of the Earth, the keeper of the deep places and special patron of engineers and those who delve, and is especially revered by dwarves. His symbol is the miner's pick.

The Dark Gods

Phrobus Orfro

Called "Father of Evil" and "Lord of Deceit," Phrobus is the seventh child of Orr and Kontifrio, which explains why seven is considered *the* unlucky number in Norfressa. No one recalls his original name; "Phrobus" ("Truth Bender") was given to him by Tomanāk when he cast Phrobus down for his treacherous attempt to wrest rulership from Orr. Following that defeat, Phrobus turned openly to the Dark and became, in fact, the opening wedge by which evil first entered Orfressa. He is the most powerful of the gods of Light or Dark after Tomanāk, and the hatred between him and Tomanāk is unthinkably bitter, but Phrobus fears his brother worse than death itself. His symbol is a flame-eyed skull.

Carnadosa Phrofressa

"The Lady of Wizardry" is the fifth child of Phrobus and Shīgū. She has become the goddess of black wizardry, but she herself might be considered totally amoral rather than evil for evil's sake. She enshrines the concept of power sought by any means and at any cost to others. Her symbol is a wizard's wand.

Fiendark Phrofro

The first-born child of Phrobus and Shīgū, Fiendark is known as "Lord of the Furies." He is cast very much in his father's image (though, fortunately, he is considerably less powerful) and all evil creatures owe him allegiance as Phrobus' deputy. Unlike Phrobus, who seeks always to pervert or conquer, however, Fiendark also delights in destruction for destruction's sake. His symbols are a flaming sword or flame-shot cloud of smoke.

Krahana Phrofressa

"The Lady of the Damned" is the fourth child of Phrobus and Shīgū and, in most ways, the most loathsome of them all. She is noted for her hideous beauty and holds dominion over the undead (which makes her Isvaria's most hated foe) and rules the hells to which the souls of those who have sold themselves to evil spend eternity. Her symbol is a splintered coffin.

Krashnark Phrofro

The second son of Phrobus and Shīgū, Krashnark is something of a disappointment to his parents. The most powerful of Phrobus' children, Krashnark (known as "Devil Master") is the god of devils and ambitious war. He is ruthless, merciless, and cruel, but personally courageous and possessed of a strong, personal code of honor, which makes him the only Dark God Tomanāk actually respects. He is, unfortunately, loyal to his father, and his power and sense of honor have made him the "enforcer" of the Dark Gods. His symbol is a flaming steward's rod.

Sharnā Phrofro

Called "Demonspawn" and "Lord of the Scorpion," Sharnā is Krashnark's younger, identical twin (a fact which pleases neither of them). Sharnā is the god of demons and the patron of assassins, the personification of cunning and deception. He is substantially less powerful than Krashnark and a total coward, and the demons who owe him allegiance hate and fear Krashnark's more powerful devils almost as much as Sharnā hates and fears his brother. His symbols are the giant scorpion (which serves as his mount) and a bleeding heart in a mailed fist.

Shīgū

Called "The Twisted One," "Queen of Hell," and "Mother of Madness," Shīgū is the wife of Phrobus. No one knows exactly where she came from, but most believe she was, in fact, a powerful demoness raised to godhood by Phrobus when he sought a mate to breed up his own pantheon to oppose that of his father. Her power is deep but subtle, her cruelty and malice are bottomless, and her favored weapon is madness. She is even more hated, loathed, and feared by mortals than Phrobus, and her worship is punishable by death in all Norfressan realms. Her symbol is a flaming spider.